# Delilah Dirk

### and the
## PILLARS of HERCULES

# Delilah Dirk

### and the
## PILLARS of HERCULES

## *Tony Cliff*

Color assistance by
Sarah Airriess, Jarad Greene, Beth Morrell,
Amanda Scurti, and Brian Cliff

First Second
*New York*

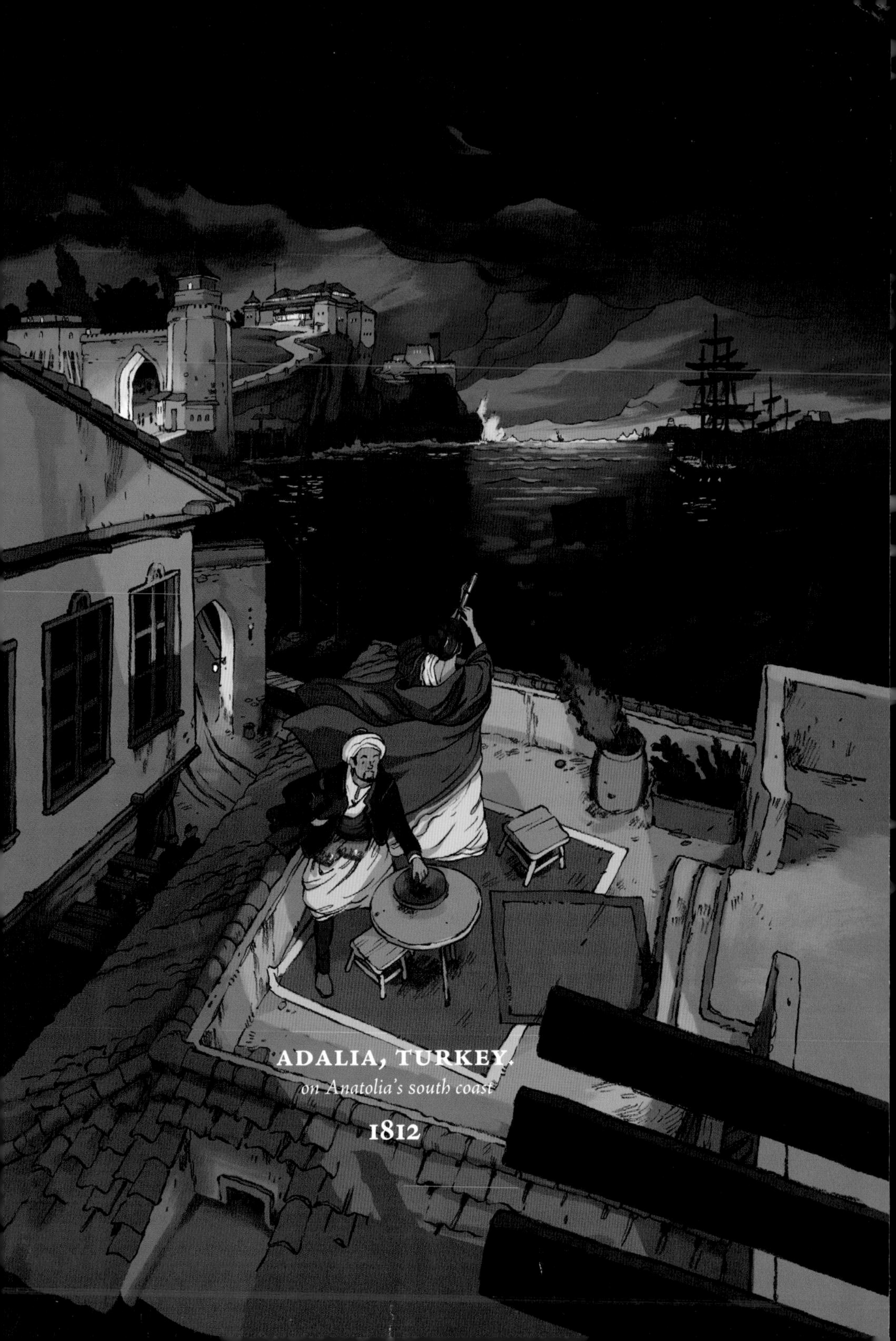
ADALIA, TURKEY.
on Anatolia's south coast
1812

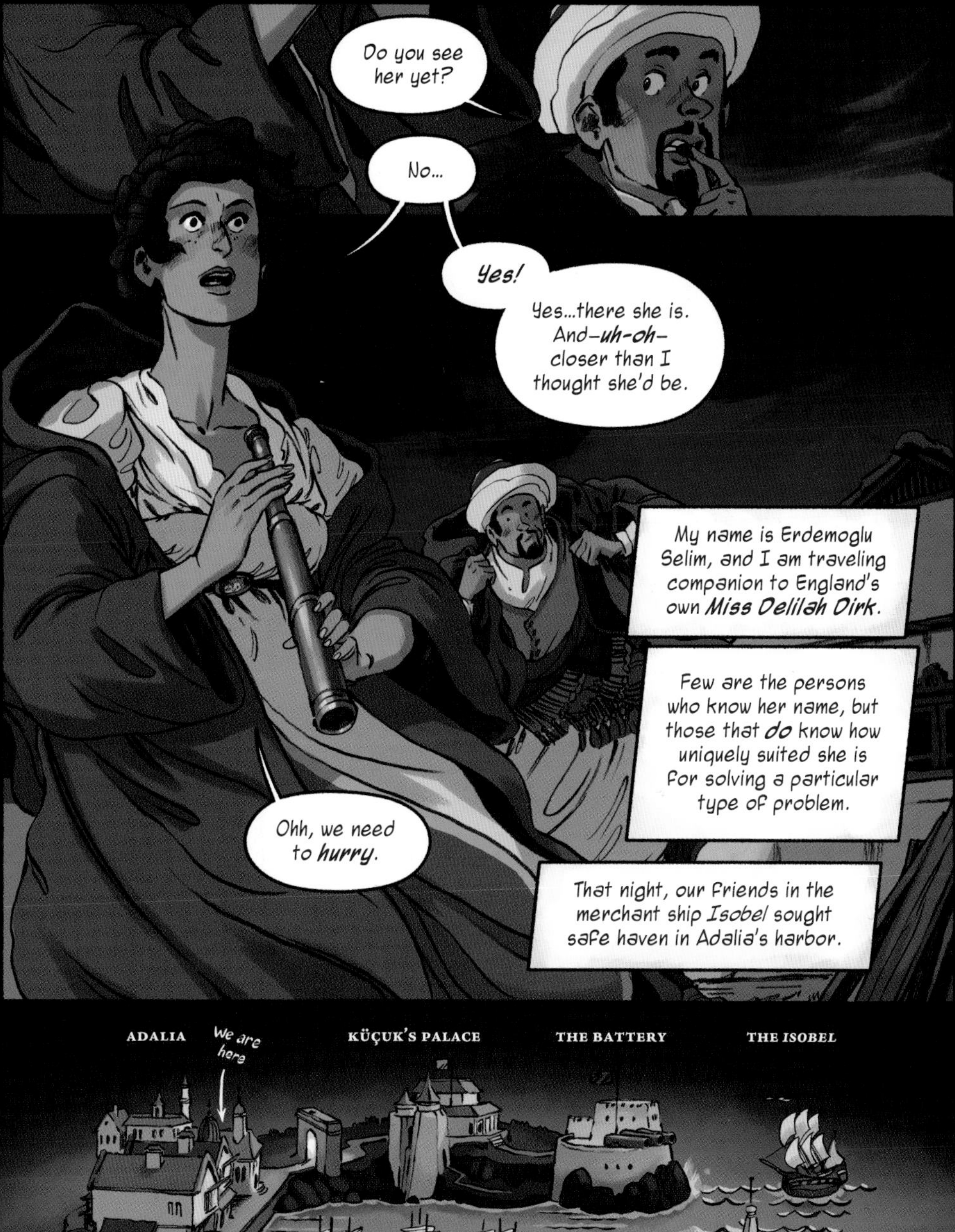
Do you see her yet?
No...
*Yes!*
Yes...there she is. And–*uh-oh*– closer than I thought she'd be.
My name is Erdemoglu Selim, and I am traveling companion to England's own *Miss Delilah Dirk*.
Few are the persons who know her name, but those that *do* know how uniquely suited she is for solving a particular type of problem.
Ohh, we need to *hurry*.
That night, our friends in the merchant ship *Isobel* sought safe haven in Adalia's harbor.
ADALIA
We are here
KÜÇUK'S PALACE
THE BATTERY
THE *ISOBEL*
But *Küçuk*, the local tyrant, cruelly protective of his own interests, would never admit the *Isobel*. His fortress battery would fire upon any unwelcome ship. We needed to disable the cannons, and the only way to get to them was by going through Küçuk's palace.

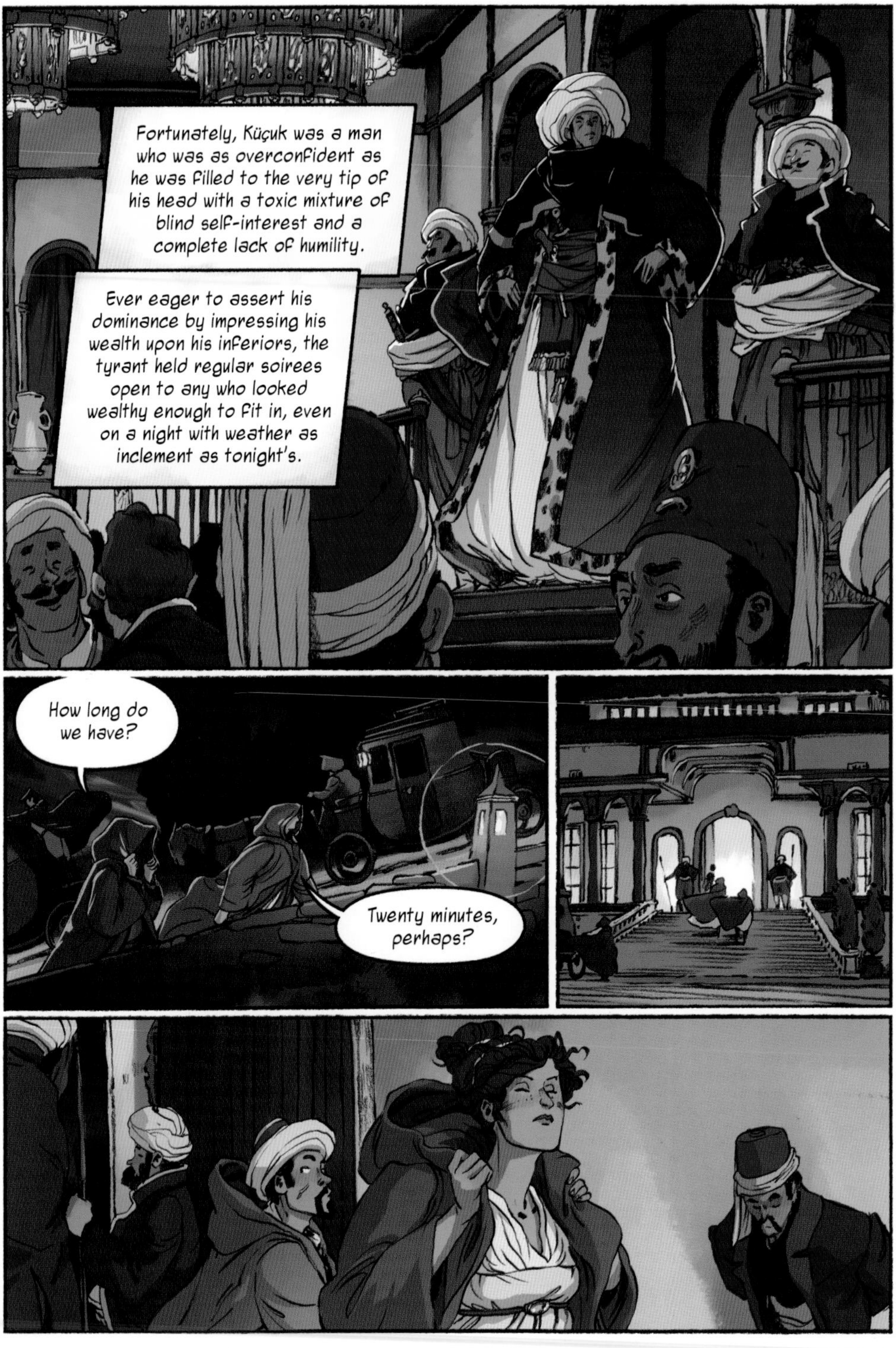
Fortunately, Küçuk was a man who was as overconfident as he was filled to the very tip of his head with a toxic mixture of blind self-interest and a complete lack of humility.
Ever eager to assert his dominance by impressing his wealth upon his inferiors, the tyrant held regular soirees open to any who looked wealthy enough to fit in, even on a night with weather as inclement as tonight's.
How long do we have?
Twenty minutes, perhaps?

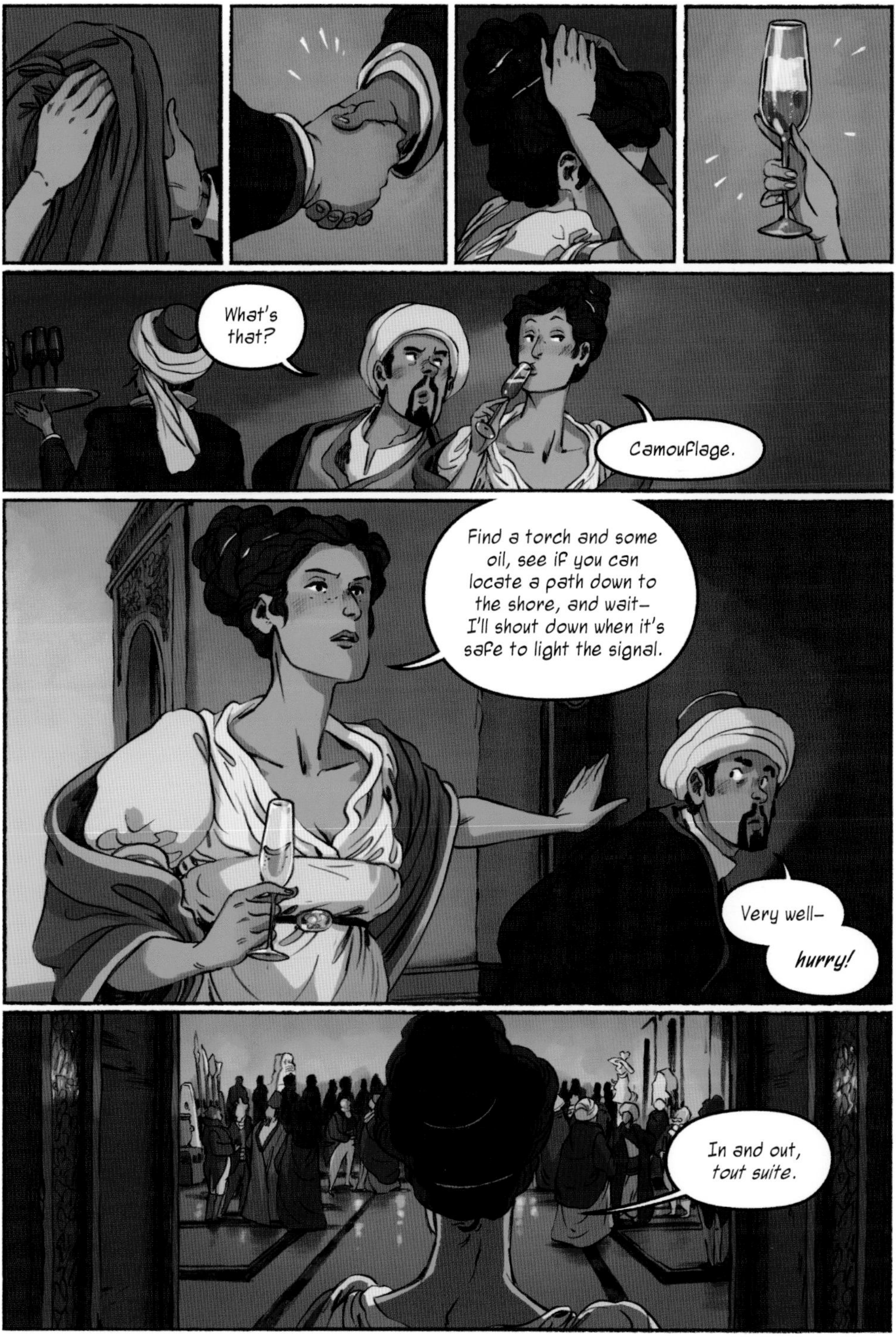
What's that?
Camouflage.
Find a torch and some oil, see if you can locate a path down to the shore, and wait– I'll shout down when it's safe to light the signal.
Very well–
hurry!
In and out, tout suite.

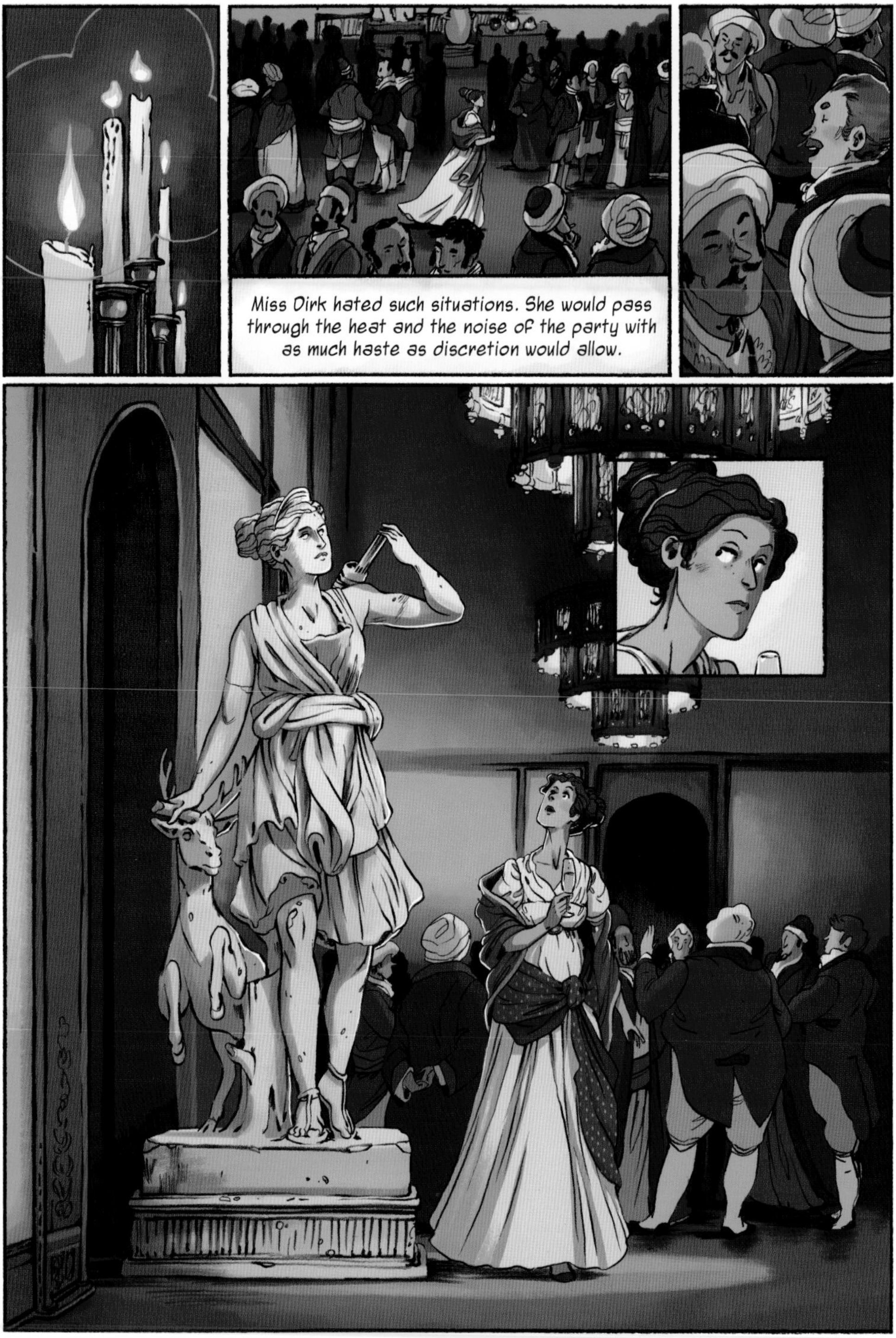
Miss Dirk hated such situations. She would pass through the heat and the noise of the party with as much haste as discretion would allow.

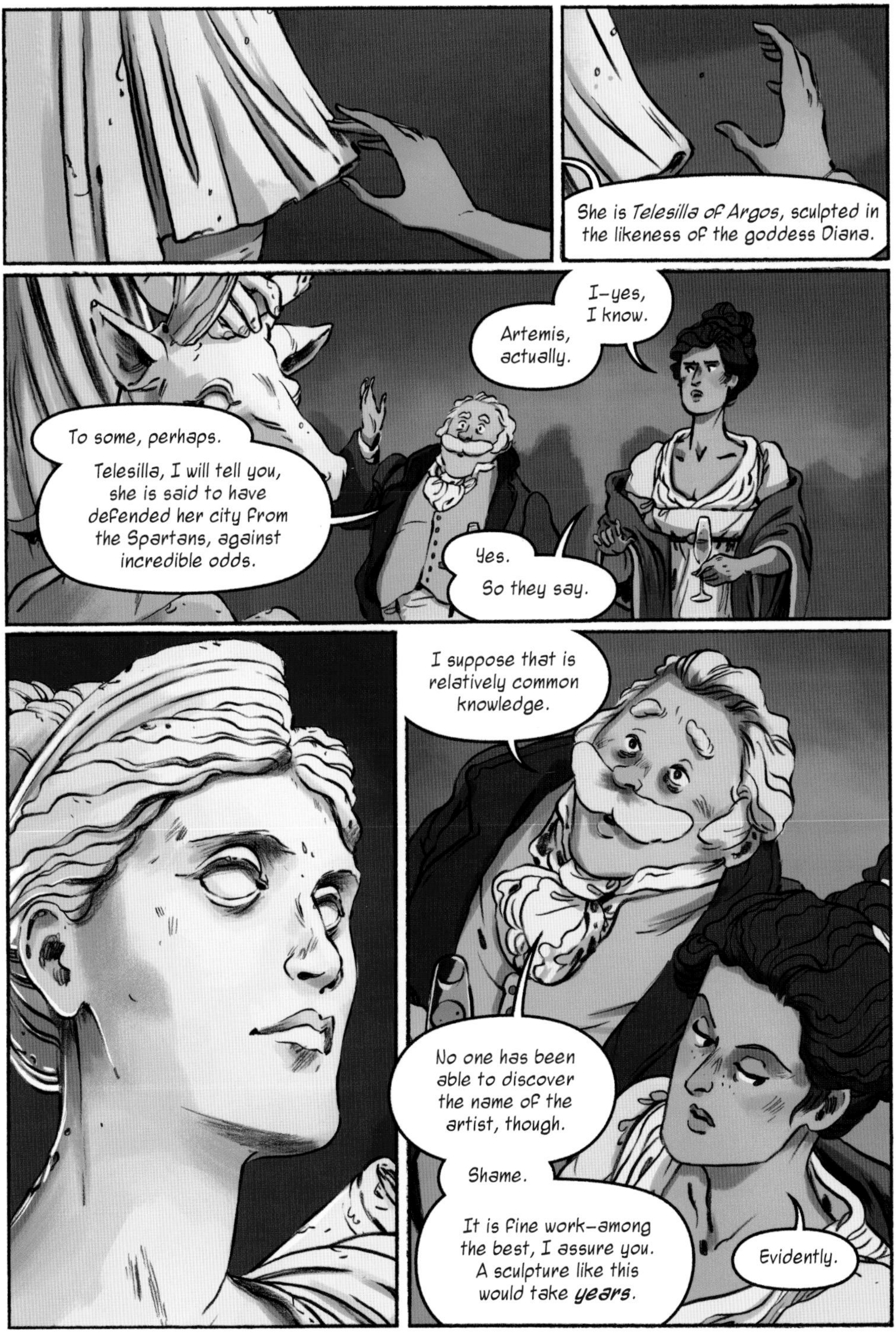
She is *Telesilla of Argos*, sculpted in the likeness of the goddess Diana.
I–yes, I know.
Artemis, actually.
To some, perhaps.
Telesilla, I will tell you, she is said to have defended her city from the Spartans, against incredible odds.
Yes.
So they say.
I suppose that is relatively common knowledge.
No one has been able to discover the name of the artist, though.
Shame.
It is fine work–among the best, I assure you. A sculpture like this would take ***years***.
Evidently.

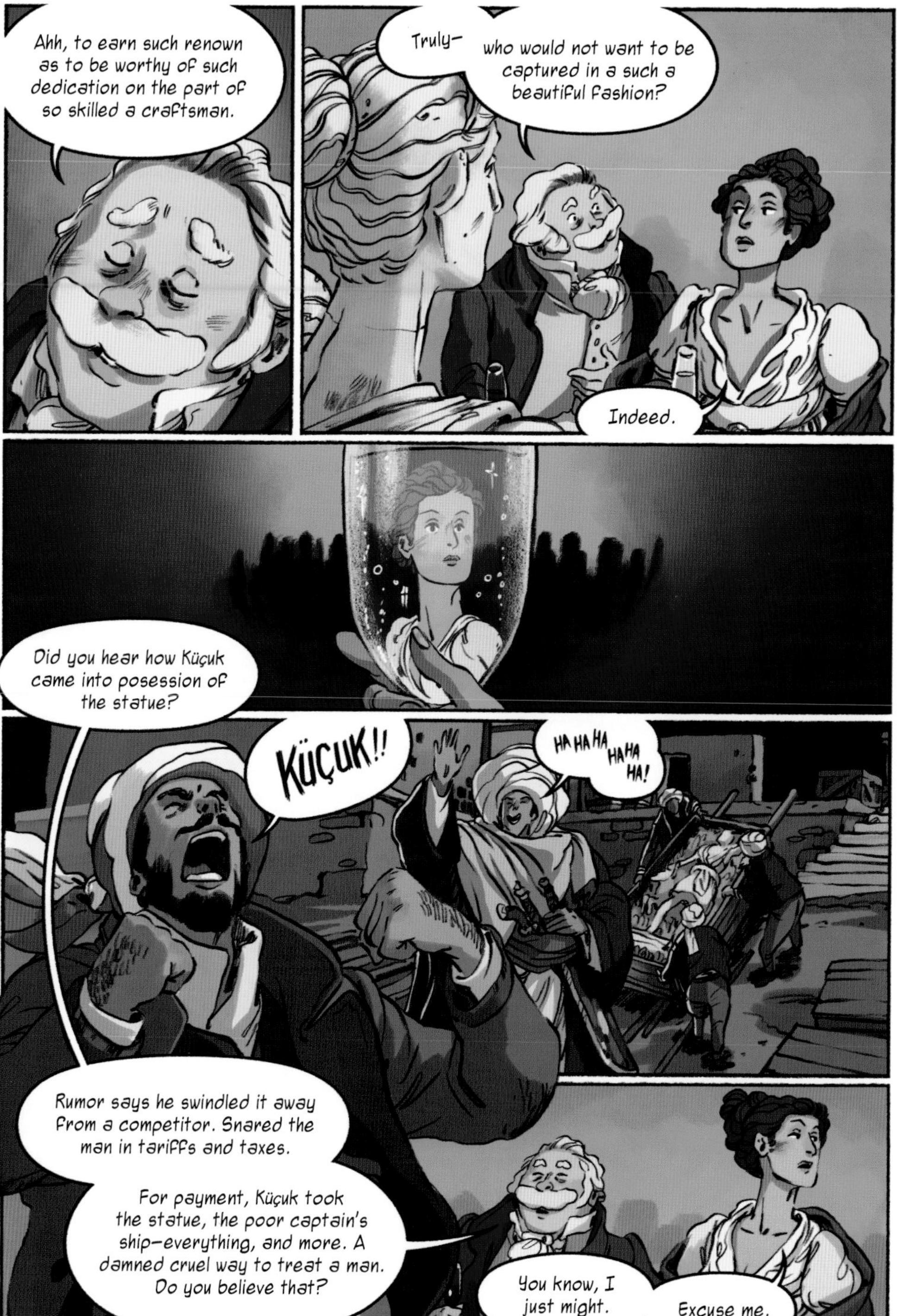
Ahh, to earn such renown as to be worthy of such dedication on the part of so skilled a craftsman.
Truly—
who would not want to be captured in a such a beautiful fashion?
Indeed.
Did you hear how Küçuk came into posession of the statue?
KÜÇUK!!
HA HA HA HA HA HA!
Rumor says he swindled it away from a competitor. Snared the man in tariffs and taxes.
For payment, Küçuk took the statue, the poor captain's ship—everything, and more. A damned cruel way to treat a man. Do you believe that?
You know, I just might.
Excuse me.

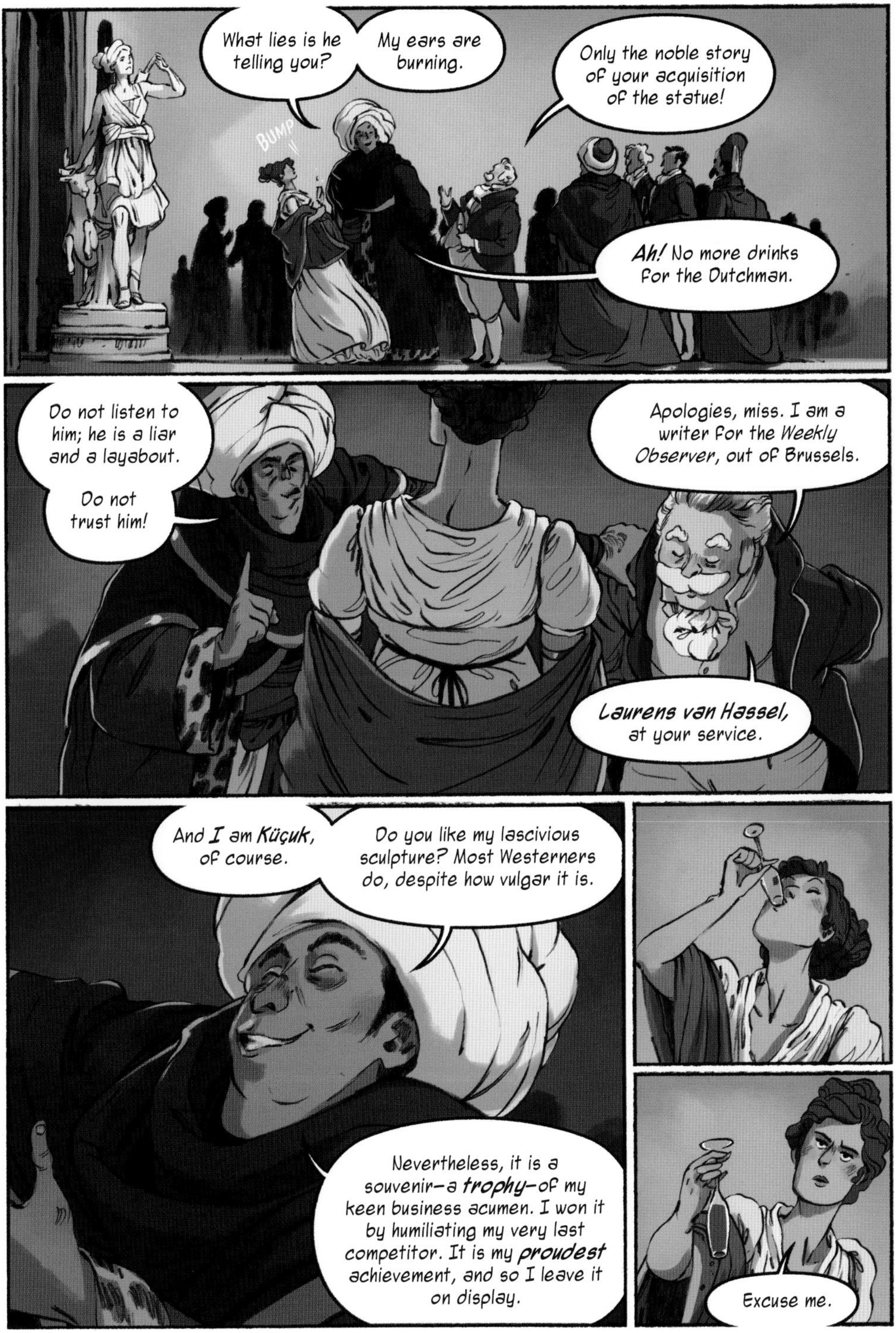
What lies is he telling you?
My ears are burning.
BUMP!!
Only the noble story of your acquisition of the statue!
Ah! No more drinks for the Outchman.
Do not listen to him; he is a liar and a layabout.
Do not trust him!
Apologies, miss. I am a writer for the Weekly Observer, out of Brussels.
Laurens van Hassel, at your service.
And I am Küçuk, of course.
Do you like my lascivious sculpture? Most Westerners do, despite how vulgar it is.
Nevertheless, it is a souvenir—a trophy—of my keen business acumen. I won it by humiliating my very last competitor. It is my proudest achievement, and so I leave it on display.
Excuse me.

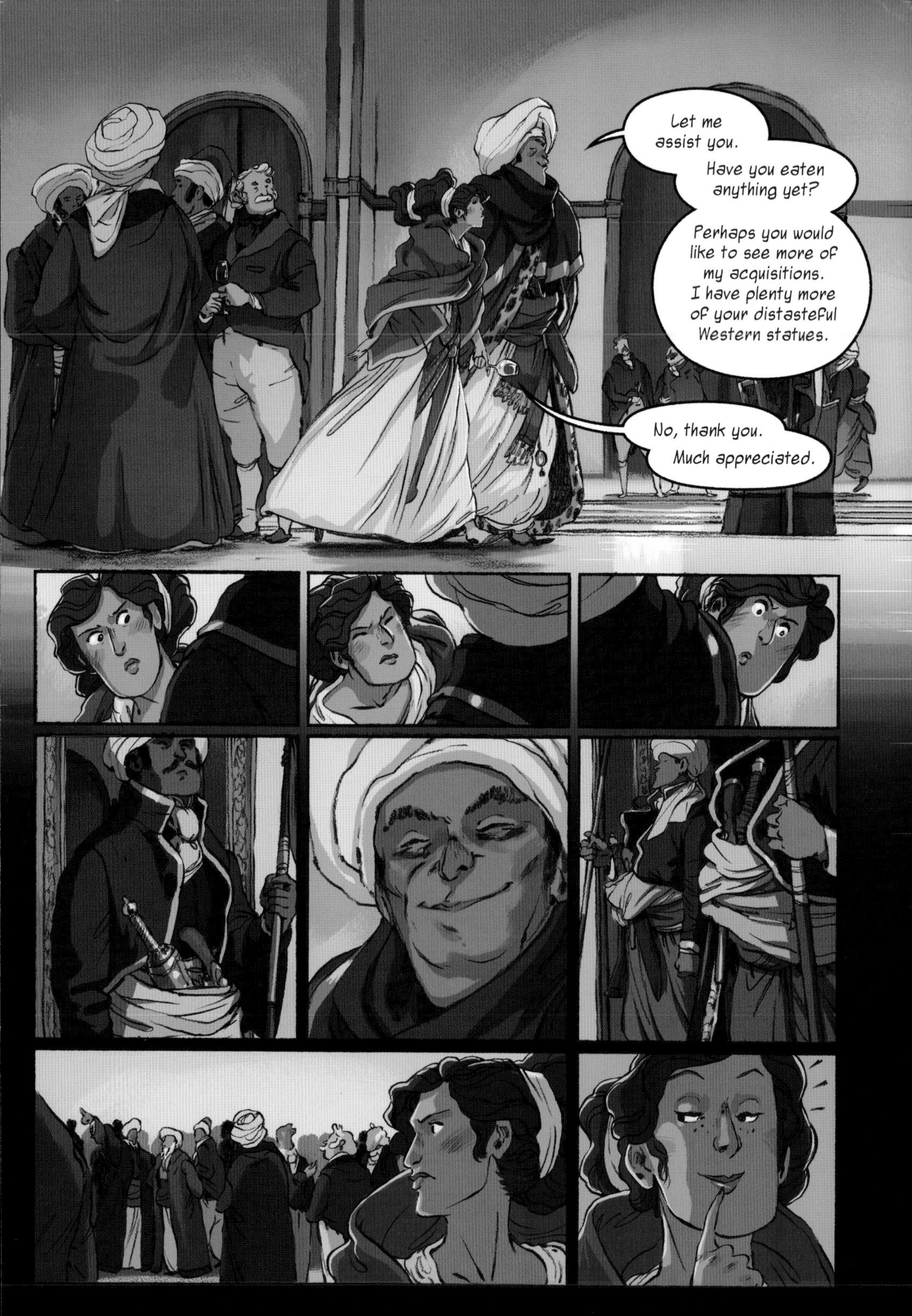
Let me assist you.
Have you eaten anything yet?
Perhaps you would like to see more of my acquisitions. I have plenty more of your distasteful Western statues.
No, thank you.
Much appreciated.

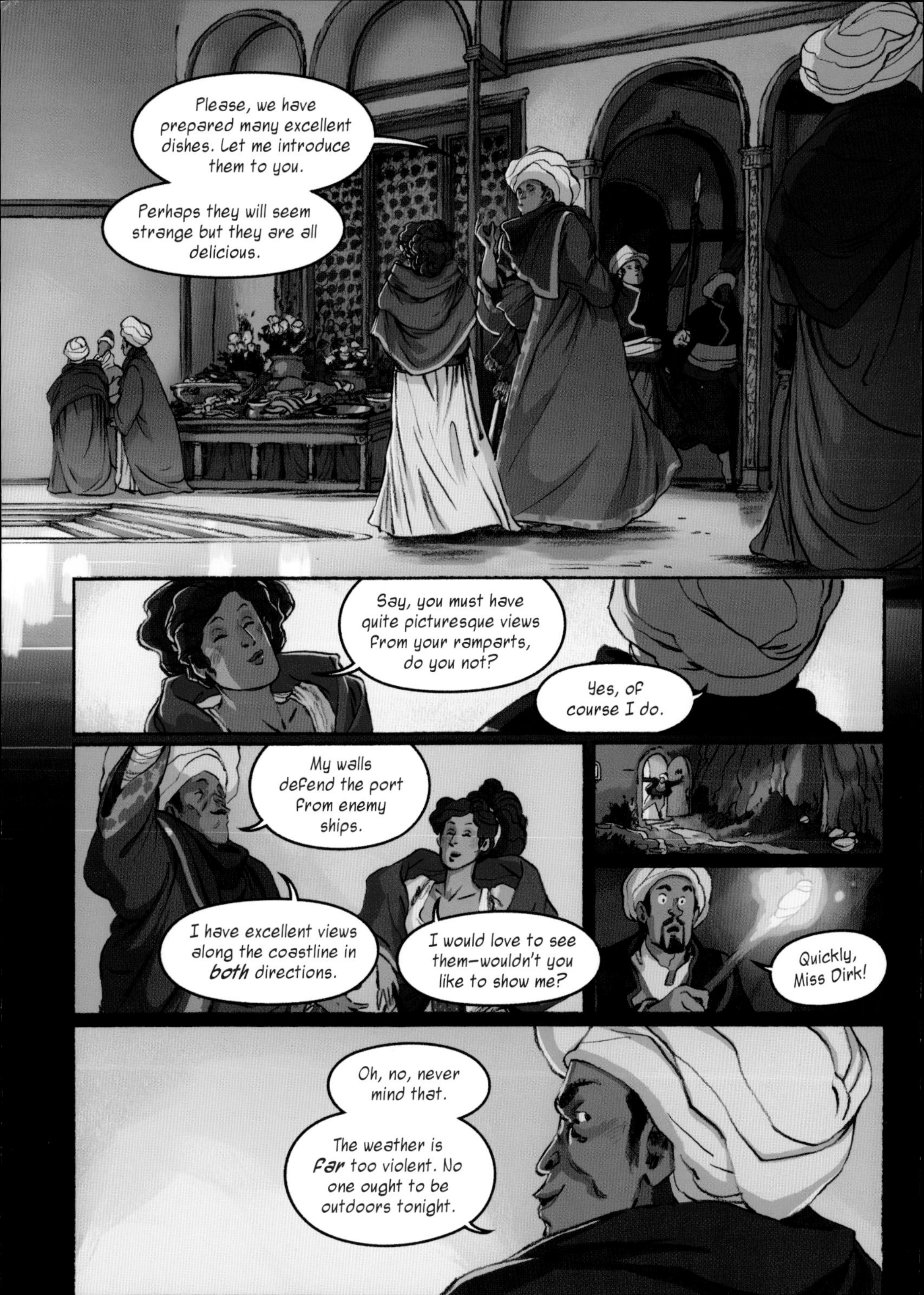
Please, we have prepared many excellent dishes. Let me introduce them to you.
Perhaps they will seem strange but they are all delicious.
Say, you must have quite picturesque views from your ramparts, do you not?
Yes, of course I do.
My walls defend the port from enemy ships.
I have excellent views along the coastline in *both* directions.
I would love to see them—wouldn't you like to show me?
Quickly, Miss Dirk!
Oh, no, never mind that.
The weather is *far* too violent. No one ought to be outdoors tonight.

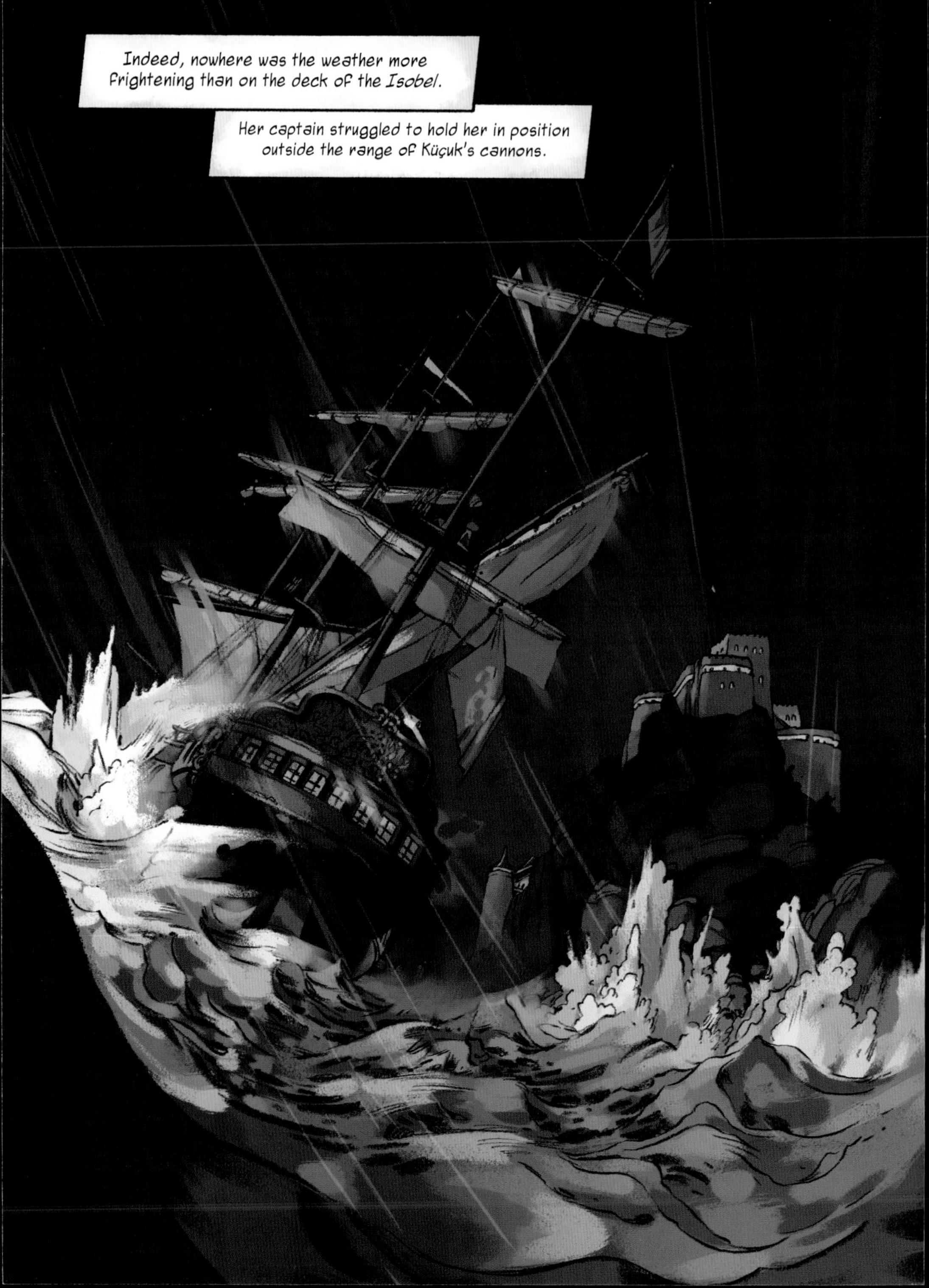
Indeed, nowhere was the weather more frightening than on the deck of the *Isobel*.
Her captain struggled to hold her in position outside the range of Küçuk's cannons.

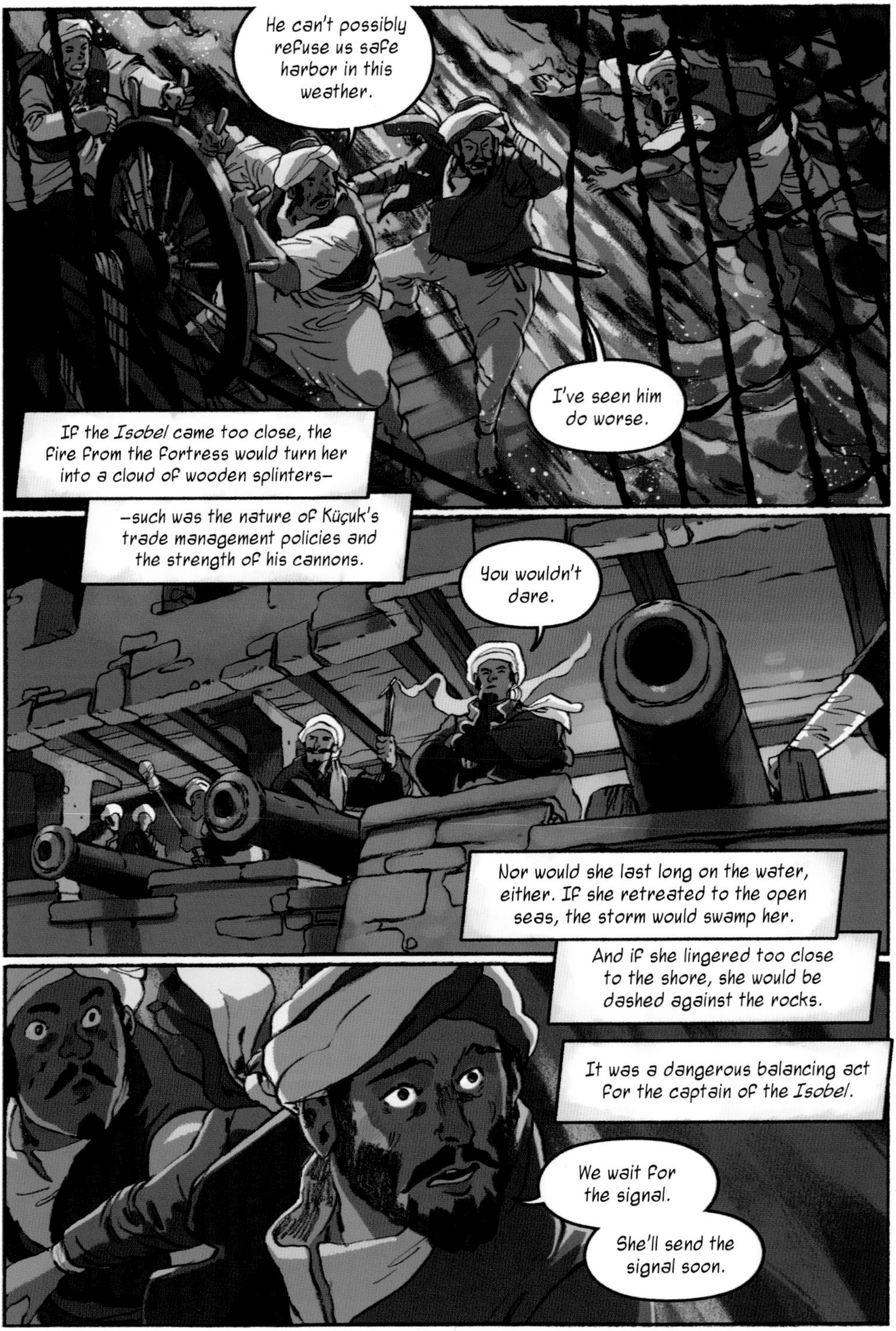

He can't possibly refuse us safe harbor in this weather.
I've seen him do worse.
If the *Isobel* came too close, the fire from the fortress would turn her into a cloud of wooden splinters–
–such was the nature of Küçuk's trade management policies and the strength of his cannons.
You wouldn't dare.
Nor would she last long on the water, either. If she retreated to the open seas, the storm would swamp her.
And if she lingered too close to the shore, she would be dashed against the rocks.
It was a dangerous balancing act for the captain of the *Isobel*.
We wait for the signal.
She'll send the signal soon.

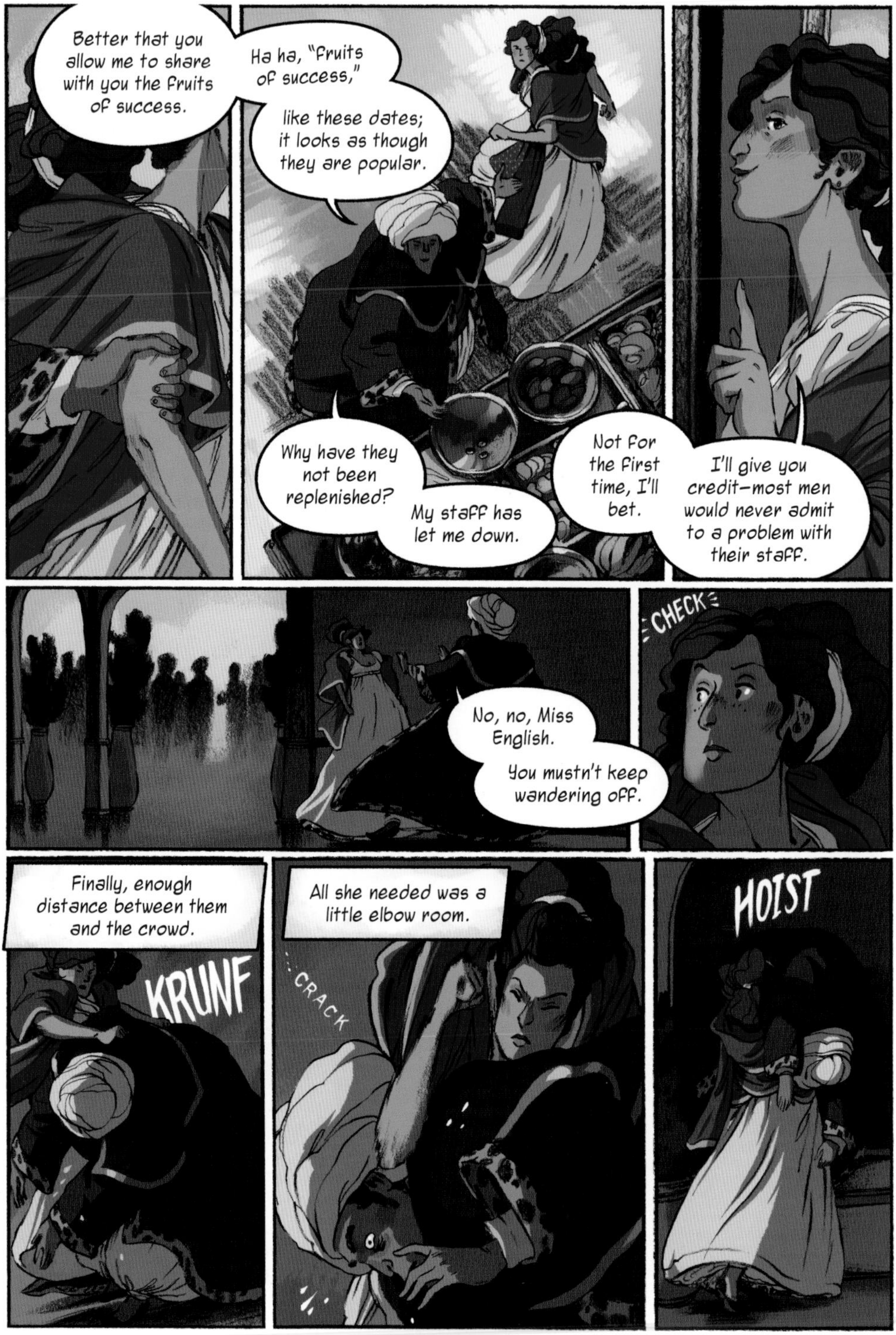
Better that you allow me to share with you the fruits of success.
Ha ha, "fruits of success,"
like these dates; it looks as though they are popular.
Why have they not been replenished?
My staff has let me down.
Not for the first time, I'll bet.
I'll give you credit—most men would never admit to a problem with their staff.
CHECK
No, no, Miss English.
You mustn't keep wandering off.
Finally, enough distance between them and the crowd.
KRUNF
All she needed was a little elbow room.
CRACK
HOIST

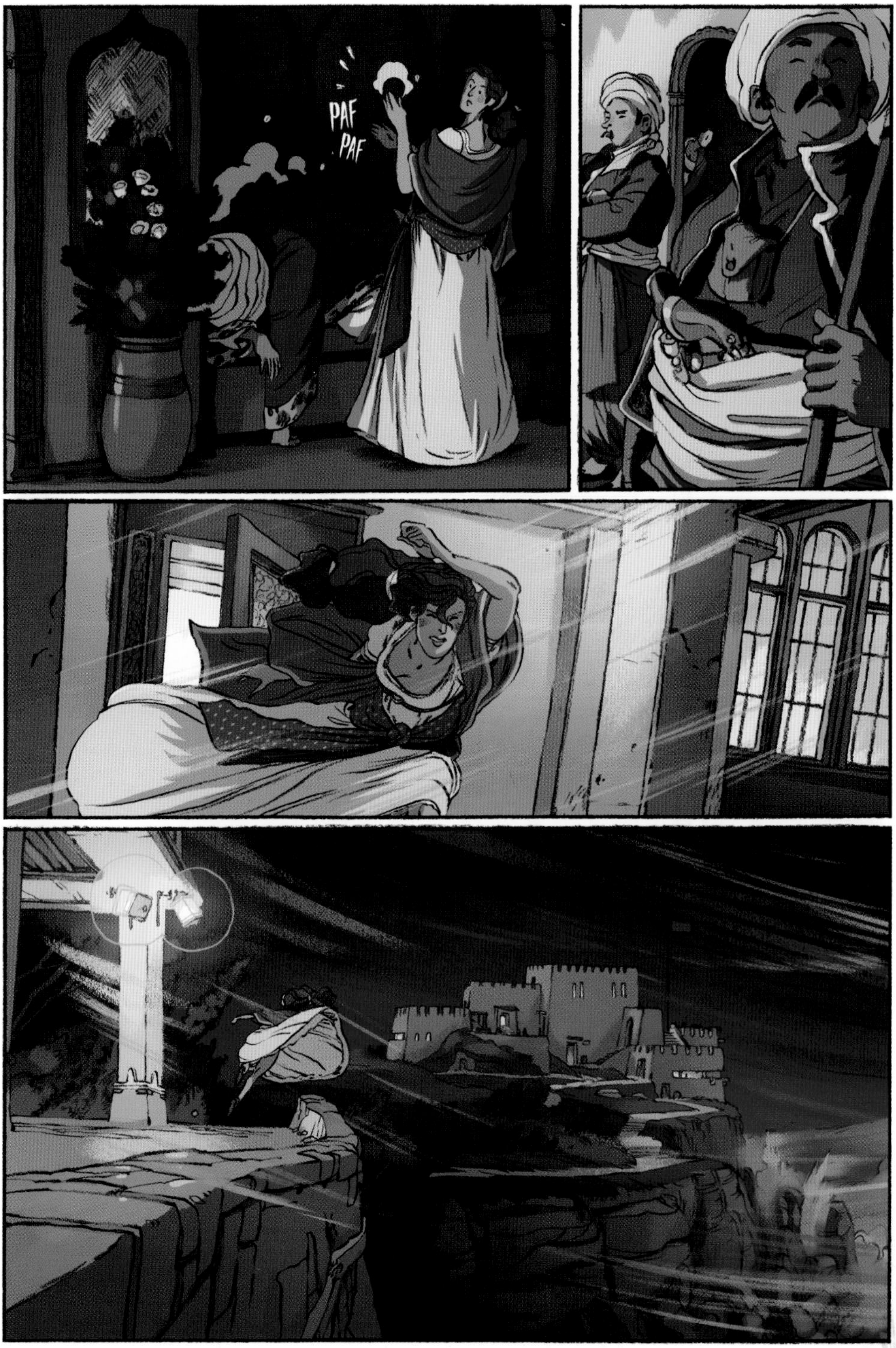
PAF
PAF

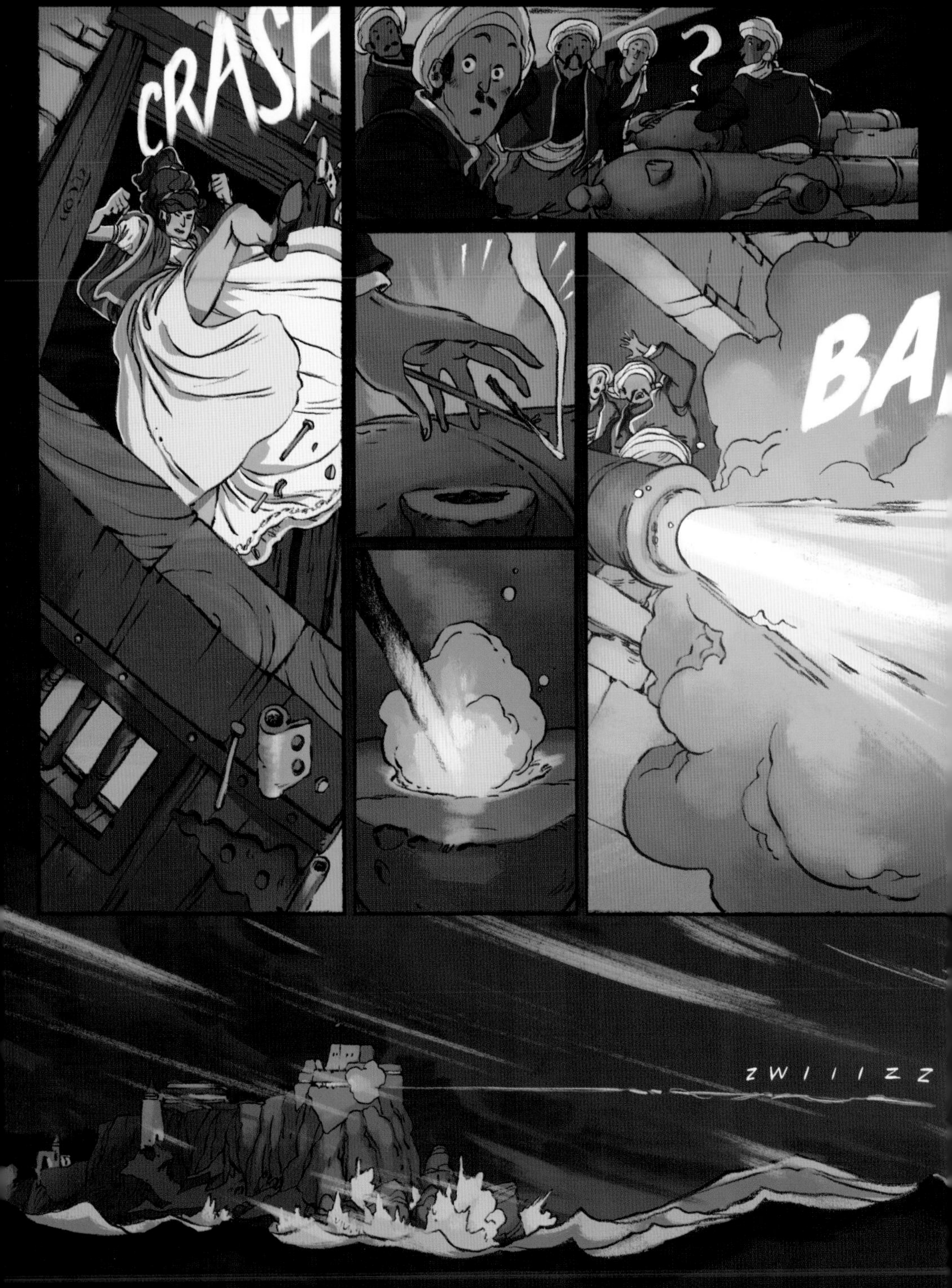
CRASH
?
BA
ZWIIIZZ

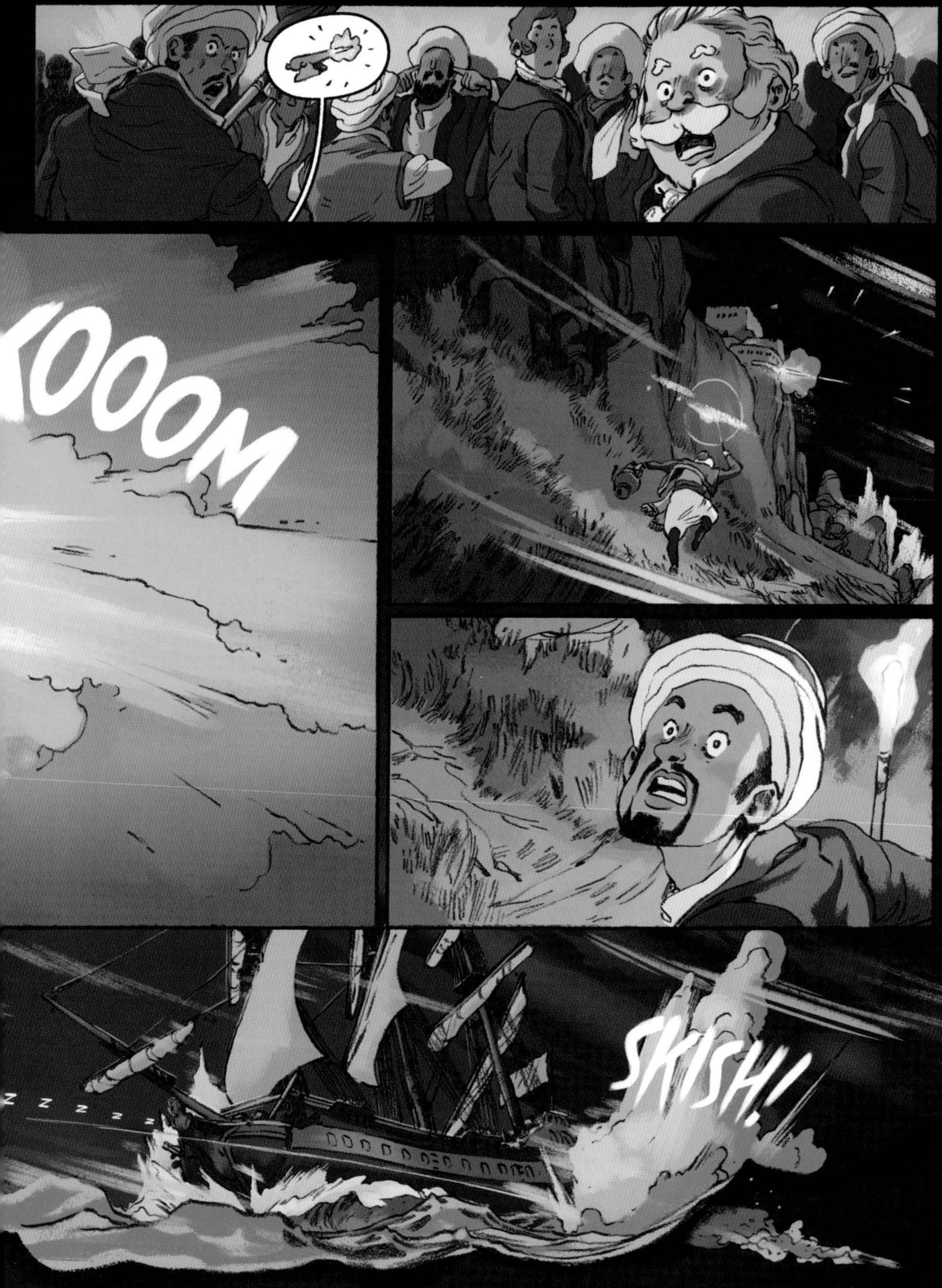
KOOOM
SKISH!

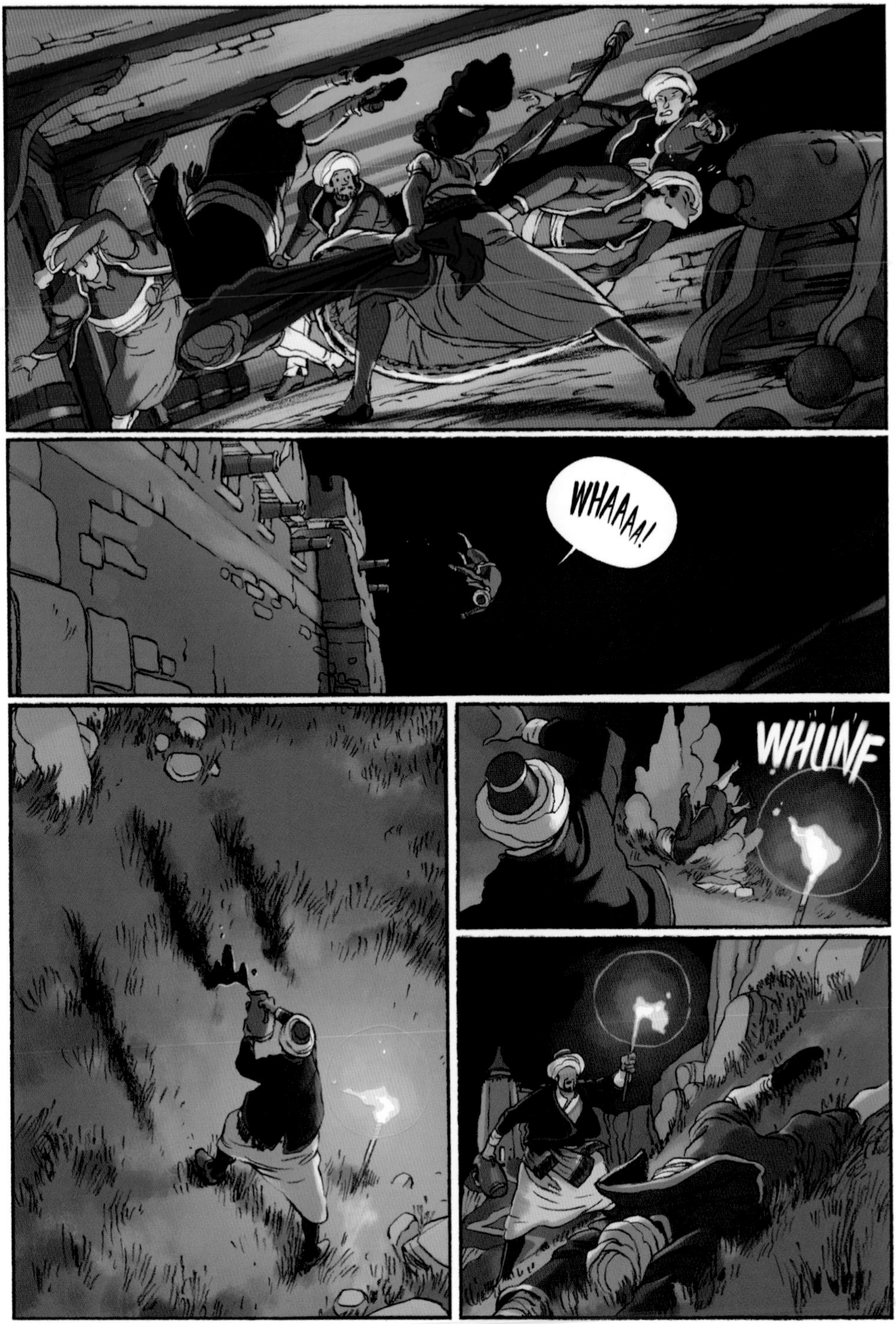
WHAAAA!
WHUNF

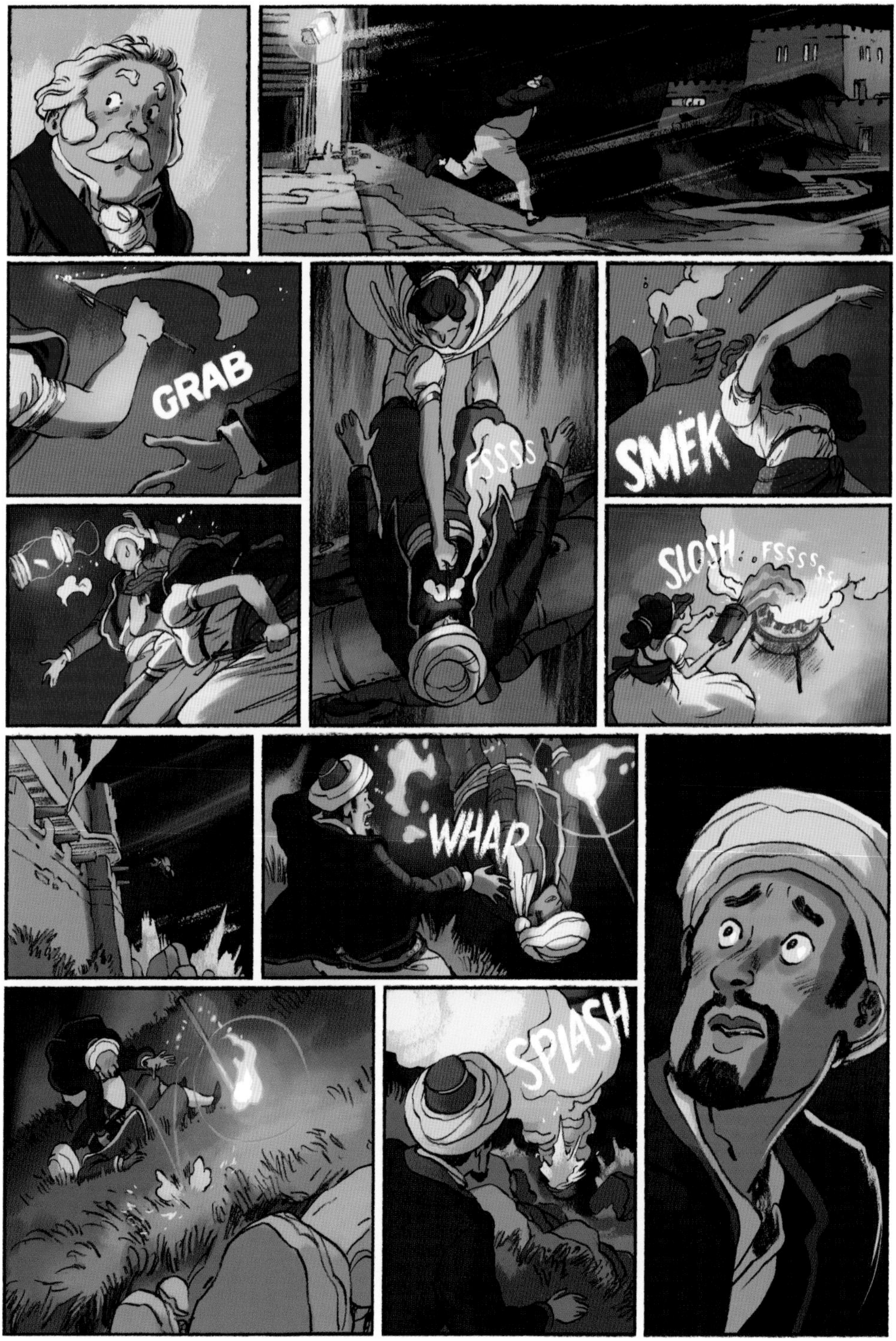
GRAB
FSSSS
SMEK
SLOSH
FSSSSSS
WHAP
SPLASH

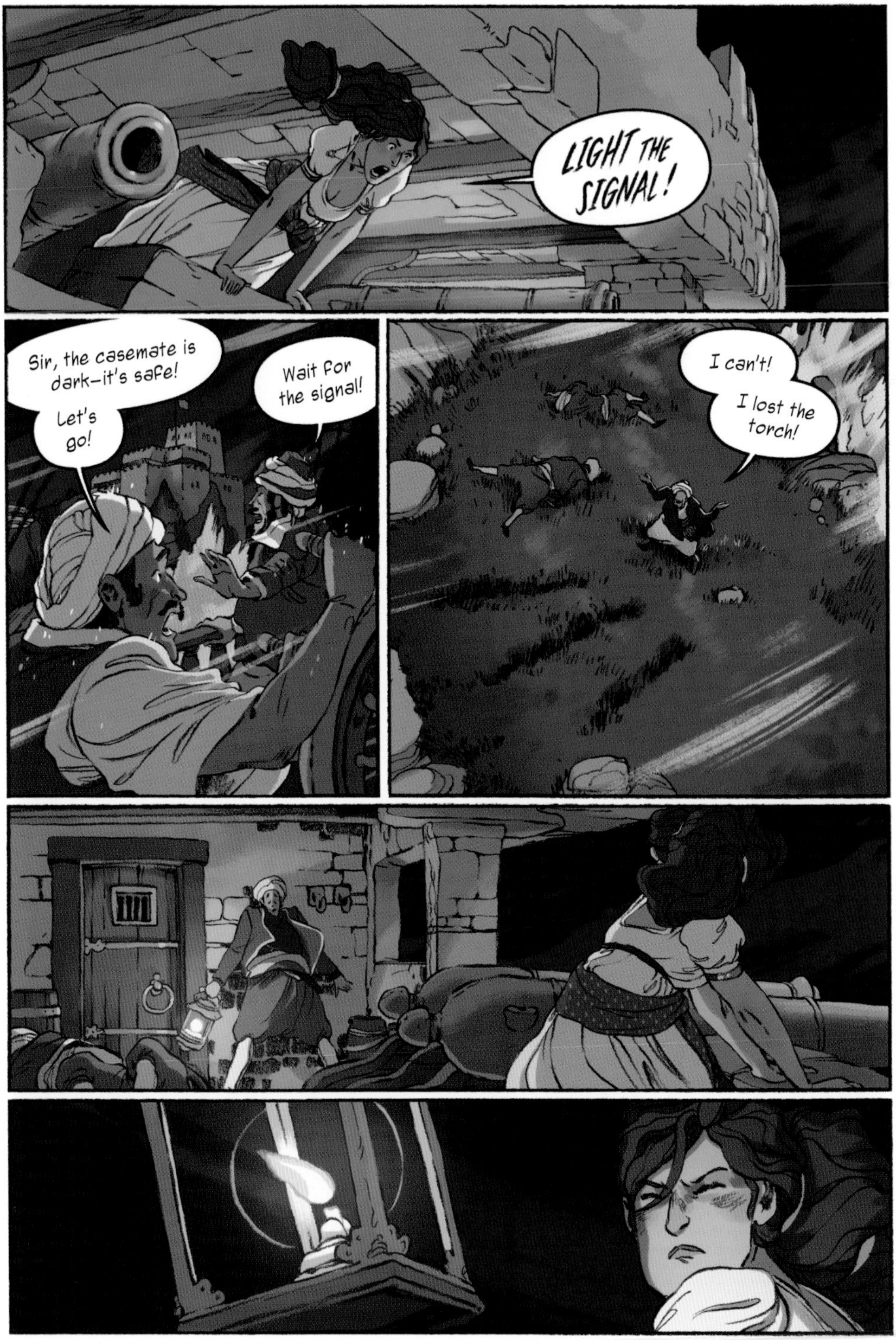
LIGHT THE SIGNAL!
Sir, the casemate is dark—it's safe!
Let's go!
Wait for the signal!
I can't!
I lost the torch!

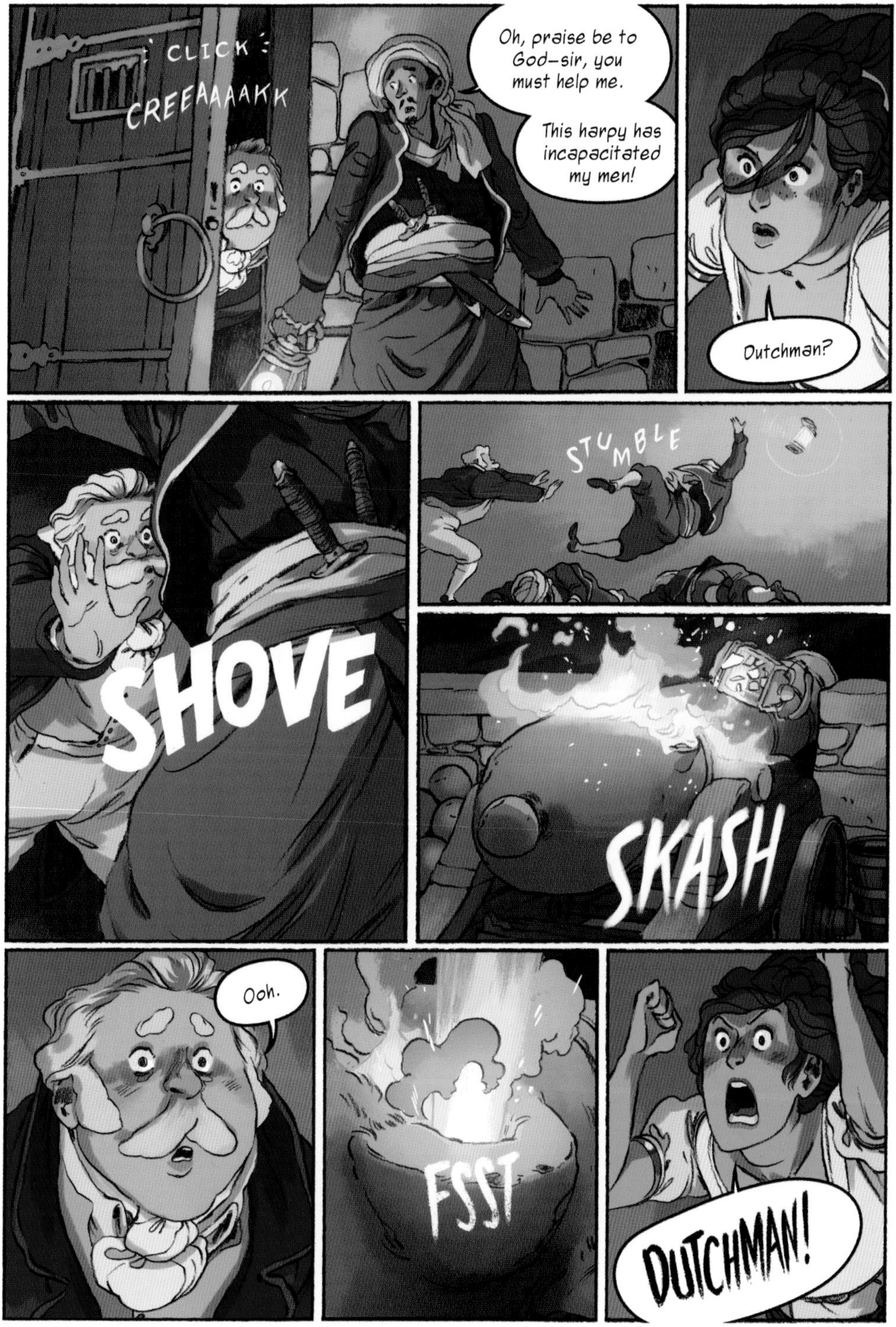
CLICK
CREEAAAAKK
Oh, praise be to God–sir, you must help me.
This harpy has incapacitated my men!
Dutchman?
SHOVE
STUMBLE
SKASH
Ooh.
FSST
DUTCHMAN!

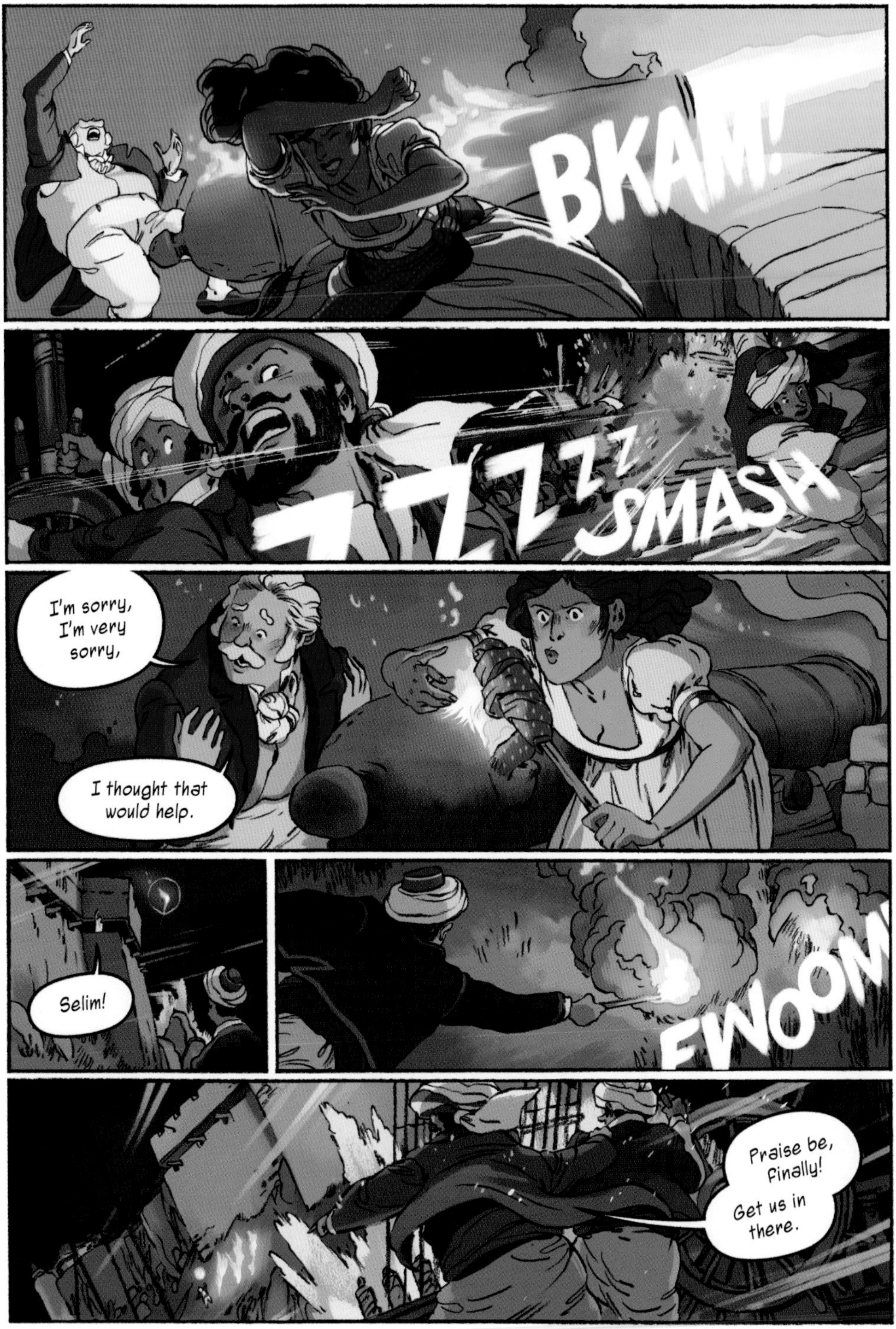
BKAM!
ZZZZZZ
SMASH
I'm sorry, I'm very sorry,
I thought that would help.
Selim!
FWOOM
Praise be, finally!
Get us in there.

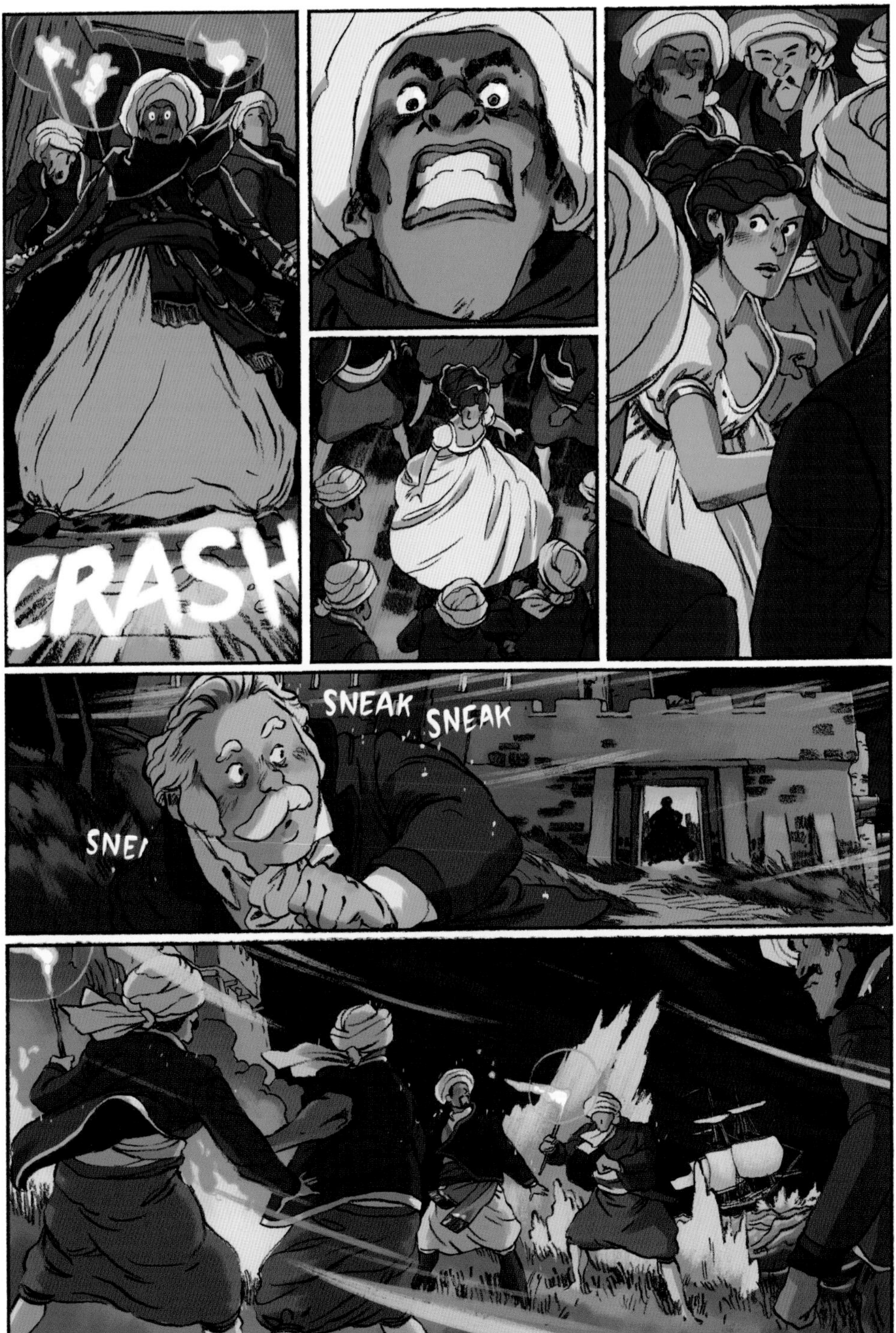
CRASH
SNEAK
SNEAK
SNEI

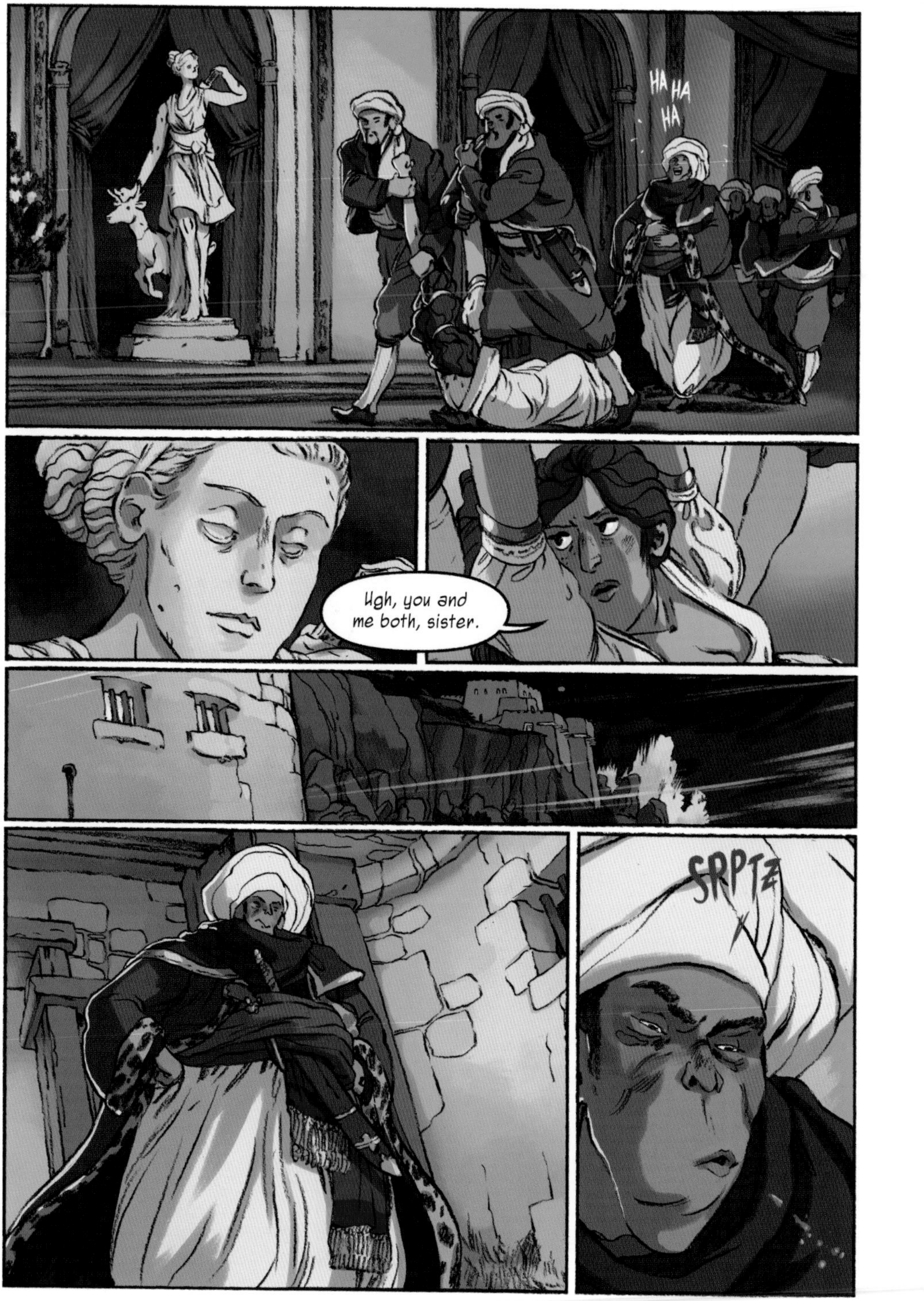
HA HA HA
Ugh, you and me both, sister.
SRPTZ

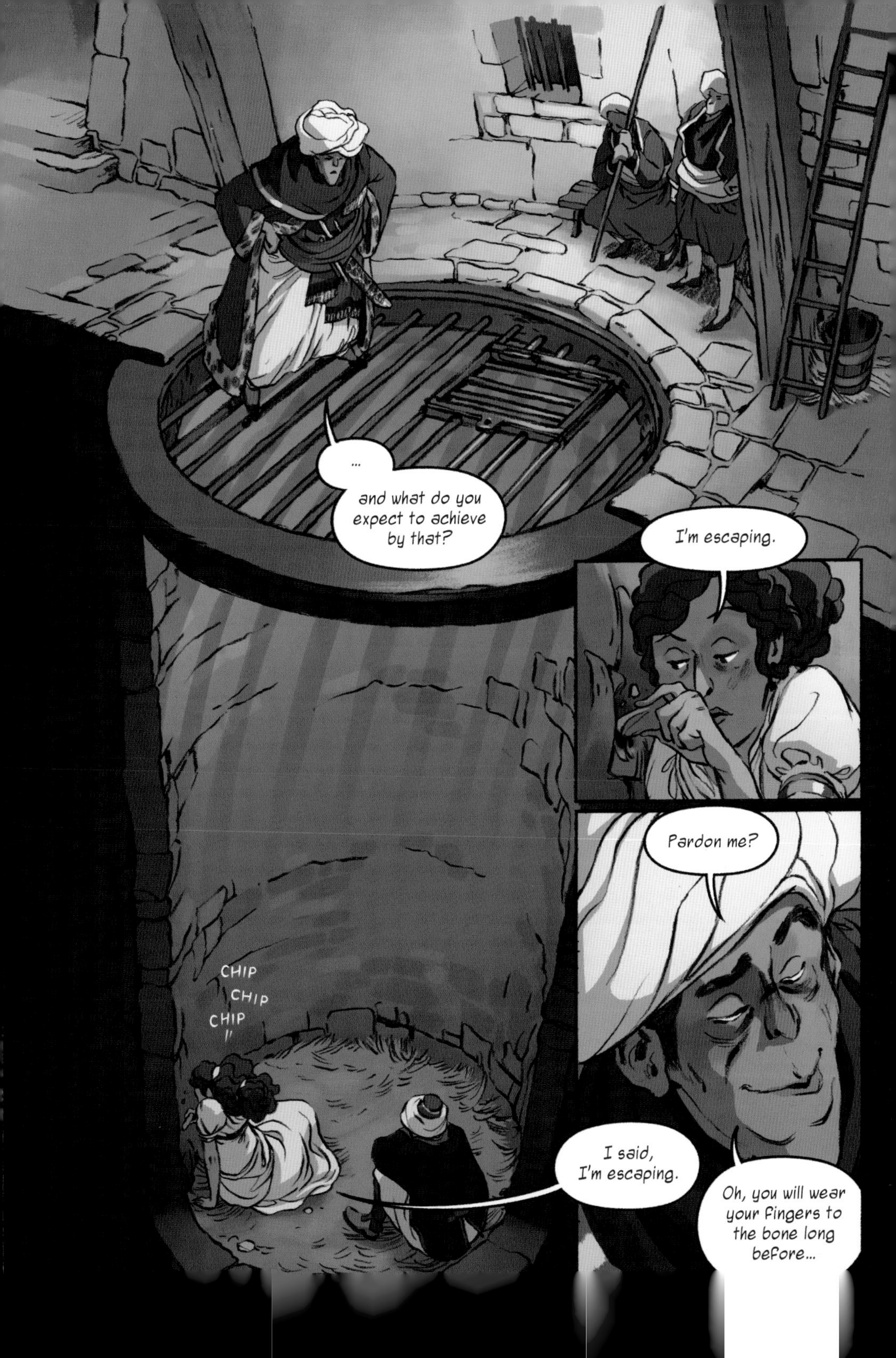
...
and what do you expect to achieve by that?
I'm escaping.
Pardon me?
CHIP
CHIP
CHIP
I said, I'm escaping.
Oh, you will wear your fingers to the bone long before...

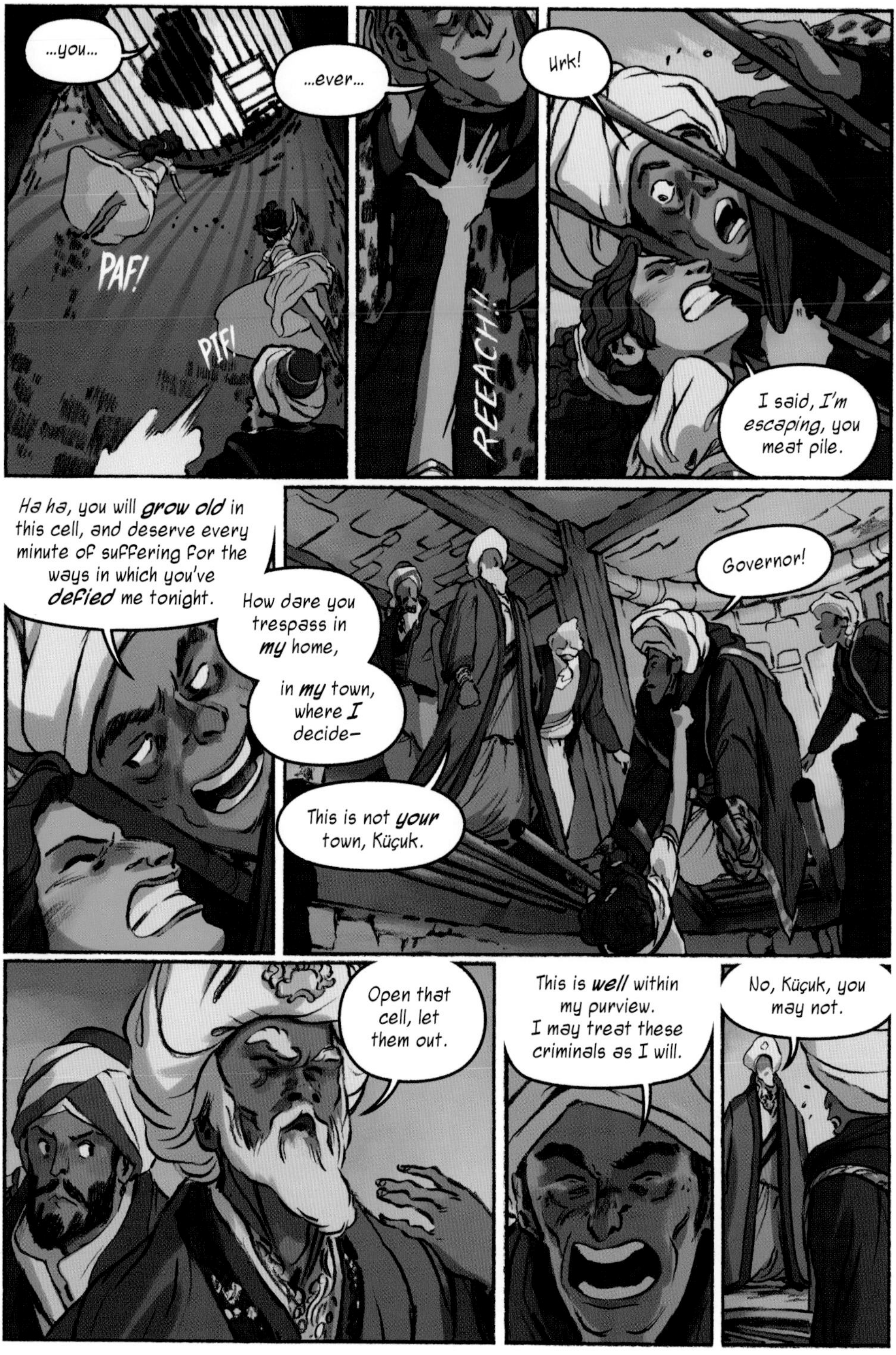
...you...
PAF!
PIF!
...ever...
REEACH!!
Urk!
I said, I'm escaping, you meat pile.
Ha ha, you will grow old in this cell, and deserve every minute of suffering for the ways in which you've defied me tonight.
How dare you trespass in my home,
in my town, where I decide—
Governor!
This is not your town, Küçuk.
Open that cell, let them out.
This is well within my purview. I may treat these criminals as I will.
No, Küçuk, you may not.

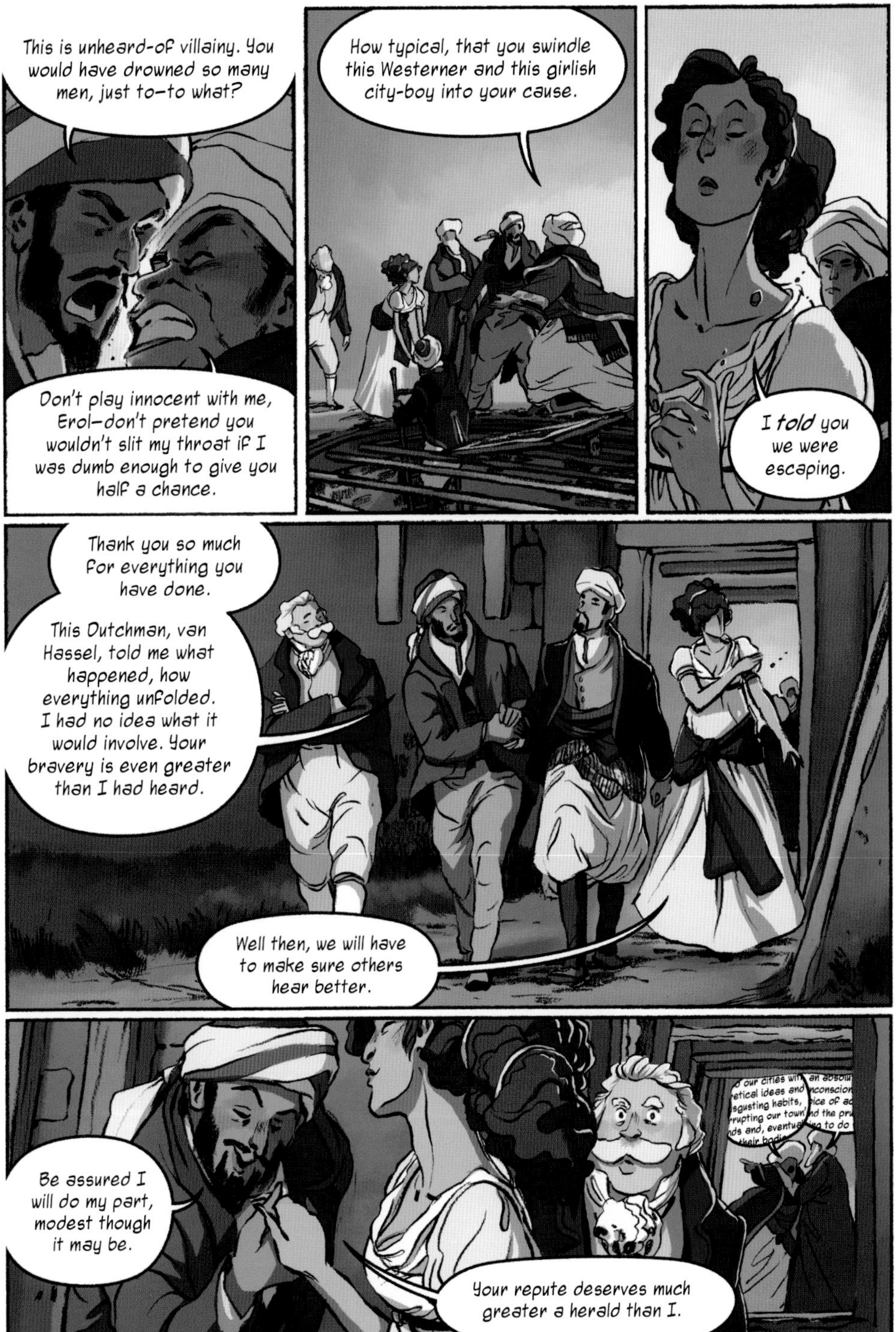
This is unheard-of villainy. You would have drowned so many men, just to—to what?
Don't play innocent with me, Erol—don't pretend you wouldn't slit my throat if I was dumb enough to give you half a chance.
How typical, that you swindle this Westerner and this girlish city-boy into your cause.
I *told* you we were escaping.
Thank you so much for everything you have done.
This Dutchman, van Hassel, told me what happened, how everything unfolded. I had no idea what it would involve. Your bravery is even greater than I had heard.
Well then, we will have to make sure others hear better.
Be assured I will do my part, modest though it may be.
Your repute deserves much greater a herald than I.

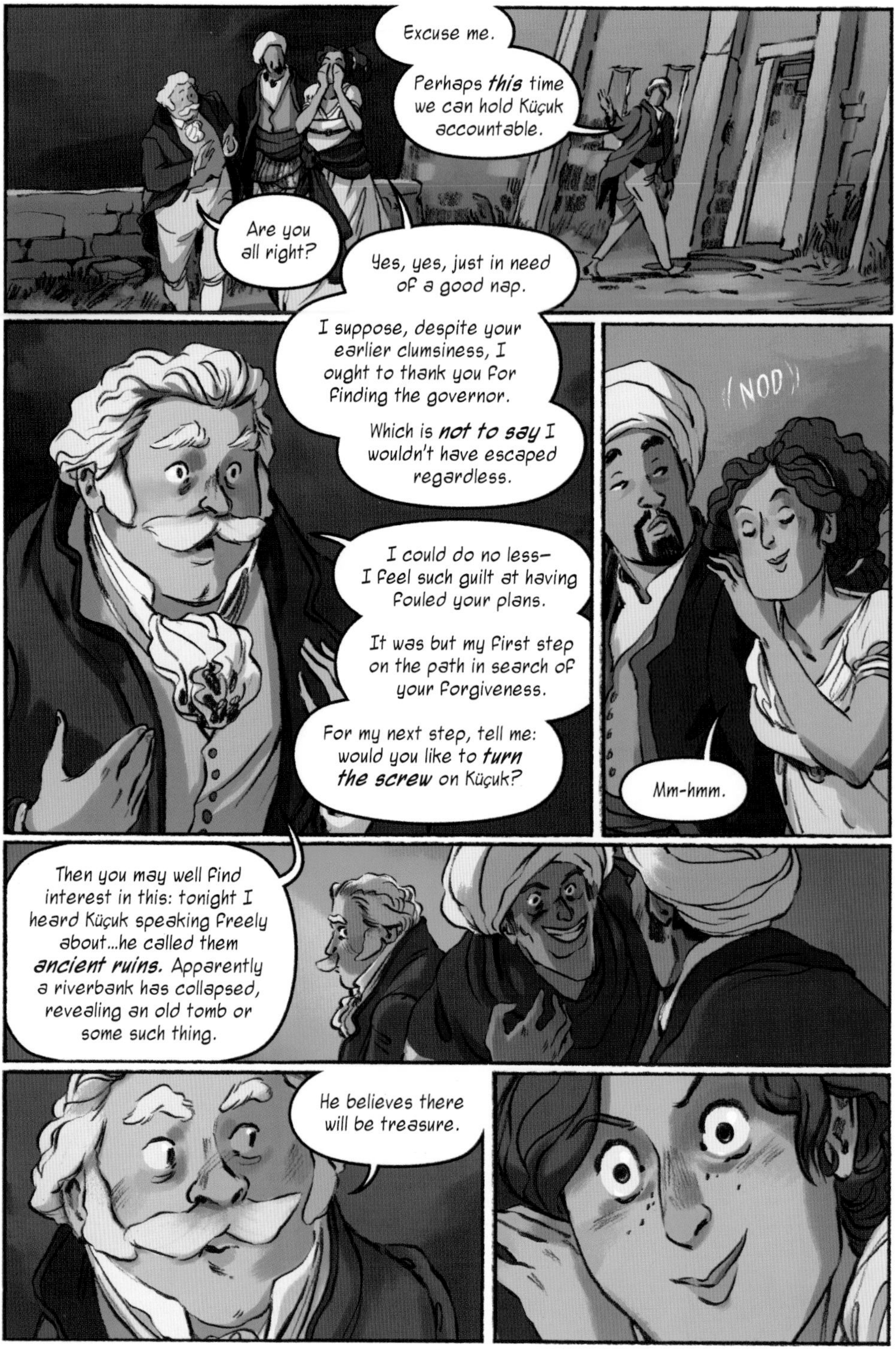
Excuse me.
Perhaps **this** time we can hold Küçuk accountable.
Are you all right?
Yes, yes, just in need of a good nap.
I suppose, despite your earlier clumsiness, I ought to thank you for finding the governor.
Which is **not to say** I wouldn't have escaped regardless.
(NOD)
I could do no less— I feel such guilt at having fouled your plans.
It was but my first step on the path in search of your forgiveness.
For my next step, tell me: would you like to **turn the screw** on Küçuk?
Mm-hmm.
Then you may well find interest in this: tonight I heard Küçuk speaking freely about...he called them **ancient ruins.** Apparently a riverbank has collapsed, revealing an old tomb or some such thing.
He believes there will be treasure.

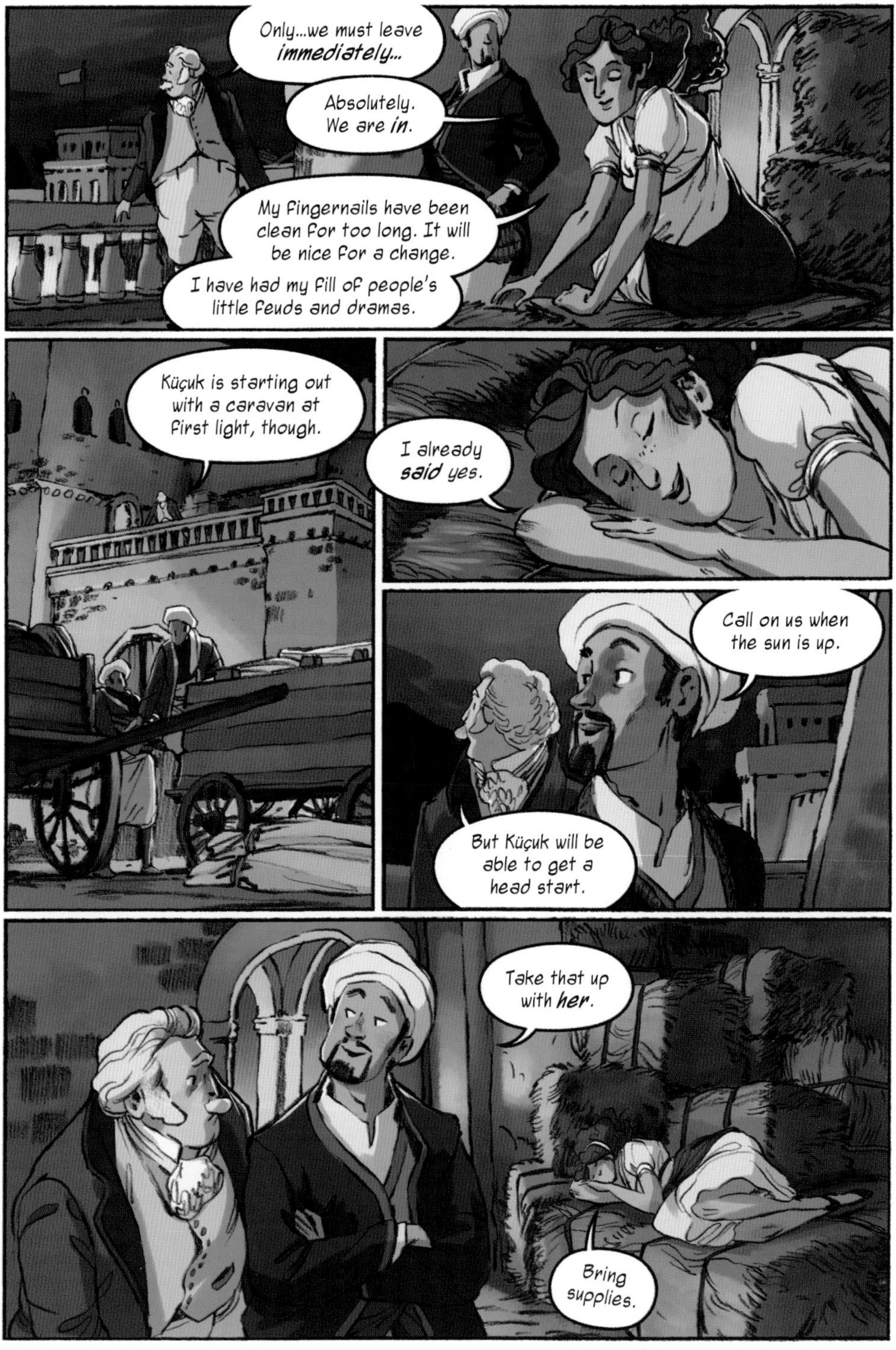
Only...we must leave immediately...
Absolutely. We are in.
My fingernails have been clean for too long. It will be nice for a change.
I have had my fill of people's little feuds and dramas.
Küçuk is starting out with a caravan at first light, though.
I already said yes.
Call on us when the sun is up.
But Küçuk will be able to get a head start.
Take that up with her.
Bring supplies.

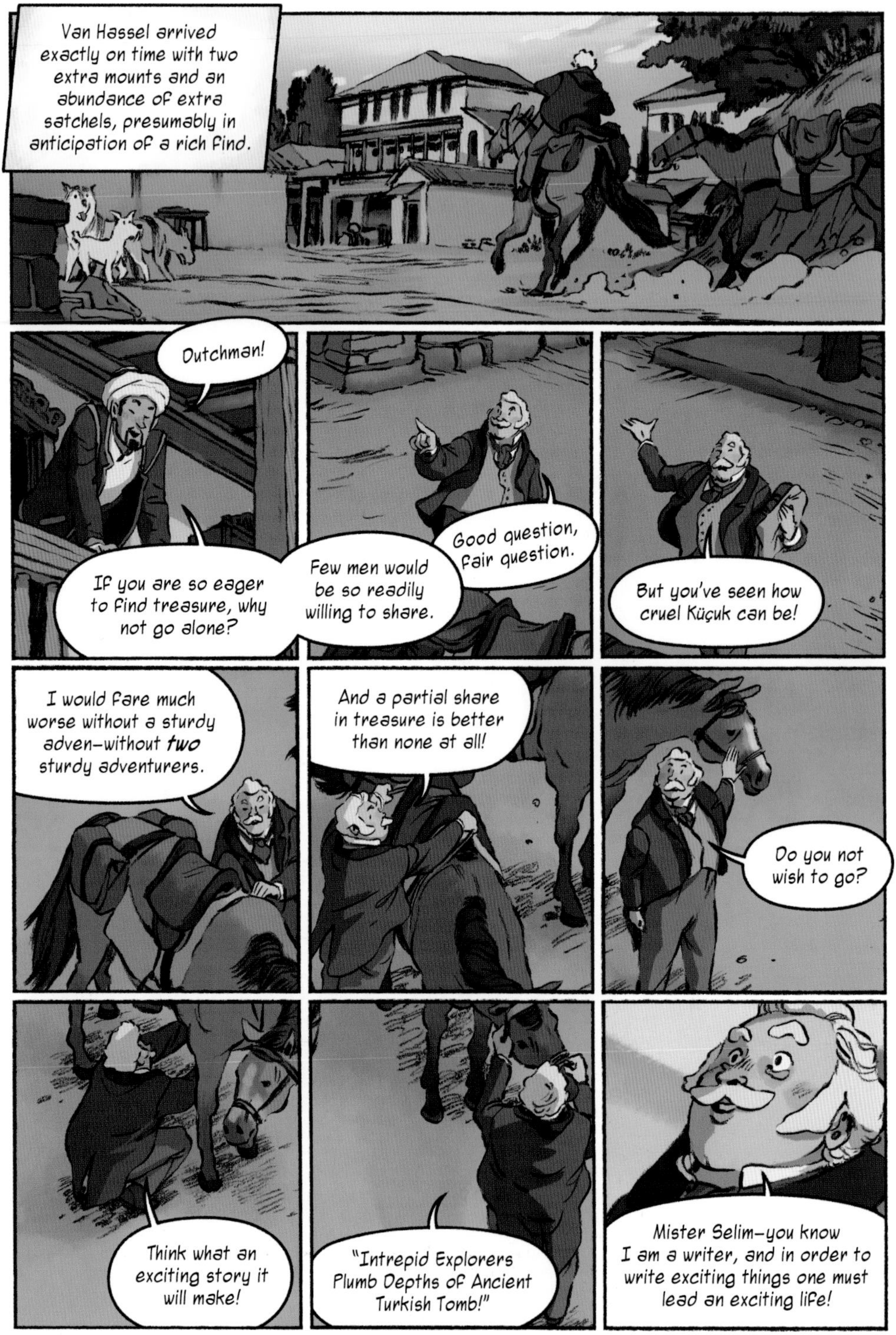

Van Hassel arrived exactly on time with two extra mounts and an abundance of extra satchels, presumably in anticipation of a rich find.
Dutchman!
If you are so eager to find treasure, why not go alone?
Few men would be so readily willing to share.
Good question, fair question.
But you've seen how cruel Küçuk can be!
I would fare much worse without a sturdy adven–without **two** sturdy adventurers.
And a partial share in treasure is better than none at all!
Do you not wish to go?
Think what an exciting story it will make!
"Intrepid Explorers Plumb Depths of Ancient Turkish Tomb!"
Mister Selim–you know I am a writer, and in order to write exciting things one must lead an exciting life!

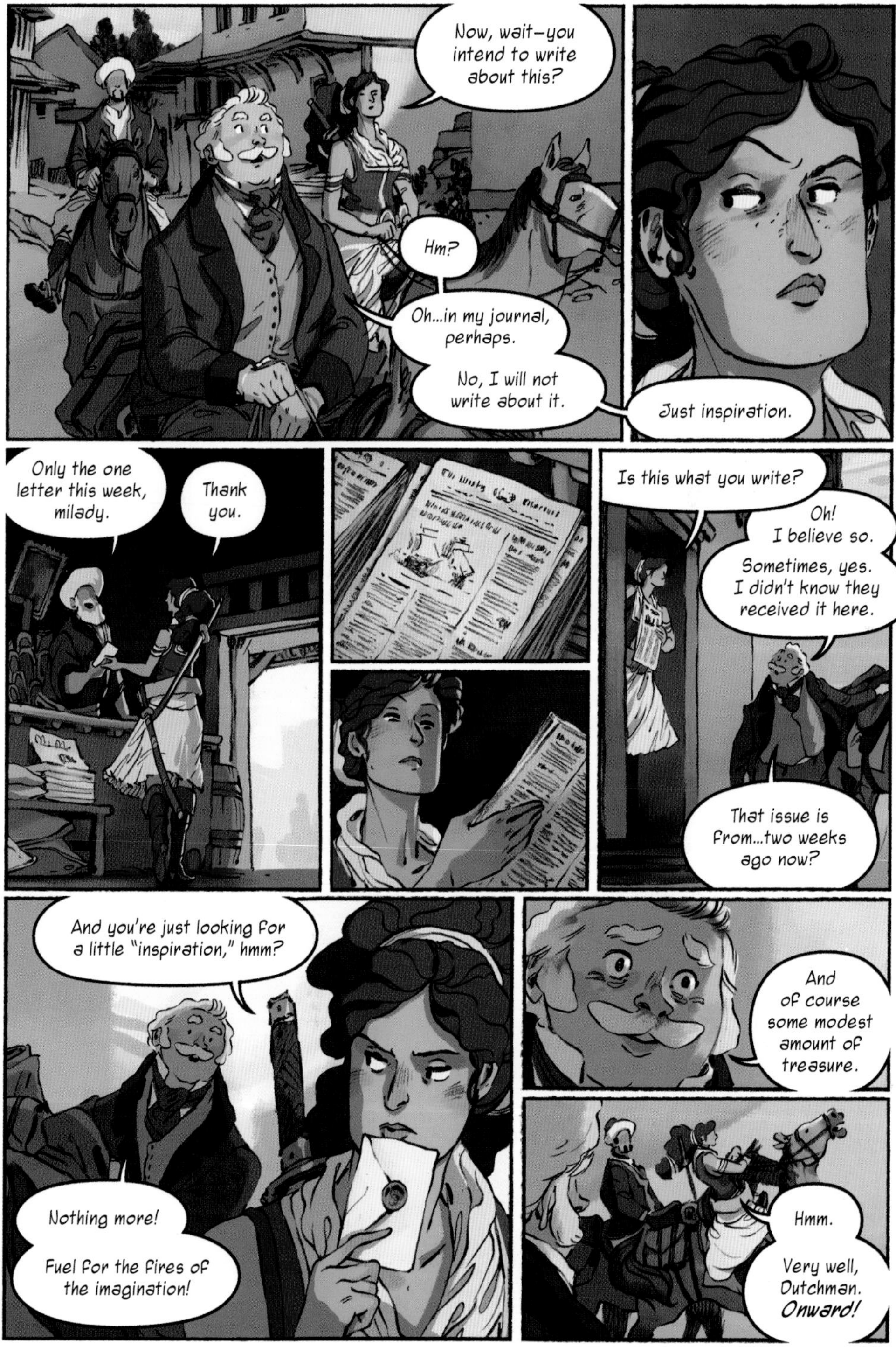
Now, wait—you intend to write about this?
Hm?
Oh...in my journal, perhaps.
No, I will not write about it.
Just inspiration.
Only the one letter this week, milady.
Thank you.
Is this what you write?
Oh! I believe so.
Sometimes, yes. I didn't know they received it here.
That issue is from...two weeks ago now?
And you're just looking for a little "inspiration," hmm?
Nothing more!
Fuel for the fires of the imagination!
And of course some modest amount of treasure.
Hmm.
Very well, Dutchman. *Onward!*

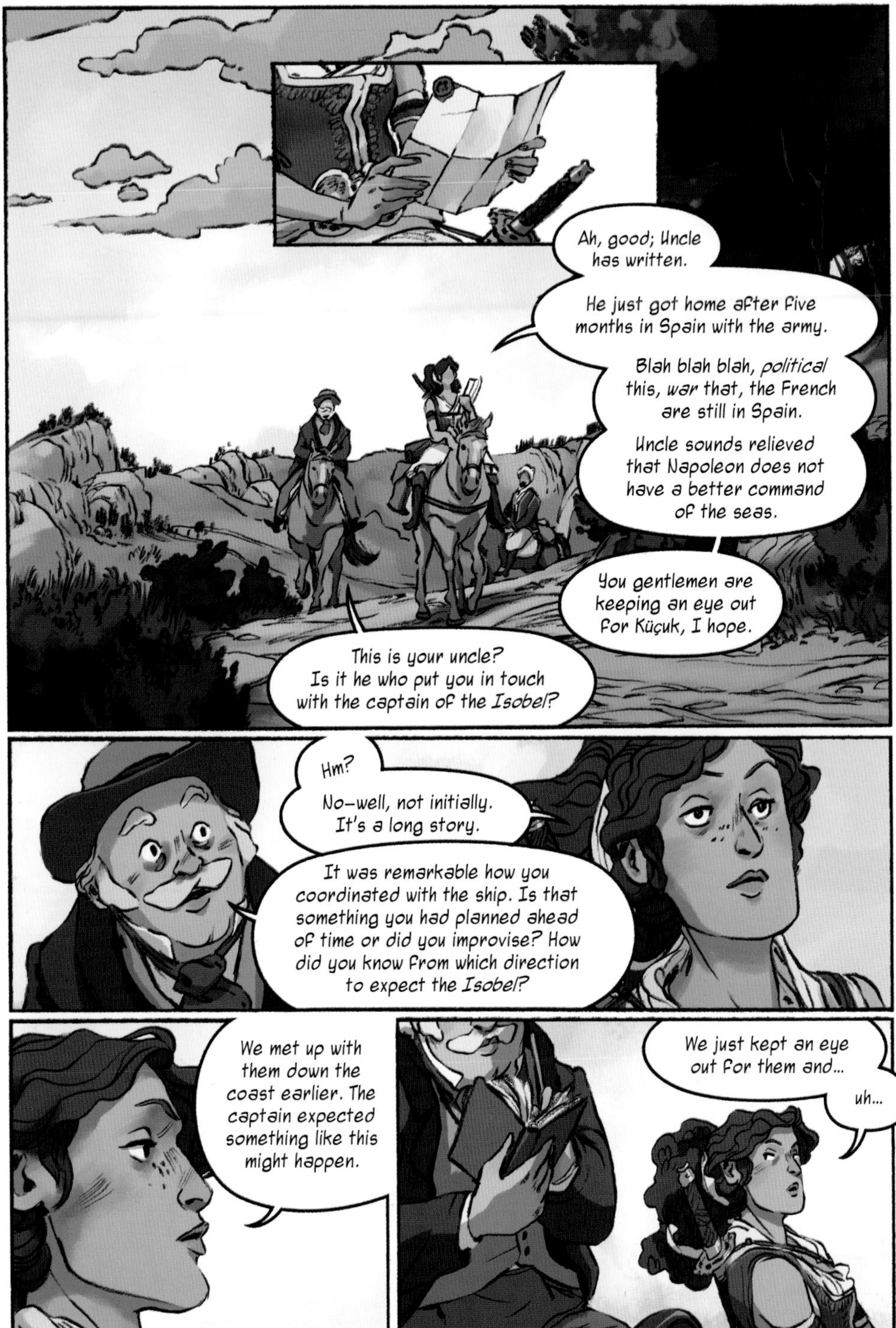

Ah, good; Uncle has written.
He just got home after five months in Spain with the army.
Blah blah blah, *political* this, *war* that, the French are still in Spain.
Uncle sounds relieved that Napoleon does not have a better command of the seas.
You gentlemen are keeping an eye out for Küçuk, I hope.
This is your uncle? Is it he who put you in touch with the captain of the *Isobel*?
Hm?
No—well, not initially. It's a long story.
It was remarkable how you coordinated with the ship. Is that something you had planned ahead of time or did you improvise? How did you know from which direction to expect the *Isobel*?
We met up with them down the coast earlier. The captain expected something like this might happen.
We just kept an eye out for them and...
uh...

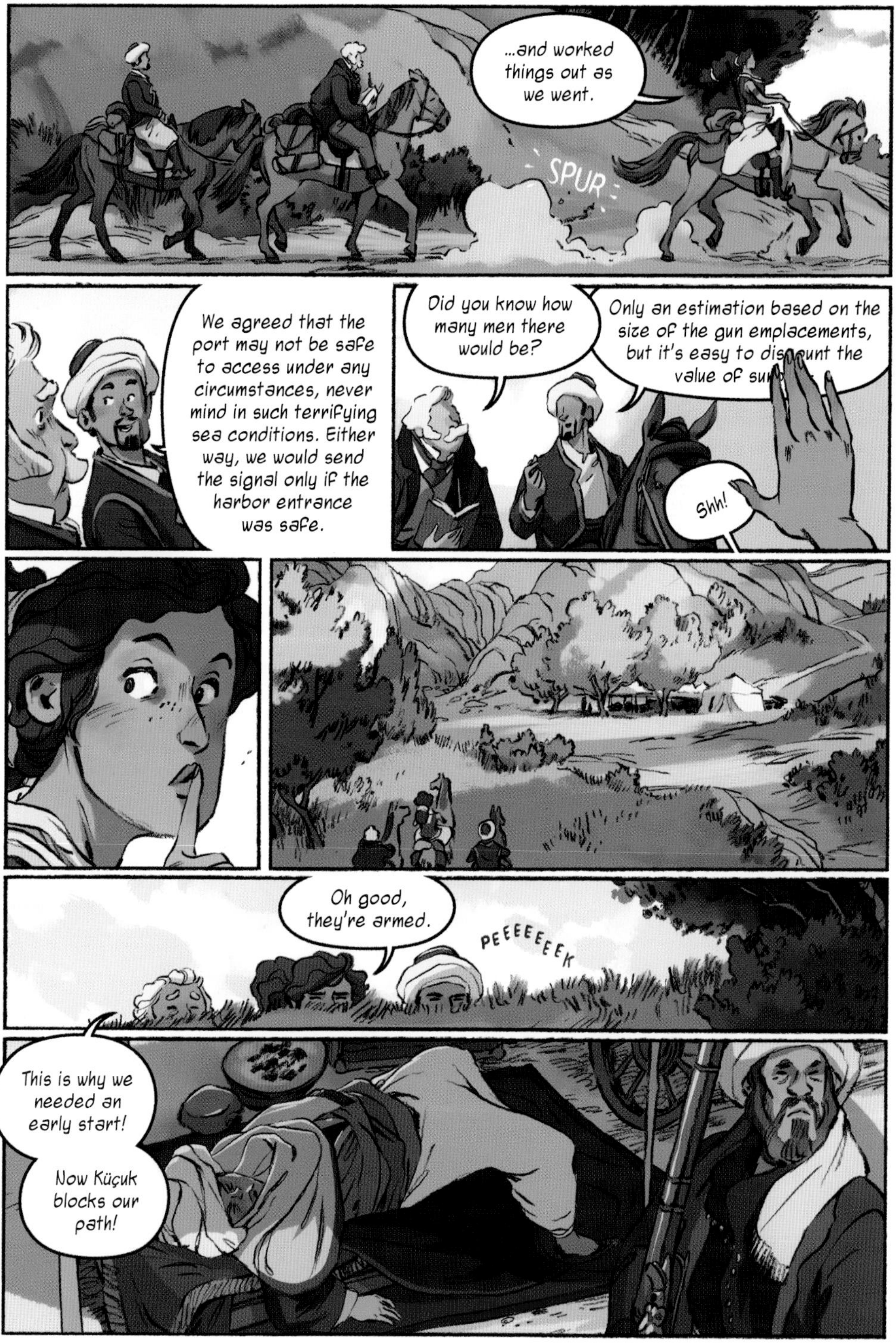
...and worked things out as we went.
SPUR
We agreed that the port may not be safe to access under any circumstances, never mind in such terrifying sea conditions. Either way, we would send the signal only if the harbor entrance was safe.
Did you know how many men there would be?
Only an estimation based on the size of the gun emplacements, but it's easy to dis unt the value of su
Shh!
Oh good, they're armed.
PEEEEEEEK
This is why we needed an early start!
Now Küçuk blocks our path!

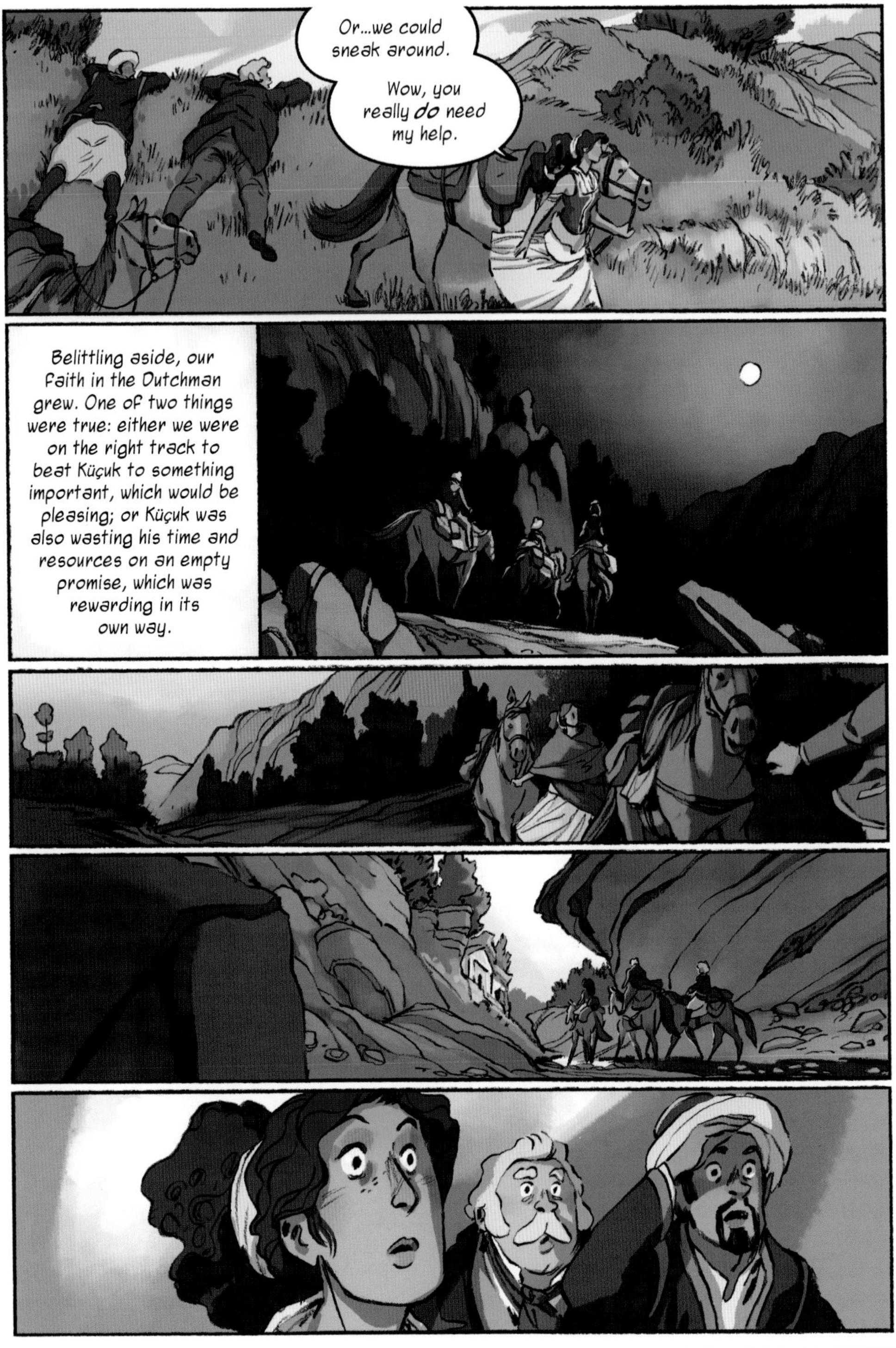
Or...we could sneak around.
Wow, you really *do* need my help.
Belittling aside, our faith in the Dutchman grew. One of two things were true: either we were on the right track to beat Küçuk to something important, which would be pleasing; or Küçuk was also wasting his time and resources on an empty promise, which was rewarding in its own way.

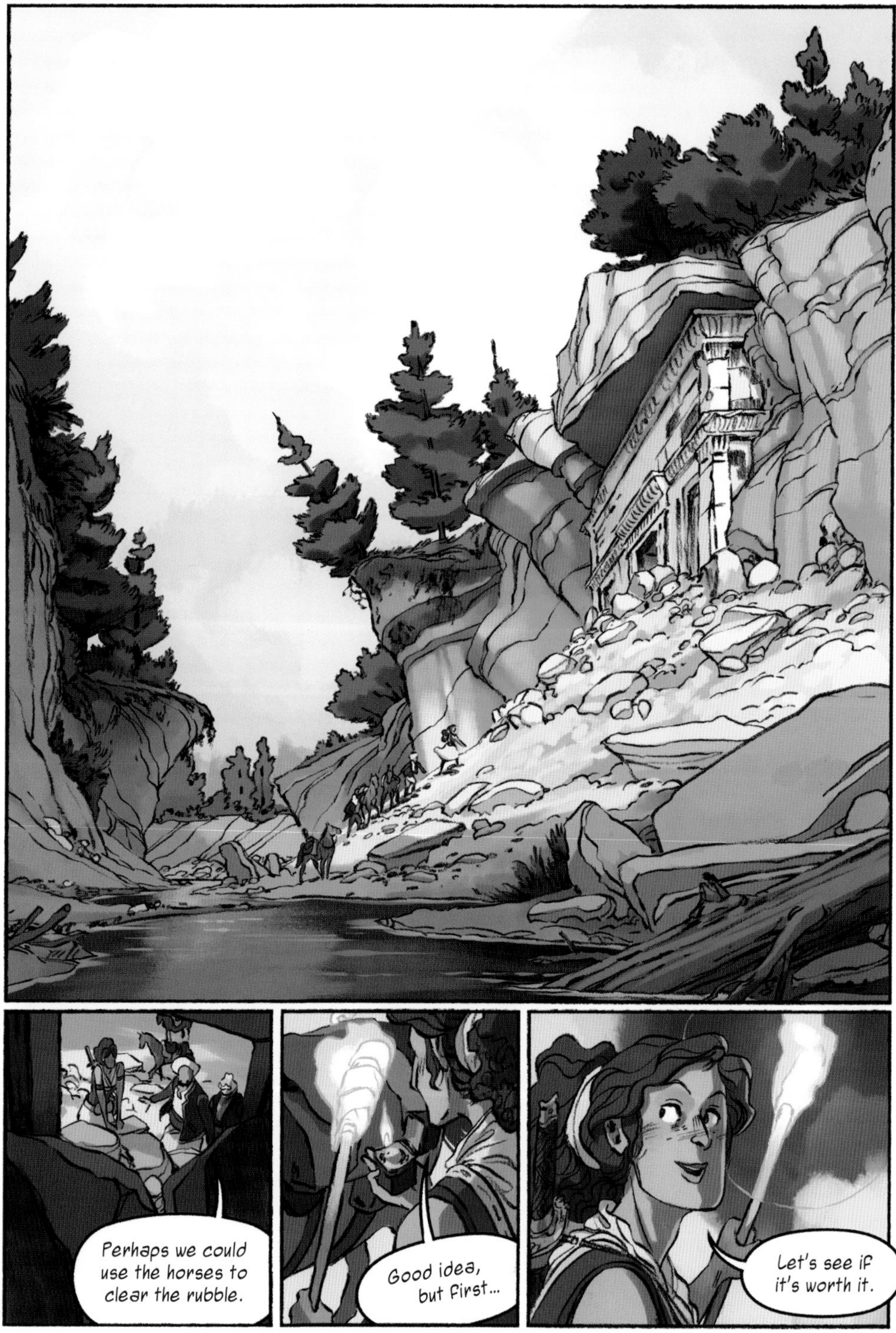
Perhaps we could use the horses to clear the rubble.
Good idea, but first...
Let's see if it's worth it.

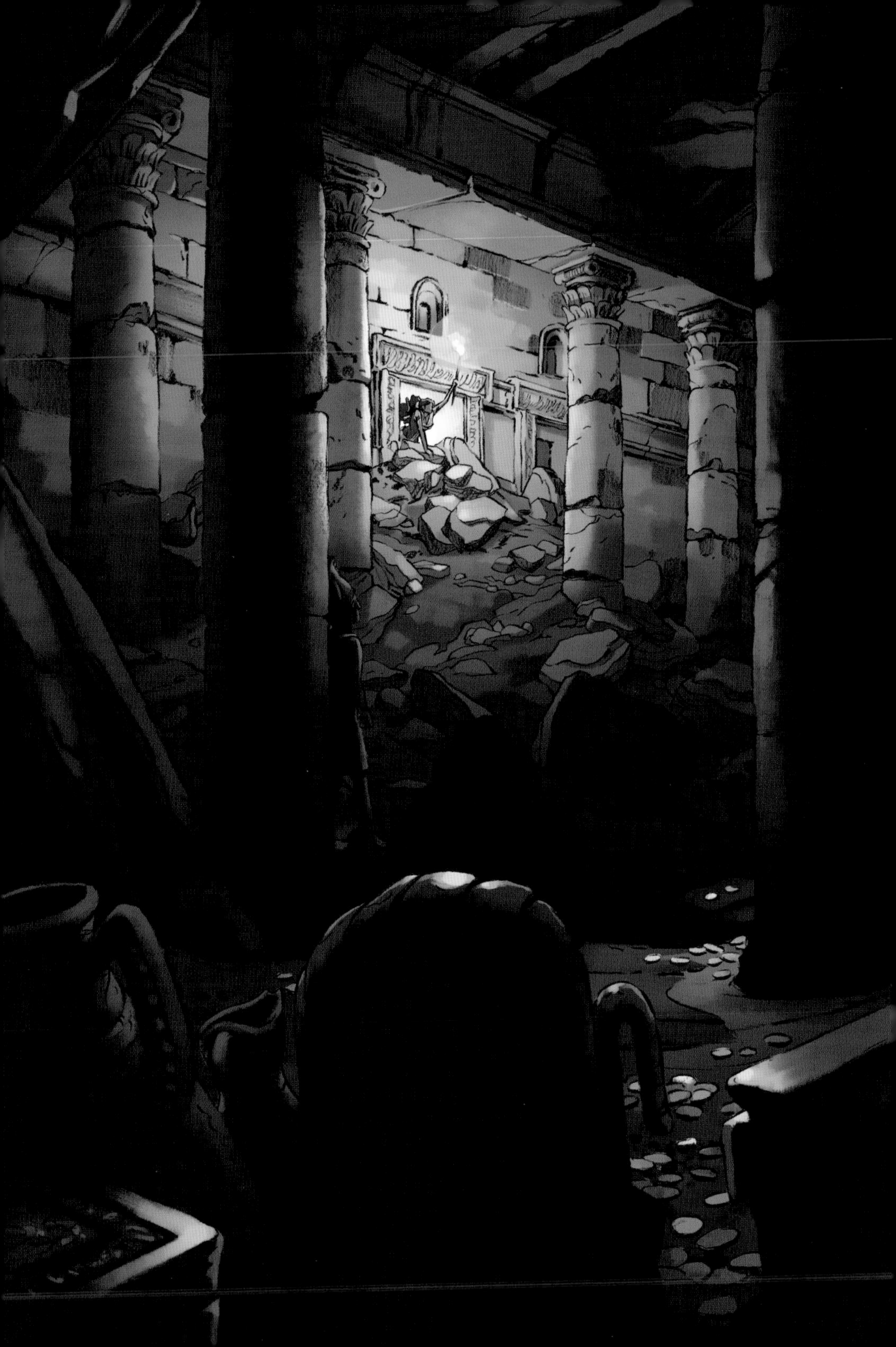

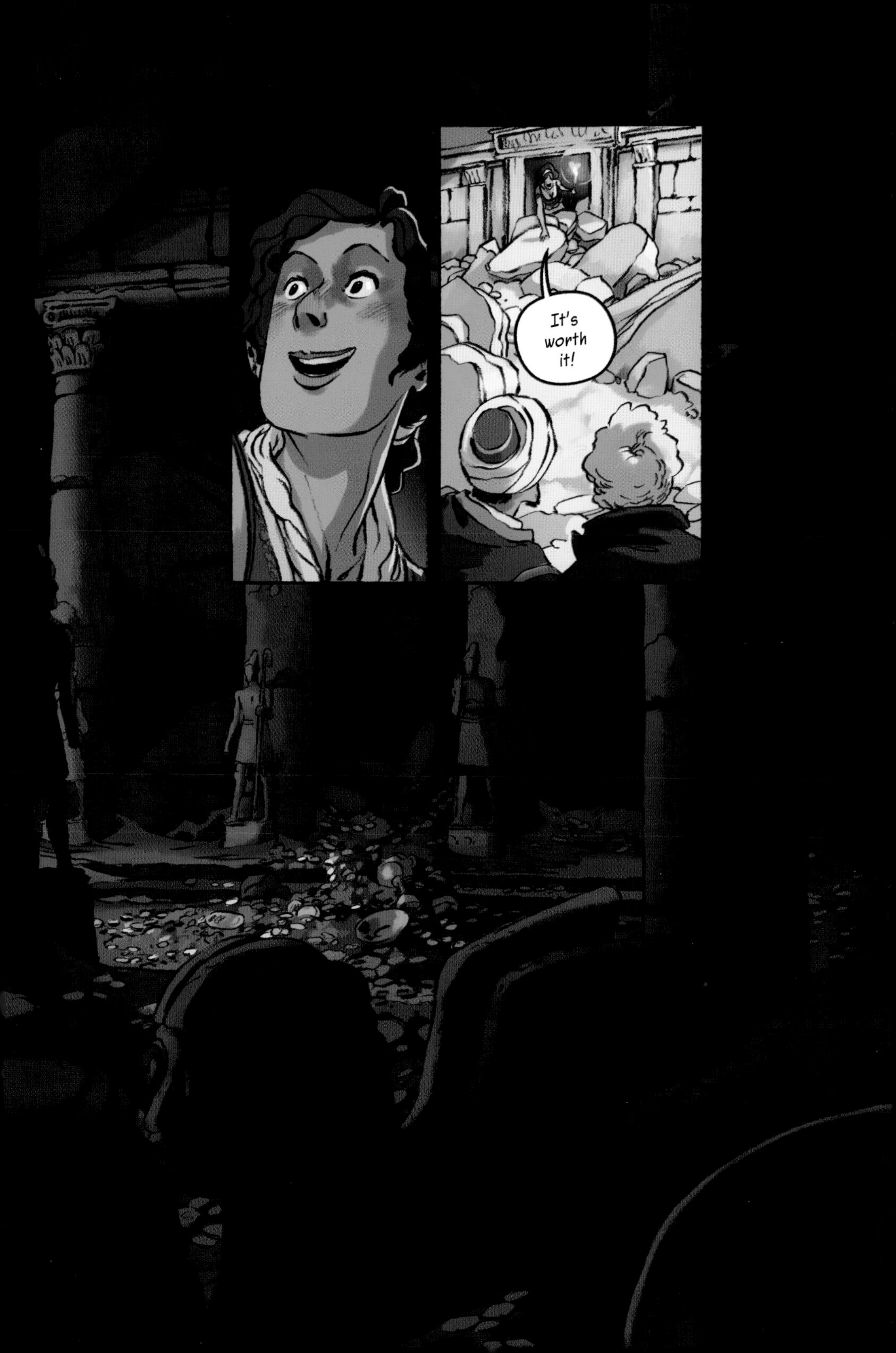
It's worth it!

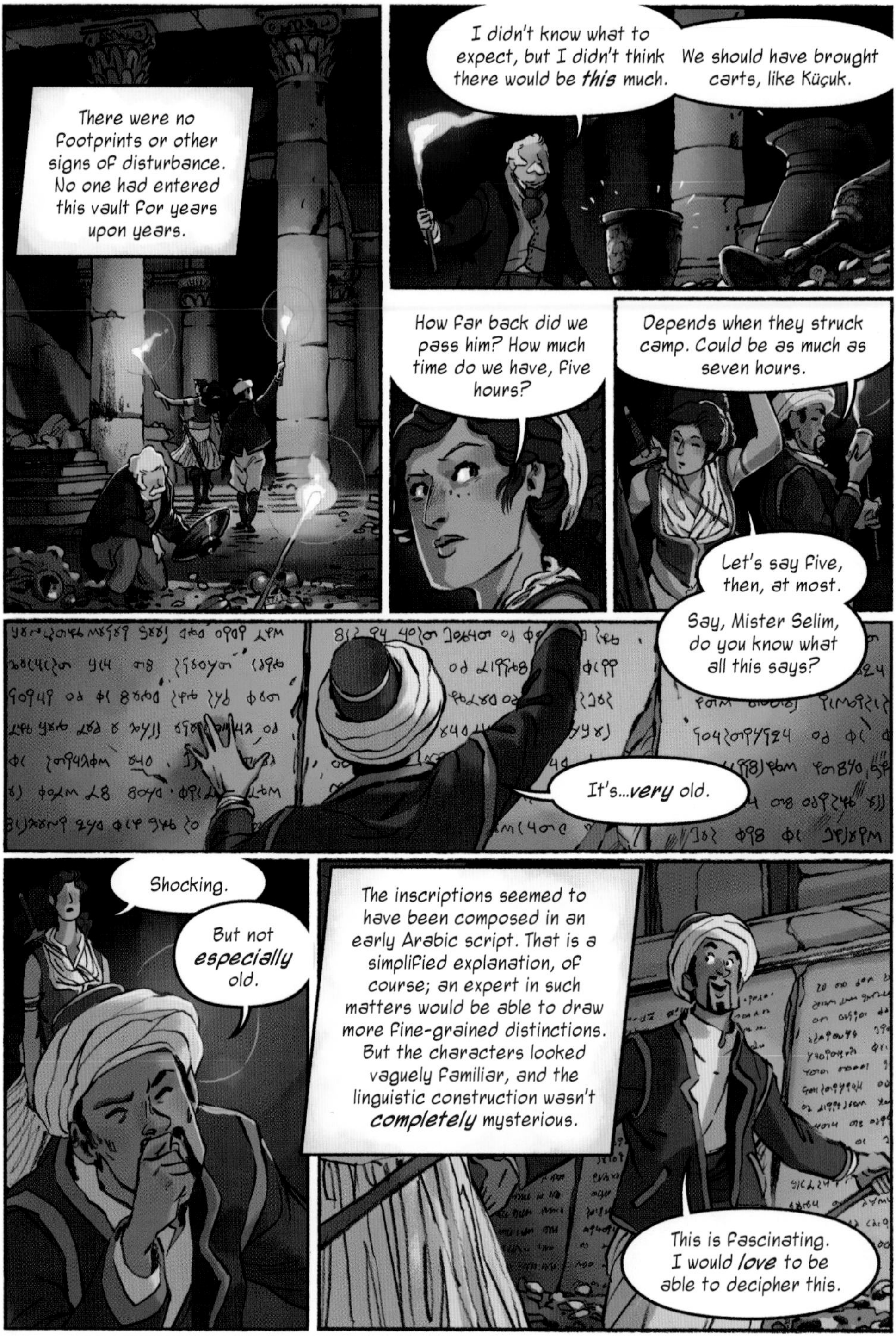
There were no footprints or other signs of disturbance. No one had entered this vault for years upon years.
I didn't know what to expect, but I didn't think there would be *this* much.
We should have brought carts, like Küçuk.
How far back did we pass him? How much time do we have, five hours?
Depends when they struck camp. Could be as much as seven hours.
Let's say five, then, at most.
Say, Mister Selim, do you know what all this says?
It's...*very* old.
Shocking.
But not *especially* old.
The inscriptions seemed to have been composed in an early Arabic script. That is a simplified explanation, of course; an expert in such matters would be able to draw more fine-grained distinctions. But the characters looked vaguely familiar, and the linguistic construction wasn't *completely* mysterious.
This is fascinating. I would *love* to be able to decipher this.

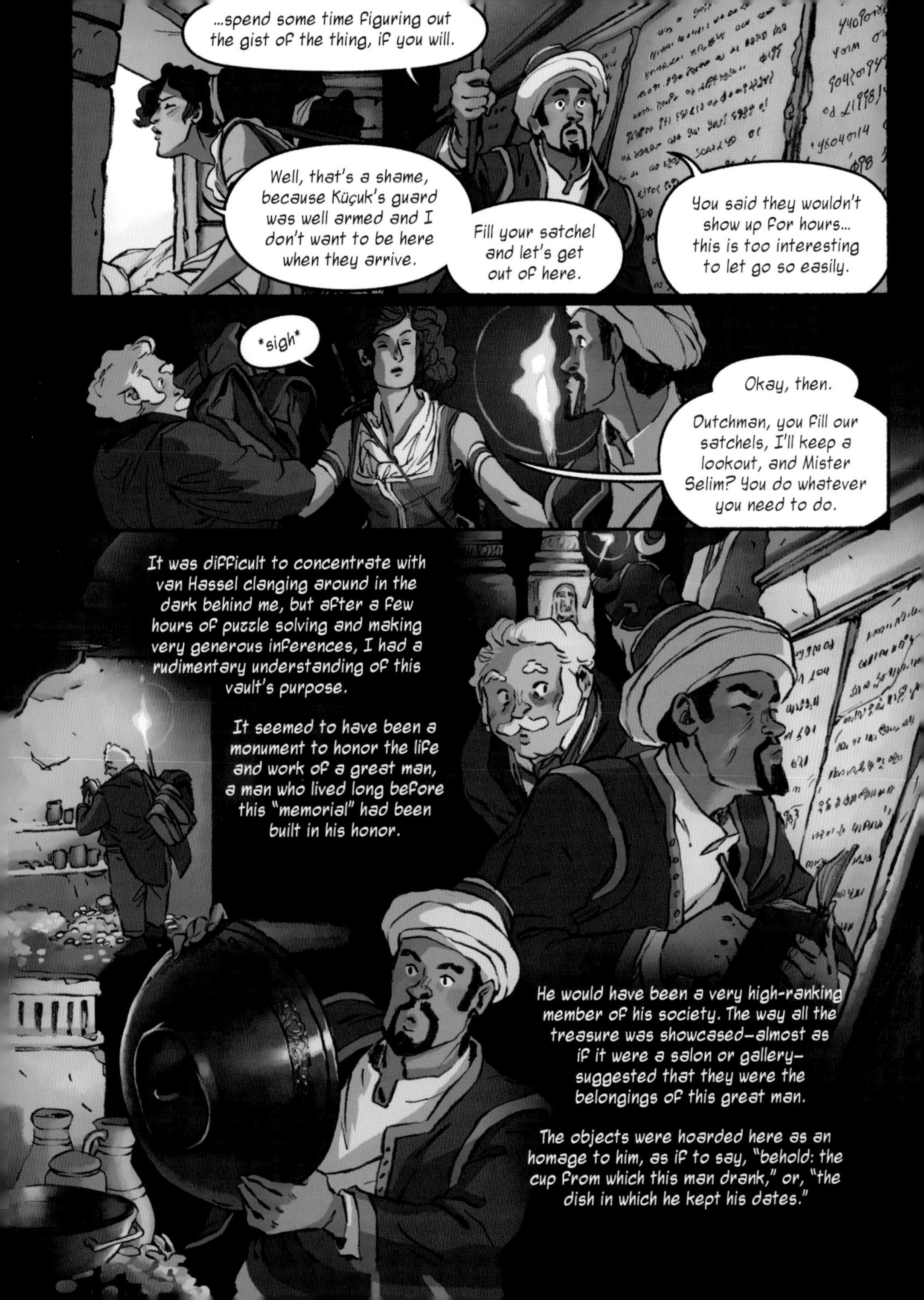
...spend some time figuring out the gist of the thing, if you will.
Well, that's a shame, because Küçuk's guard was well armed and I don't want to be here when they arrive.
Fill your satchel and let's get out of here.
You said they wouldn't show up for hours... this is too interesting to let go so easily.
*sigh*
Okay, then.
Dutchman, you fill our satchels, I'll keep a lookout, and Mister Selim? You do whatever you need to do.
It was difficult to concentrate with van Hassel clanging around in the dark behind me, but after a few hours of puzzle solving and making very generous inferences, I had a rudimentary understanding of this vault's purpose.
It seemed to have been a monument to honor the life and work of a great man, a man who lived long before this "memorial" had been built in his honor.
He would have been a very high-ranking member of his society. The way all the treasure was showcased—almost as if it were a salon or gallery—suggested that they were the belongings of this great man.
The objects were hoarded here as an homage to him, as if to say, "behold: the cup from which this man drank," or, "the dish in which he kept his dates."

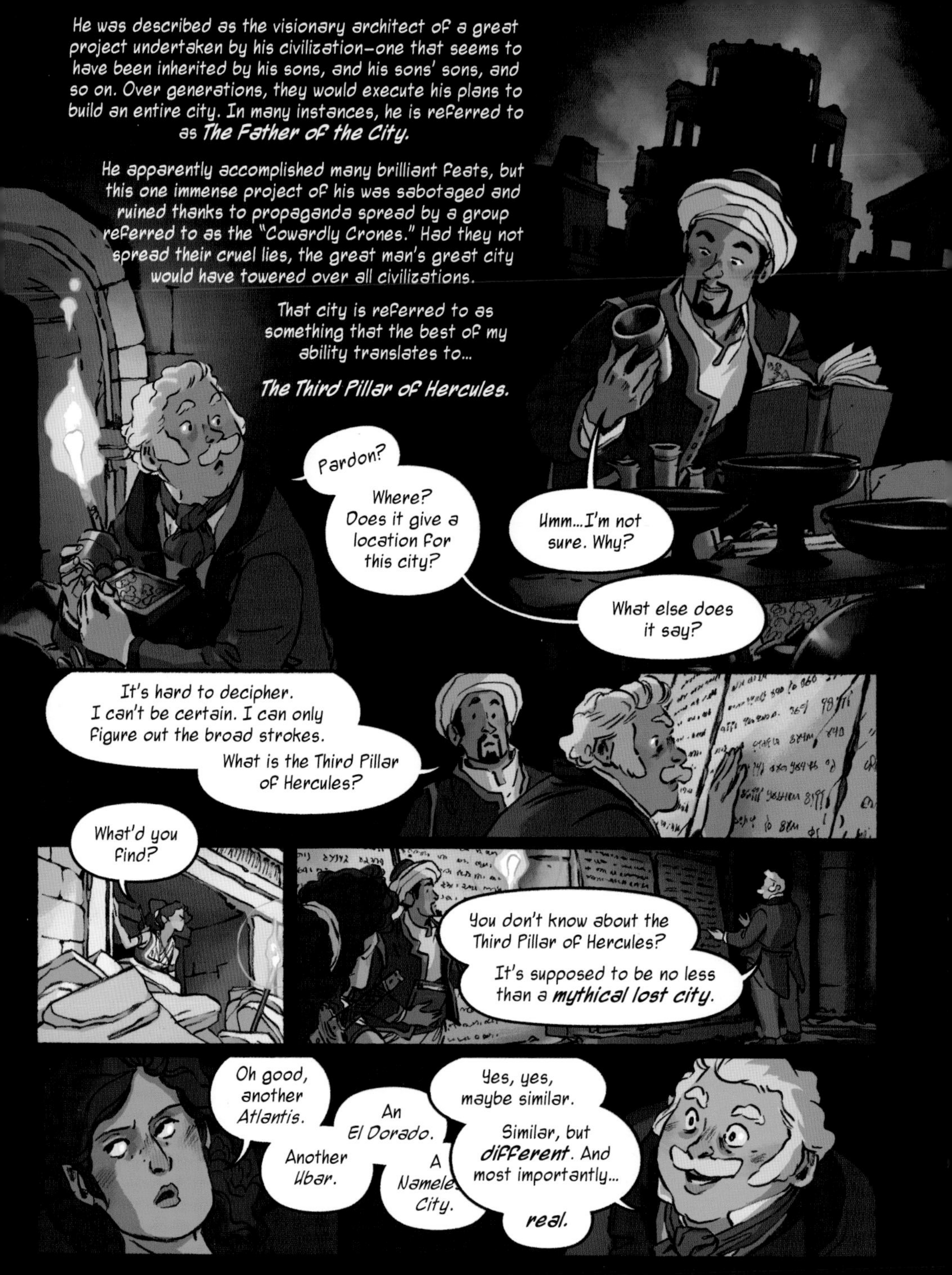
He was described as the visionary architect of a great project undertaken by his civilization—one that seems to have been inherited by his sons, and his sons' sons, and so on. Over generations, they would execute his plans to build an entire city. In many instances, he is referred to as *The Father of the City.*
He apparently accomplished many brilliant feats, but this one immense project of his was sabotaged and ruined thanks to propaganda spread by a group referred to as the "Cowardly Crones." Had they not spread their cruel lies, the great man's great city would have towered over all civilizations.
That city is referred to as something that the best of my ability translates to...
*The Third Pillar of Hercules.*
Pardon?
Where? Does it give a location for this city?
Umm...I'm not sure. Why?
What else does it say?
It's hard to decipher. I can't be certain. I can only figure out the broad strokes.
What is the Third Pillar of Hercules?
What'd you find?
You don't know about the Third Pillar of Hercules?
It's supposed to be no less than a ***mythical lost city***.
Oh good, another *Atlantis*.
An *El Dorado*.
Another *Ubar*.
A *Nameless City*.
Yes, yes, maybe similar.
Similar, but ***different***. And most importantly...
***real.***

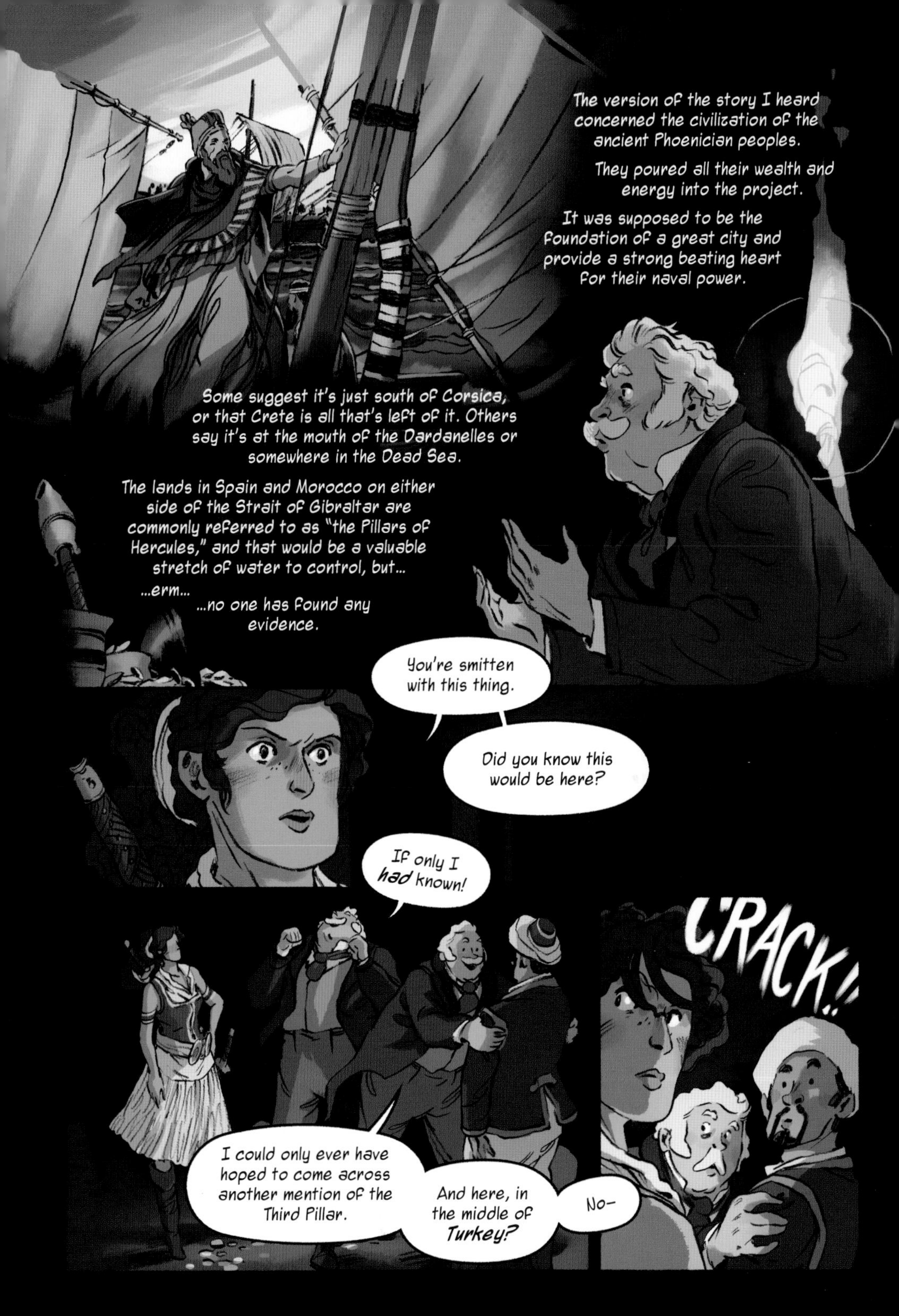

The version of the story I heard concerned the civilization of the ancient Phoenician peoples.
They poured all their wealth and energy into the project.
It was supposed to be the foundation of a great city and provide a strong beating heart for their naval power.
Some suggest it's just south of Corsica, or that Crete is all that's left of it. Others say it's at the mouth of the Dardanelles or somewhere in the Dead Sea.
The lands in Spain and Morocco on either side of the Strait of Gibraltar are commonly referred to as "the Pillars of Hercules," and that would be a valuable stretch of water to control, but...
...erm...
...no one has found any evidence.
You're smitten with this thing.
Did you know this would be here?
If only I *had* known!
I could only ever have hoped to come across another mention of the Third Pillar.
And here, in the middle of *Turkey?*
No–
CRACK!!

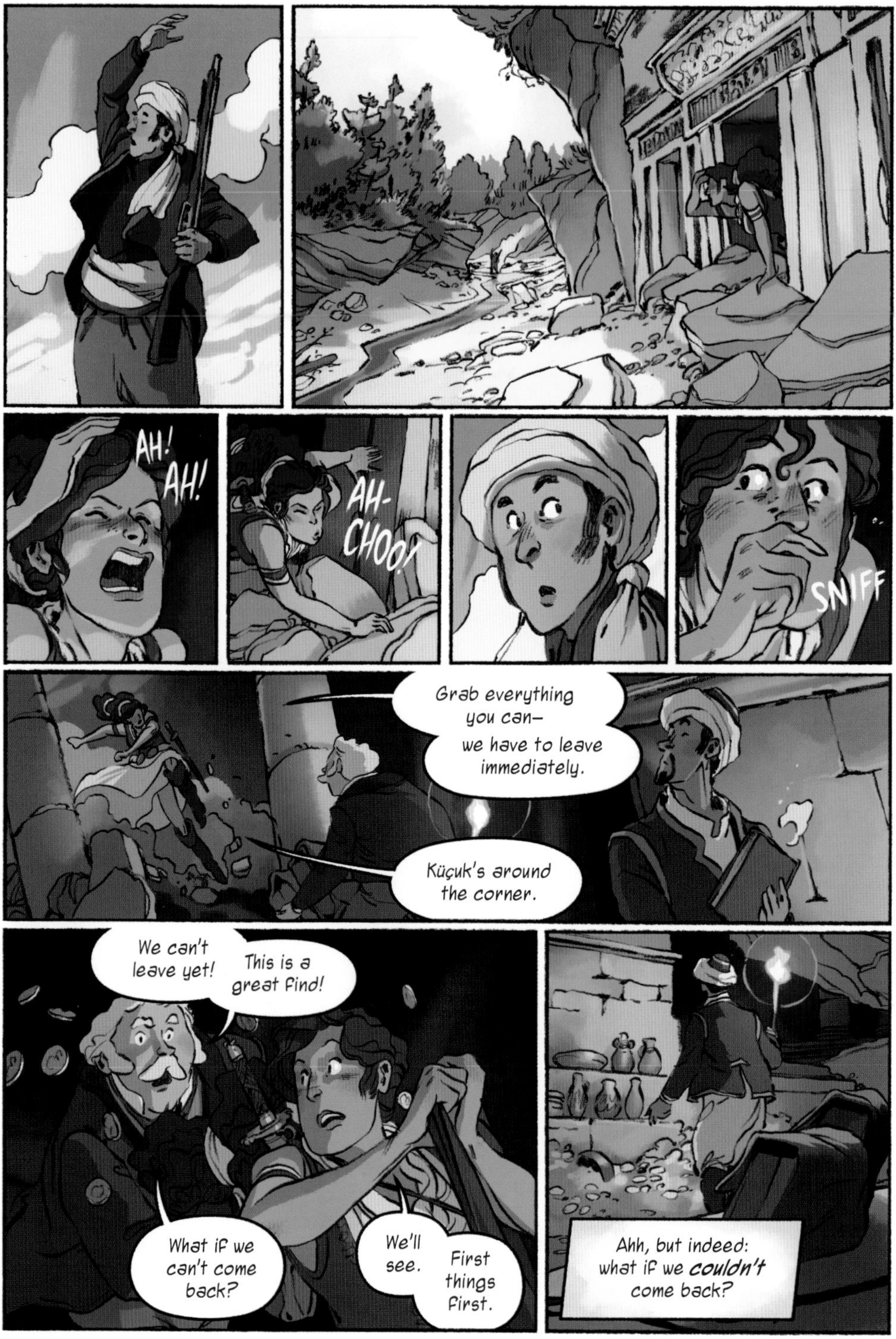

AH! AH!
AH-CHOO!
SNIFF
Grab everything you can—
we have to leave immediately.
Küçuk's around the corner.
We can't leave yet!
This is a great find!
What if we can't come back?
We'll see.
First things first.
Ahh, but indeed: what if we *couldn't* come back?

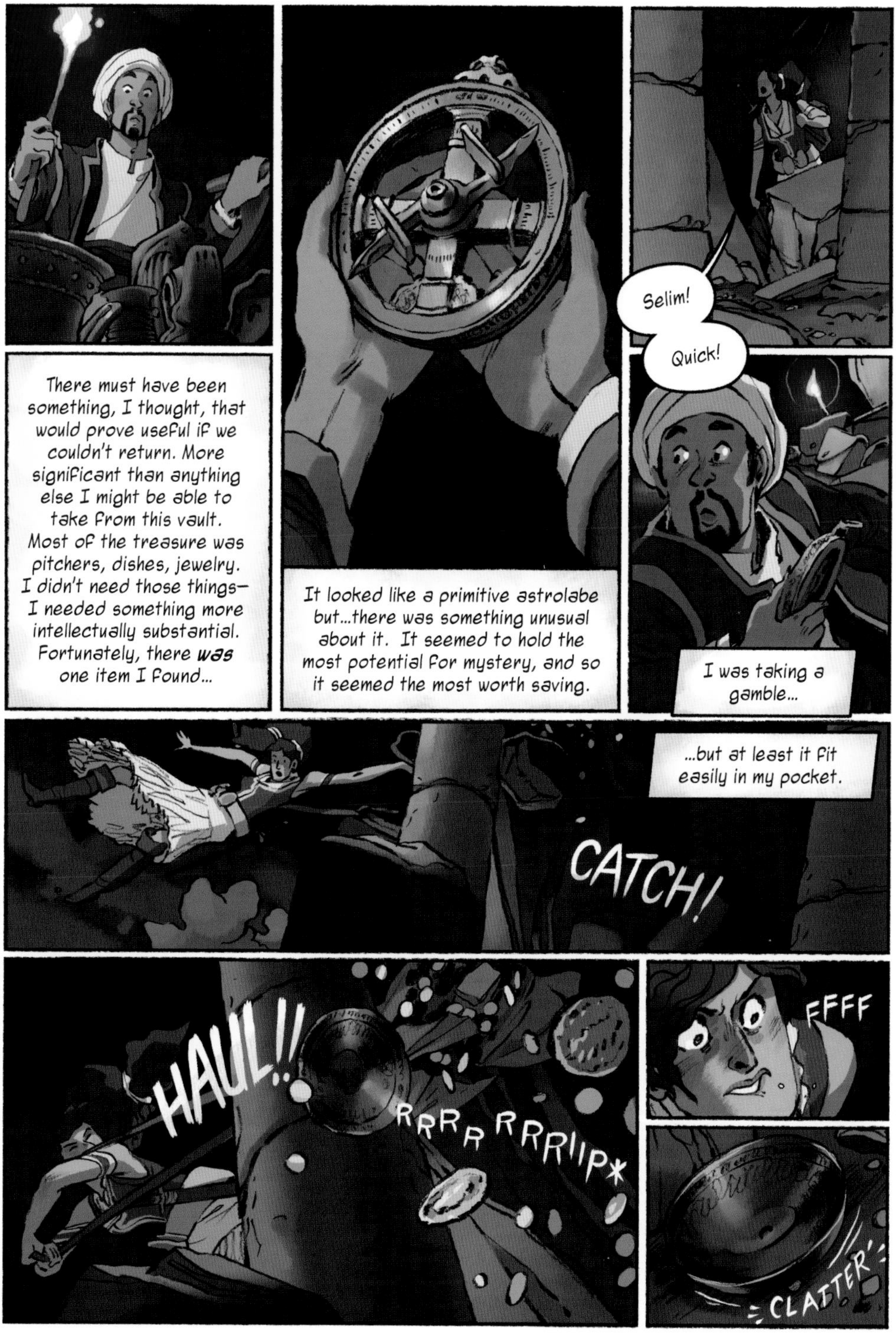
There must have been something, I thought, that would prove useful if we couldn't return. More significant than anything else I might be able to take from this vault. Most of the treasure was pitchers, dishes, jewelry. I didn't need those things— I needed something more intellectually substantial. Fortunately, there *was* one item I found...
It looked like a primitive astrolabe but...there was something unusual about it. It seemed to hold the most potential for mystery, and so it seemed the most worth saving.
Selim!
Quick!
I was taking a gamble...
...but at least it fit easily in my pocket.
CATCH!
HAUL!!
RRRR RRRIIP*
FFFF
CLATTER

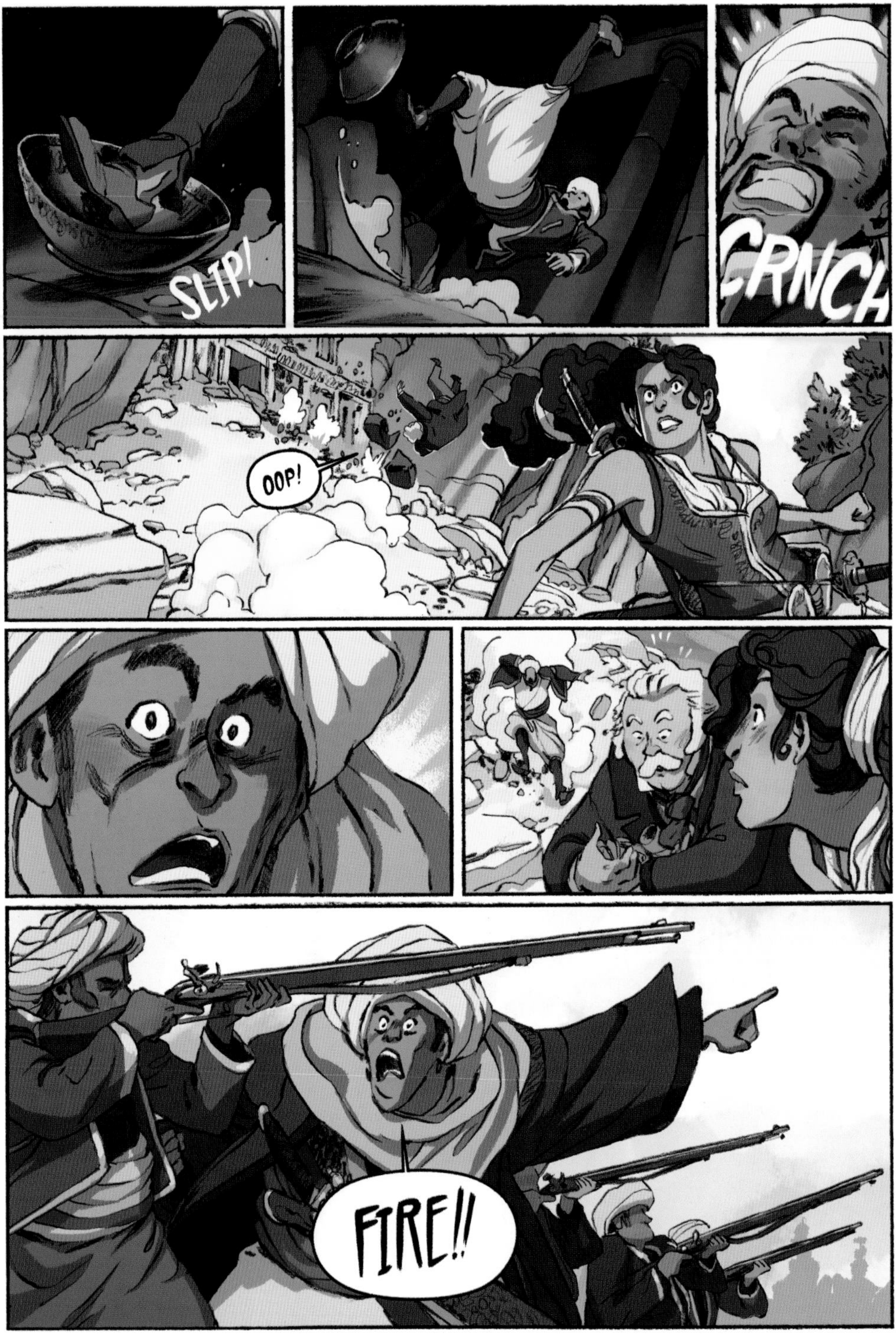
SLIP!
CRNCH
OOP!
FIRE!!

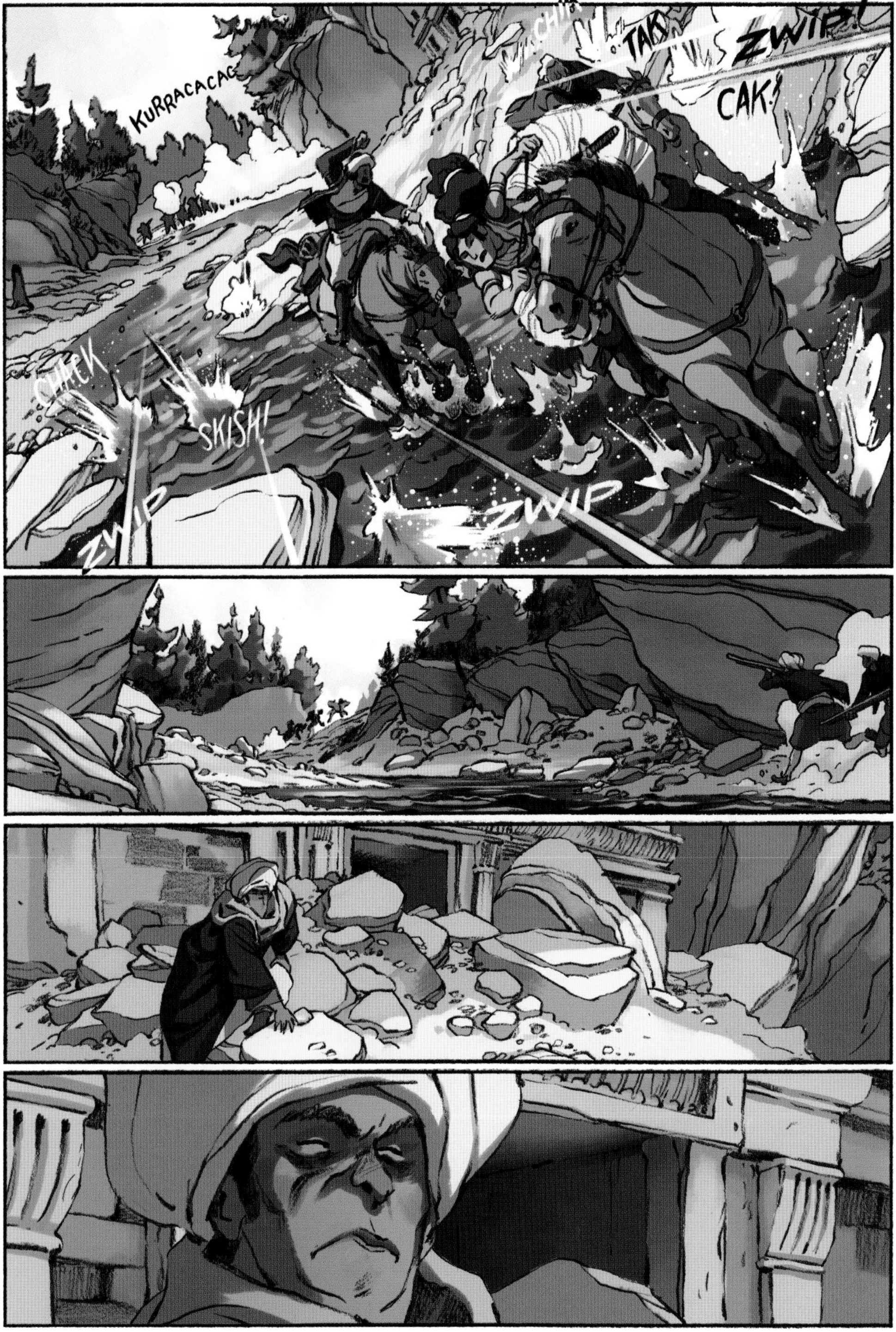
KURRACACAC
WHCHIK
TAK
ZWIP!
CAK!
CHACK
SKISH!
ZWIP
ZWIP

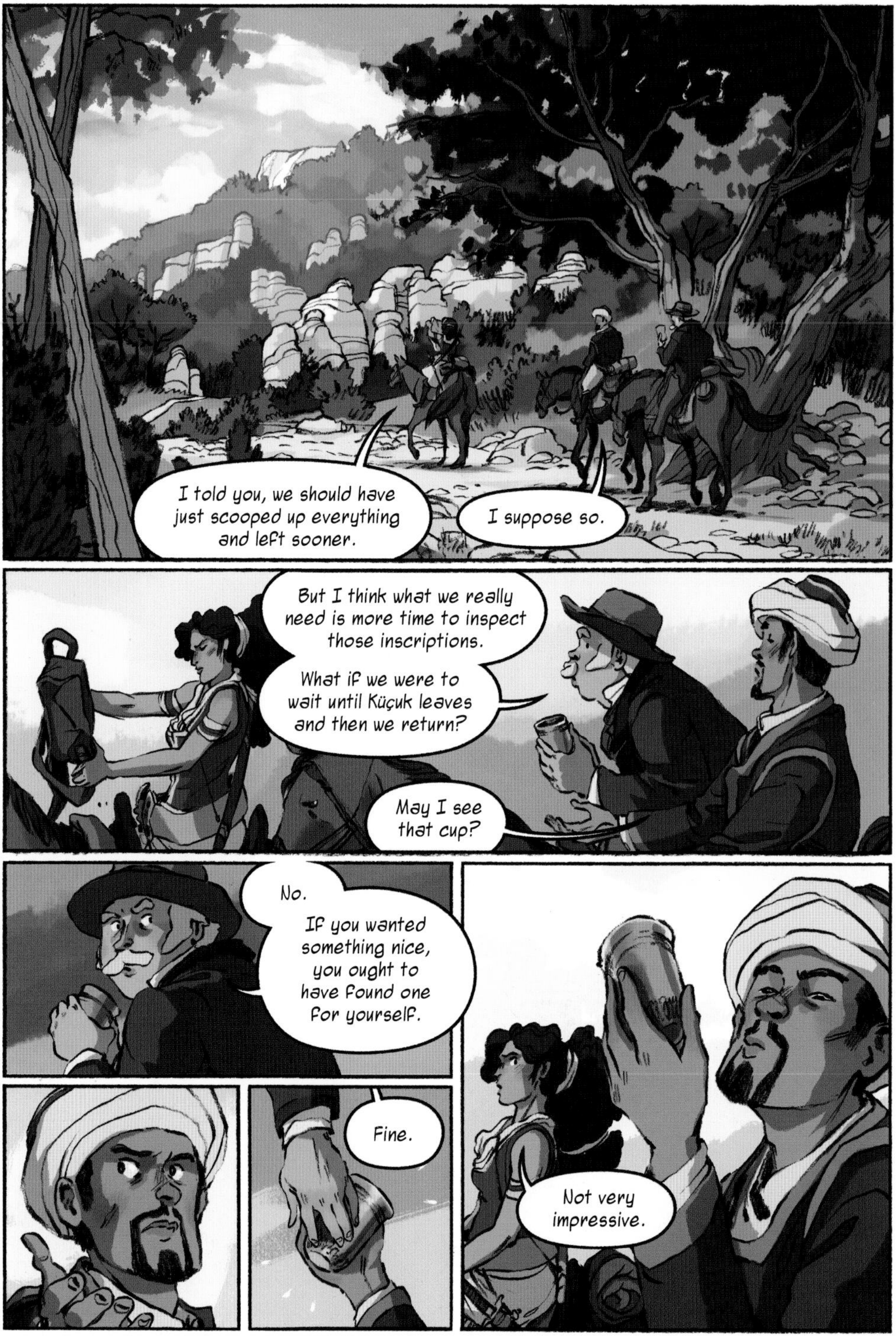
I told you, we should have just scooped up everything and left sooner.
I suppose so.
But I think what we really need is more time to inspect those inscriptions.
What if we were to wait until Küçuk leaves and then we return?
May I see that cup?
No.
If you wanted something nice, you ought to have found one for yourself.
Fine.
Not very impressive.

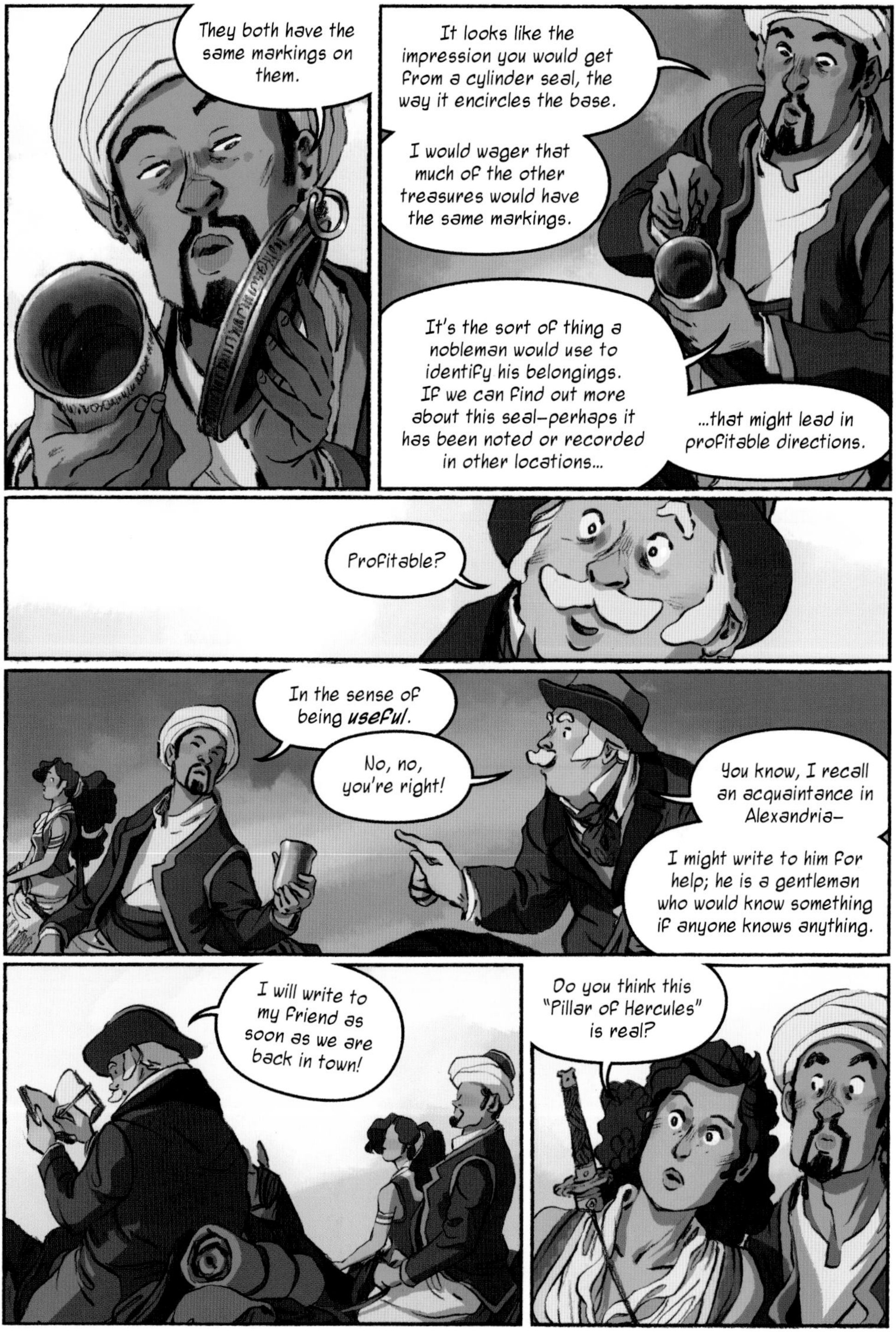
They both have the same markings on them.
It looks like the impression you would get from a cylinder seal, the way it encircles the base.
I would wager that much of the other treasures would have the same markings.
It's the sort of thing a nobleman would use to identify his belongings. If we can find out more about this seal—perhaps it has been noted or recorded in other locations...
...that might lead in profitable directions.
Profitable?
In the sense of being *useful*.
No, no, you're right!
You know, I recall an acquaintance in Alexandria—
I might write to him for help; he is a gentleman who would know something if anyone knows anything.
I will write to my friend as soon as we are back in town!
Do you think this "Pillar of Hercules" is real?

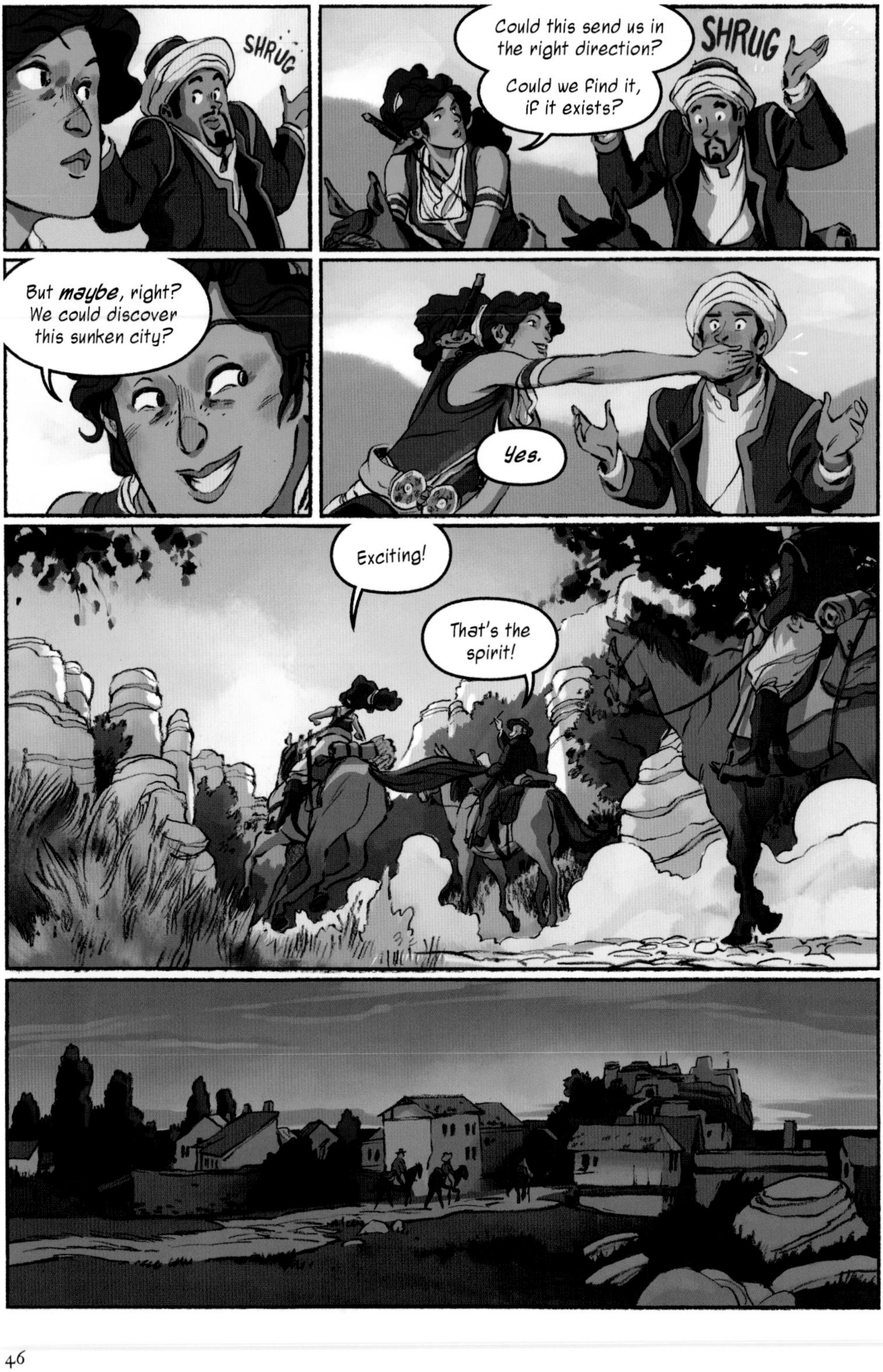
SHRUG
Could this send us in the right direction?
Could we find it, if it exists?
SHRUG
But *maybe*, right? We could discover this sunken city?
*Yes.*
Exciting!
That's the spirit!

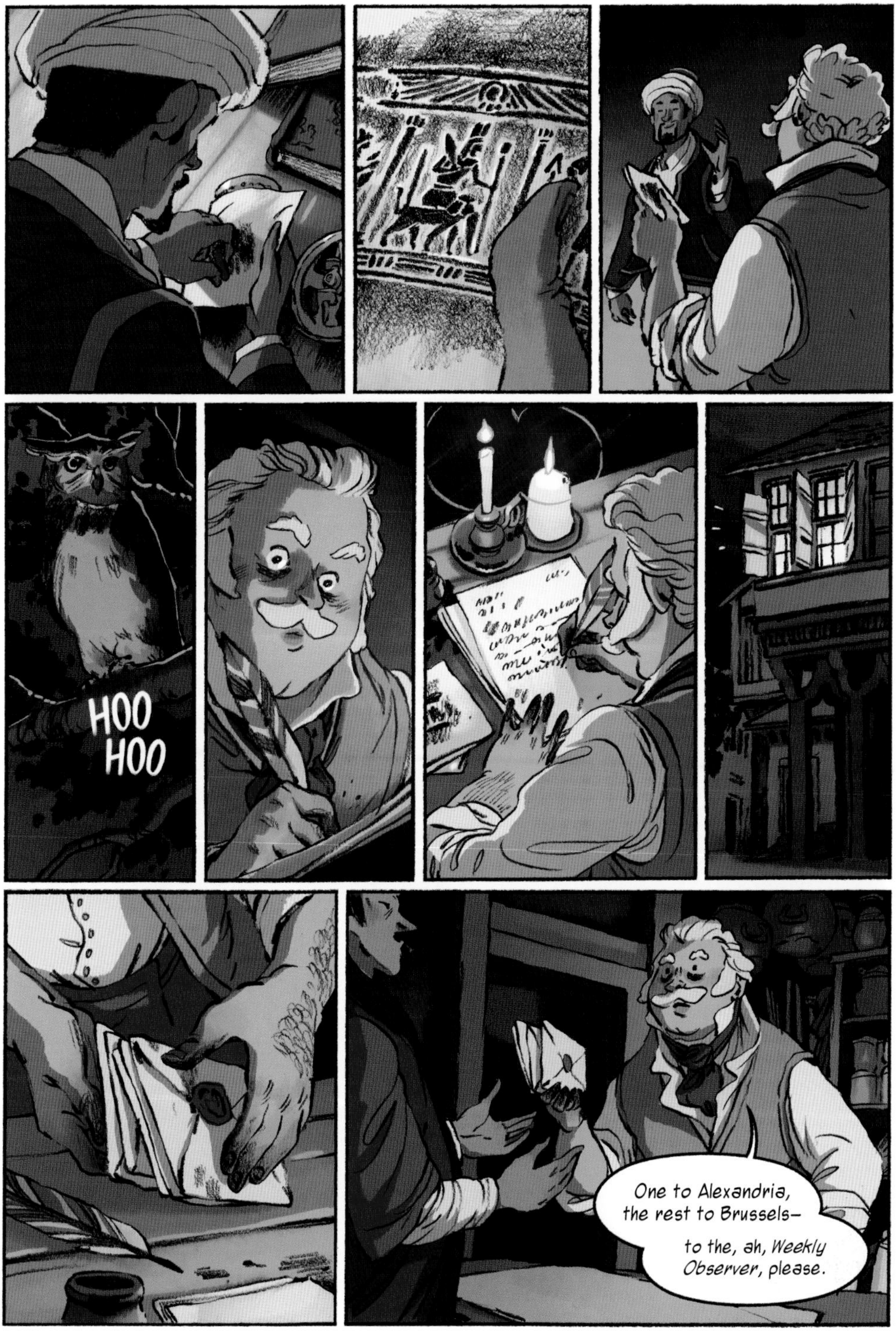
HOO
HOO
One to Alexandria,
the rest to Brussels—
to the, ah, *Weekly Observer*, please.

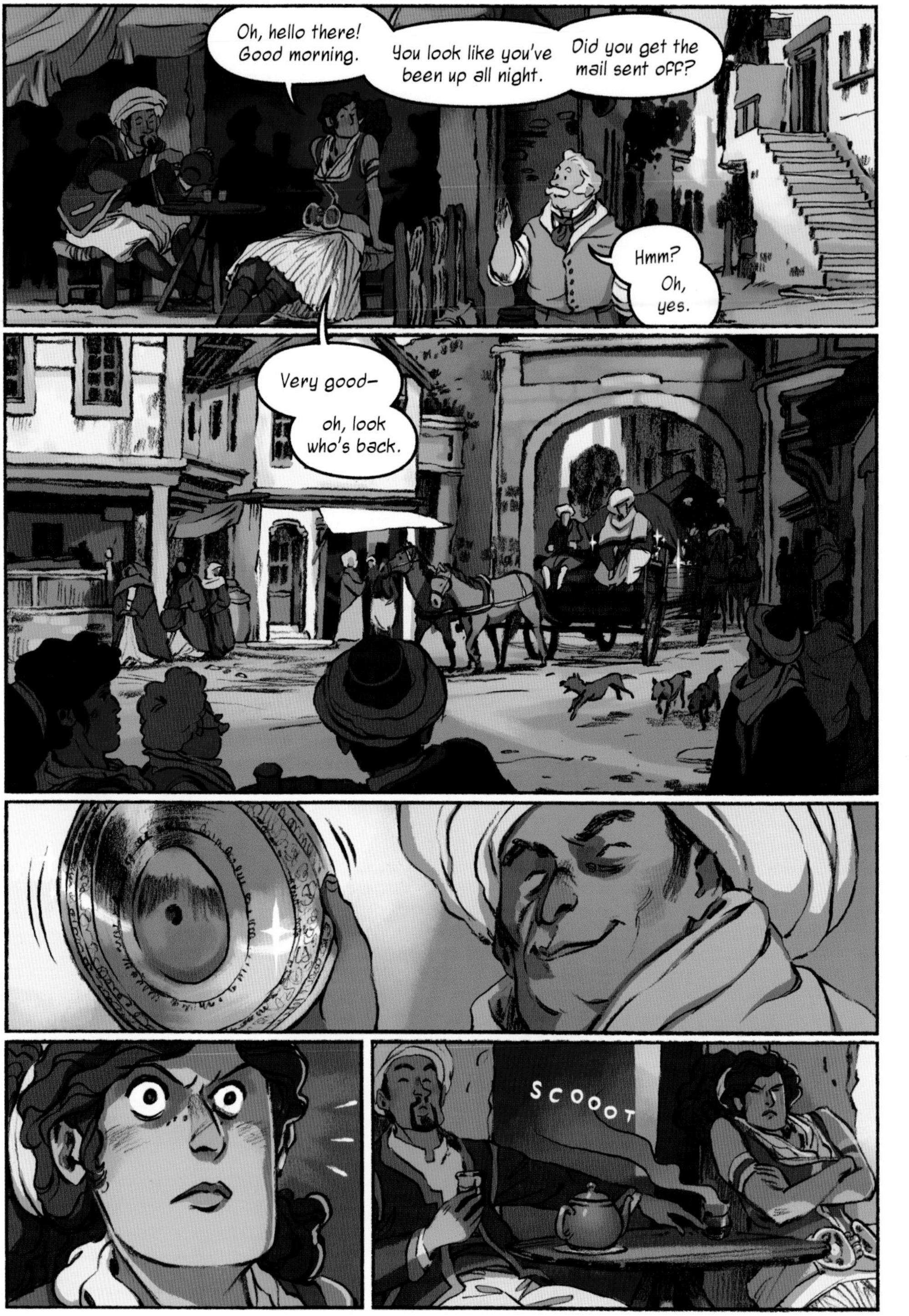
Oh, hello there! Good morning.
You look like you've been up all night.
Did you get the mail sent off?
Hmm? Oh, yes.
Very good—
oh, look who's back.
SCOOOT

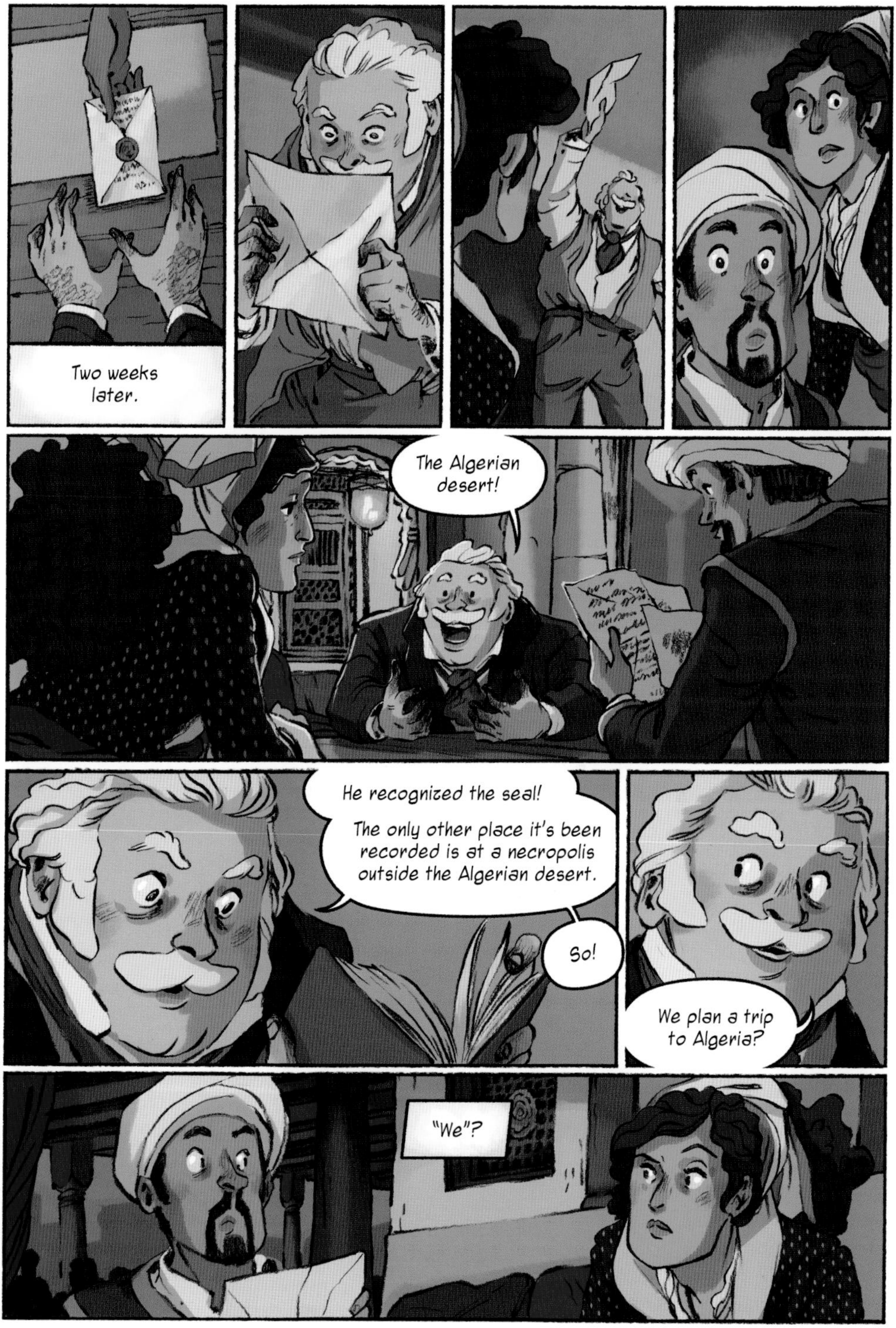
Two weeks later.
The Algerian desert!
He recognized the seal!
The only other place it's been recorded is at a necropolis outside the Algerian desert.
So!
We plan a trip to Algeria?
"We"?

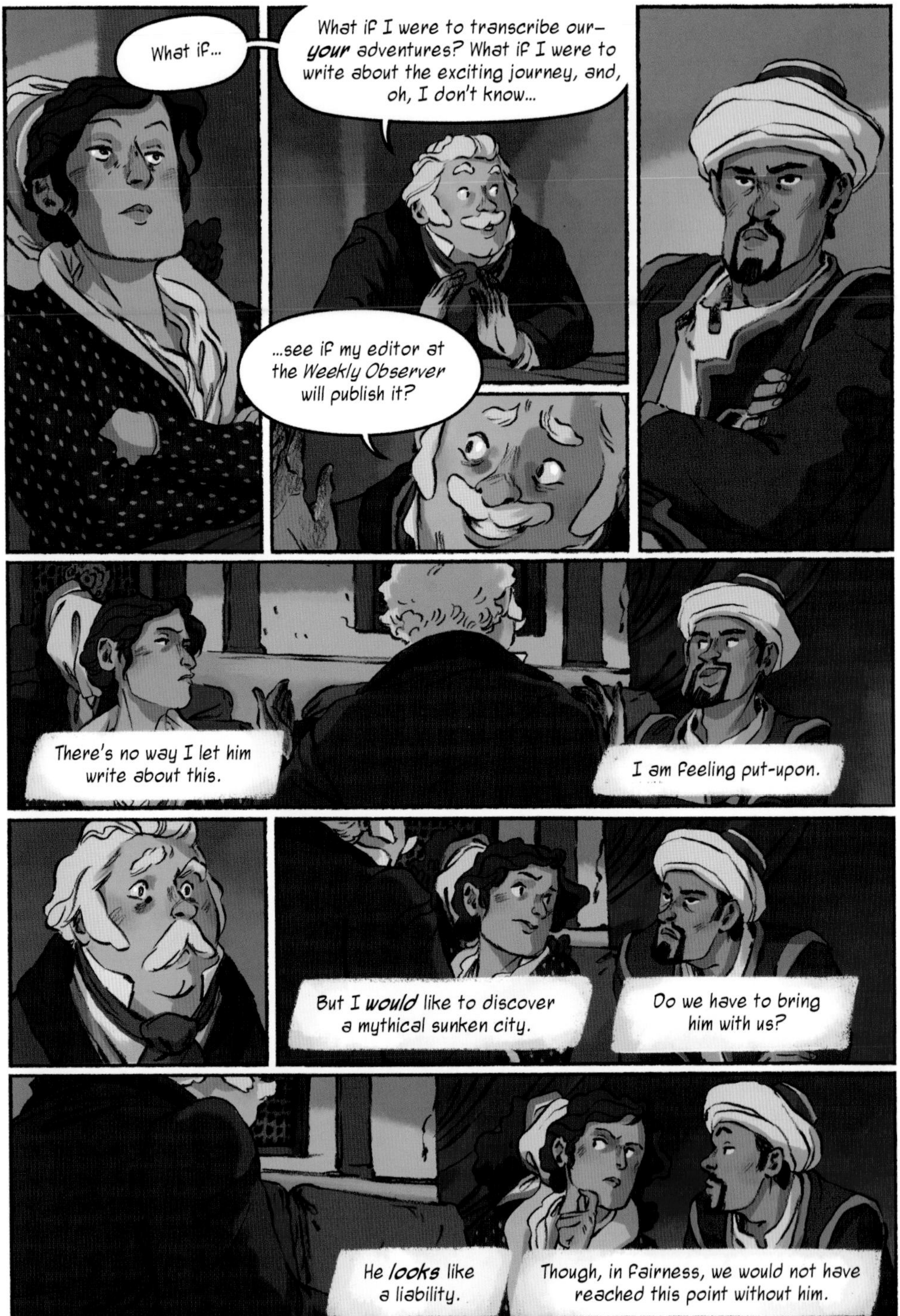
What if...
What if I were to transcribe our—*your* adventures? What if I were to write about the exciting journey, and, oh, I don't know...
...see if my editor at the *Weekly Observer* will publish it?
There's no way I let him write about this.
I am feeling put-upon.
But I *would* like to discover a mythical sunken city.
Do we have to bring him with us?
He *looks* like a liability.
Though, in fairness, we would not have reached this point without him.

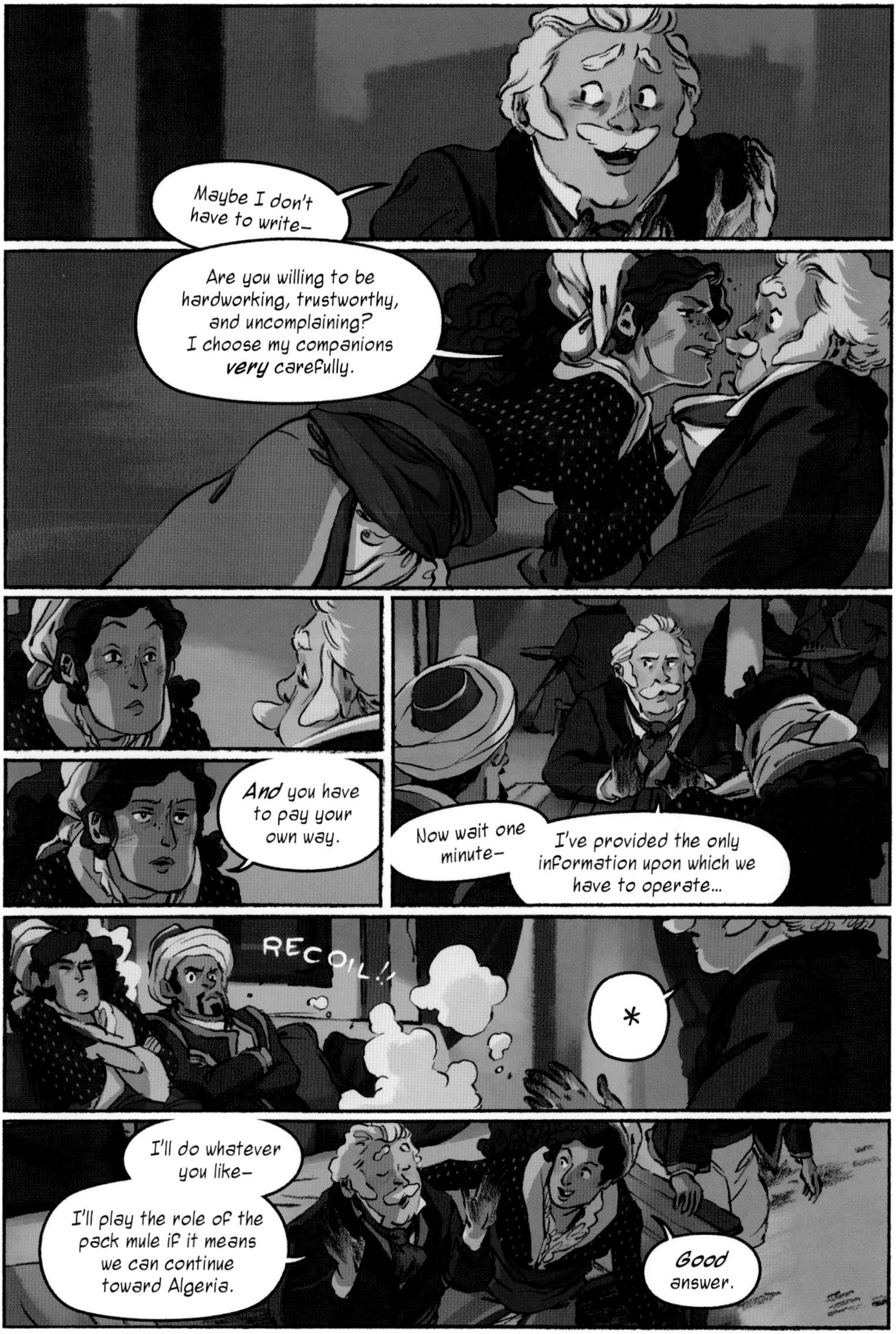
Maybe I don't have to write–
Are you willing to be hardworking, trustworthy, and uncomplaining? I choose my companions *very* carefully.
*And* you have to pay your own way.
Now wait one minute–
I've provided the only information upon which we have to operate...
RECOIL!!
*
I'll do whatever you like–
I'll play the role of the pack mule if it means we can continue toward Algeria.
*Good* answer.

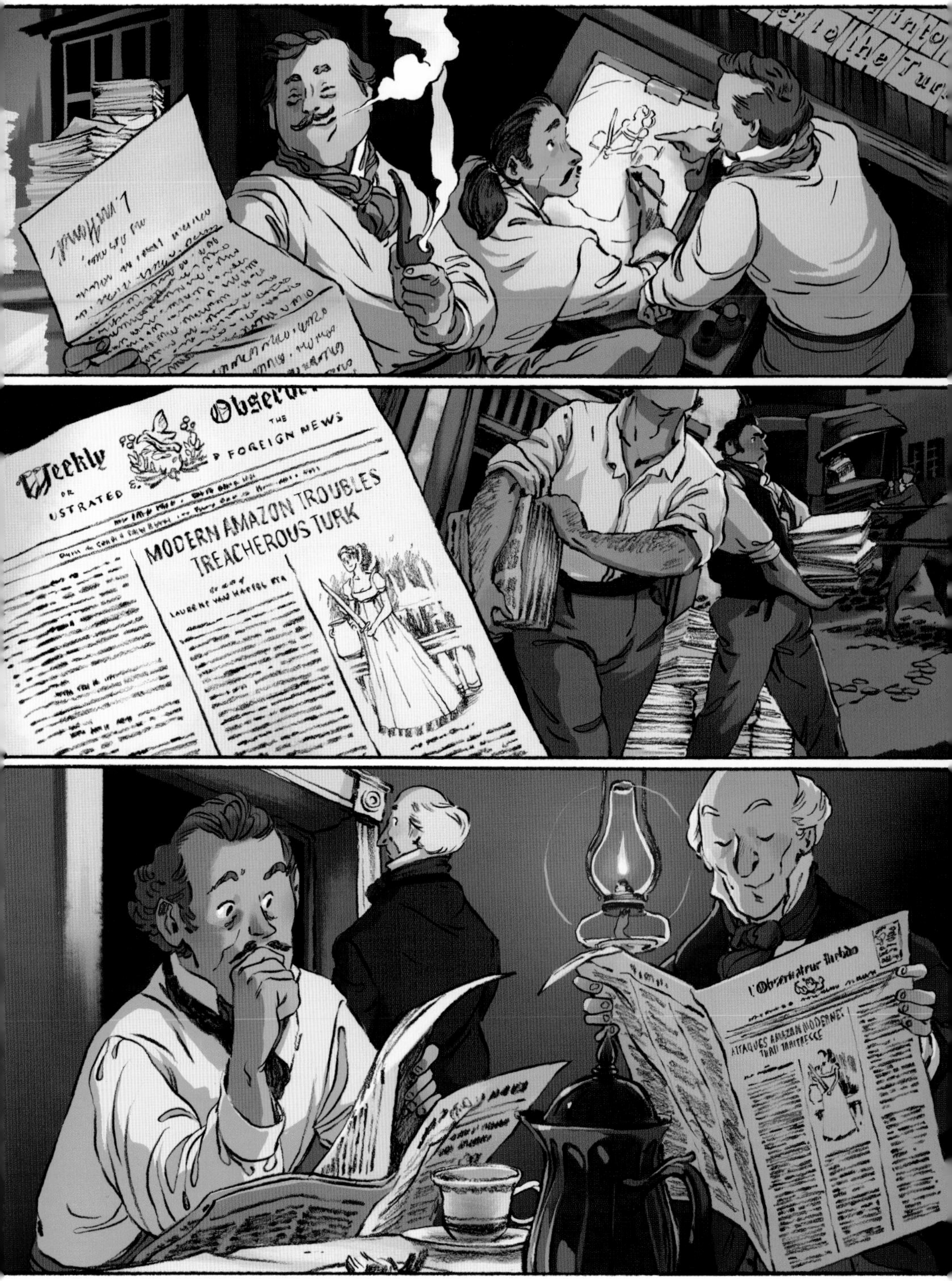
into
the Tur
Weekly
OR
USTRATED
THE
FOREIGN NEWS
MODERN AMAZON TROUBLES
TREACHEROUS TURK

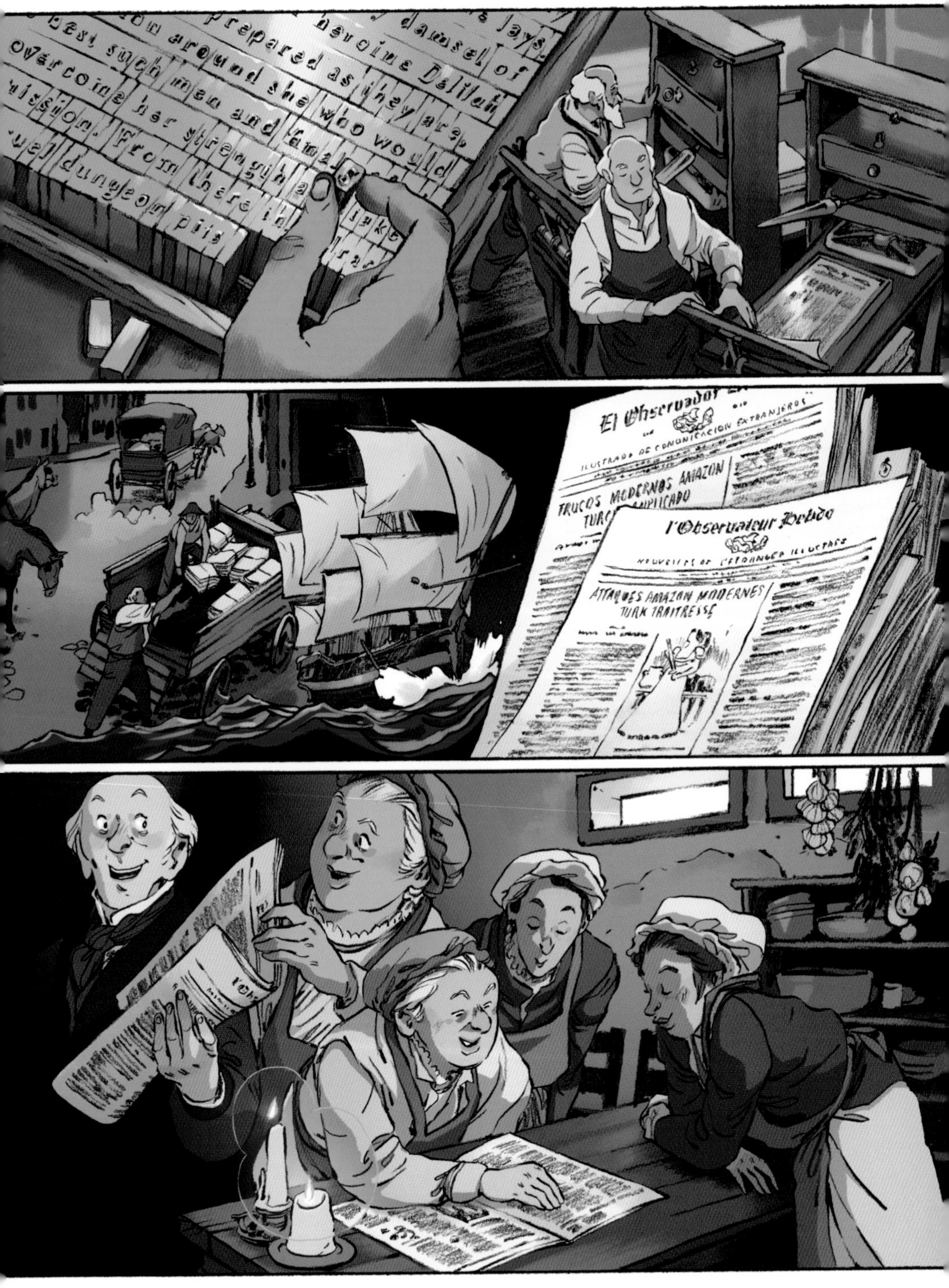
El Observador
ILUSTRADO DE COMUNICACION EXTRANJEROS
TRUCOS MODERNOS AMAZON
ATTAQUES AMAZON MODERNES
TURK TRAITRESSE

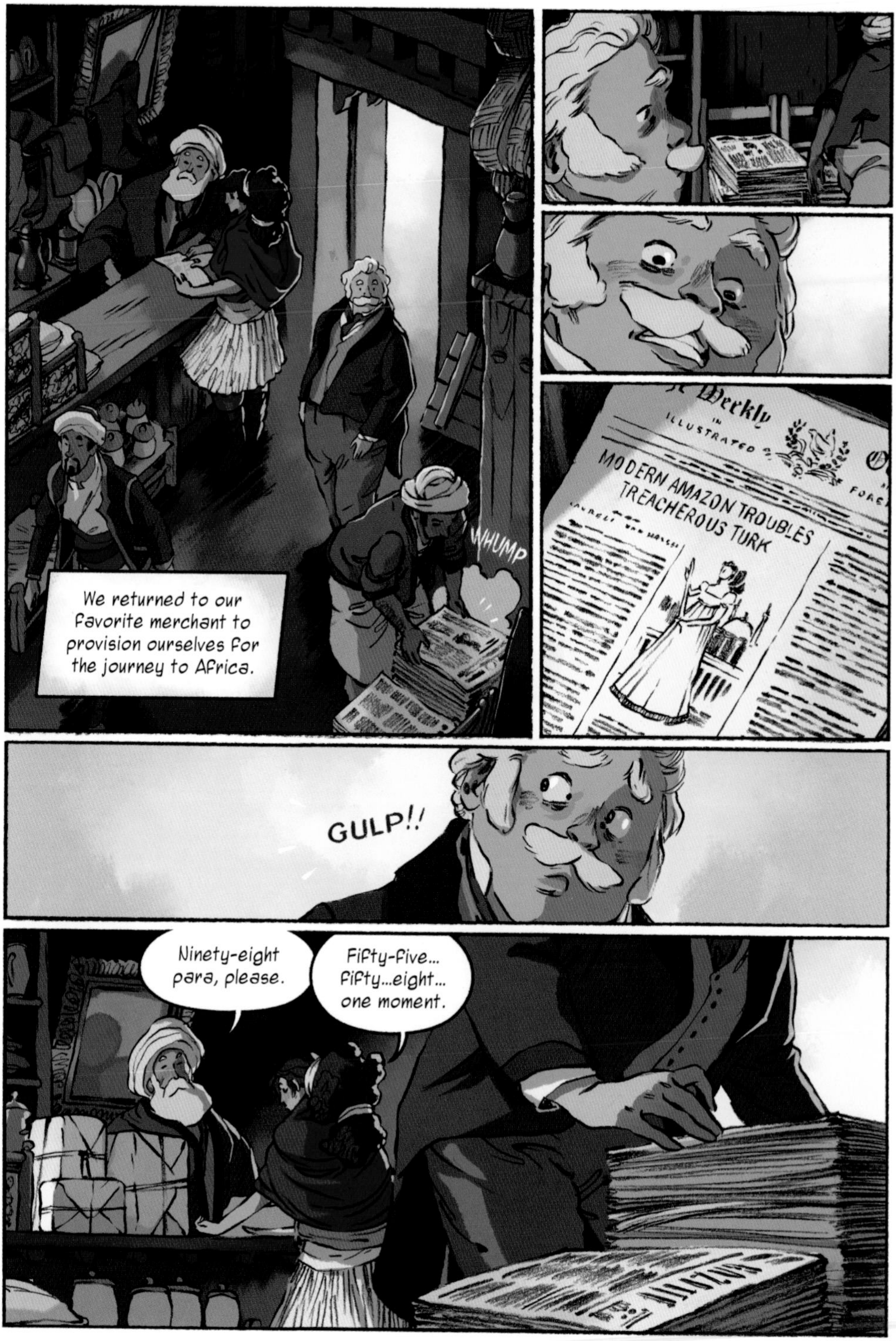
We returned to our favorite merchant to provision ourselves for the journey to Africa.
WHUMP
Weekly
ILLUSTRATED
MODERN AMAZON TROUBLES TREACHEROUS TURK
GULP!!
Ninety-eight para, please.
Fifty-five... fifty...eight... one moment.

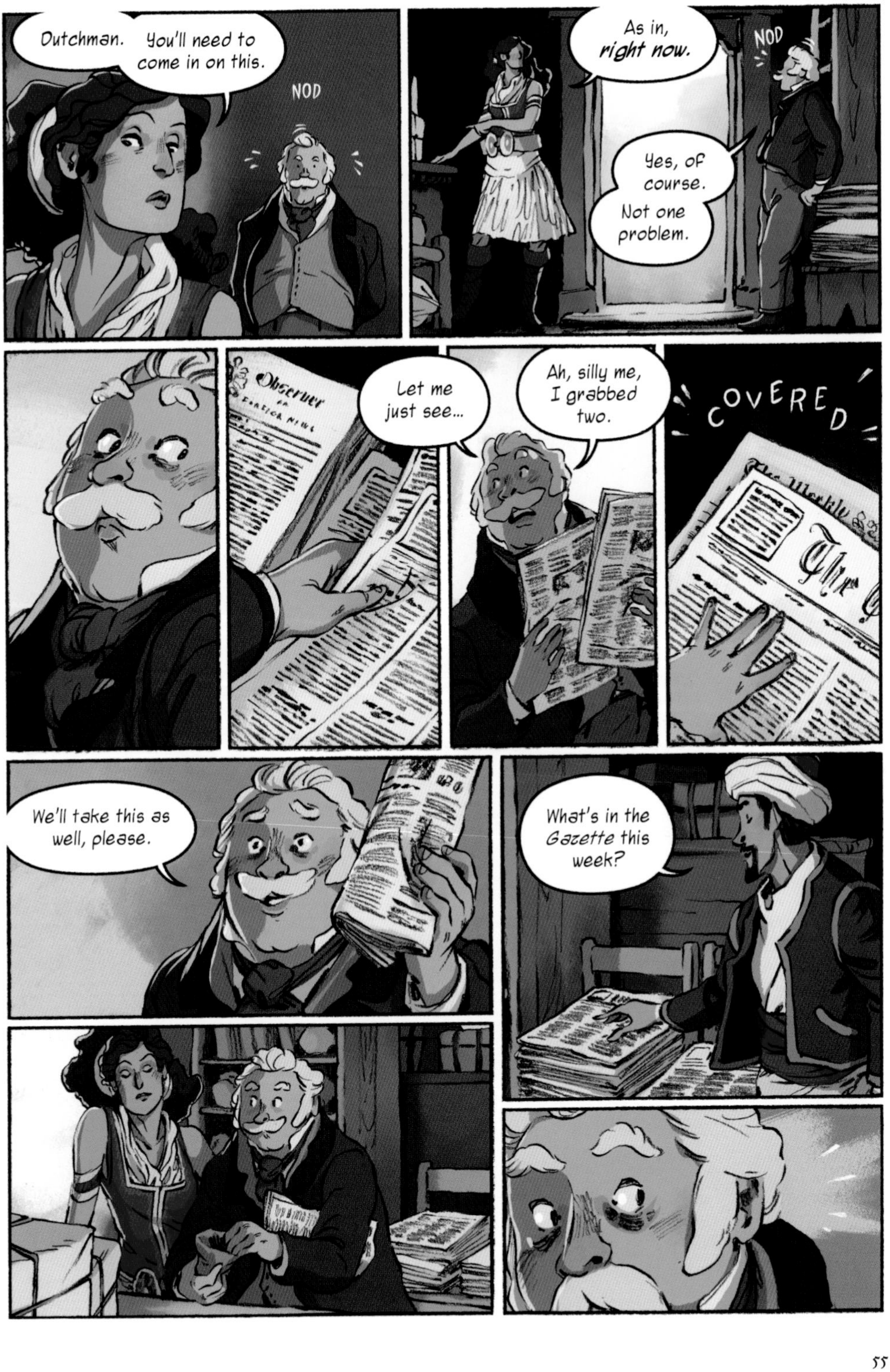
Dutchman.
You'll need to come in on this.
NOD
As in, right now.
NOD
Yes, of course.
Not one problem.
Observer
Let me just see...
Ah, silly me, I grabbed two.
COVERED
We'll take this as well, please.
What's in the Gazette this week?

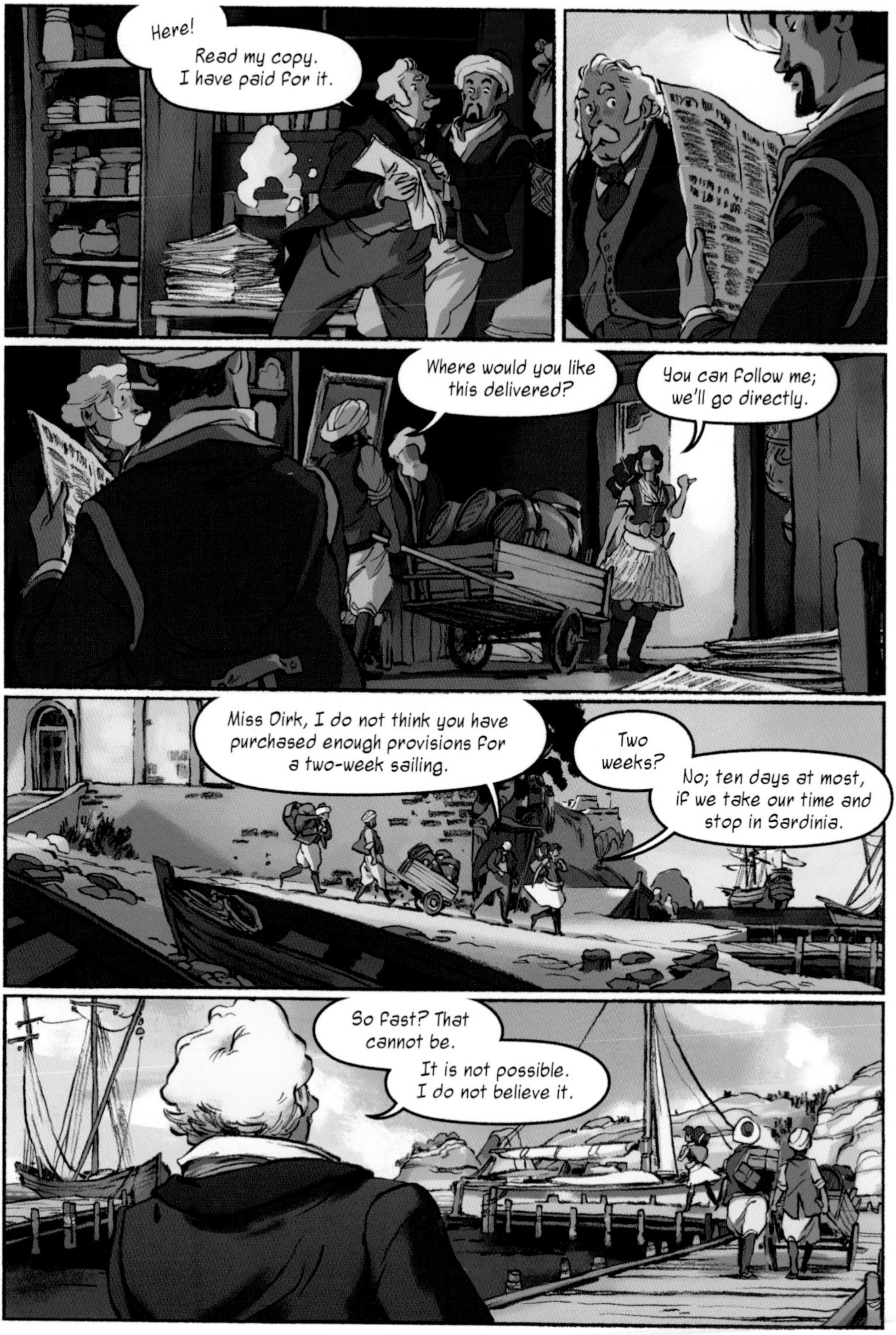
Here!
Read my copy. I have paid for it.
Where would you like this delivered?
You can follow me; we'll go directly.
Miss Dirk, I do not think you have purchased enough provisions for a two-week sailing.
Two weeks?
No; ten days at most, if we take our time and stop in Sardinia.
So fast? That cannot be.
It is not possible. I do not believe it.

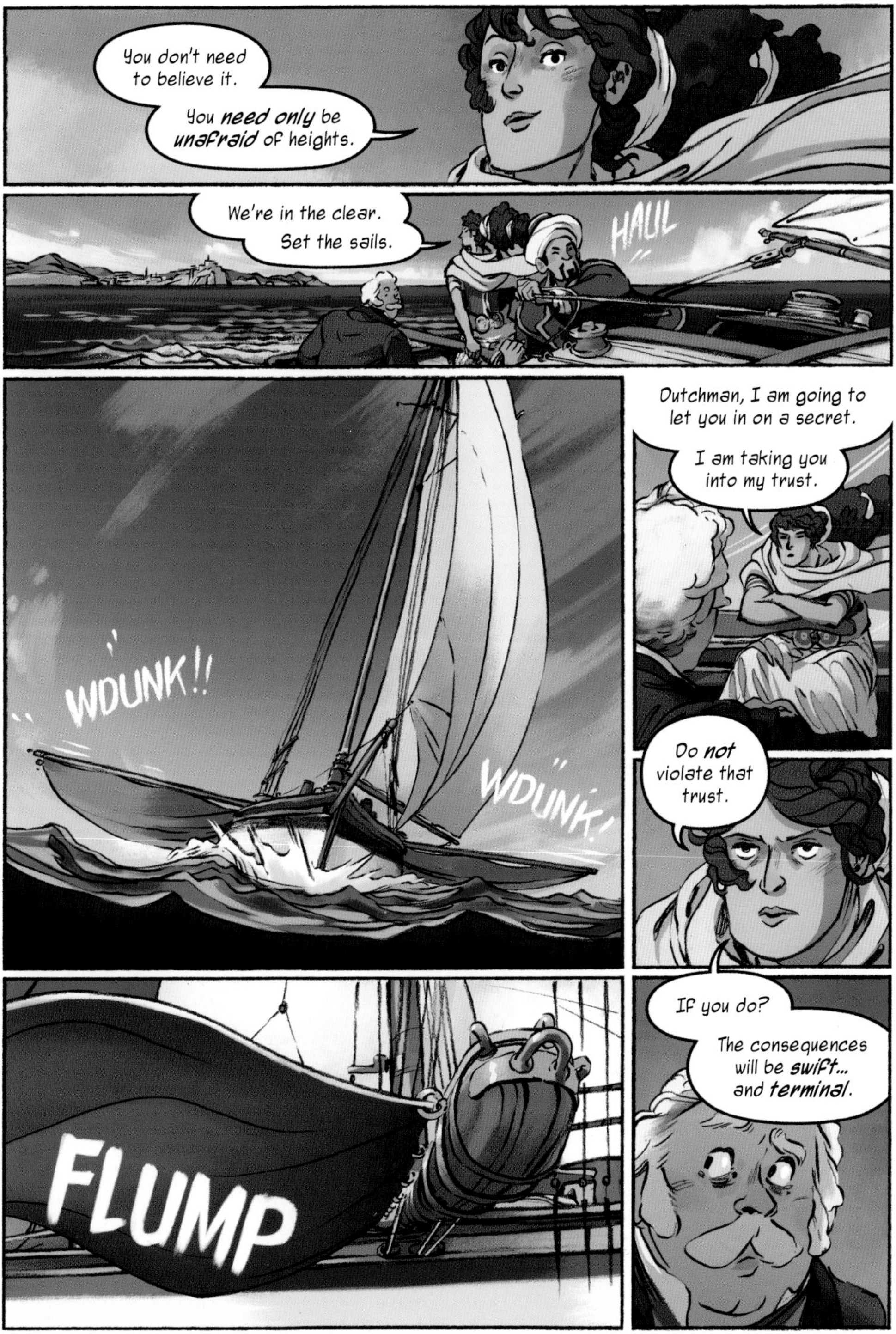
You don't need to believe it.
You need only be unafraid of heights.
We're in the clear. Set the sails.
HAUL
WDUNK!!
WDUNK!
Dutchman, I am going to let you in on a secret.
I am taking you into my trust.
Do not violate that trust.
FLUMP
If you do?
The consequences will be swift... and terminal.

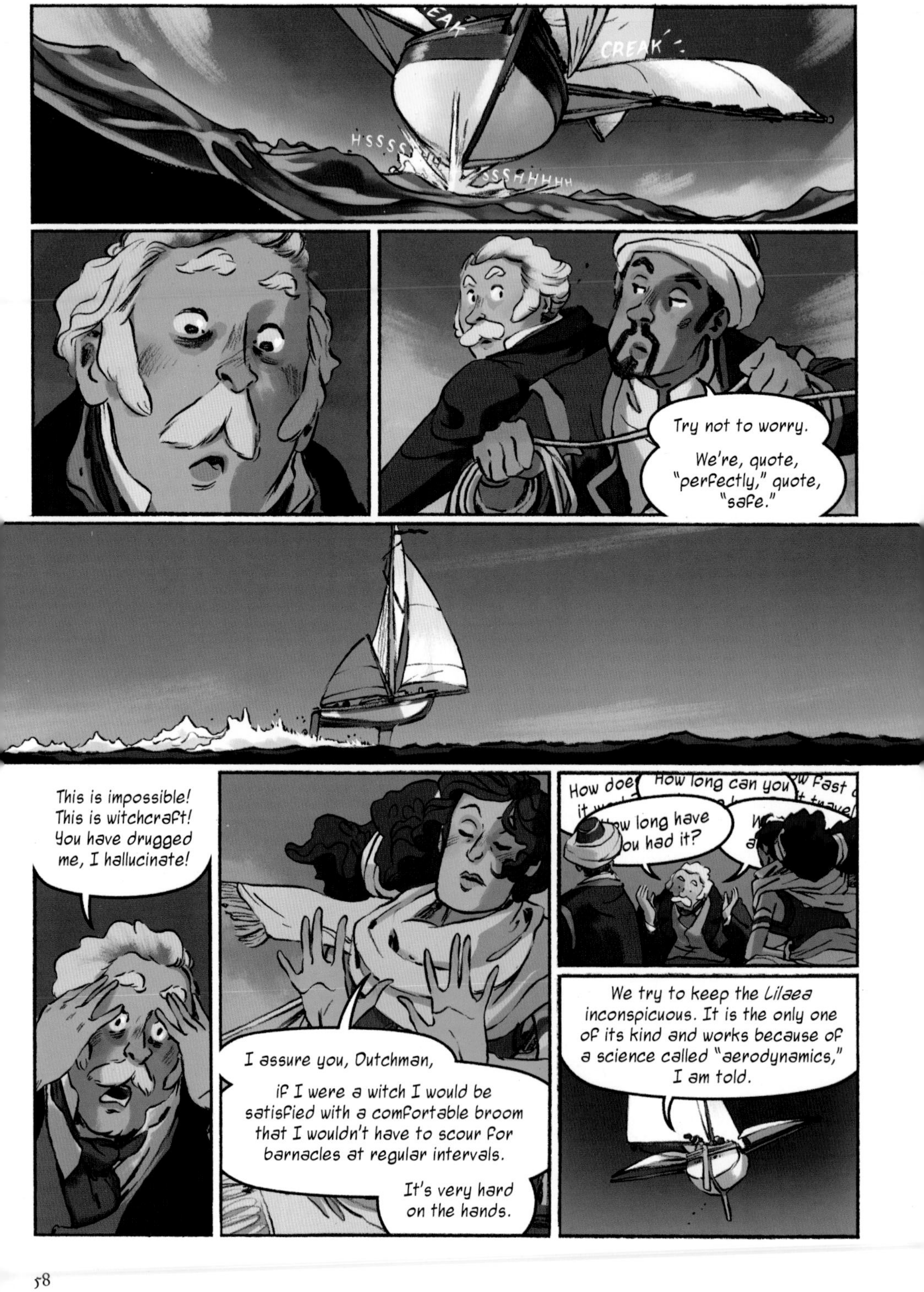
CREAK
CREAK
HSSSS
SSSHHHHH
Try not to worry.
We're, quote, "perfectly," quote, "safe."
This is impossible! This is witchcraft! You have drugged me, I hallucinate!
I assure you, Dutchman,
if I were a witch I would be satisfied with a comfortable broom that I wouldn't have to scour for barnacles at regular intervals.
It's very hard on the hands.
How doe
How long can you
w fast
ow long have
ou had it?
We try to keep the *Lilaea* inconspicuous. It is the only one of its kind and works because of a science called "aerodynamics," I am told.

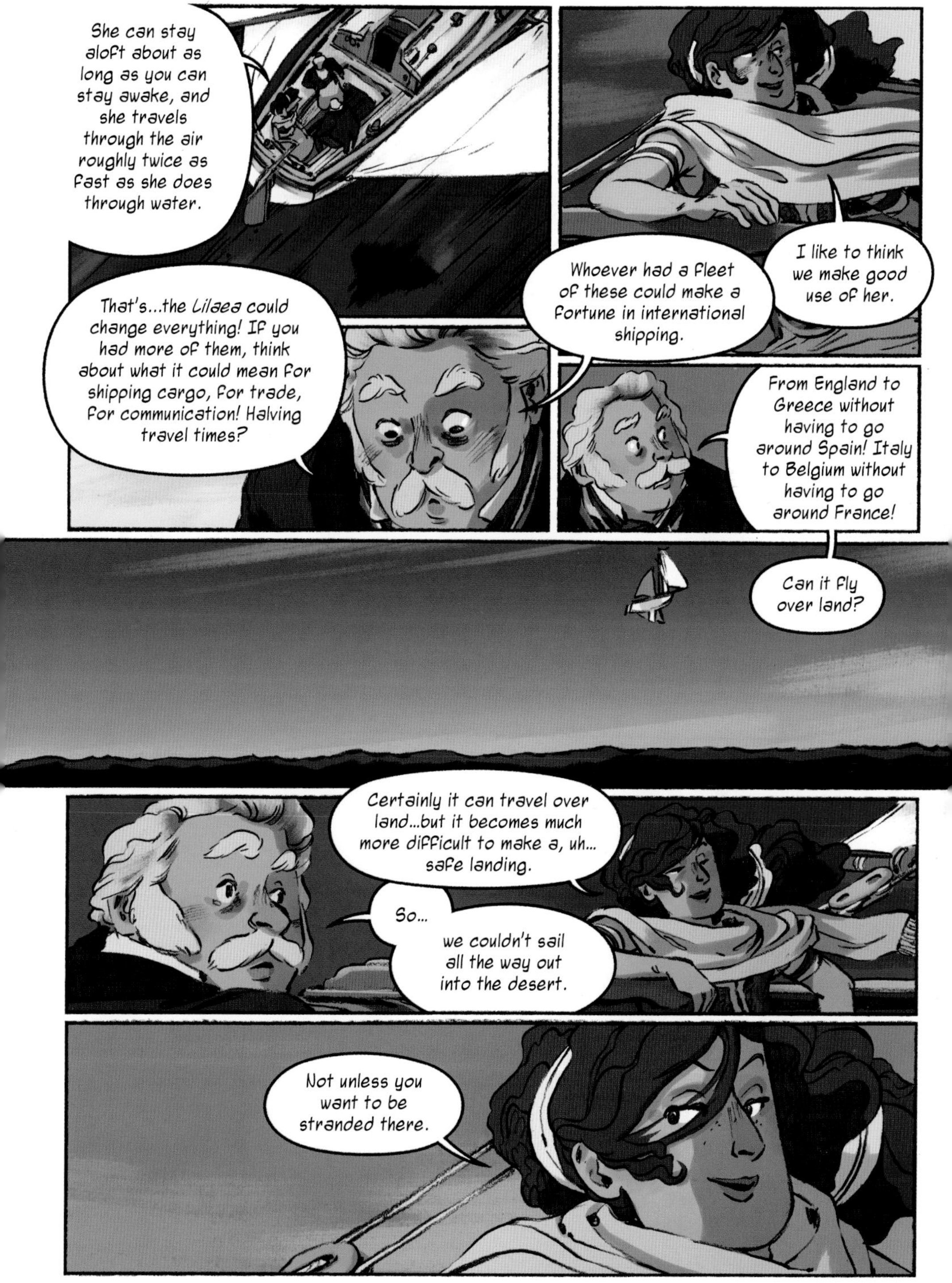
She can stay aloft about as long as you can stay awake, and she travels through the air roughly twice as fast as she does through water.
I like to think we make good use of her.
That's...the *Lilaea* could change everything! If you had more of them, think about what it could mean for shipping cargo, for trade, for communication! Halving travel times?
Whoever had a fleet of these could make a fortune in international shipping.
From England to Greece without having to go around Spain! Italy to Belgium without having to go around France!
Can it fly over land?
Certainly it can travel over land...but it becomes much more difficult to make a, uh... safe landing.
So...
we couldn't sail all the way out into the desert.
Not unless you want to be stranded there.

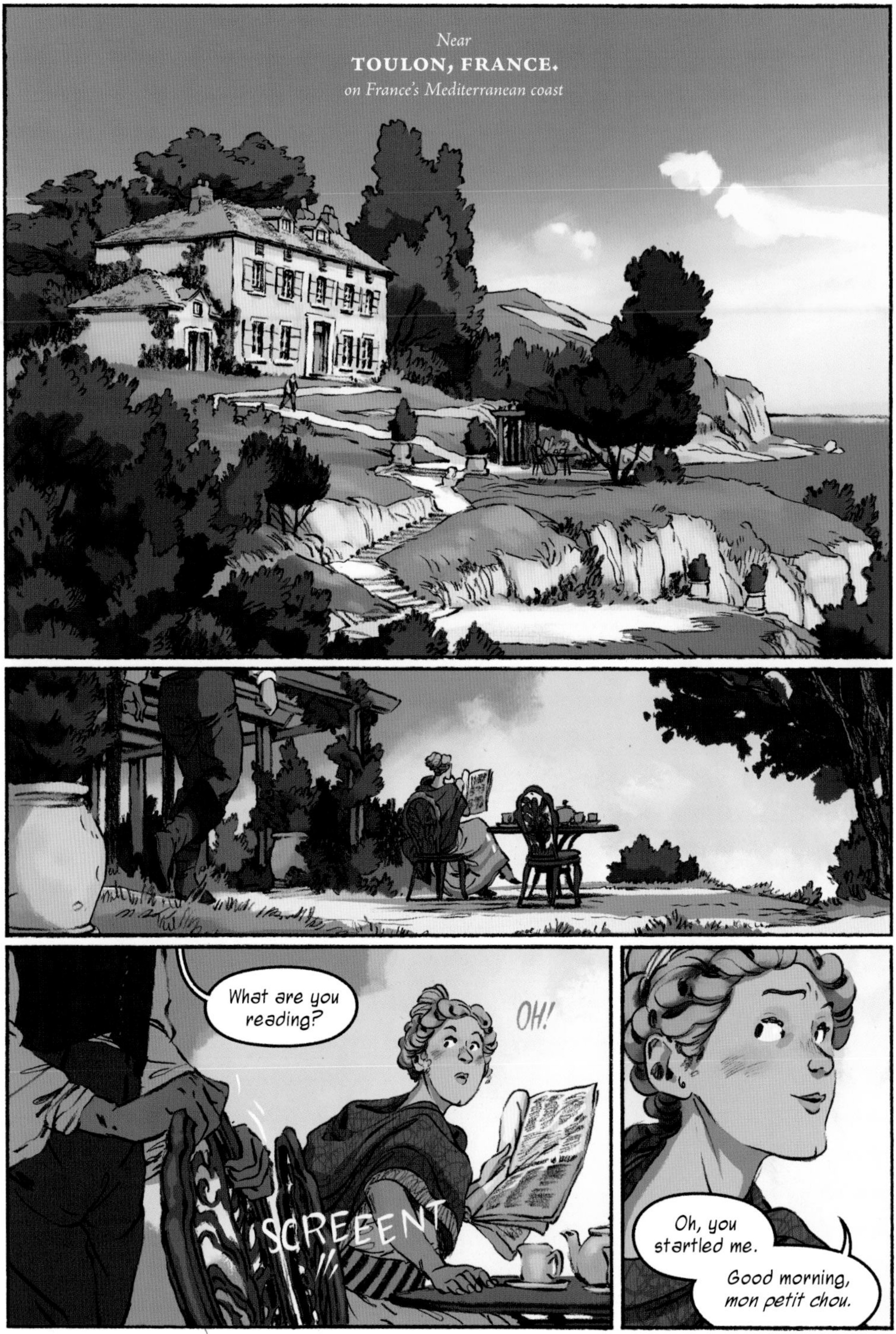
Near
TOULON, FRANCE.
on France's Mediterranean coast
What are you reading?
OH!
SCREEENT
Oh, you startled me.
Good morning, mon petit chou.

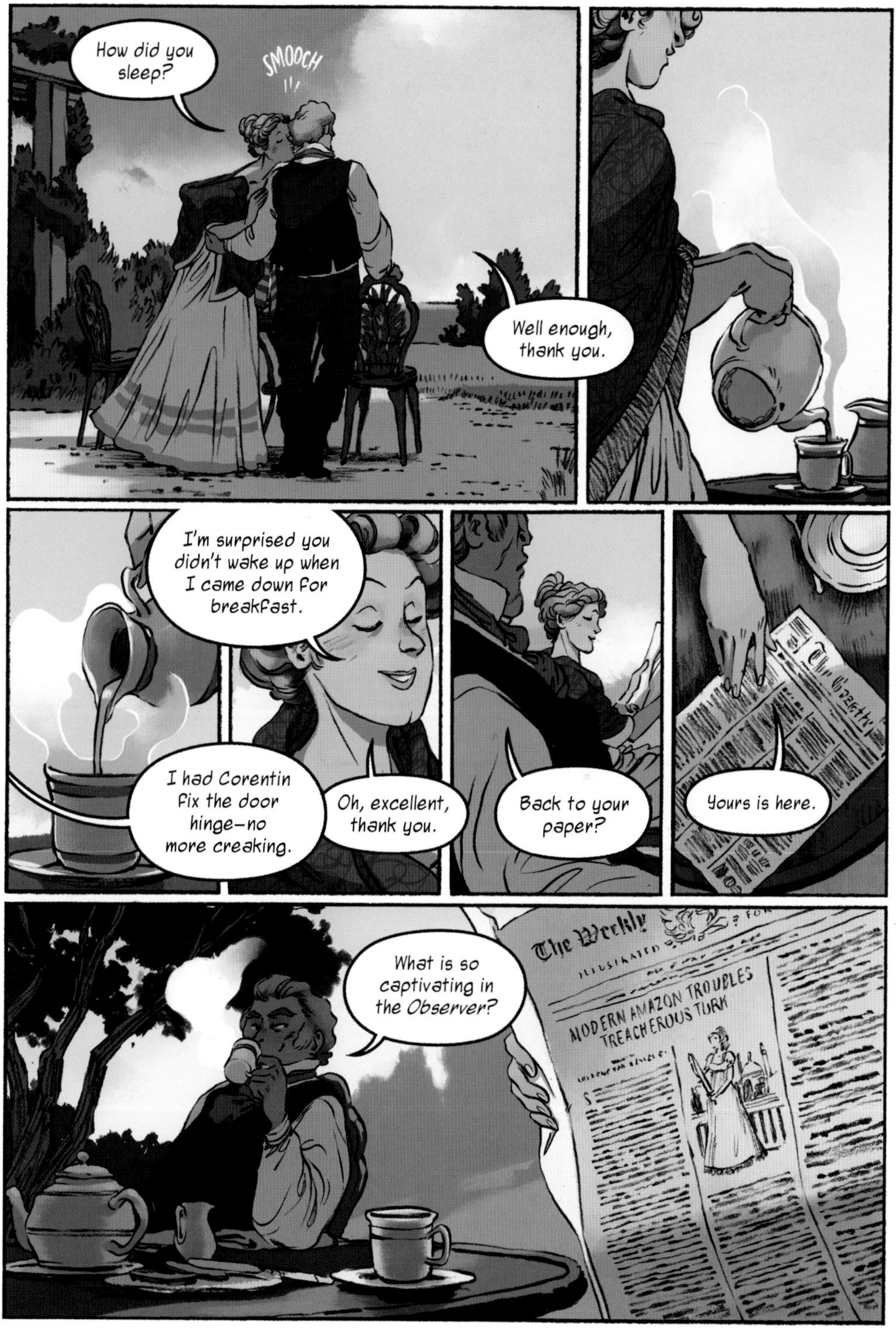
How did you sleep?
SMOOCH
Well enough, thank you.
I'm surprised you didn't wake up when I came down for breakfast.
I had Corentin fix the door hinge—no more creaking.
Oh, excellent, thank you.
Back to your paper?
Yours is here.
The Weekly
MODERN AMAZON TROUBLES TREACHEROUS TURK
What is so captivating in the *Observer*?

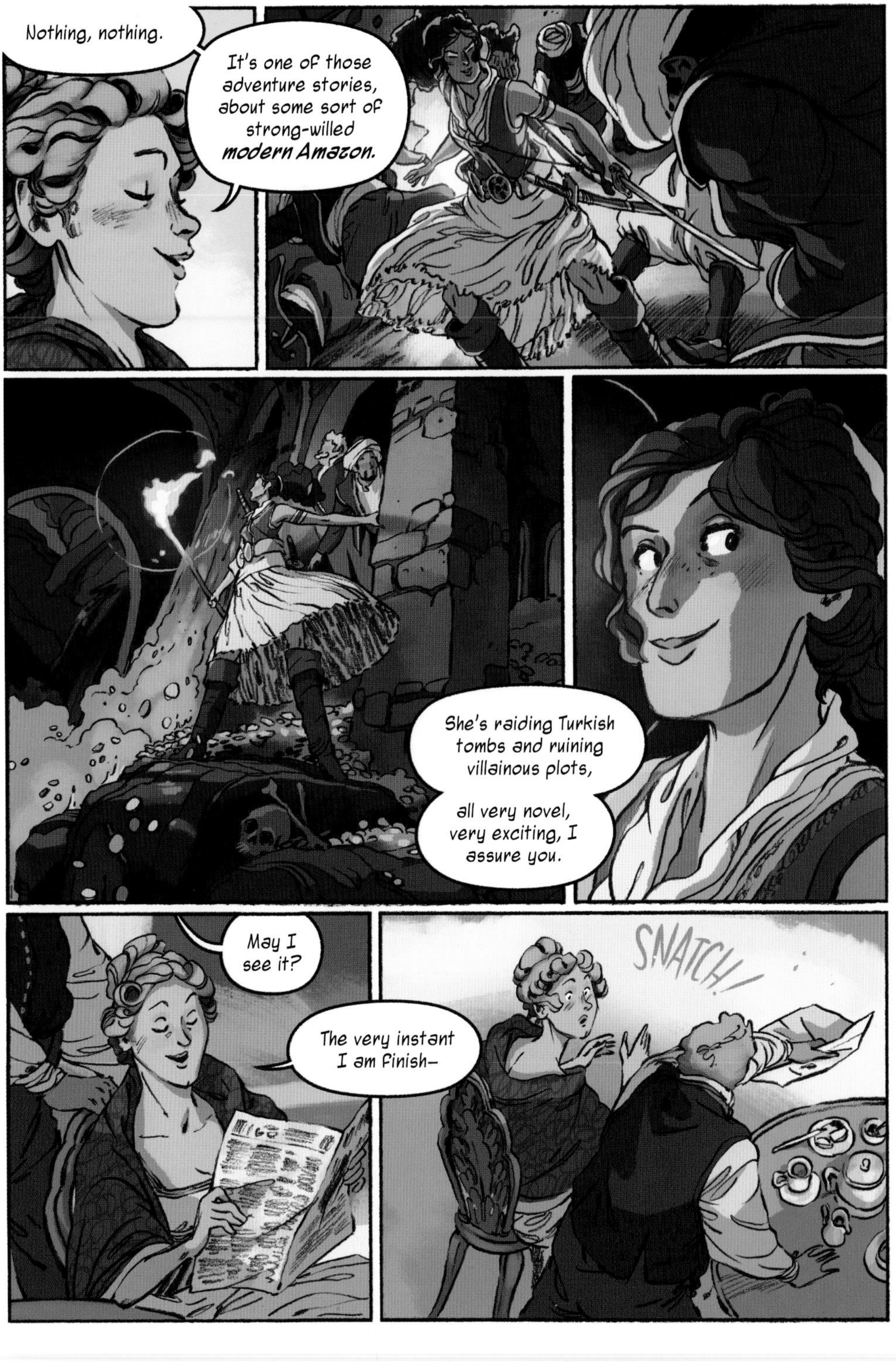
Nothing, nothing.
It's one of those adventure stories, about some sort of strong-willed ***modern Amazon.***
She's raiding Turkish tombs and ruining villainous plots,
all very novel, very exciting, I assure you.
May I see it?
The very instant I am finish–
SNATCH!

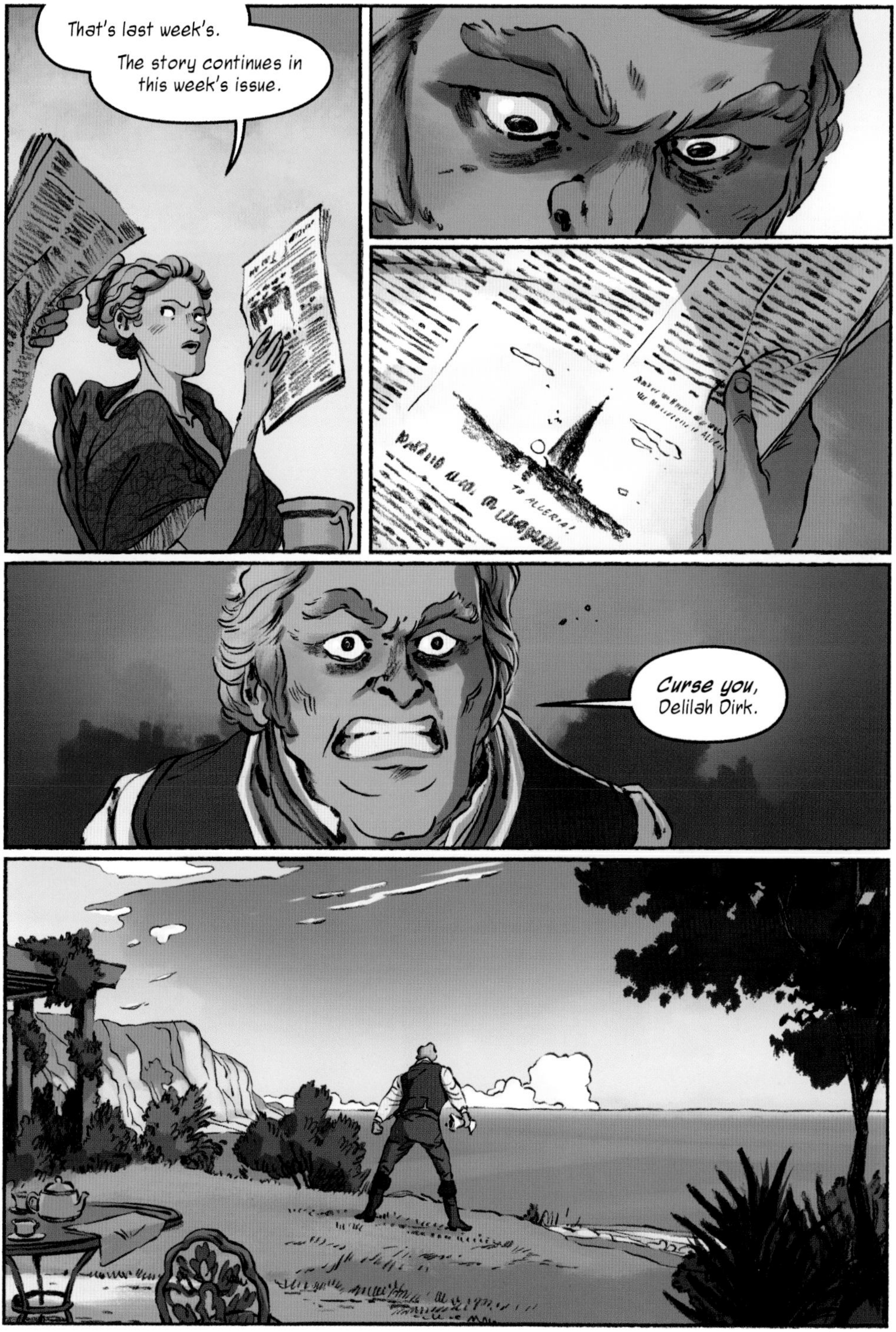
That's last week's.
The story continues in this week's issue.
Curse you, Delilah Dirk.

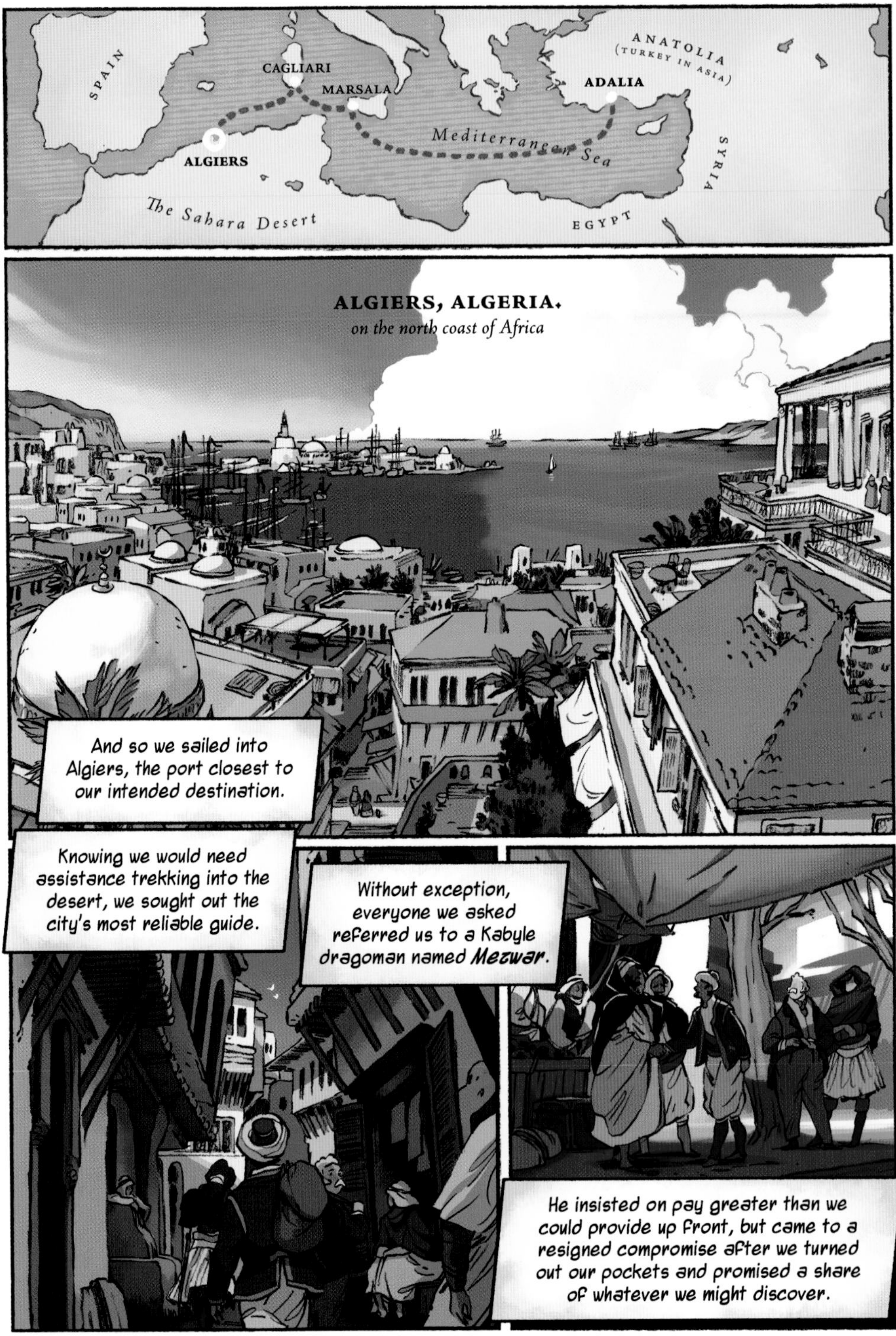
ANATOLIA
(TURKEY IN ASIA)
SPAIN
CAGLIARI
MARSALA
ADALIA
ALGIERS
Mediterranean Sea
SYRIA
The Sahara Desert
EGYPT
ALGIERS, ALGERIA.
on the north coast of Africa
And so we sailed into Algiers, the port closest to our intended destination.
Knowing we would need assistance trekking into the desert, we sought out the city's most reliable guide.
Without exception, everyone we asked referred us to a Kabyle dragoman named Mezwar.
He insisted on pay greater than we could provide up front, but came to a resigned compromise after we turned out our pockets and promised a share of whatever we might discover.

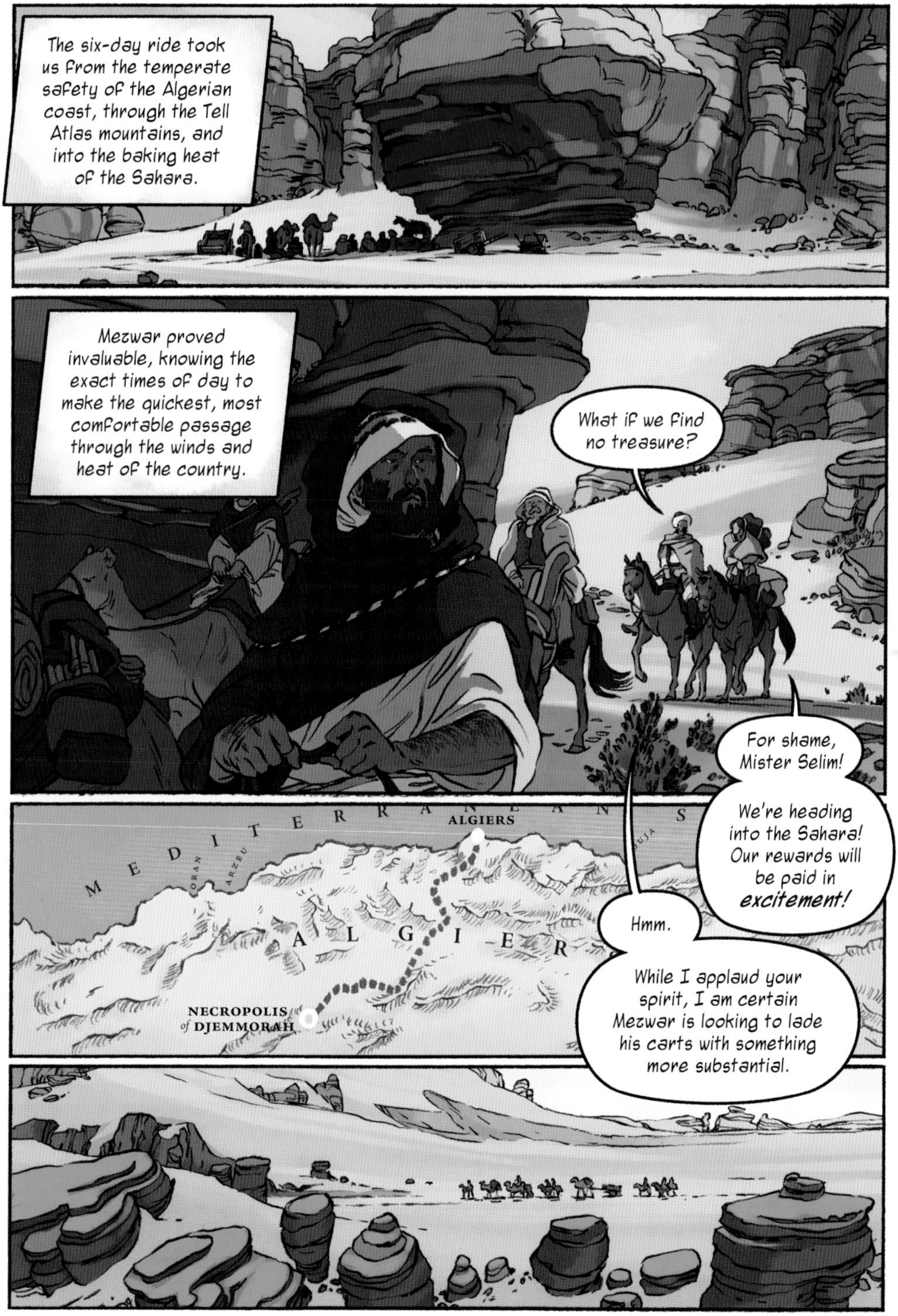
The six-day ride took us from the temperate safety of the Algerian coast, through the Tell Atlas mountains, and into the baking heat of the Sahara.
Mezwar proved invaluable, knowing the exact times of day to make the quickest, most comfortable passage through the winds and heat of the country.
What if we find no treasure?
For shame, Mister Selim!
We're heading into the Sahara! Our rewards will be paid in ***excitement!***
Hmm.
While I applaud your spirit, I am certain Mezwar is looking to lade his carts with something more substantial.
MEDITERRANEAN S
ALGIERS
ORAN
ARZEU
ALGIERS
NECROPOLIS of DJEMMORAH

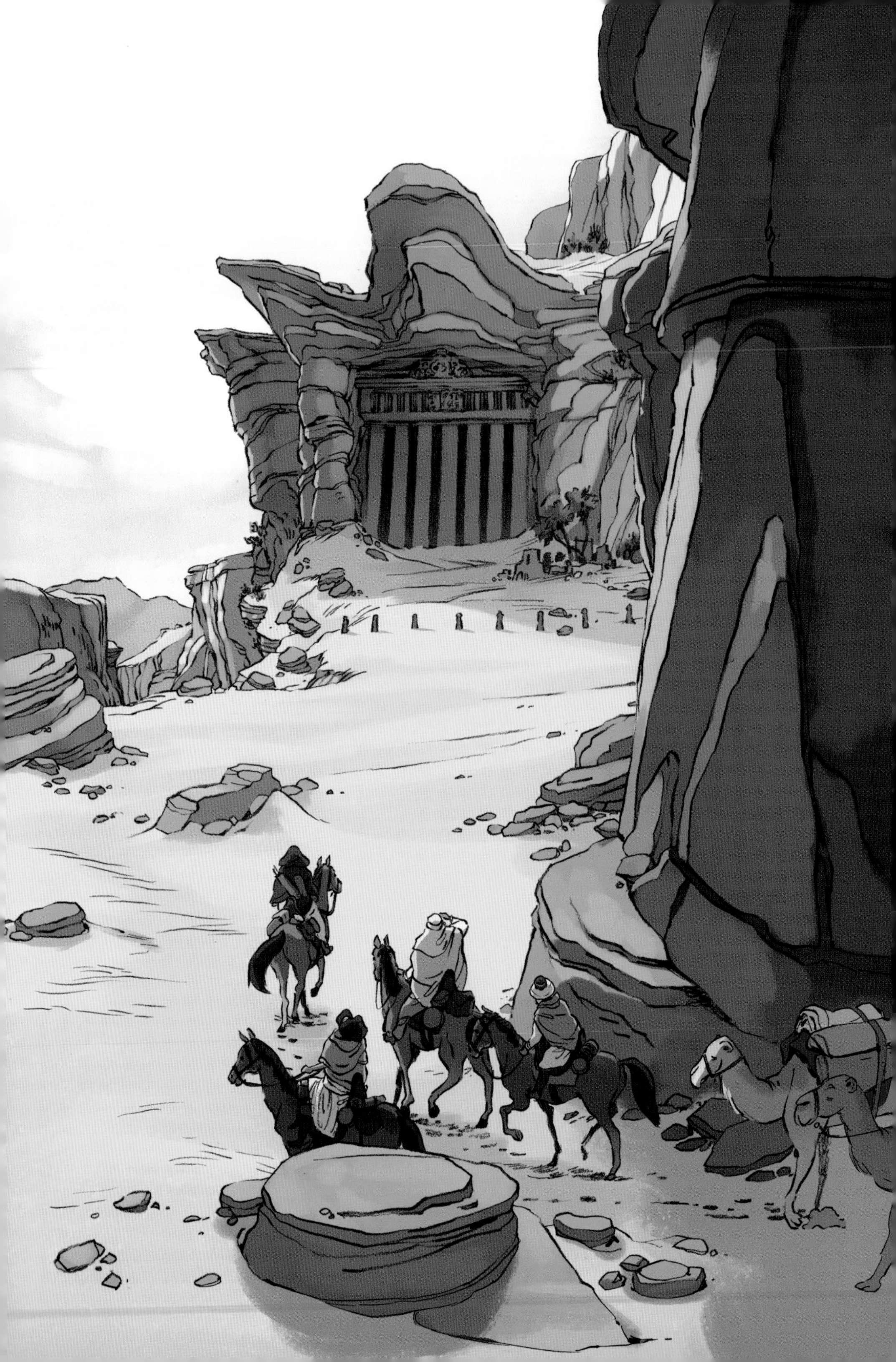

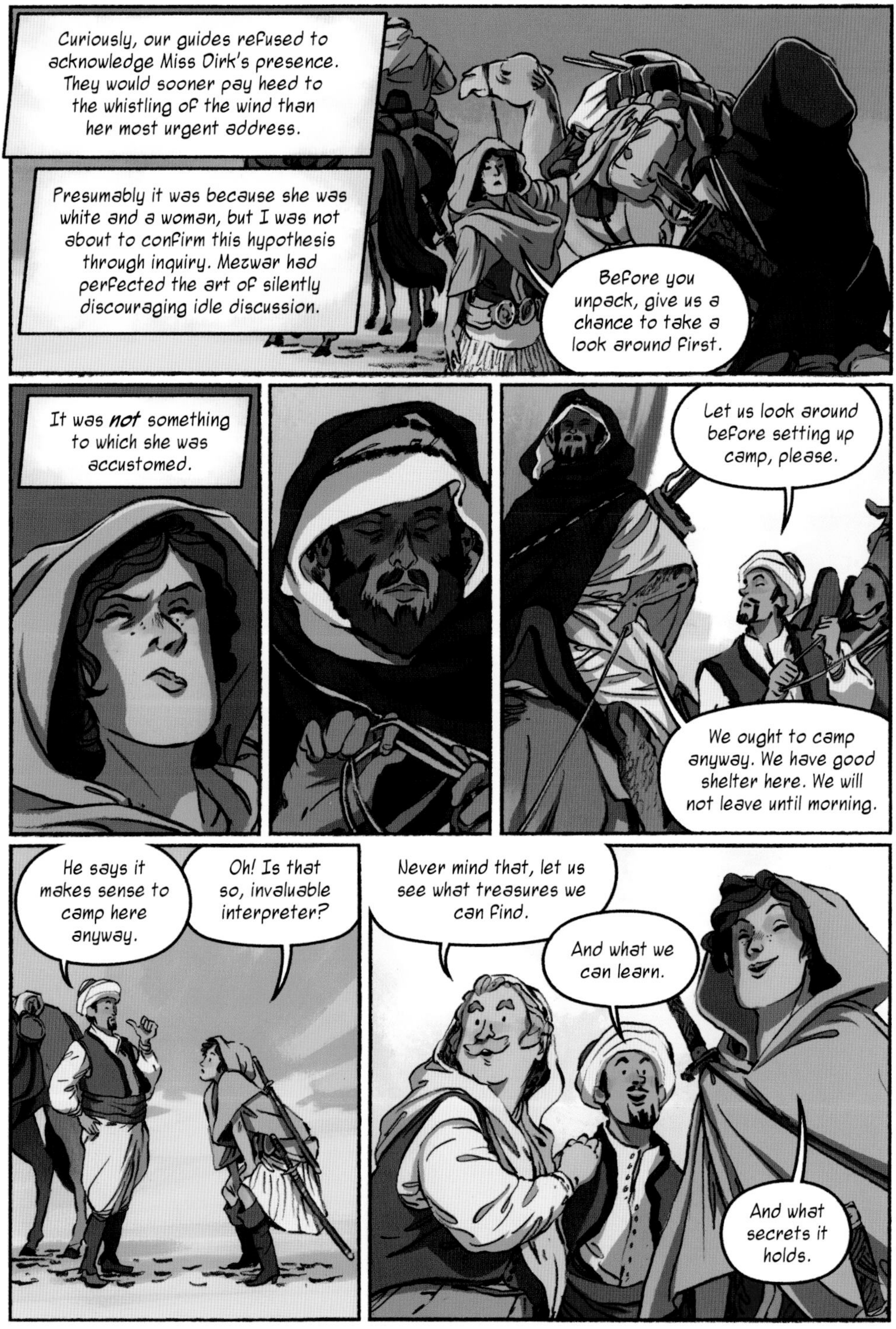
Curiously, our guides refused to acknowledge Miss Dirk's presence. They would sooner pay heed to the whistling of the wind than her most urgent address.
Presumably it was because she was white and a woman, but I was not about to confirm this hypothesis through inquiry. Mezwar had perfected the art of silently discouraging idle discussion.
Before you unpack, give us a chance to take a look around first.
It was *not* something to which she was accustomed.
Let us look around before setting up camp, please.
We ought to camp anyway. We have good shelter here. We will not leave until morning.
He says it makes sense to camp here anyway.
Oh! Is that so, invaluable interpreter?
Never mind that, let us see what treasures we can find.
And what we can learn.
And what secrets it holds.

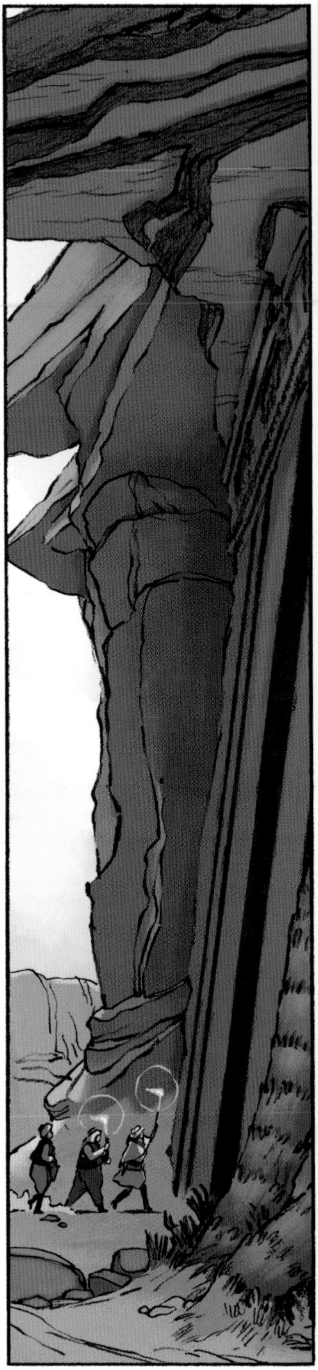

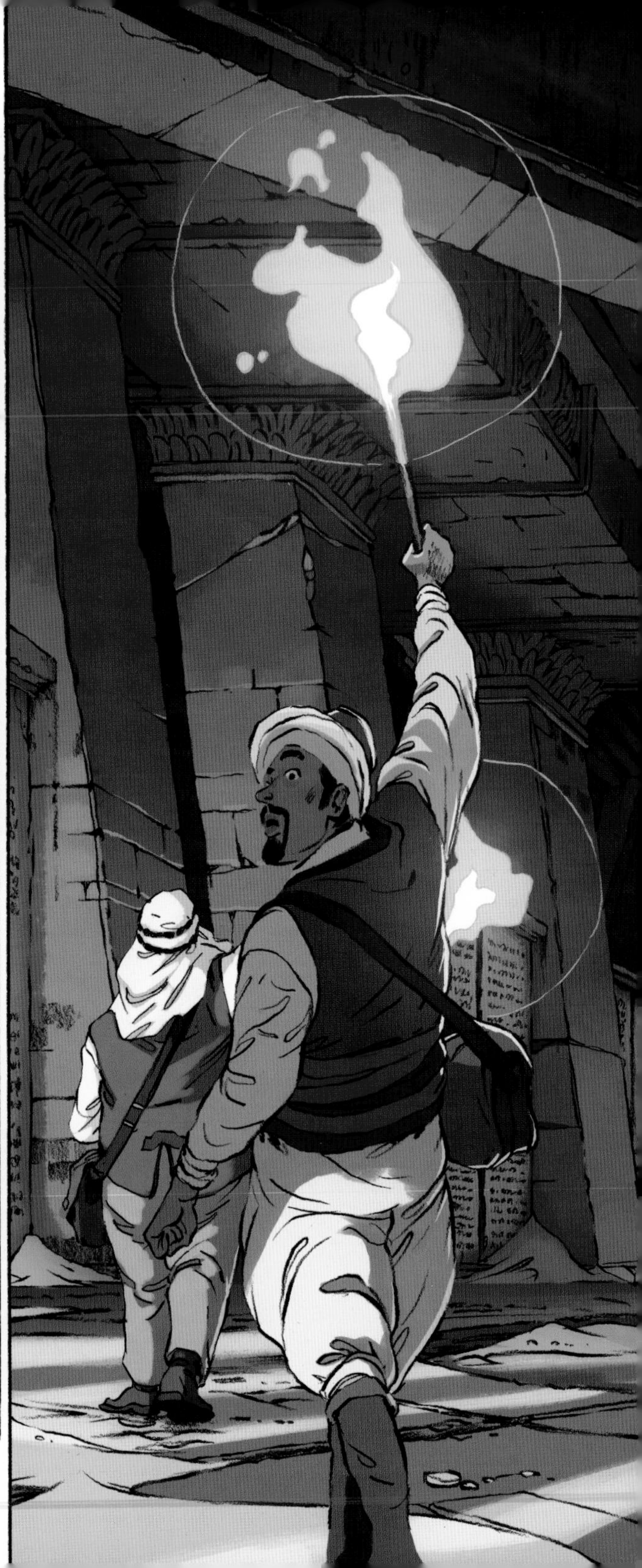

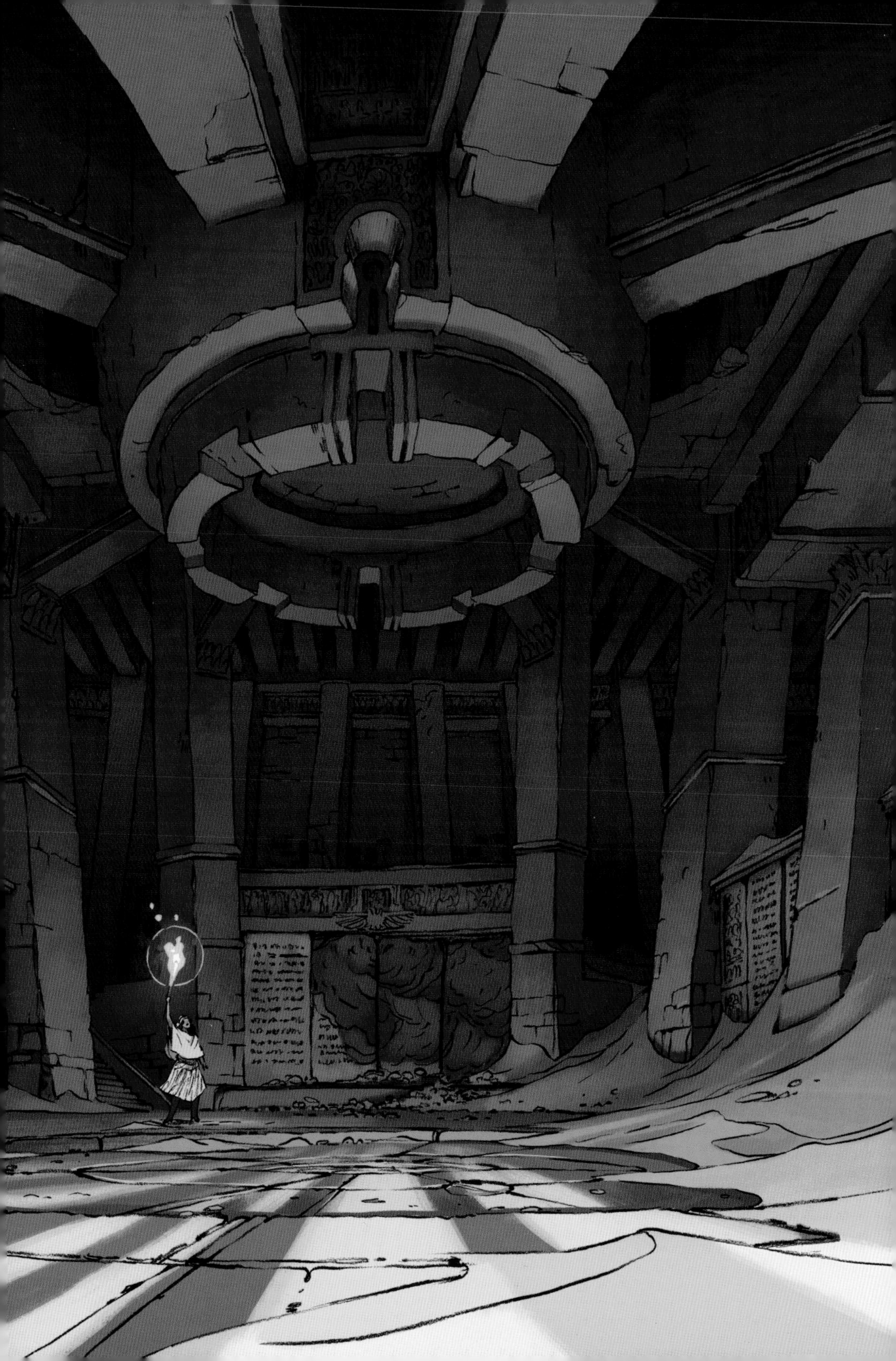

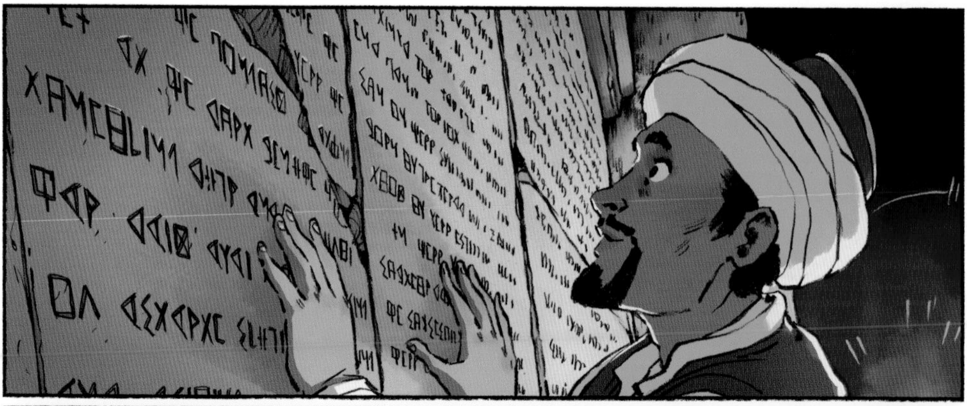

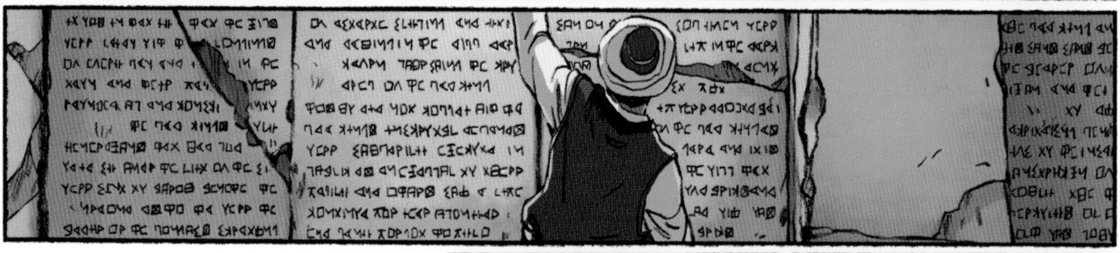

We spent the afternoon exploring the vast, magnificent necropolis. The Dutchman immediately confirmed that no, there was nothing in the way of treasure.

Meanwhile, I made some headway in deciphering the inscriptions on the walls. We were on the right track—they described the building of a great city at the cost of many years, many generations, and many ***lives***. It was a tale of immense sacrifice.

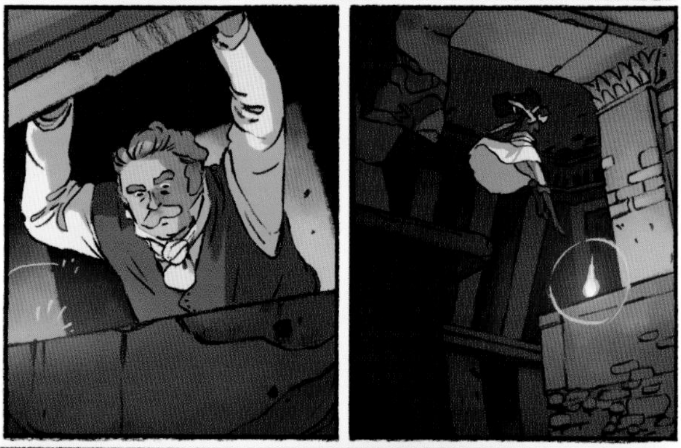

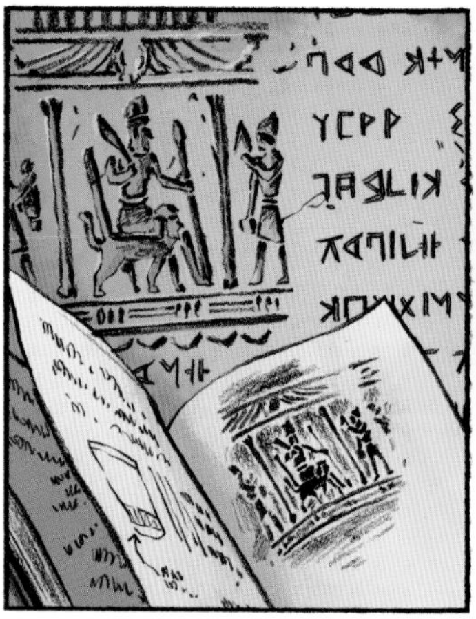

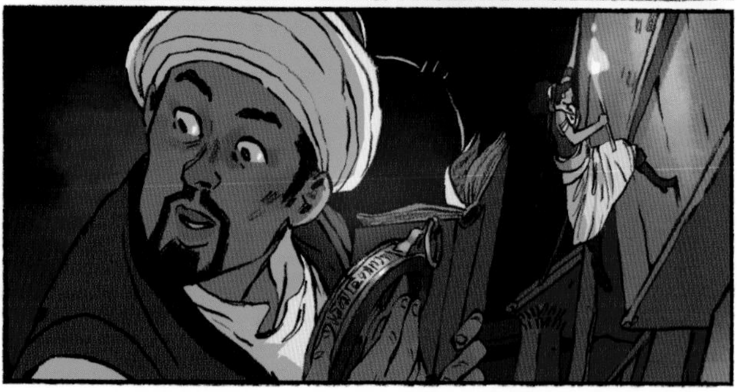

But this story differed from that of the vault in Turkey. Here, "The Father of the City" was no visionary, but a despotic slave driver who tricked his people into building his immense, impossible underground city.

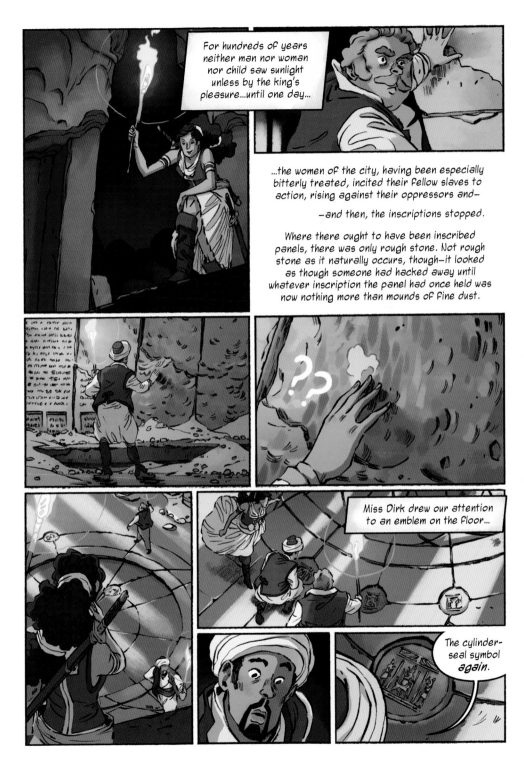

For hundreds of years neither man nor woman nor child saw sunlight unless by the king's pleasure...until one day...

...the women of the city, having been especially bitterly treated, incited their fellow slaves to action, rising against their oppressors and—

—and then, the inscriptions stopped.

Where there ought to have been inscribed panels, there was only rough stone. Not rough stone as it naturally occurs, though—it looked as though someone had hacked away until whatever inscription the panel had once held was now nothing more than mounds of fine dust.

??

Miss Dirk drew our attention to an emblem on the floor...

The cylinder-seal symbol *again*.

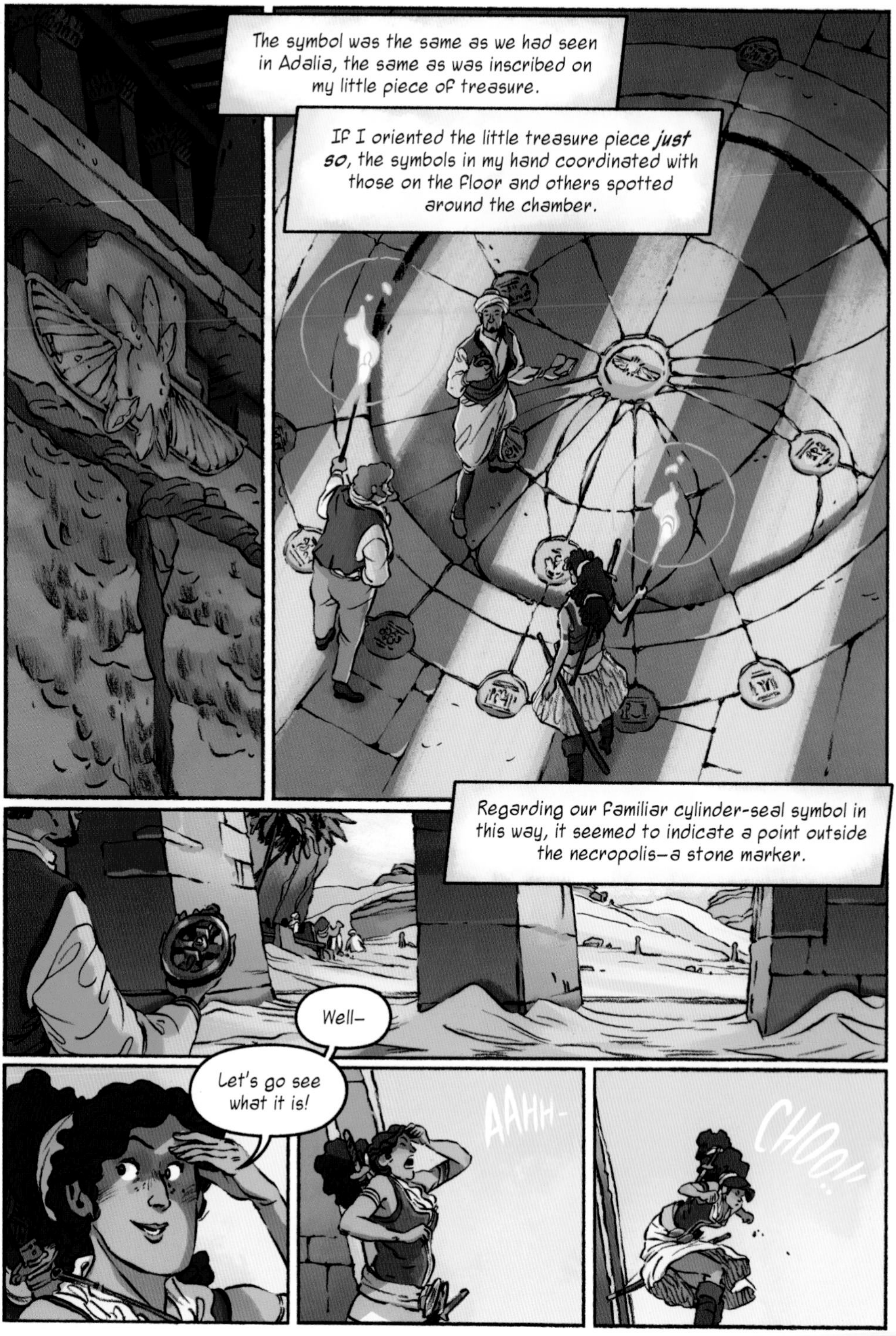
The symbol was the same as we had seen in Adalia, the same as was inscribed on my little piece of treasure.
If I oriented the little treasure piece ***just so***, the symbols in my hand coordinated with those on the floor and others spotted around the chamber.
Regarding our familiar cylinder-seal symbol in this way, it seemed to indicate a point outside the necropolis—a stone marker.
Well—
Let's go see what it is!
AAHH-
CHOO!!

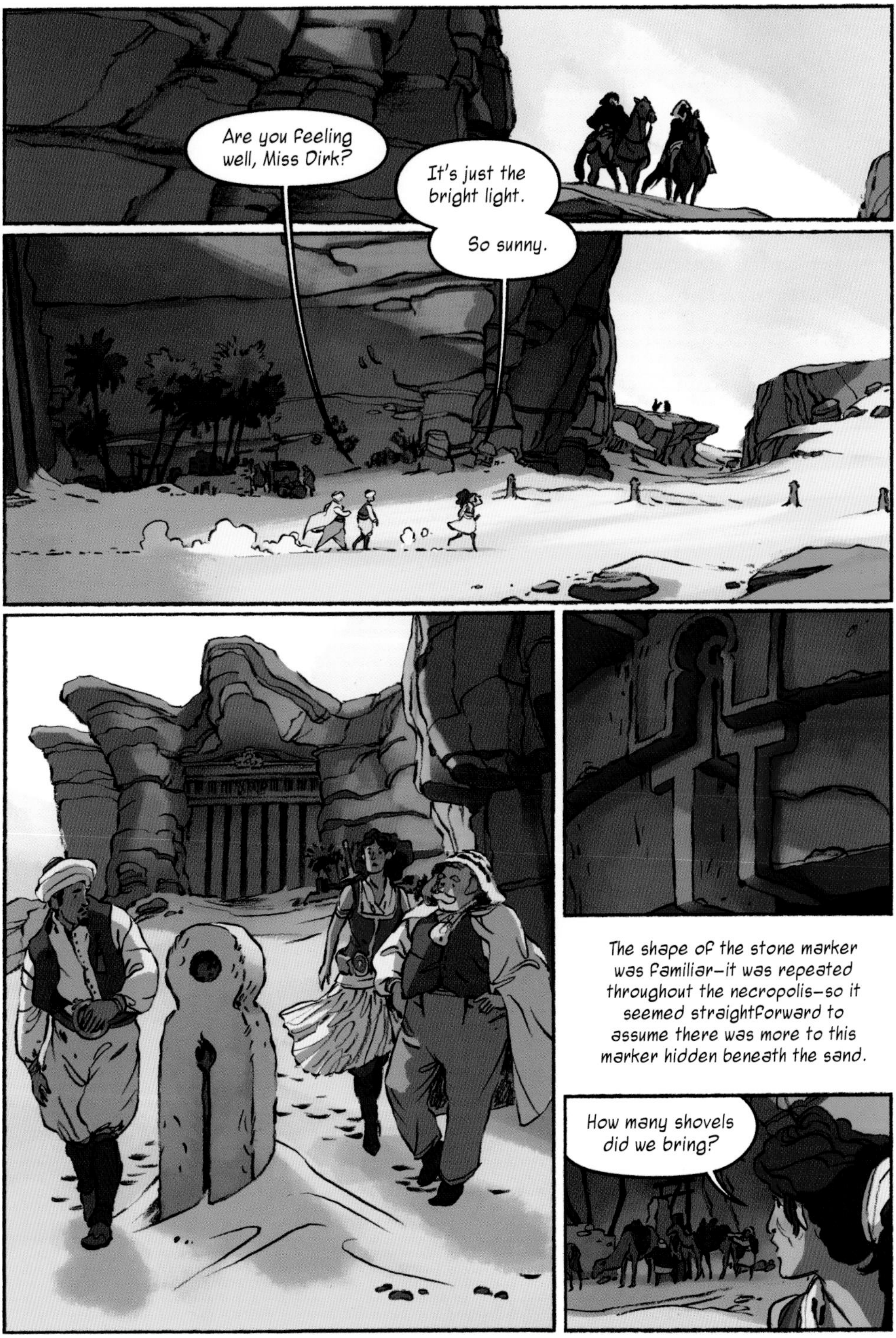
Are you feeling well, Miss Dirk?
It's just the bright light.
So sunny.
The shape of the stone marker was familiar—it was repeated throughout the necropolis—so it seemed straightforward to assume there was more to this marker hidden beneath the sand.
How many shovels did we bring?

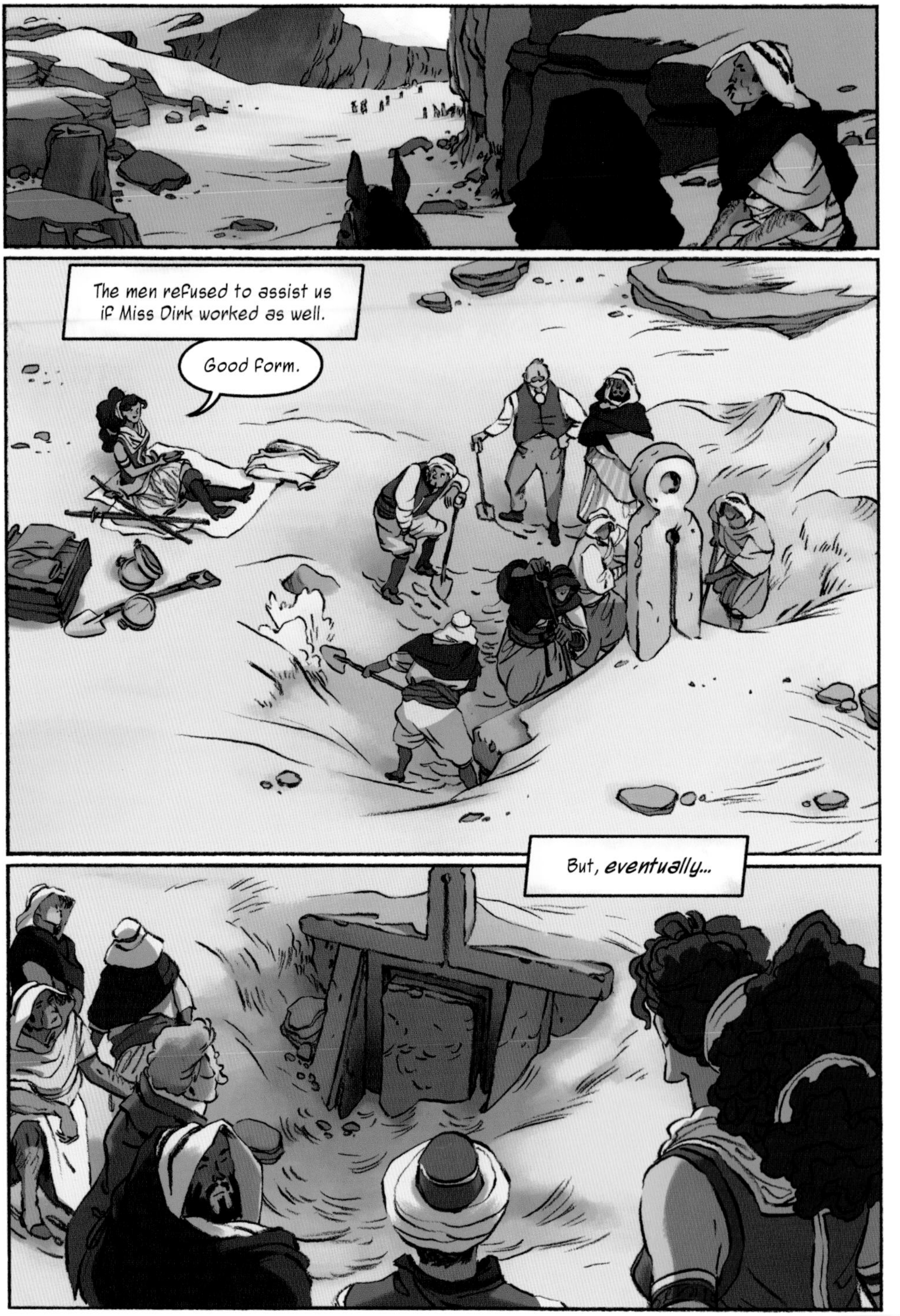
The men refused to assist us if Miss Dirk worked as well.
Good form.
But, *eventually*...

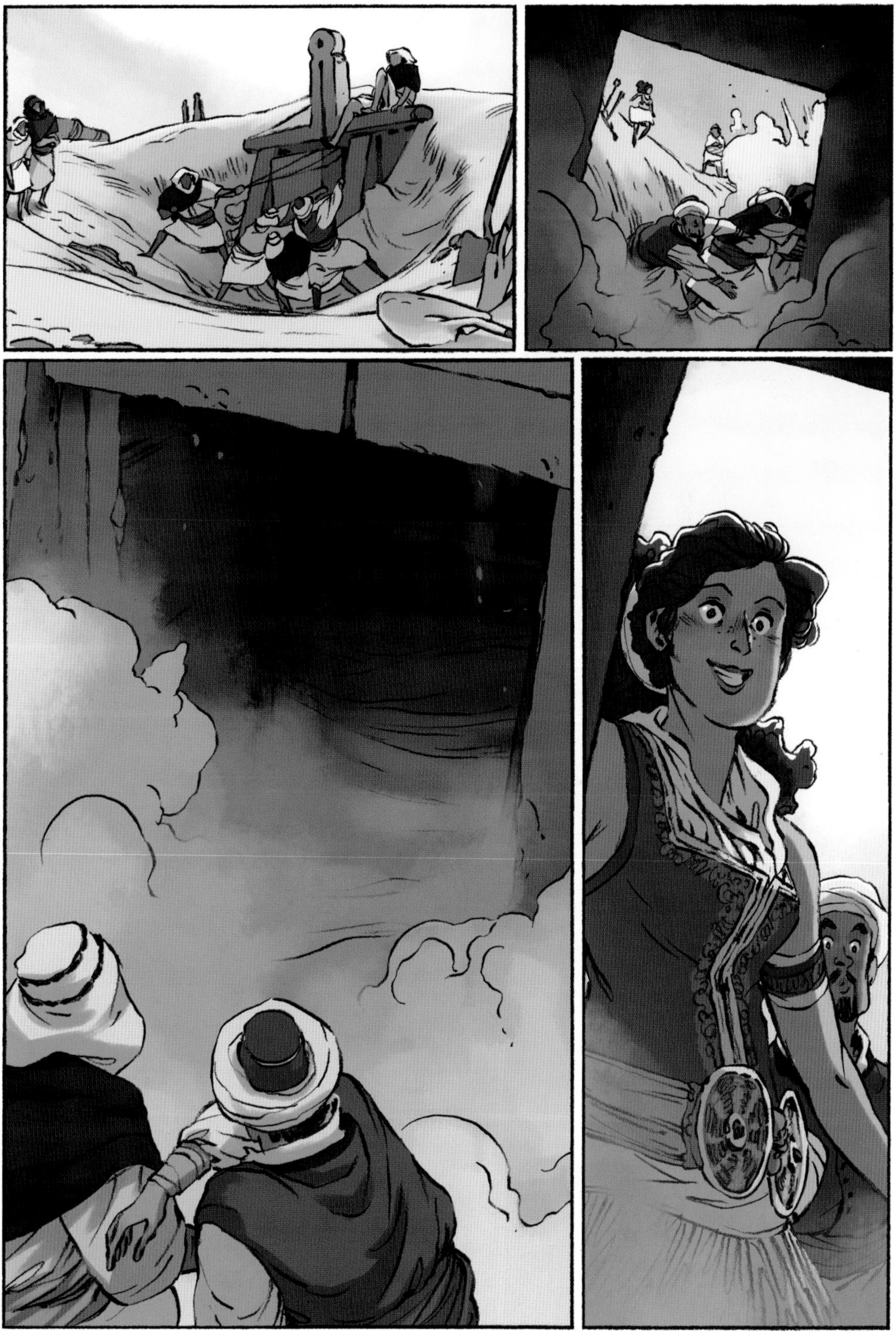

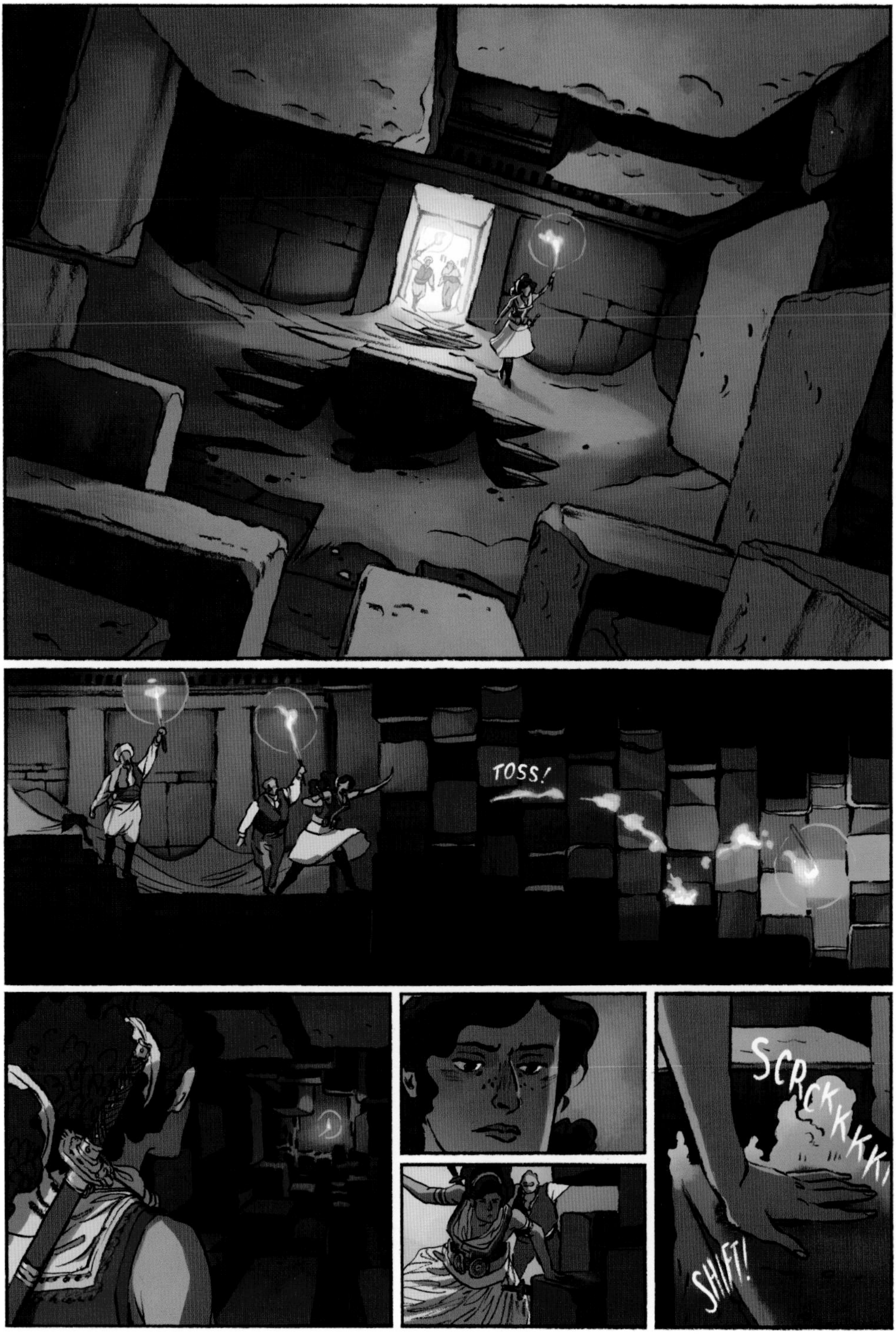
TOSS!
SCRCKKKK!
SHIFT!

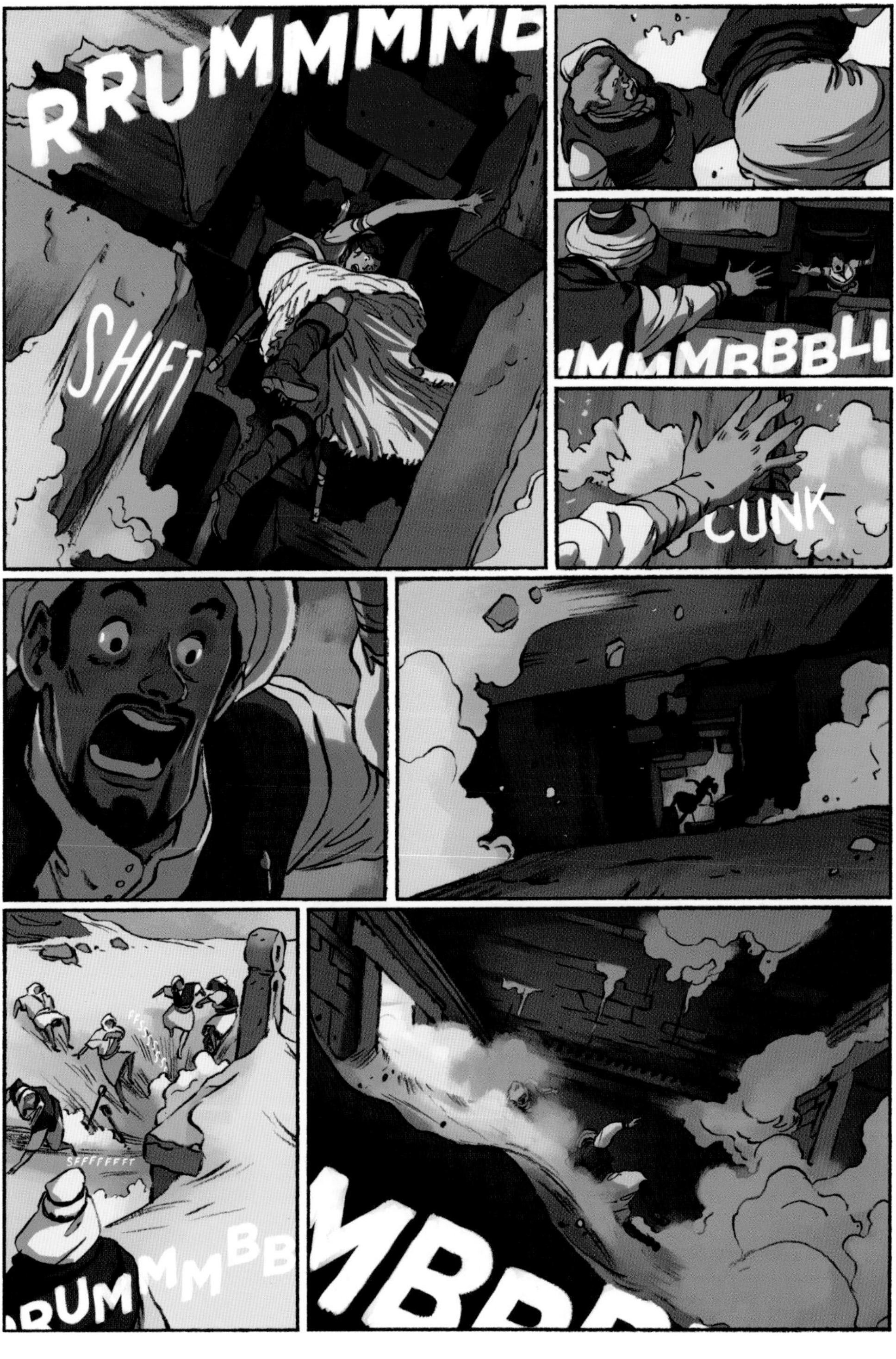
RRUMMMMMB
SHIFT
MMMMBBBLL
CUNK
FSSSSSS
SFFFFFFFT
RUMMMBB
MBBB

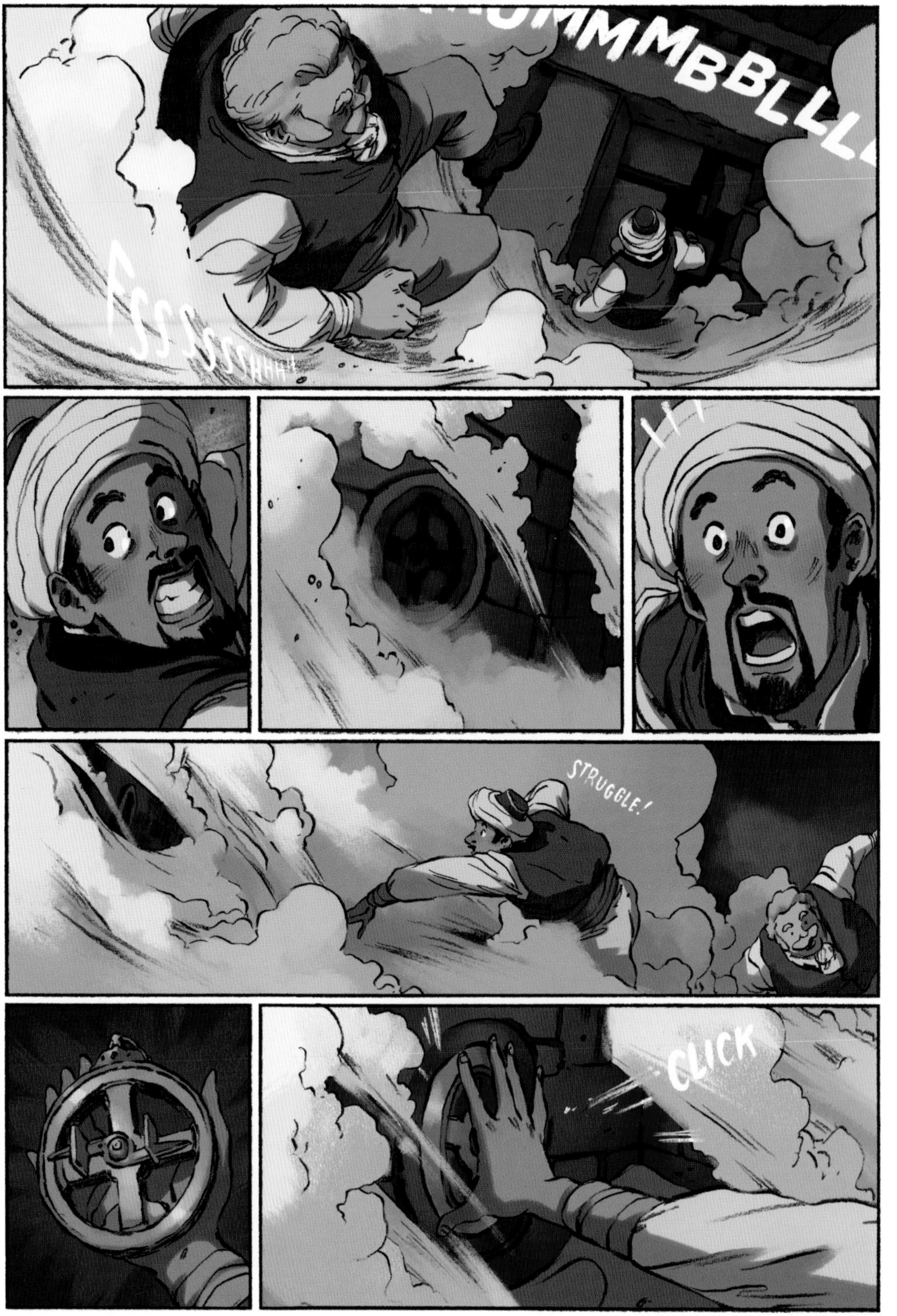
...UMMMMBBLLLL
FSSSSSSHHH!!
STRUGGLE!
CLICK

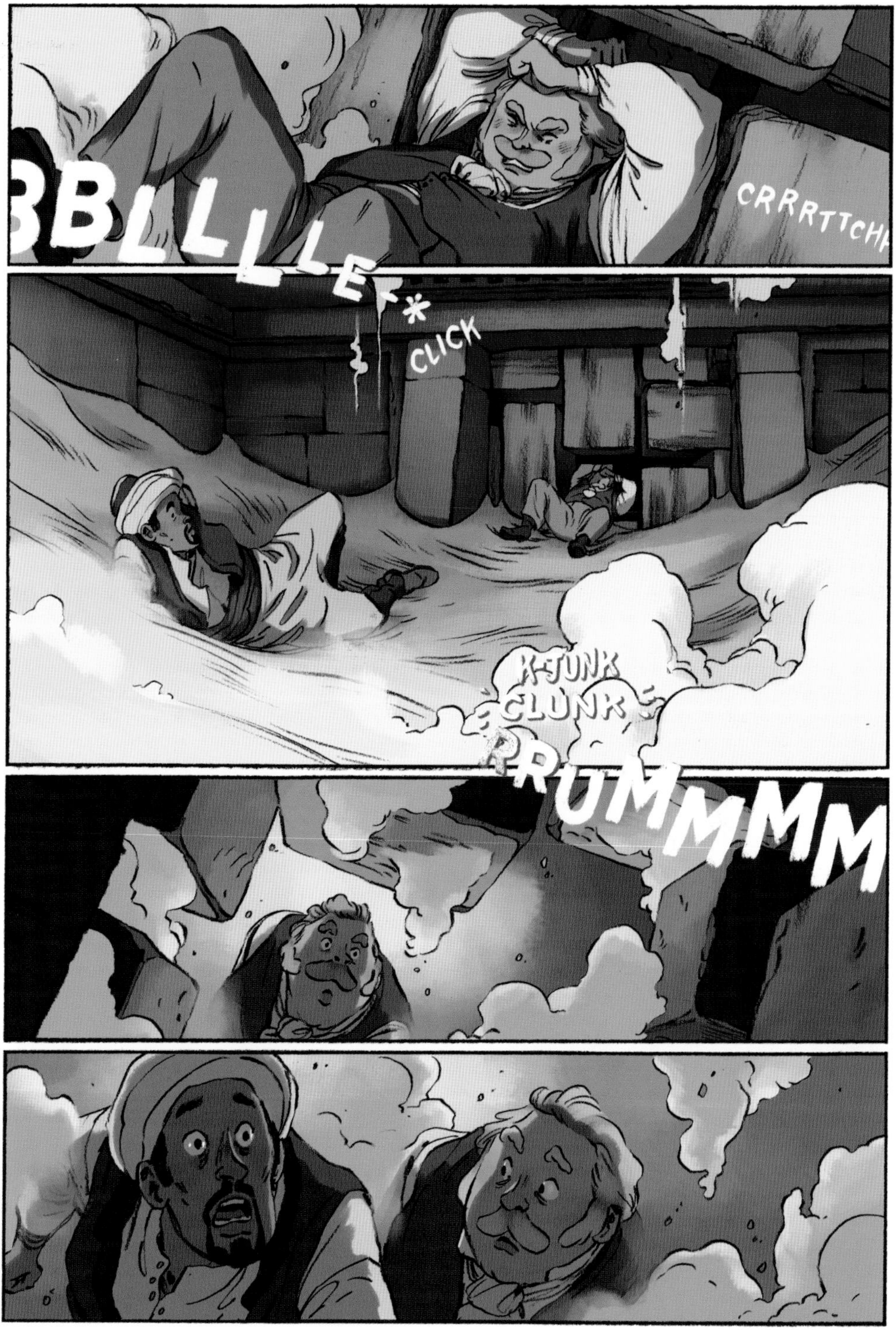
BBLLLLE-
CRRRTTCHF
*CLICK
K-TUNK
CLUNK
RRUMMMMM

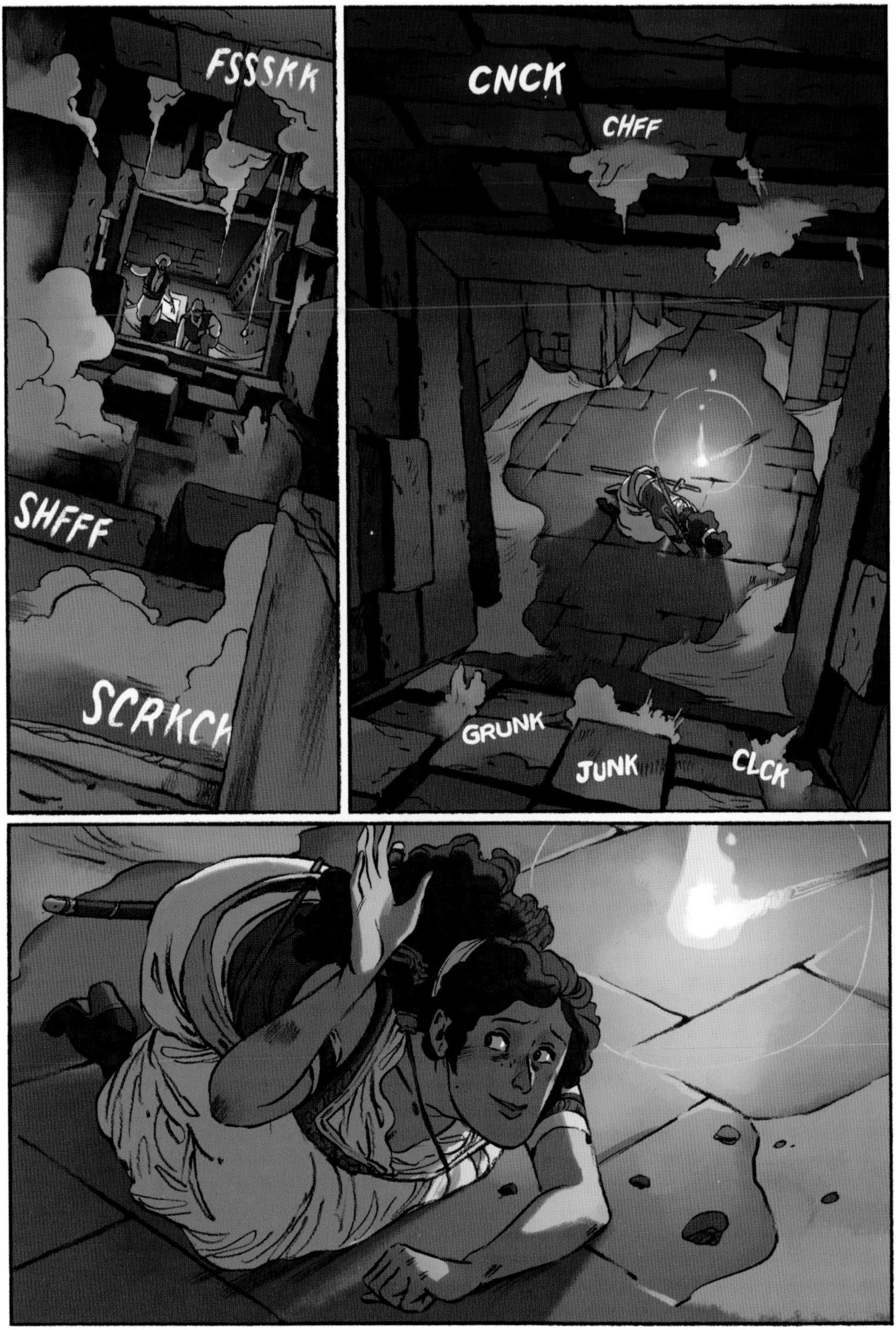
FSSSKK
SHFFF
SCRKCH
CNCK
CHFF
GRUNK
JUNK
CLCK

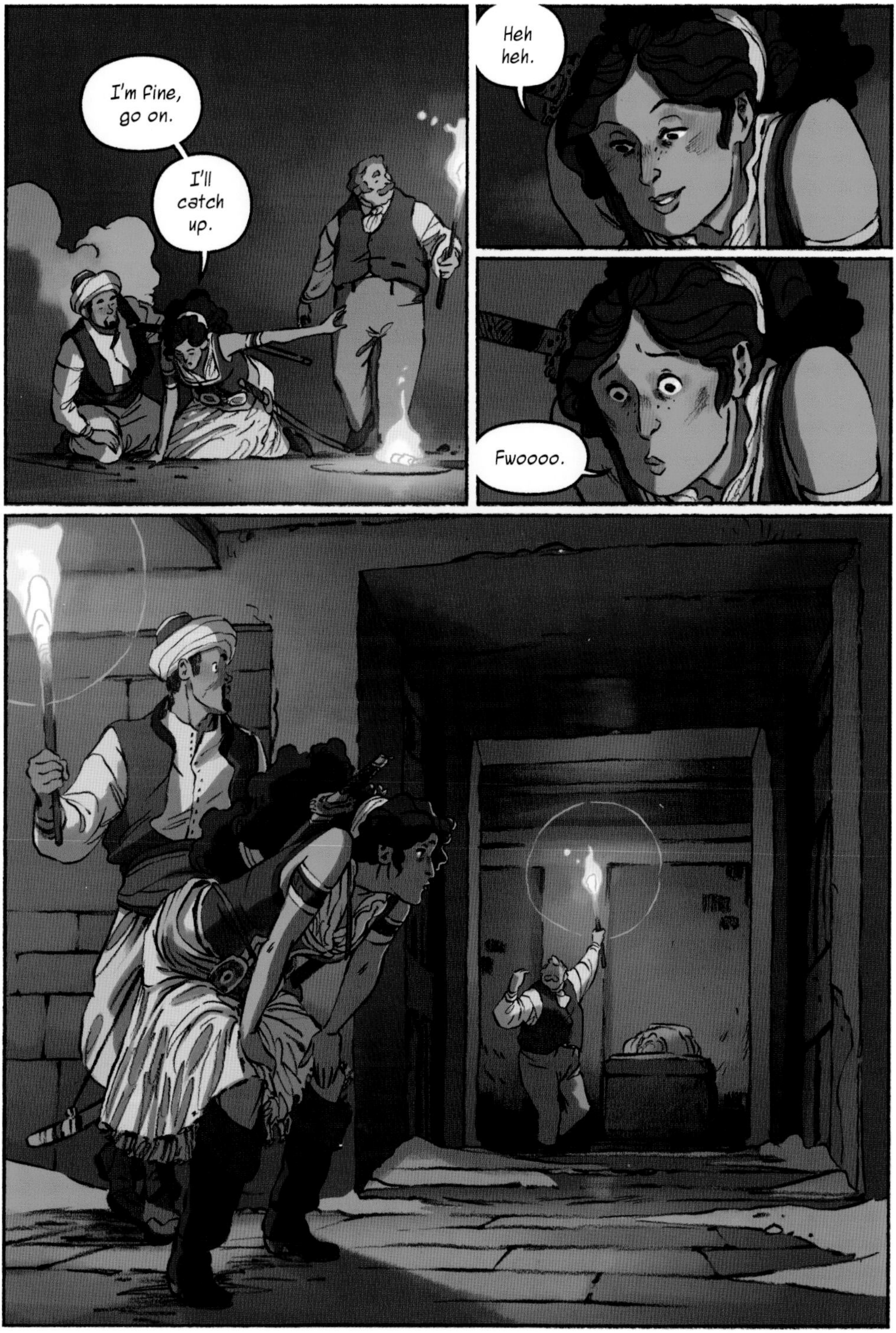
I'm fine, go on.
I'll catch up.
Heh heh.
Fwoooo.

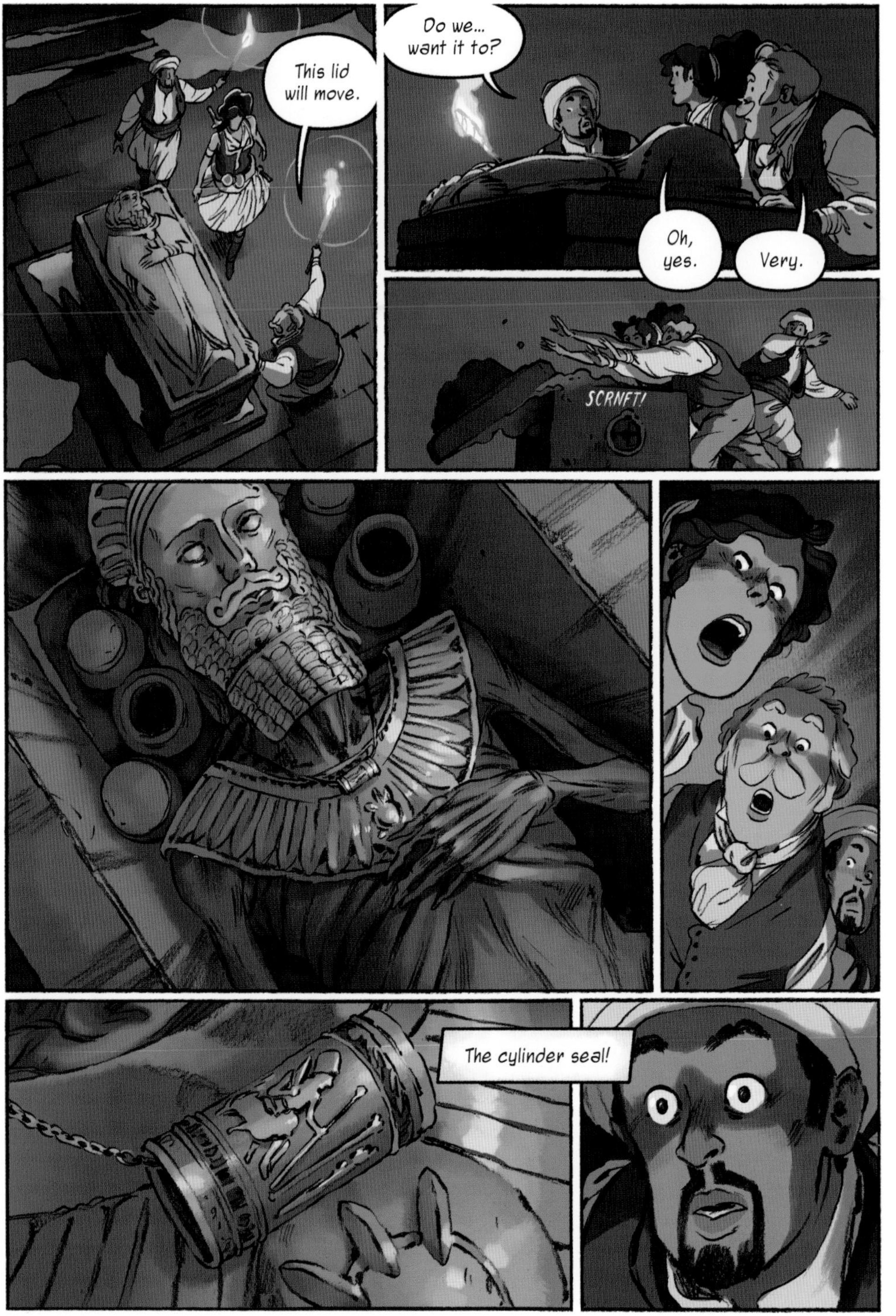
This lid will move.
Do we... want it to?
Oh, yes.
Very.
SCRNFT!
The cylinder seal!

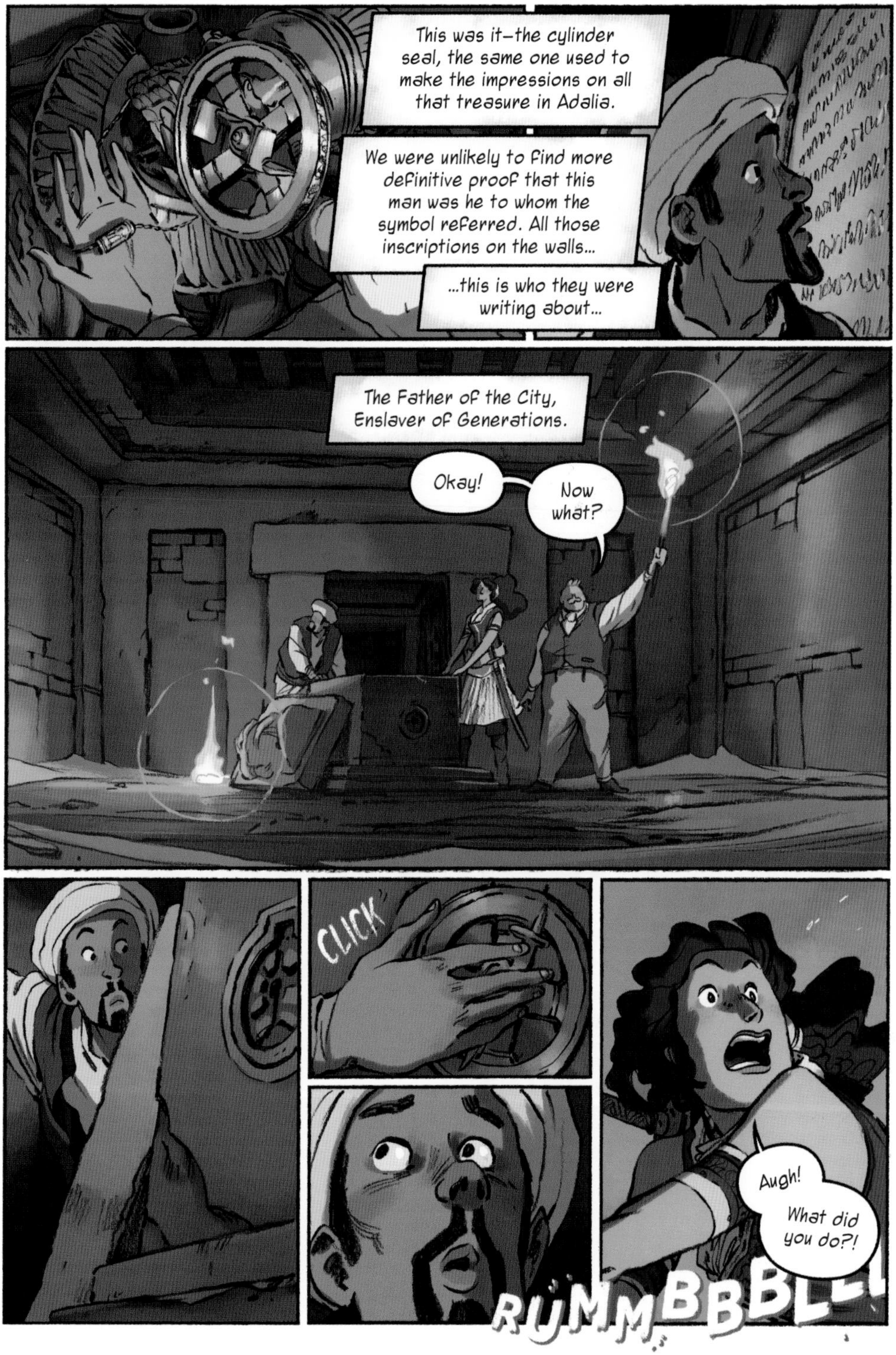

This was it—the cylinder seal, the same one used to make the impressions on all that treasure in Adalia.
We were unlikely to find more definitive proof that this man was he to whom the symbol referred. All those inscriptions on the walls...
...this is who they were writing about...
The Father of the City, Enslaver of Generations.
Okay!
Now what?
CLICK
Augh!
What did you do?!
RUMMBBBLE

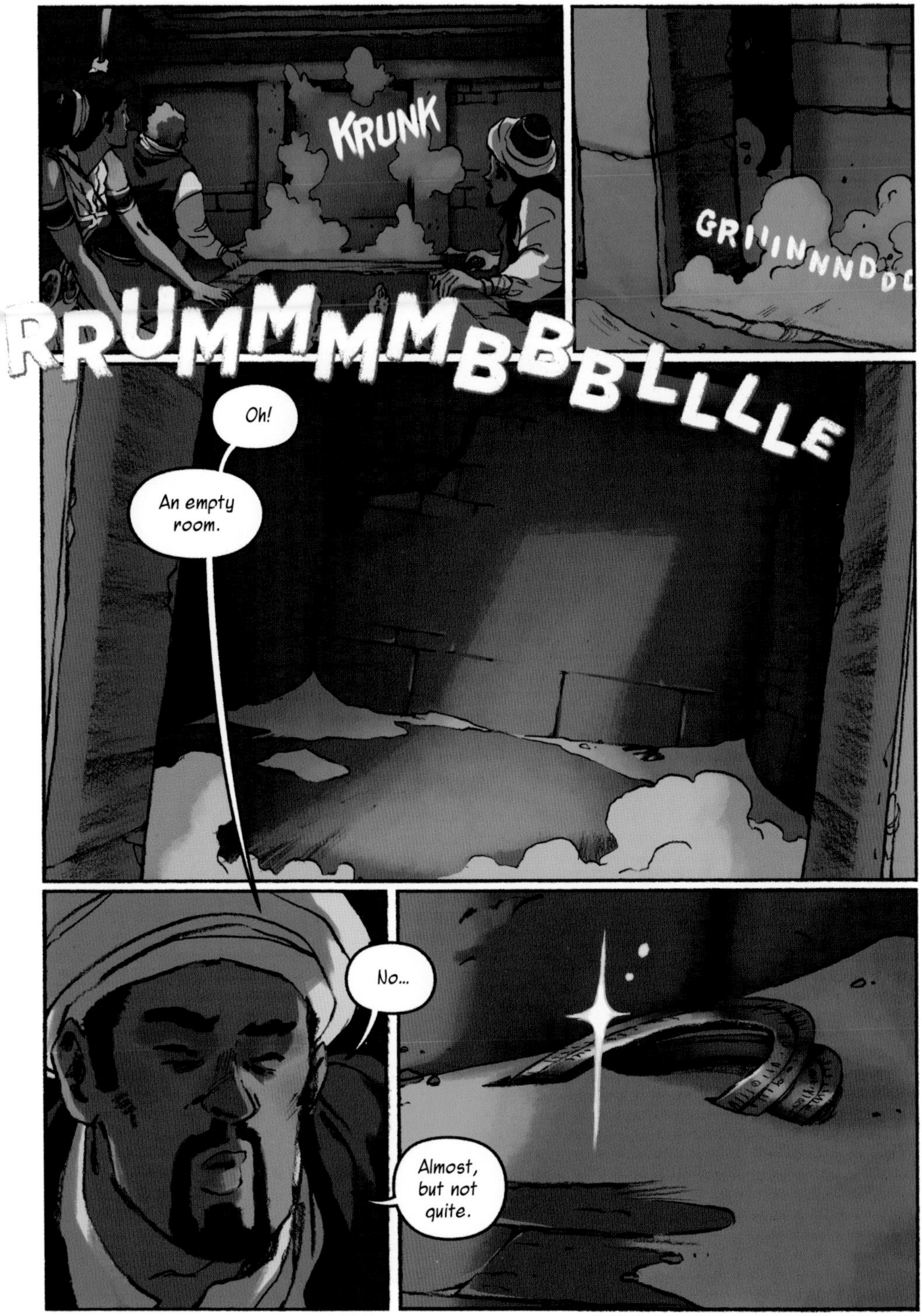
KRUNK
GRIIINNNDDD
RRUMMMMMBBBLLLLE
Oh!
An empty room.
No...
Almost, but not quite.

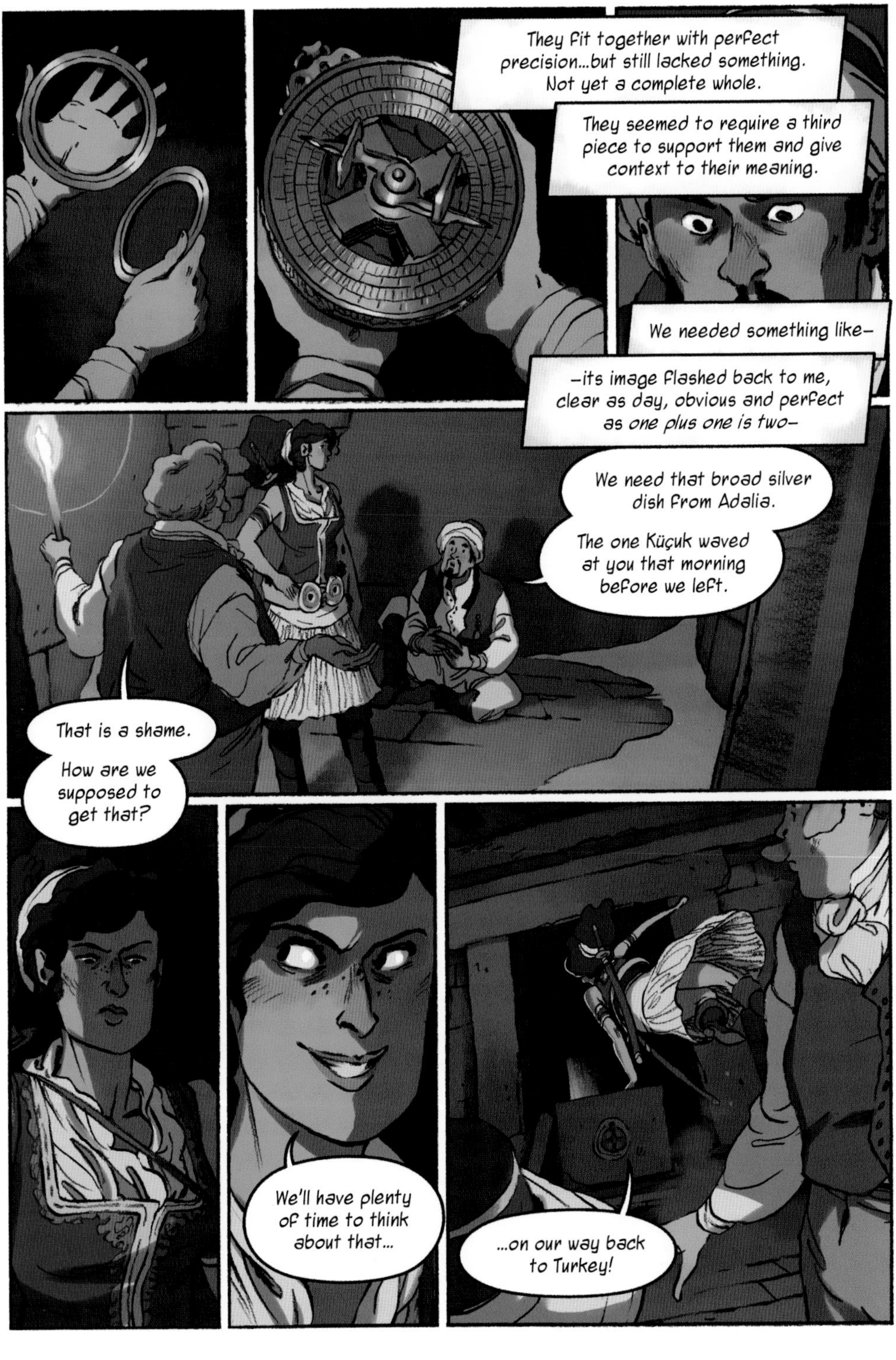

They fit together with perfect precision...but still lacked something. Not yet a complete whole.
They seemed to require a third piece to support them and give context to their meaning.
We needed something like—
—its image flashed back to me, clear as day, obvious and perfect as *one plus one is two*—
We need that broad silver dish from Adalia.
The one Küçuk waved at you that morning before we left.
That is a shame.
How are we supposed to get that?
We'll have plenty of time to think about that...
...on our way back to Turkey!

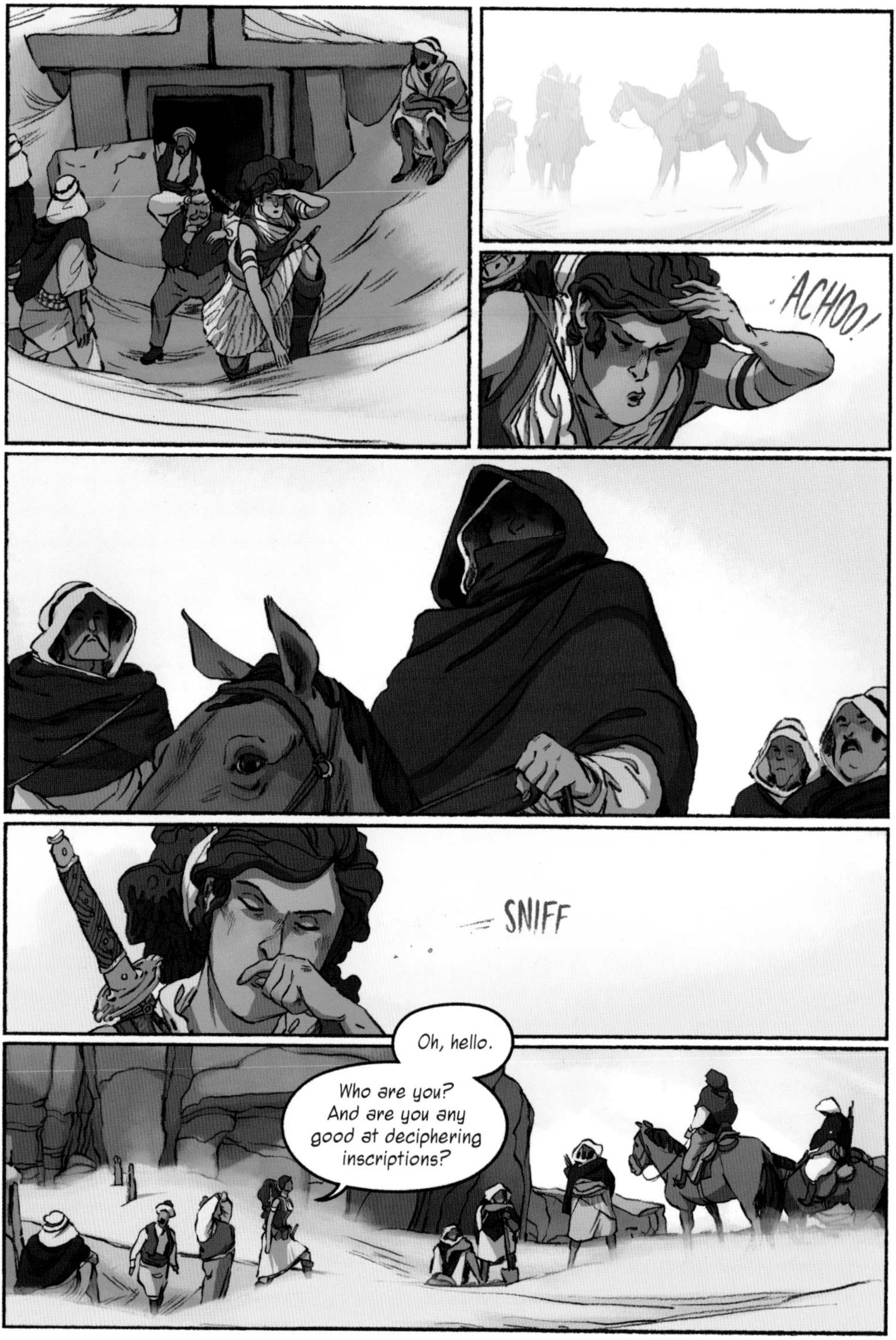
ACHOO!
SNIFF
Oh, hello.
Who are you? And are you any good at deciphering inscriptions?

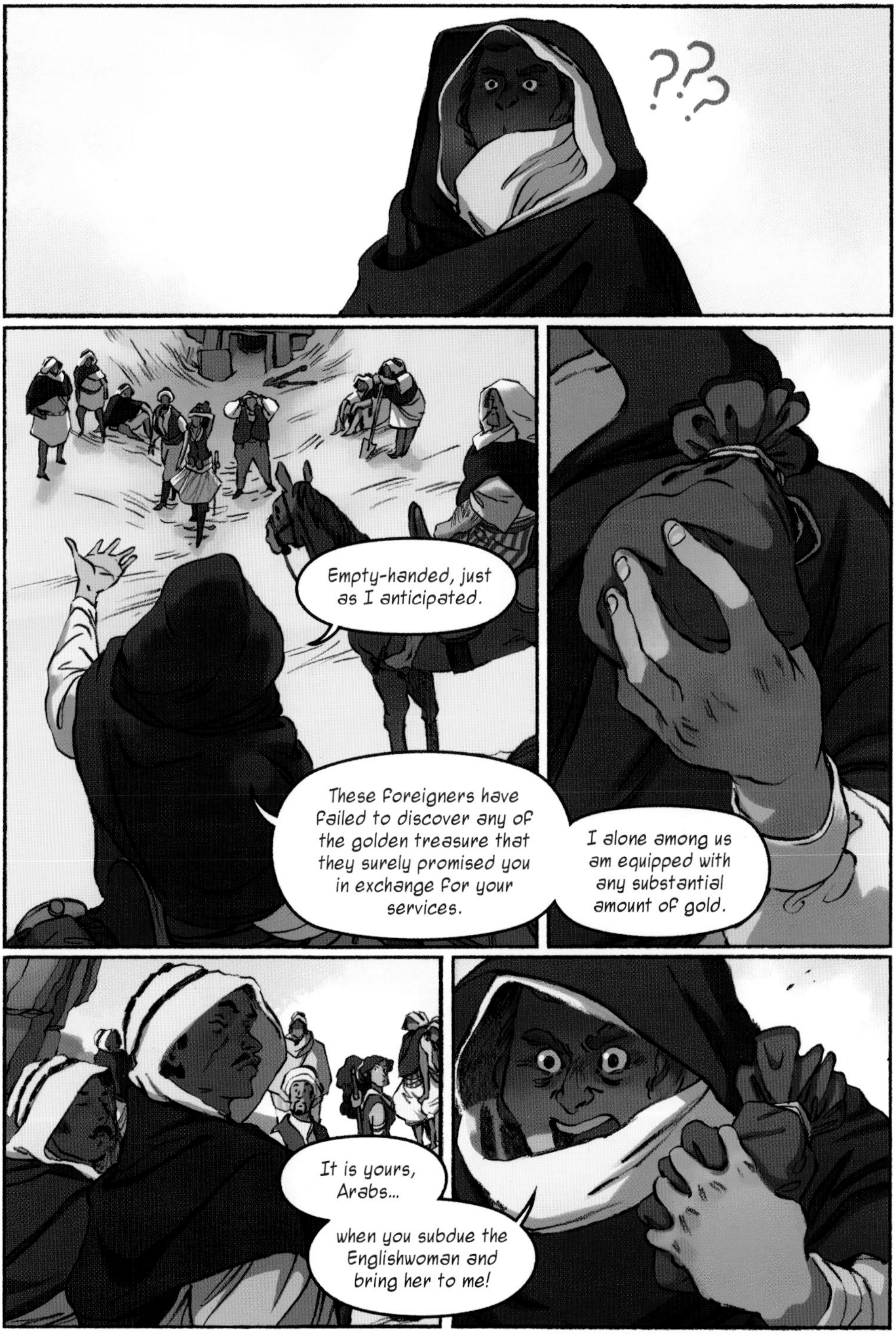
???
Empty-handed, just as I anticipated.
These foreigners have failed to discover any of the golden treasure that they surely promised you in exchange for your services.
I alone among us am equipped with any substantial amount of gold.
It is yours, Arabs...
when you subdue the Englishwoman and bring her to me!

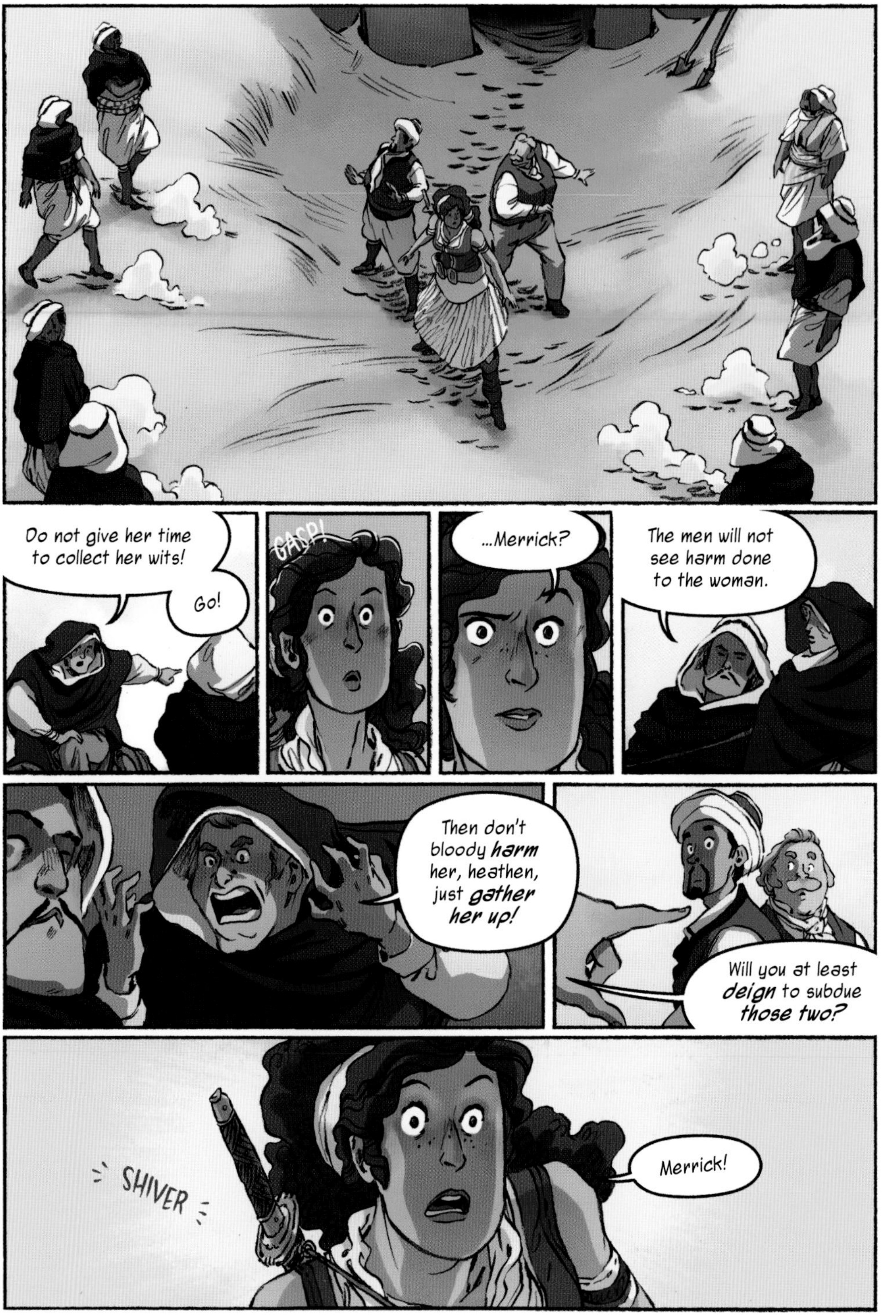
Do not give her time to collect her wits!
Go!
GASP!
...Merrick?
The men will not see harm done to the woman.
Then don't bloody harm her, heathen, just gather her up!
Will you at least deign to subdue those two?
SHIVER
Merrick!

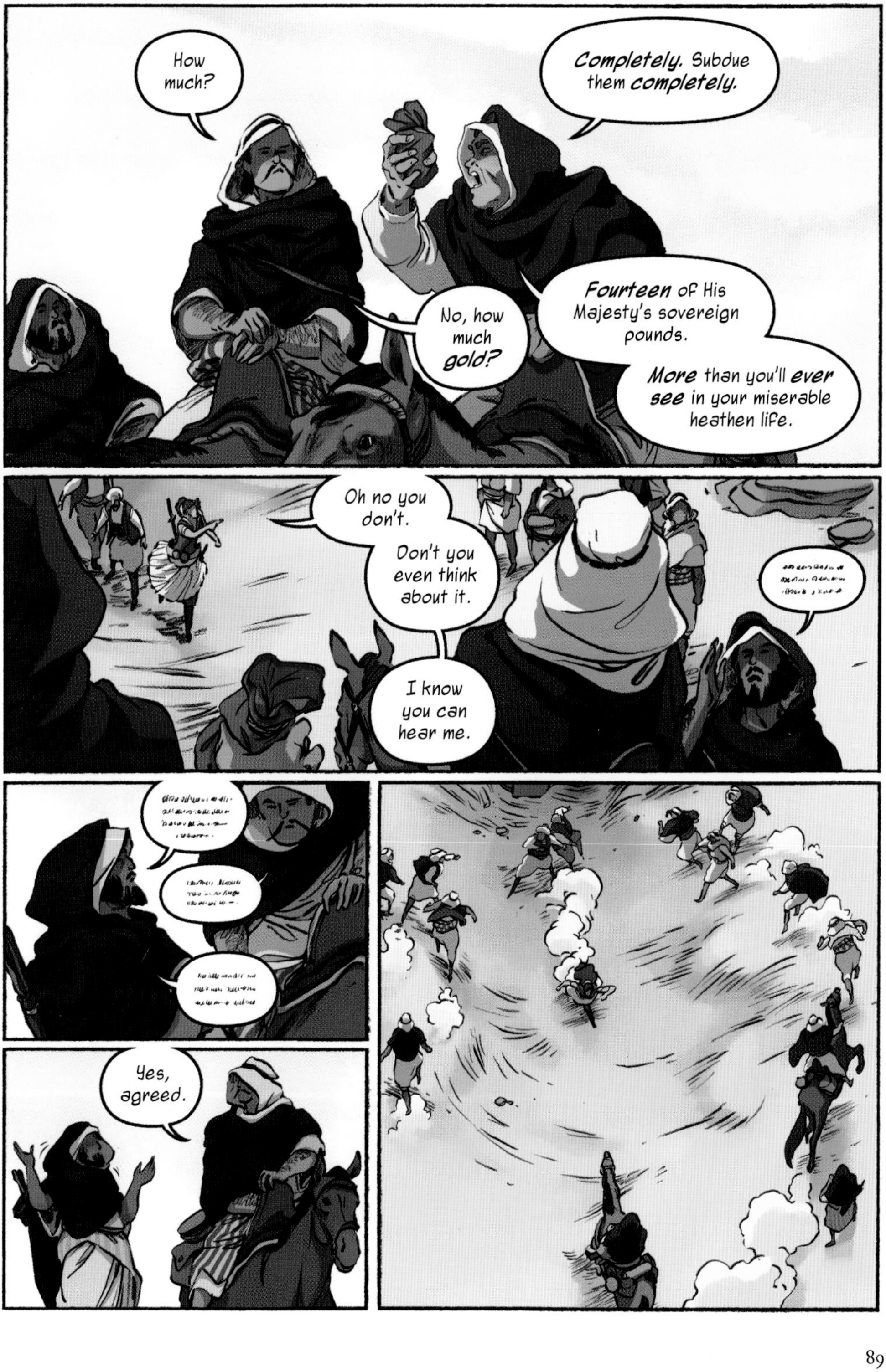
How much?
Completely. Subdue them completely.
No, how much gold?
Fourteen of His Majesty's sovereign pounds.
More than you'll ever see in your miserable heathen life.
Oh no you don't.
Don't you even think about it.
I know you can hear me.
Yes, agreed.

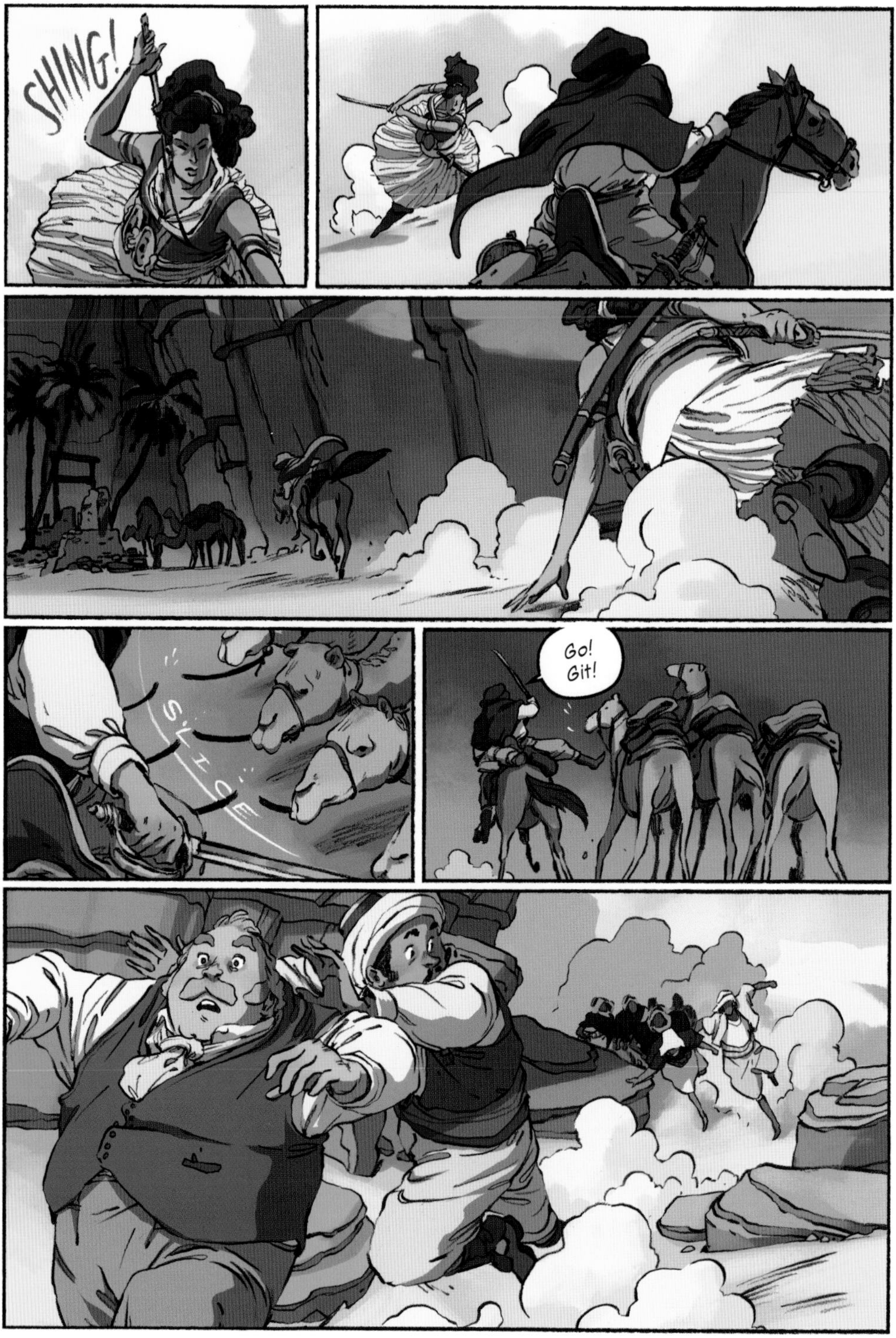
SHING!
SLICE
Go! Git!

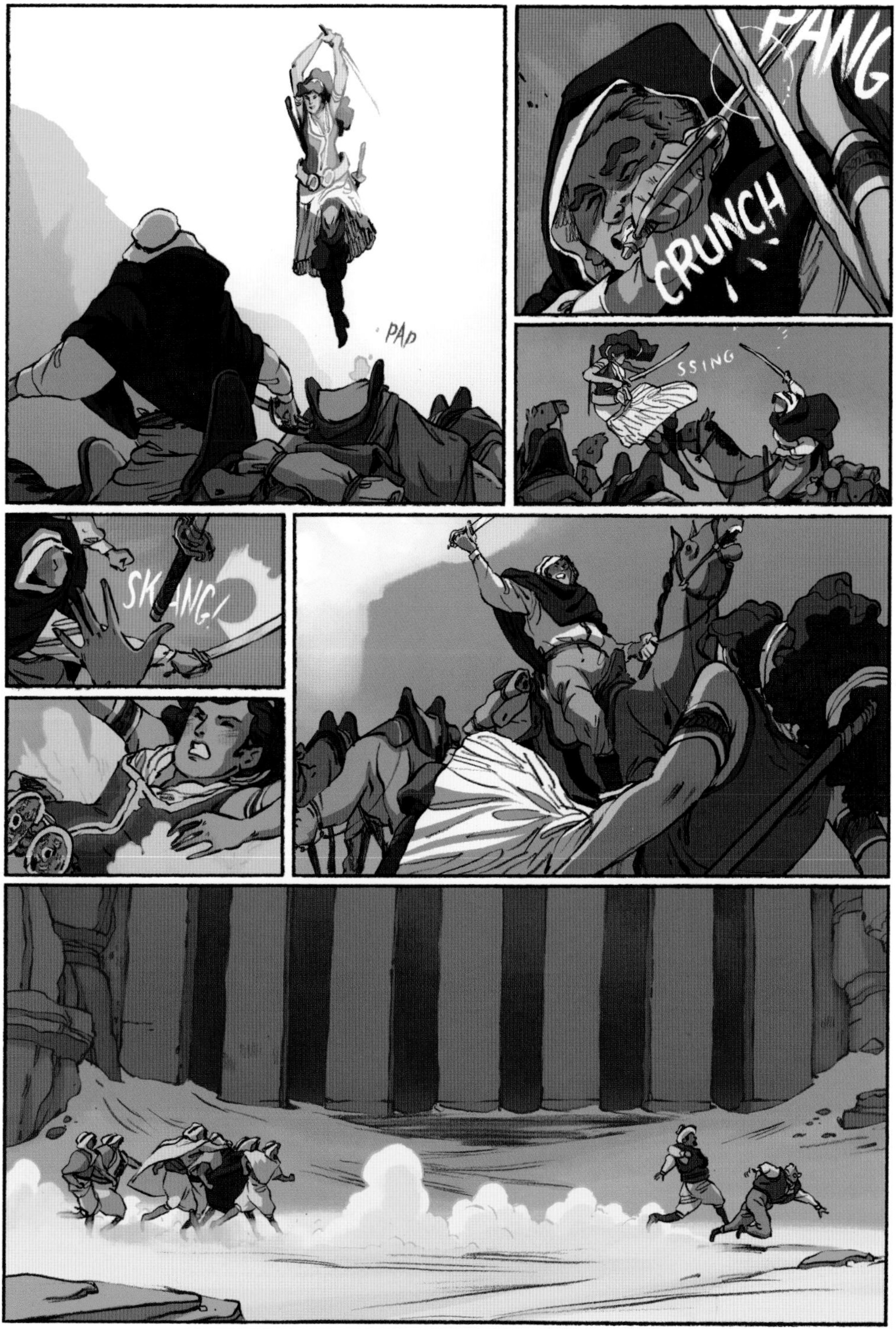
PAP
PANG
CRUNCH
SSING
SKANG!

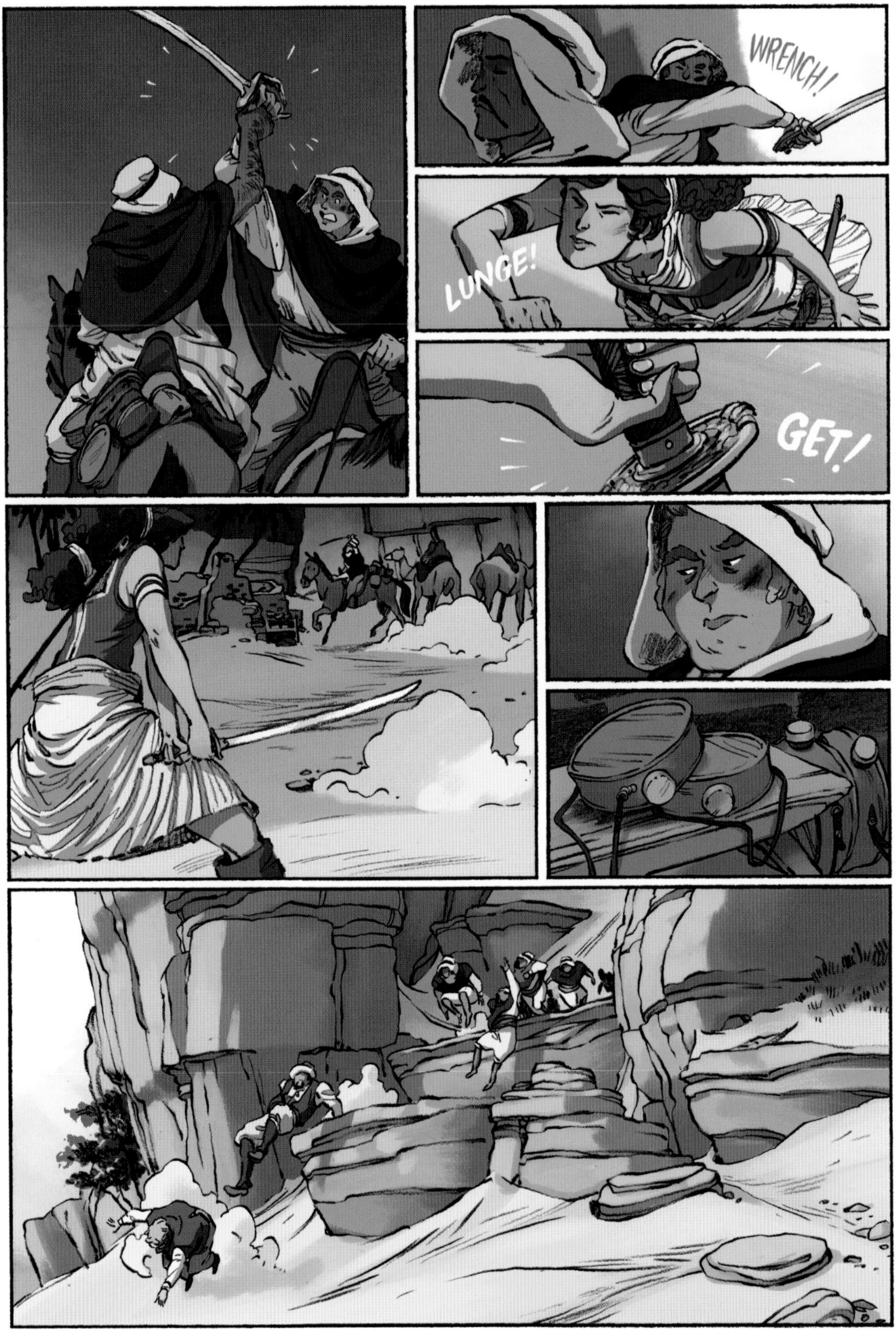
WRENCH!
LUNGE!
GET!

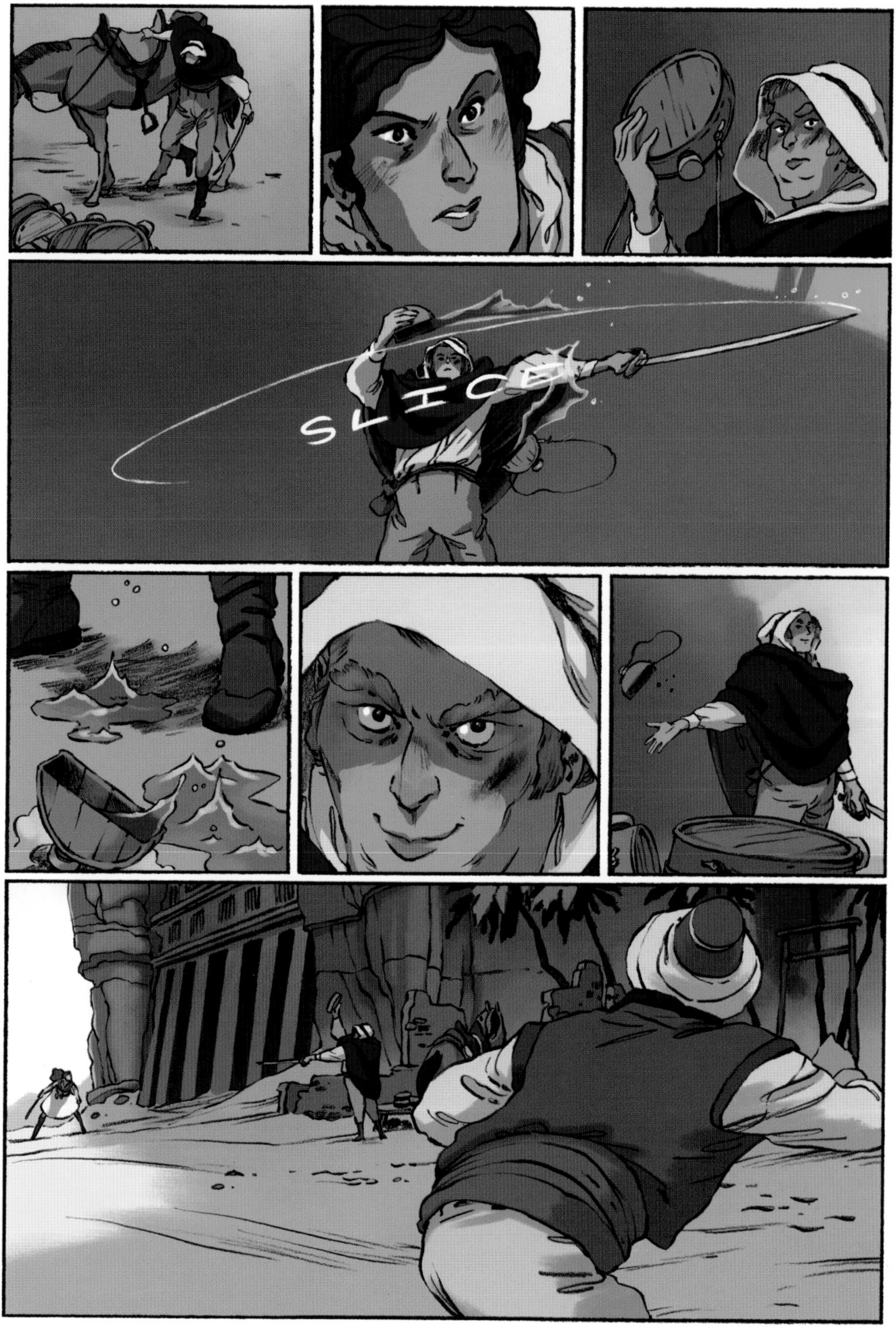
SLICE

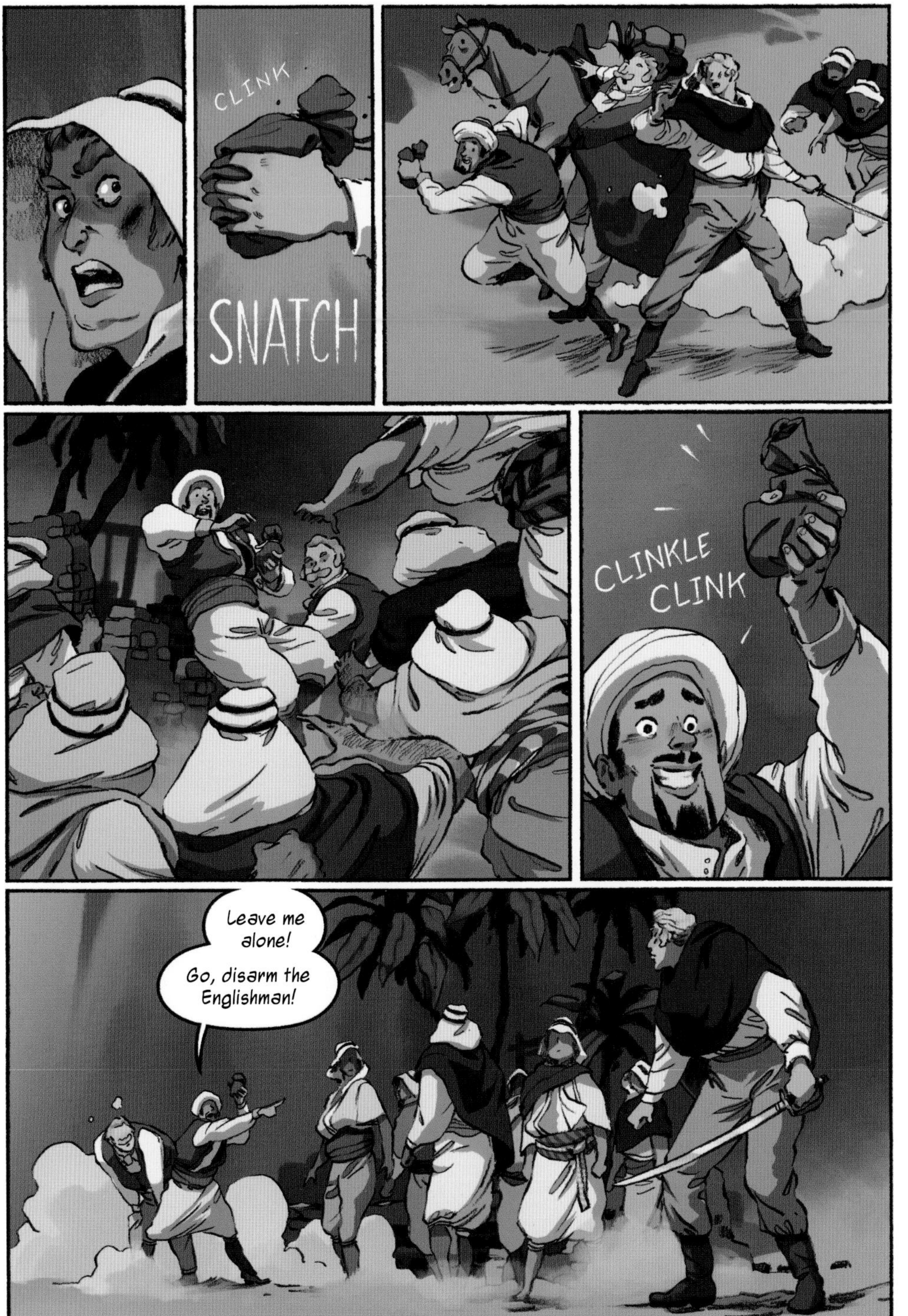
CLINK
SNATCH
CLINKLE
CLINK
Leave me alone!
Go, disarm the Englishman!

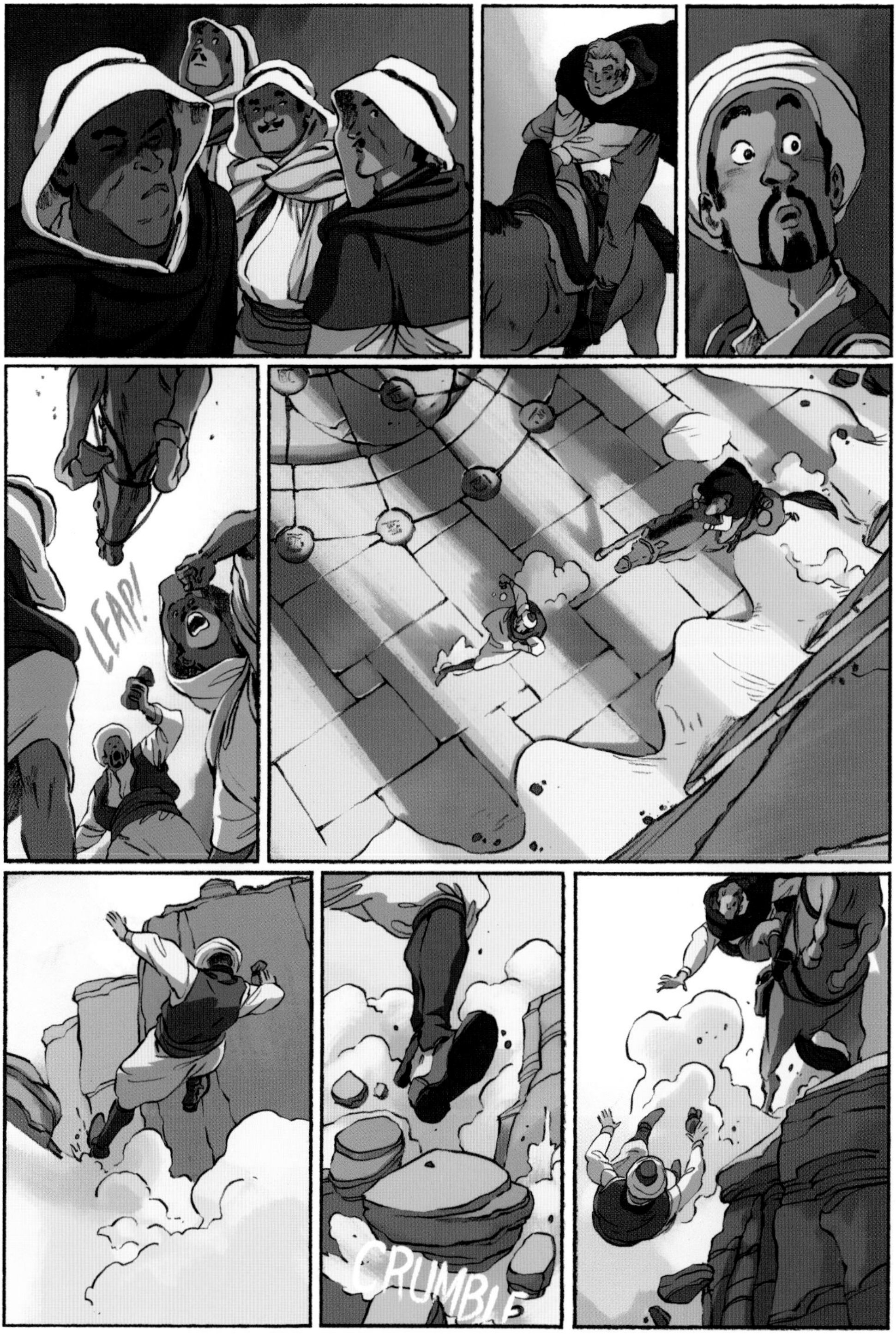
LEAP!
CRUMBLE

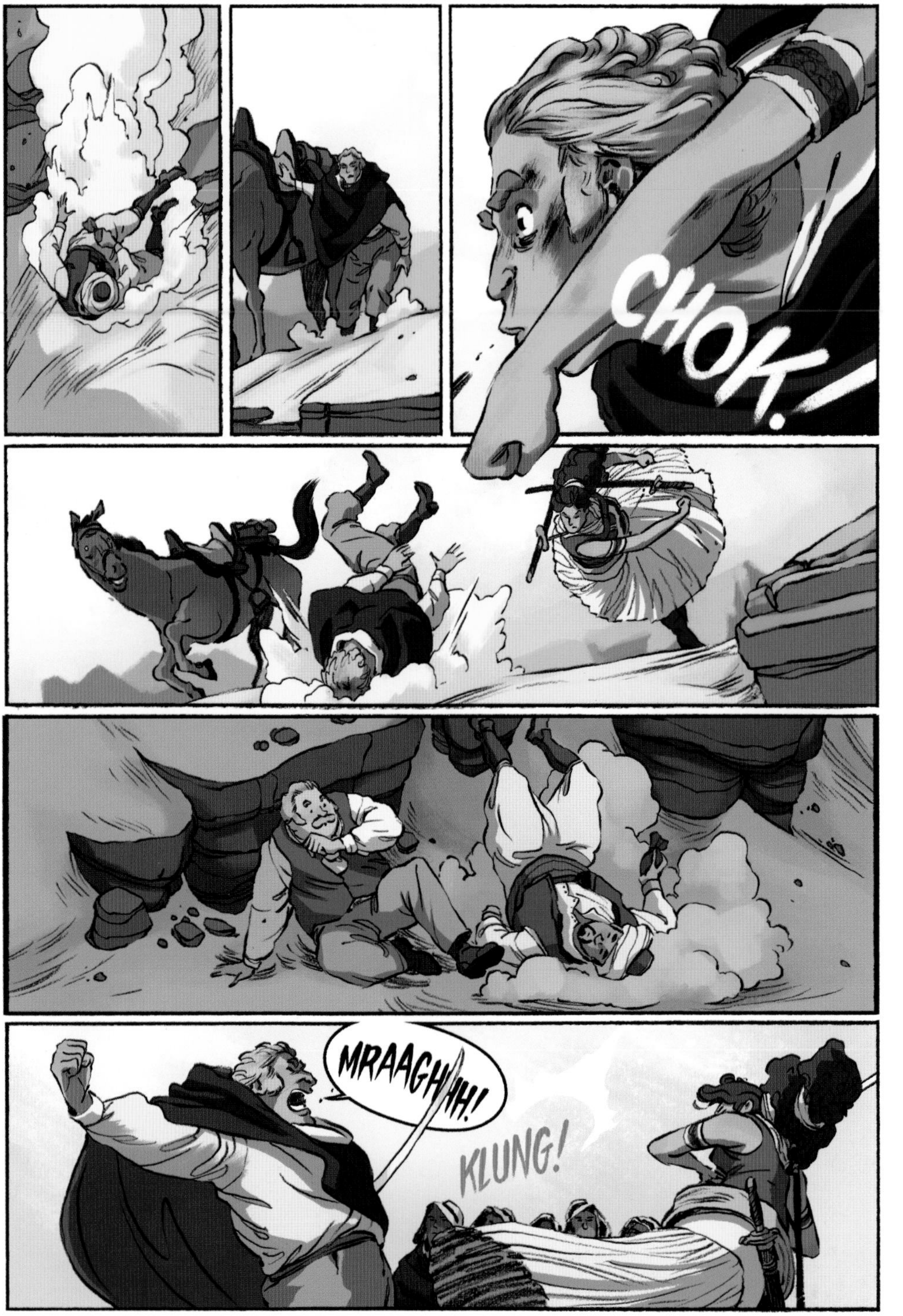
CHOK!
MRAAGHHH!
KLUNG!

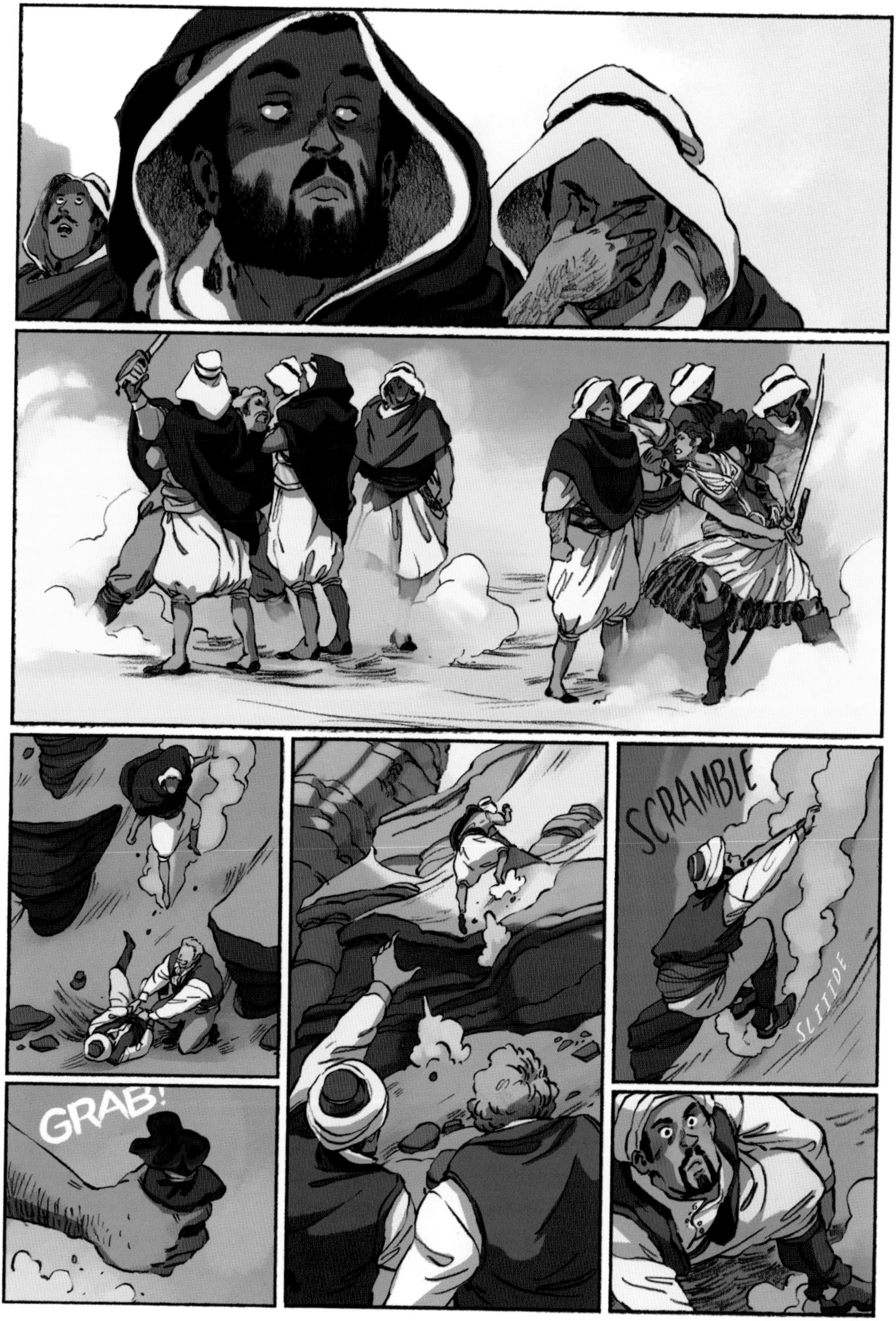
SCRAMBLE
SLIIIDE
GRAB!

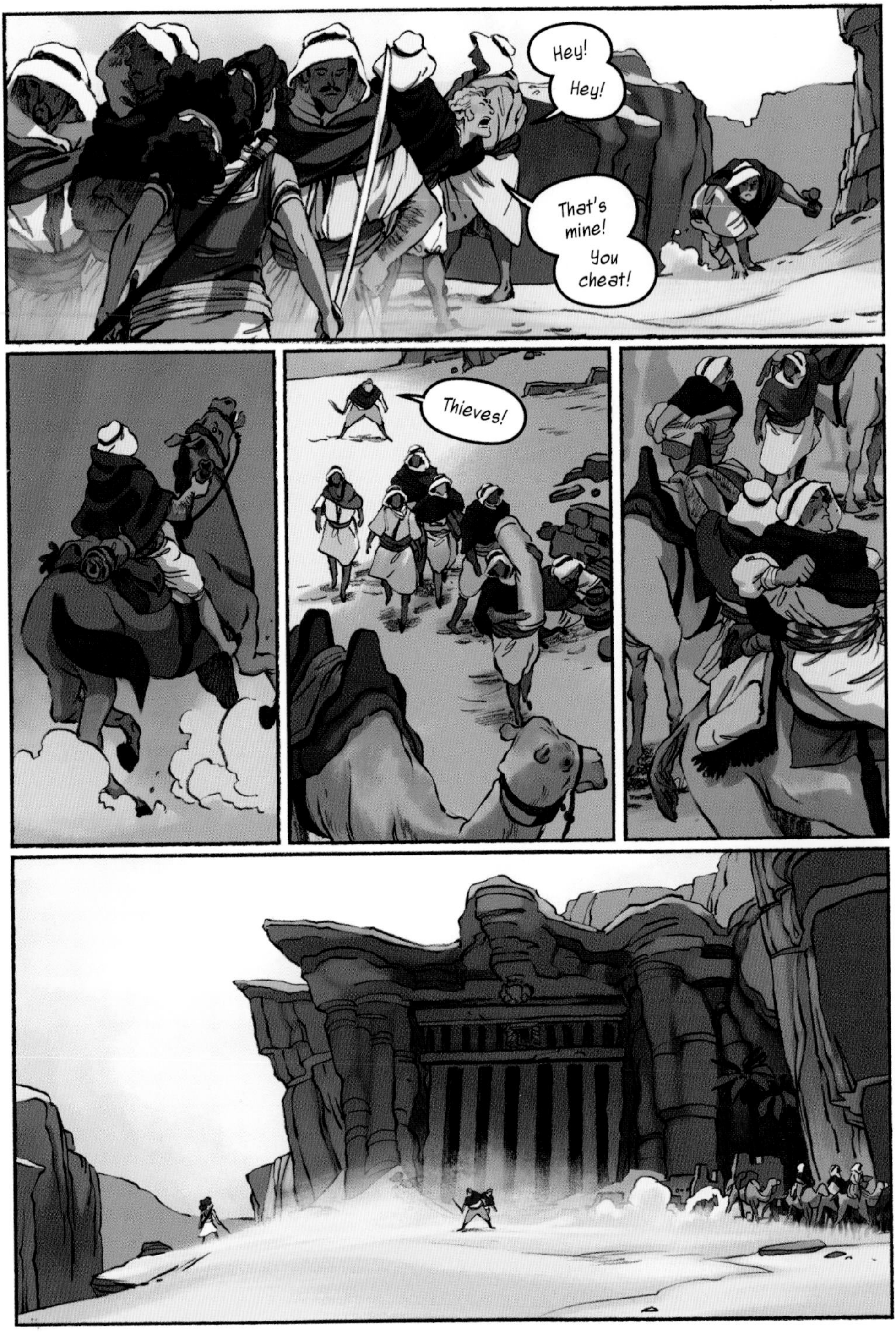
Hey!
Hey!
That's mine!
You cheat!
Thieves!

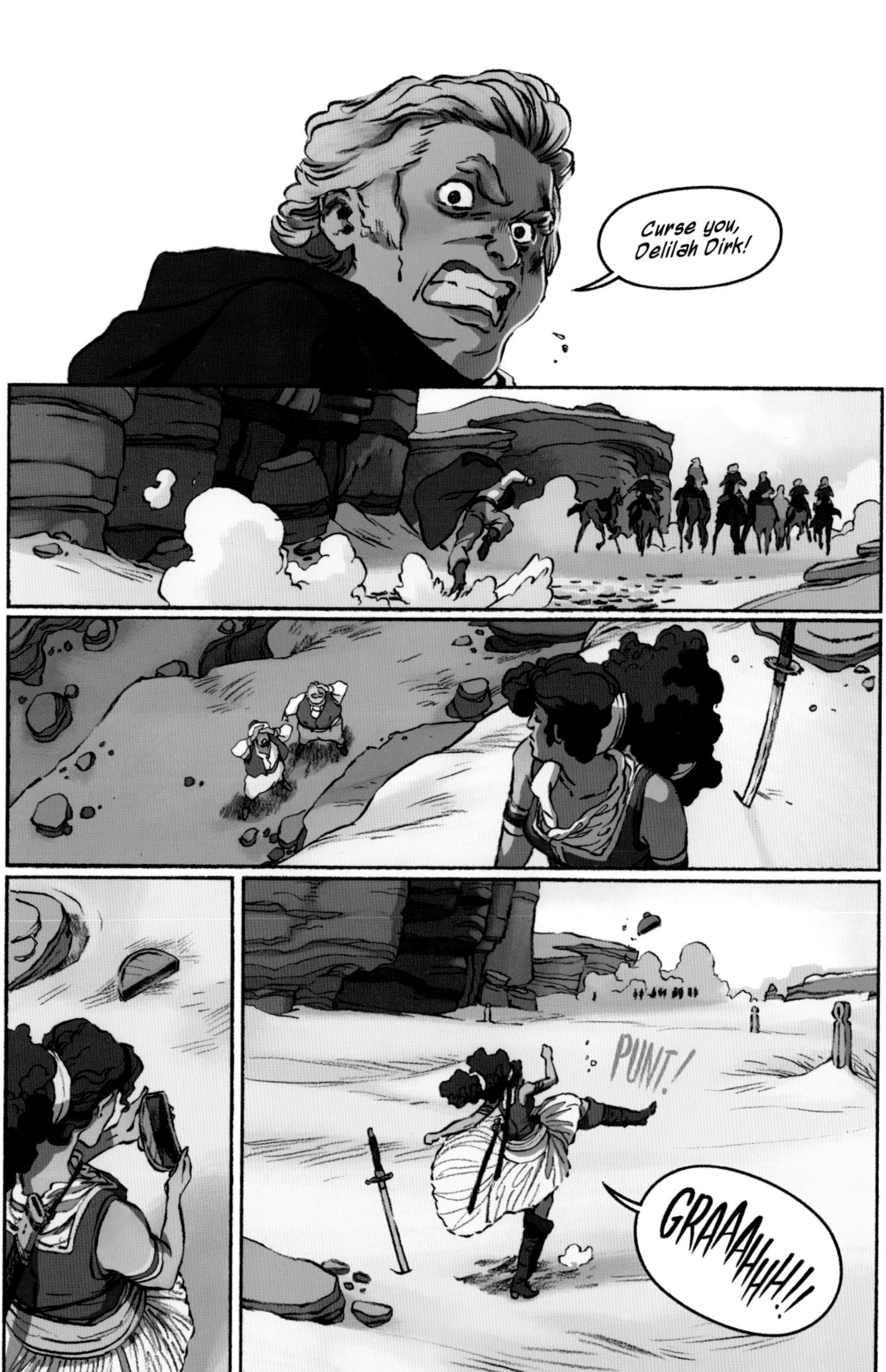
Curse you, Delilah Dirk!
PUNT!
GRAAAHHH!!

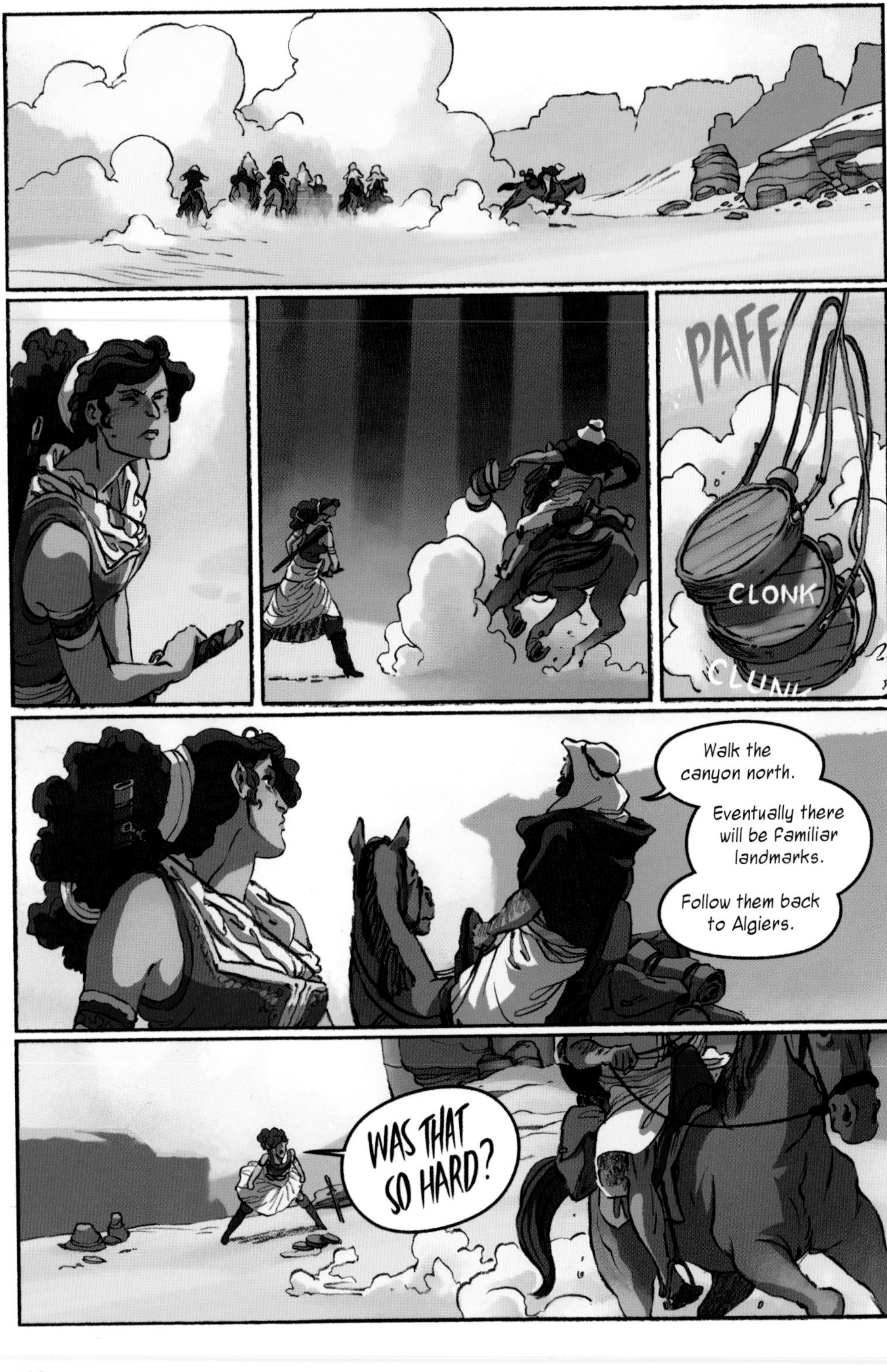
PAFF
CLONK
CLUNK
Walk the canyon north.
Eventually there will be familiar landmarks.
Follow them back to Algiers.
WAS THAT SO HARD?

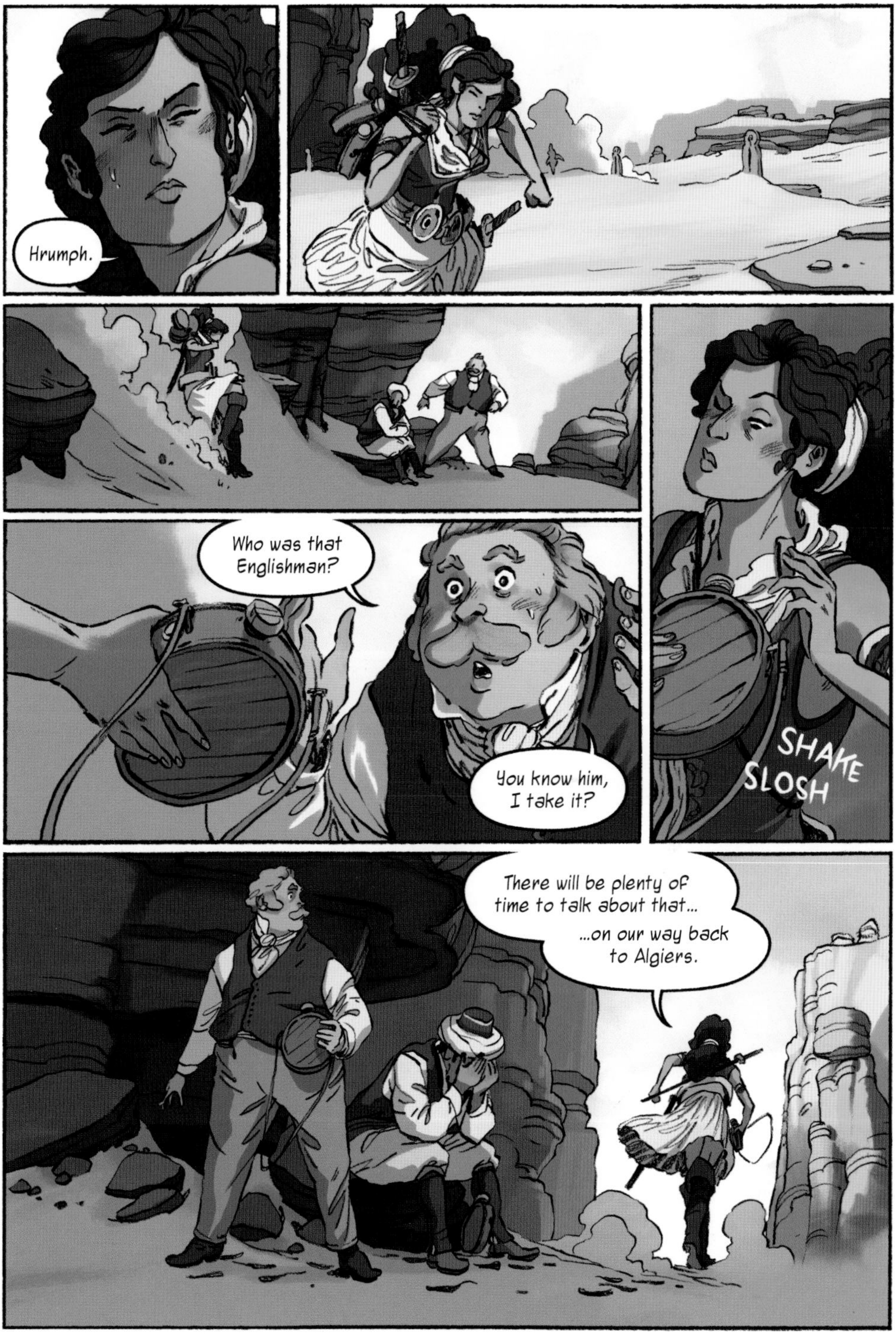
Hrumph.
Who was that Englishman?
You know him, I take it?
SHAKE
SLOSH
There will be plenty of time to talk about that...
...on our way back to Algiers.

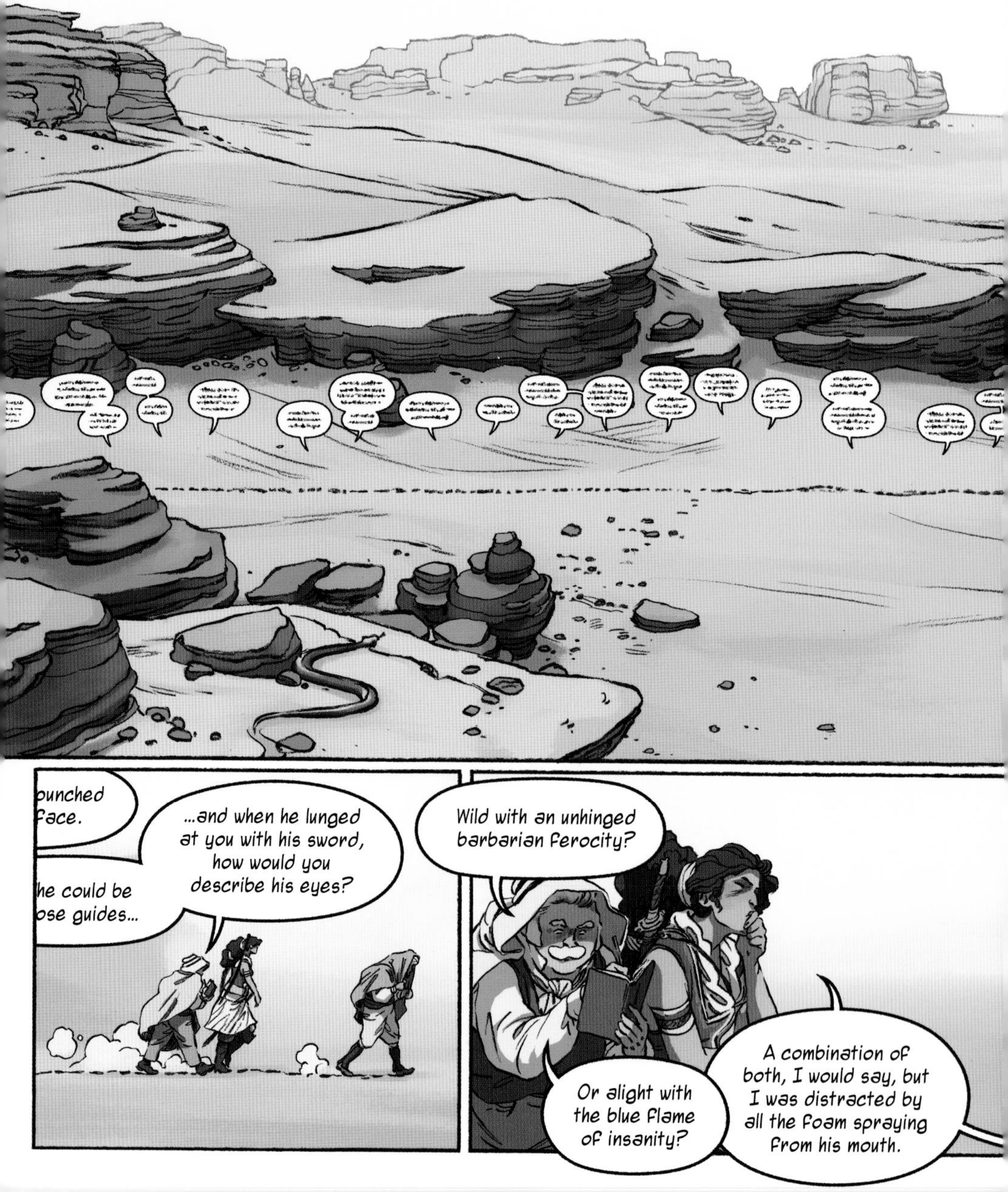
unched
face.
...and when he lunged at you with his sword, how would you describe his eyes?
he could be
ose guides...
Wild with an unhinged barbarian ferocity?
Or alight with the blue flame of insanity?
A combination of both, I would say, but I was distracted by all the foam spraying from his mouth.

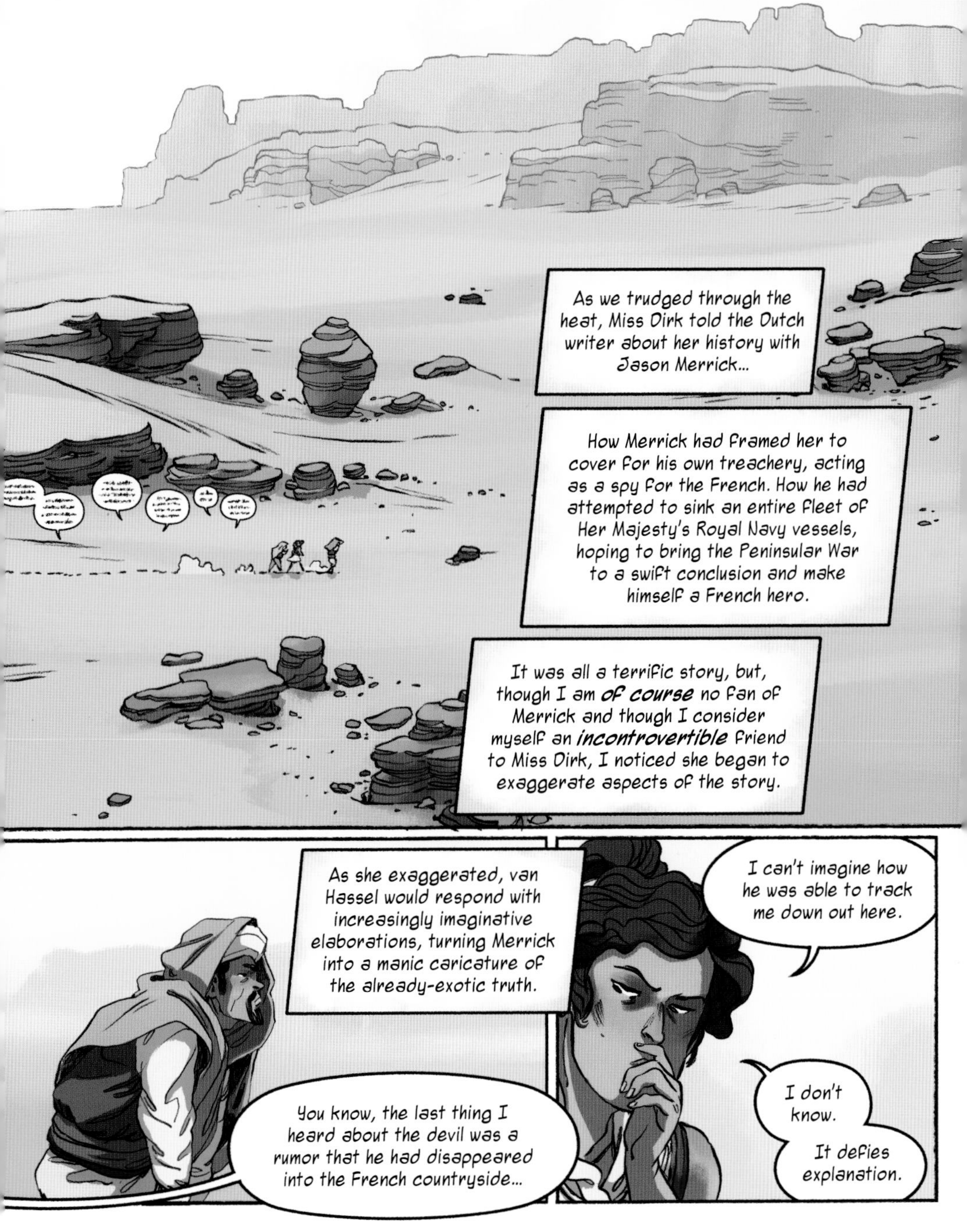

As we trudged through the heat, Miss Dirk told the Dutch writer about her history with Jason Merrick...
How Merrick had framed her to cover for his own treachery, acting as a spy for the French. How he had attempted to sink an entire fleet of Her Majesty's Royal Navy vessels, hoping to bring the Peninsular War to a swift conclusion and make himself a French hero.
It was all a terrific story, but, though I am *of course* no fan of Merrick and though I consider myself an *incontrovertible* friend to Miss Dirk, I noticed she began to exaggerate aspects of the story.
As she exaggerated, van Hassel would respond with increasingly imaginative elaborations, turning Merrick into a manic caricature of the already-exotic truth.
You know, the last thing I heard about the devil was a rumor that he had disappeared into the French countryside...
I can't imagine how he was able to track me down out here.
I don't know.
It defies explanation.

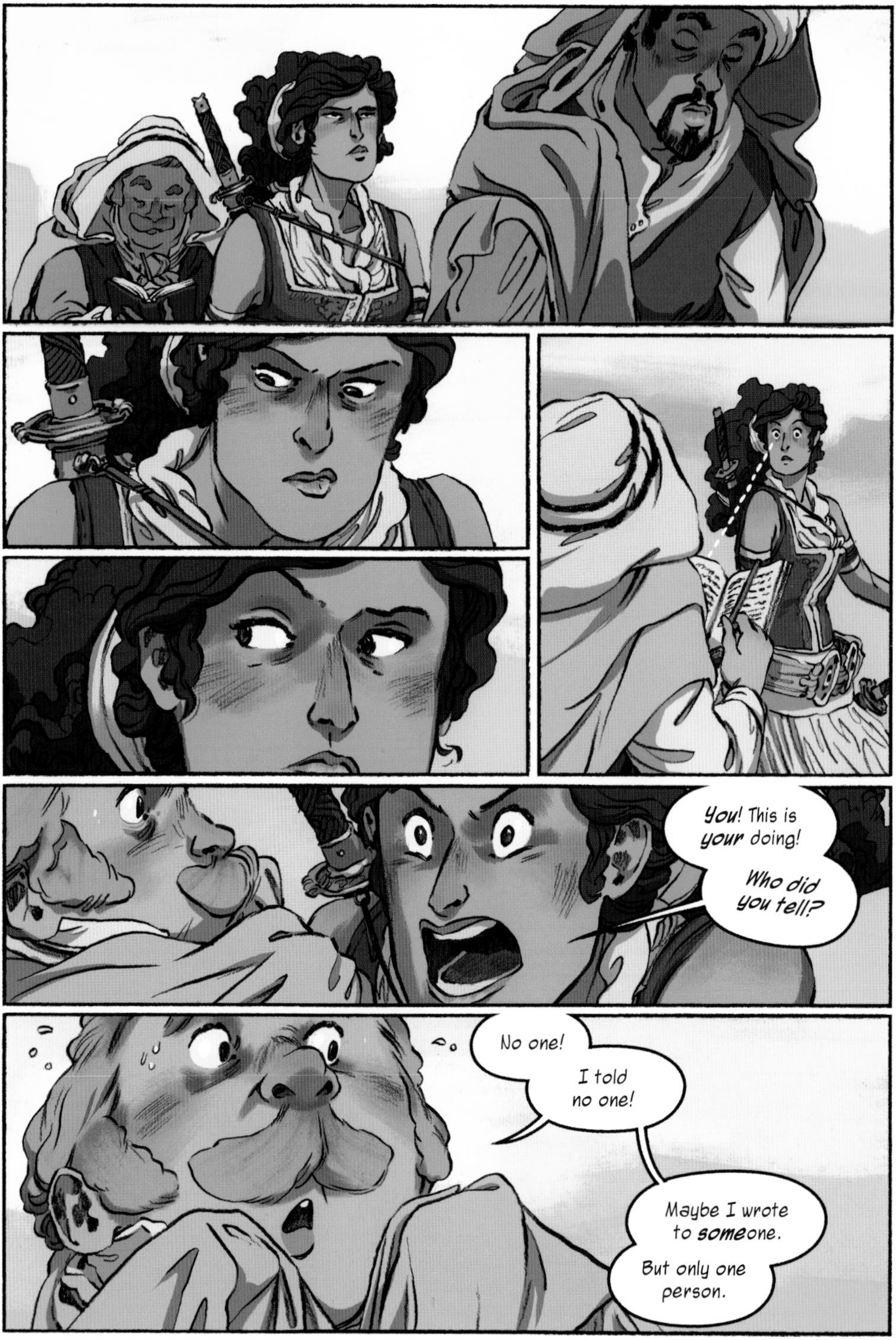
You! This is your doing!
Who did you tell?
No one!
I told no one!
Maybe I wrote to someone.
But only one person.

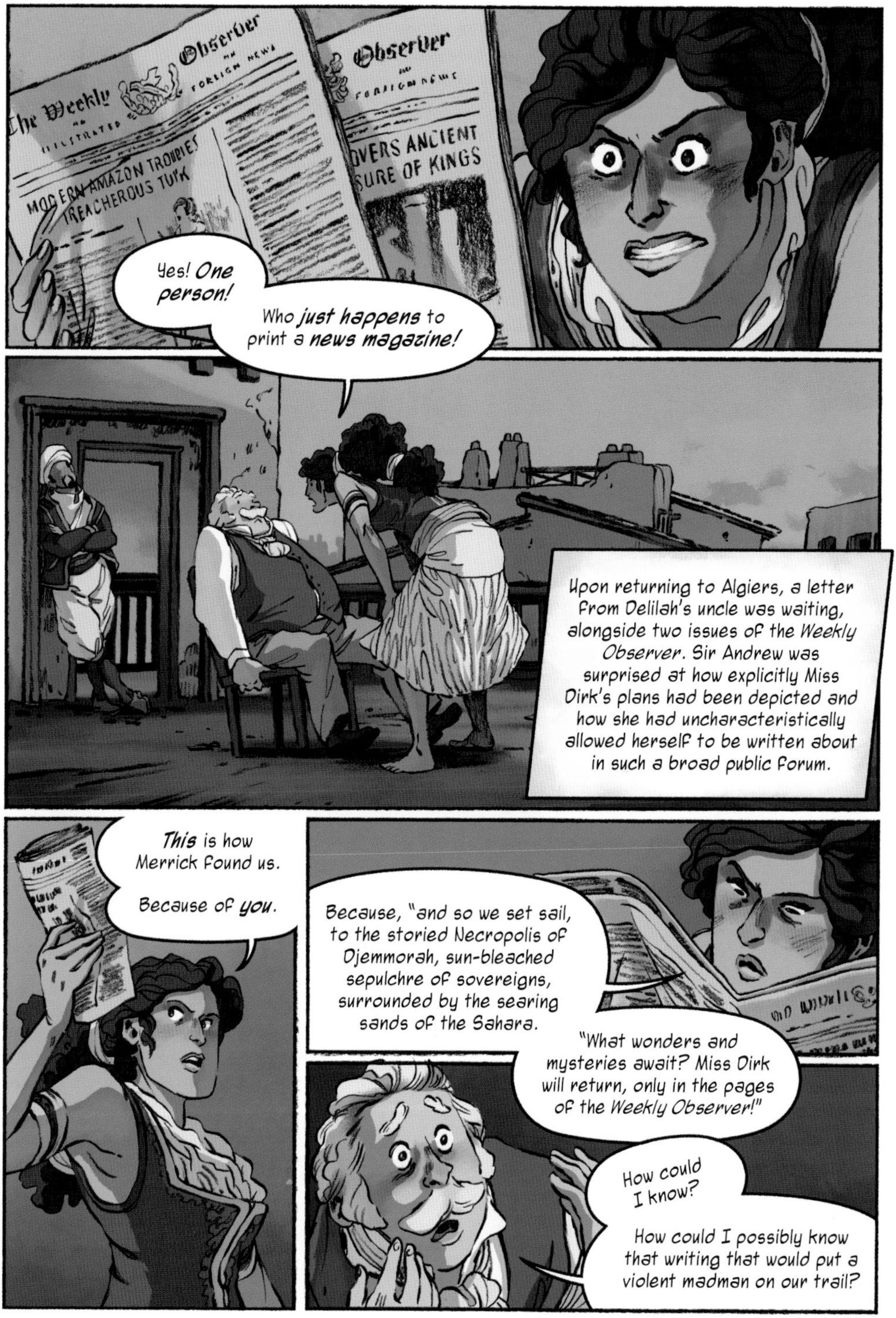
The Weekly Illustrated Observer and Foreign News
MODERN AMAZON TROPHIES
TREACHEROUS TURK
Observer and Foreign News
OVERS ANCIENT
SURE OF KINGS
Yes! *One person!*
Who ***just happens*** to print a ***news magazine!***
Upon returning to Algiers, a letter from Delilah's uncle was waiting, alongside two issues of the *Weekly Observer*. Sir Andrew was surprised at how explicitly Miss Dirk's plans had been depicted and how she had uncharacteristically allowed herself to be written about in such a broad public forum.
***This*** is how Merrick found us.
Because of ***you***.
Because, "and so we set sail, to the storied Necropolis of Djemmorah, sun-bleached sepulchre of sovereigns, surrounded by the searing sands of the Sahara.
"What wonders and mysteries await? Miss Dirk will return, only in the pages of the *Weekly Observer!*"
How could I know?
How could I possibly know that writing that would put a violent madman on our trail?

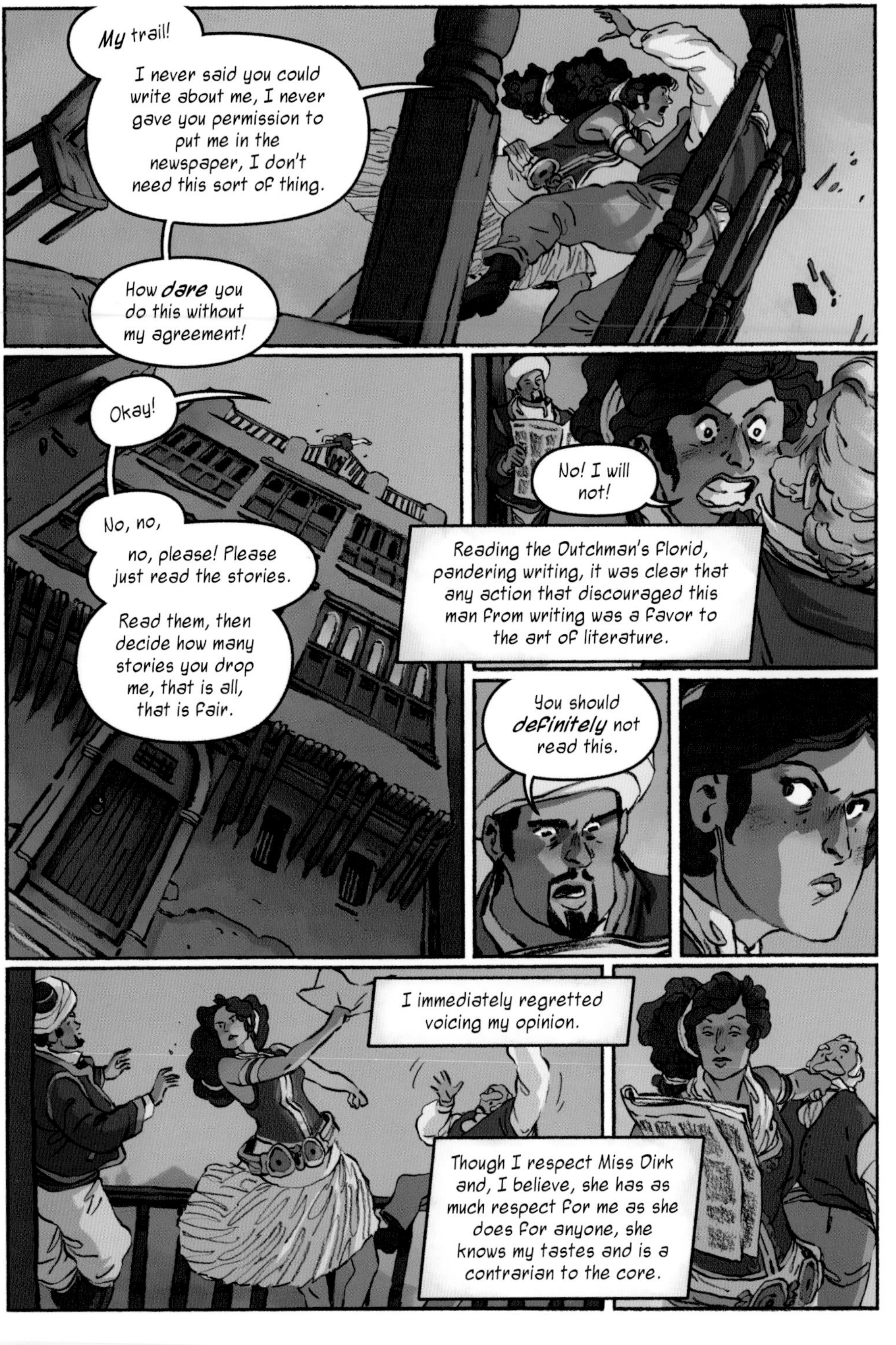
My trail!
I never said you could write about me, I never gave you permission to put me in the newspaper, I don't need this sort of thing.
How dare you do this without my agreement!
Okay!
No, no,
no, please! Please just read the stories.
Read them, then decide how many stories you drop me, that is all, that is fair.
No! I will not!
Reading the Dutchman's florid, pandering writing, it was clear that any action that discouraged this man from writing was a favor to the art of literature.
You should definitely not read this.
I immediately regretted voicing my opinion.
Though I respect Miss Dirk and, I believe, she has as much respect for me as she does for anyone, she knows my tastes and is a contrarian to the core.

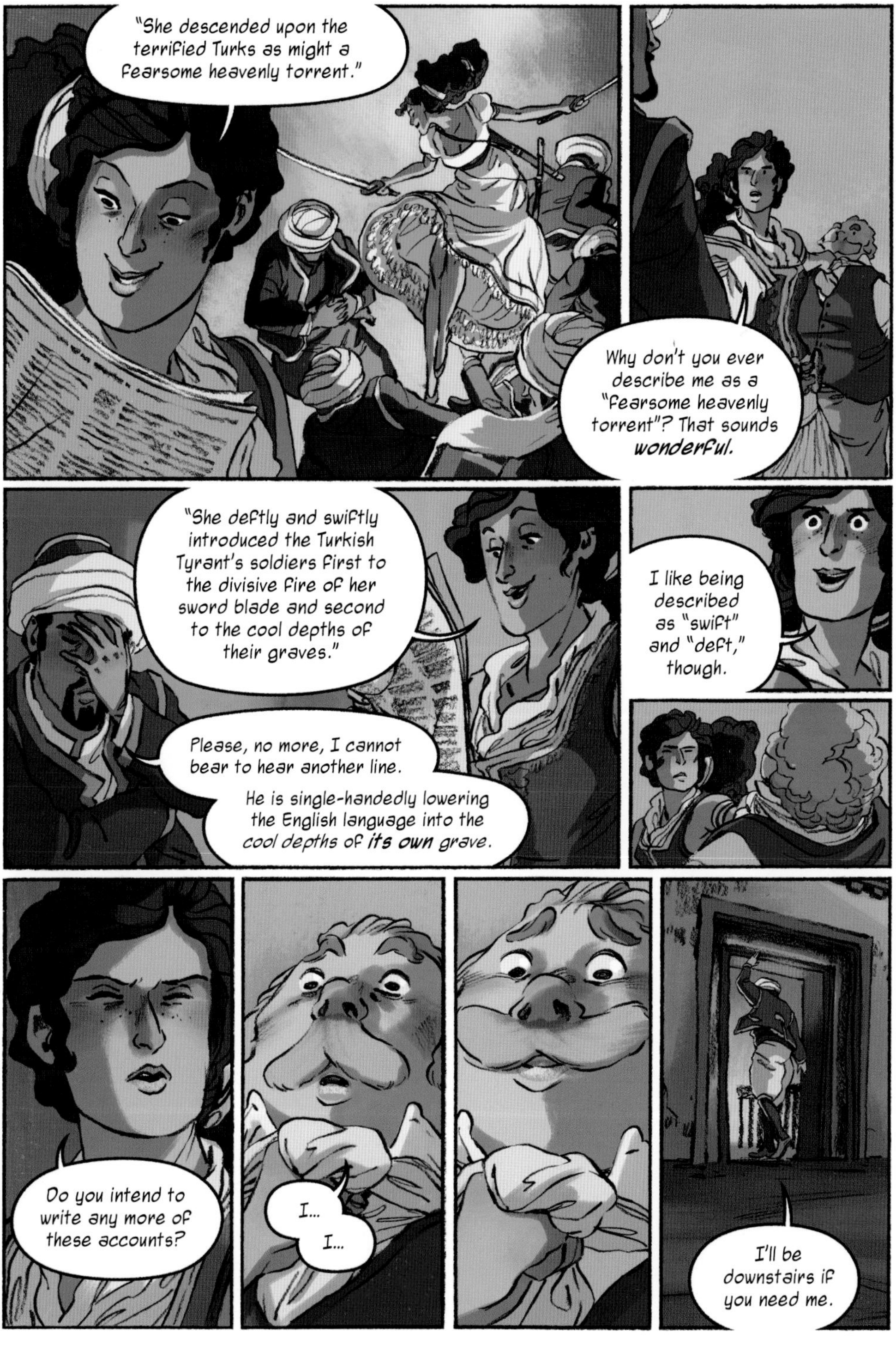
"She descended upon the terrified Turks as might a fearsome heavenly torrent."
Why don't you ever describe me as a "fearsome heavenly torrent"? That sounds **wonderful.**
"She deftly and swiftly introduced the Turkish Tyrant's soldiers first to the divisive fire of her sword blade and second to the cool depths of their graves."
I like being described as "swift" and "deft," though.
Please, no more, I cannot bear to hear another line.
He is single-handedly lowering the English language into the *cool depths of* ***its own*** *grave.*
Do you intend to write any more of these accounts?
I... I...
I'll be downstairs if you need me.

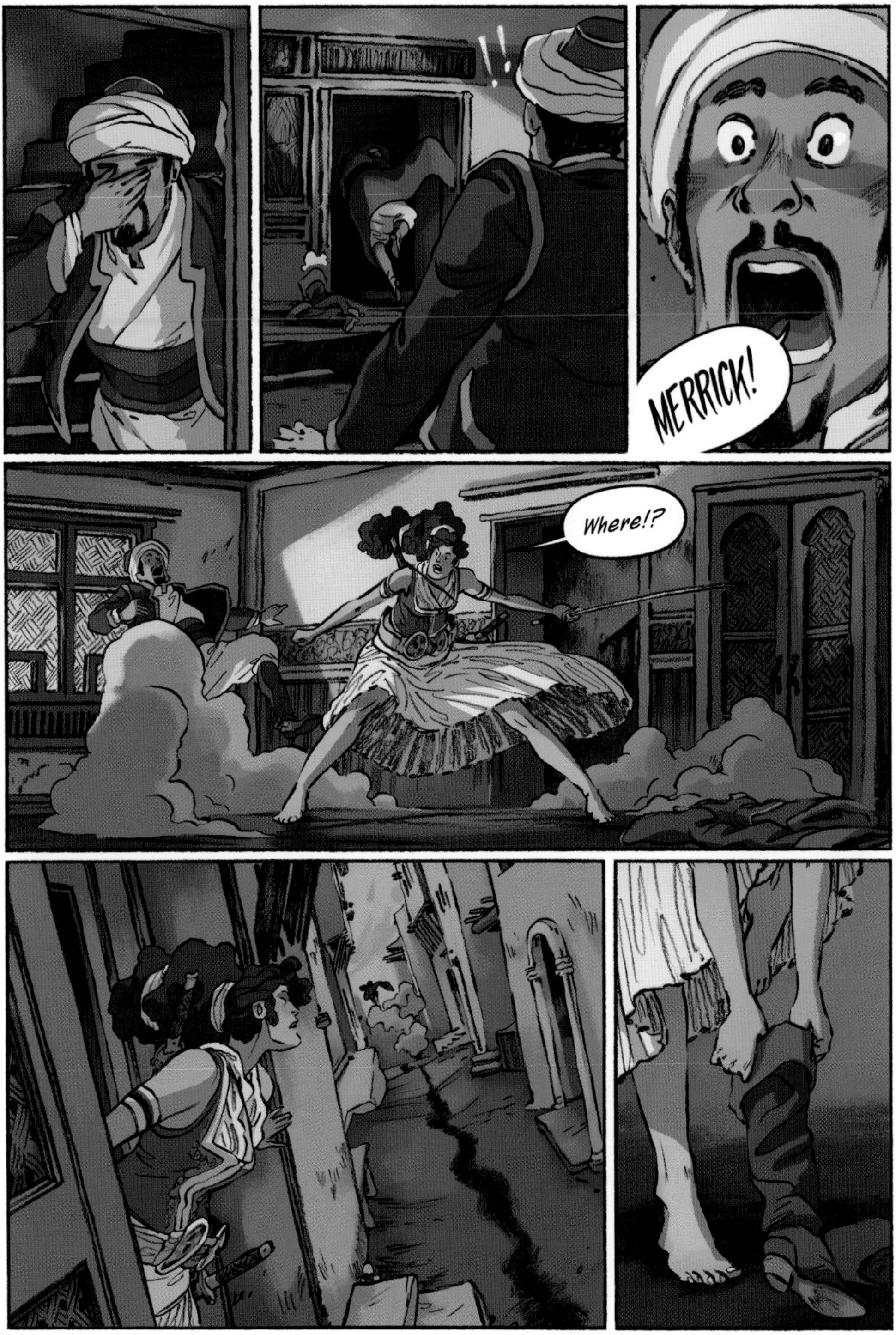
!!
MERRICK!
Where!?

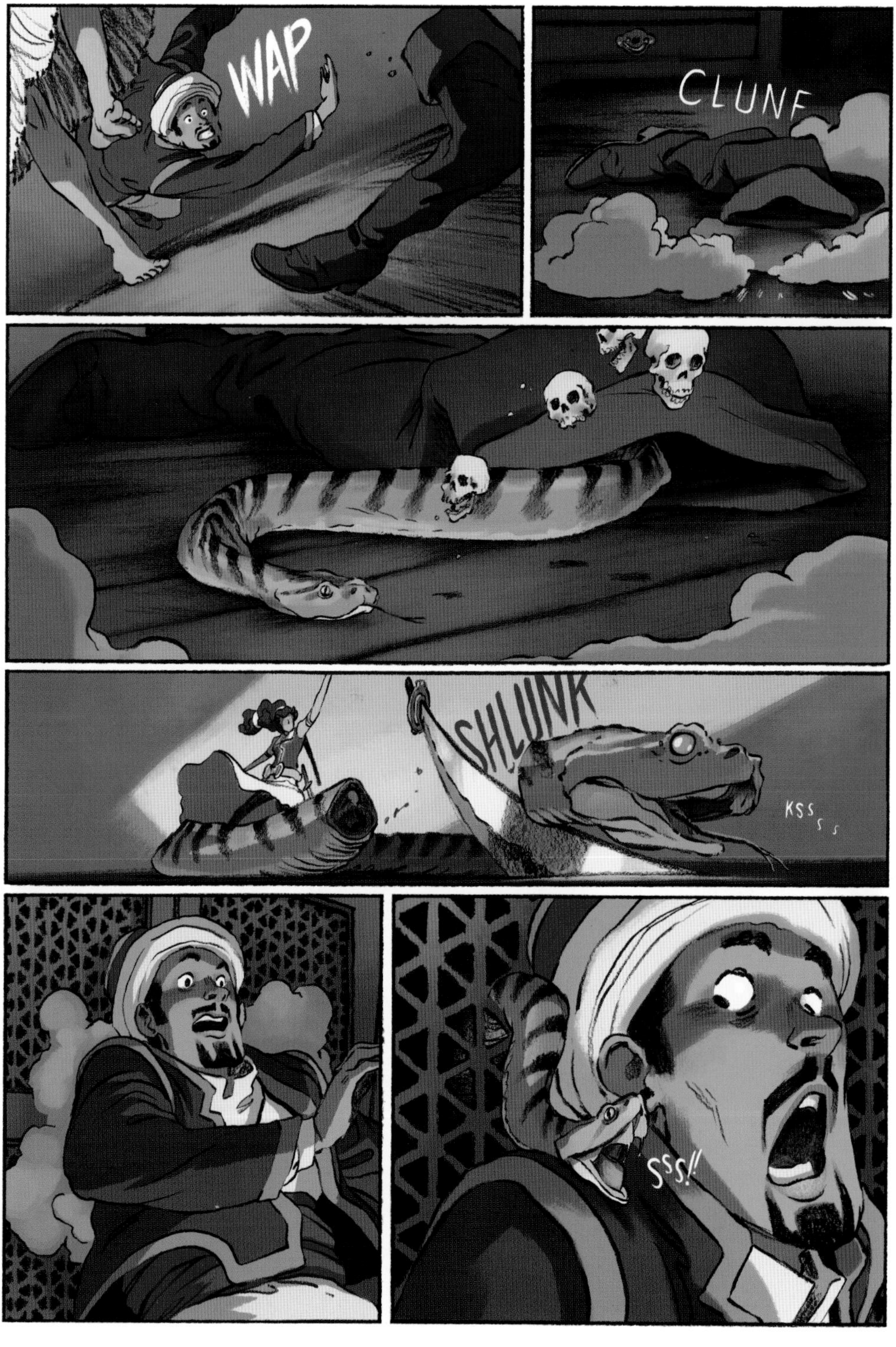
WAP
CLUNF
SHLUNK
KSSSS
SSS!!

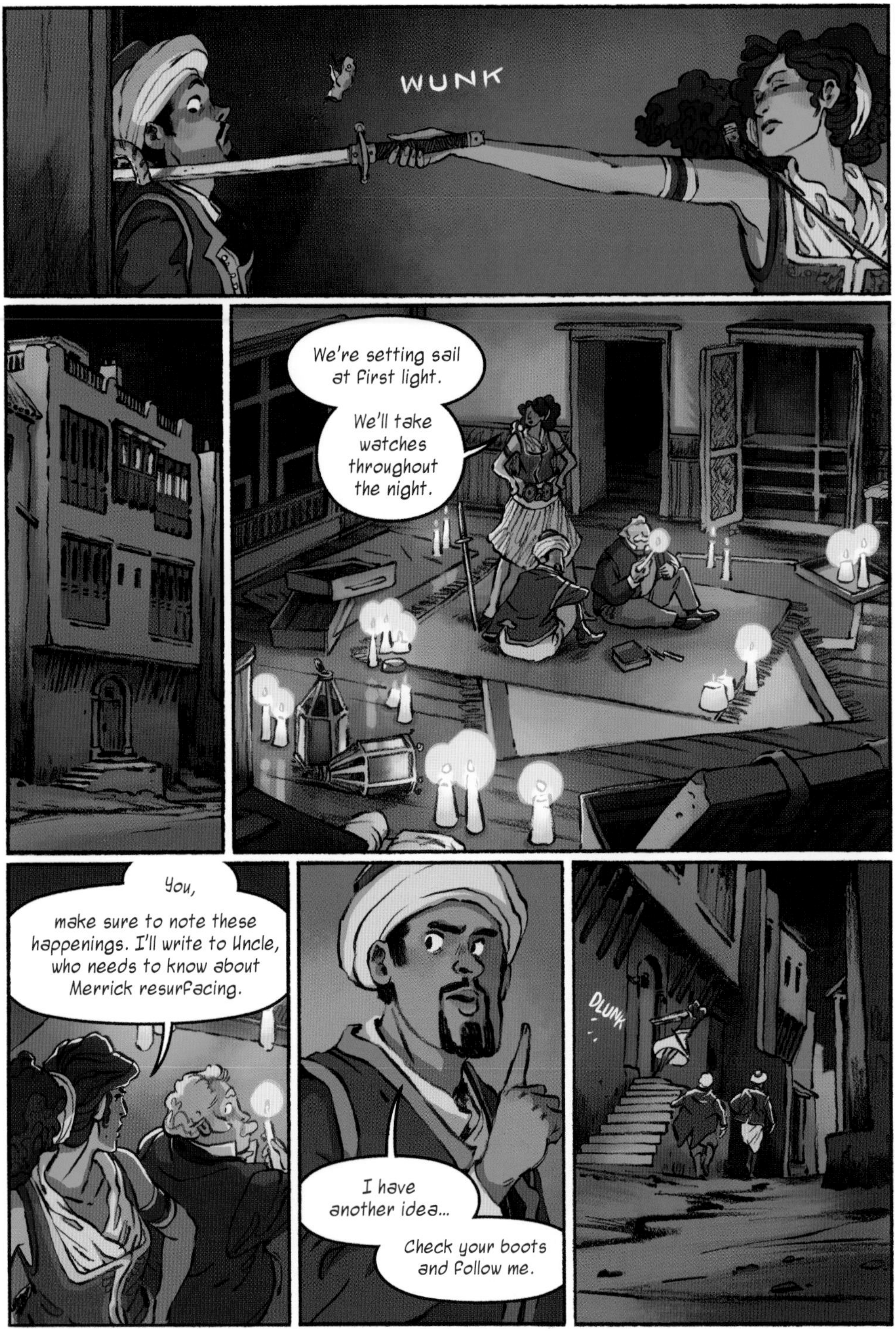
WUNK
We're setting sail at first light.
We'll take watches throughout the night.
You,
make sure to note these happenings. I'll write to Uncle, who needs to know about Merrick resurfacing.
I have another idea...
Check your boots and follow me.
DLUNK

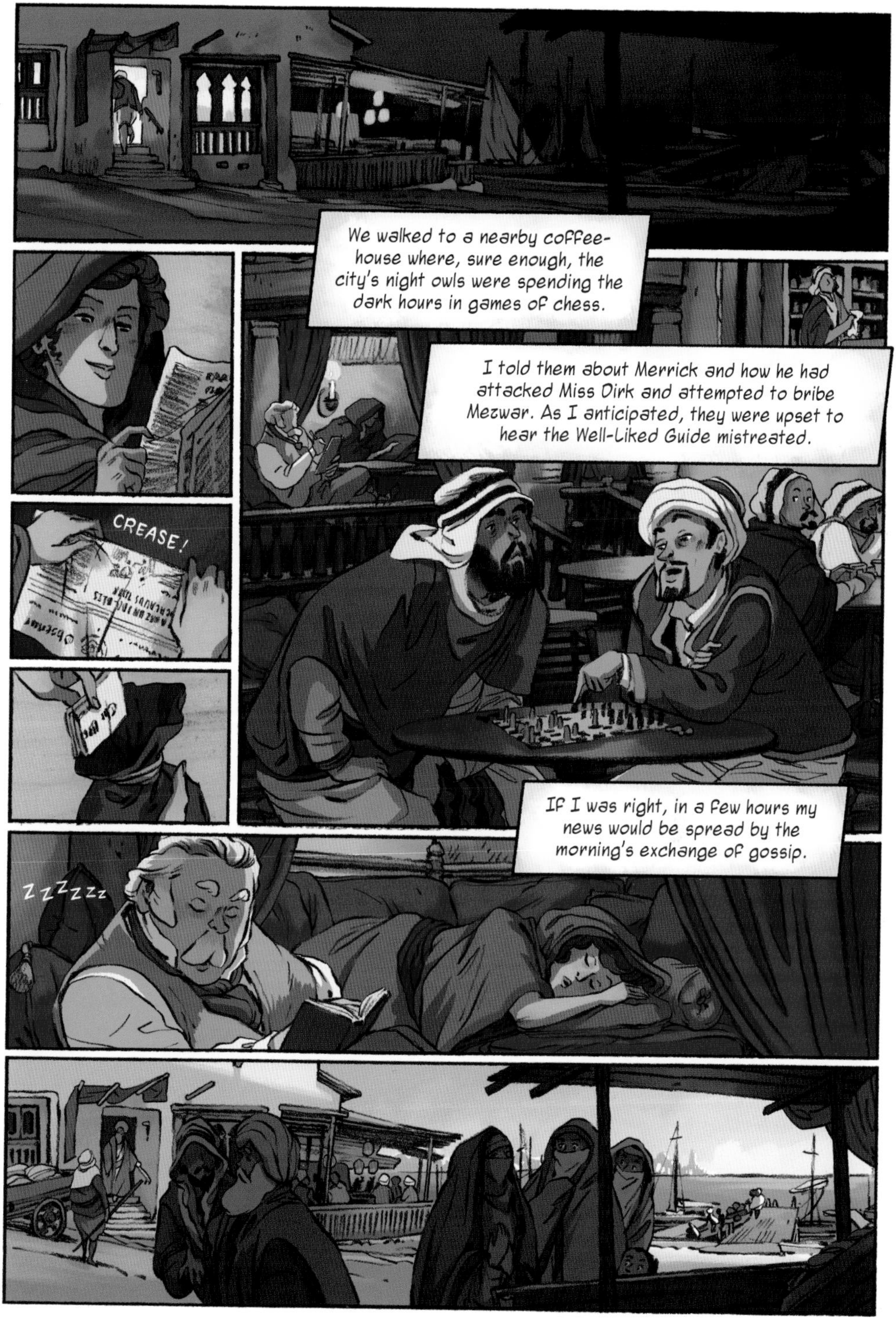

We walked to a nearby coffee-house where, sure enough, the city's night owls were spending the dark hours in games of chess.
I told them about Merrick and how he had attacked Miss Dirk and attempted to bribe Mezwar. As I anticipated, they were upset to hear the Well-Liked Guide mistreated.
CREASE!
If I was right, in a few hours my news would be spread by the morning's exchange of gossip.
ZZZZZZ

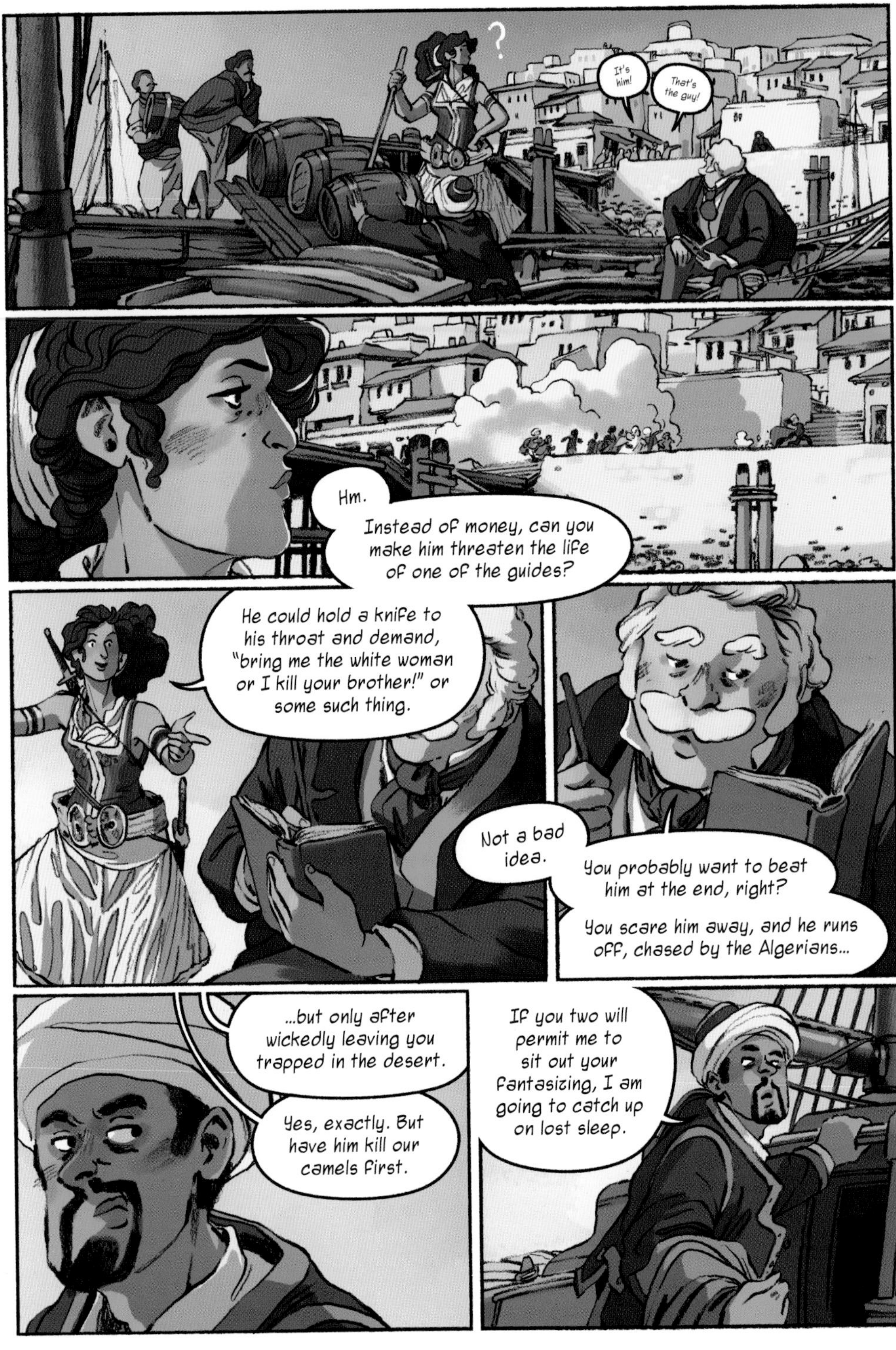
?
It's him!
That's the guy!
Hm.
Instead of money, can you make him threaten the life of one of the guides?
He could hold a knife to his throat and demand, "bring me the white woman or I kill your brother!" or some such thing.
Not a bad idea.
You probably want to beat him at the end, right?
You scare him away, and he runs off, chased by the Algerians...
...but only after wickedly leaving you trapped in the desert.
Yes, exactly. But have him kill our camels first.
If you two will permit me to sit out your fantasizing, I am going to catch up on lost sleep.

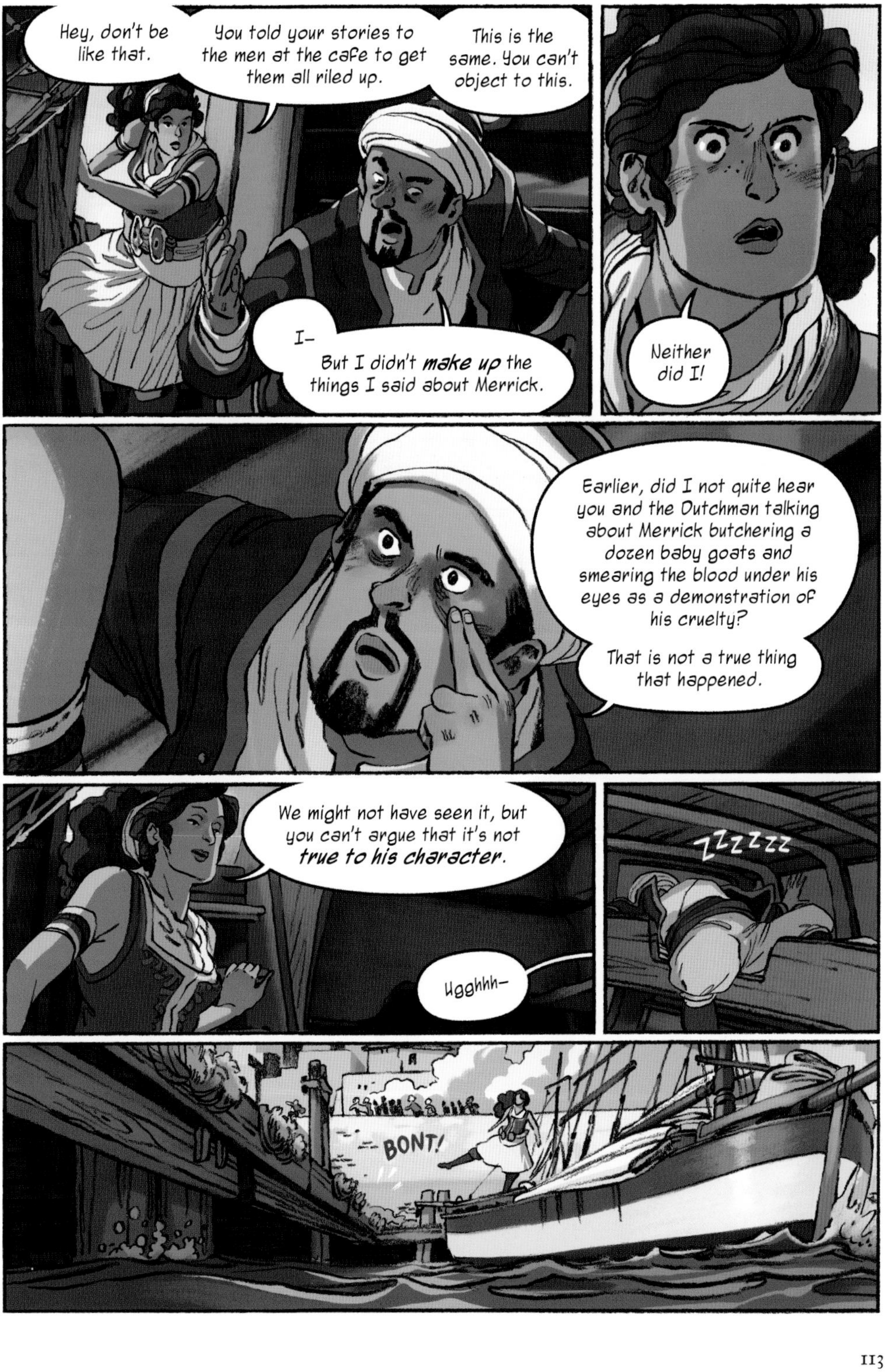
Hey, don't be like that.
You told your stories to the men at the cafe to get them all riled up.
This is the same. You can't object to this.
I–
But I didn't ***make up*** the things I said about Merrick.
Neither did I!
Earlier, did I not quite hear you and the Dutchman talking about Merrick butchering a dozen baby goats and smearing the blood under his eyes as a demonstration of his cruelty?
That is not a true thing that happened.
We might not have seen it, but you can't argue that it's not ***true to his character***.
Ugghhh–
ZZZZZZ
BONT!

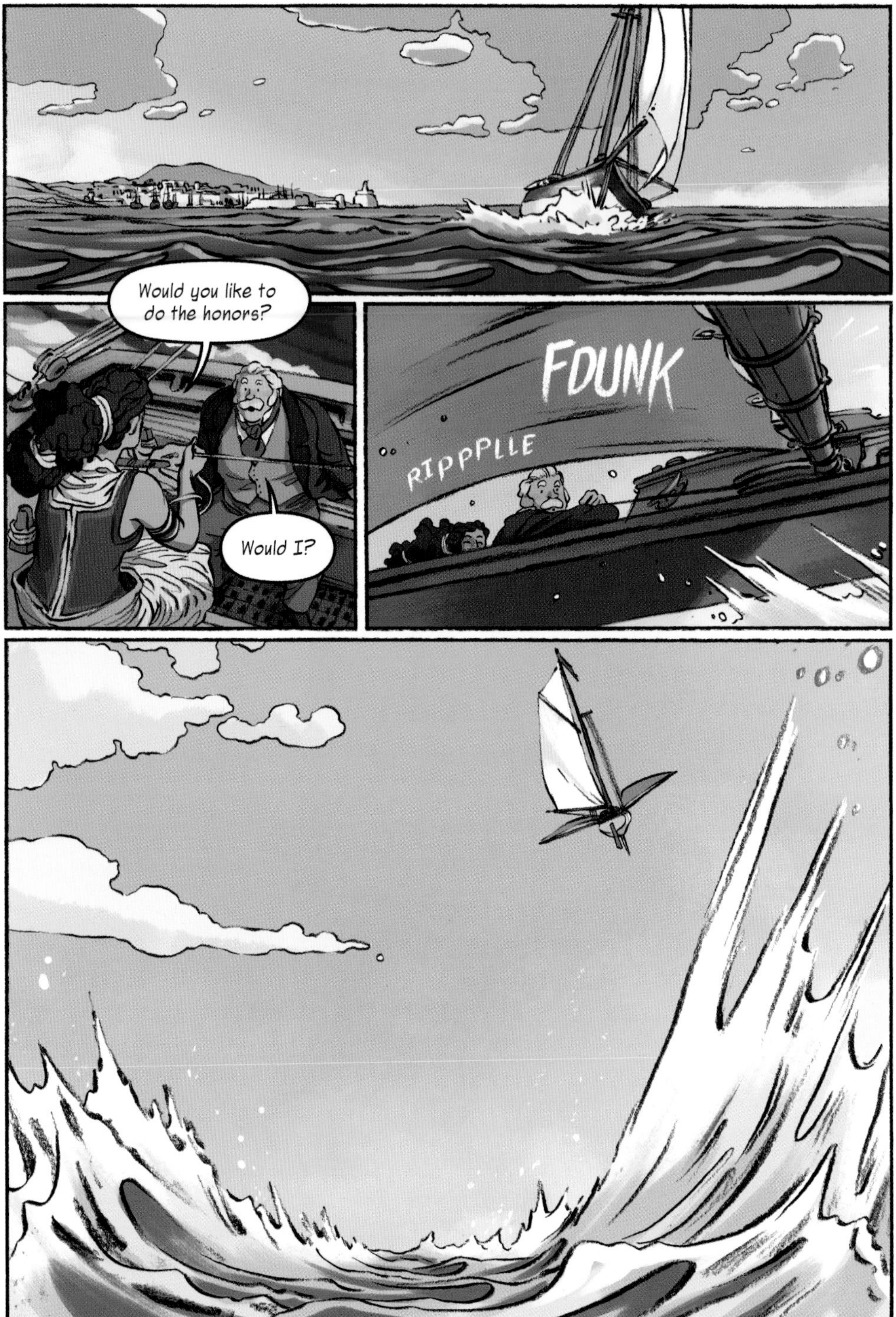

Would you like to do the honors?
Would I?
FDUNK
RIPPPLLE

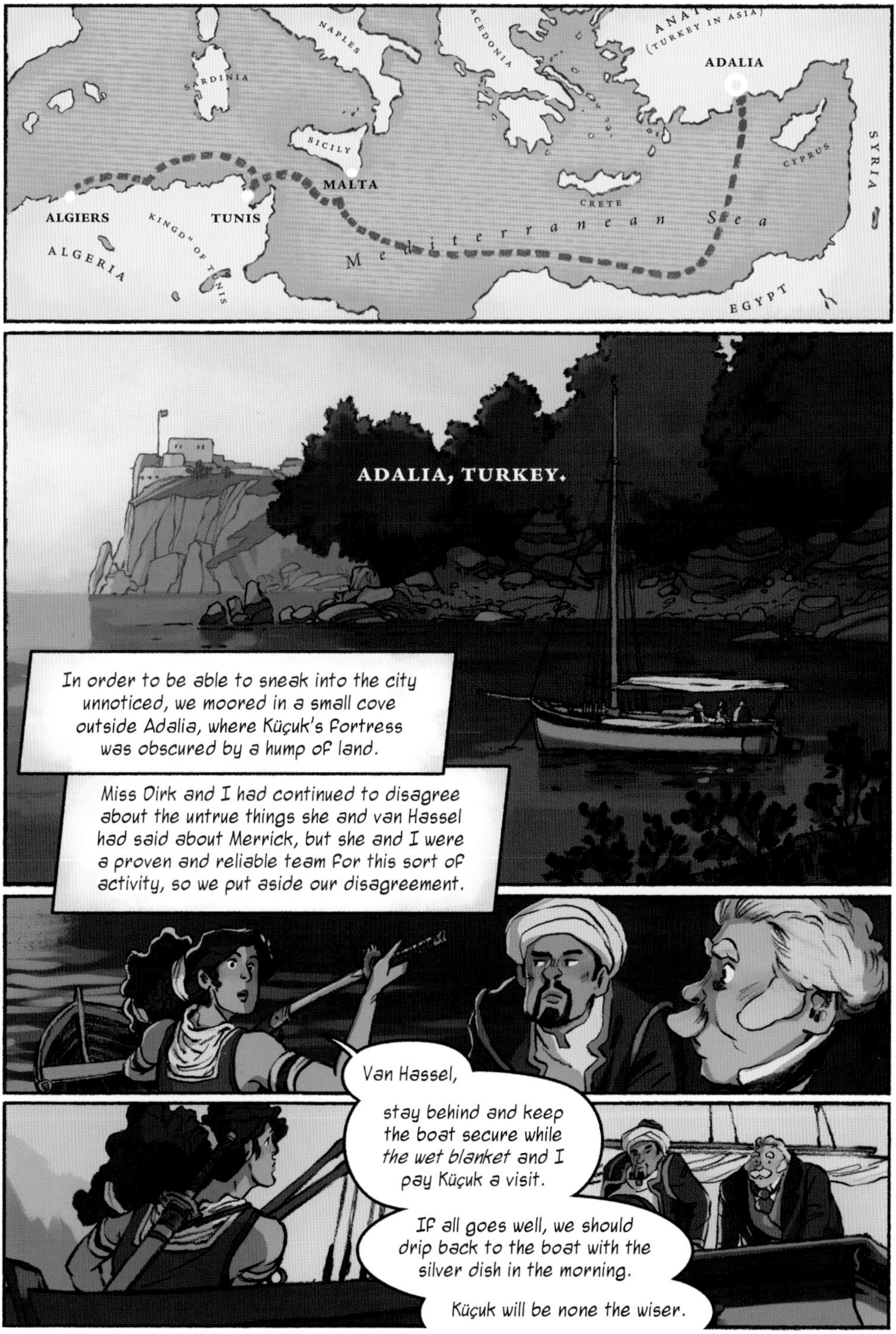

NAPLES
SARDINIA
MACEDONIA
ANATOLIA
(TURKEY IN ASIA)
ADALIA
SICILY
MALTA
CYPRUS
SYRIA
CRETE
ALGIERS
TUNIS
KINGDM OF TUNIS
ALGERIA
Mediterranean Sea
EGYPT
ADALIA, TURKEY.
In order to be able to sneak into the city unnoticed, we moored in a small cove outside Adalia, where Küçuk's fortress was obscured by a hump of land.
Miss Dirk and I had continued to disagree about the untrue things she and van Hassel had said about Merrick, but she and I were a proven and reliable team for this sort of activity, so we put aside our disagreement.
Van Hassel,
stay behind and keep the boat secure while *the wet blanket* and I pay Küçuk a visit.
If all goes well, we should drip back to the boat with the silver dish in the morning.
Küçuk will be none the wiser.

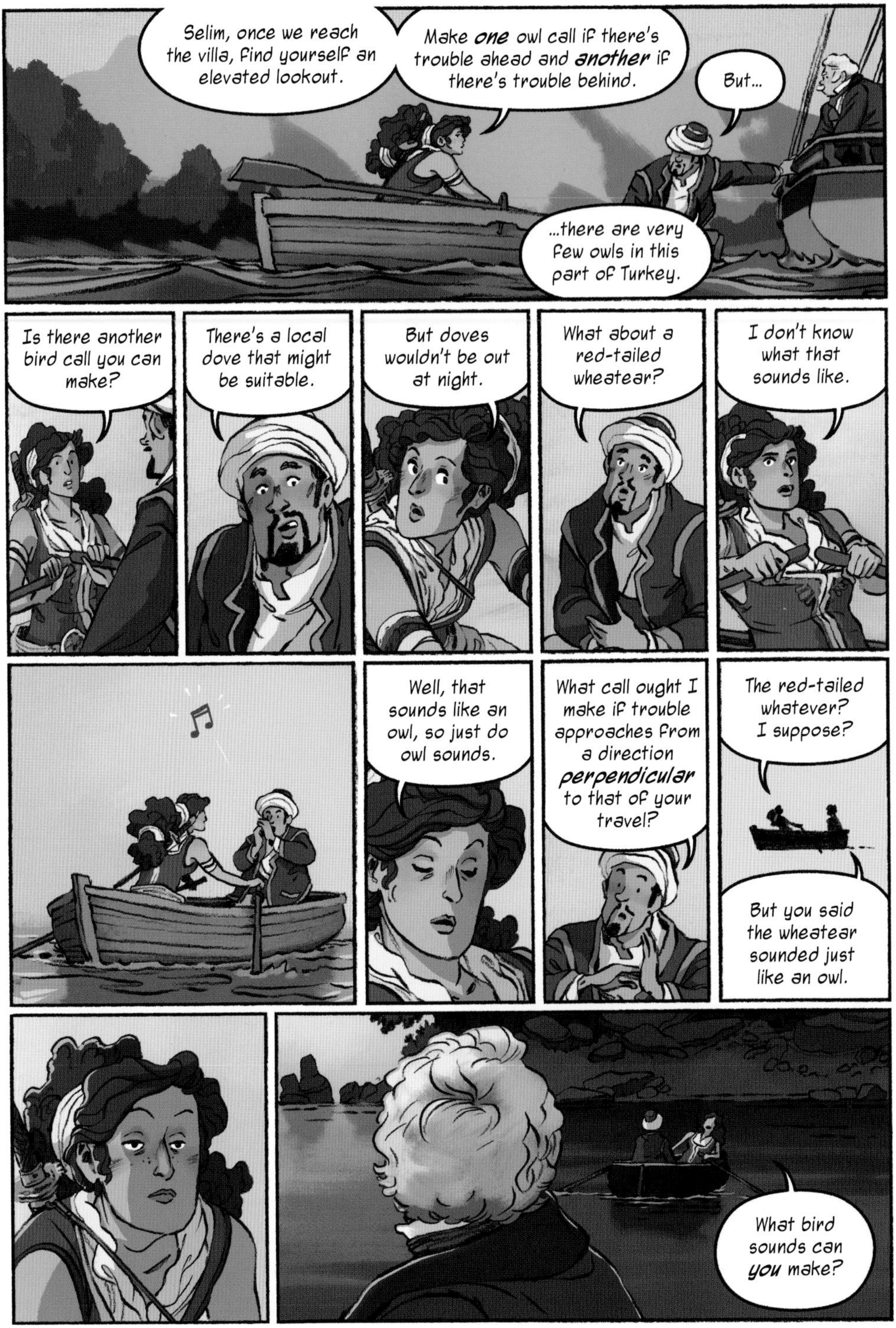
Selim, once we reach the villa, find yourself an elevated lookout.
Make **one** owl call if there's trouble ahead and **another** if there's trouble behind.
But...
...there are very few owls in this part of Turkey.
Is there another bird call you can make?
There's a local dove that might be suitable.
But doves wouldn't be out at night.
What about a red-tailed wheatear?
I don't know what that sounds like.
Well, that sounds like an owl, so just do owl sounds.
What call ought I make if trouble approaches from a direction **perpendicular** to that of your travel?
The red-tailed whatever? I suppose?
But you said the wheatear sounded just like an owl.
What bird sounds can **you** make?

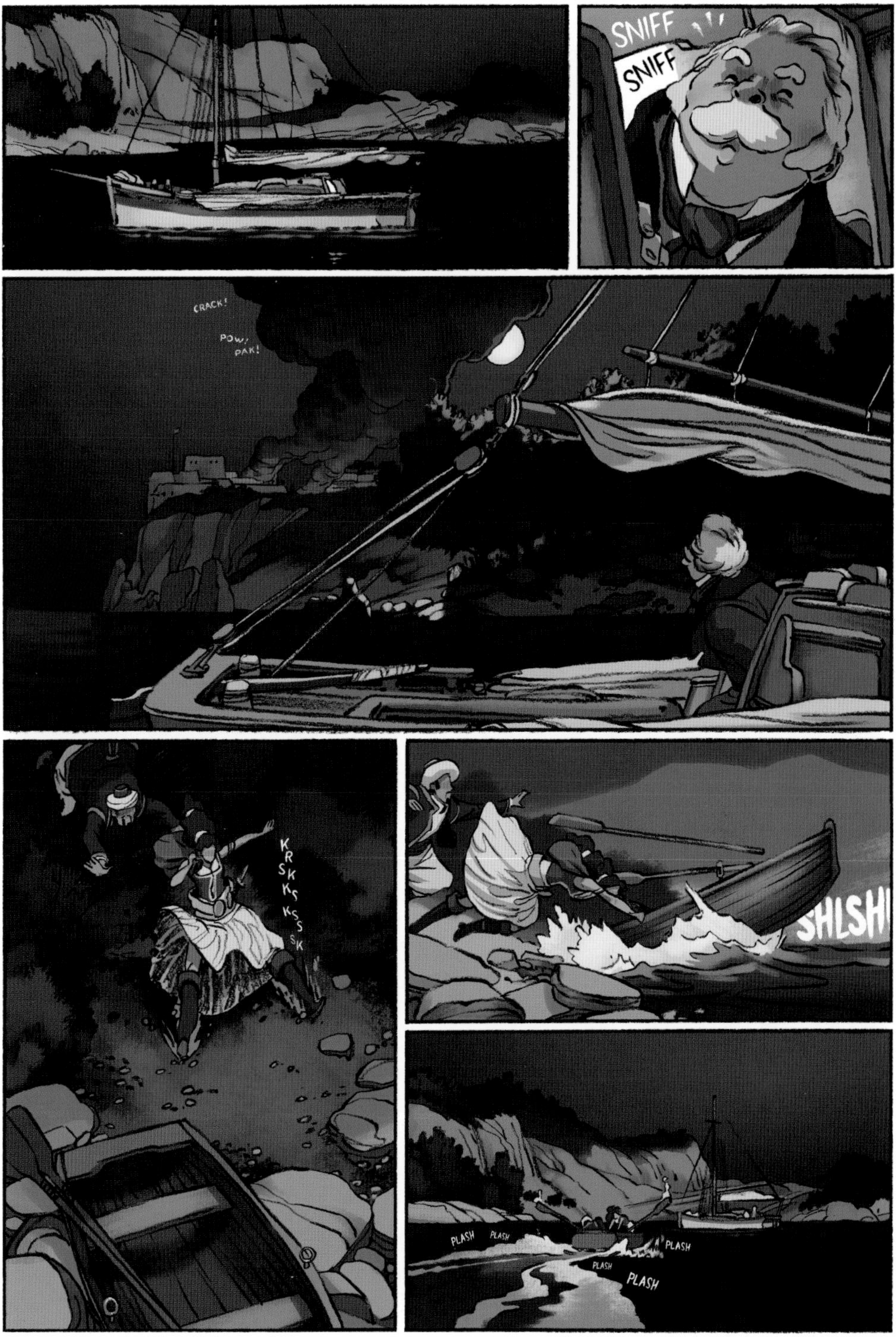
SNIFF
SNIFF
CRACK!
POW, PAK!
KRSKKSKSSSK
SHLSH
PLASH PLASH
PLASH
PLASH
PLASH

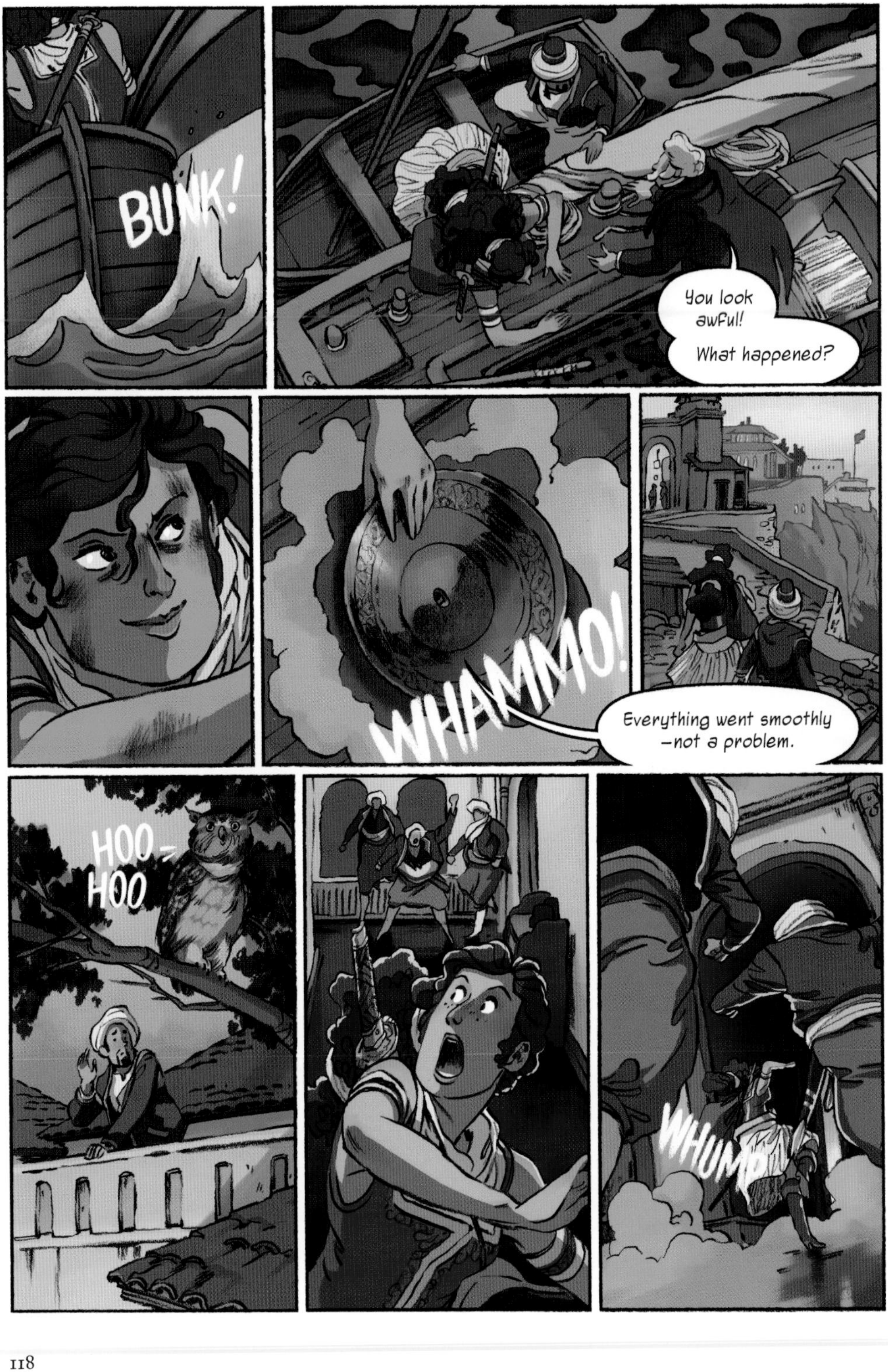
BUNK!
You look awful!
What happened?
WHAMMO!
Everything went smoothly
—not a problem.
HOO-
HOO
WHUMP

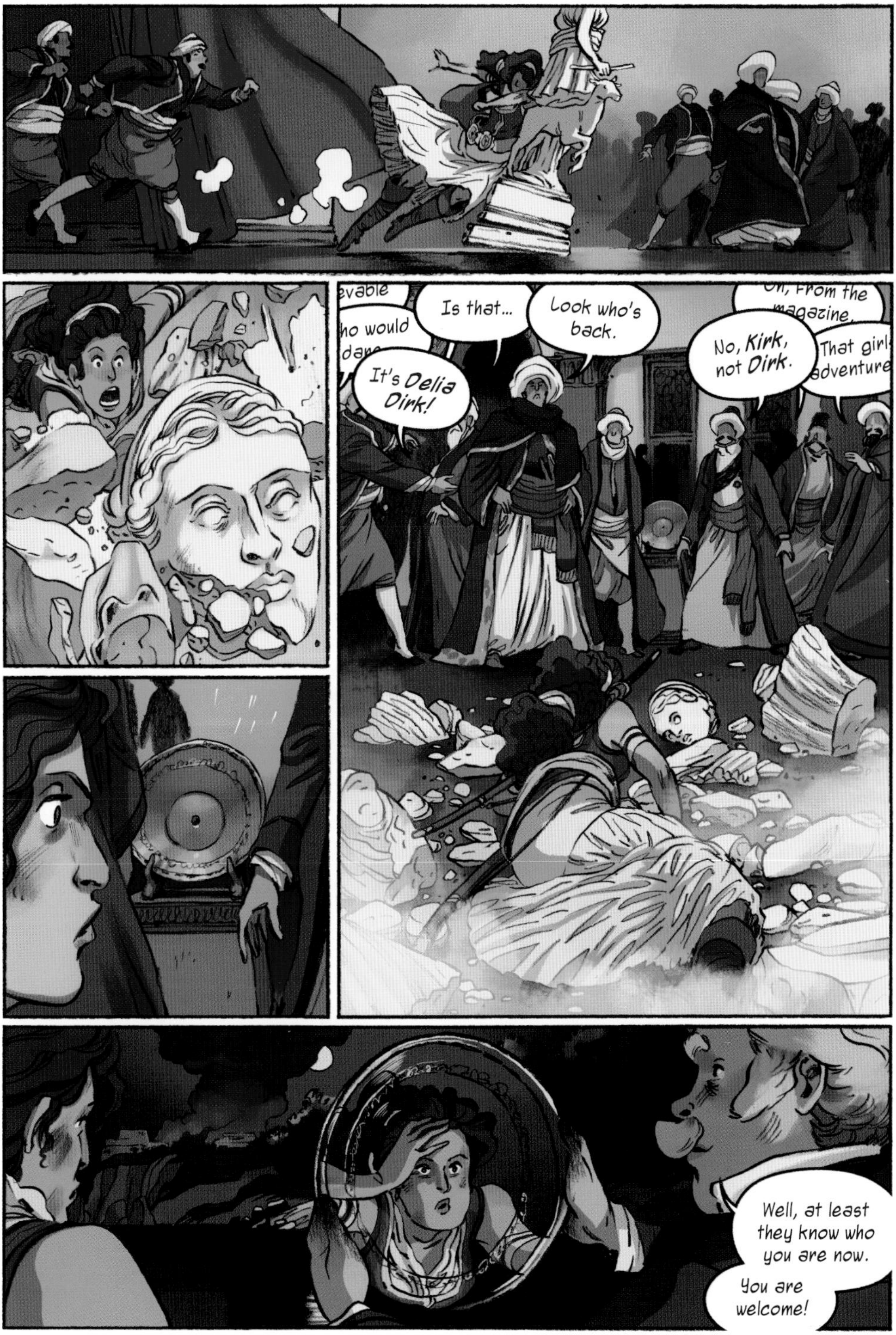

Is that...
Look who's back.
It's Delia Dirk!
No, Kirk, not Dirk.
Well, at least they know who you are now.
You are welcome!

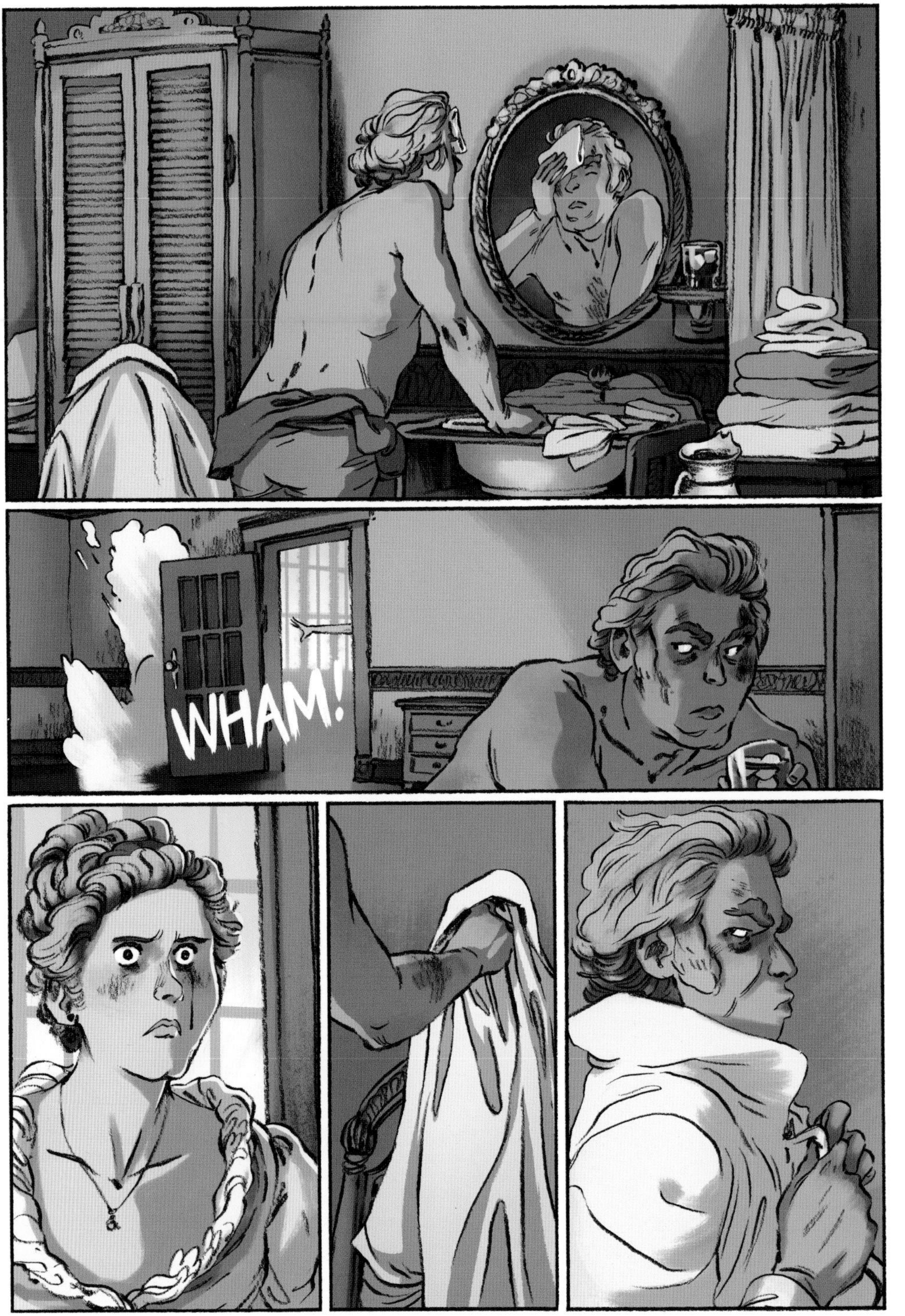
WHAM!

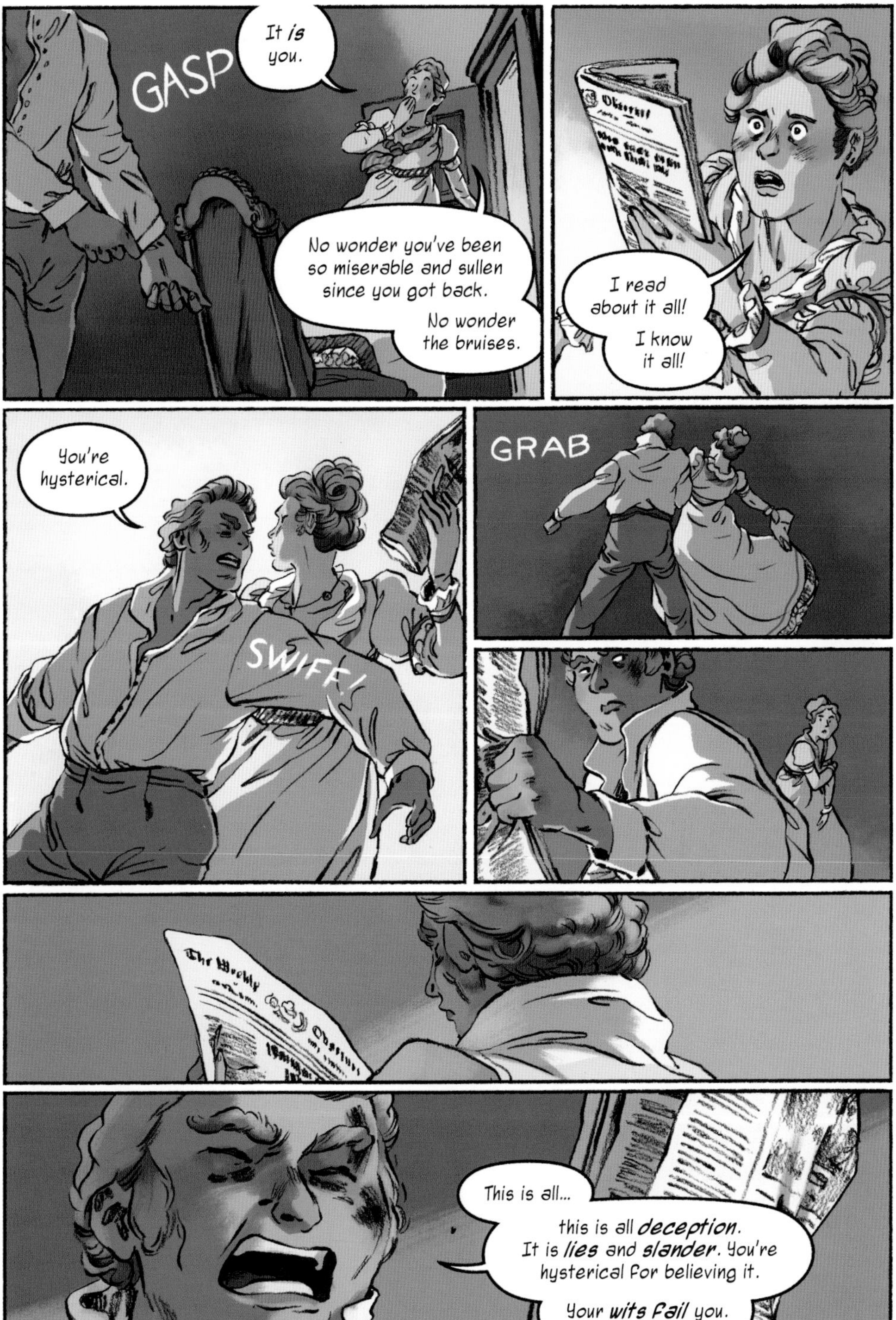
GASP
It *is* you.
No wonder you've been so miserable and sullen since you got back.
No wonder the bruises.
I read about it all!
I know it all!
You're hysterical.
SWIFF!
GRAB
This is all...
this is all ***deception***. It is ***lies*** and ***slander***. You're hysterical for believing it.
Your ***wits fail*** you.

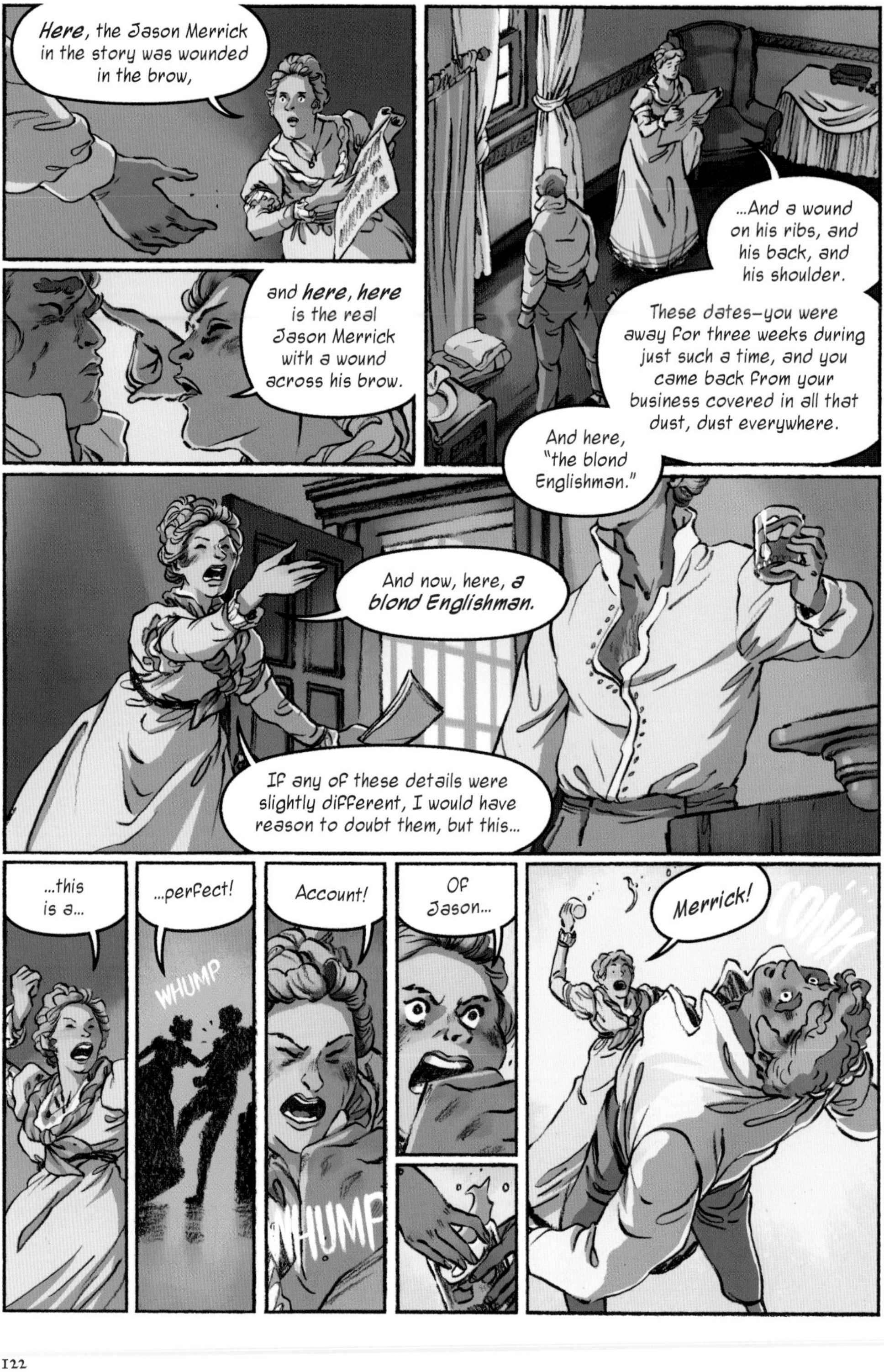

*Here*, the Jason Merrick in the story was wounded in the brow,
and *here, here* is the real Jason Merrick with a wound across his brow.
...And a wound on his ribs, and his back, and his shoulder.
These dates—you were away for three weeks during just such a time, and you came back from your business covered in all that dust, dust everywhere.
And here, "the blond Englishman."
And now, here, *a blond Englishman.*
If any of these details were slightly different, I would have reason to doubt them, but this...
...this is a...
...perfect!
WHUMP
Account!
WHUMP
Of Jason...
Merrick!
CONK

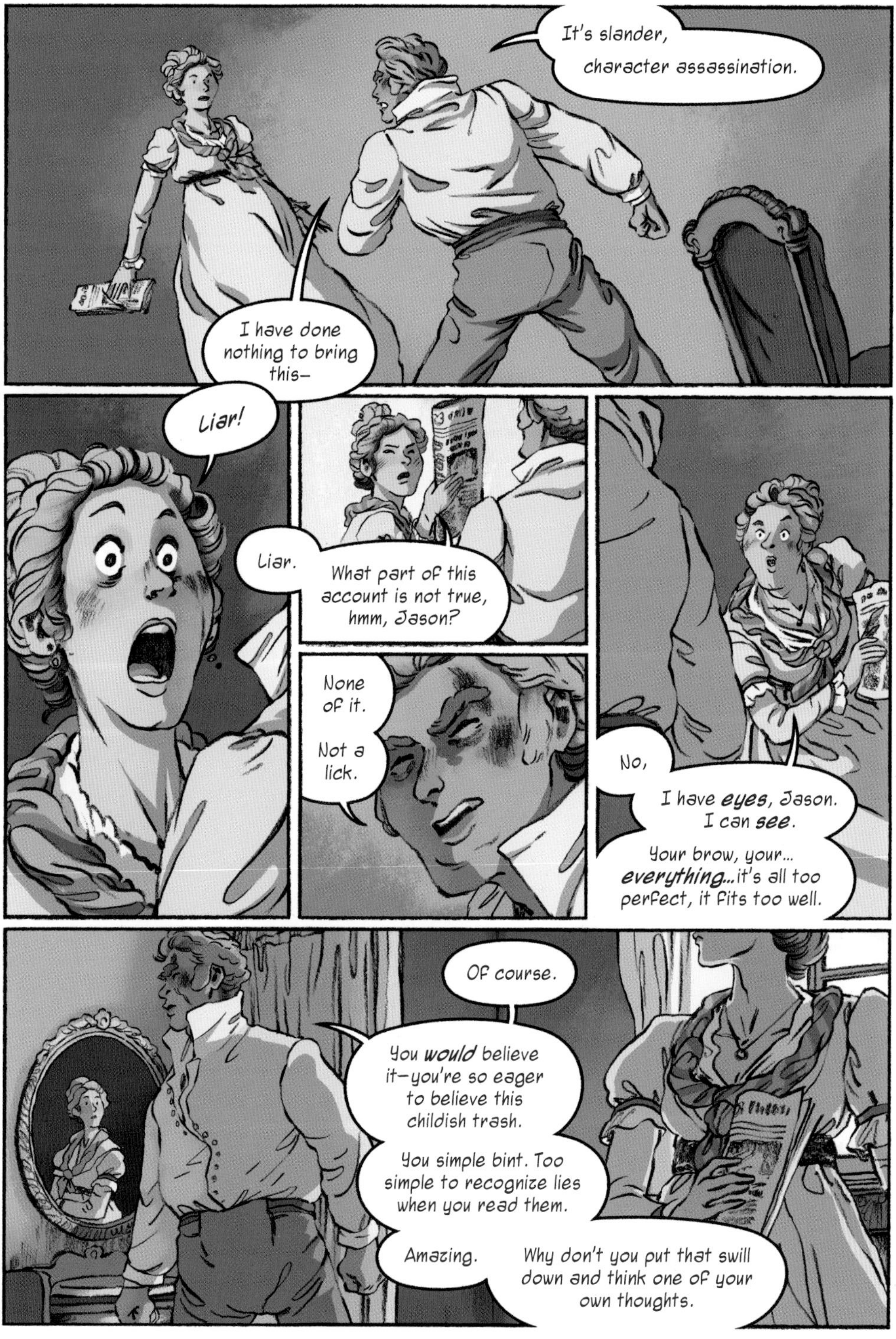
It's slander,
character assassination.
I have done nothing to bring this–
Liar!
Liar.
What part of this account is not true, hmm, Jason?
None of it.
Not a lick.
No,
I have *eyes*, Jason. I can *see*.
Your brow, your... *everything*... it's all too perfect, it fits too well.
Of course.
You *would* believe it–you're so eager to believe this childish trash.
You simple bint. Too simple to recognize lies when you read them.
Amazing.
Why don't you put that swill down and think one of your own thoughts.

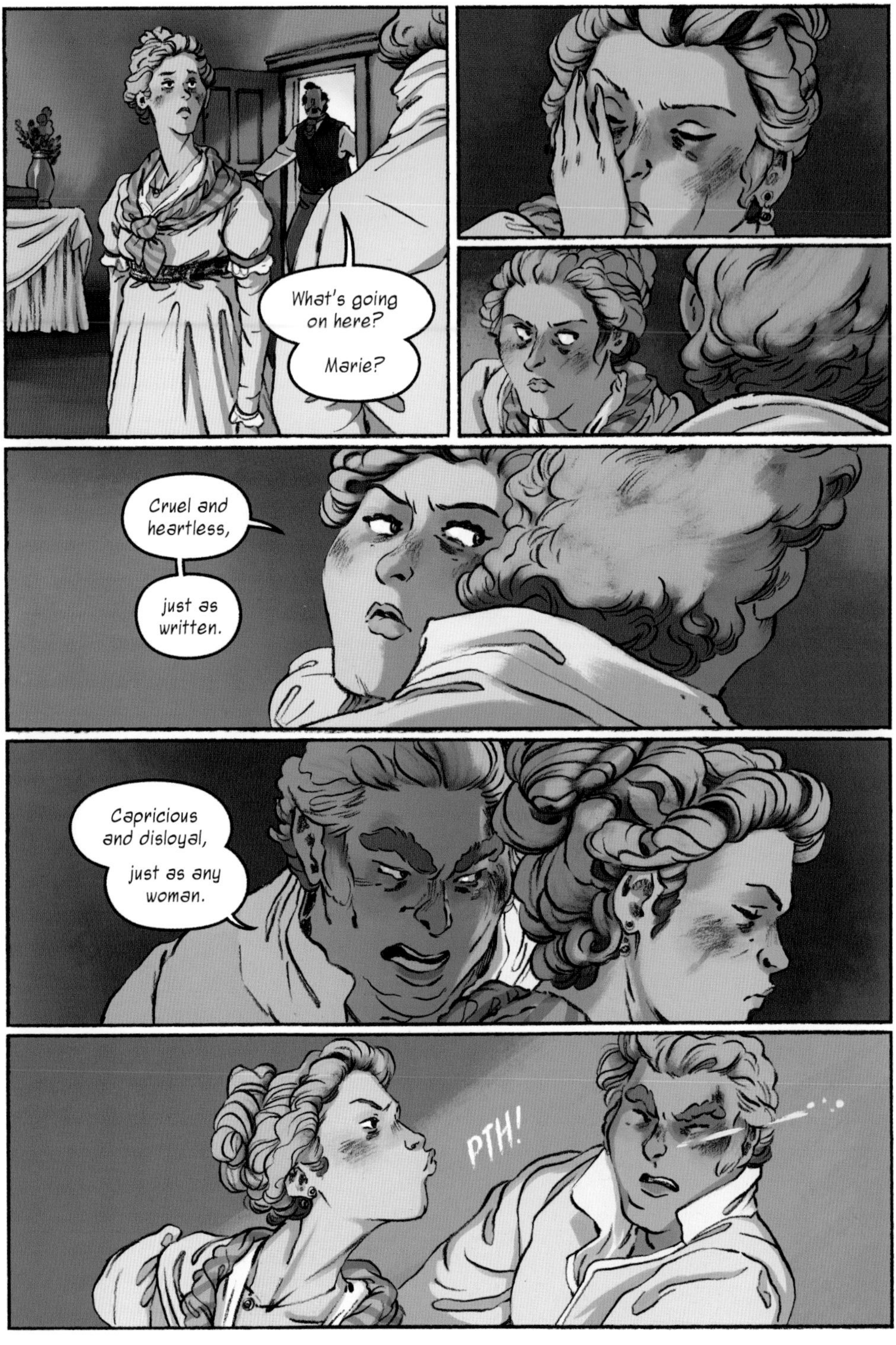
What's going on here?
Marie?
Cruel and heartless,
just as written.
Capricious and disloyal,
just as any woman.
PTH!

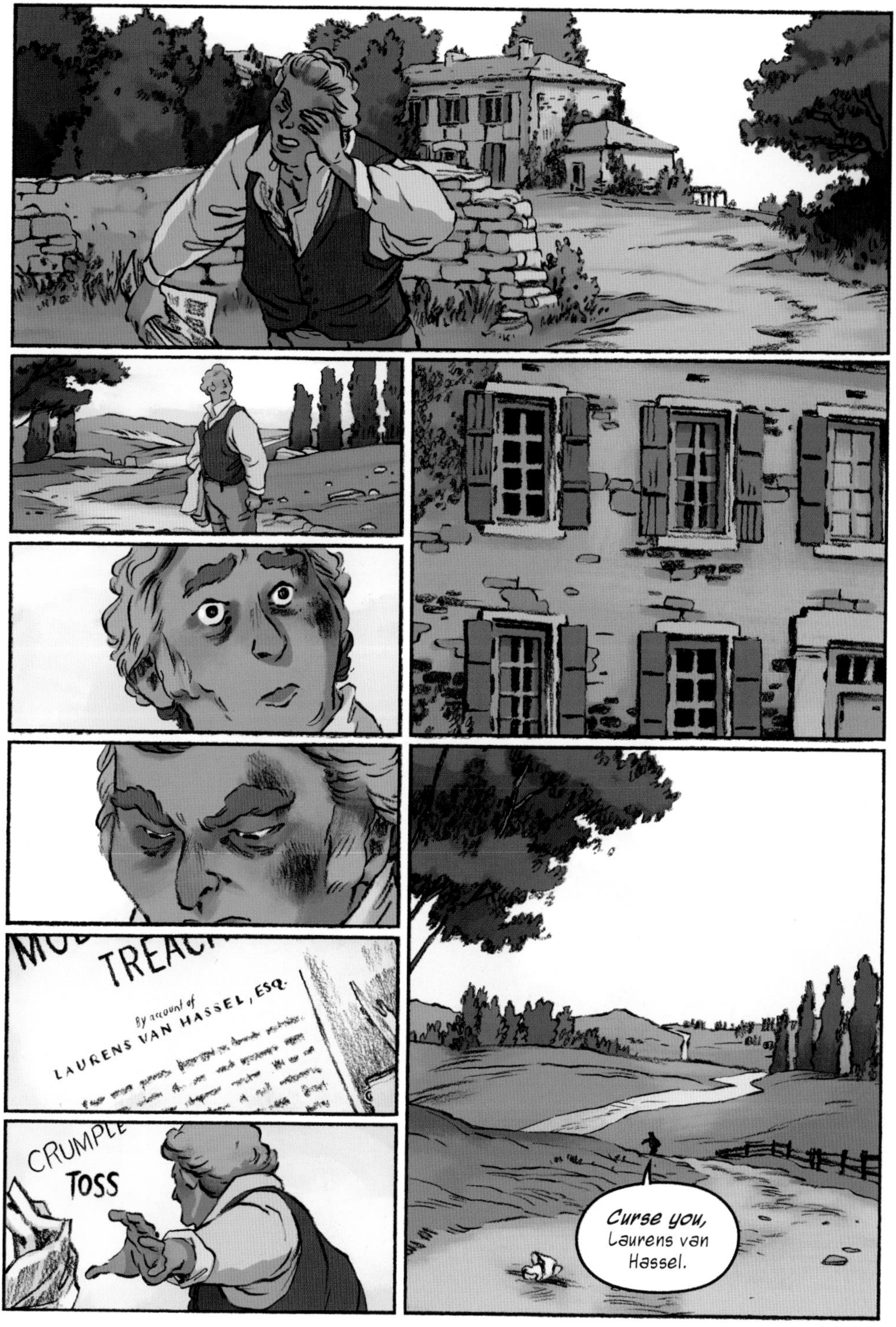
TREACH
By account of
LAURENS VAN HASSEL, ESQ.
CRUMPLE
TOSS
Curse you, Laurens van Hassel.

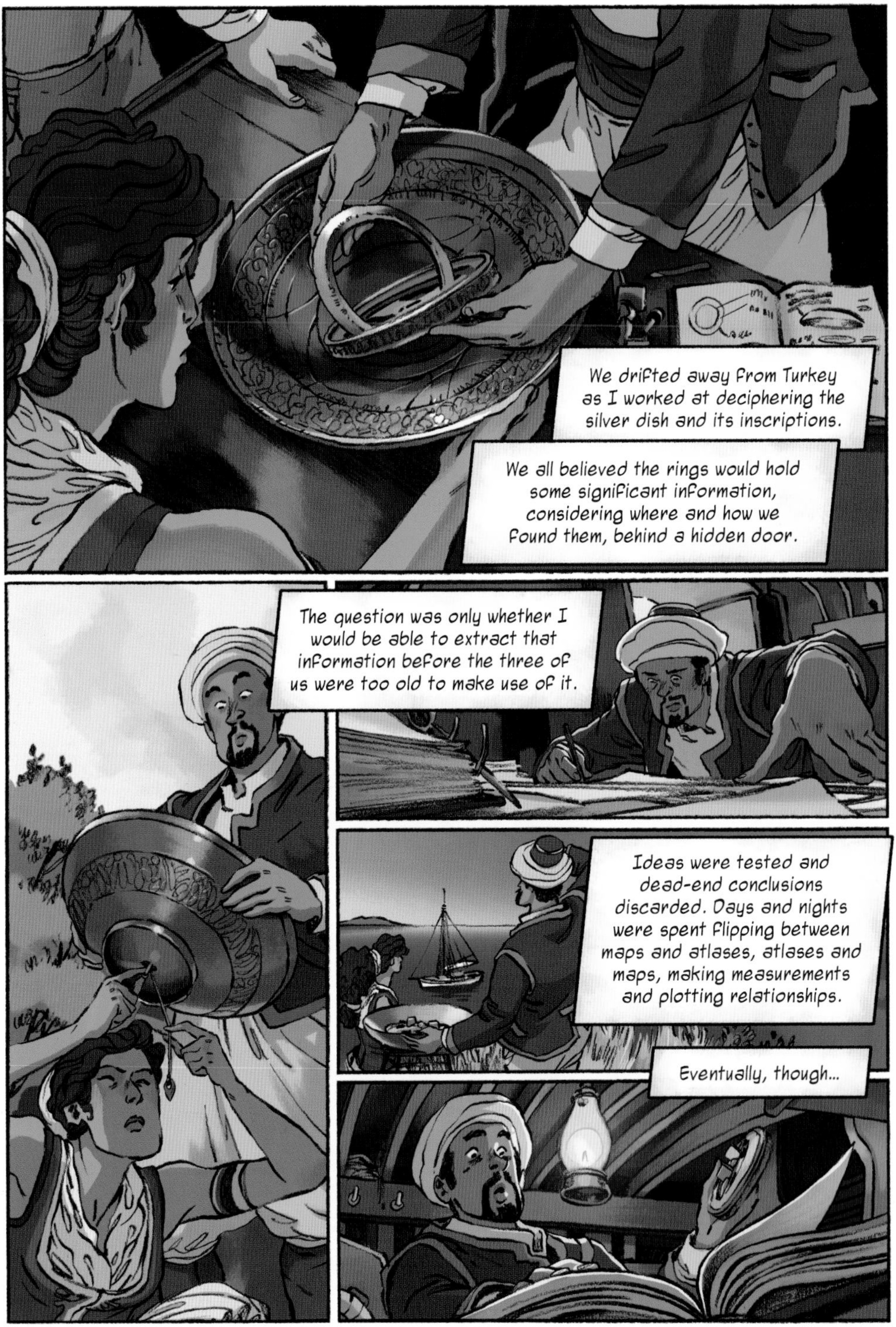
We drifted away from Turkey as I worked at deciphering the silver dish and its inscriptions.
We all believed the rings would hold some significant information, considering where and how we found them, behind a hidden door.
The question was only whether I would be able to extract that information before the three of us were too old to make use of it.
Ideas were tested and dead-end conclusions discarded. Days and nights were spent flipping between maps and atlases, atlases and maps, making measurements and plotting relationships.
Eventually, though...

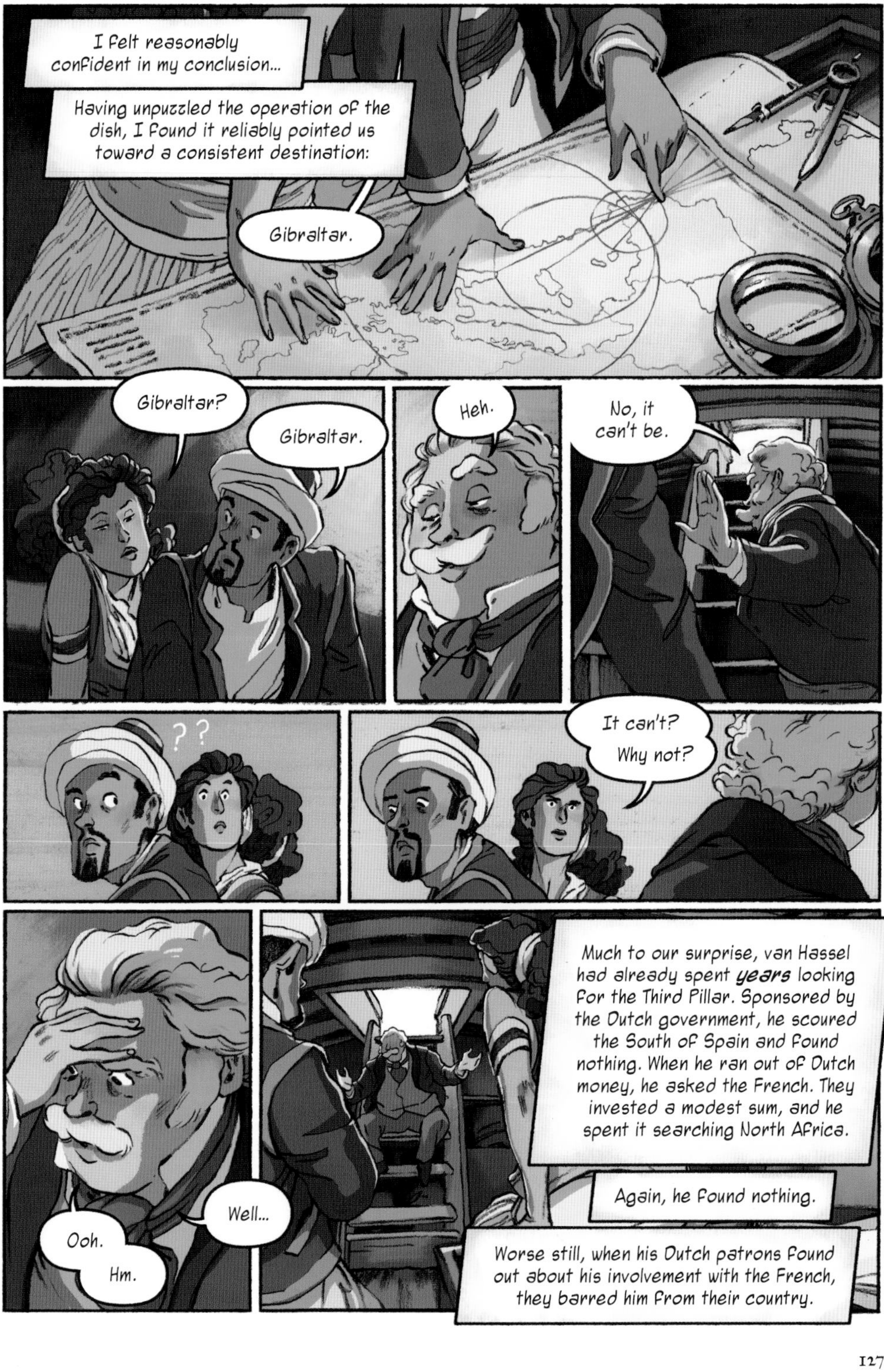
I felt reasonably confident in my conclusion...
Having unpuzzled the operation of the dish, I found it reliably pointed us toward a consistent destination:
Gibraltar.
Gibraltar?
Gibraltar.
Heh.
No, it can't be.
? ?
It can't?
Why not?
Ooh.
Hm.
Well...
Much to our surprise, van Hassel had already spent *years* looking for the Third Pillar. Sponsored by the Dutch government, he scoured the South of Spain and found nothing. When he ran out of Dutch money, he asked the French. They invested a modest sum, and he spent it searching North Africa.
Again, he found nothing.
Worse still, when his Dutch patrons found out about his involvement with the French, they barred him from their country.

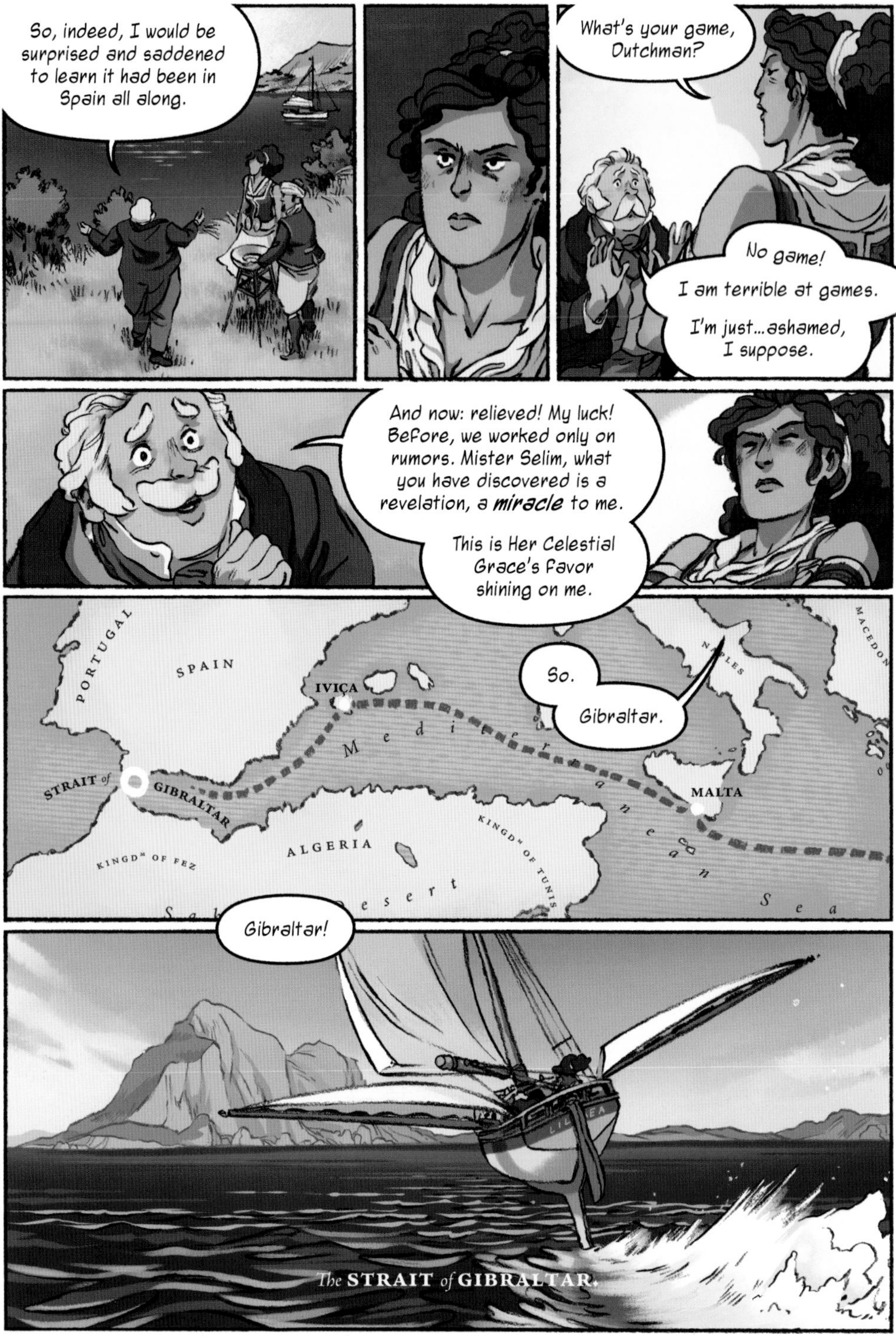
So, indeed, I would be surprised and saddened to learn it had been in Spain all along.
What's your game, Dutchman?
No game!
I am terrible at games.
I'm just...ashamed, I suppose.
And now: relieved! My luck! Before, we worked only on rumors. Mister Selim, what you have discovered is a revelation, a *miracle* to me.
This is Her Celestial Grace's favor shining on me.
PORTUGAL
SPAIN
IVIÇA
MACEDON
So.
Gibraltar.
Mediterranean Sea
STRAIT of GIBRALTAR
MALTA
ALGERIA
KINGDm OF FEZ
KINGDm OF TUNIS
Gibraltar!
The STRAIT of GIBRALTAR.

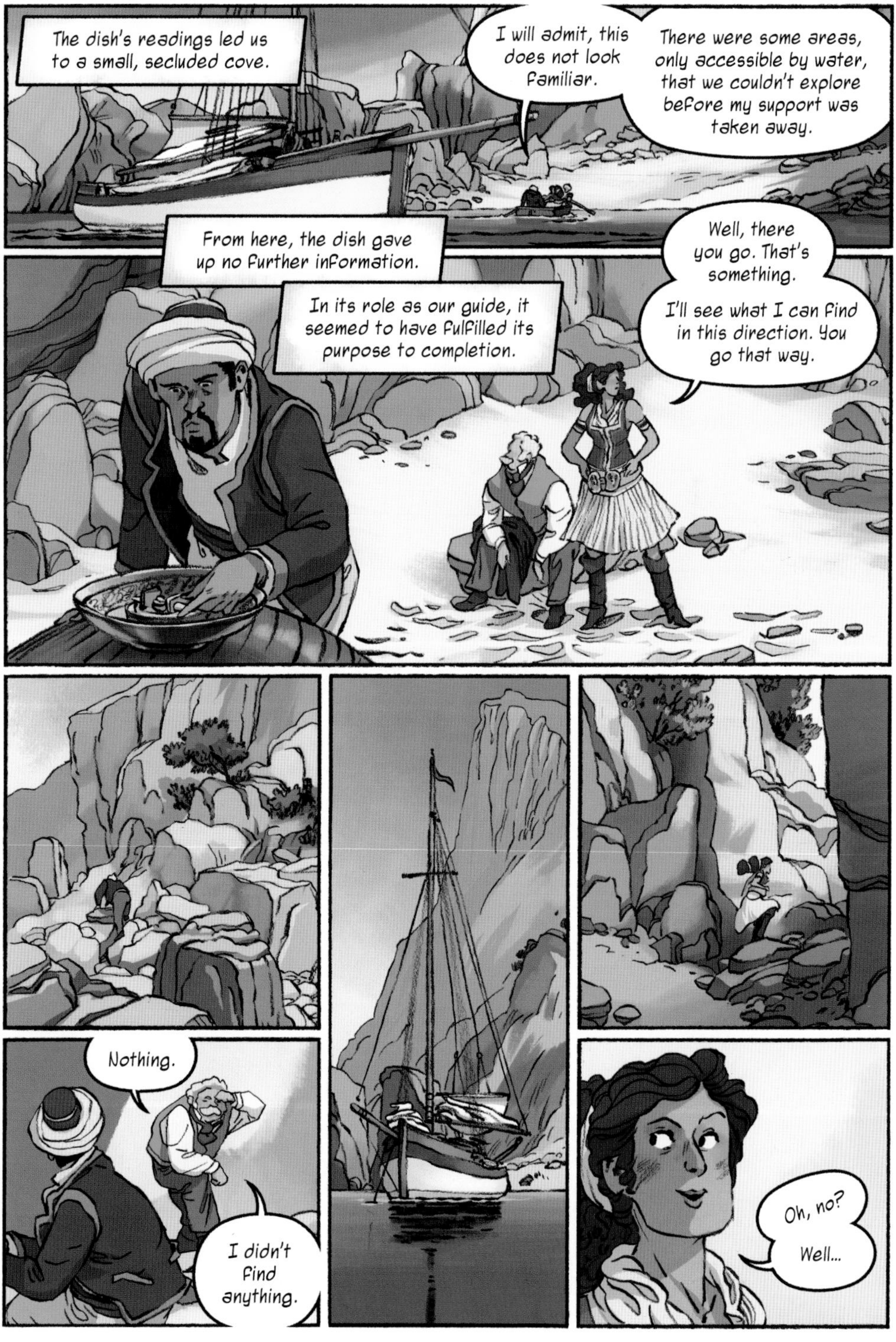

The dish's readings led us to a small, secluded cove.
I will admit, this does not look familiar.
There were some areas, only accessible by water, that we couldn't explore before my support was taken away.
From here, the dish gave up no further information.
In its role as our guide, it seemed to have fulfilled its purpose to completion.
Well, there you go. That's something.
I'll see what I can find in this direction. You go that way.
Nothing.
I didn't find anything.
Oh, no?
Well...

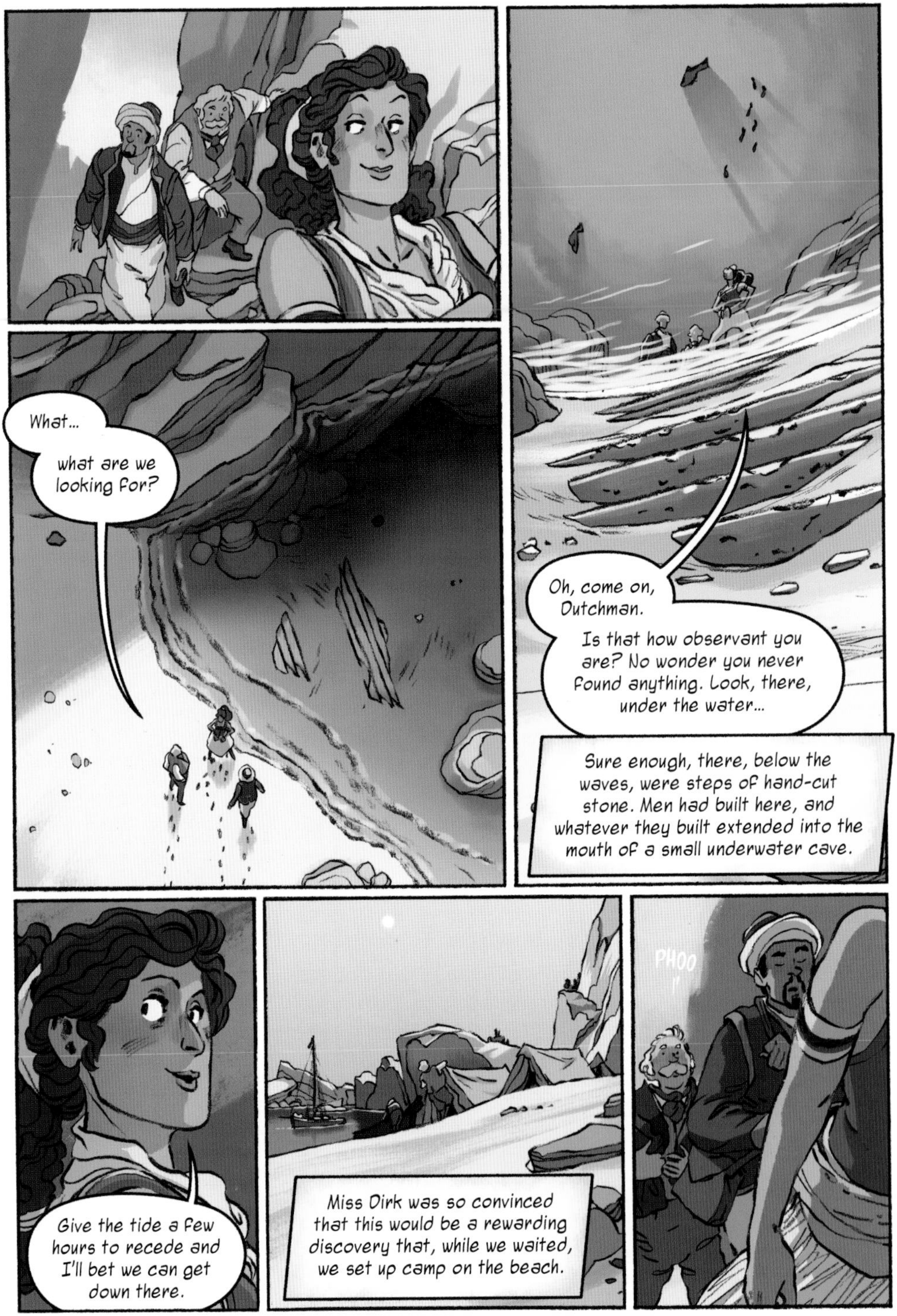

What...
what are we looking for?
Oh, come on, Dutchman.
Is that how observant you are? No wonder you never found anything. Look, there, under the water...
Sure enough, there, below the waves, were steps of hand-cut stone. Men had built here, and whatever they built extended into the mouth of a small underwater cave.
Give the tide a few hours to recede and I'll bet we can get down there.
Miss Dirk was so convinced that this would be a rewarding discovery that, while we waited, we set up camp on the beach.
PHOO

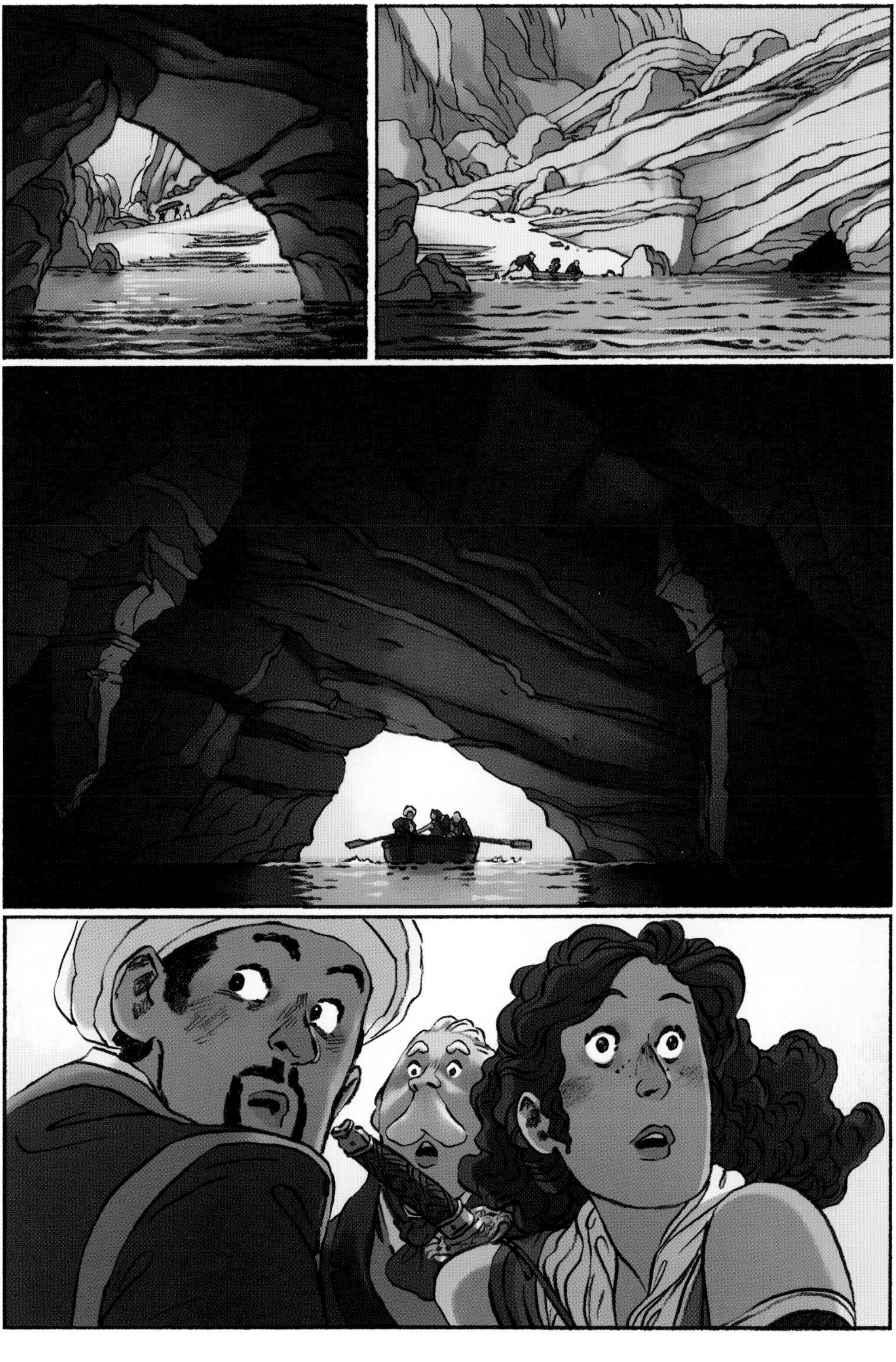

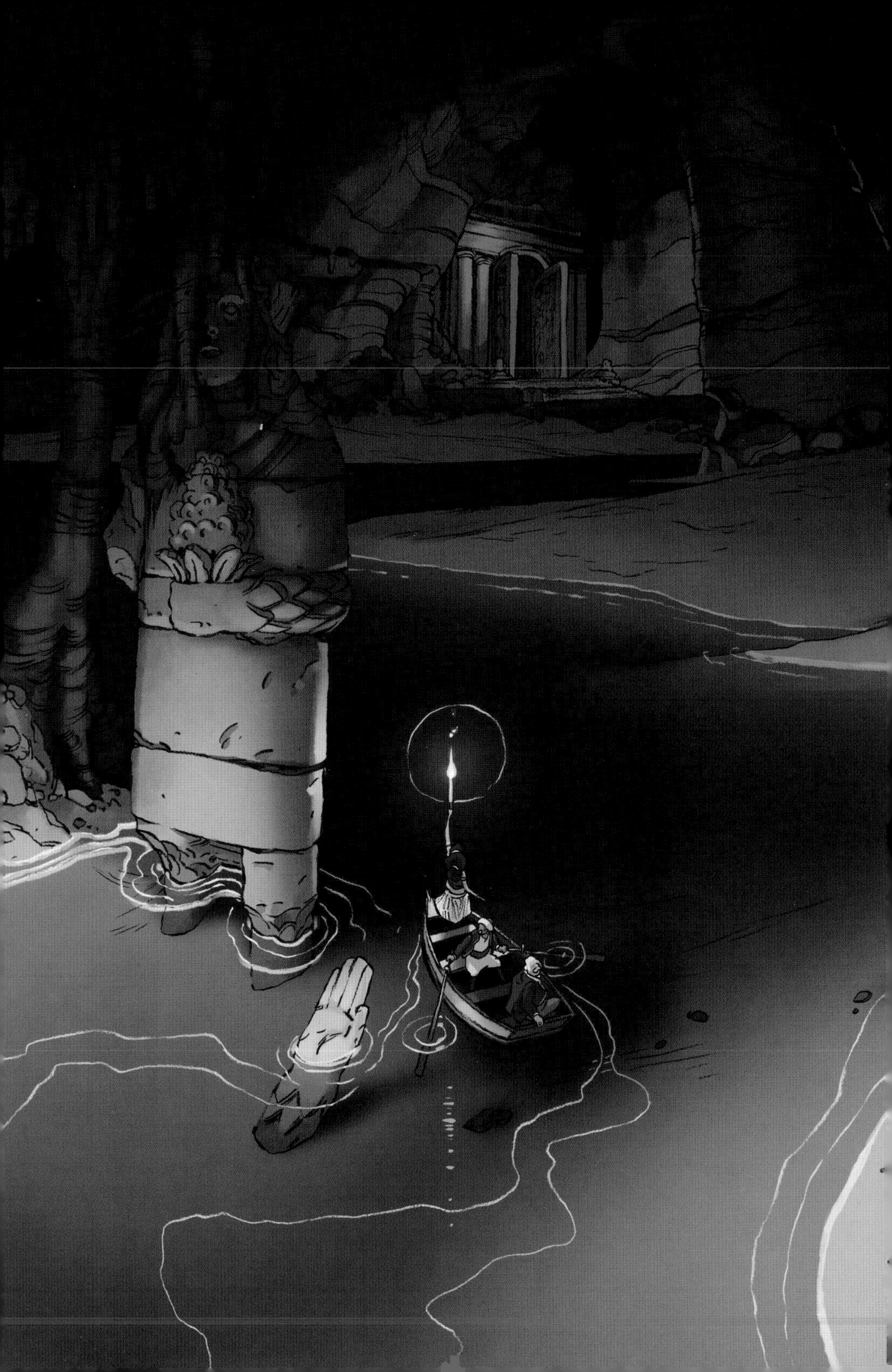

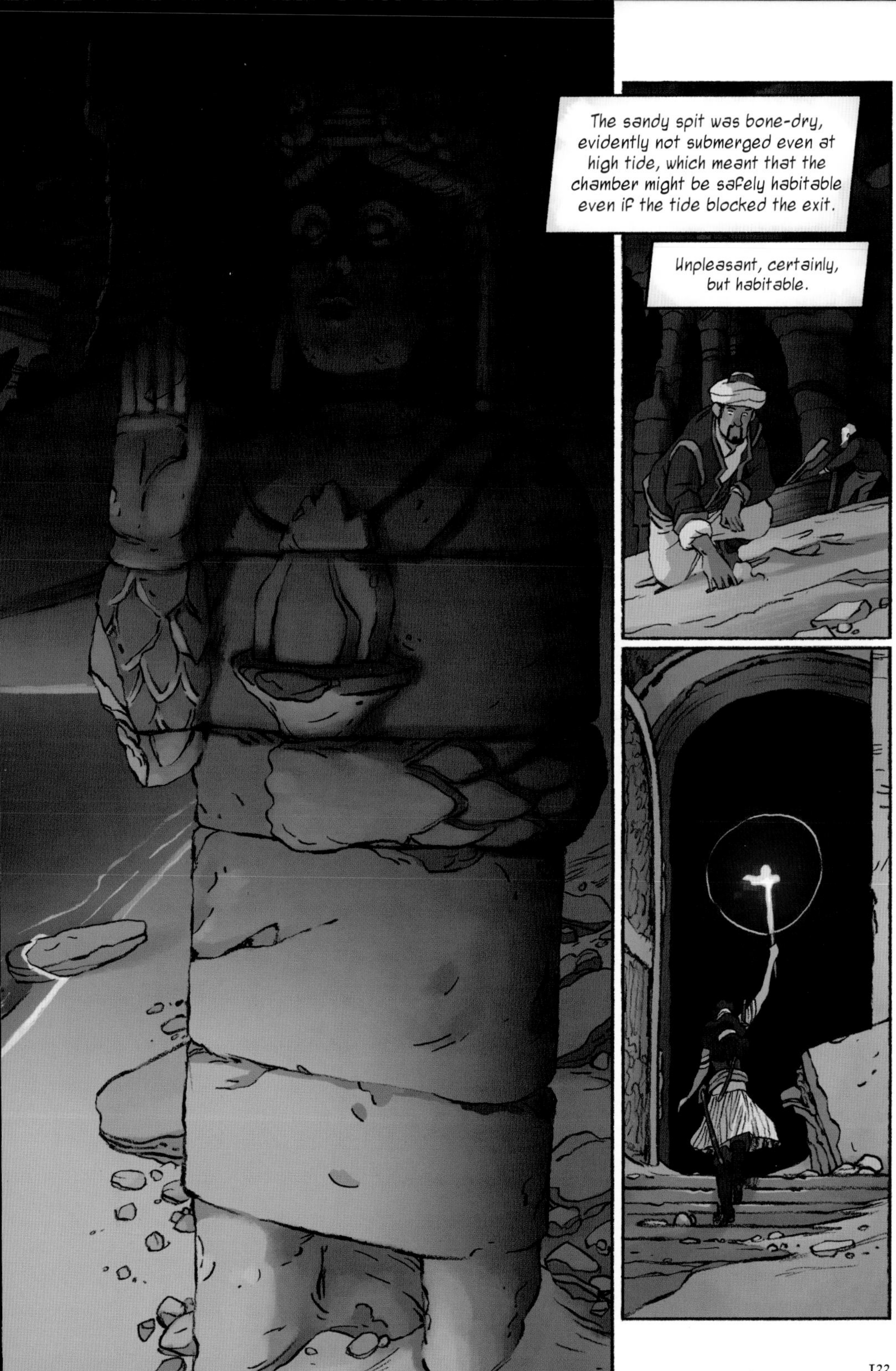
The sandy spit was bone-dry, evidently not submerged even at high tide, which meant that the chamber might be safely habitable even if the tide blocked the exit.
Unpleasant, certainly, but habitable.

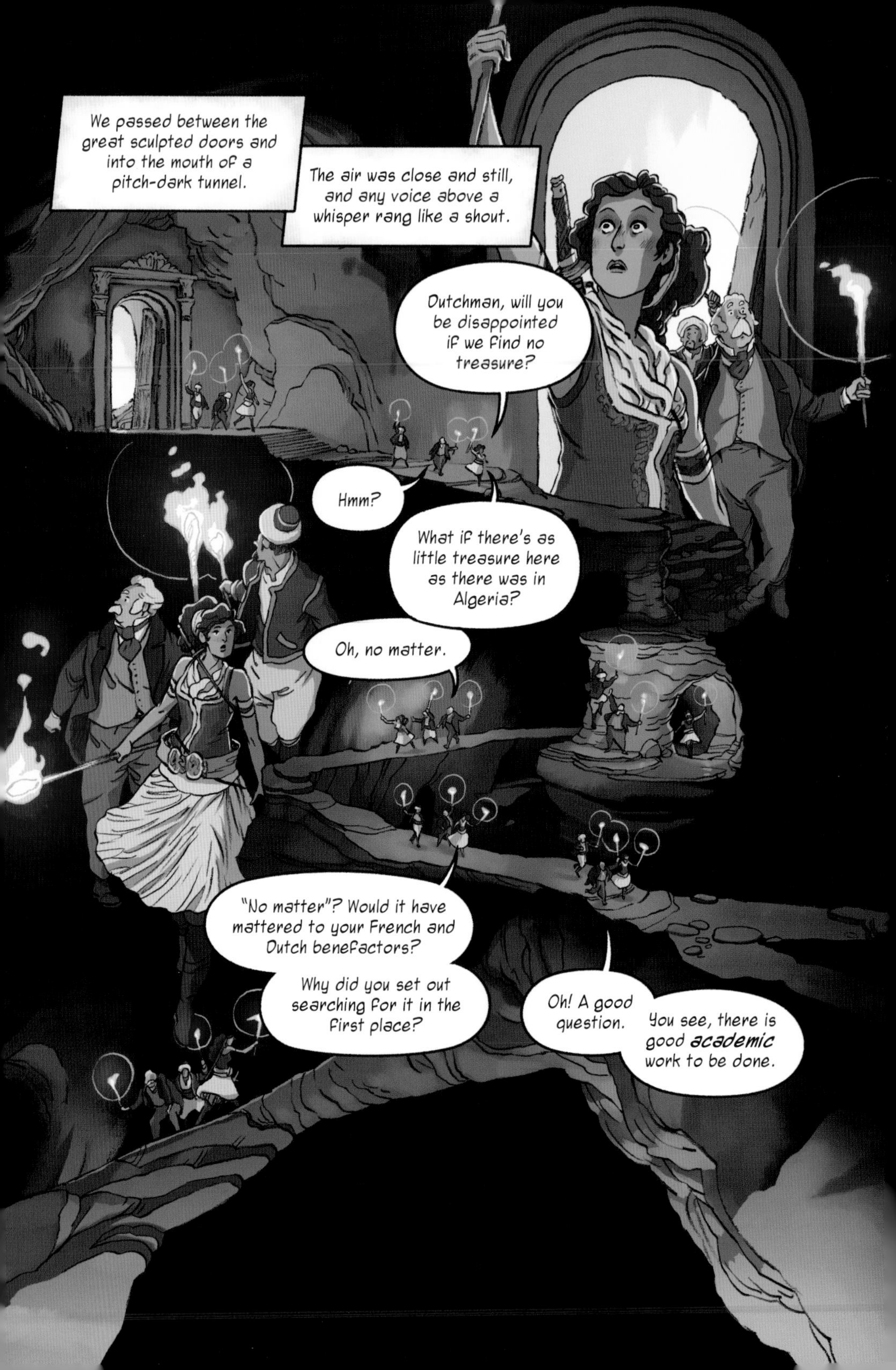
We passed between the great sculpted doors and into the mouth of a pitch-dark tunnel.
The air was close and still, and any voice above a whisper rang like a shout.
Dutchman, will you be disappointed if we find no treasure?
Hmm?
What if there's as little treasure here as there was in Algeria?
Oh, no matter.
"No matter"? Would it have mattered to your French and Dutch benefactors?
Why did you set out searching for it in the first place?
Oh! A good question.
You see, there is good academic work to be done.

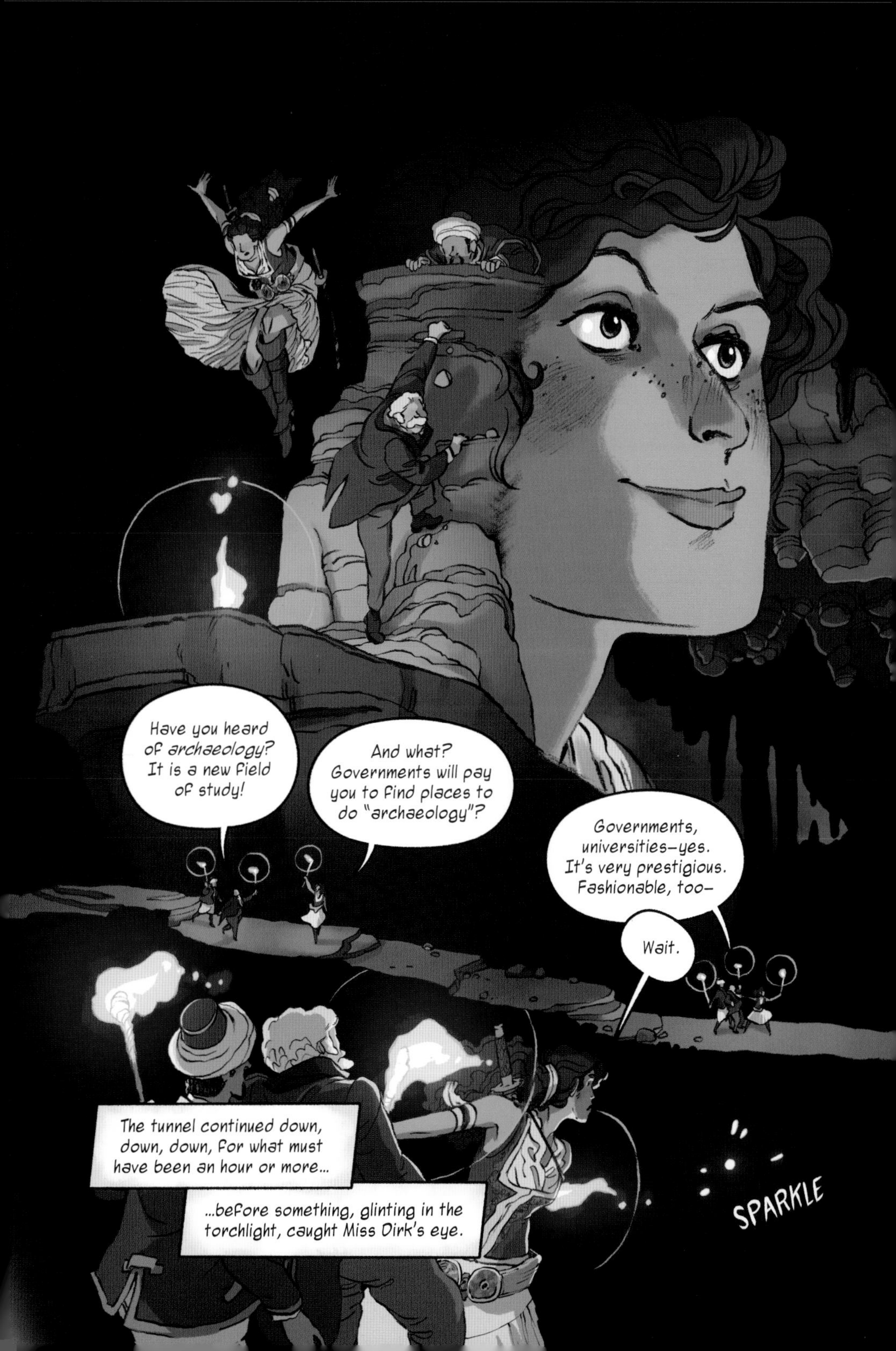
Have you heard of *archaeology*? It is a new field of study!
And what? Governments will pay you to find places to do "archaeology"?
Governments, universities–yes. It's very prestigious. Fashionable, too–
Wait.
The tunnel continued down, down, down, for what must have been an hour or more...
...before something, glinting in the torchlight, caught Miss Dirk's eye.
SPARKLE

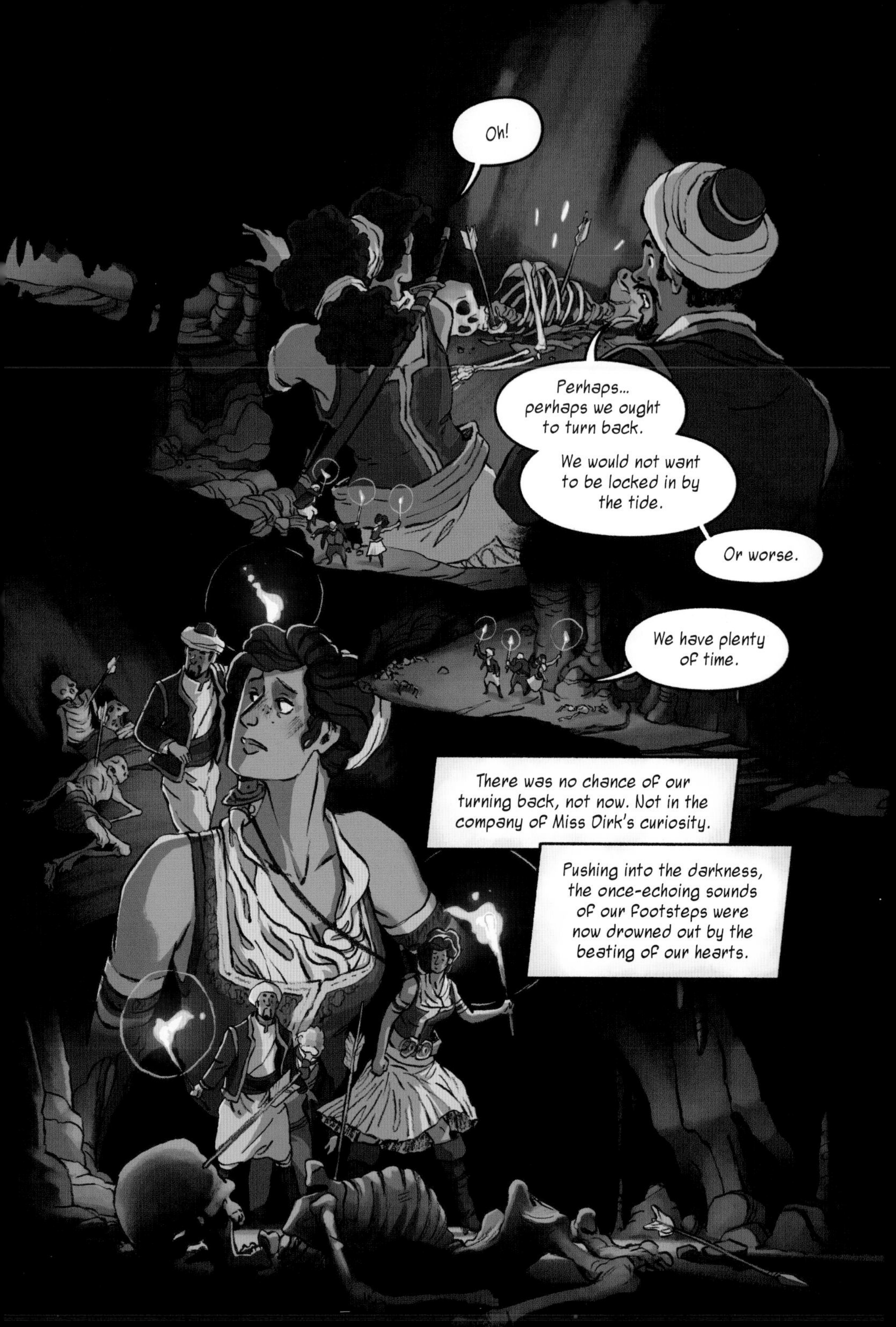
Oh!
Perhaps... perhaps we ought to turn back.
We would not want to be locked in by the tide.
Or worse.
We have plenty of time.
There was no chance of our turning back, not now. Not in the company of Miss Dirk's curiosity.
Pushing into the darkness, the once-echoing sounds of our footsteps were now drowned out by the beating of our hearts.

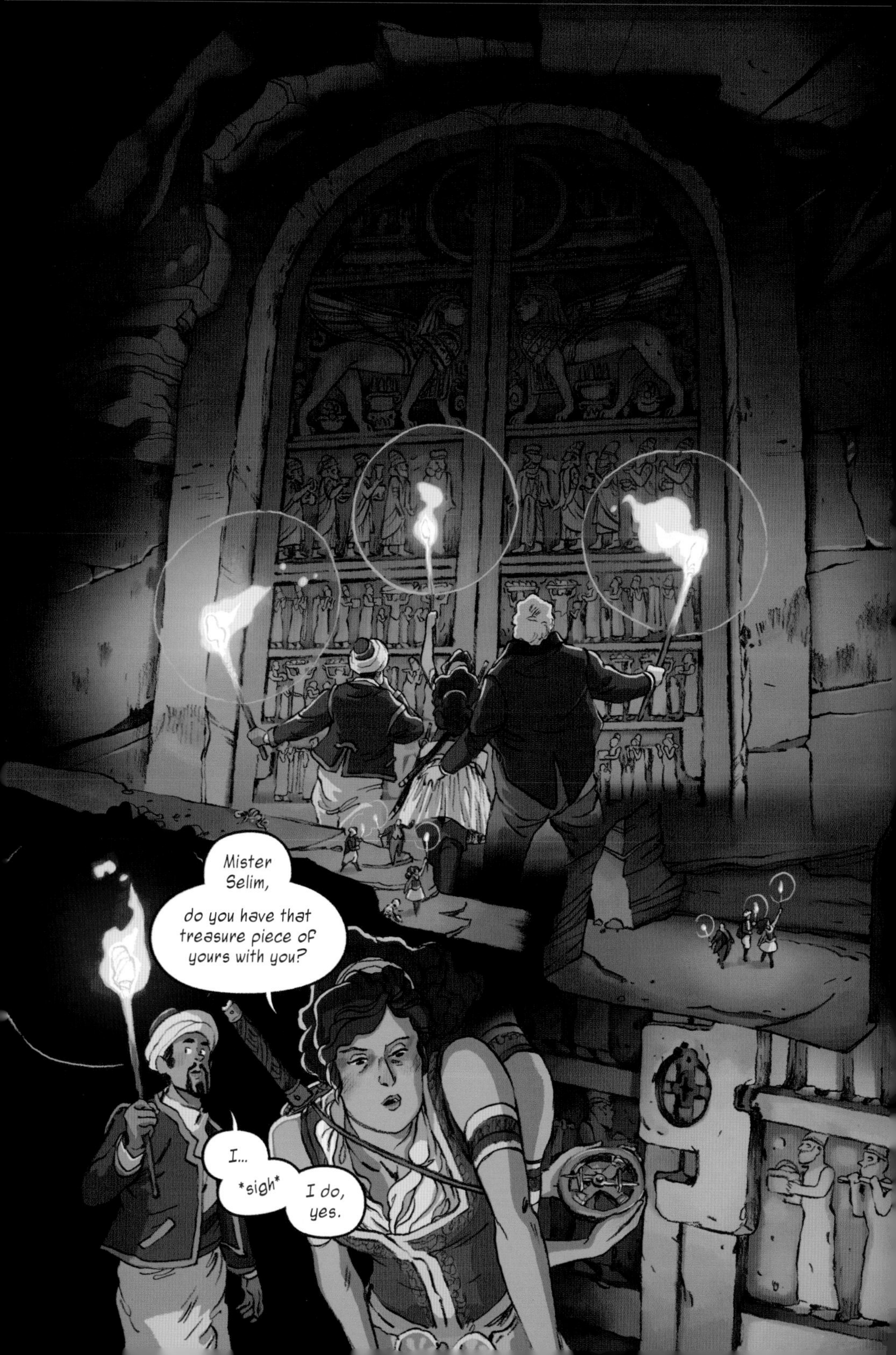

Mister Selim,
do you have that treasure piece of yours with you?
I...
*sigh*
I do, yes.

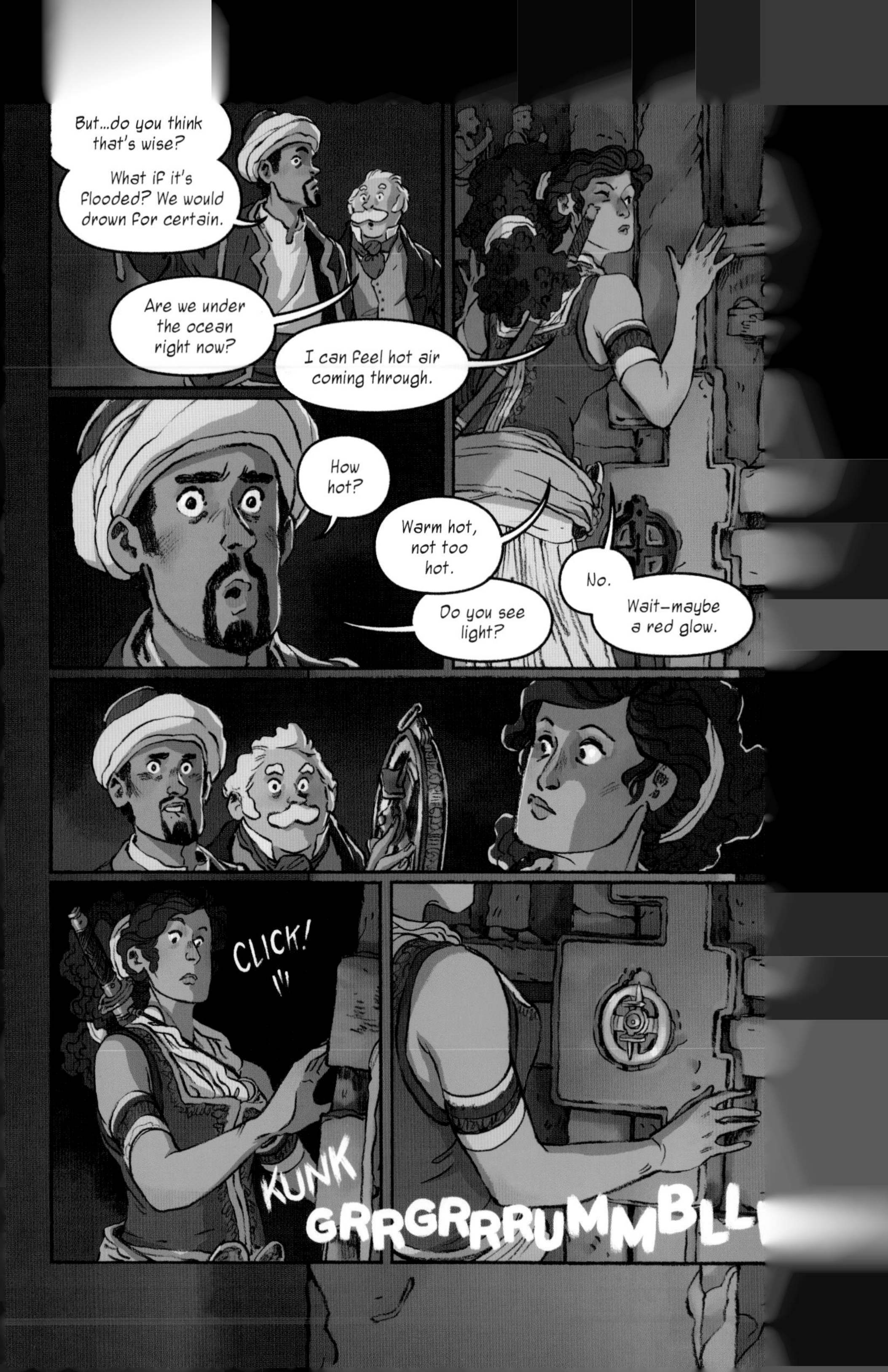

But...do you think that's wise?
What if it's flooded? We would drown for certain.
Are we under the ocean right now?
I can feel hot air coming through.
How hot?
Warm hot, not too hot.
Do you see light?
No.
Wait—maybe a red glow.
CLICK!
KUNK
GRRGRRRUMMBLL

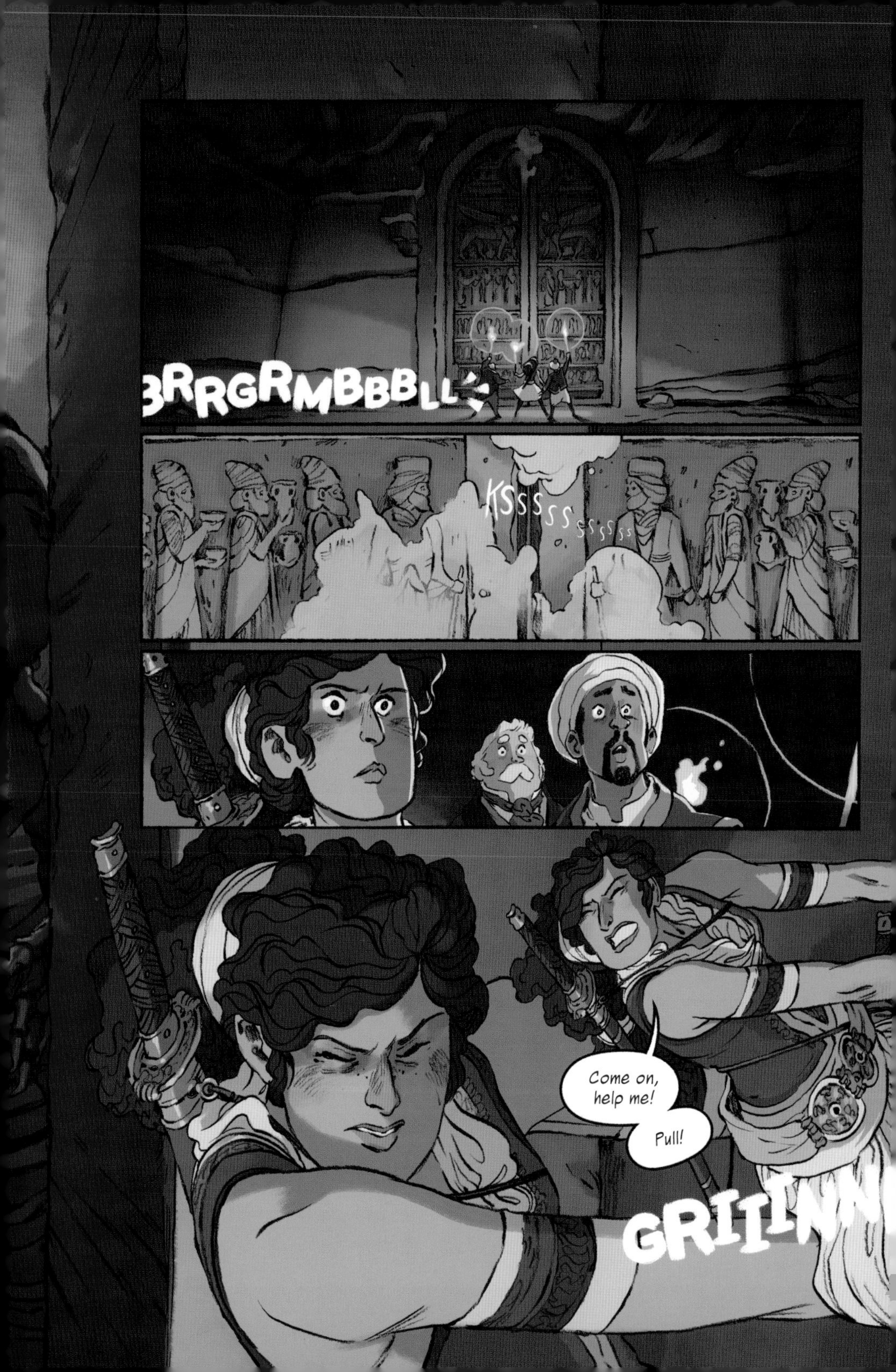
BRRGRMBBBLL
KSSSSSSSSSSS
Come on, help me!
Pull!
GRIIINN

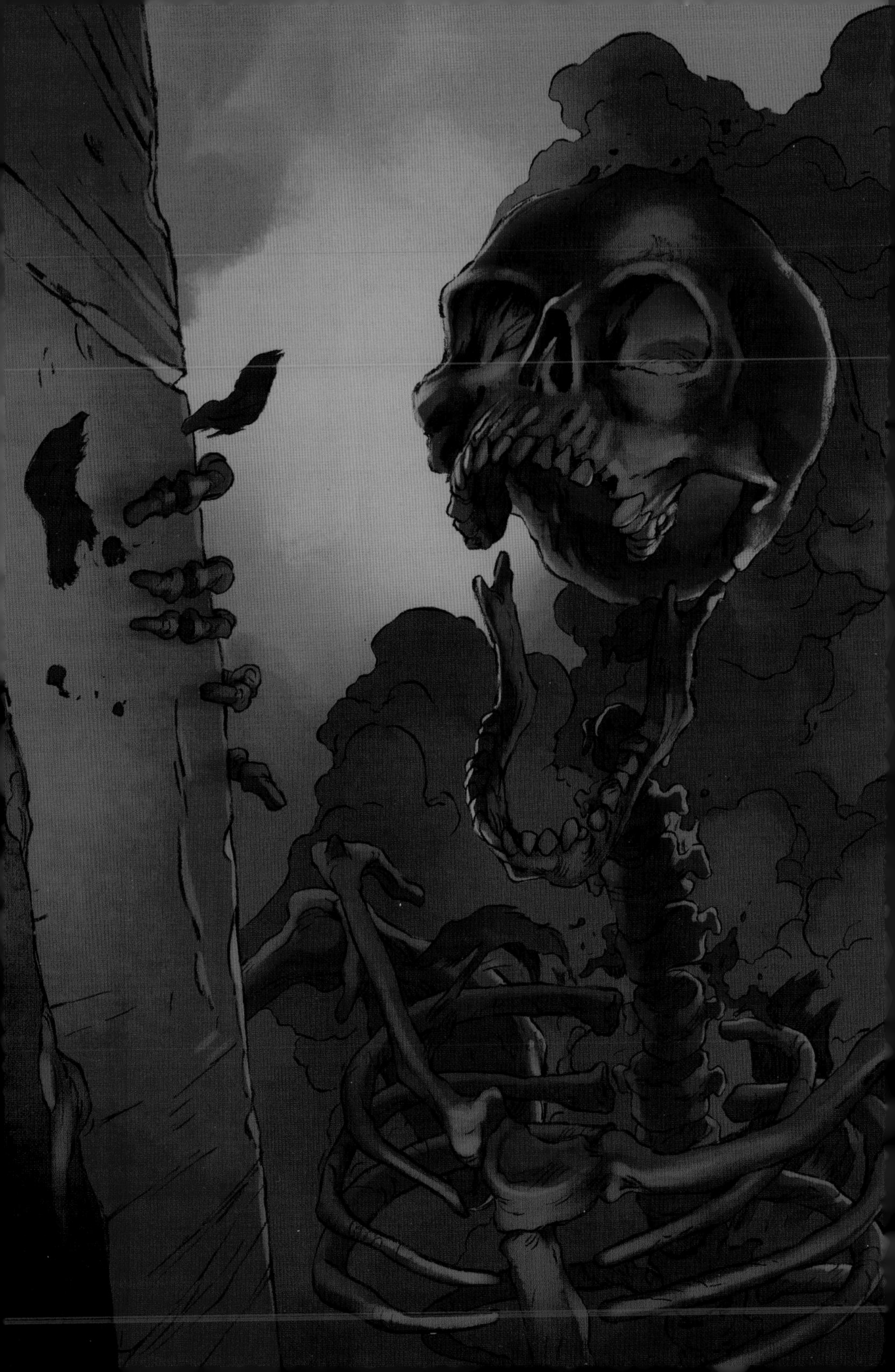

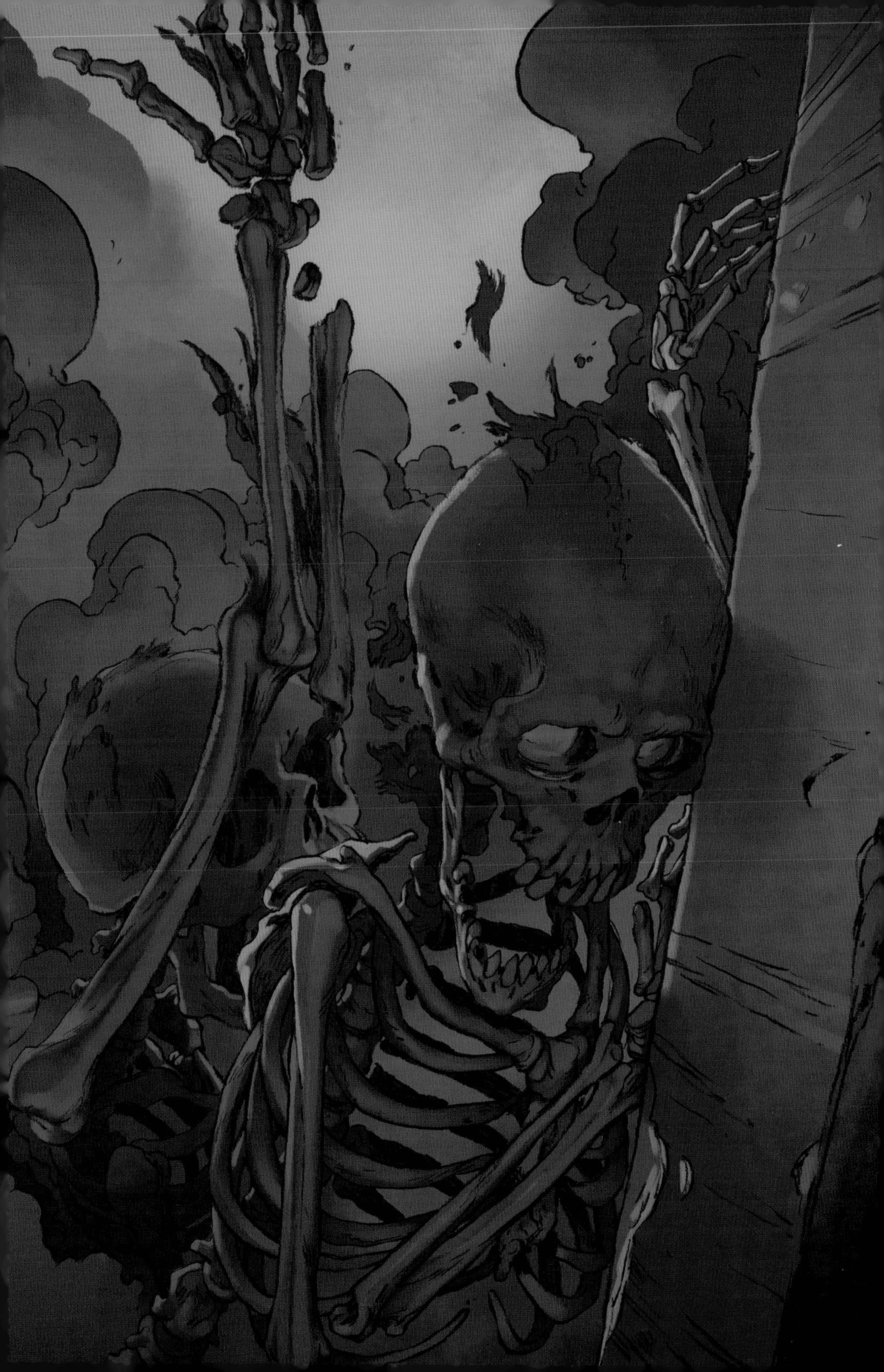

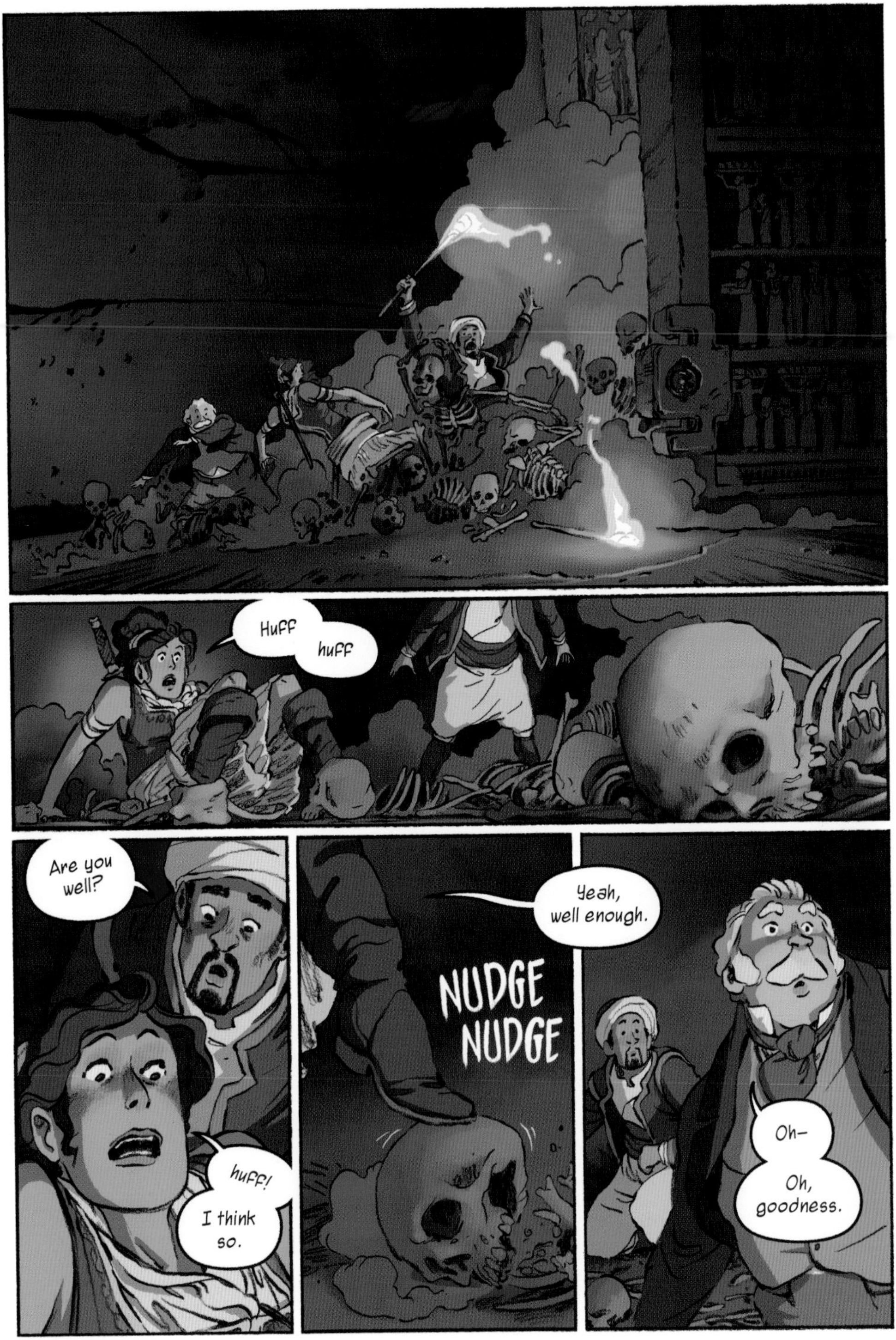
Huff
huff
Are you well?
huff!
I think so.
NUDGE
NUDGE
Yeah, well enough.
Oh–
Oh, goodness.

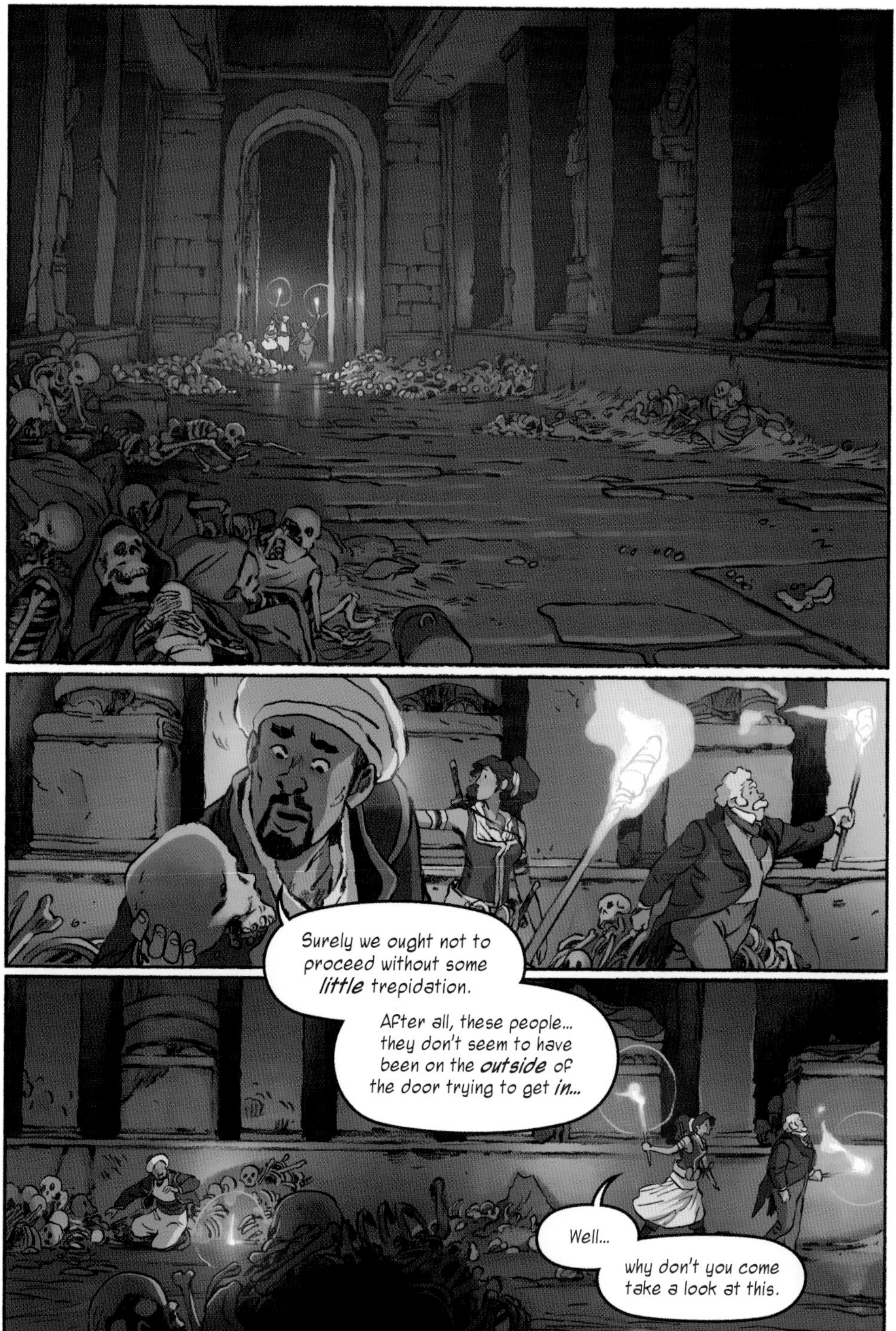
Surely we ought not to proceed without some *little* trepidation.
After all, these people... they don't seem to have been on the *outside* of the door trying to get *in*...
Well...
why don't you come take a look at this.

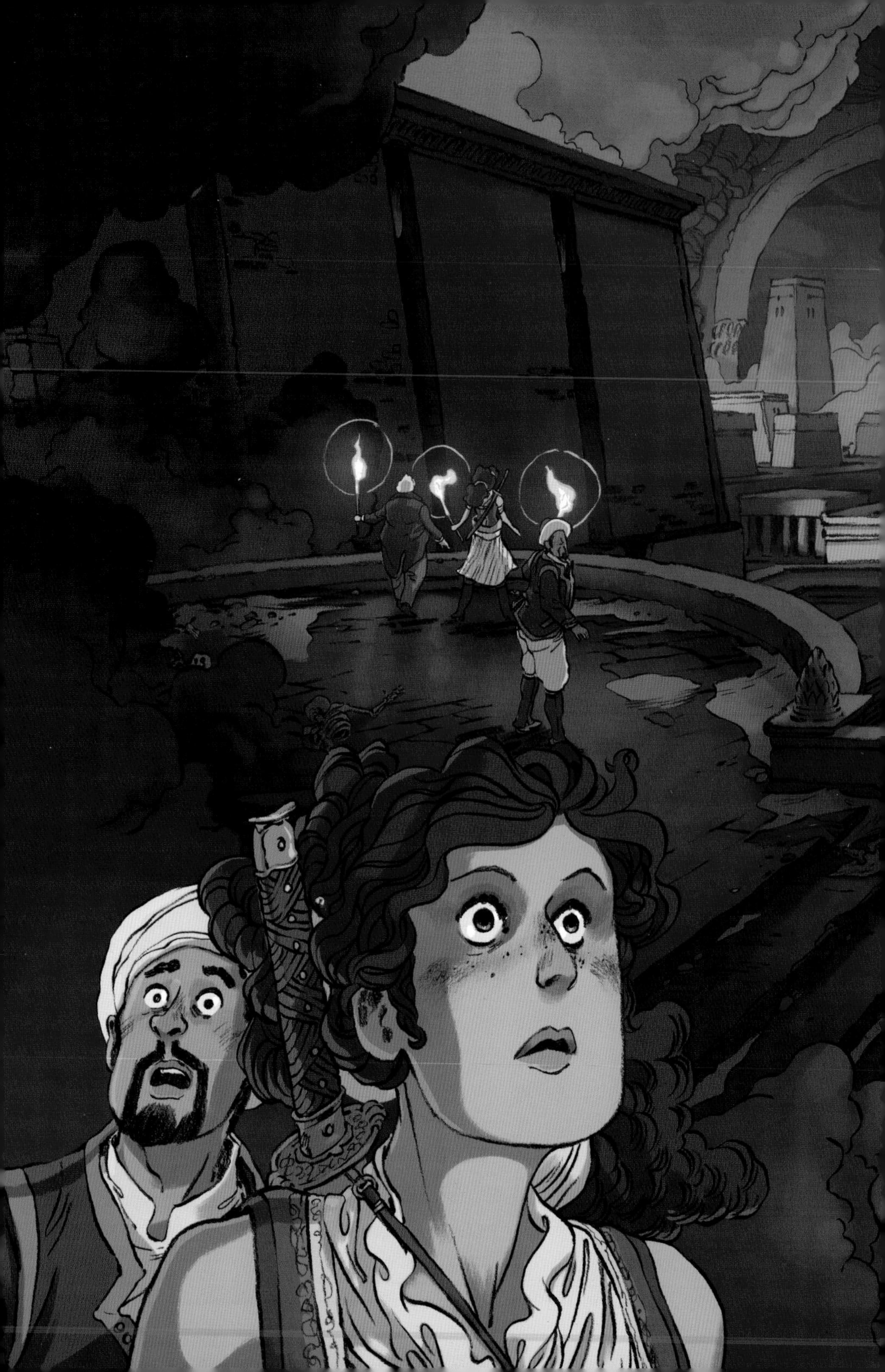

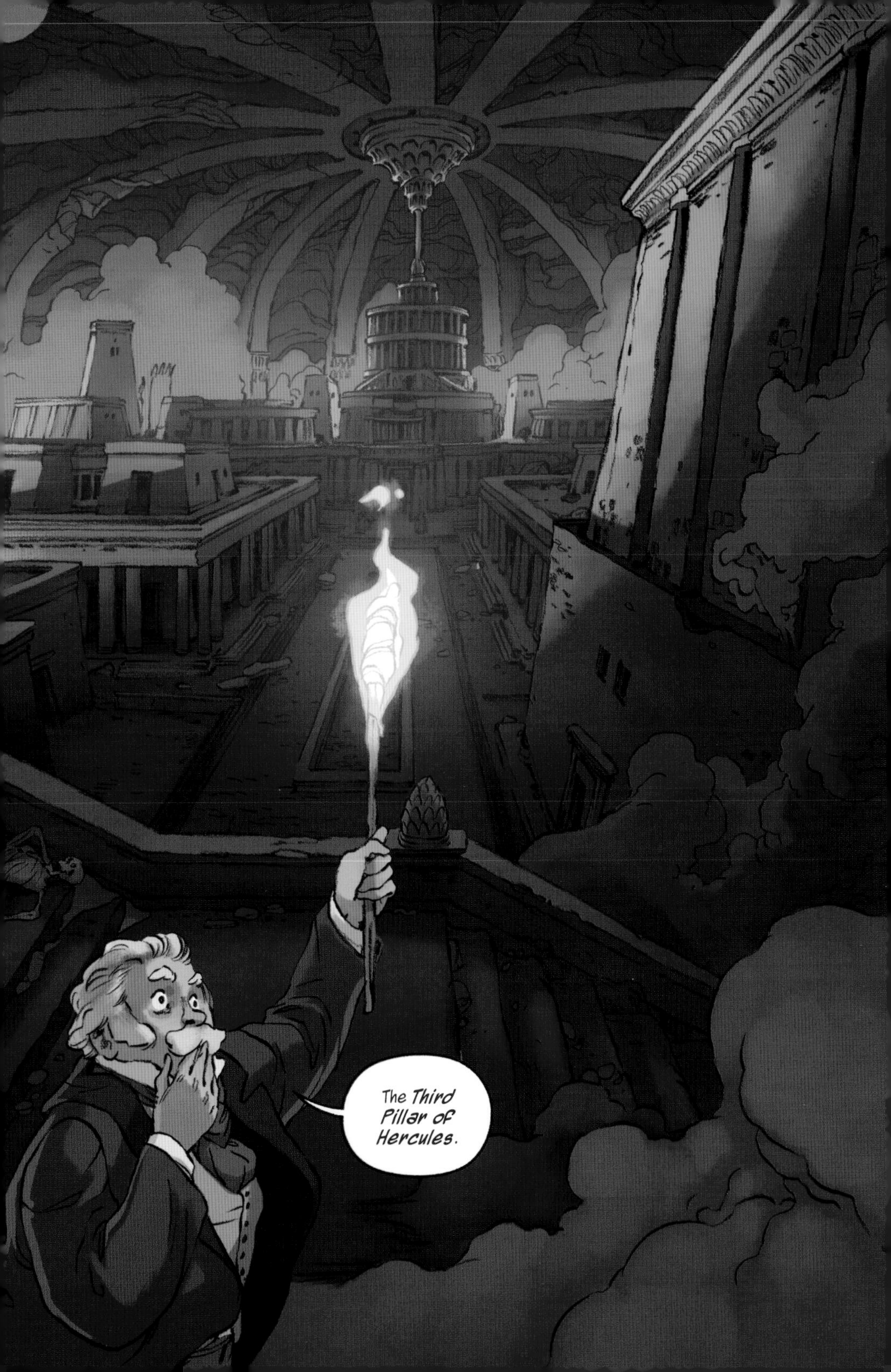
The *Third Pillar of Hercules*.

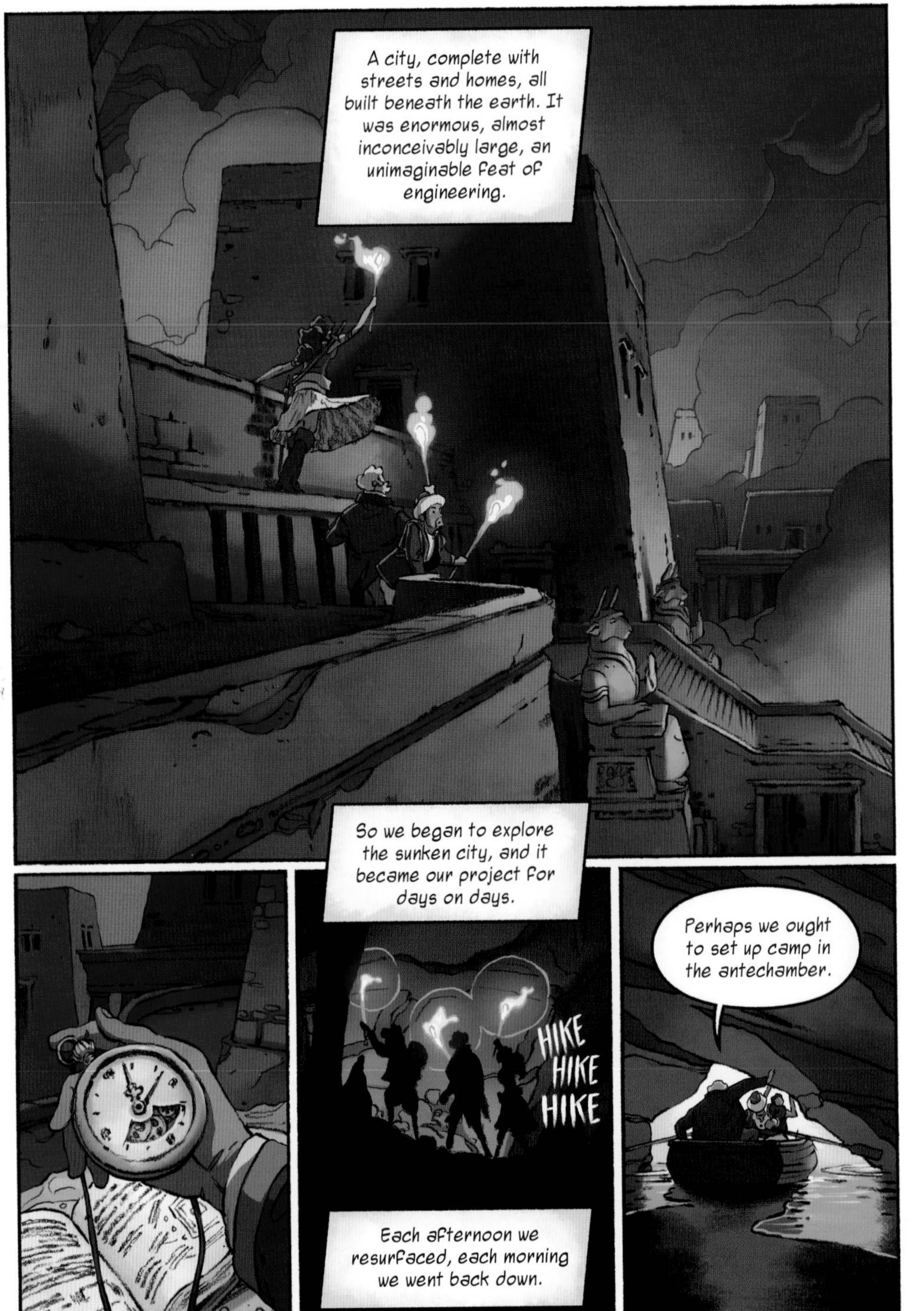
A city, complete with streets and homes, all built beneath the earth. It was enormous, almost inconceivably large, an unimaginable feat of engineering.
So we began to explore the sunken city, and it became our project for days on days.
HIKE HIKE HIKE
Each afternoon we resurfaced, each morning we went back down.
Perhaps we ought to set up camp in the antechamber.

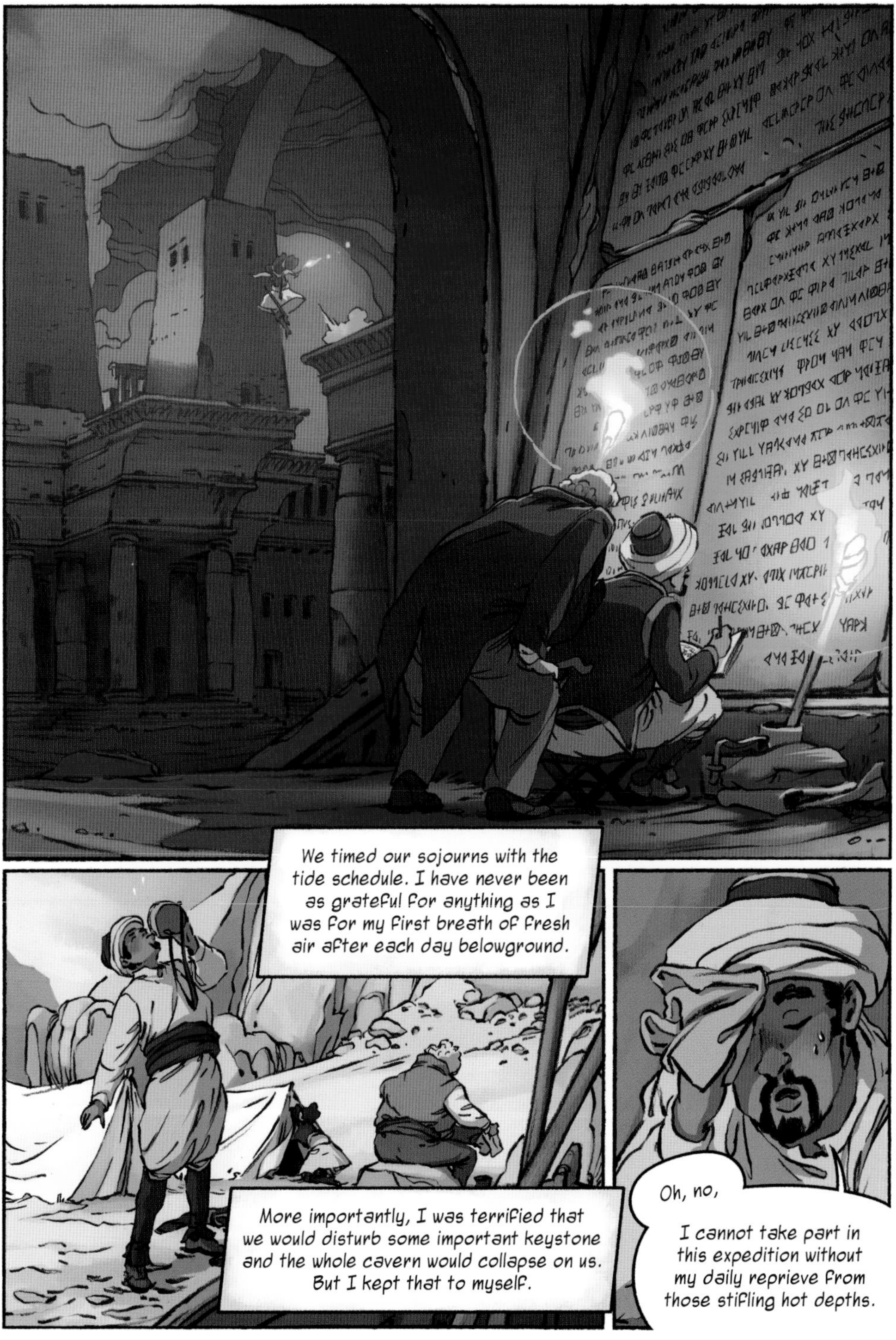
We timed our sojourns with the tide schedule. I have never been as grateful for anything as I was for my first breath of fresh air after each day belowground.
More importantly, I was terrified that we would disturb some important keystone and the whole cavern would collapse on us. But I kept that to myself.
Oh, no,
I cannot take part in this expedition without my daily reprieve from those stifling hot depths.

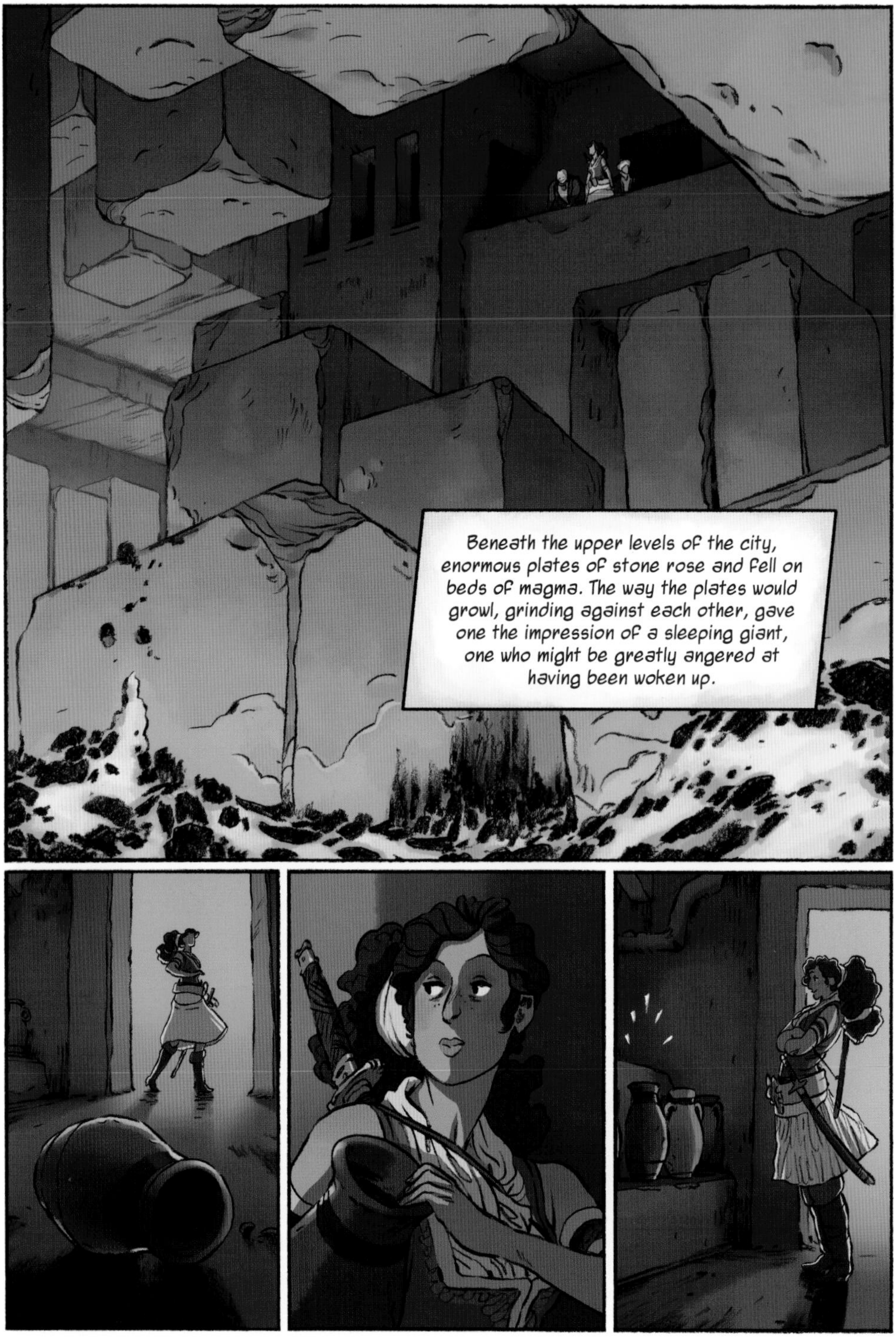
Beneath the upper levels of the city, enormous plates of stone rose and fell on beds of magma. The way the plates would growl, grinding against each other, gave one the impression of a sleeping giant, one who might be greatly angered at having been woken up.

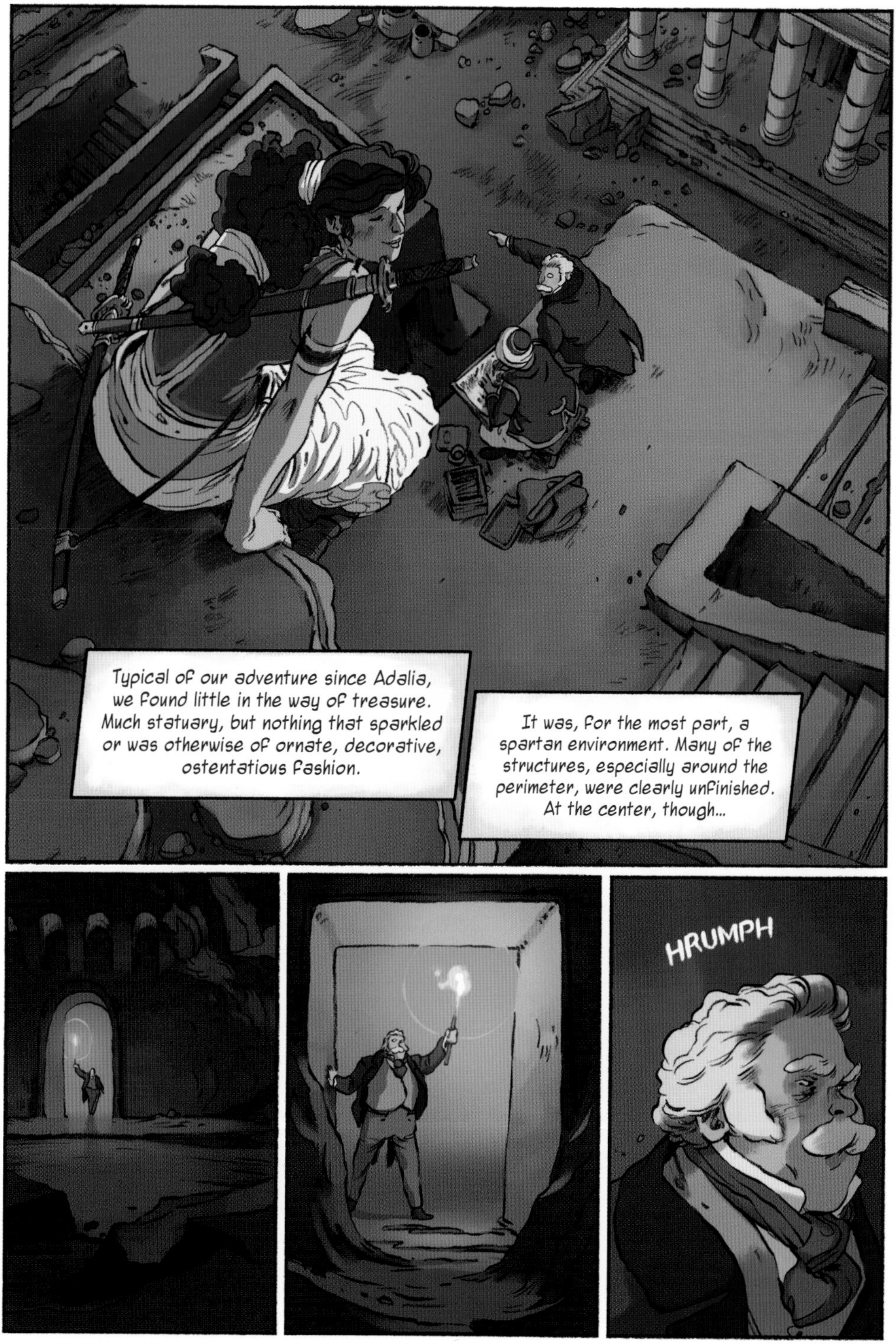
Typical of our adventure since Adalia, we found little in the way of treasure. Much statuary, but nothing that sparkled or was otherwise of ornate, decorative, ostentatious fashion.
It was, for the most part, a spartan environment. Many of the structures, especially around the perimeter, were clearly unfinished. At the center, though...
HRUMPH

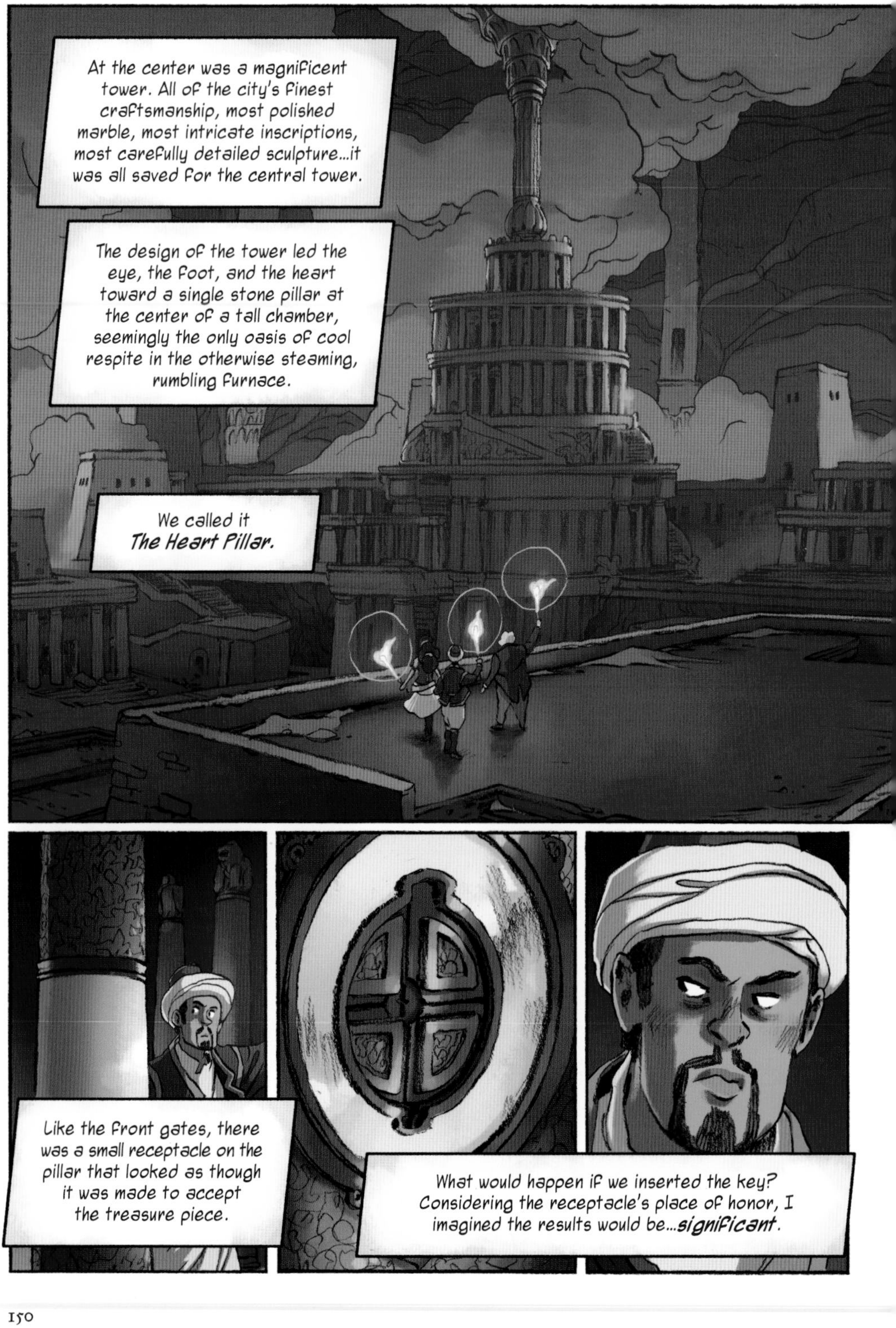
At the center was a magnificent tower. All of the city's finest craftsmanship, most polished marble, most intricate inscriptions, most carefully detailed sculpture...it was all saved for the central tower.
The design of the tower led the eye, the foot, and the heart toward a single stone pillar at the center of a tall chamber, seemingly the only oasis of cool respite in the otherwise steaming, rumbling furnace.
We called it *The Heart Pillar.*
Like the front gates, there was a small receptacle on the pillar that looked as though it was made to accept the treasure piece.
What would happen if we inserted the key? Considering the receptacle's place of honor, I imagined the results would be...***significant***.

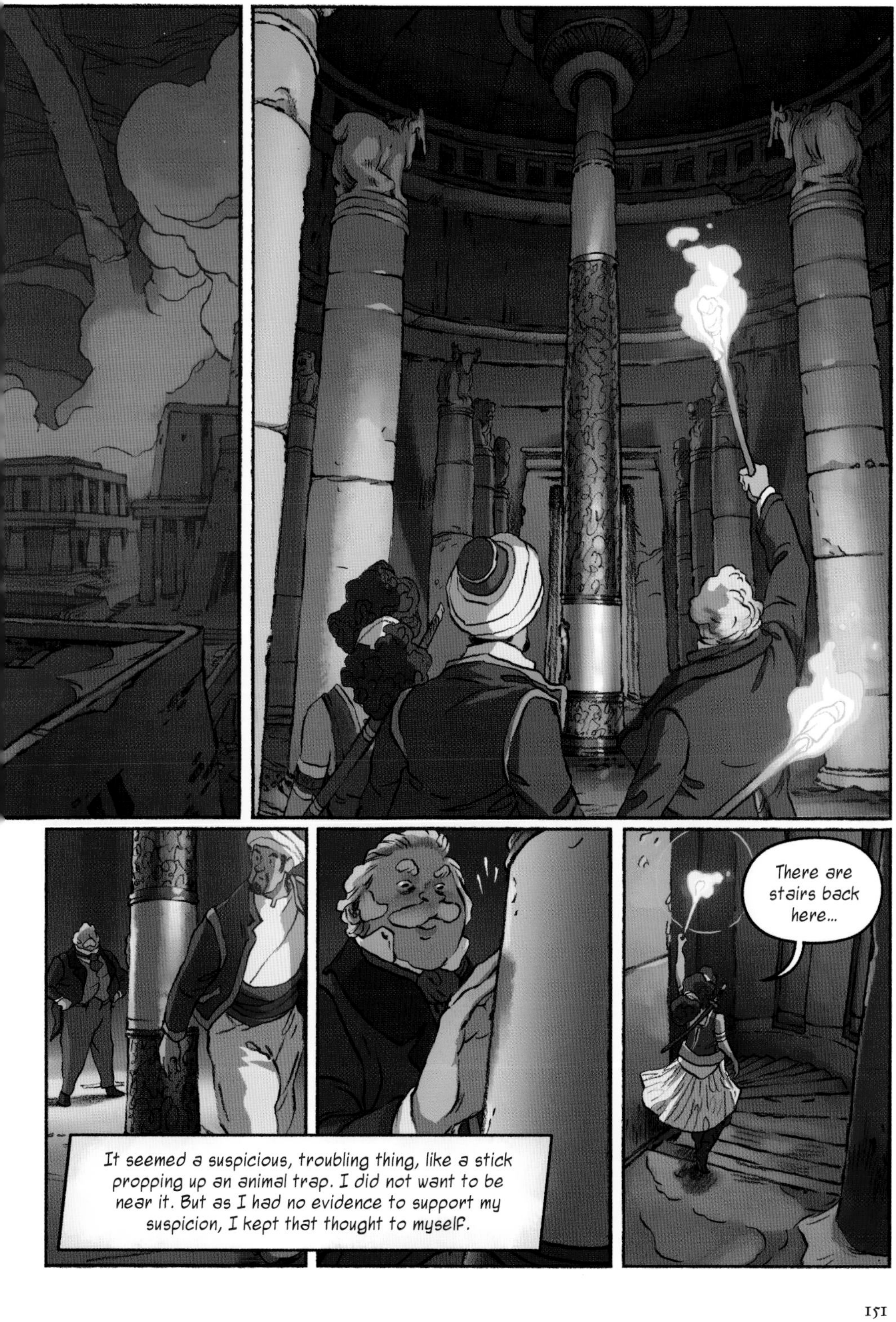

It seemed a suspicious, troubling thing, like a stick propping up an animal trap. I did not want to be near it. But as I had no evidence to support my suspicion, I kept that thought to myself.
There are stairs back here...

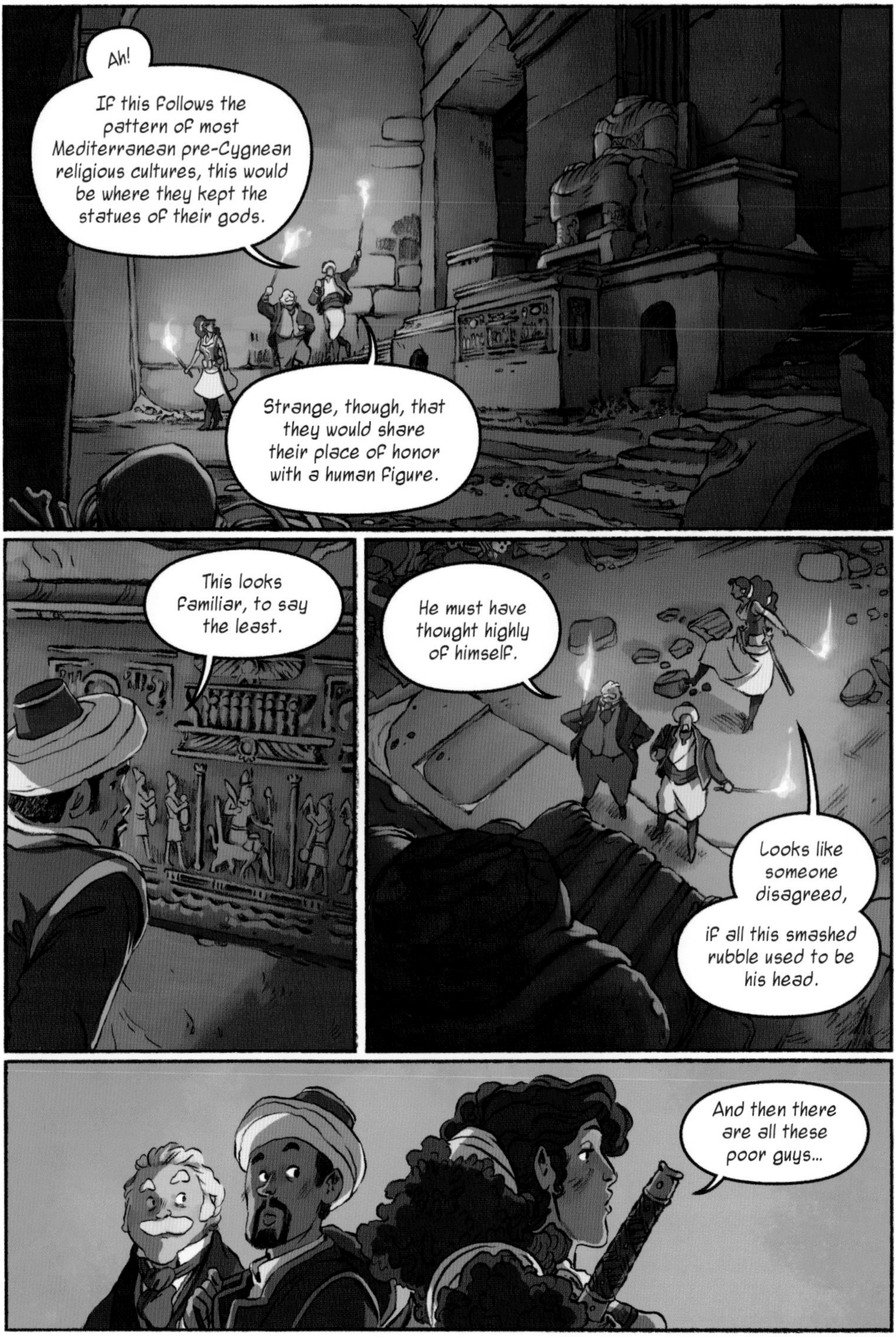

Ah!
If this follows the pattern of most Mediterranean pre-Cygnean religious cultures, this would be where they kept the statues of their gods.
Strange, though, that they would share their place of honor with a human figure.
This looks familiar, to say the least.
He must have thought highly of himself.
Looks like someone disagreed,
if all this smashed rubble used to be his head.
And then there are all these poor guys...

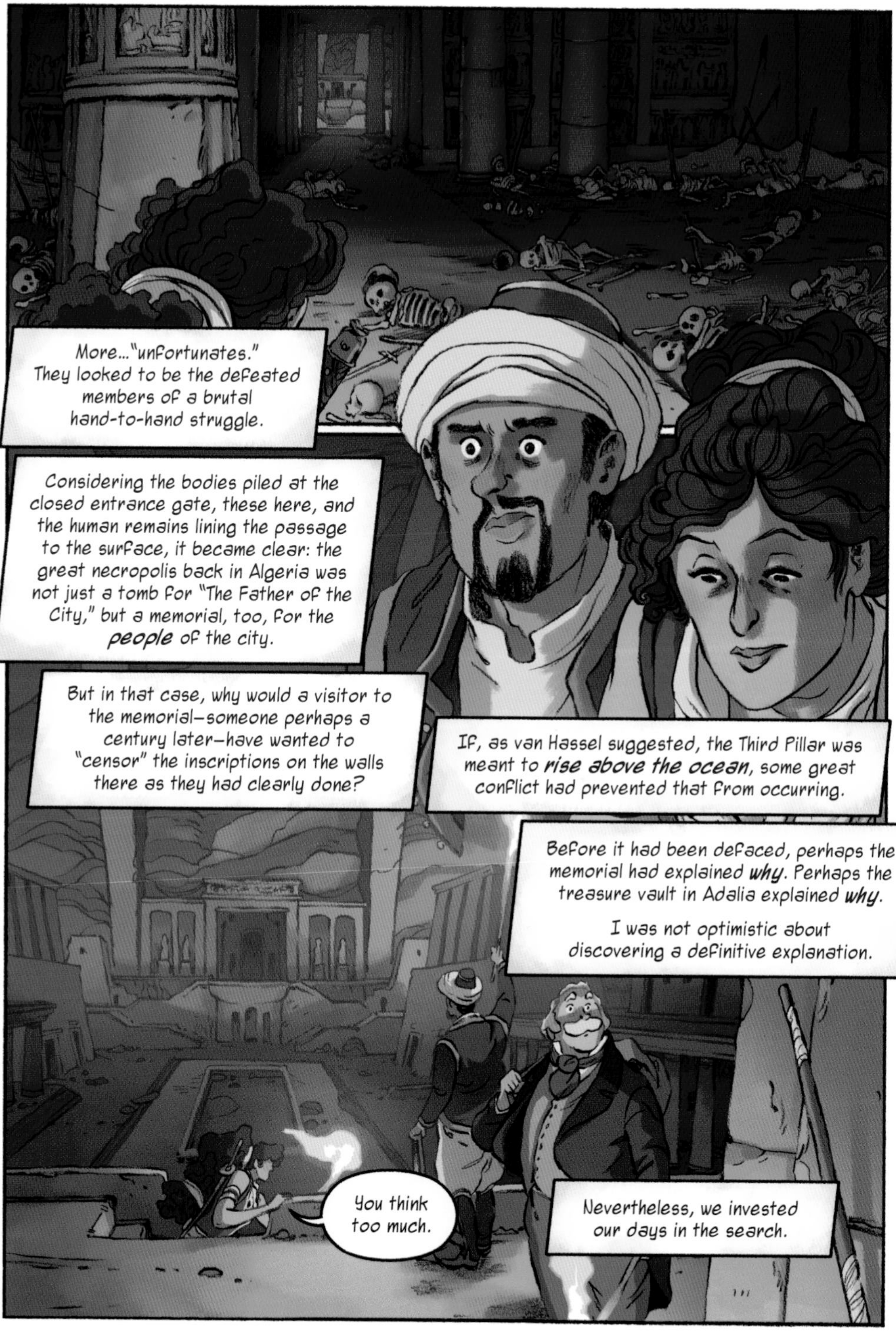

More..."unfortunates." They looked to be the defeated members of a brutal hand-to-hand struggle.
Considering the bodies piled at the closed entrance gate, these here, and the human remains lining the passage to the surface, it became clear: the great necropolis back in Algeria was not just a tomb for "The Father of the City," but a memorial, too, for the *people* of the city.
But in that case, why would a visitor to the memorial–someone perhaps a century later–have wanted to "censor" the inscriptions on the walls there as they had clearly done?
If, as van Hassel suggested, the Third Pillar was meant to *rise above the ocean*, some great conflict had prevented that from occurring.
Before it had been defaced, perhaps the memorial had explained *why*. Perhaps the treasure vault in Adalia explained *why*.
I was not optimistic about discovering a definitive explanation.
You think too much.
Nevertheless, we invested our days in the search.

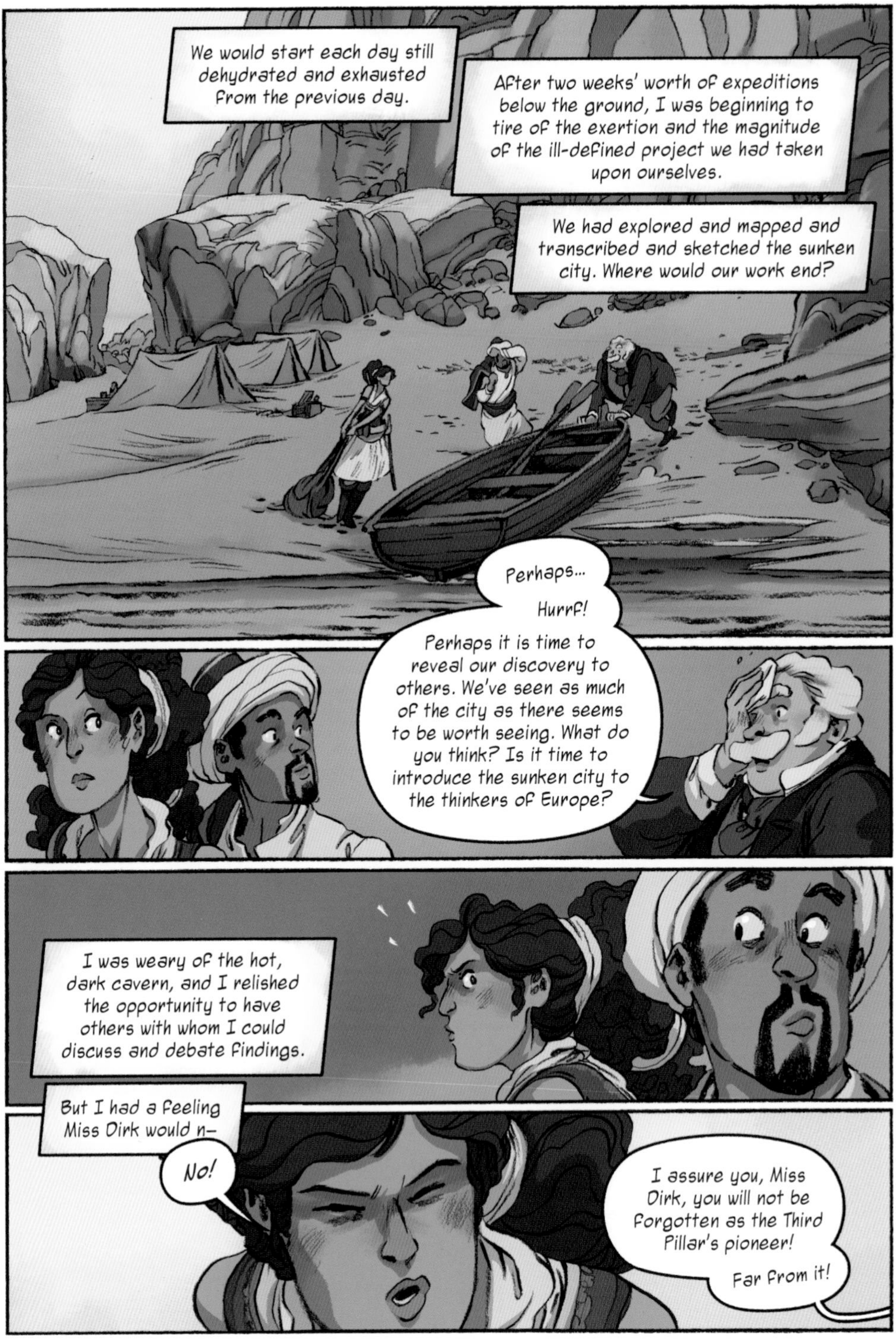

We would start each day still dehydrated and exhausted from the previous day.
After two weeks' worth of expeditions below the ground, I was beginning to tire of the exertion and the magnitude of the ill-defined project we had taken upon ourselves.
We had explored and mapped and transcribed and sketched the sunken city. Where would our work end?
Perhaps...
Hurrf!
Perhaps it is time to reveal our discovery to others. We've seen as much of the city as there seems to be worth seeing. What do you think? Is it time to introduce the sunken city to the thinkers of Europe?
I was weary of the hot, dark cavern, and I relished the opportunity to have others with whom I could discuss and debate findings.
But I had a feeling Miss Dirk would n—
No!
I assure you, Miss Dirk, you will not be forgotten as the Third Pillar's pioneer!
Far from it!

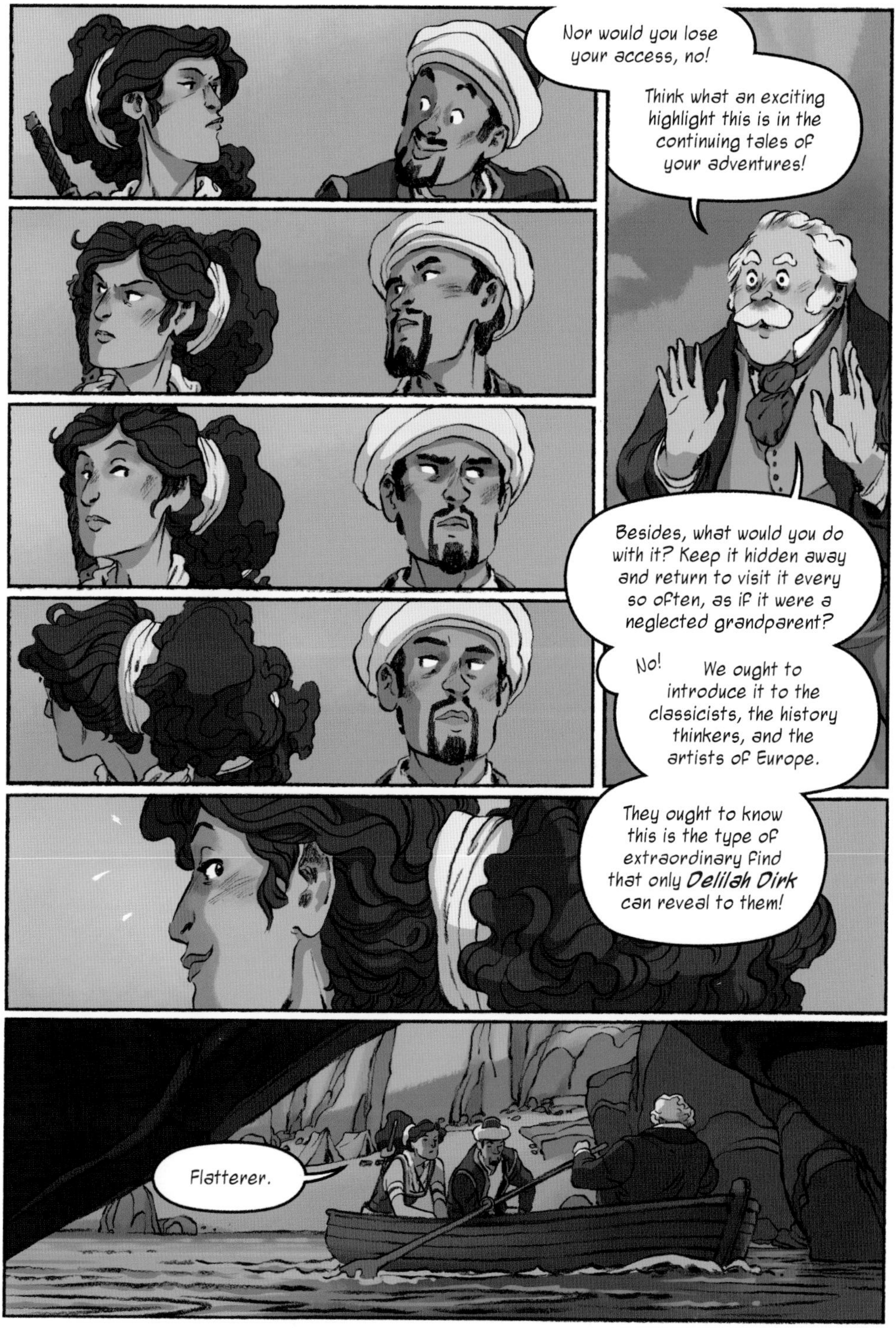
Nor would you lose your access, no!
Think what an exciting highlight this is in the continuing tales of your adventures!
Besides, what would you do with it? Keep it hidden away and return to visit it every so often, as if it were a neglected grandparent?
No!
We ought to introduce it to the classicists, the history thinkers, and the artists of Europe.
They ought to know this is the type of extraordinary find that only *Delilah Dirk* can reveal to them!
Flatterer.

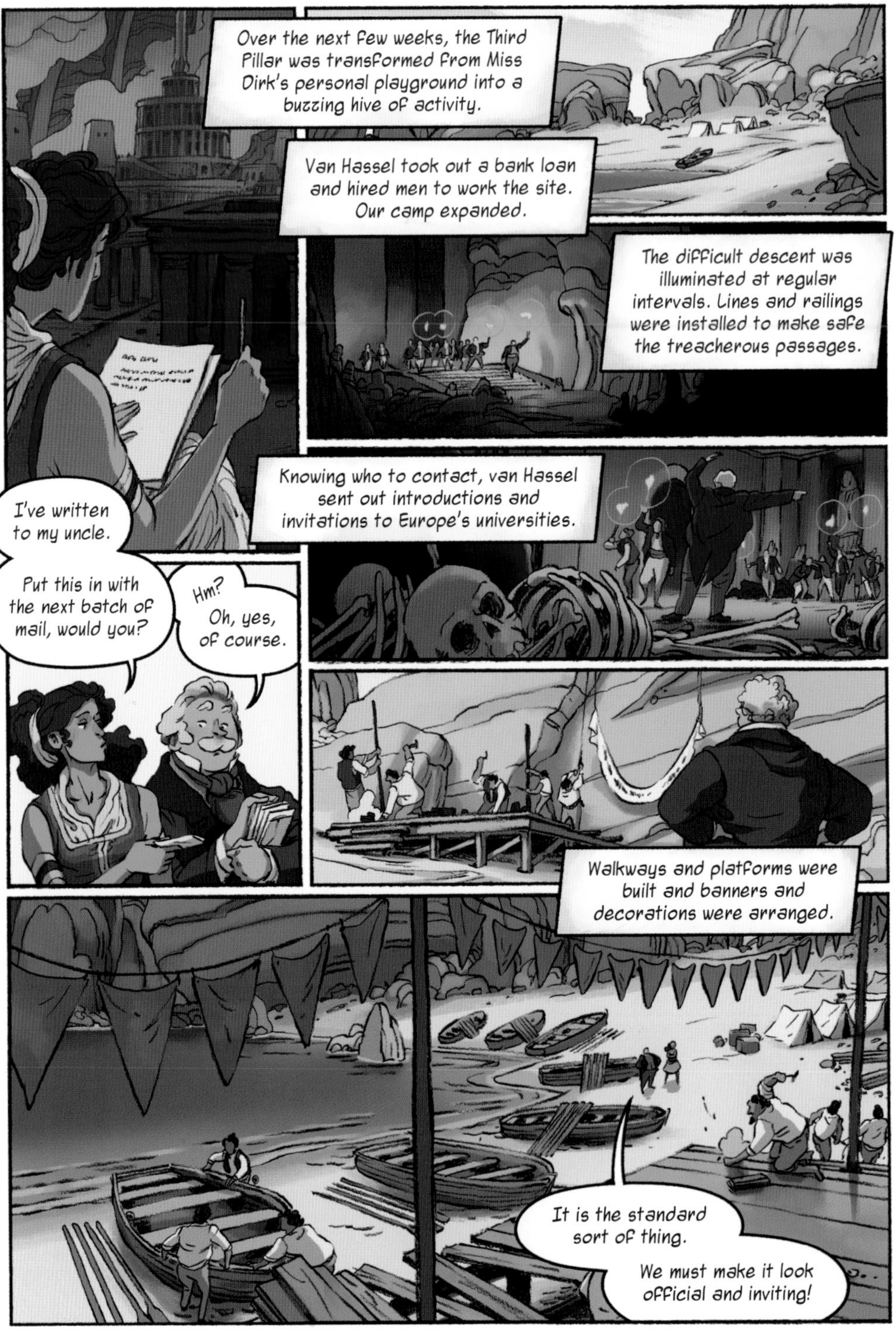
Over the next few weeks, the Third Pillar was transformed from Miss Dirk's personal playground into a buzzing hive of activity.
Van Hassel took out a bank loan and hired men to work the site. Our camp expanded.
The difficult descent was illuminated at regular intervals. Lines and railings were installed to make safe the treacherous passages.
Knowing who to contact, van Hassel sent out introductions and invitations to Europe's universities.
I've written to my uncle.
Put this in with the next batch of mail, would you?
Hm?
Oh, yes, of course.
Walkways and platforms were built and banners and decorations were arranged.
It is the standard sort of thing.
We must make it look official and inviting!

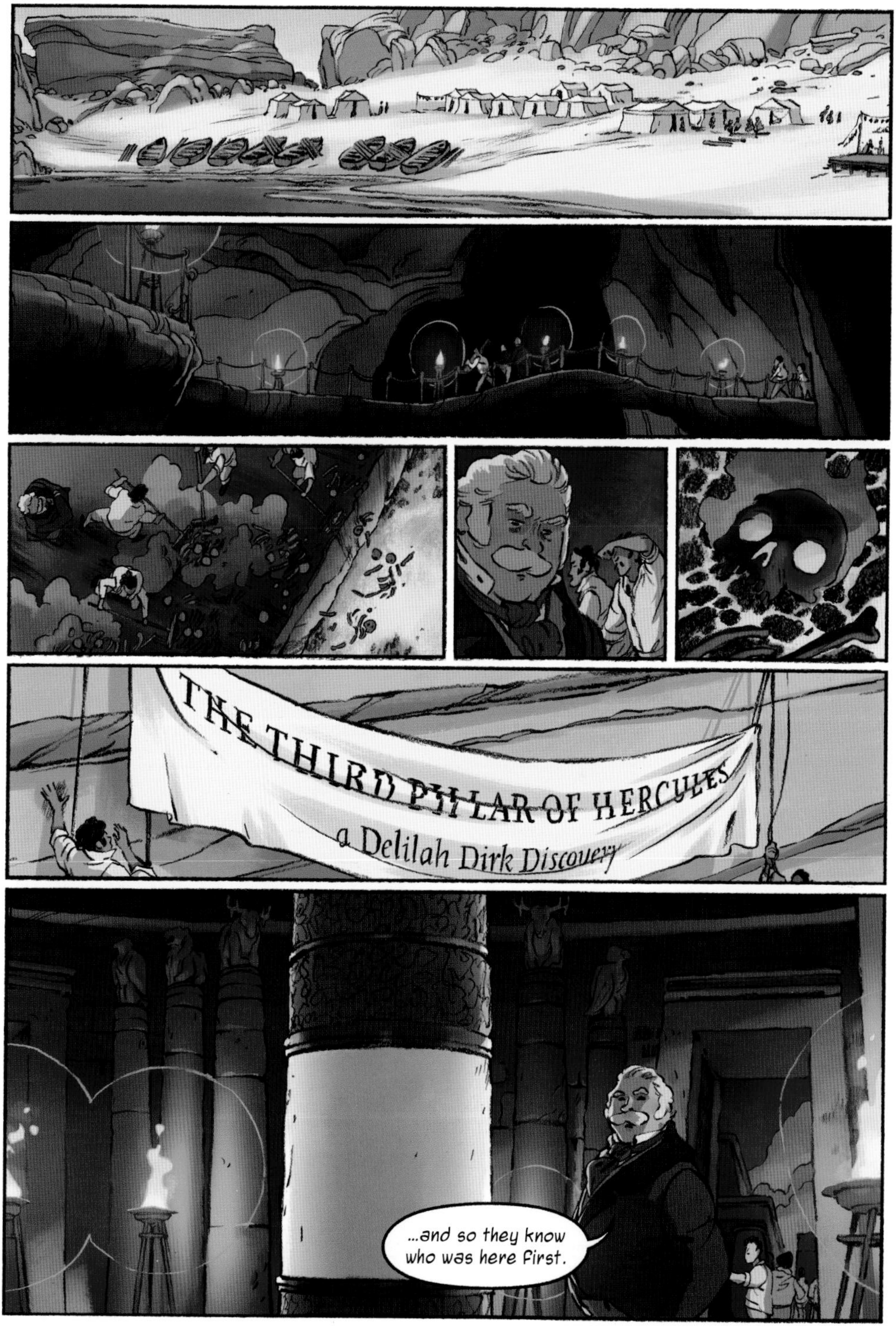
THE THIRD PILLAR OF HERCULES
a Delilah Dirk Discovery
...and so they know who was here first.

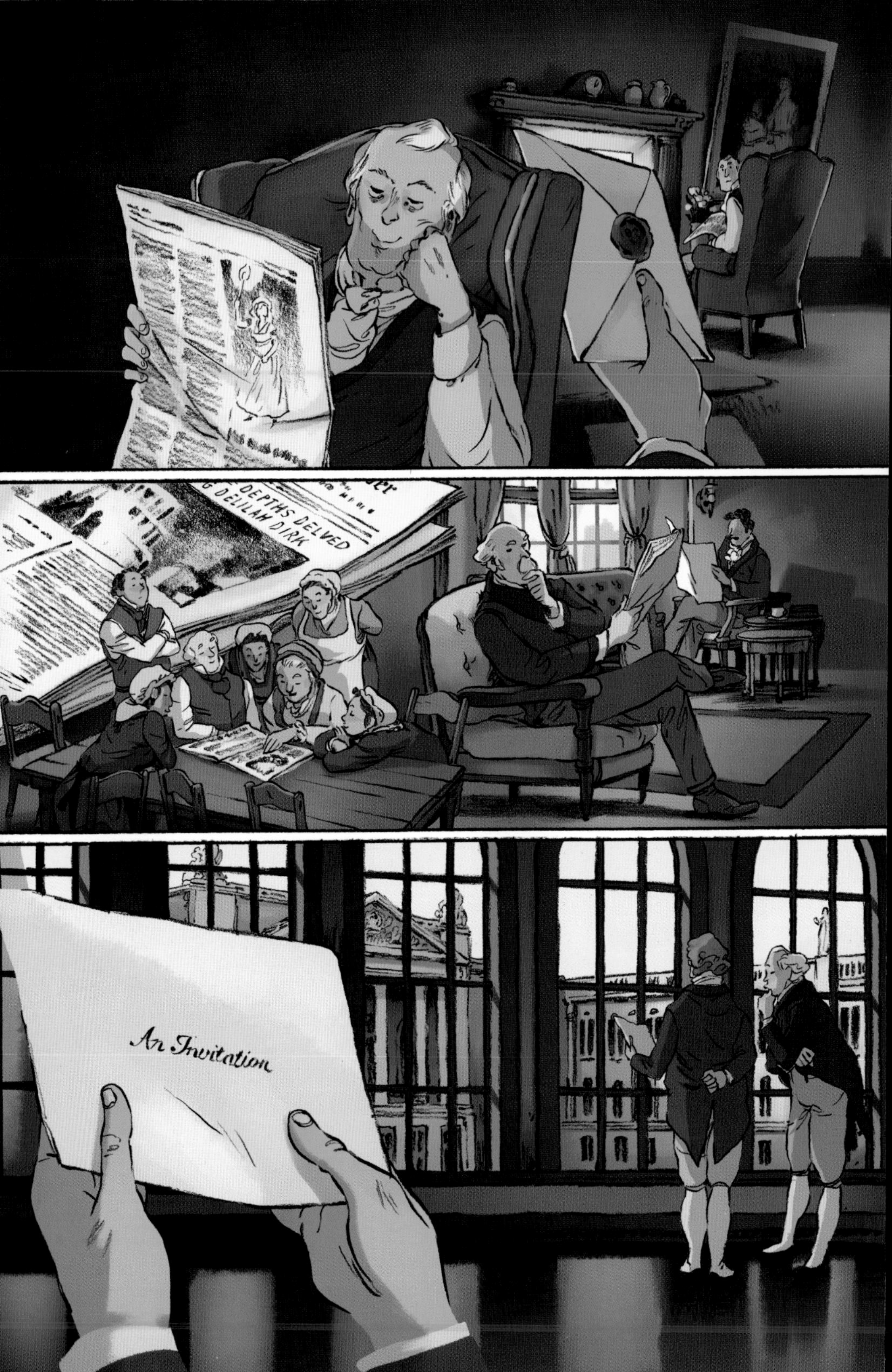
DEPTHS DELVED
G DELILAH DIRK
An Invitation

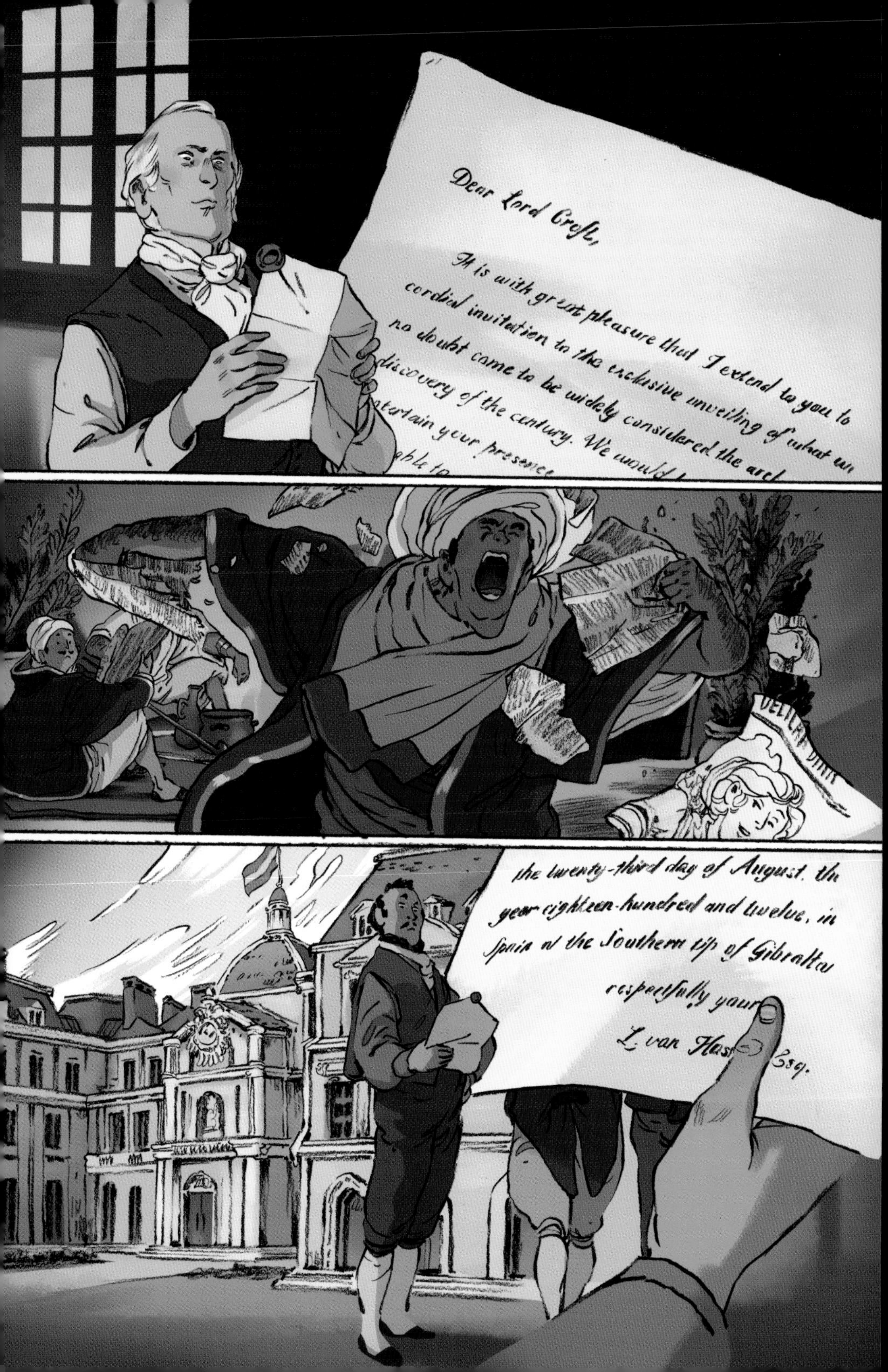
Dear Lord Croft,
It is with great pleasure that I extend to you to cordial invitation to the exclusive unveiling of what un no doubt come to be widely considered the arch discovery of the century. We would
ntertain your presence
the twenty-third day of August, the year eighteen-hundred and twelve, in Spain at the Southern tip of Gibraltar
respectfully your
L. van Has Esq.

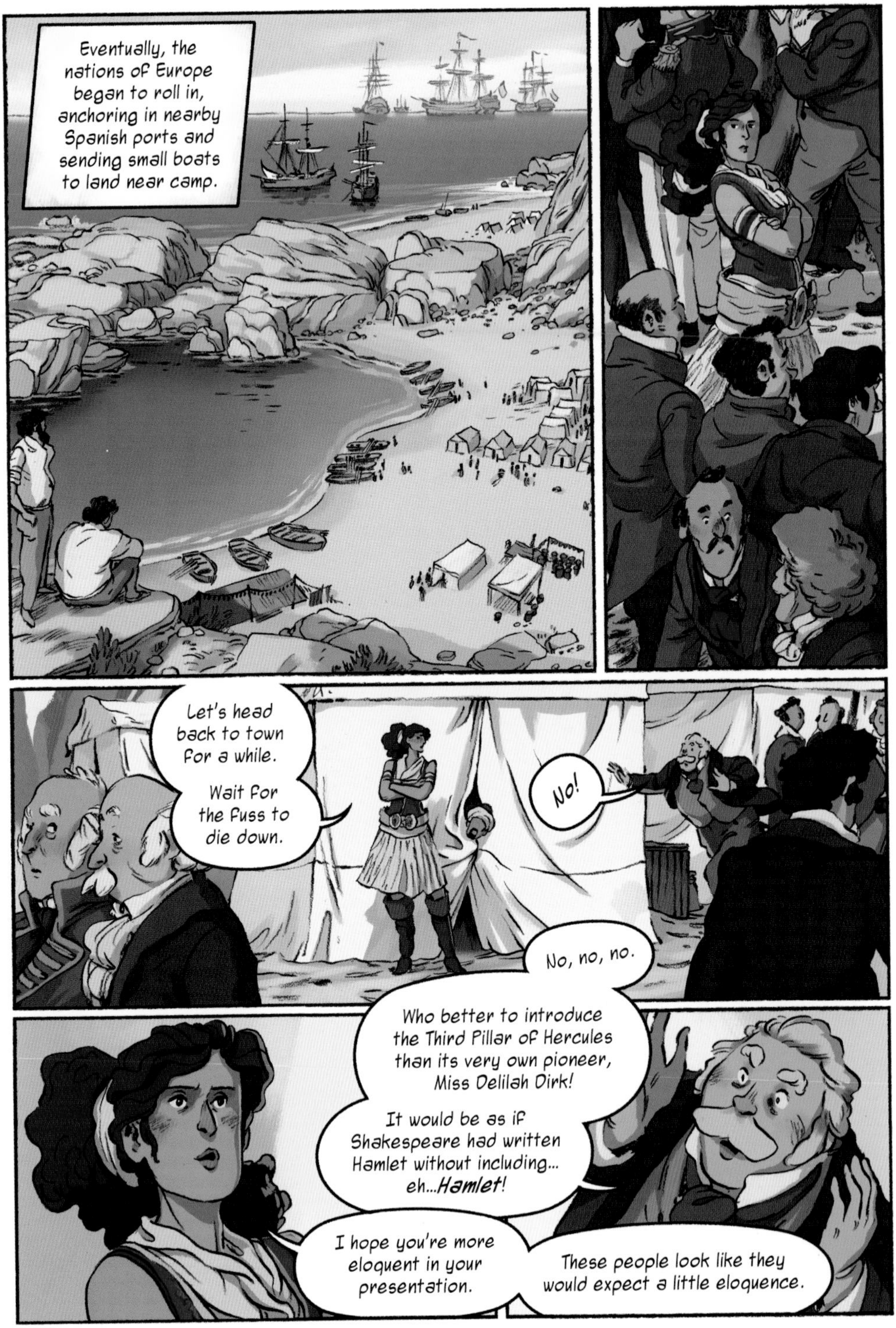
Eventually, the nations of Europe began to roll in, anchoring in nearby Spanish ports and sending small boats to land near camp.
Let's head back to town for a while.
Wait for the fuss to die down.
No!
No, no, no.
Who better to introduce the Third Pillar of Hercules than its very own pioneer, Miss Delilah Dirk!
It would be as if Shakespeare had written Hamlet without including... eh...*Hamlet*!
I hope you're more eloquent in your presentation.
These people look like they would expect a little eloquence.

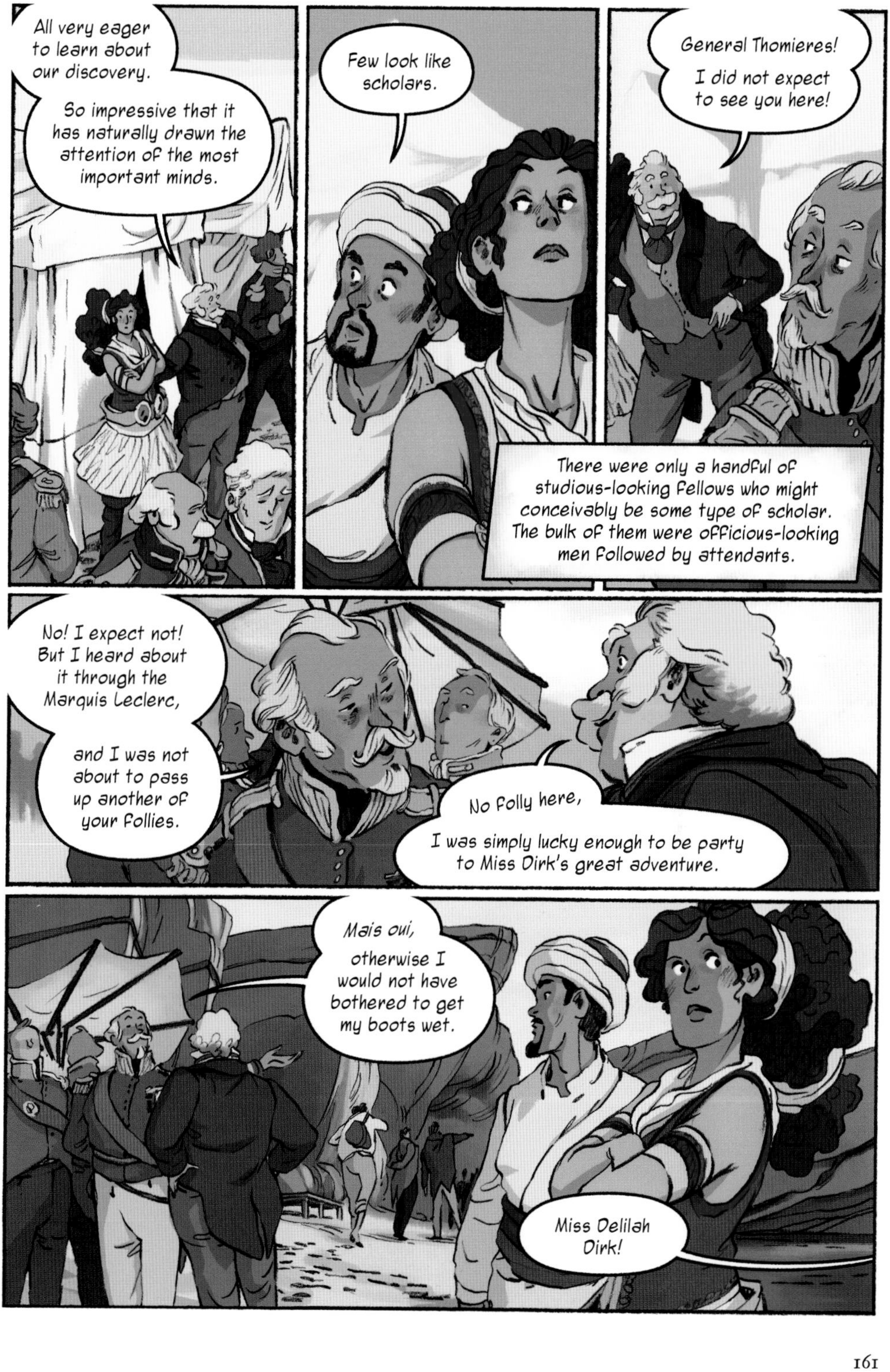

All very eager to learn about our discovery.
So impressive that it has naturally drawn the attention of the most important minds.
Few look like scholars.
General Thomieres!
I did not expect to see you here!
There were only a handful of studious-looking fellows who might conceivably be some type of scholar. The bulk of them were officious-looking men followed by attendants.
No! I expect not! But I heard about it through the Marquis Leclerc,
and I was not about to pass up another of your follies.
No folly here,
I was simply lucky enough to be party to Miss Dirk's great adventure.
Mais oui,
otherwise I would not have bothered to get my boots wet.
Miss Delilah Dirk!

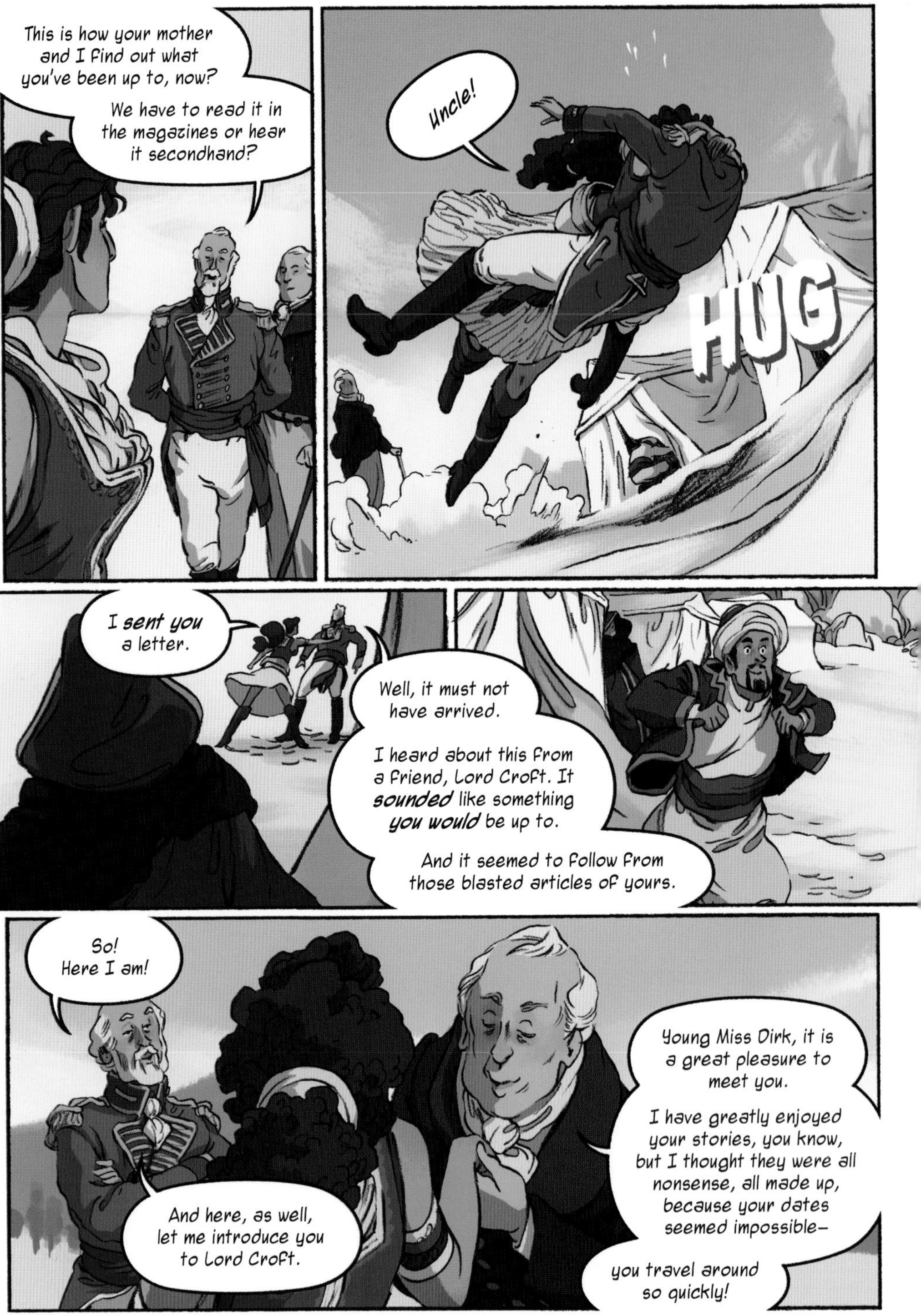

This is how your mother and I find out what you've been up to, now?
We have to read it in the magazines or hear it secondhand?
Uncle!
HUG
I *sent you* a letter.
Well, it must not have arrived.
I heard about this from a friend, Lord Croft. It ***sounded*** like something ***you would*** be up to.
And it seemed to follow from those blasted articles of yours.
So! Here I am!
And here, as well, let me introduce you to Lord Croft.
Young Miss Dirk, it is a great pleasure to meet you.
I have greatly enjoyed your stories, you know, but I thought they were all nonsense, all made up, because your dates seemed impossible–
you travel around so quickly!

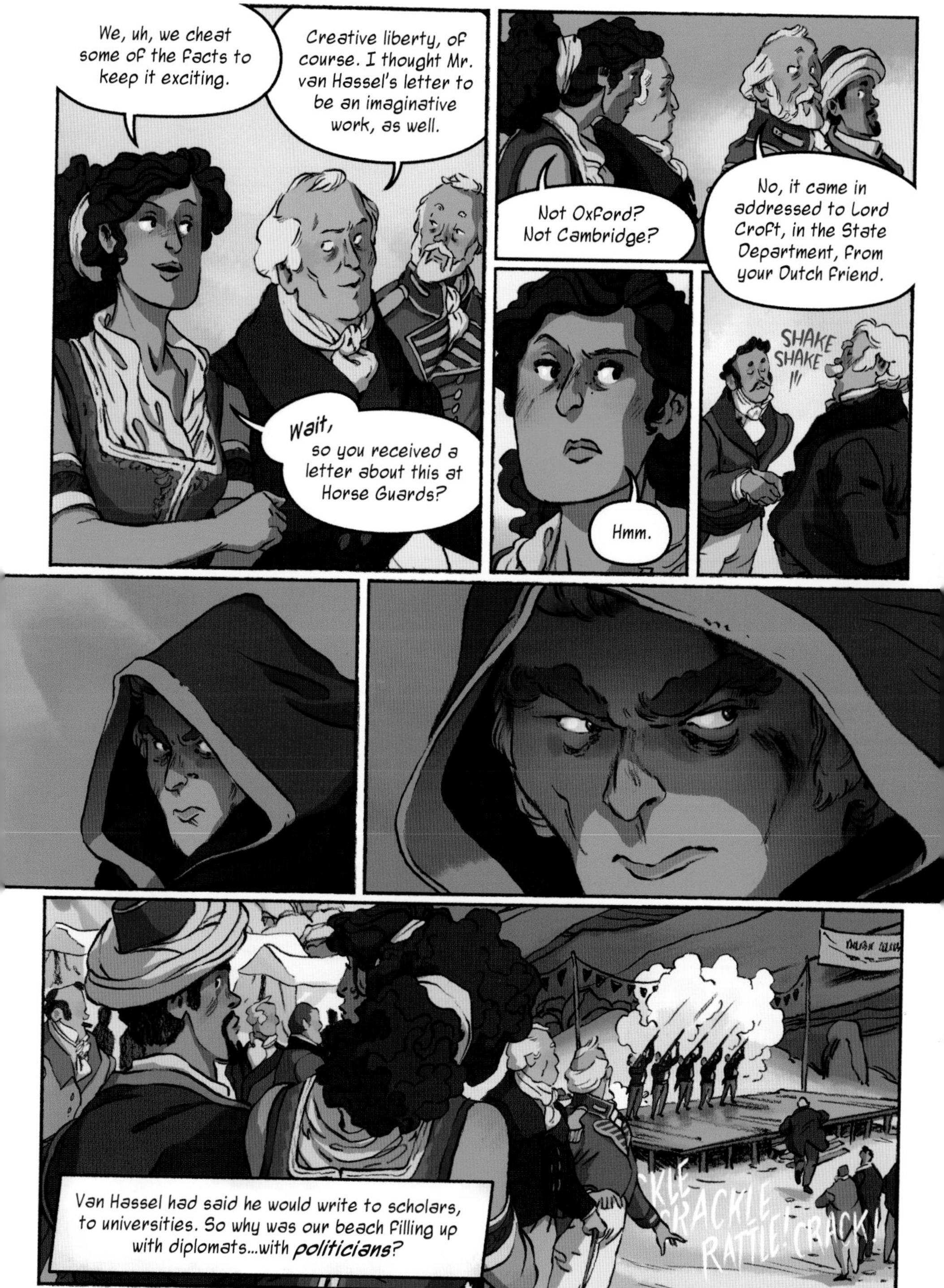
We, uh, we cheat some of the facts to keep it exciting.
Creative liberty, of course. I thought Mr. van Hassel's letter to be an imaginative work, as well.
Wait, so you received a letter about this at Horse Guards?
Not Oxford? Not Cambridge?
No, it came in addressed to Lord Croft, in the State Department, from your Dutch friend.
SHAKE SHAKE
Hmm.
Van Hassel had said he would write to scholars, to universities. So why was our beach filling up with diplomats...with *politicians*?
CRACKLE RATTLE! CRACK!

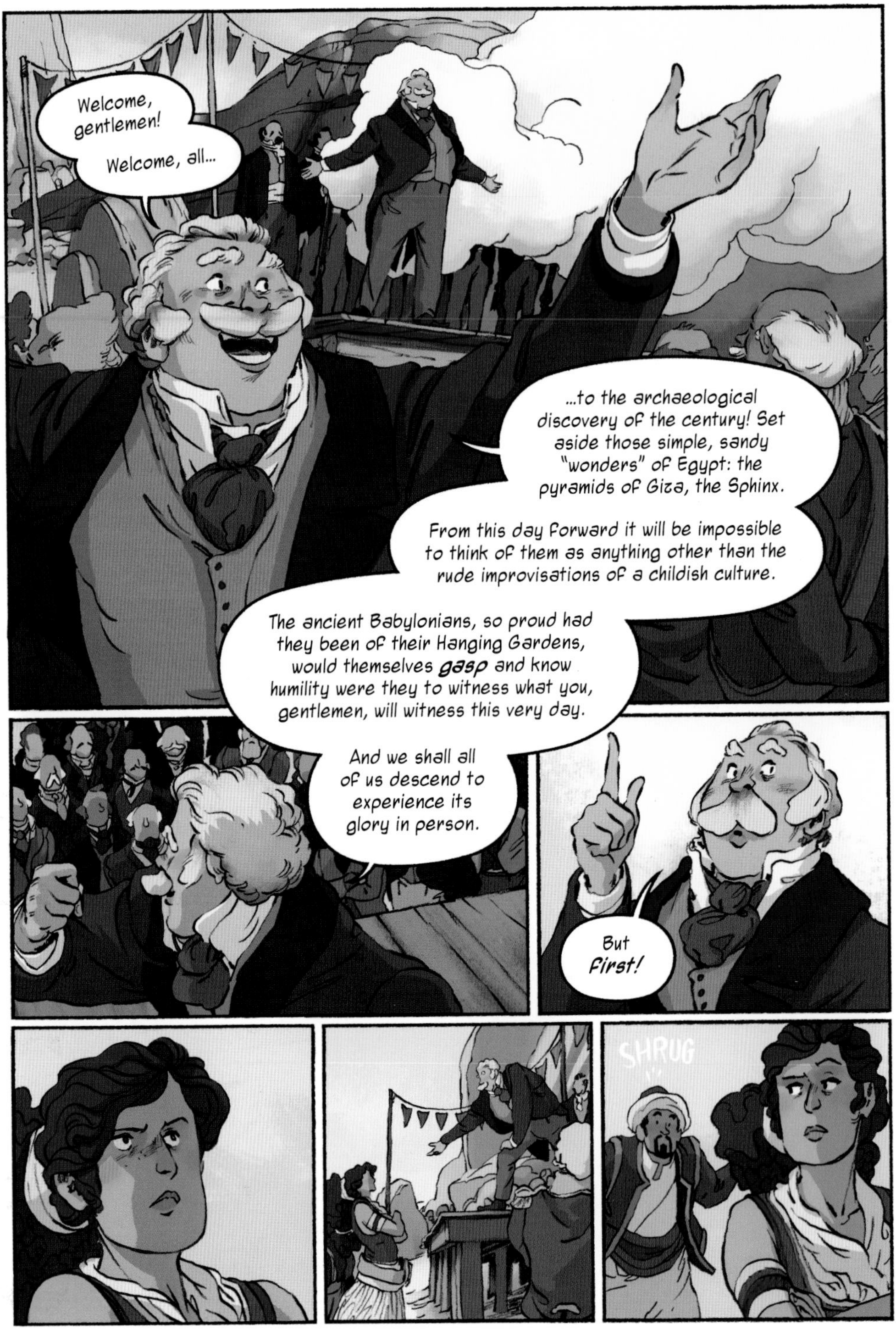

Welcome, gentlemen!
Welcome, all...
...to the archaeological discovery of the century! Set aside those simple, sandy "wonders" of Egypt: the pyramids of Giza, the Sphinx.
From this day forward it will be impossible to think of them as anything other than the rude improvisations of a childish culture.
The ancient Babylonians, so proud had they been of their Hanging Gardens, would themselves *gasp* and know humility were they to witness what you, gentlemen, will witness this very day.
And we shall all of us descend to experience its glory in person.
But *first!*
SHRUG

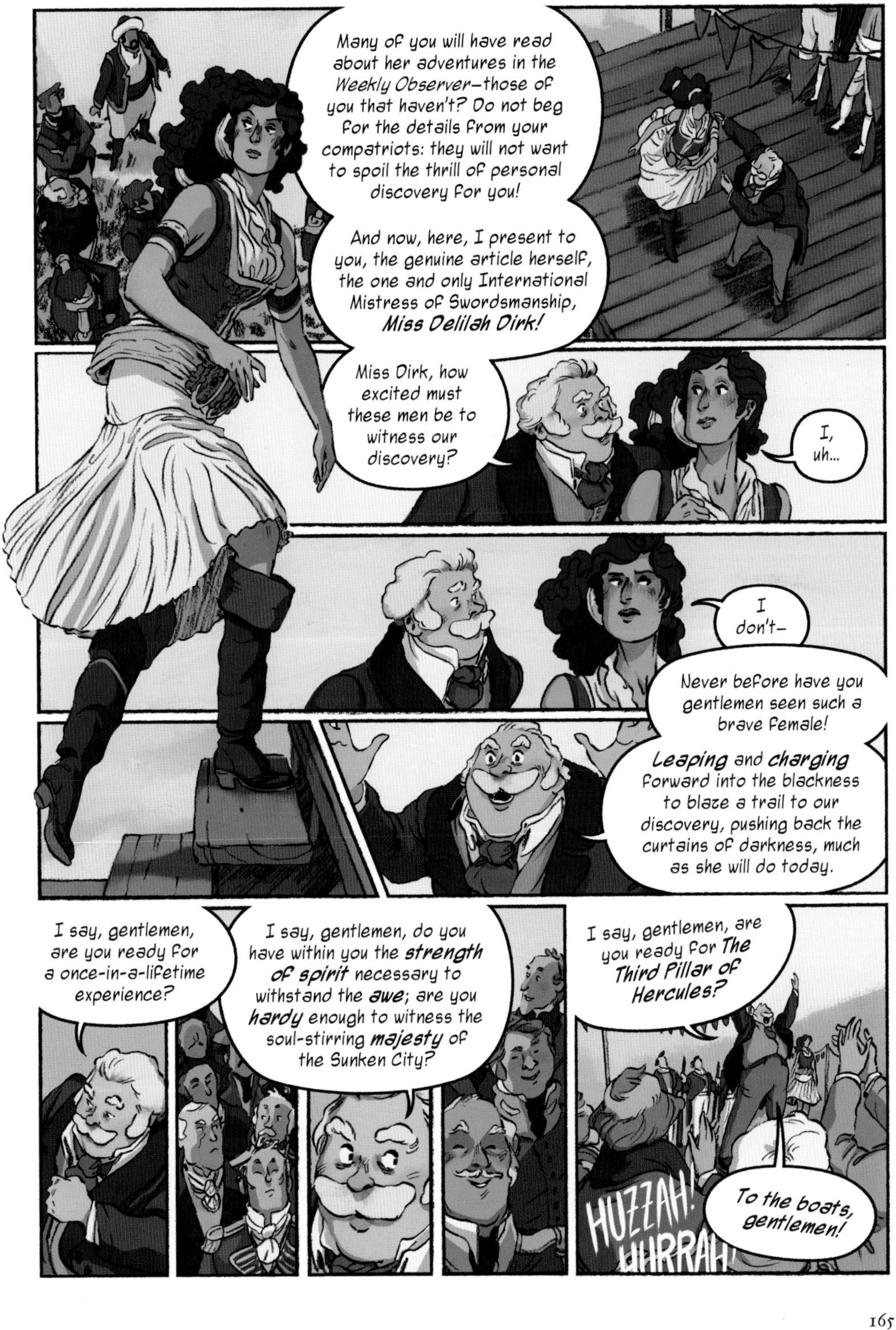
Many of you will have read about her adventures in the *Weekly Observer*—those of you that haven't? Do not beg for the details from your compatriots: they will not want to spoil the thrill of personal discovery for you!
And now, here, I present to you, the genuine article herself, the one and only International Mistress of Swordsmanship, ***Miss Delilah Dirk!***
Miss Dirk, how excited must these men be to witness our discovery?
I, uh...
I don't—
Never before have you gentlemen seen such a brave female!
***Leaping*** and ***charging*** forward into the blackness to blaze a trail to our discovery, pushing back the curtains of darkness, much as she will do today.
I say, gentlemen, are you ready for a once-in-a-lifetime experience?
I say, gentlemen, do you have within you the ***strength of spirit*** necessary to withstand the ***awe***; are you ***hardy*** enough to witness the soul-stirring ***majesty*** of the Sunken City?
I say, gentlemen, are you ready for ***The Third Pillar of Hercules?***
HUZZAH!
UHRRAH!
*To the boats, gentlemen!*

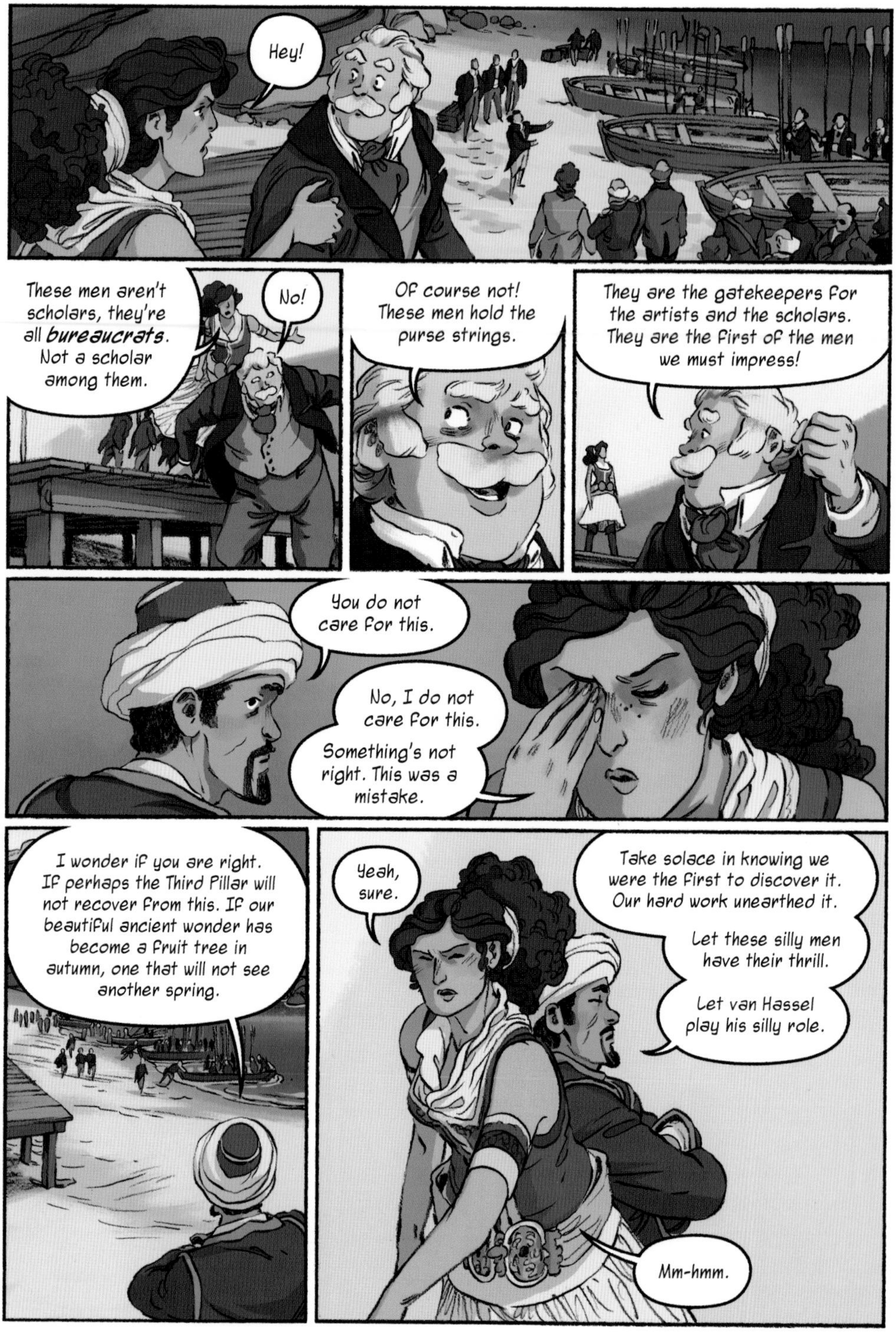
Hey!
These men aren't scholars, they're all ***bureaucrats***. Not a scholar among them.
No!
Of course not! These men hold the purse strings.
They are the gatekeepers for the artists and the scholars. They are the first of the men we must impress!
You do not care for this.
No, I do not care for this.
Something's not right. This was a mistake.
I wonder if you are right. If perhaps the Third Pillar will not recover from this. If our beautiful ancient wonder has become a fruit tree in autumn, one that will not see another spring.
Yeah, sure.
Take solace in knowing we were the first to discover it. Our hard work unearthed it.
Let these silly men have their thrill.
Let van Hassel play his silly role.
Mm-hmm.

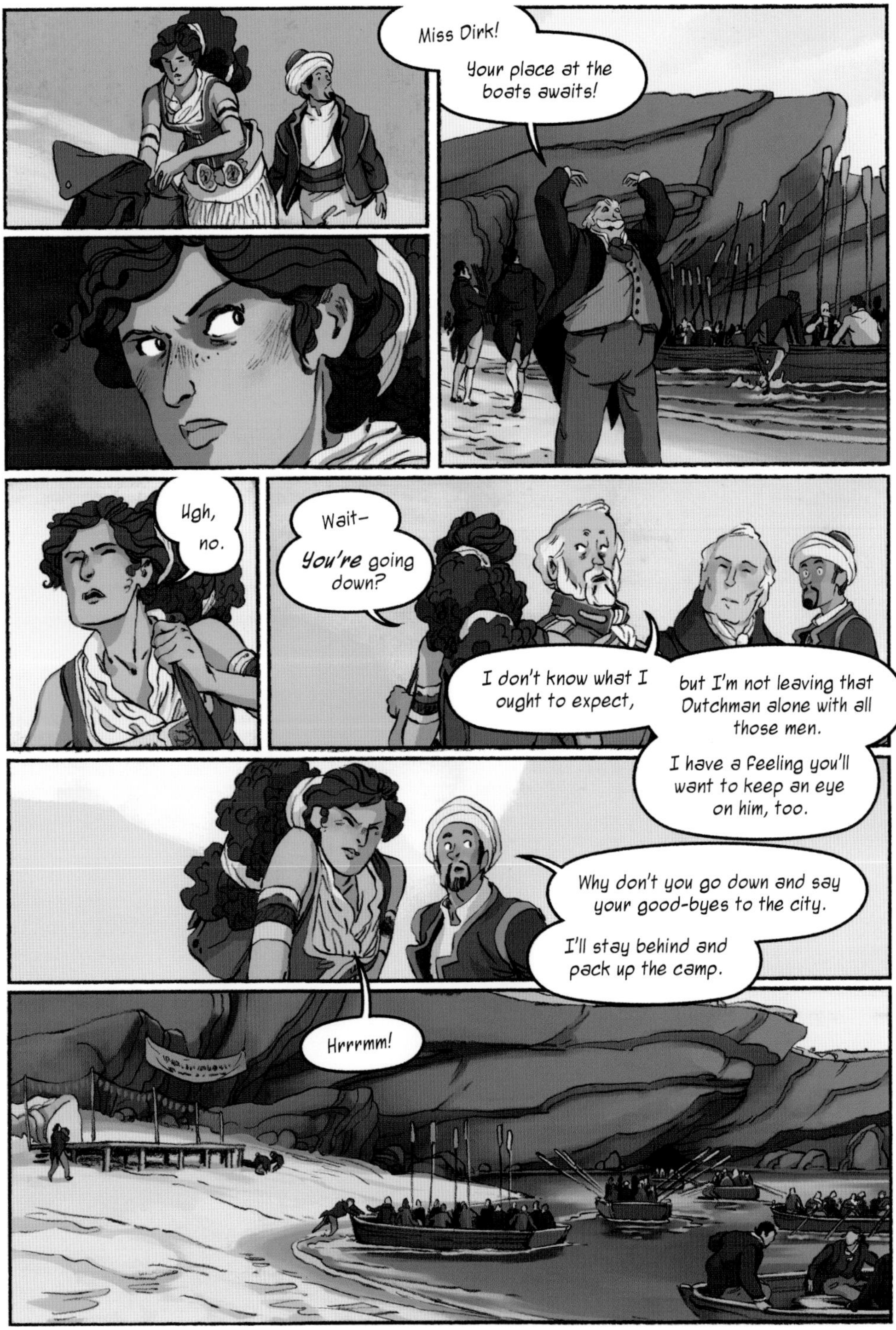

Miss Dirk!
Your place at the boats awaits!
Ugh, no.
Wait–
You're going down?
I don't know what I ought to expect,
but I'm not leaving that Dutchman alone with all those men.
I have a feeling you'll want to keep an eye on him, too.
Why don't you go down and say your good-byes to the city.
I'll stay behind and pack up the camp.
Hrrrmm!

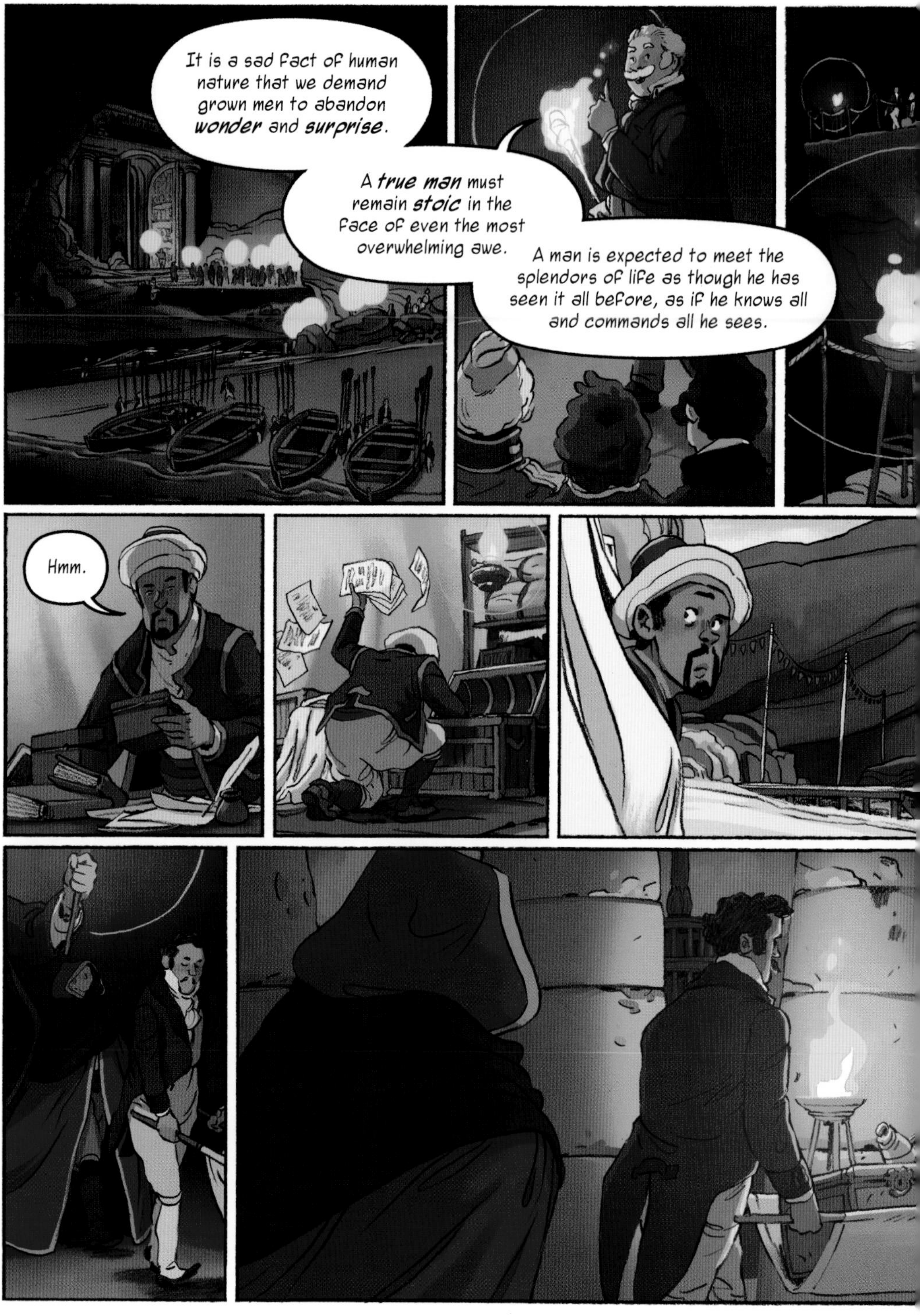
It is a sad fact of human nature that we demand grown men to abandon *wonder* and *surprise*.
A *true man* must remain *stoic* in the face of even the most overwhelming awe.
A man is expected to meet the splendors of life as though he has seen it all before, as if he knows all and commands all he sees.
Hmm.

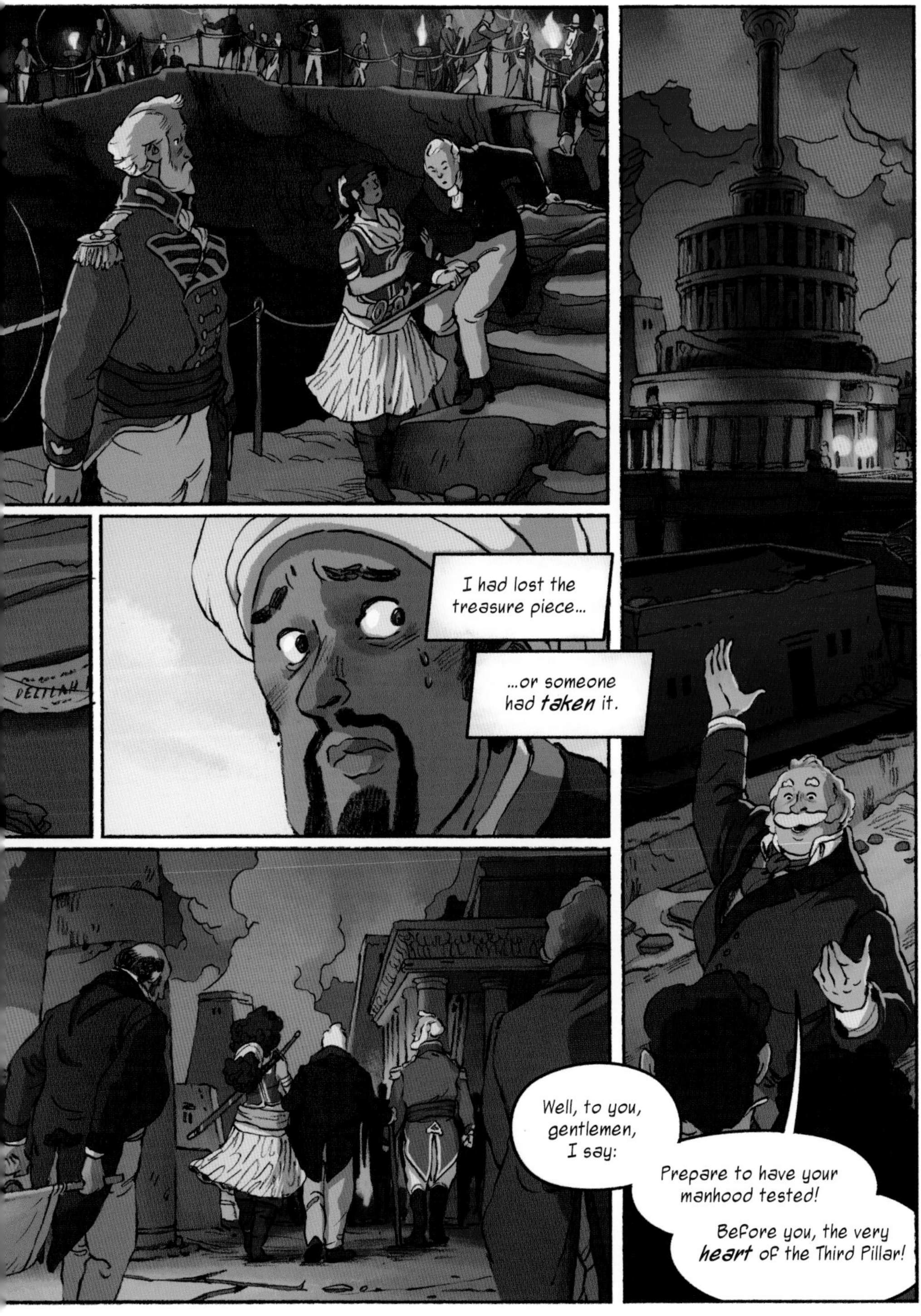
DELILAH
I had lost the treasure piece...
...or someone had *taken* it.
Well, to you, gentlemen, I say:
Prepare to have your manhood tested!
Before you, the very *heart* of the Third Pillar!

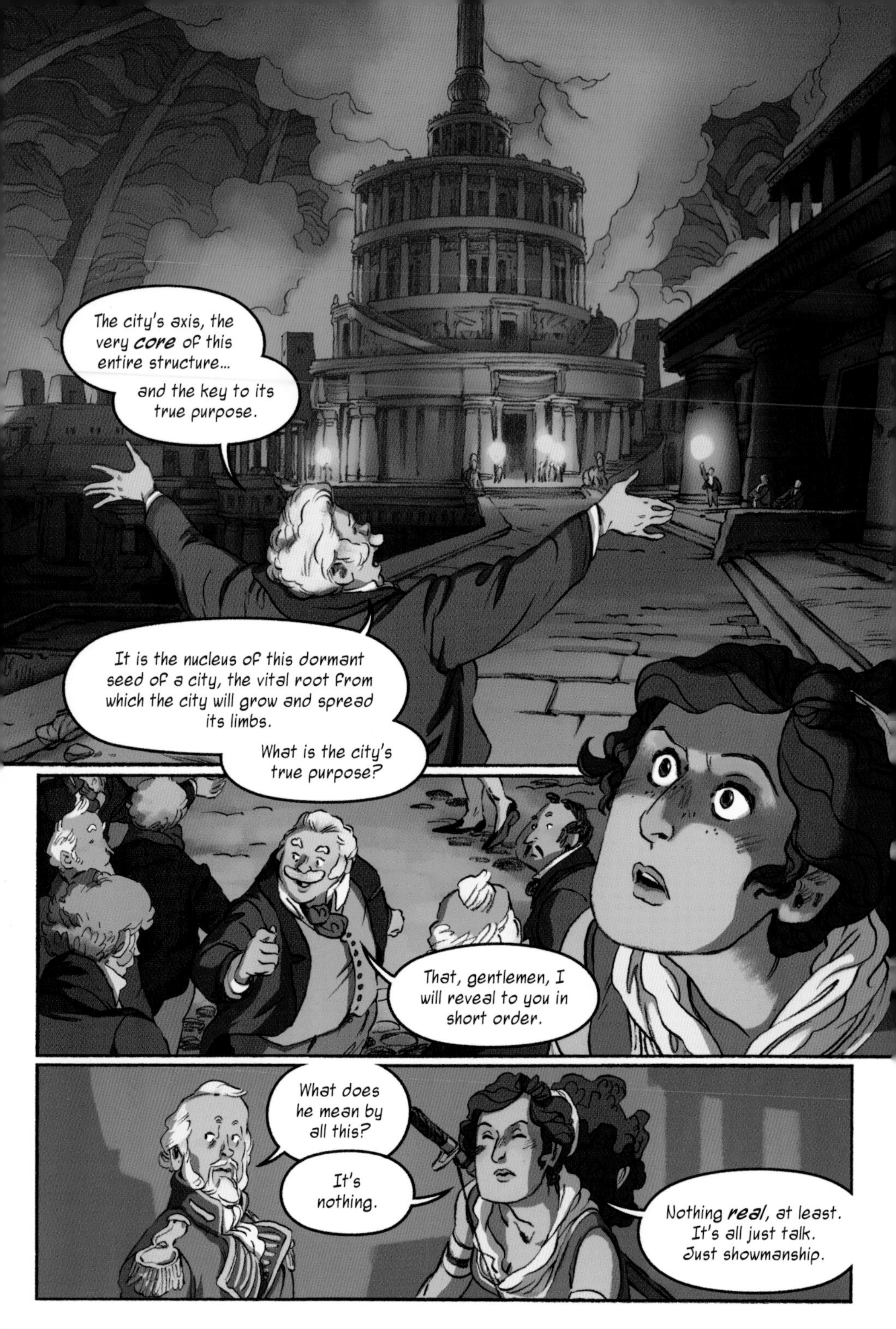
The city's axis, the very **core** of this entire structure...
and the key to its true purpose.
It is the nucleus of this dormant seed of a city, the vital root from which the city will grow and spread its limbs.
What is the city's true purpose?
That, gentlemen, I will reveal to you in short order.
What does he mean by all this?
It's nothing.
Nothing **real**, at least. It's all just talk. Just showmanship.

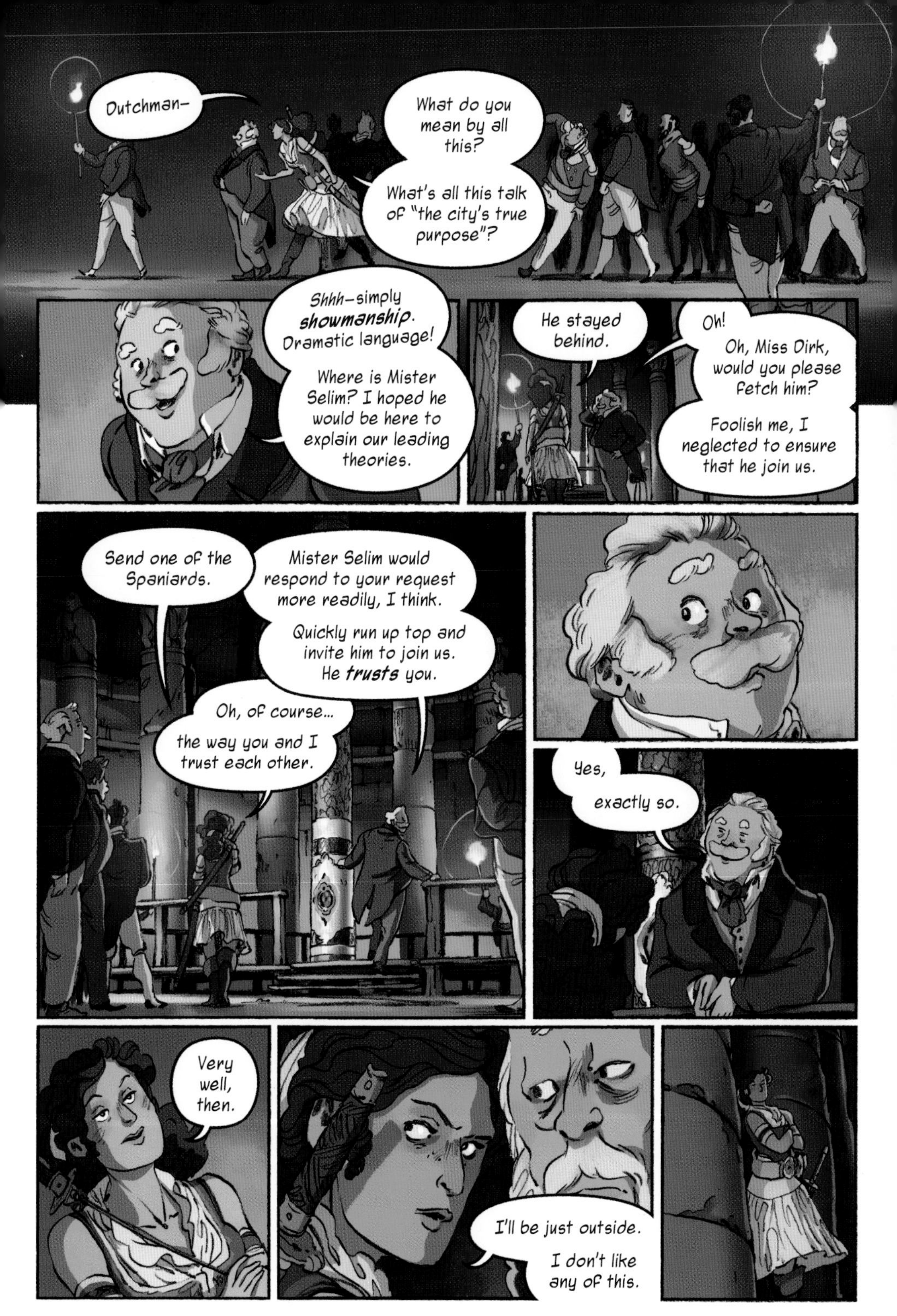
Dutchman–
What do you mean by all this?
What's all this talk of "the city's true purpose"?
Shhh—simply **showmanship**. Dramatic language!
Where is Mister Selim? I hoped he would be here to explain our leading theories.
He stayed behind.
Oh!
Oh, Miss Dirk, would you please fetch him?
Foolish me, I neglected to ensure that he join us.
Send one of the Spaniards.
Mister Selim would respond to your request more readily, I think.
Quickly run up top and invite him to join us. He **trusts** you.
Oh, of course...
the way you and I trust each other.
Yes,
exactly so.
Very well, then.
I'll be just outside.
I don't like any of this.

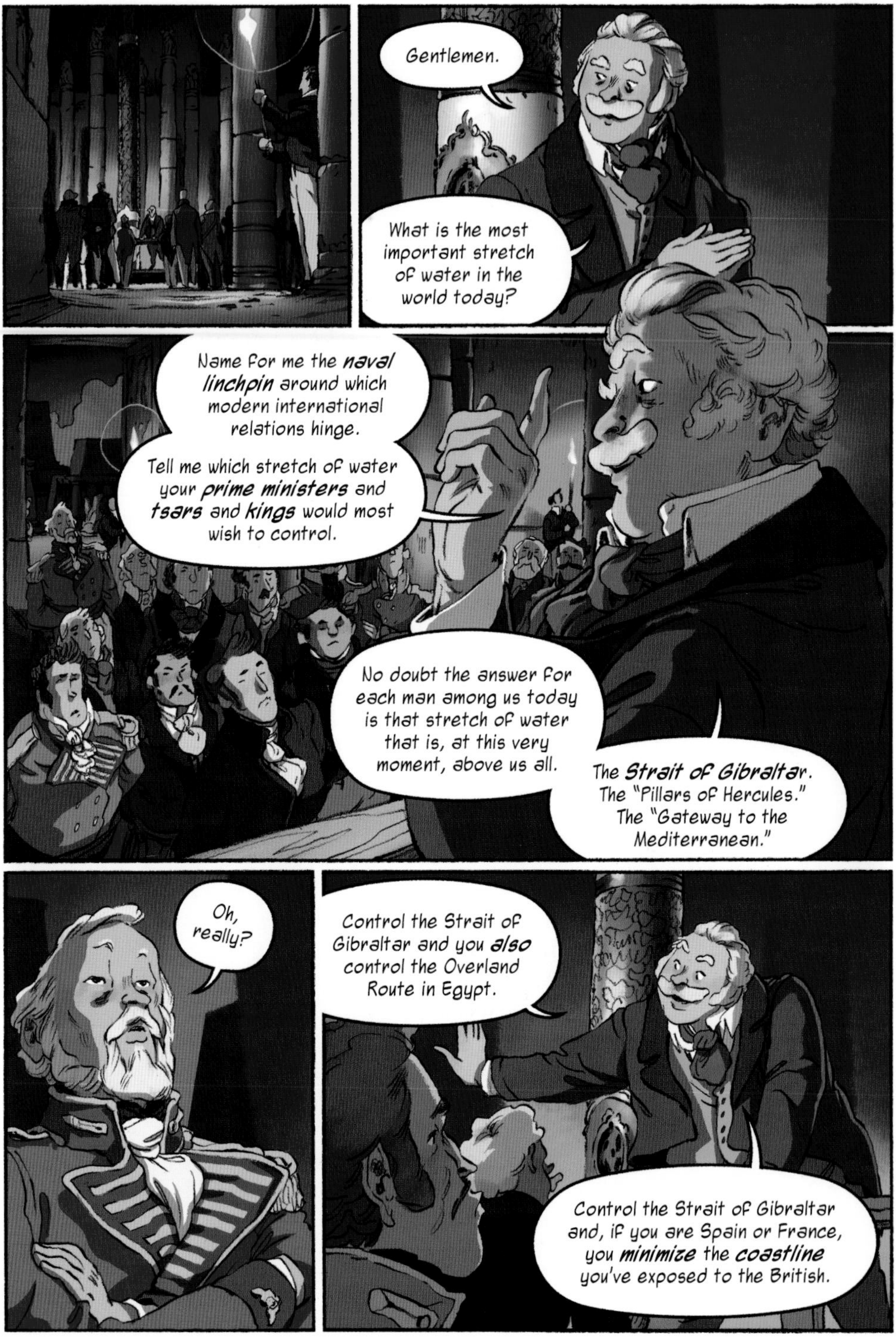
Gentlemen.
What is the most important stretch of water in the world today?
Name for me the *naval linchpin* around which modern international relations hinge.
Tell me which stretch of water your *prime ministers* and *tsars* and *kings* would most wish to control.
No doubt the answer for each man among us today is that stretch of water that is, at this very moment, above us all.
The *Strait of Gibraltar*. The "Pillars of Hercules." The "Gateway to the Mediterranean."
Oh, really?
Control the Strait of Gibraltar and you *also* control the Overland Route in Egypt.
Control the Strait of Gibraltar and, if you are Spain or France, you *minimize* the *coastline* you've exposed to the British.

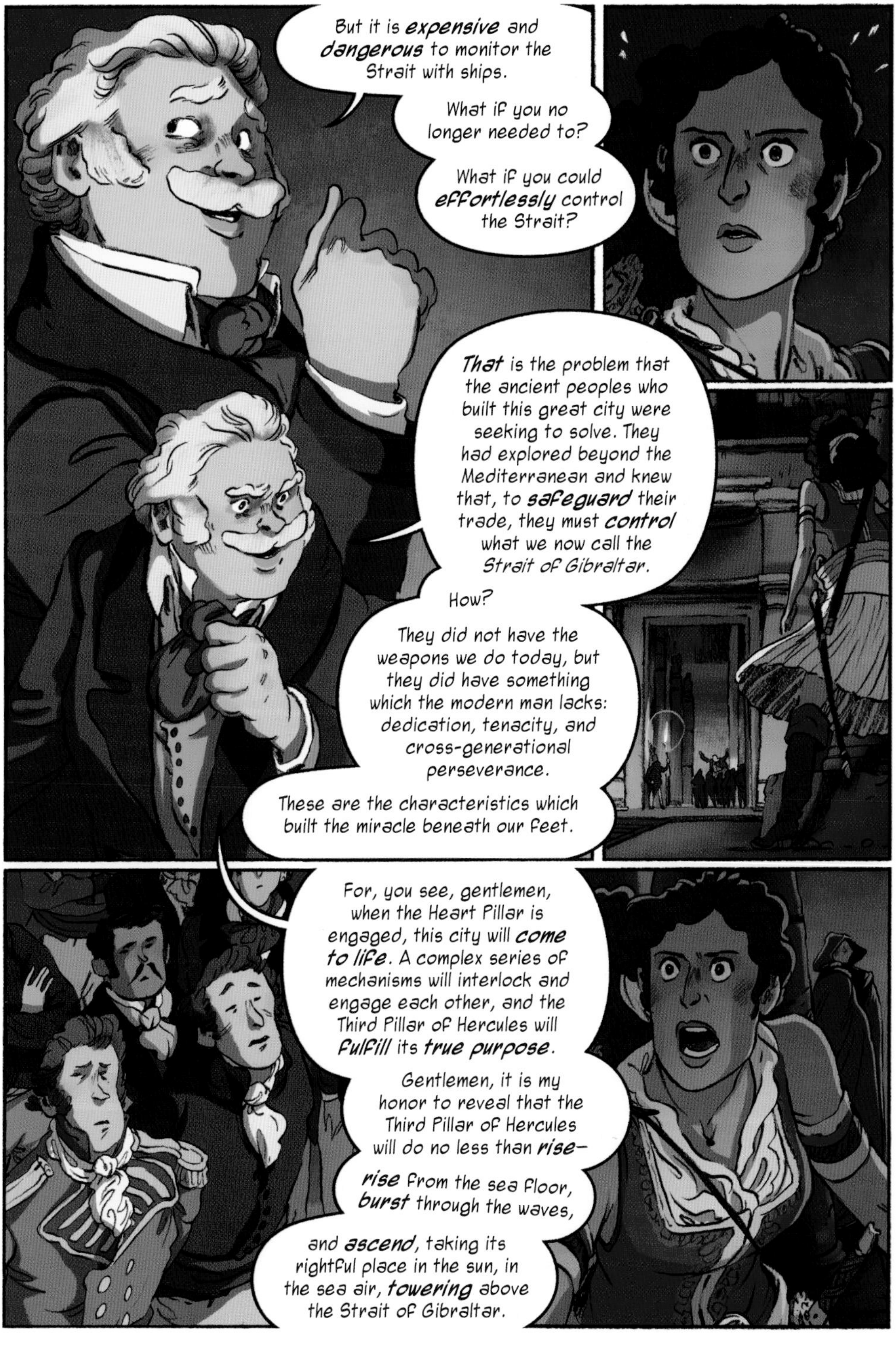
But it is ***expensive*** and ***dangerous*** to monitor the Strait with ships.
What if you no longer needed to?
What if you could ***effortlessly*** control the Strait?
***That*** is the problem that the ancient peoples who built this great city were seeking to solve. They had explored beyond the Mediterranean and knew that, to ***safeguard*** their trade, they must ***control*** what we now call the *Strait of Gibraltar*.
How?
They did not have the weapons we do today, but they did have something which the modern man lacks: dedication, tenacity, and cross-generational perseverance.
These are the characteristics which built the miracle beneath our feet.
For, you see, gentlemen, when the Heart Pillar is engaged, this city will ***come to life***. A complex series of mechanisms will interlock and engage each other, and the Third Pillar of Hercules will ***fulfill*** its ***true purpose***.
Gentlemen, it is my honor to reveal that the Third Pillar of Hercules will do no less than ***rise***—
***rise*** from the sea floor, ***burst*** through the waves,
and ***ascend***, taking its rightful place in the sun, in the sea air, ***towering*** above the Strait of Gibraltar.

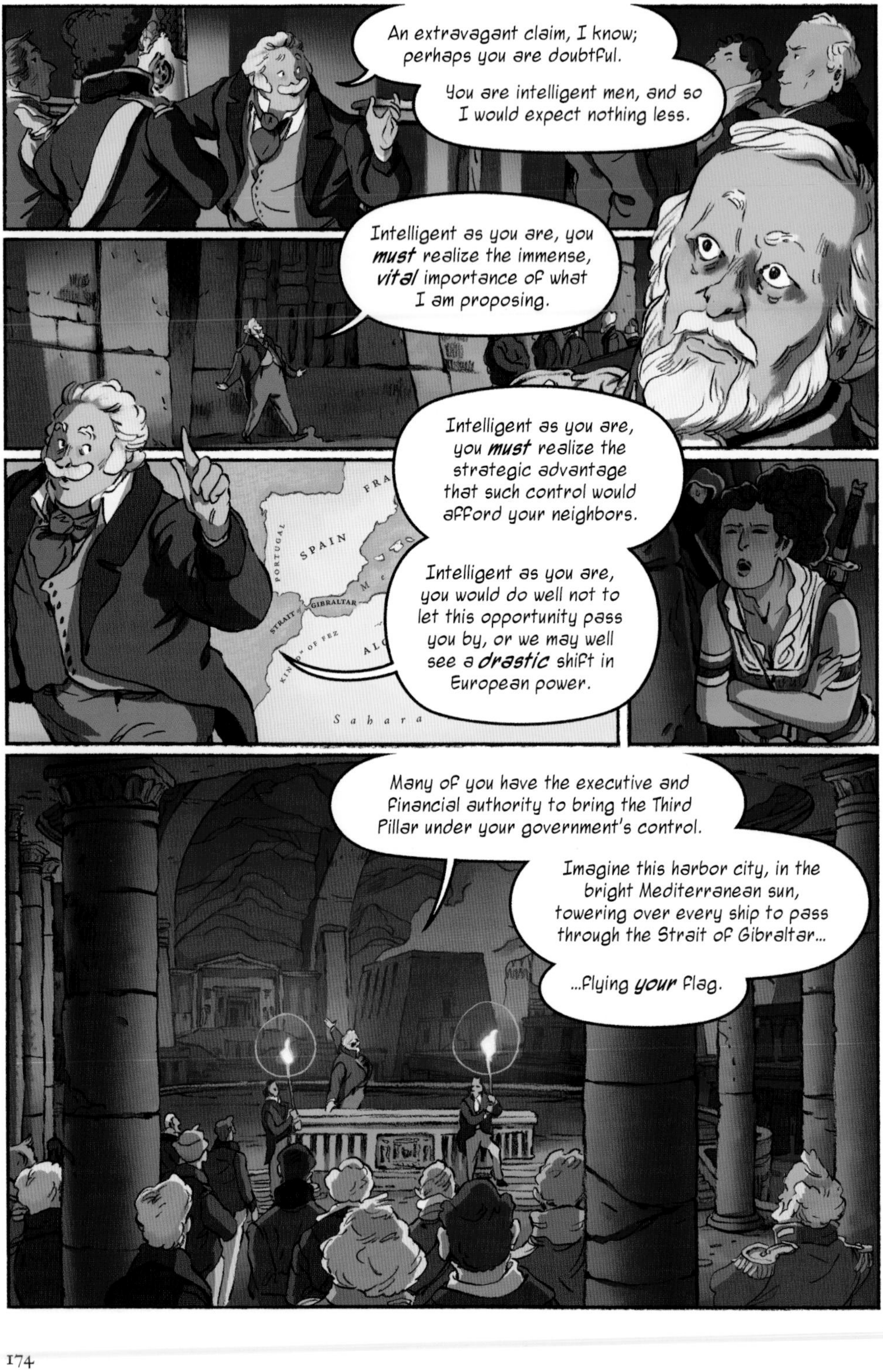
An extravagant claim, I know; perhaps you are doubtful.
You are intelligent men, and so I would expect nothing less.
Intelligent as you are, you **must** realize the immense, ***vital*** importance of what I am proposing.
Intelligent as you are, you **must** realize the strategic advantage that such control would afford your neighbors.
PORTUGAL
SPAIN
STRAIT
GIBRALTAR
Sahara
Intelligent as you are, you would do well not to let this opportunity pass you by, or we may well see a ***drastic*** shift in European power.
Many of you have the executive and financial authority to bring the Third Pillar under your government's control.
Imagine this harbor city, in the bright Mediterranean sun, towering over every ship to pass through the Strait of Gibraltar...
...flying **your** flag.

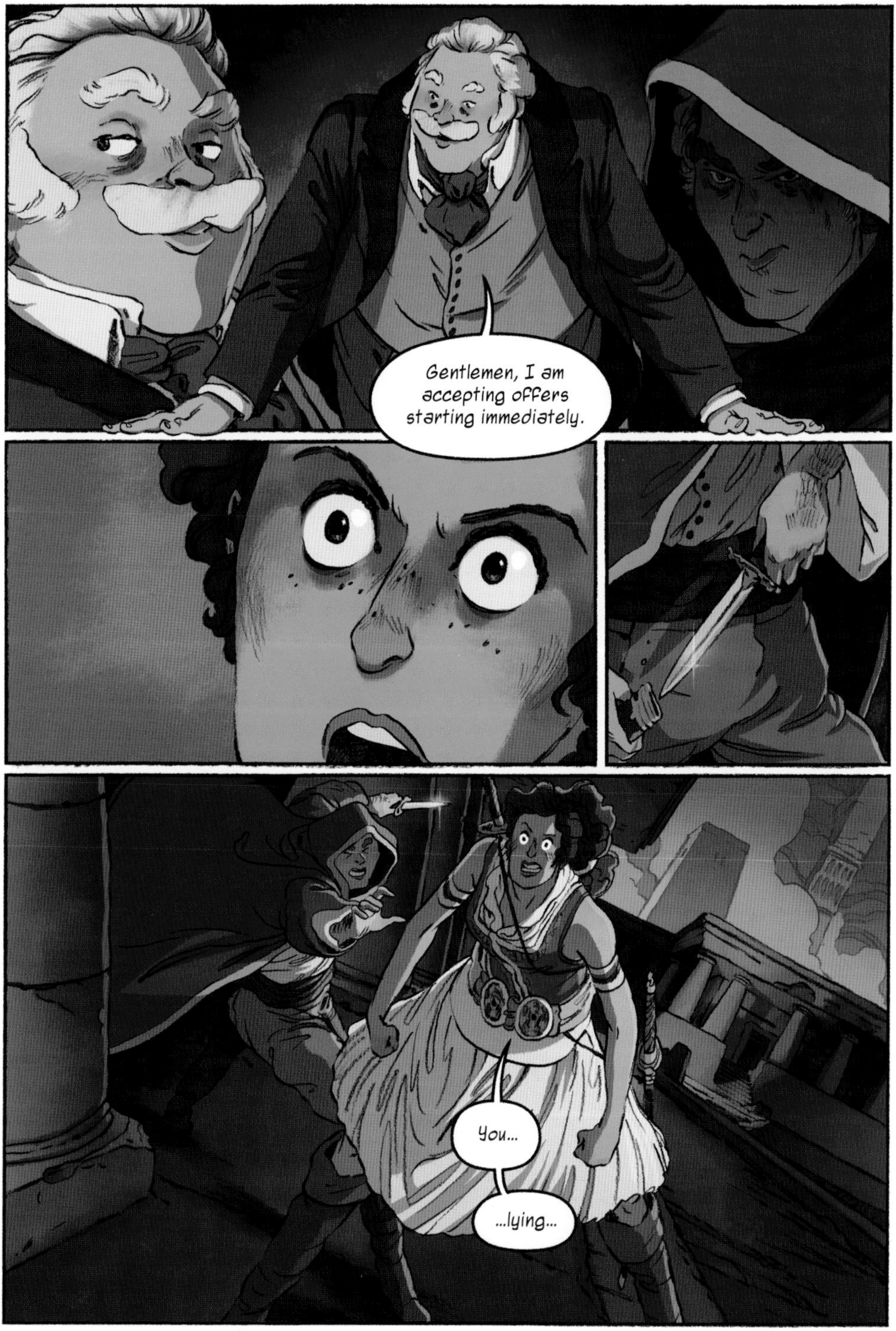
Gentlemen, I am accepting offers starting immediately.
You...
...lying...

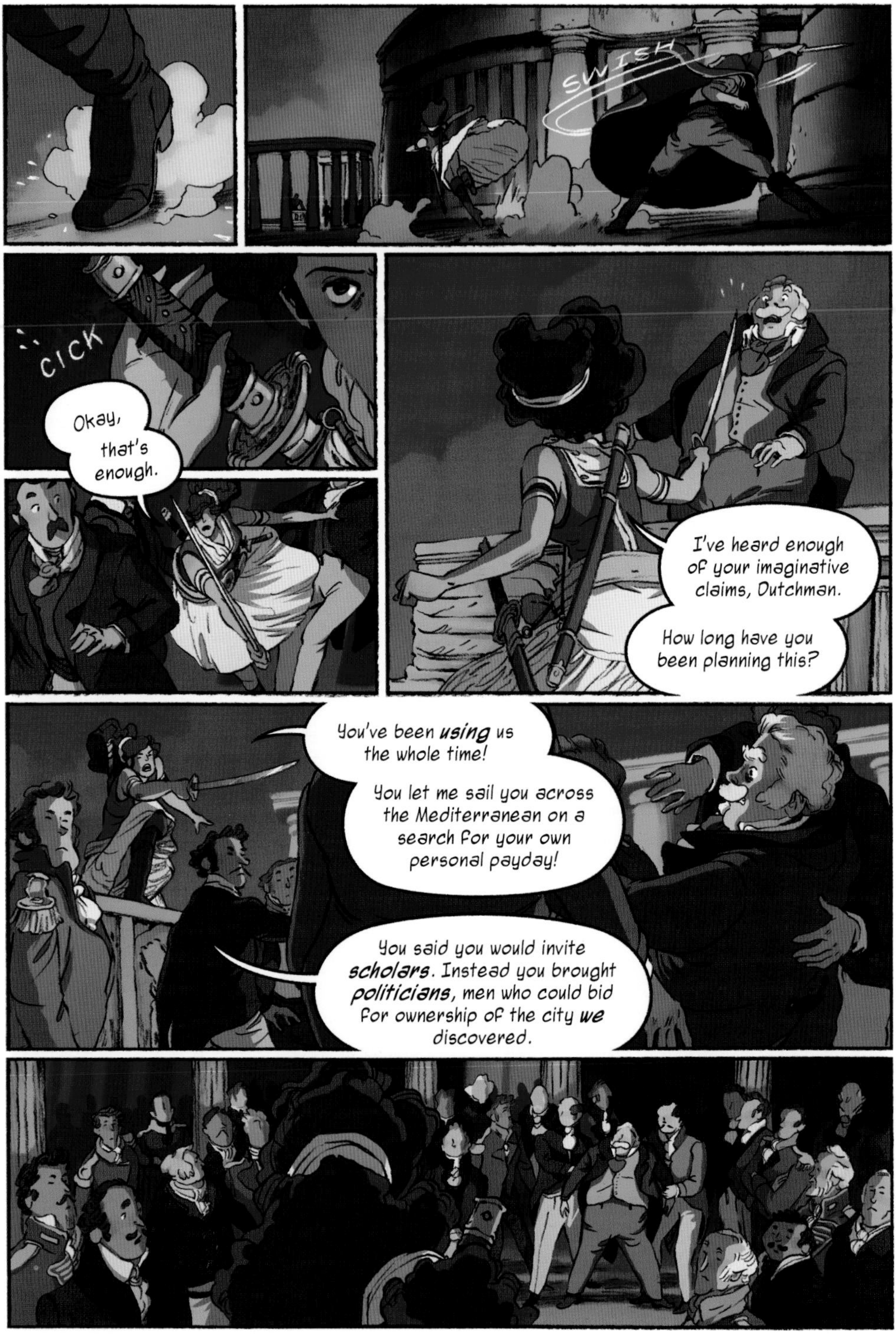
SWISH
CICK
Okay, that's enough.
I've heard enough of your imaginative claims, Dutchman.
How long have you been planning this?
You've been **using** us the whole time!
You let me sail you across the Mediterranean on a search for your own personal payday!
You said you would invite **scholars**. Instead you brought **politicians**, men who could bid for ownership of the city **we** discovered.

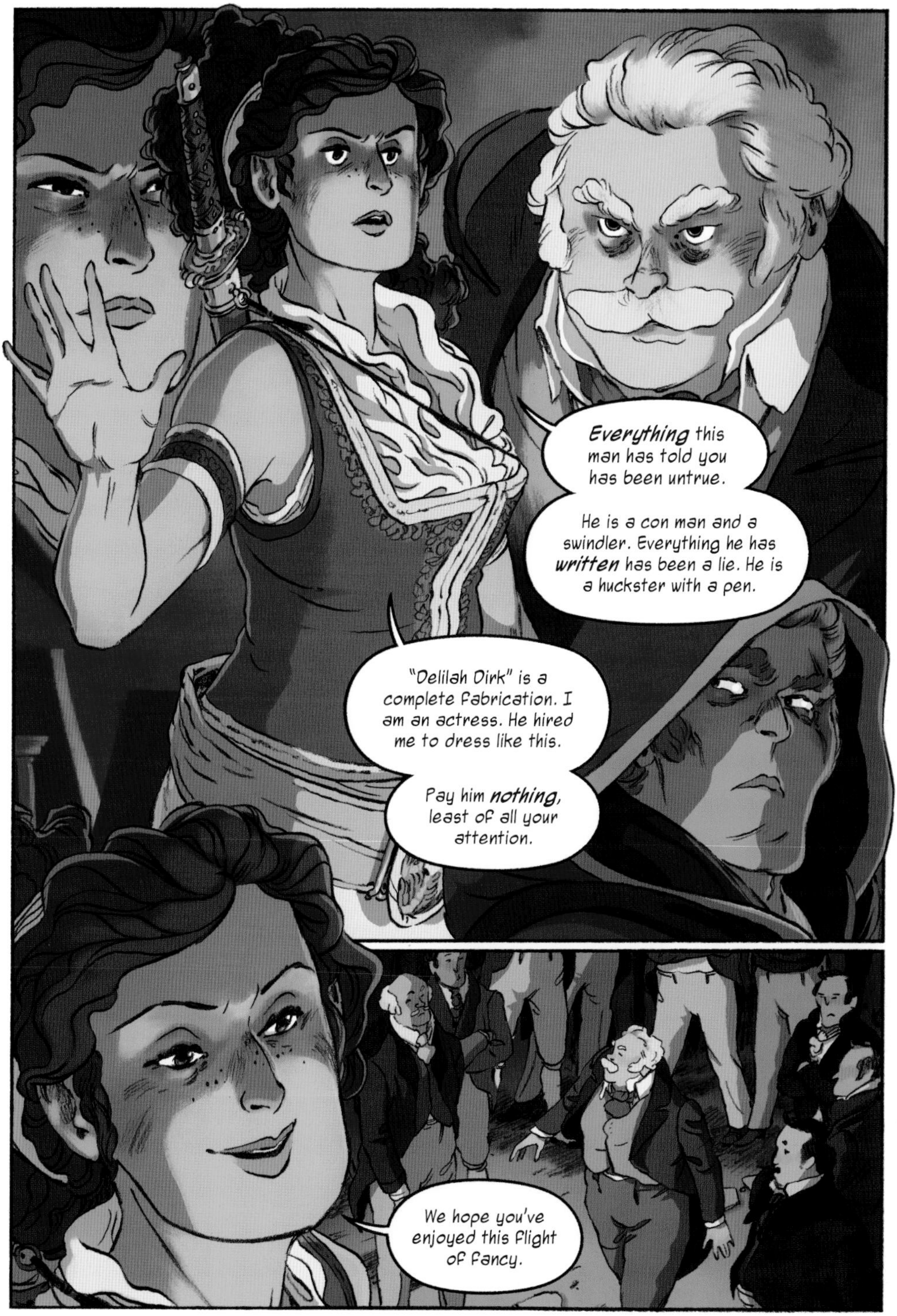
*Everything* this man has told you has been untrue.
He is a con man and a swindler. Everything he has *written* has been a lie. He is a huckster with a pen.
"Delilah Dirk" is a complete fabrication. I am an actress. He hired me to dress like this.
Pay him *nothing,* least of all your attention.
We hope you've enjoyed this flight of fancy.

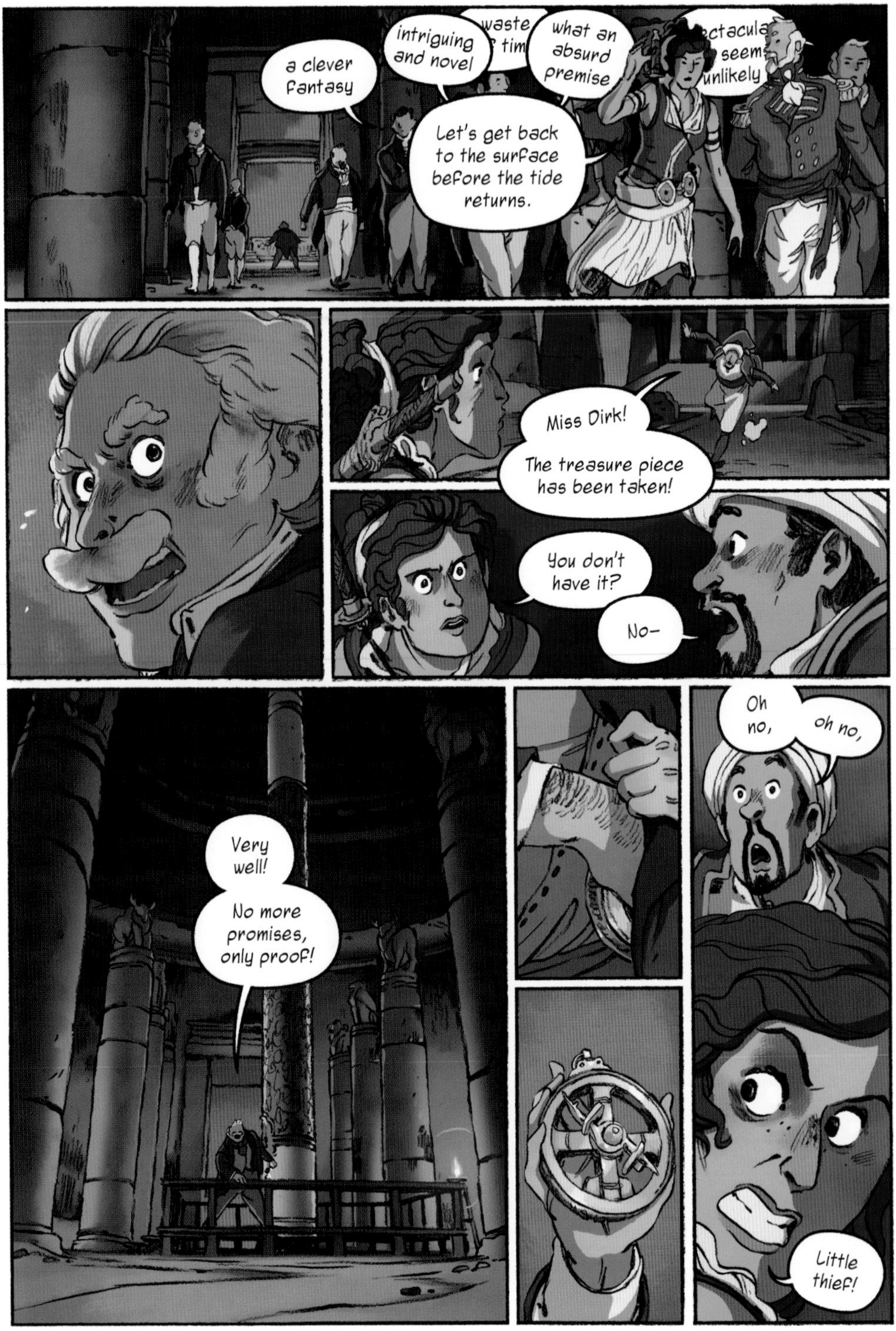
a clever fantasy
intriguing and novel
waste … tim
what an absurd premise
ectacula … seem … unlikely
Let's get back to the surface before the tide returns.
Miss Dirk!
The treasure piece has been taken!
You don't have it?
No-
Very well!
No more promises, only proof!
Oh no,
oh no,
Little thief!

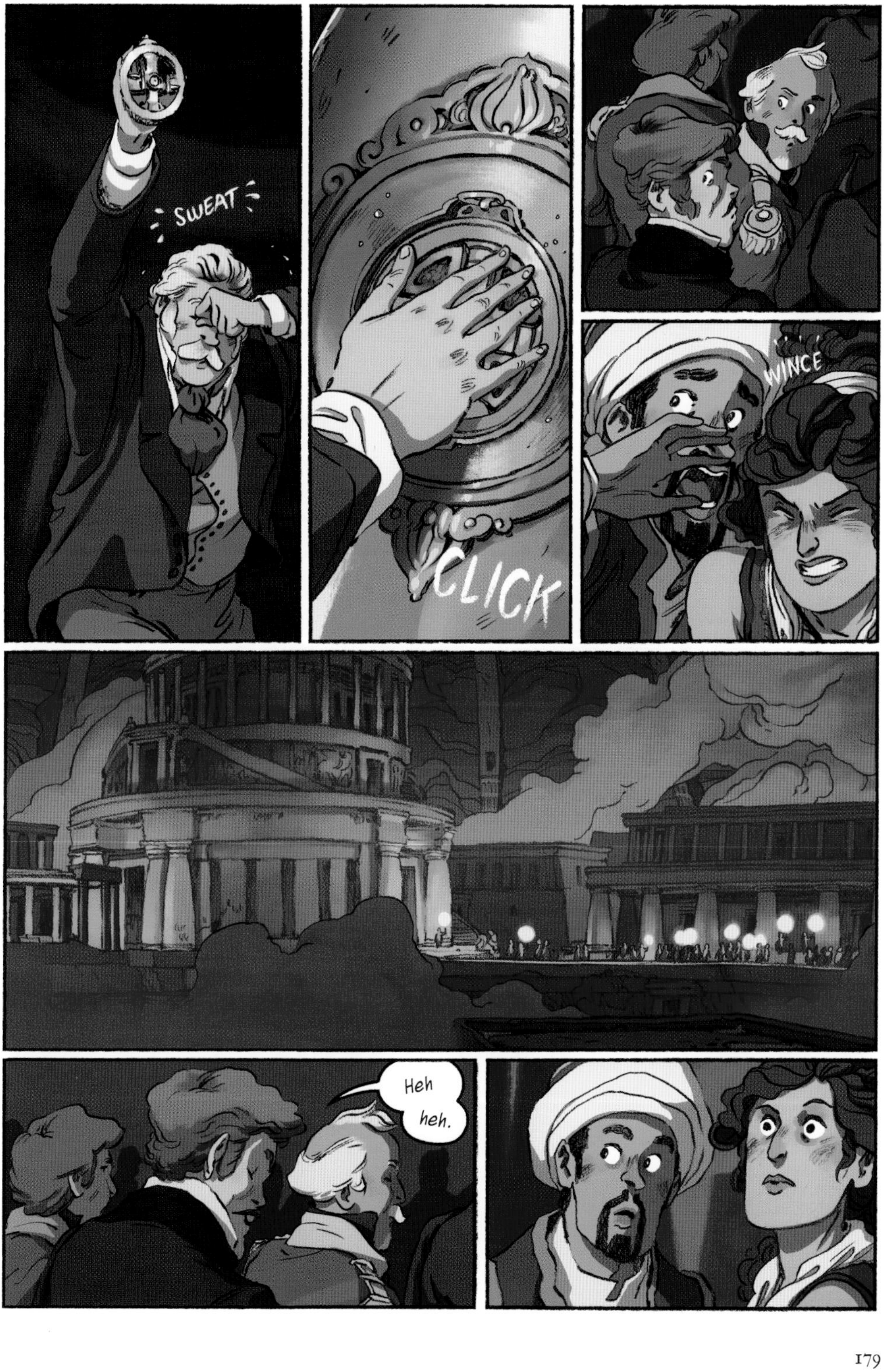
SWEAT
CLICK
WINCE
Heh heh.

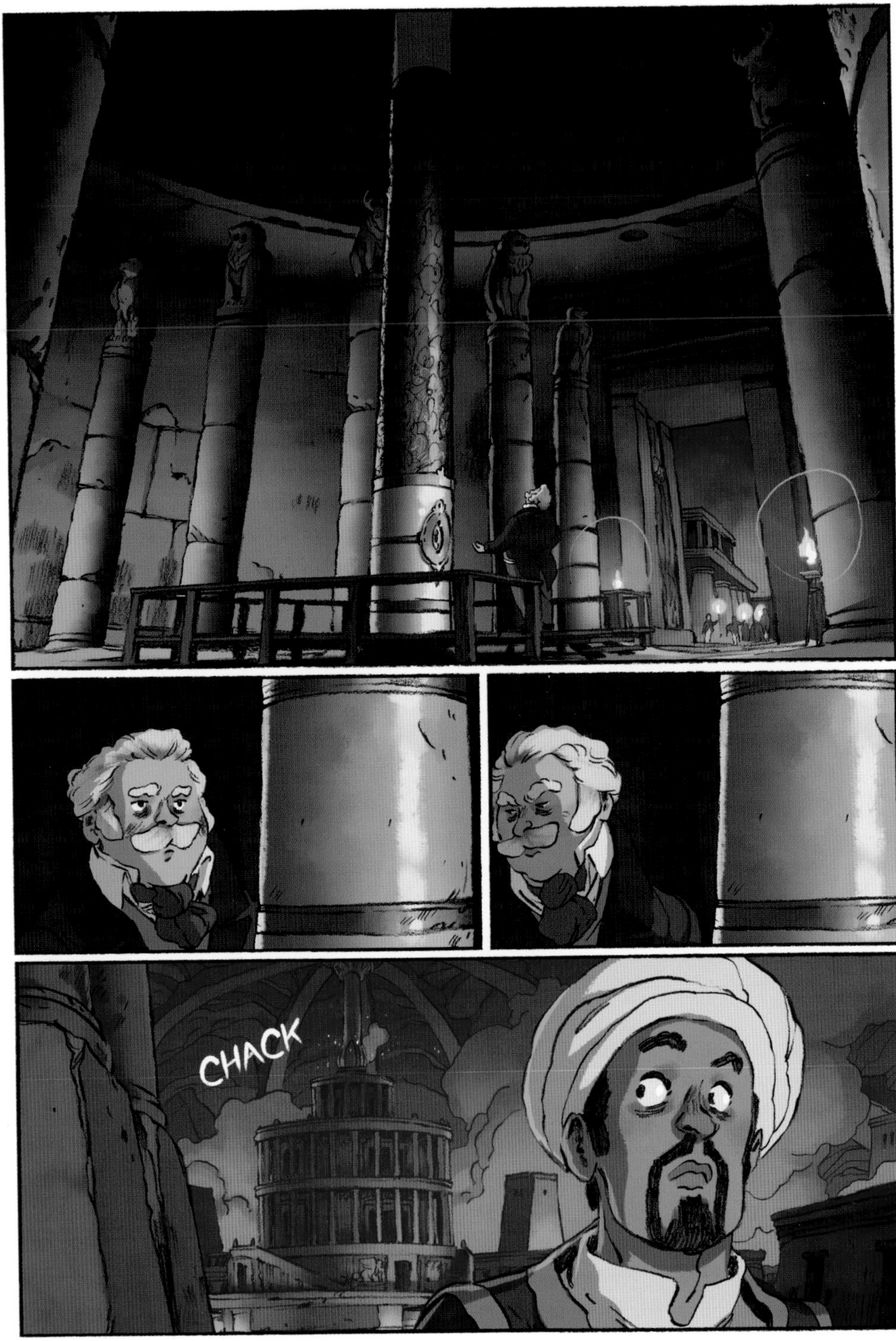
CHACK

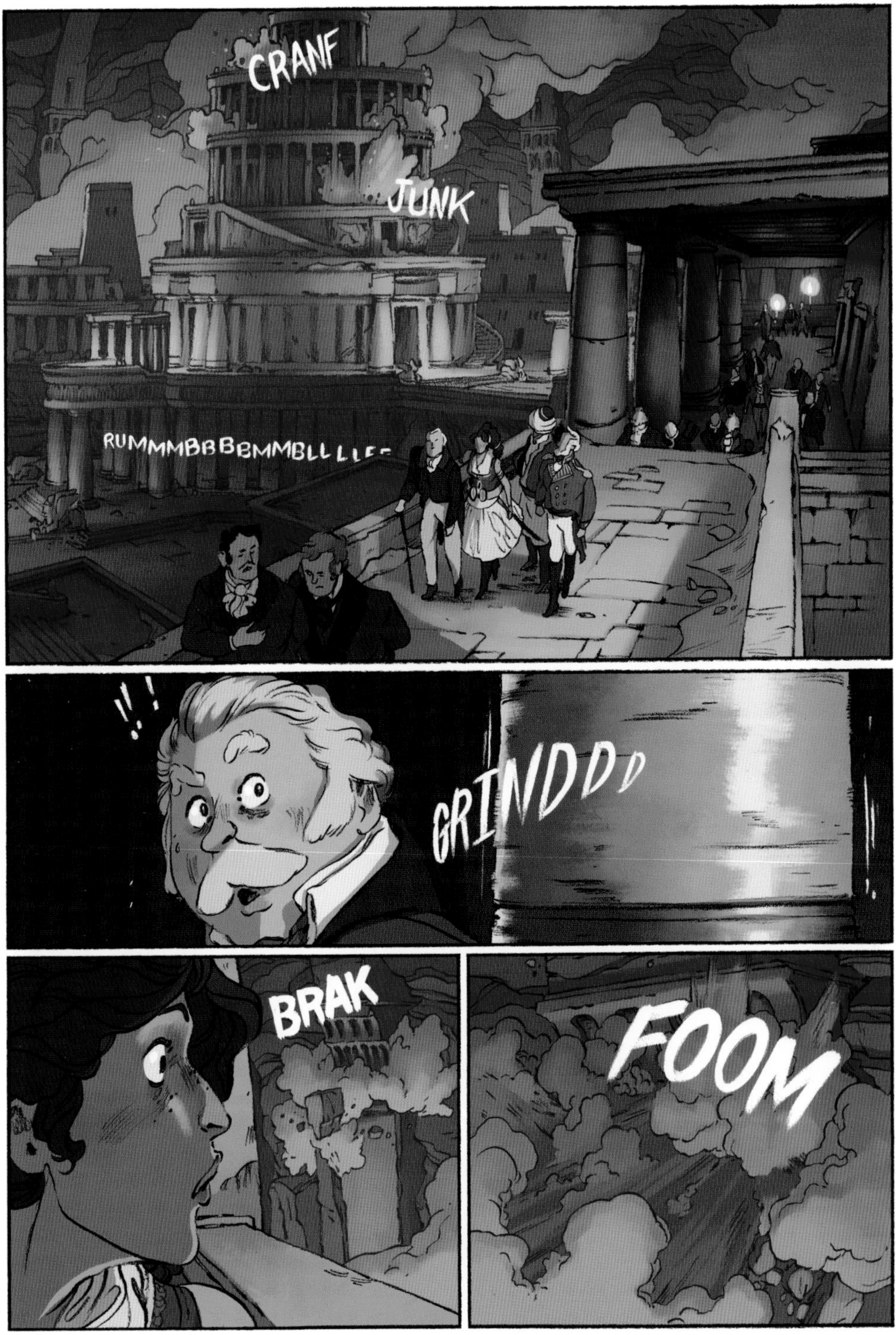
CRANF
JUNK
RUMMMBBBBMMBLLLLE
!!!
GRINDDD
BRAK
FOOM

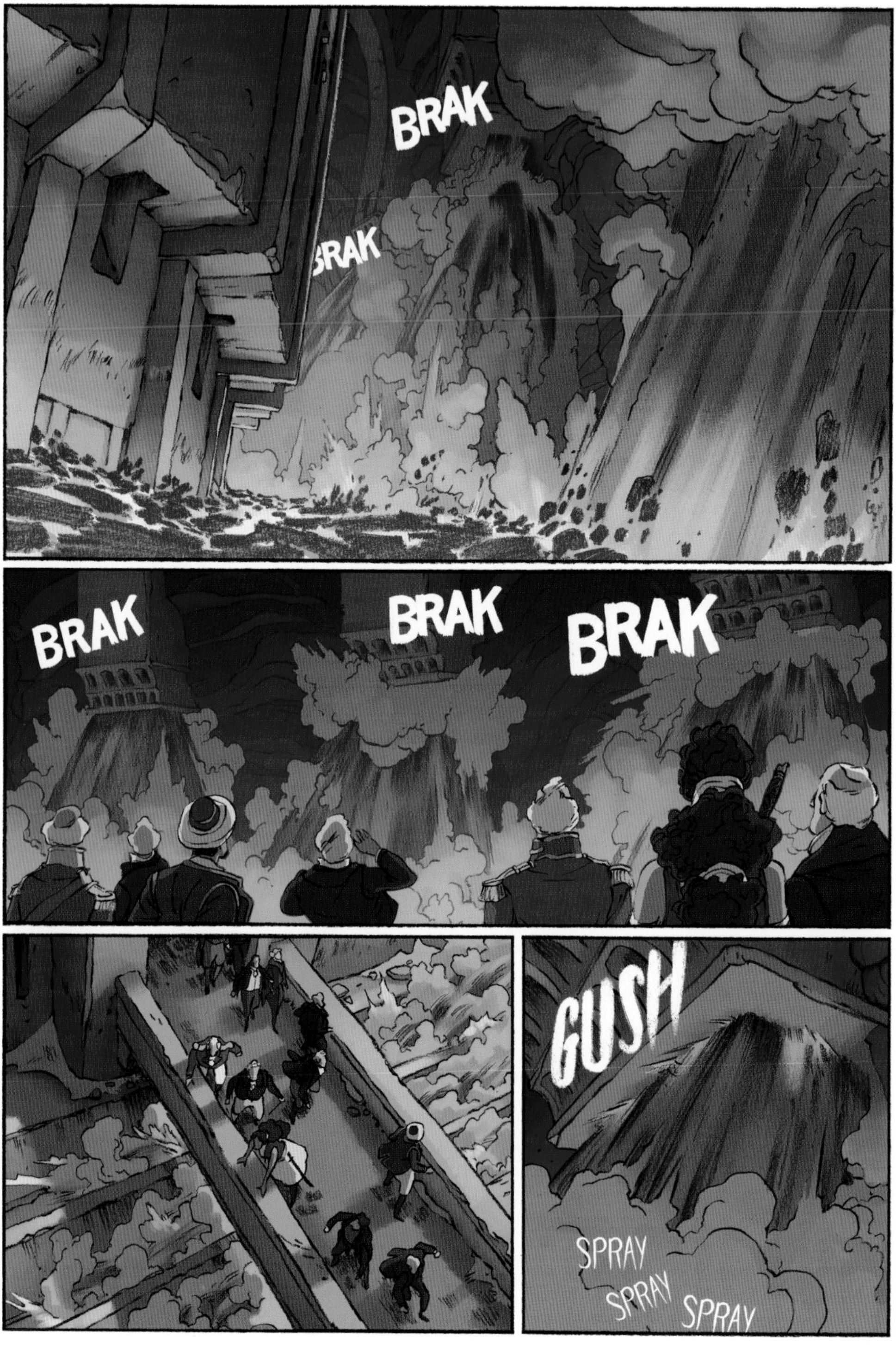
BRAK
BRAK
BRAK
BRAK
BRAK
GUSH
SPRAY
SPRAY
SPRAY

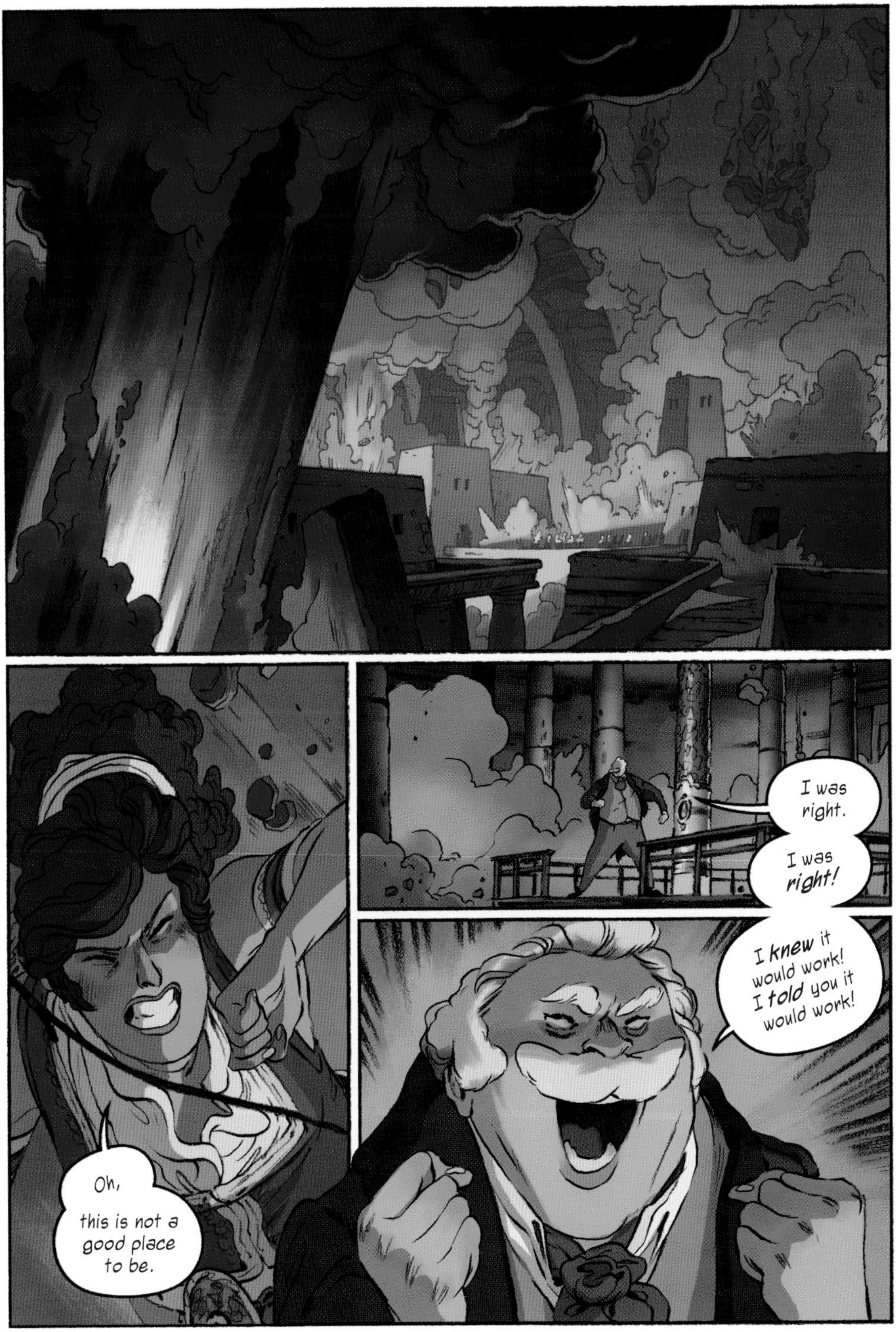
I was right.
I was *right!*
I *knew* it would work! I *told* you it would work!
Oh,
this is not a good place to be.

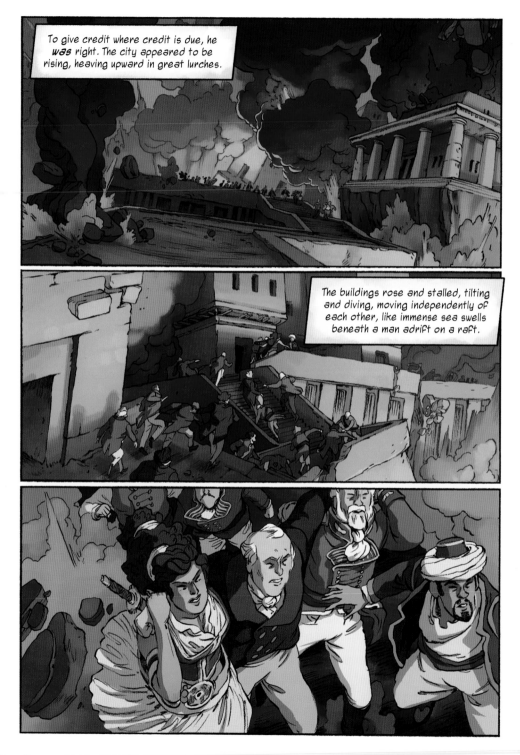

To give credit where credit is due, he *was* right. The city appeared to be rising, heaving upward in great lurches.

The buildings rose and stalled, tilting and diving, moving independently of each other, like immense sea swells beneath a man adrift on a raft.

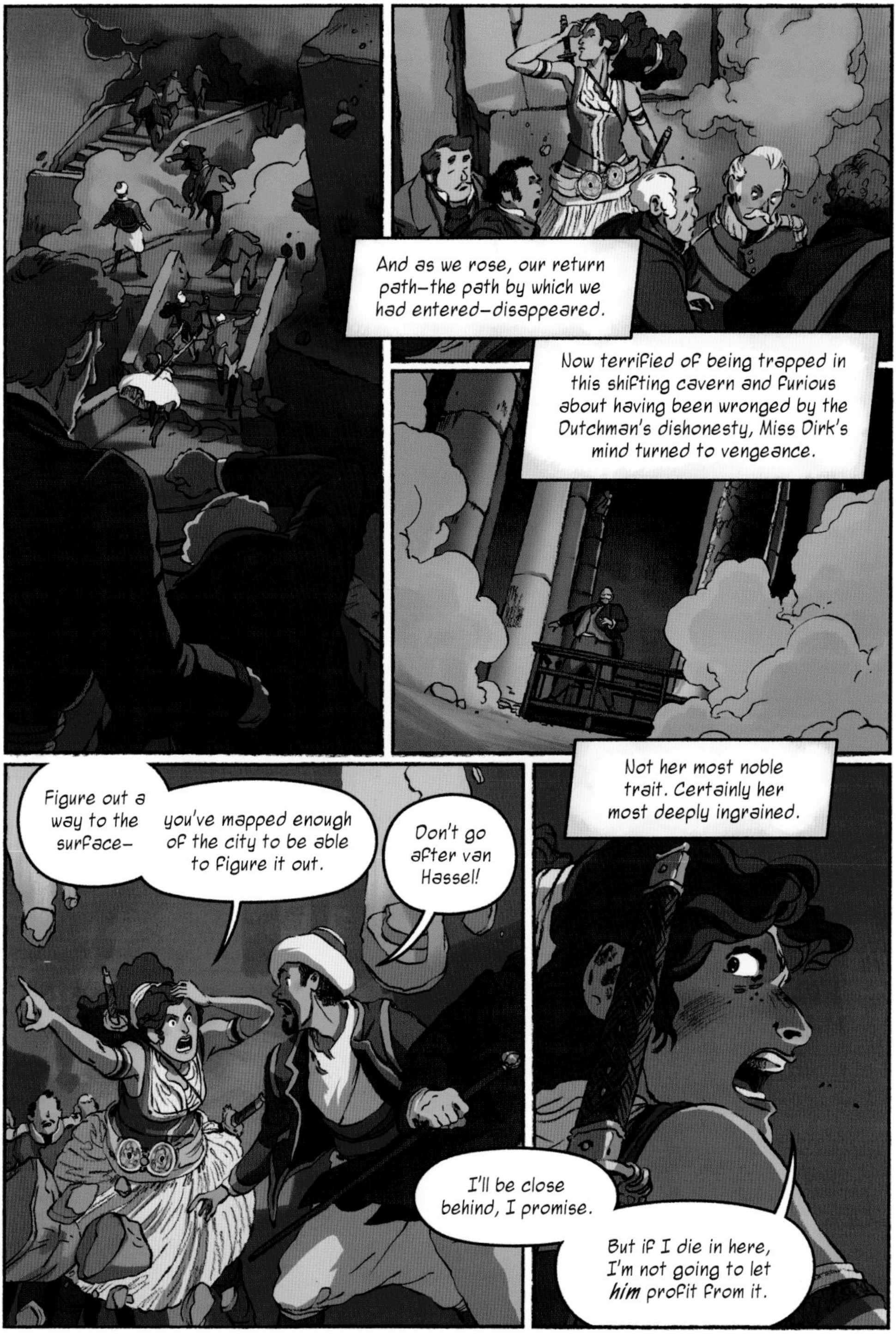
And as we rose, our return path—the path by which we had entered—disappeared.
Now terrified of being trapped in this shifting cavern and furious about having been wronged by the Dutchman's dishonesty, Miss Dirk's mind turned to vengeance.
Figure out a way to the surface—
you've mapped enough of the city to be able to figure it out.
Don't go after van Hassel!
Not her most noble trait. Certainly her most deeply ingrained.
I'll be close behind, I promise.
But if I die in here, I'm not going to let *him* profit from it.

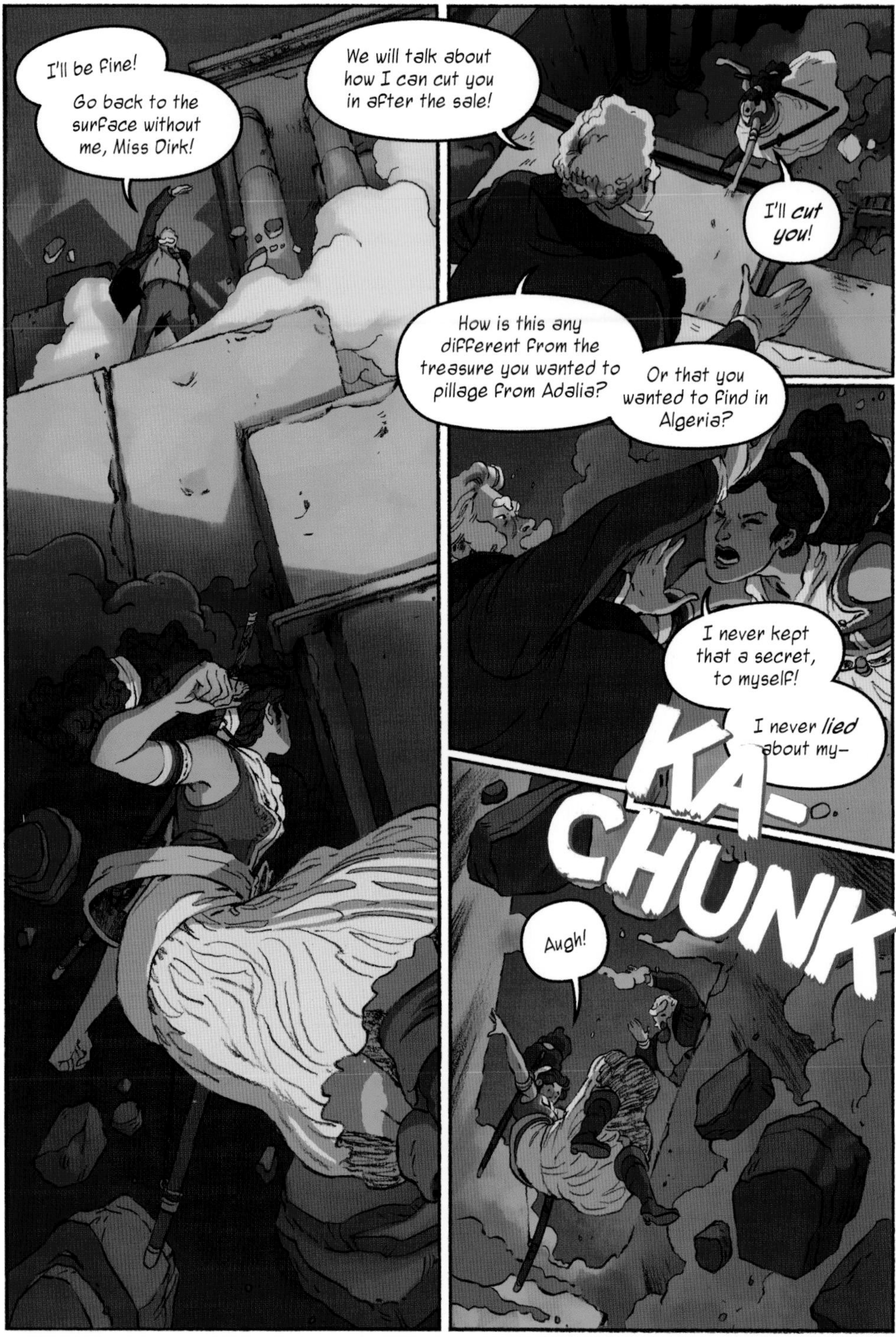
I'll be fine!
Go back to the surface without me, Miss Dirk!
We will talk about how I can cut you in after the sale!
I'll *cut you*!
How is this any different from the treasure you wanted to pillage from Adalia?
Or that you wanted to find in Algeria?
I never kept that a secret, to myself!
I never *lied* about my–
KA-CHUNK
Augh!

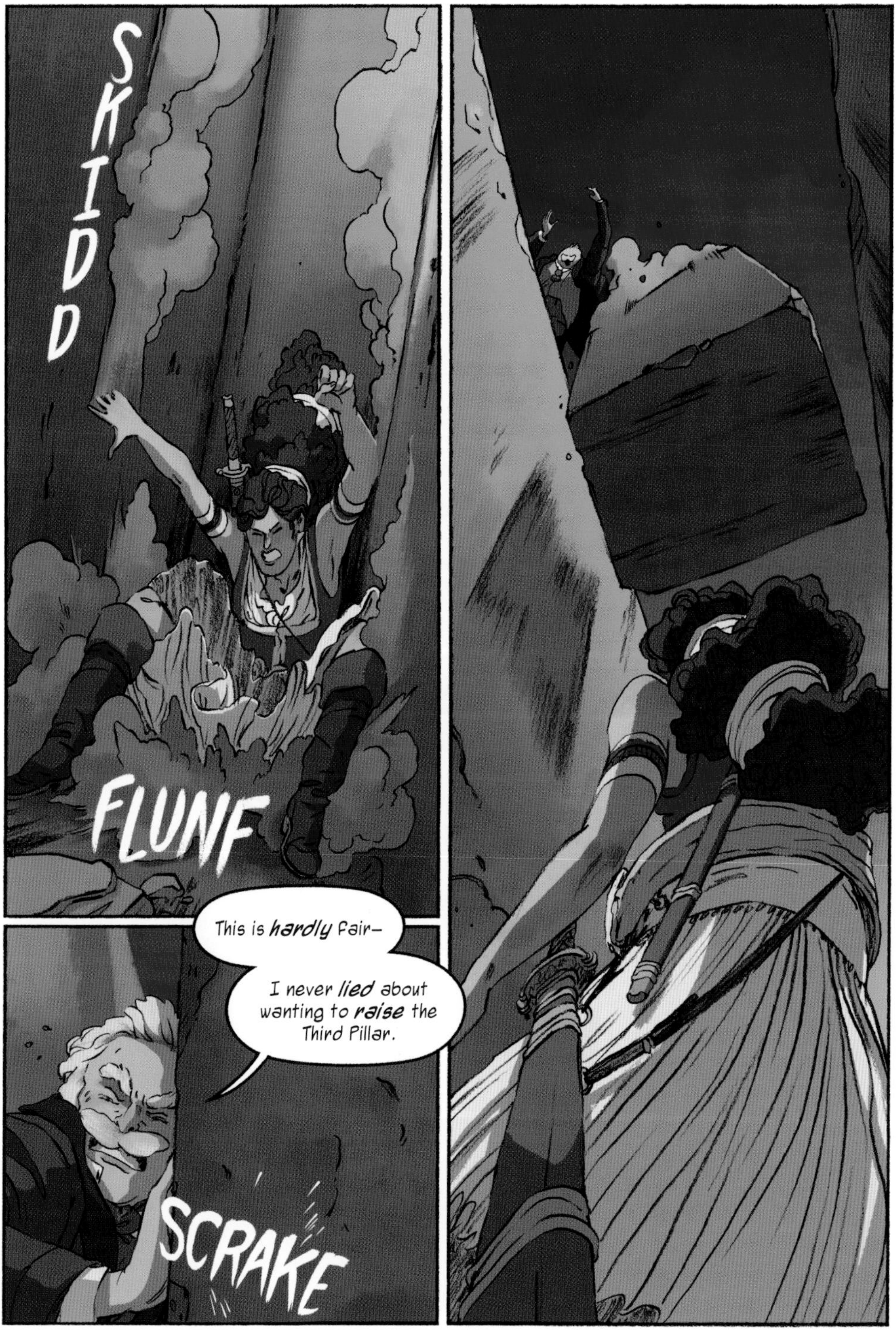
SKIDD
FLUNF
This is *hardly* fair–
I never *lied* about wanting to *raise* the Third Pillar.
SCRAKE

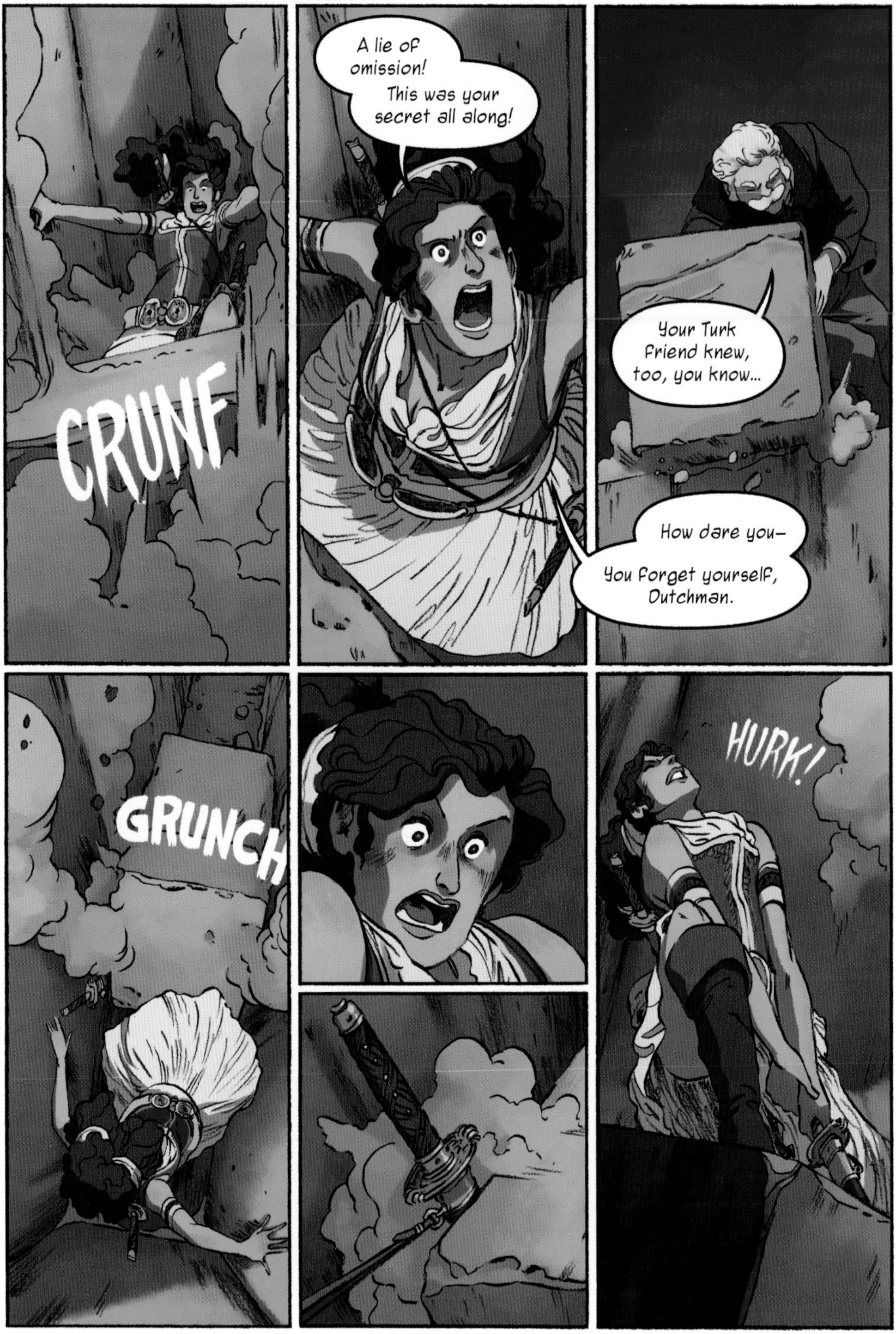
CRUNF
A lie of omission!
This was your secret all along!
Your Turk friend knew, too, you know...
How dare you—
You forget yourself, Dutchman.
GRUNCH
HURK!

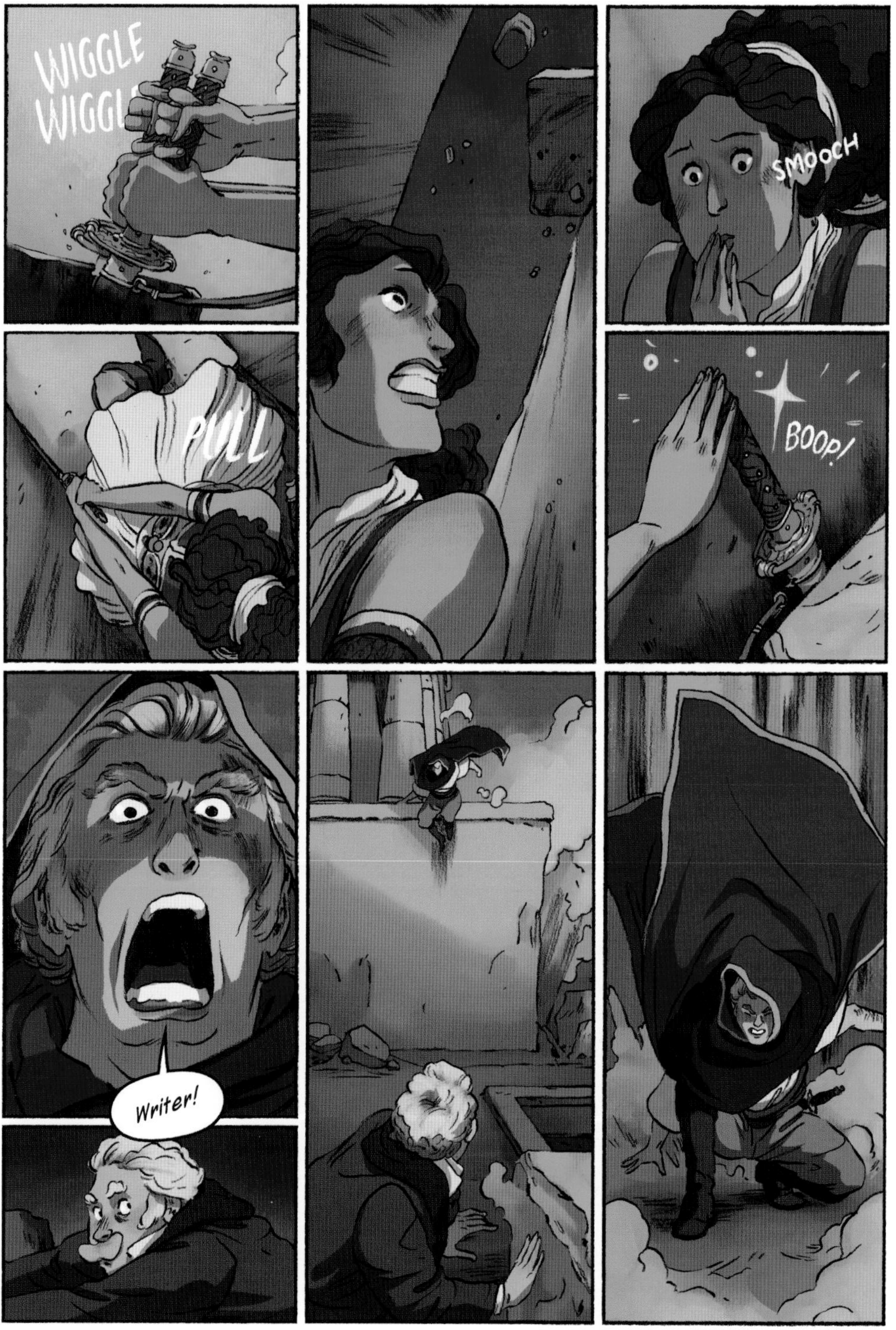
WIGGLE
WIGGL
SMOOCH
PULL
BOOP!
Writer!

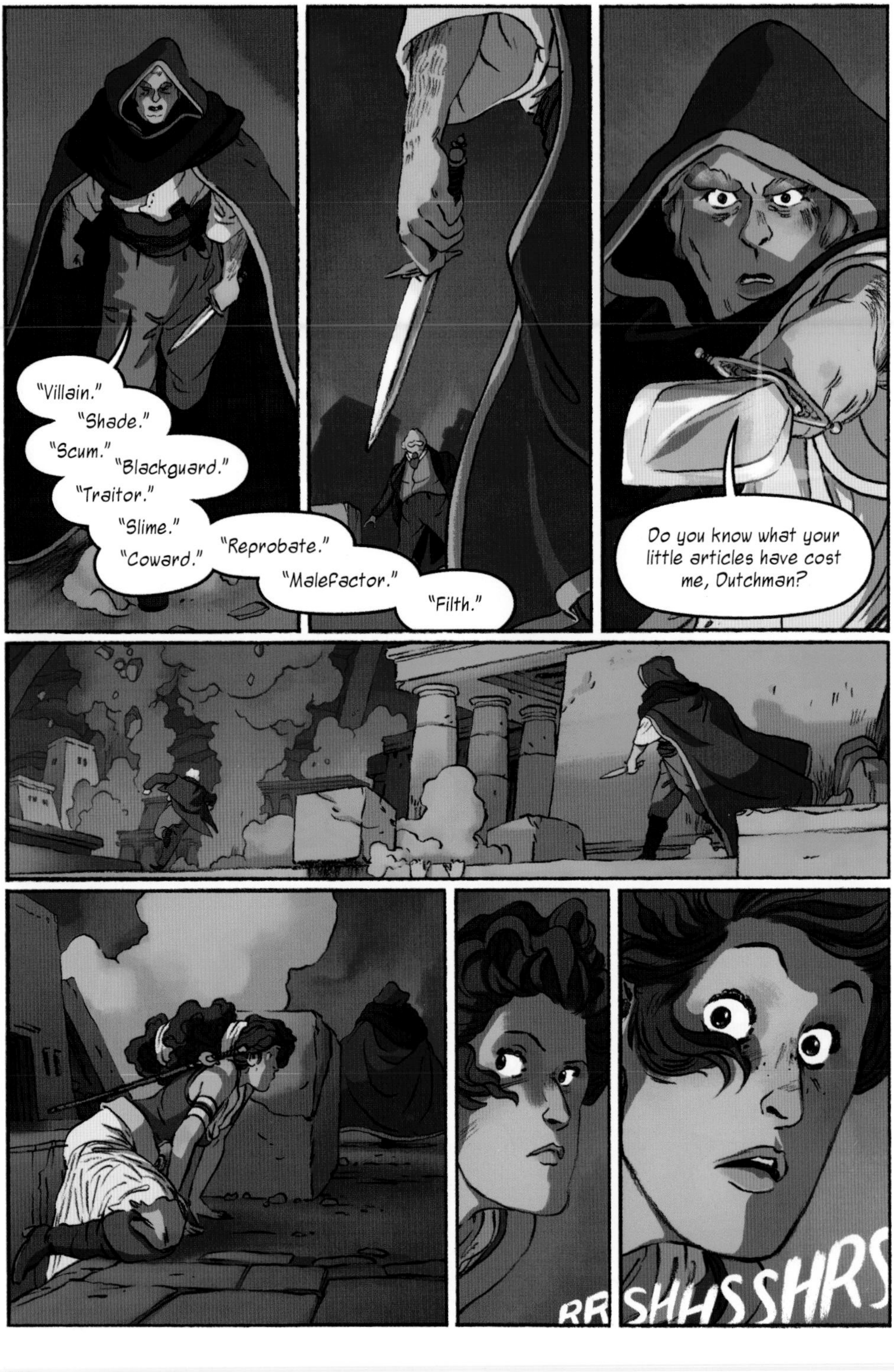
"Villain."
"Shade."
"Scum."
"Blackguard."
"Traitor."
"Slime."
"Coward."
"Reprobate."
"Malefactor."
"Filth."
Do you know what your little articles have cost me, Dutchman?
RRSHHSSHRS

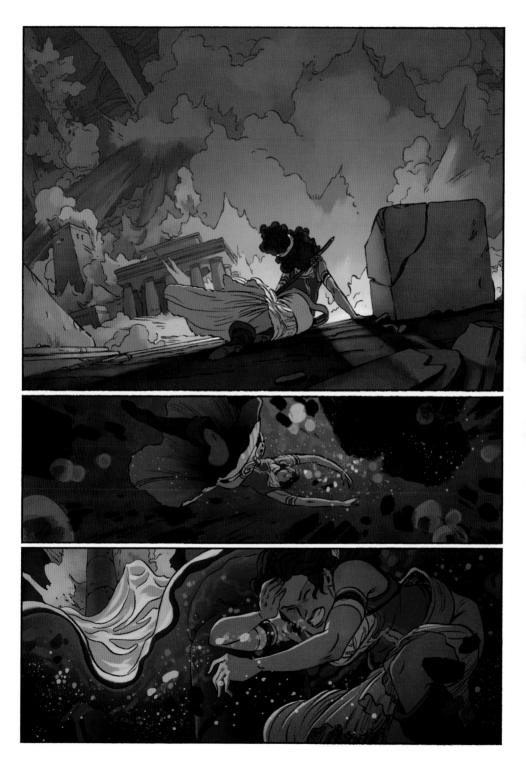

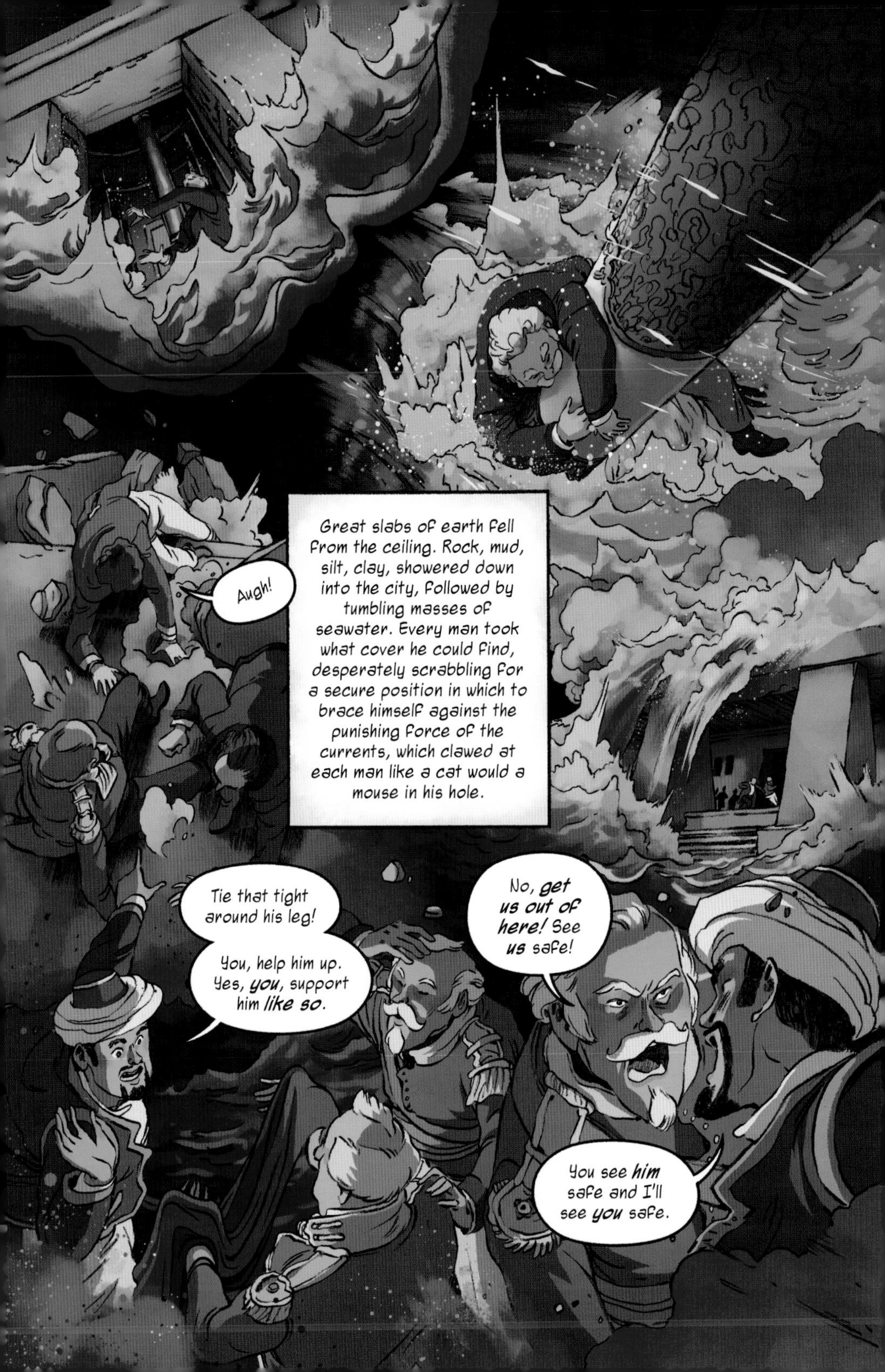
Great slabs of earth fell from the ceiling. Rock, mud, silt, clay, showered down into the city, followed by tumbling masses of seawater. Every man took what cover he could find, desperately scrabbling for a secure position in which to brace himself against the punishing force of the currents, which clawed at each man like a cat would a mouse in his hole.
Augh!
Tie that tight around his leg!
You, help him up. Yes, *you*, support him *like so*.
No, *get us out of here!* See *us* safe!
You see *him* safe and I'll see *you* safe.

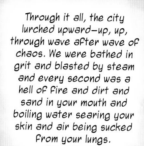

Through it all, the city lurched upward—up, up, through wave after wave of chaos. We were bathed in grit and blasted by steam and every second was a hell of fire and dirt and sand in your mouth and boiling water searing your skin and air being sucked from your lungs.

And when it finally ended...*sunlight*.

Do you know who I am?

No!

And that gives me a certain amount of liberty that I'm sure you are unaccustomed to seeing in others!

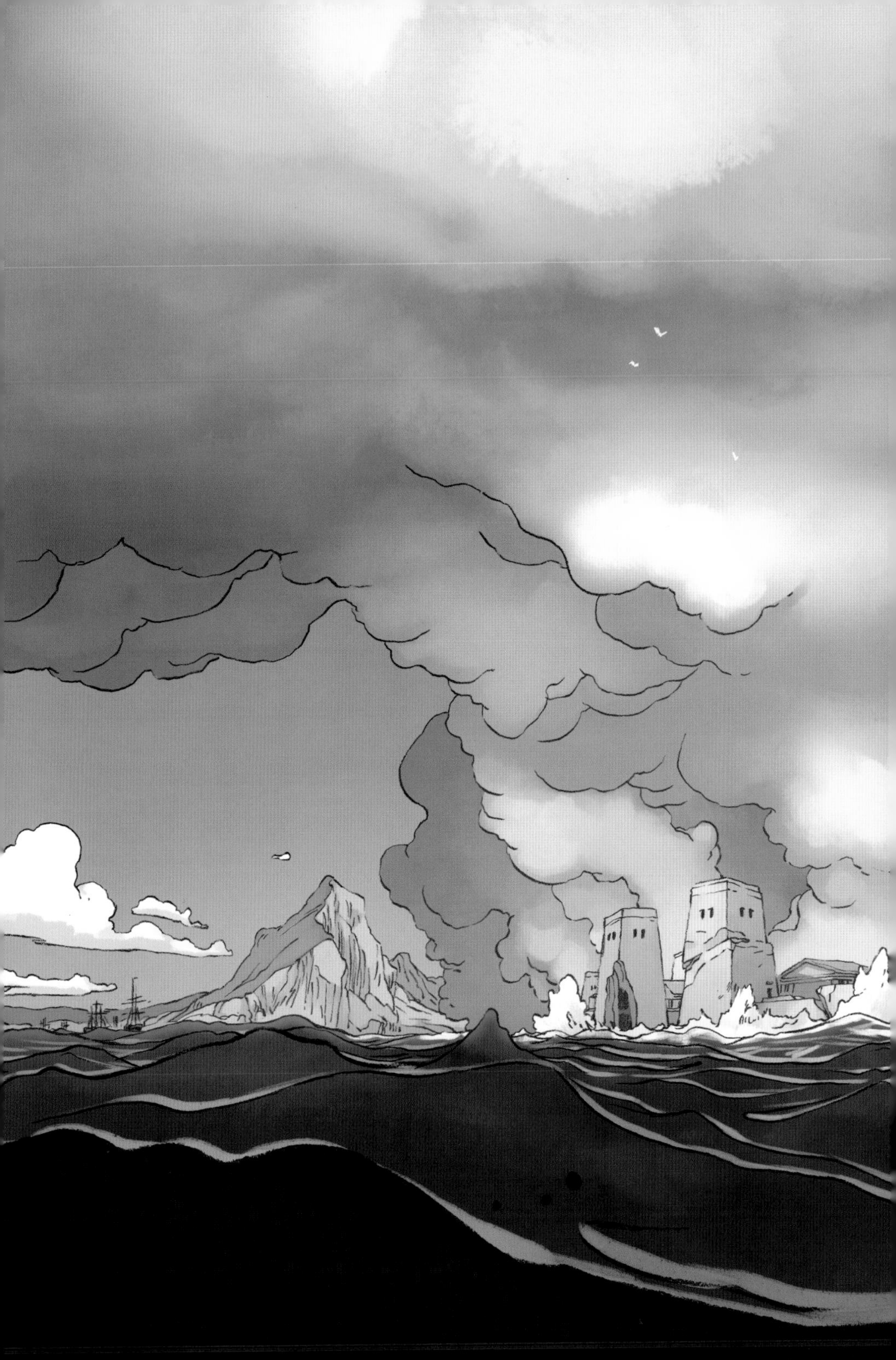

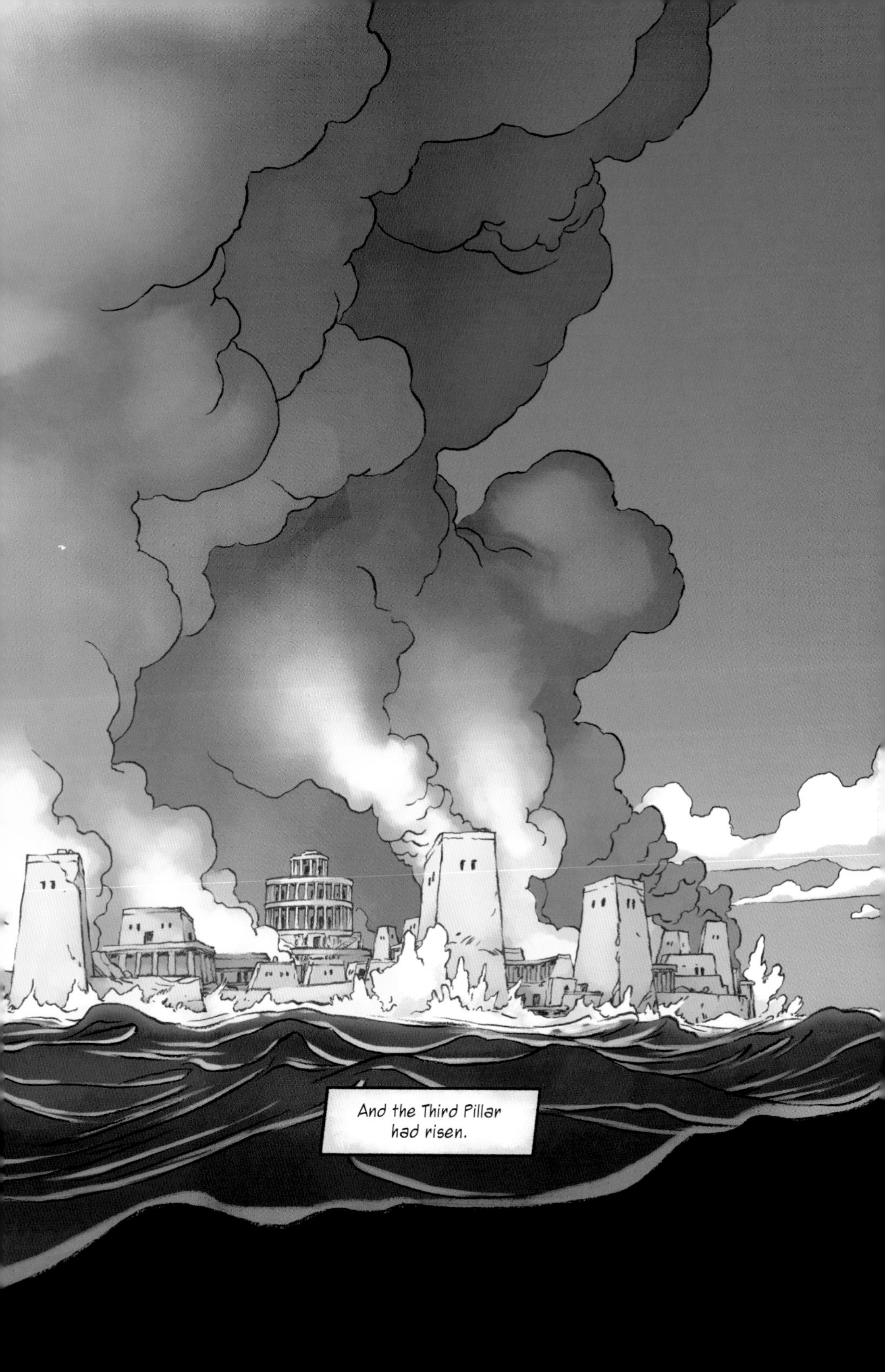
And the Third Pillar had risen.

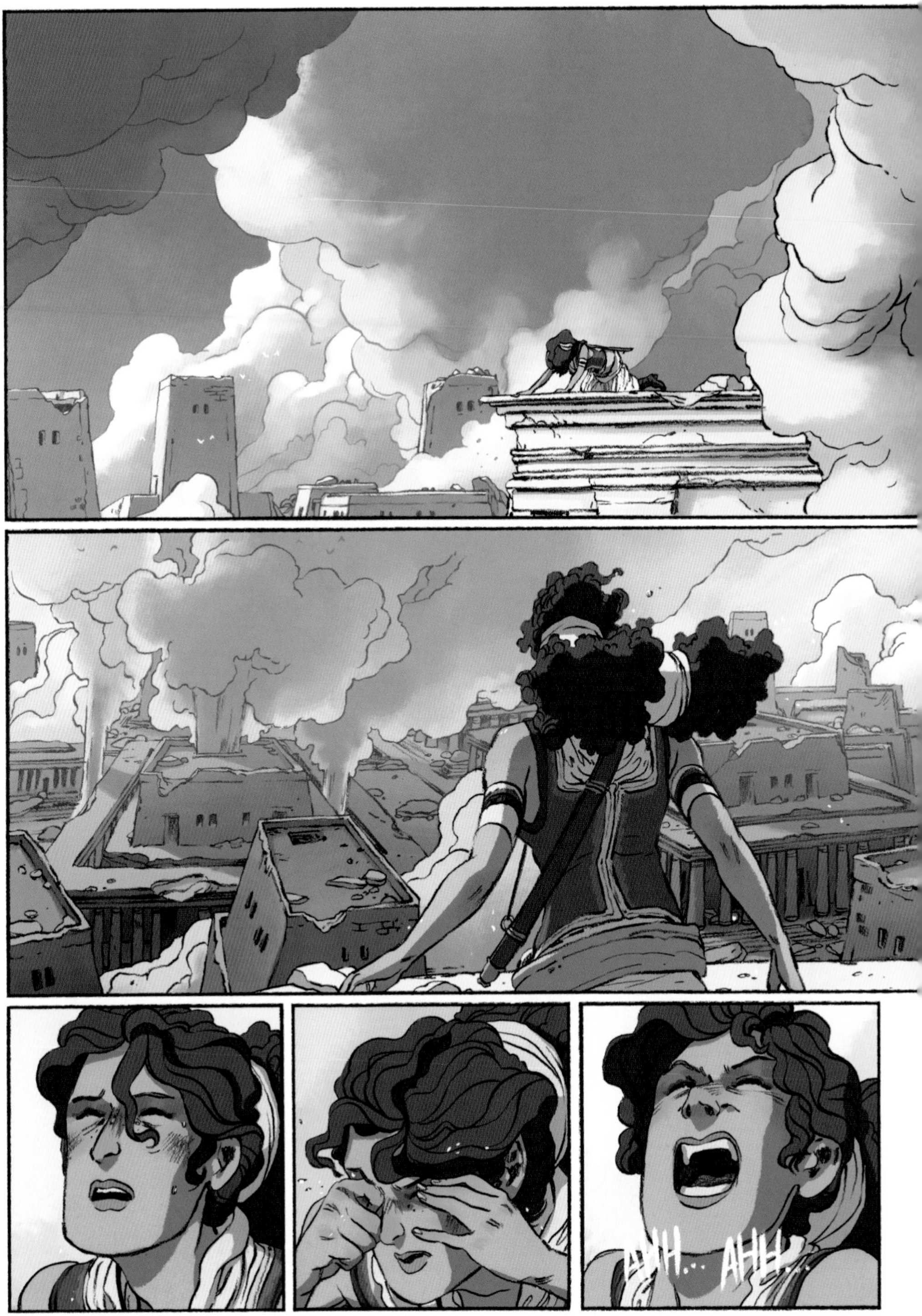
AHH... AHH...

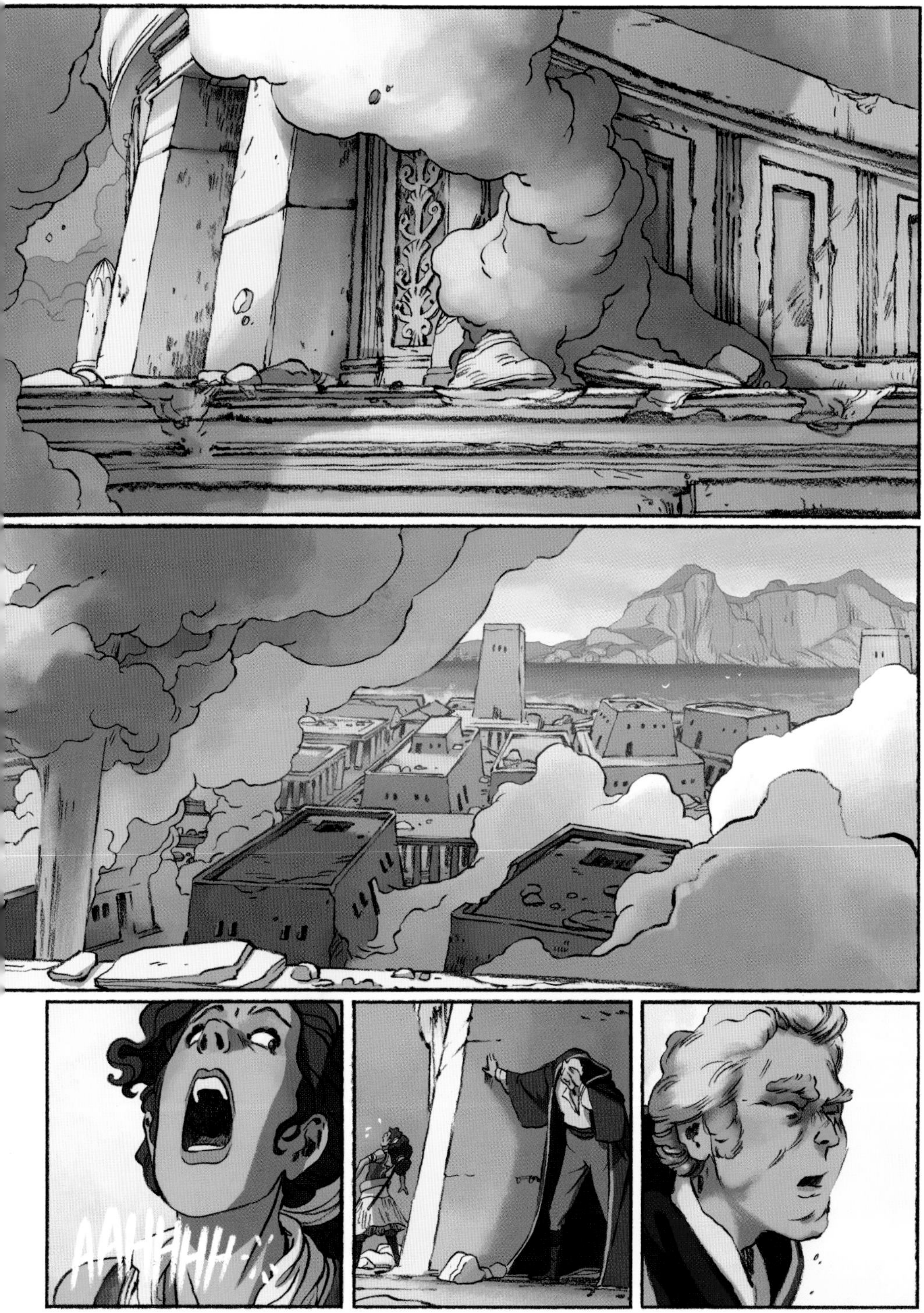
AAHHHH...!

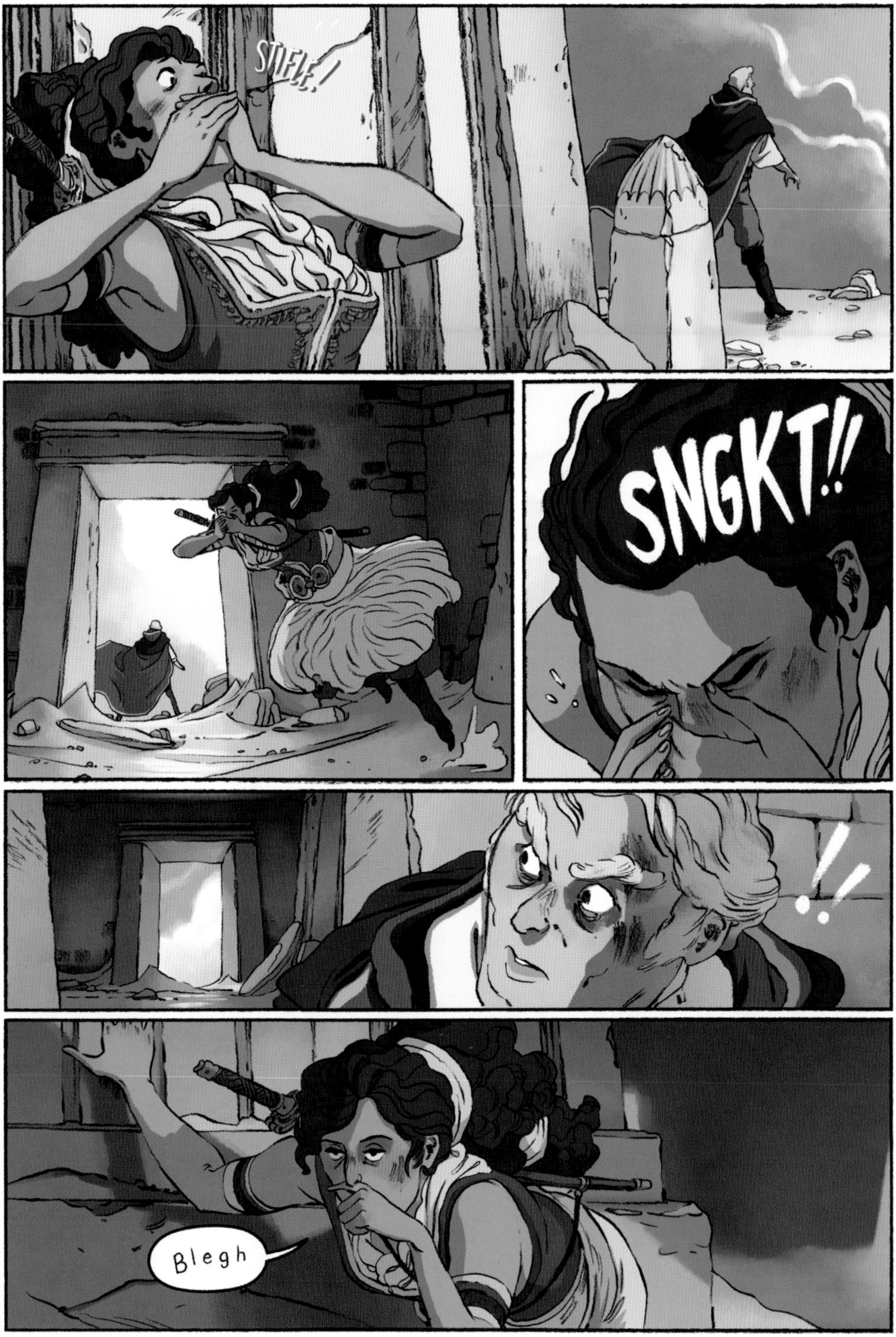
STIFLE!
SNGKT!!
Blegh

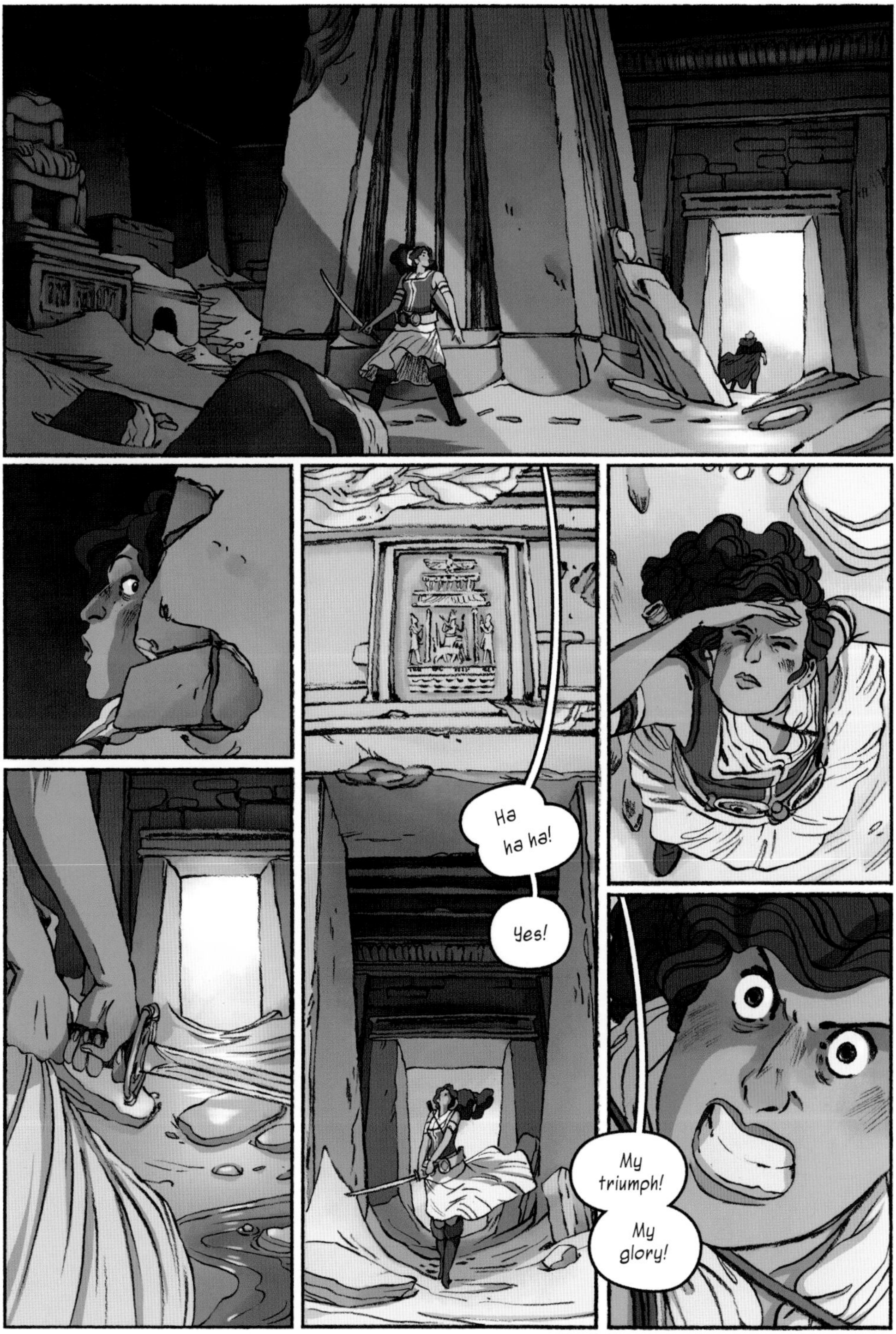
Ha
ha ha!
Yes!
My triumph!
My glory!

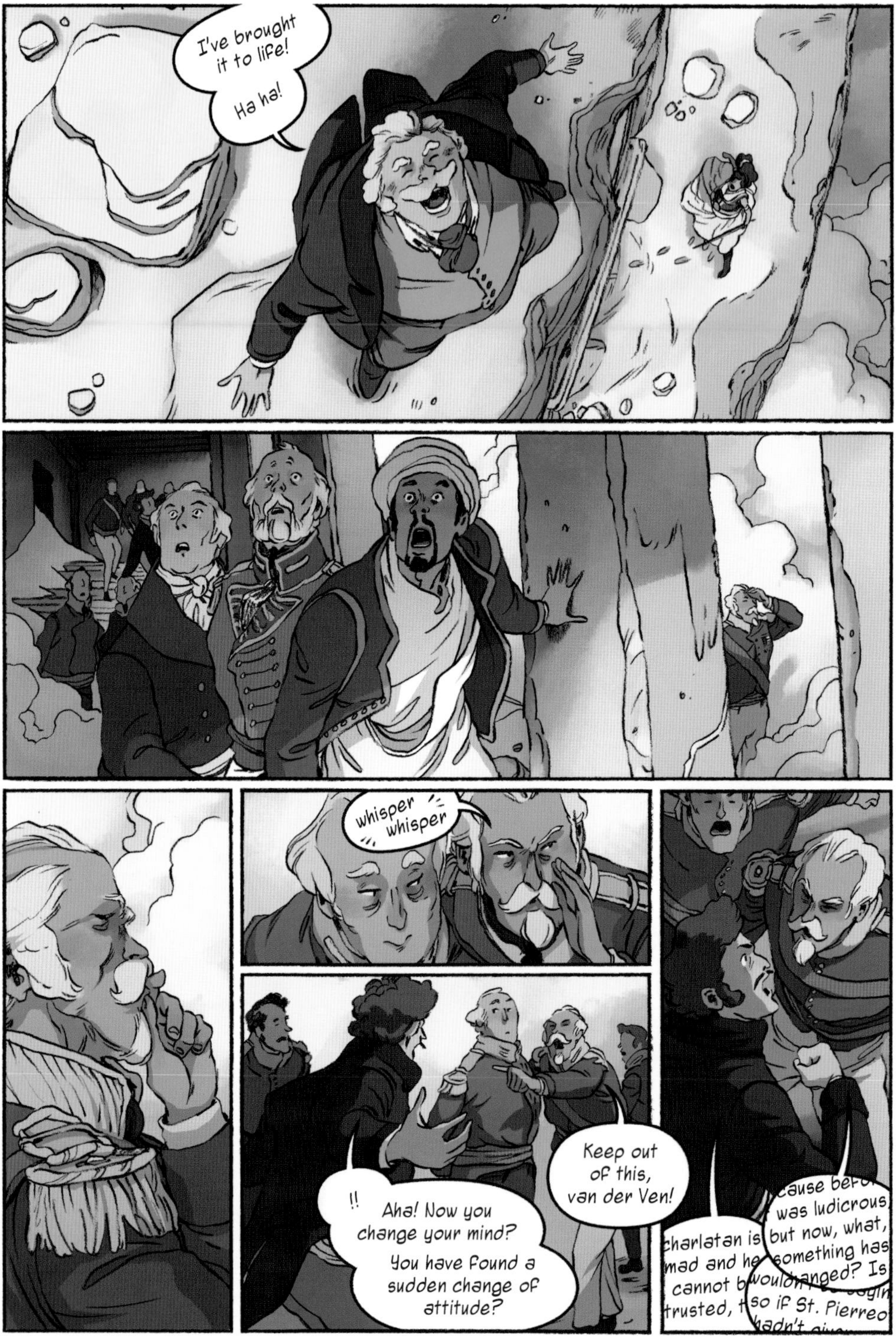
I've brought it to life!
Ha ha!
whisper whisper
!!
Aha! Now you change your mind?
You have found a sudden change of attitude?
Keep out of this, van der Ven!
charlatan is mad and he cannot b trusted, t
cause befo was ludicrous, but now, what, something has changed? Is so if St. Pierre

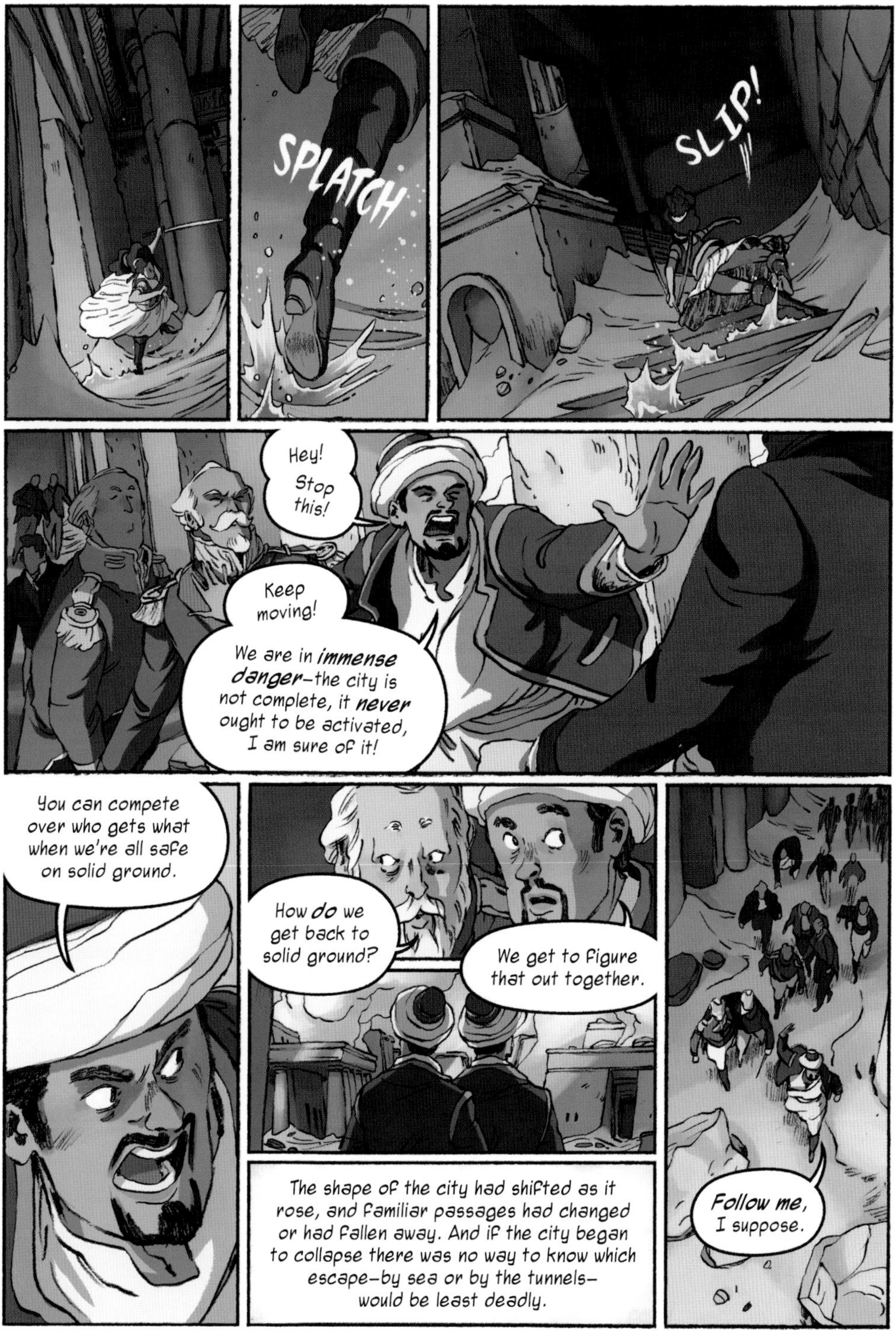
SPLATCH
SLIP!
Hey! Stop this!
Keep moving!
We are in *immense danger*—the city is not complete, it *never* ought to be activated, I am sure of it!
You can compete over who gets what when we're all safe on solid ground.
How *do* we get back to solid ground?
We get to figure that out together.
The shape of the city had shifted as it rose, and familiar passages had changed or had fallen away. And if the city began to collapse there was no way to know which escape—by sea or by the tunnels—would be least deadly.
*Follow me*, I suppose.

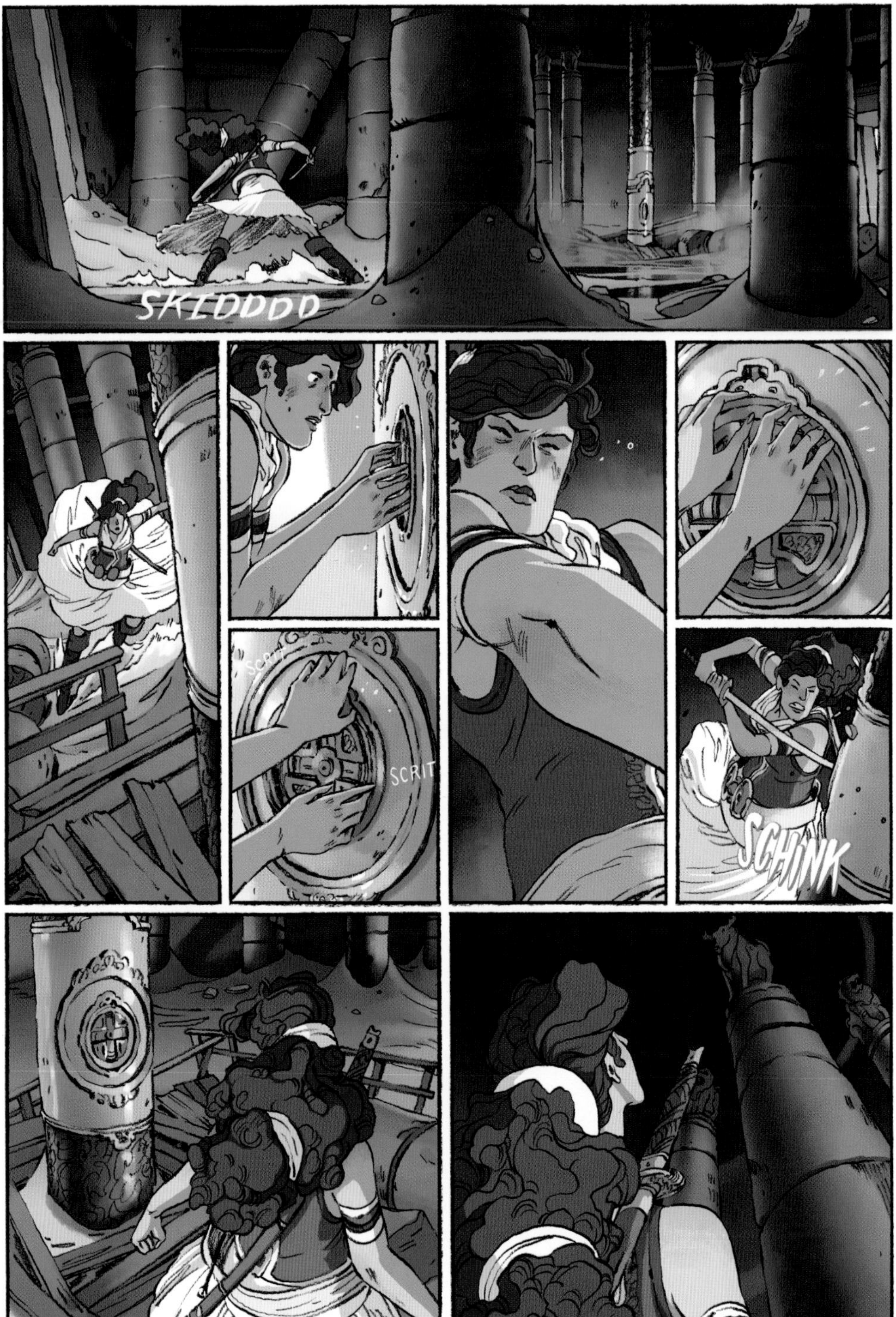
SKIDDDD
SCRIT
SCRIT
SCHINK

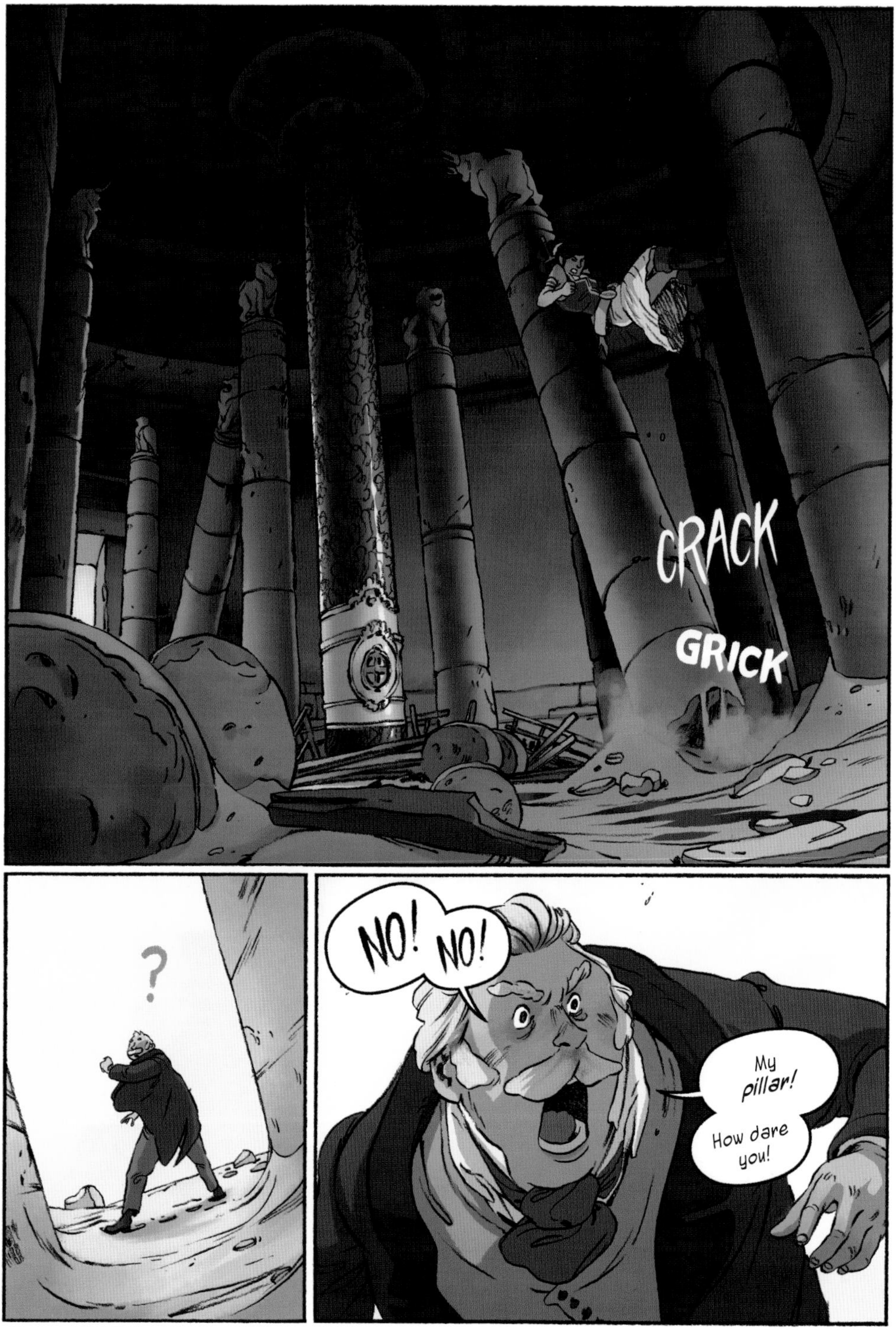
CRACK
GRICK
?
NO! NO!
My pillar!
How dare you!

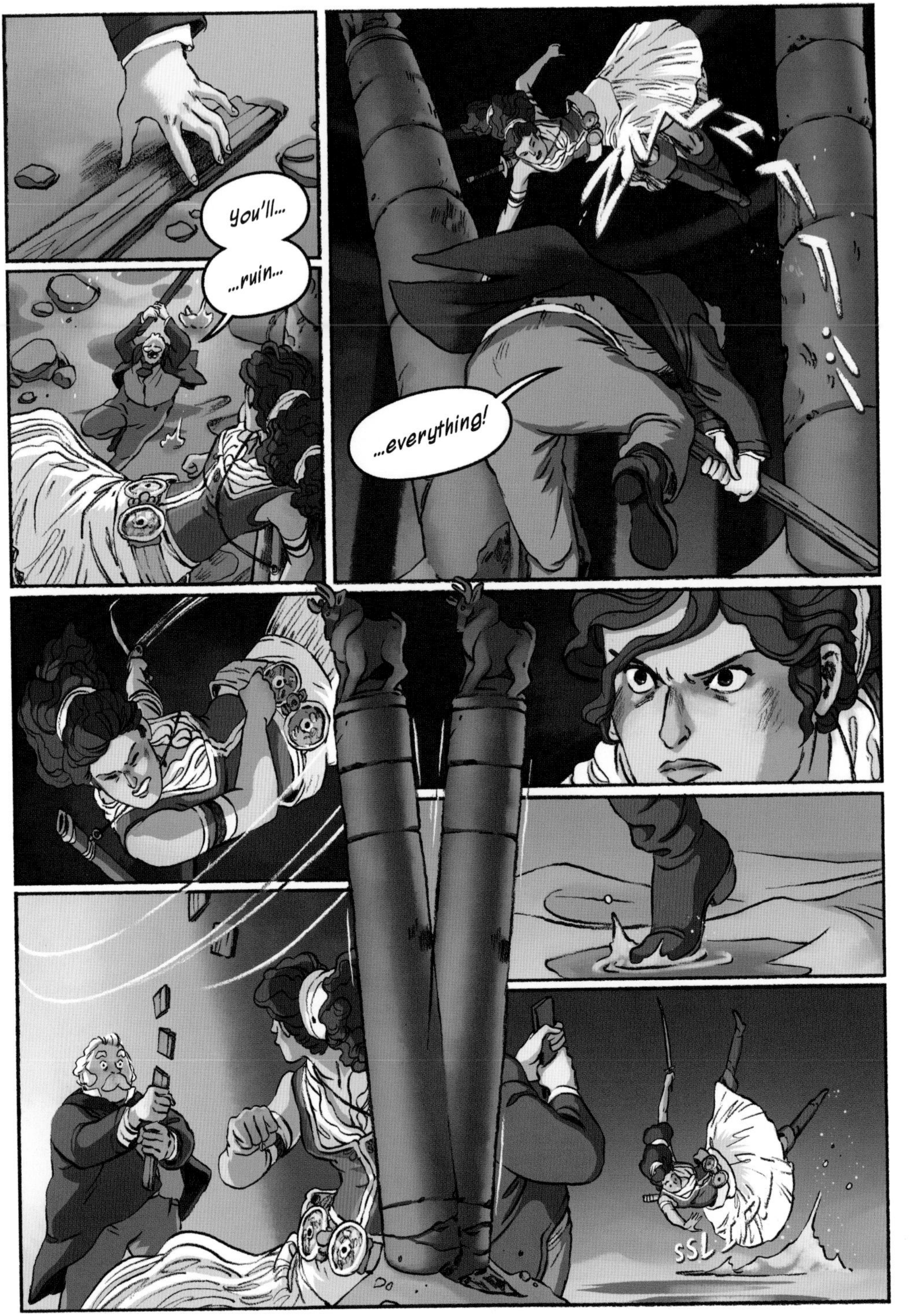
You'll...
...ruin...
...everything!
SSL

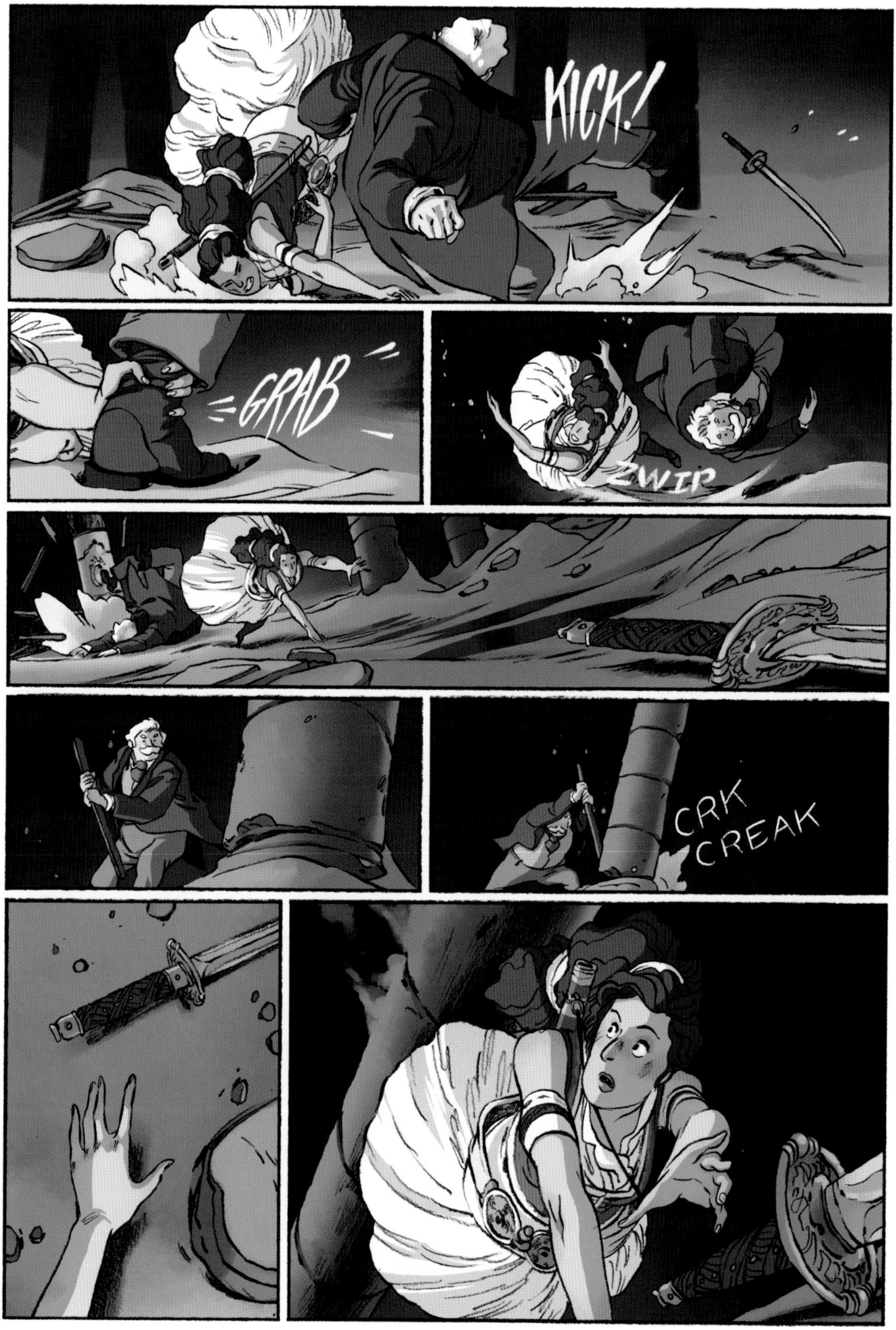
KICK!
GRAB
ZWIP
CRK
CREAK

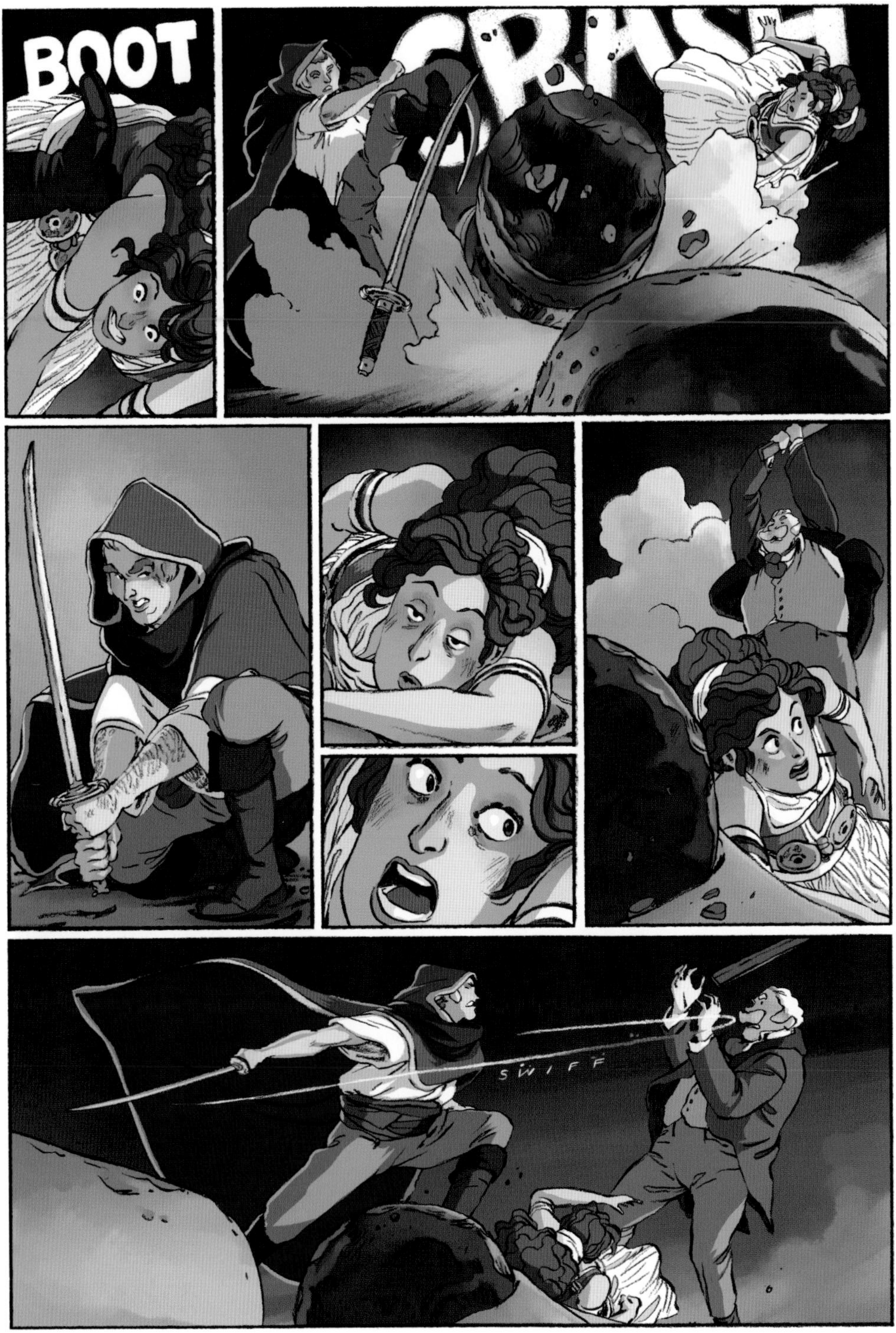
BOOT
CRASH
SWIFF

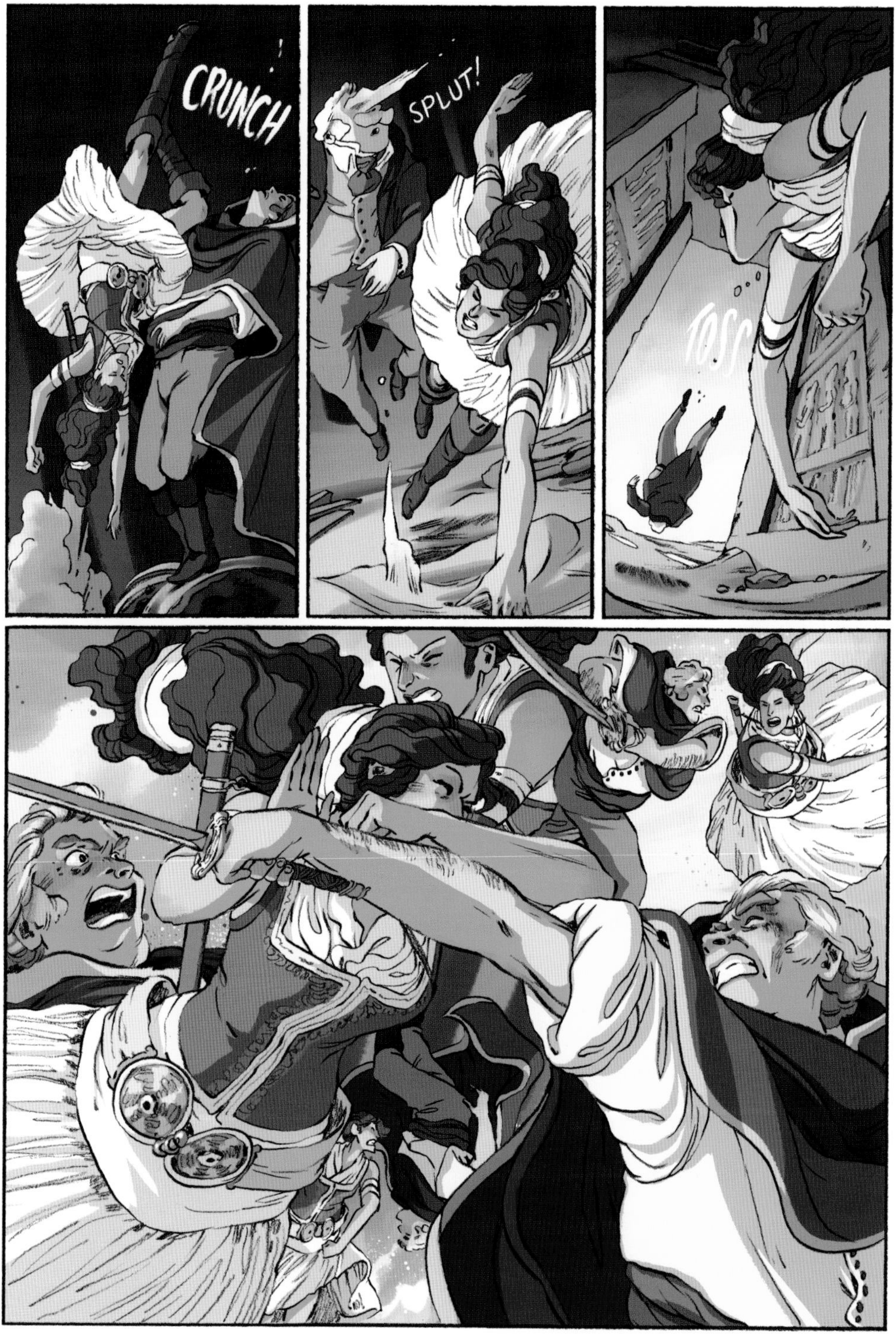
CRUNCH
SPLUT!
TOSS

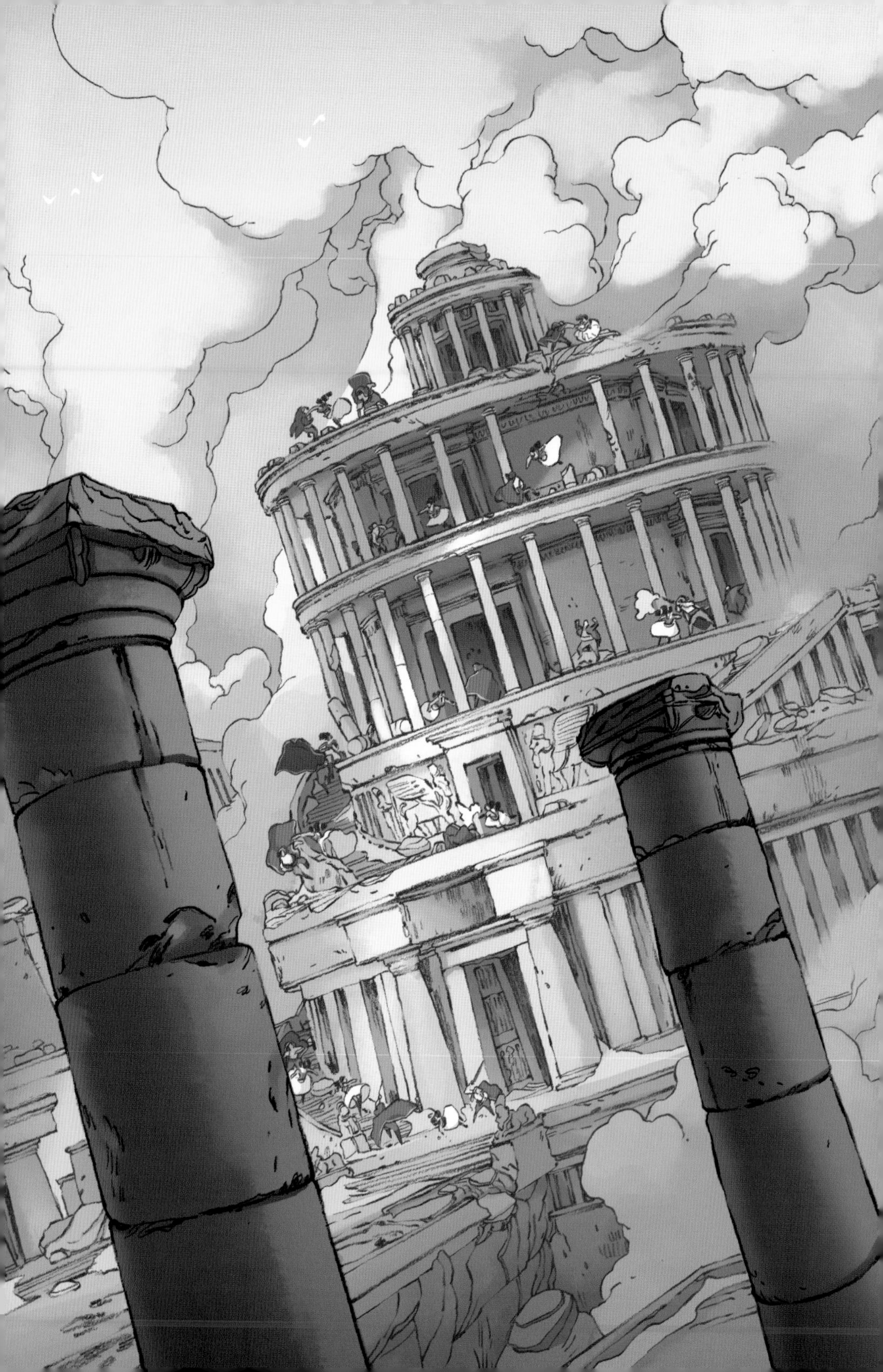

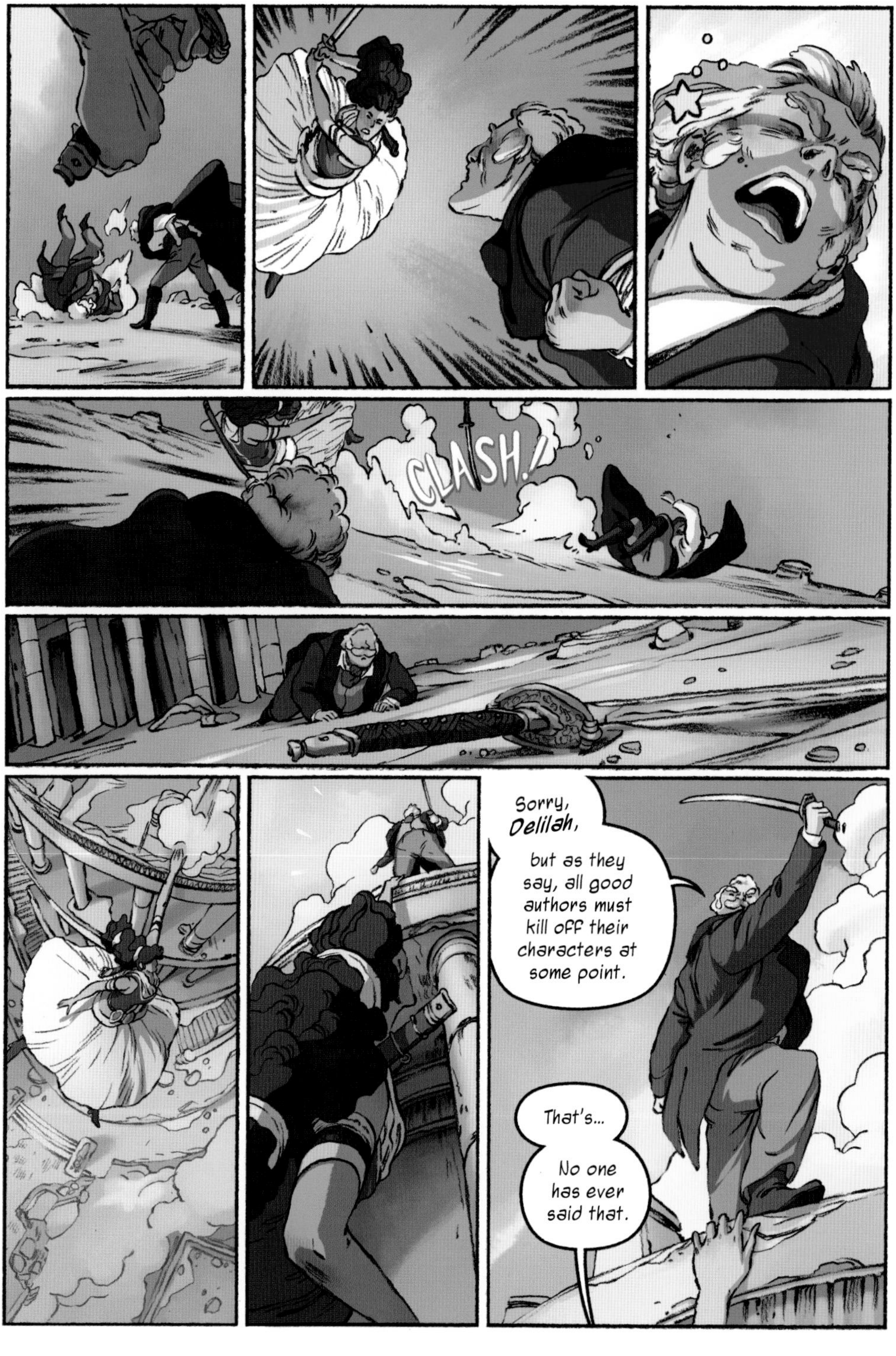
CLASH!!
Sorry, Delilah,
but as they say, all good authors must kill off their characters at some point.
That's...
No one has ever said that.

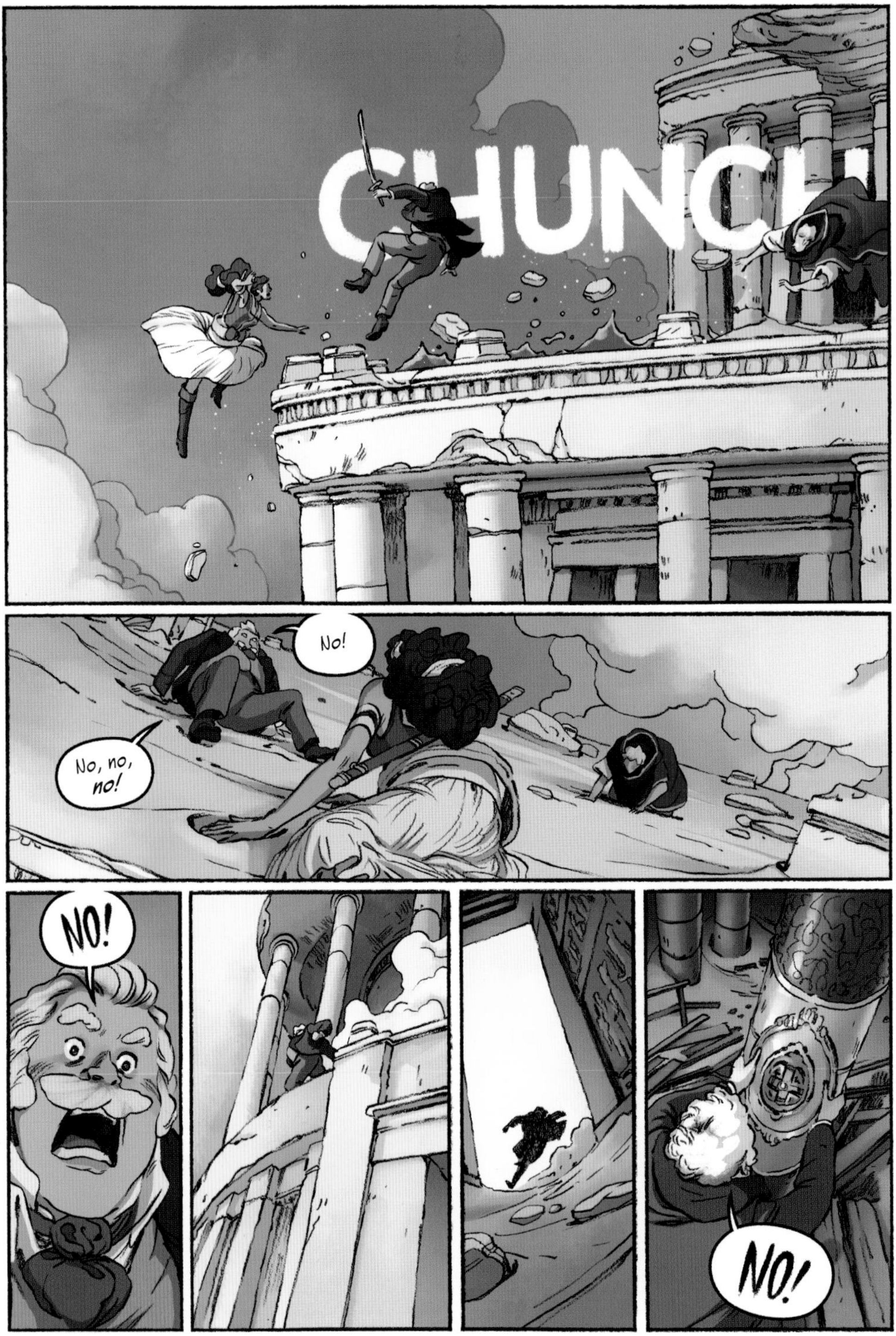
CHUNCH
No!
No, no, no!
NO!
NO!

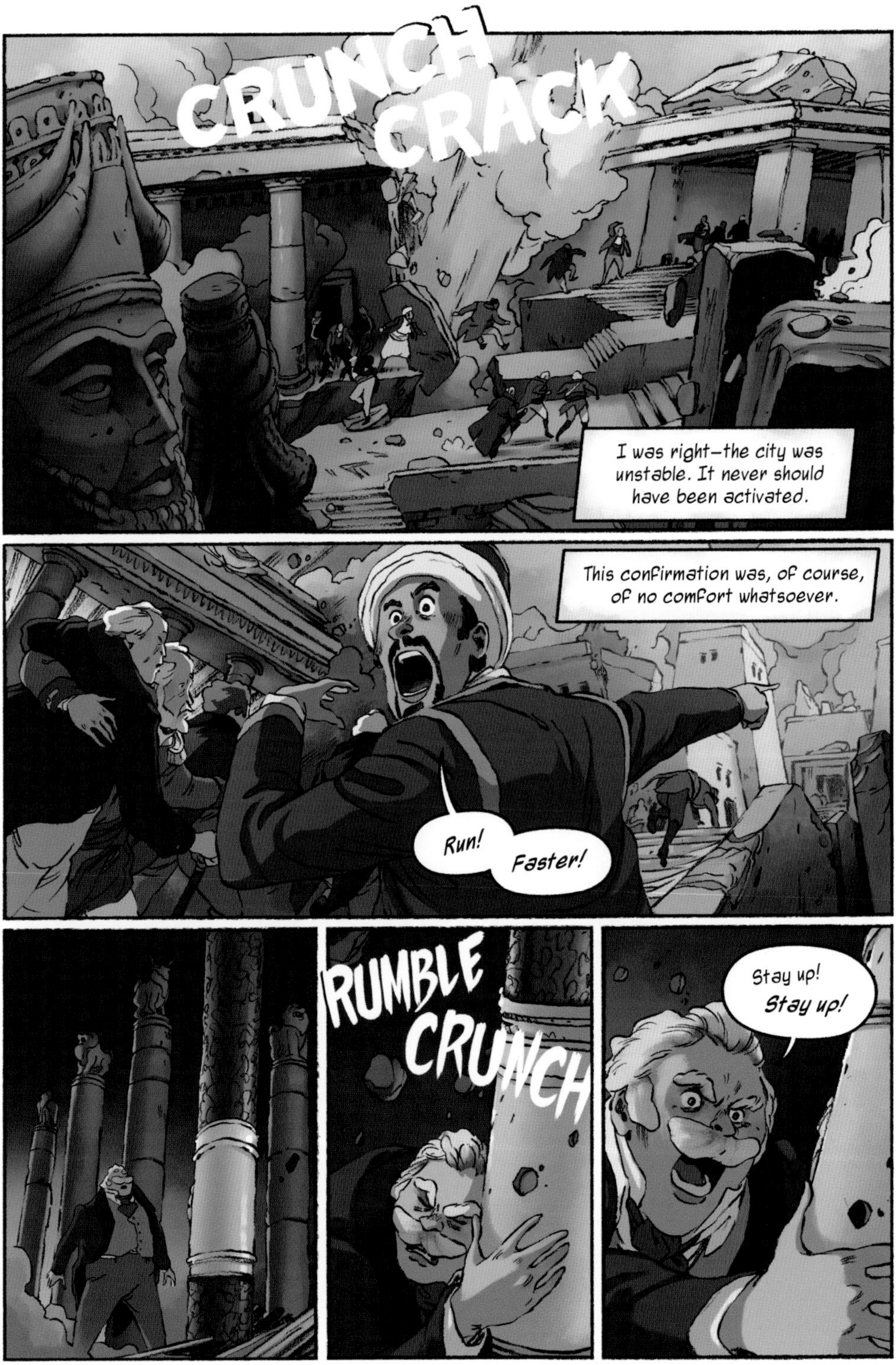
CRUNCH
CRACK
I was right—the city was unstable. It never should have been activated.
This confirmation was, of course, of no comfort whatsoever.
Run!
Faster!
RUMBLE
CRUNCH
Stay up!
Stay up!

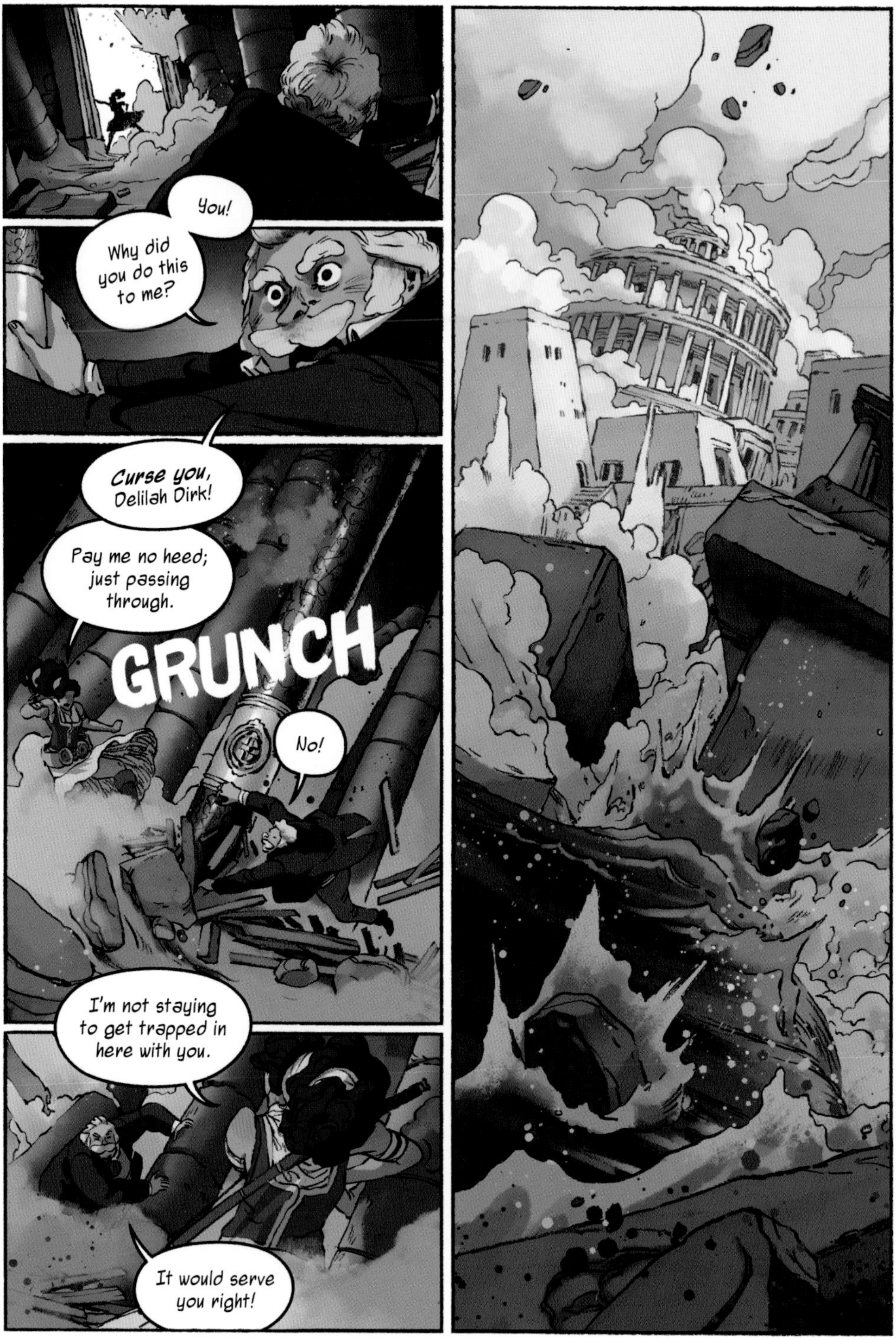
You!
Why did you do this to me?
Curse you, Delilah Dirk!
Pay me no heed; just passing through.
GRUNCH
No!
I'm not staying to get trapped in here with you.
It would serve you right!

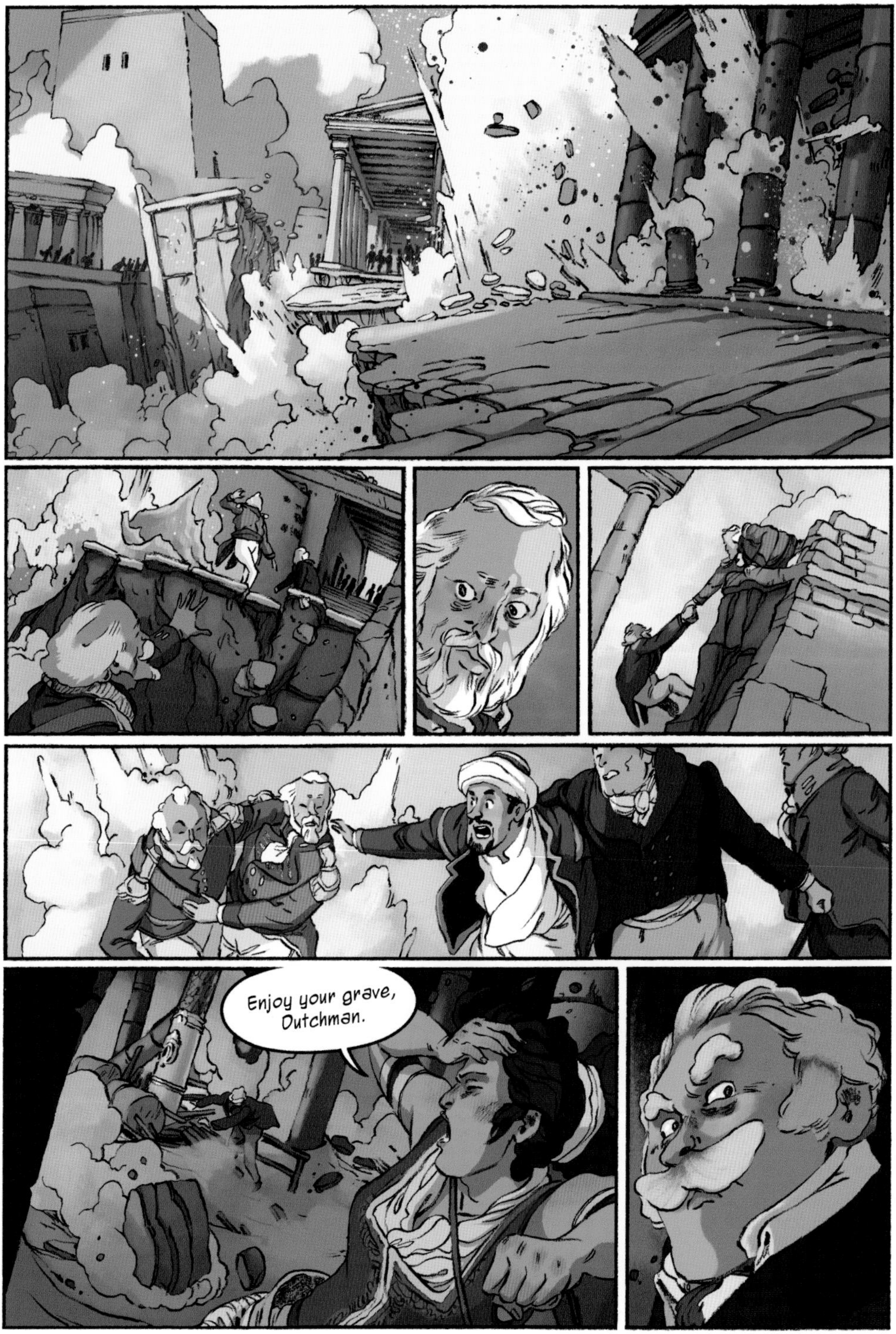
Enjoy your grave, Dutchman.

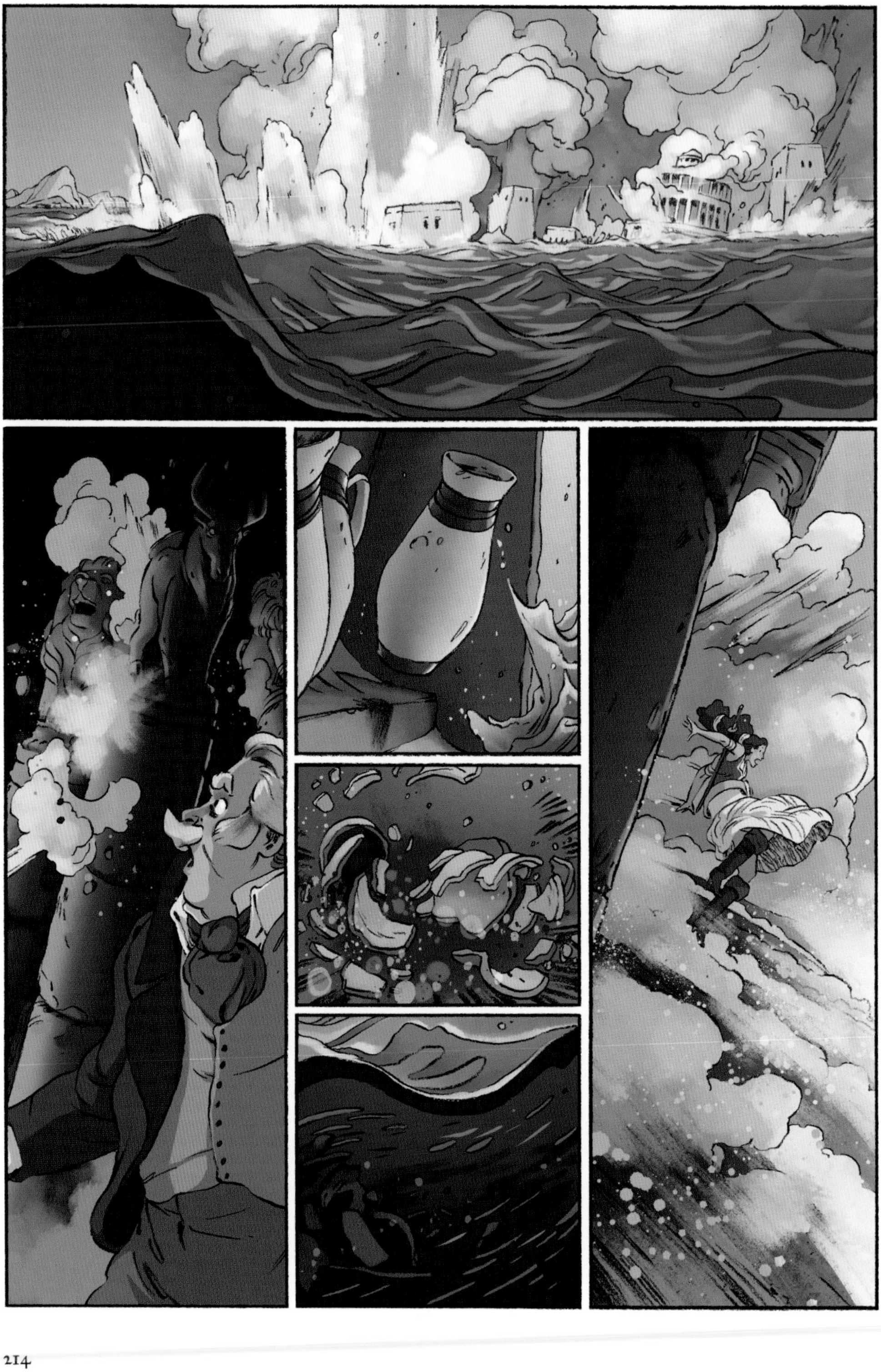

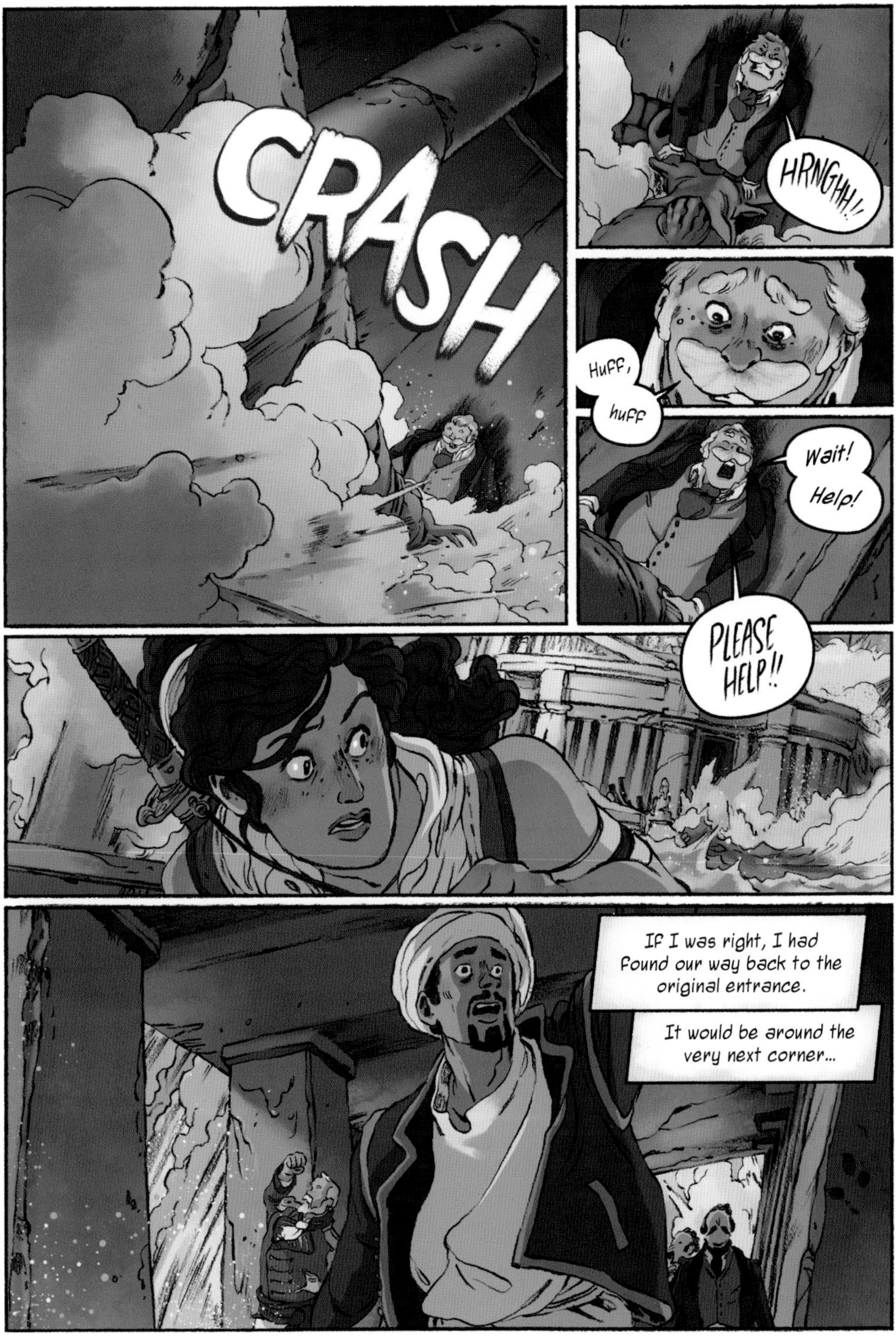
CRASH
HRNGHH!!
Huff,
huff
Wait!
Help!
PLEASE HELP!!
If I was right, I had found our way back to the original entrance.
It would be around the very next corner...

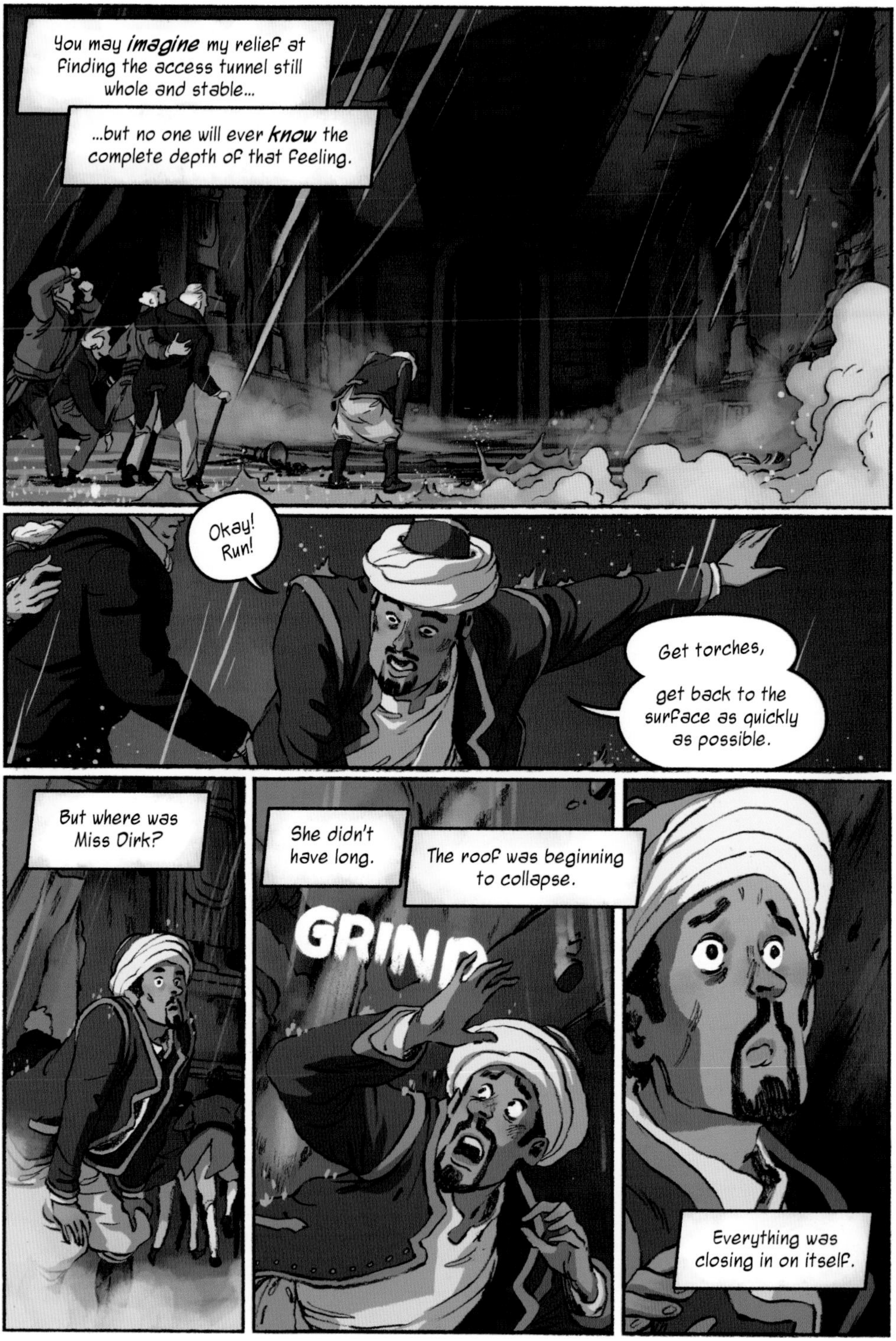
You may *imagine* my relief at finding the access tunnel still whole and stable...
...but no one will ever *know* the complete depth of that feeling.
Okay! Run!
Get torches,
get back to the surface as quickly as possible.
But where was Miss Dirk?
She didn't have long.
The roof was beginning to collapse.
GRIND
Everything was closing in on itself.

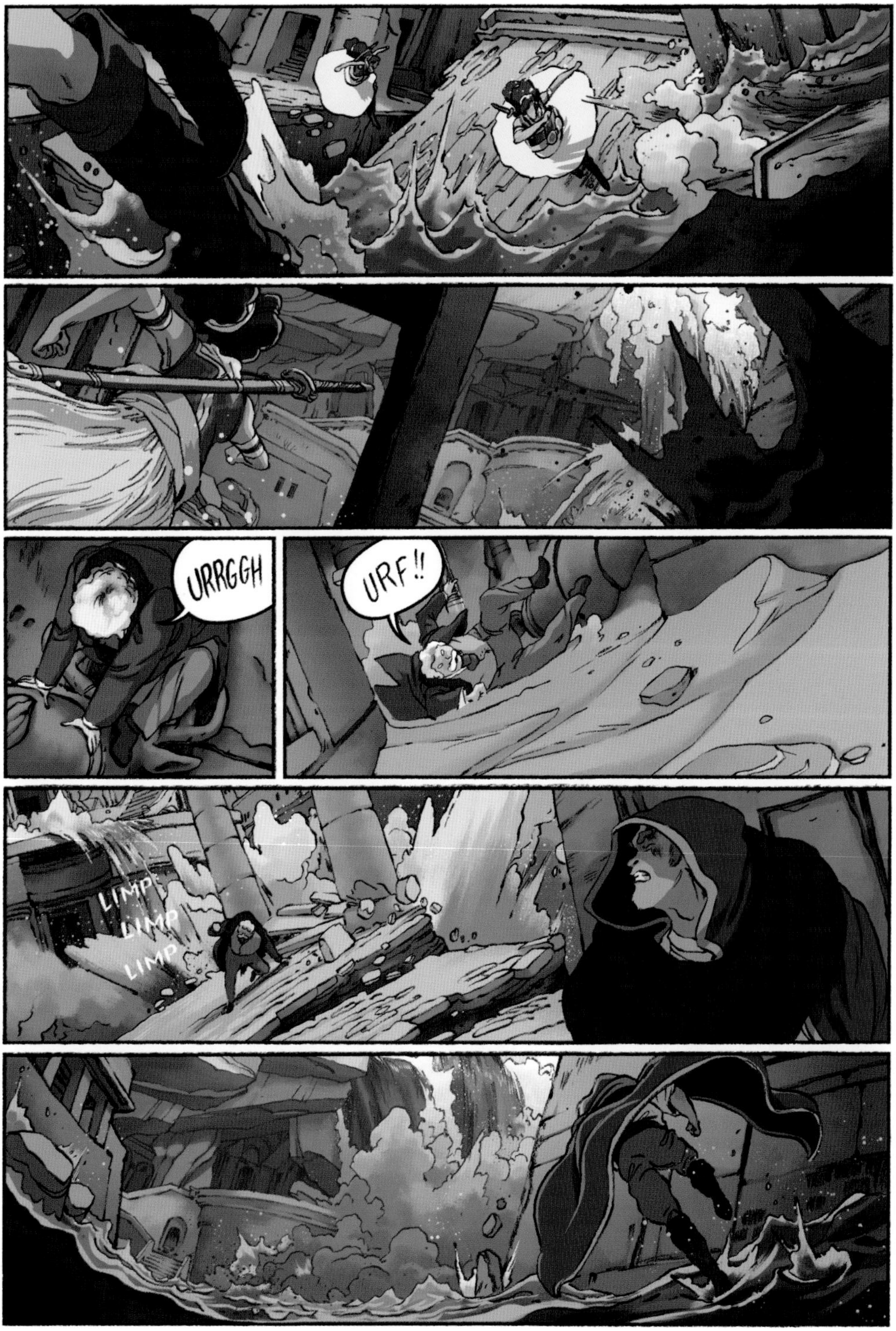
URRGGH
URF!!
LIMP
LIMP
LIMP

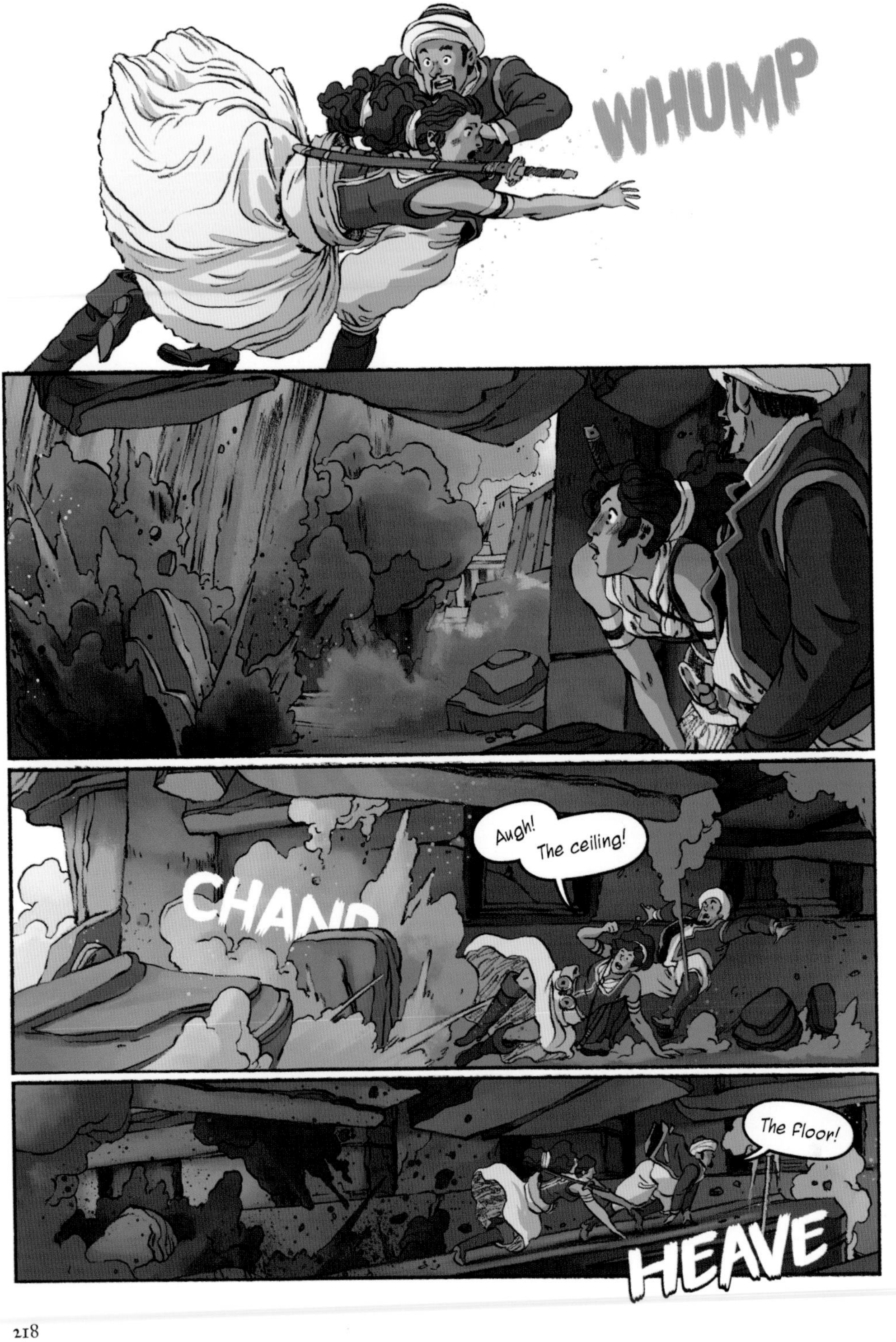
WHUMP
Augh!
The ceiling!
CHAND
The floor!
HEAVE

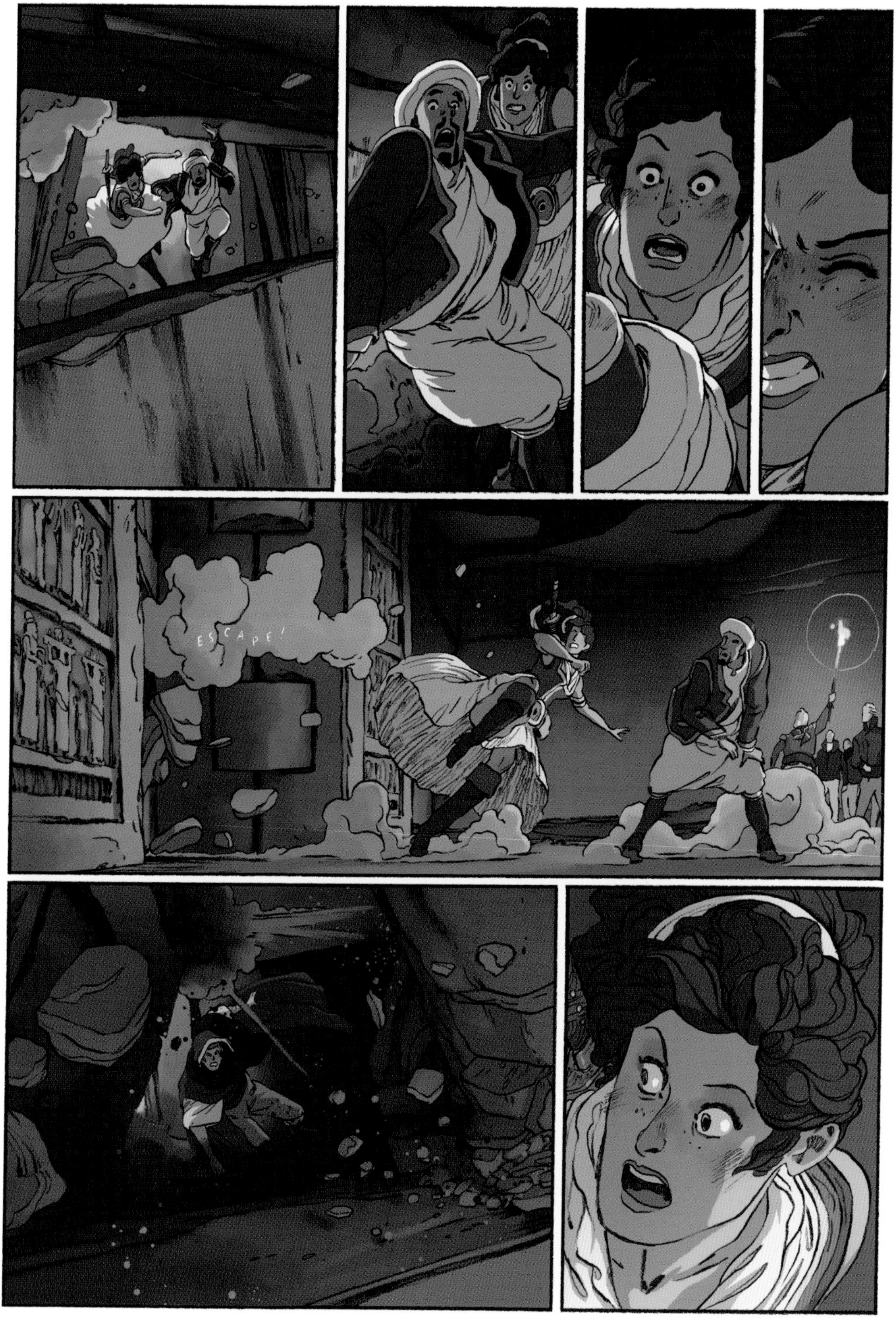
ESCAPE!

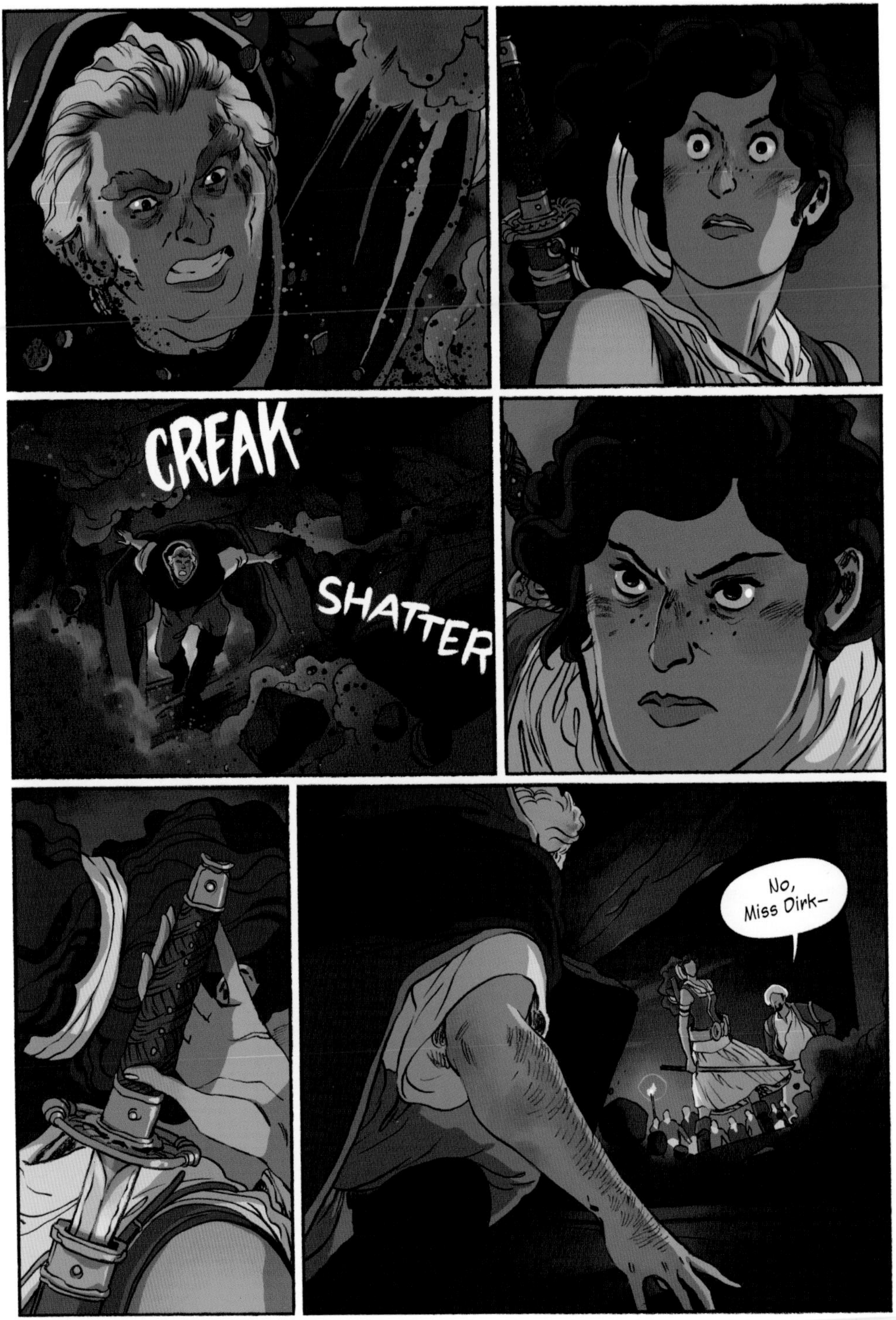
CREAK
SHATTER
No, Miss Dirk—

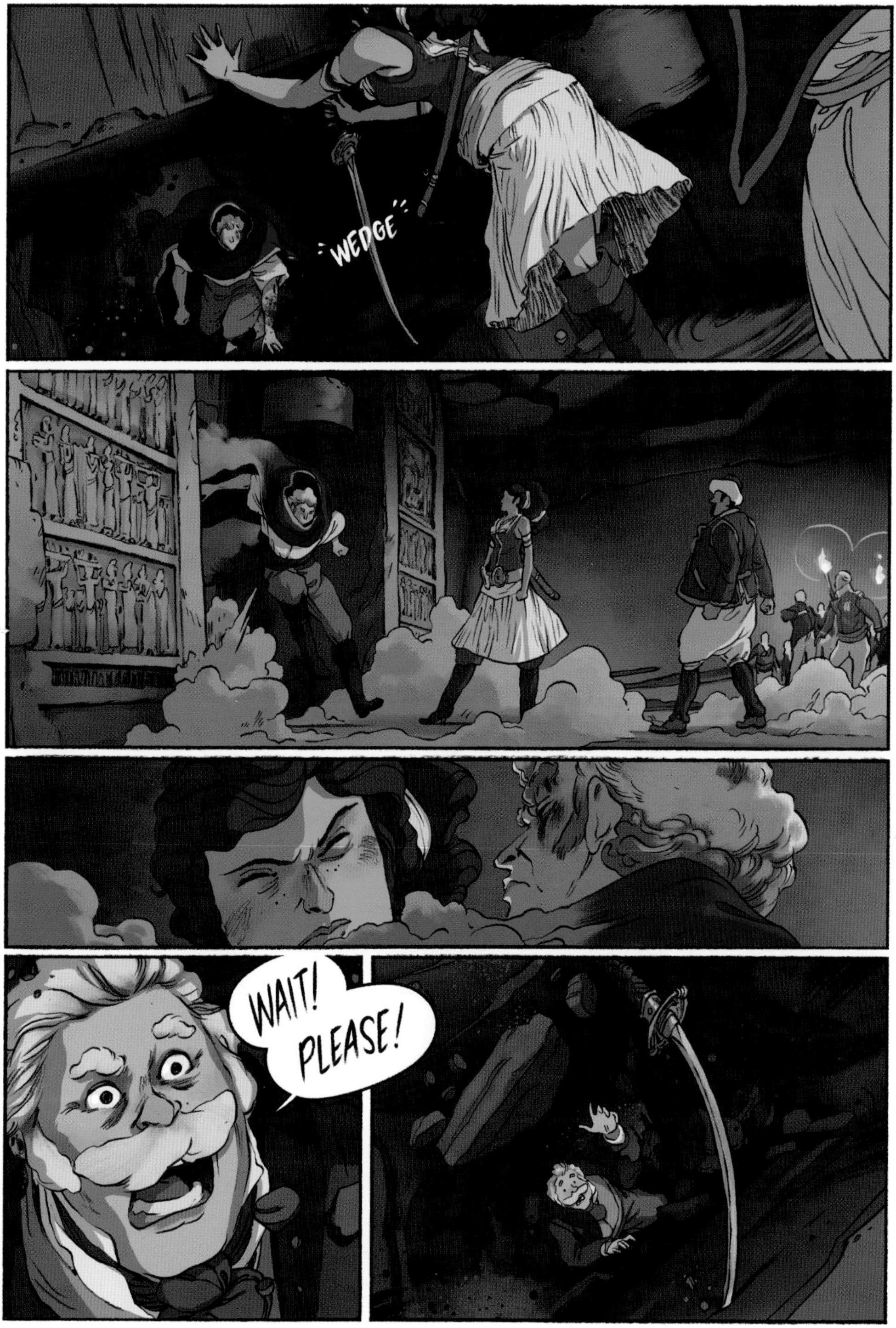
WEDGE
WAIT! PLEASE!

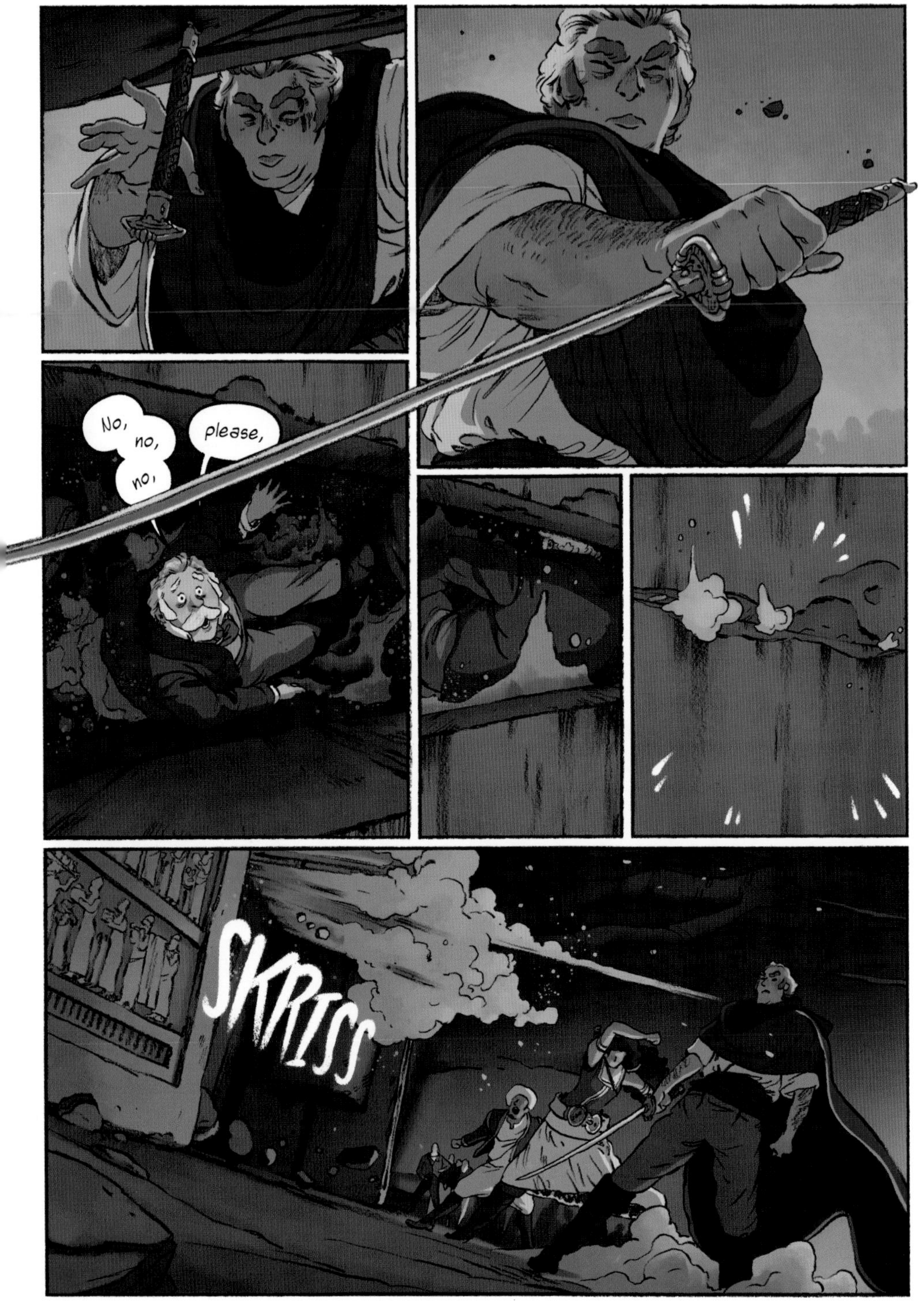
No,
no,
no,
please,
SKRISS

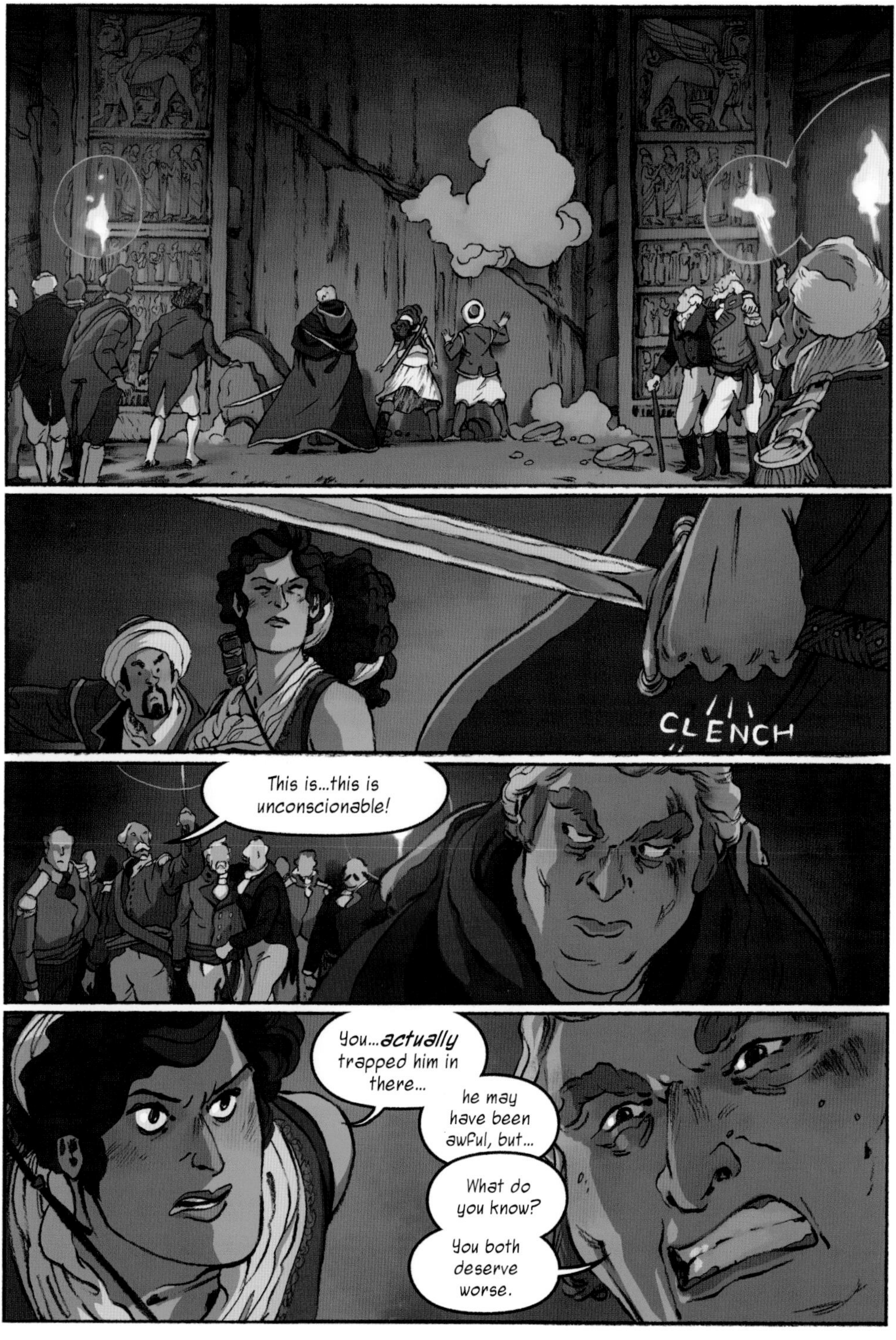
CLENCH
This is...this is unconscionable!
You...actually trapped him in there...
he may have been awful, but...
What do you know?
You both deserve worse.

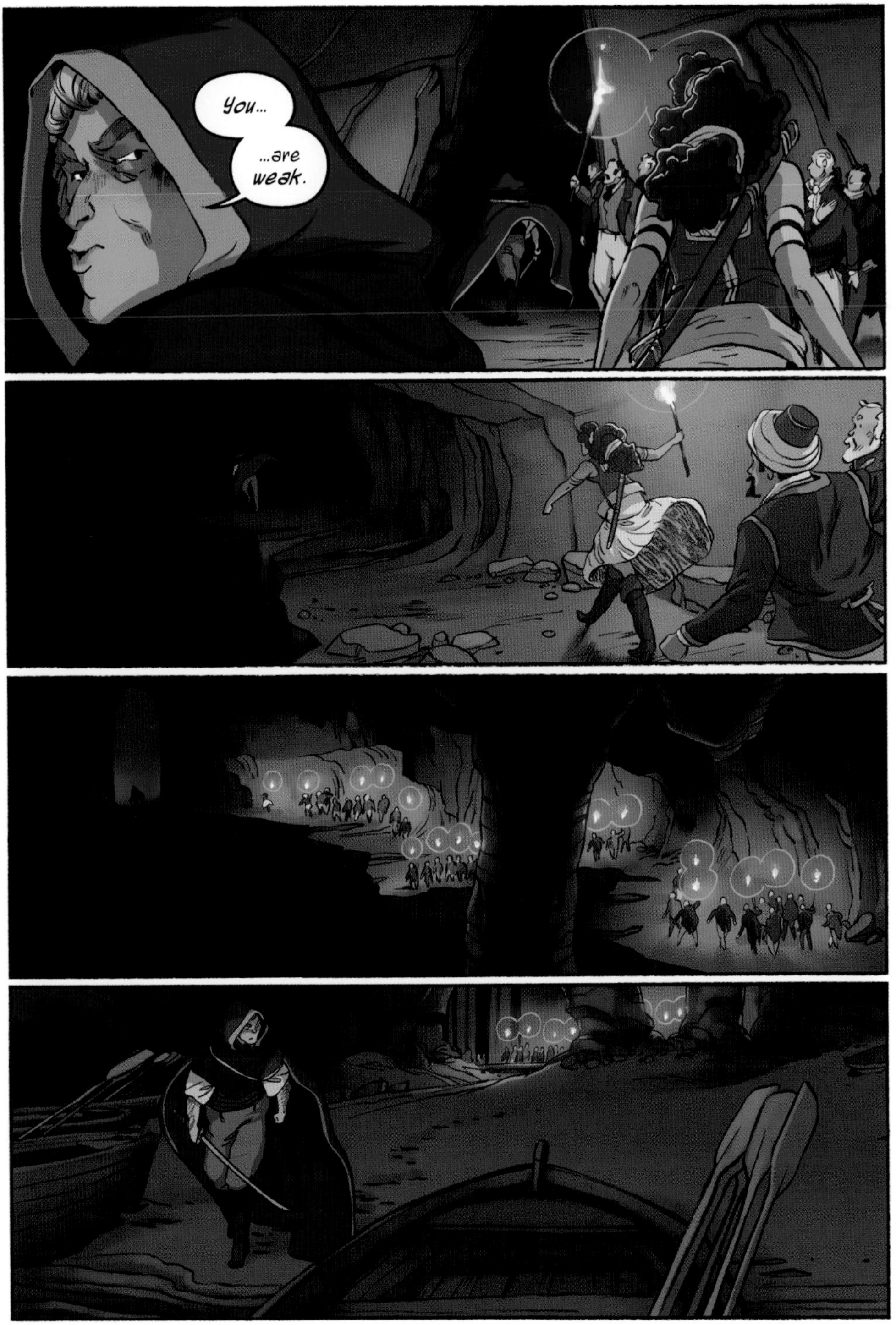
You...
...are weak.

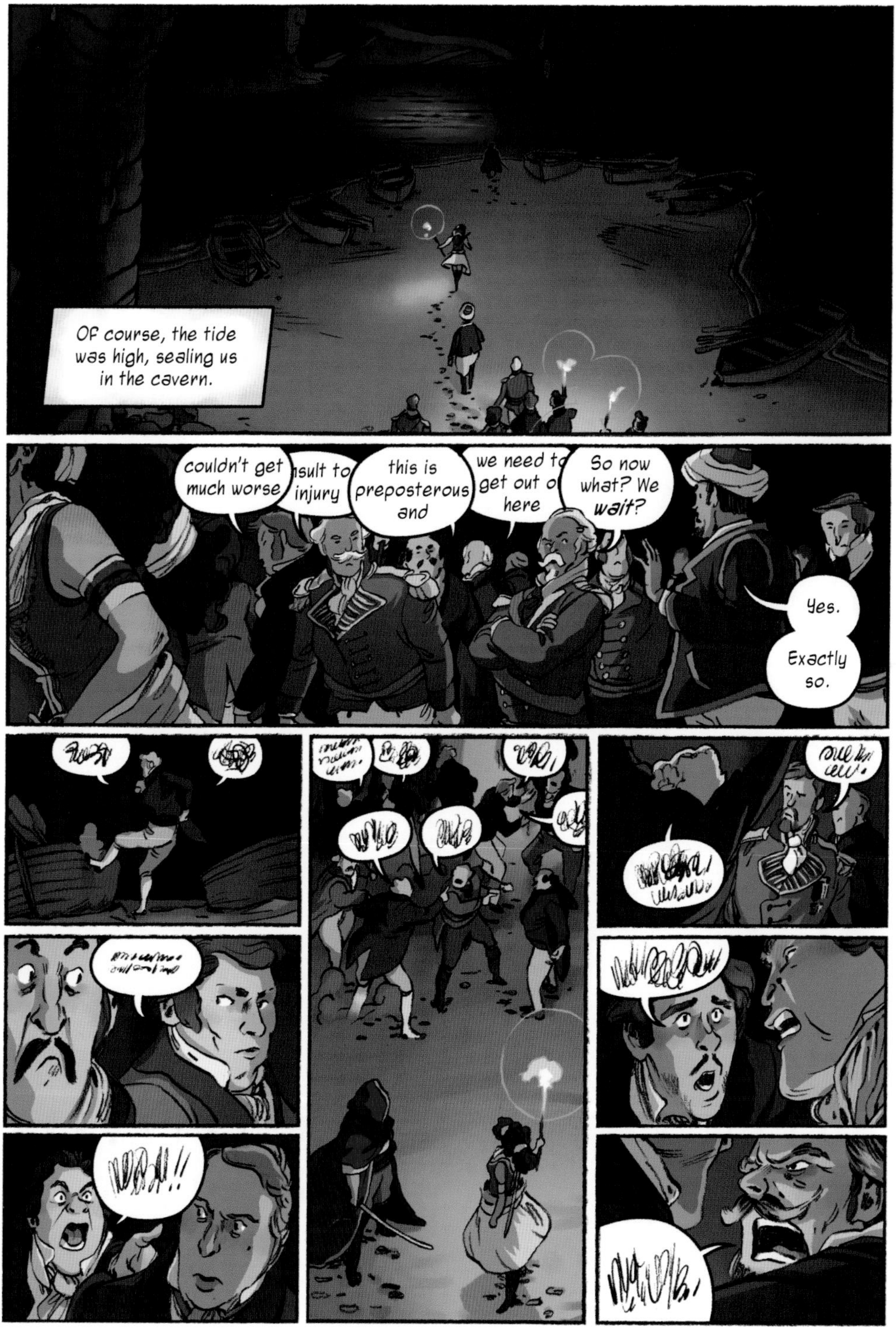

Of course, the tide was high, sealing us in the cavern.
couldn't get much worse
nsult to injury
this is preposterous and
we need to get out o here
So now what? We *wait?*
Yes.
Exactly so.

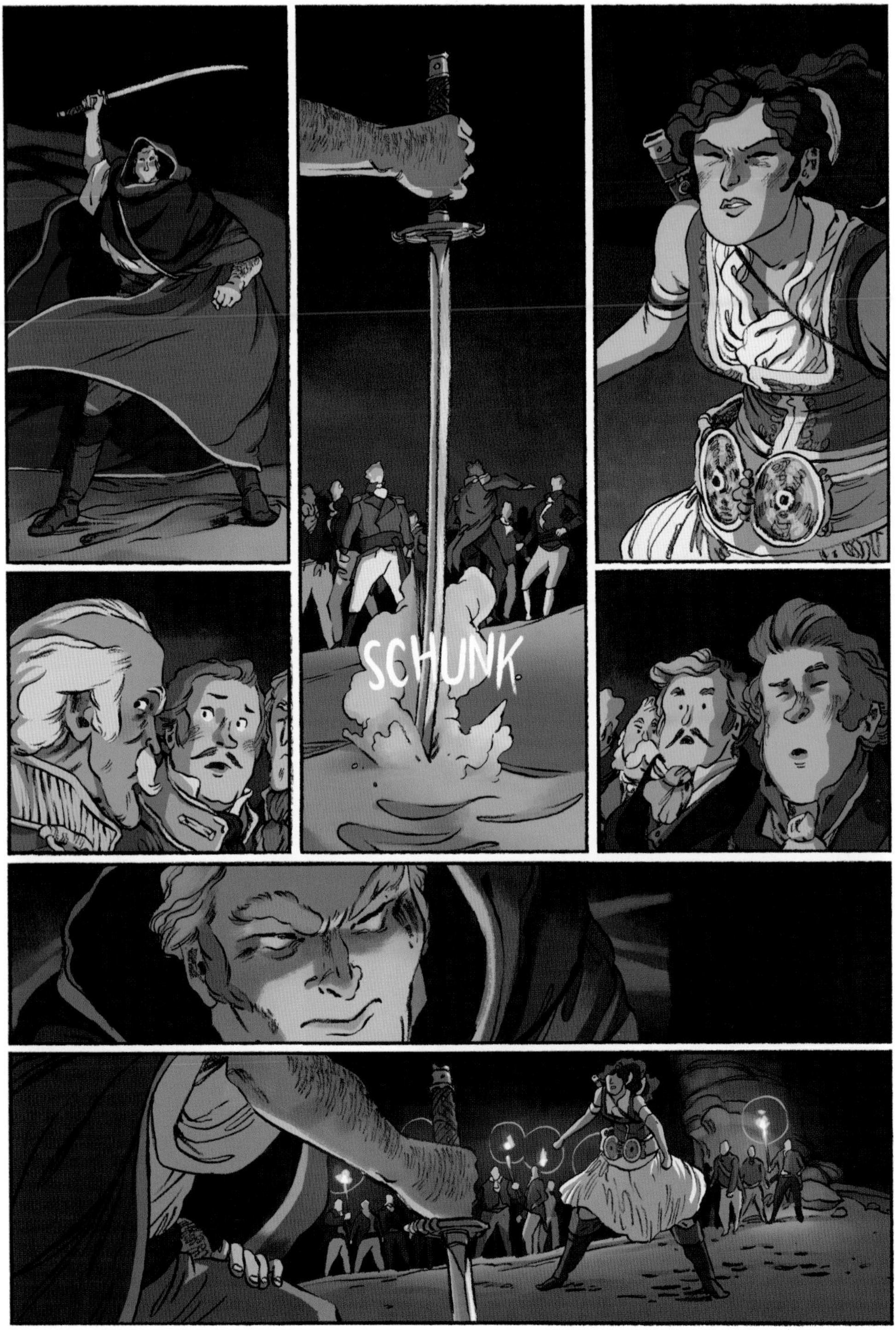
SCHUNK

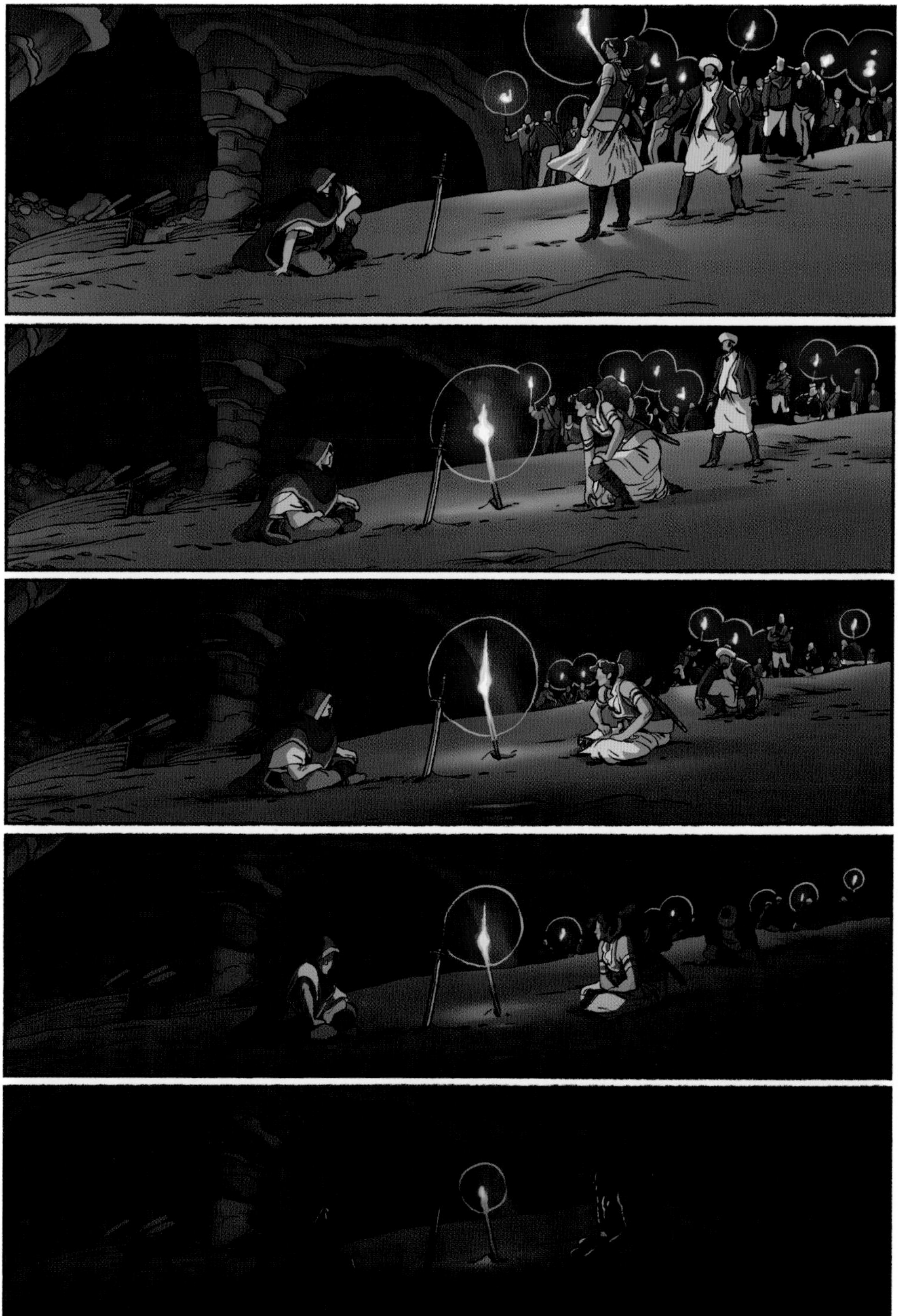

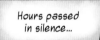

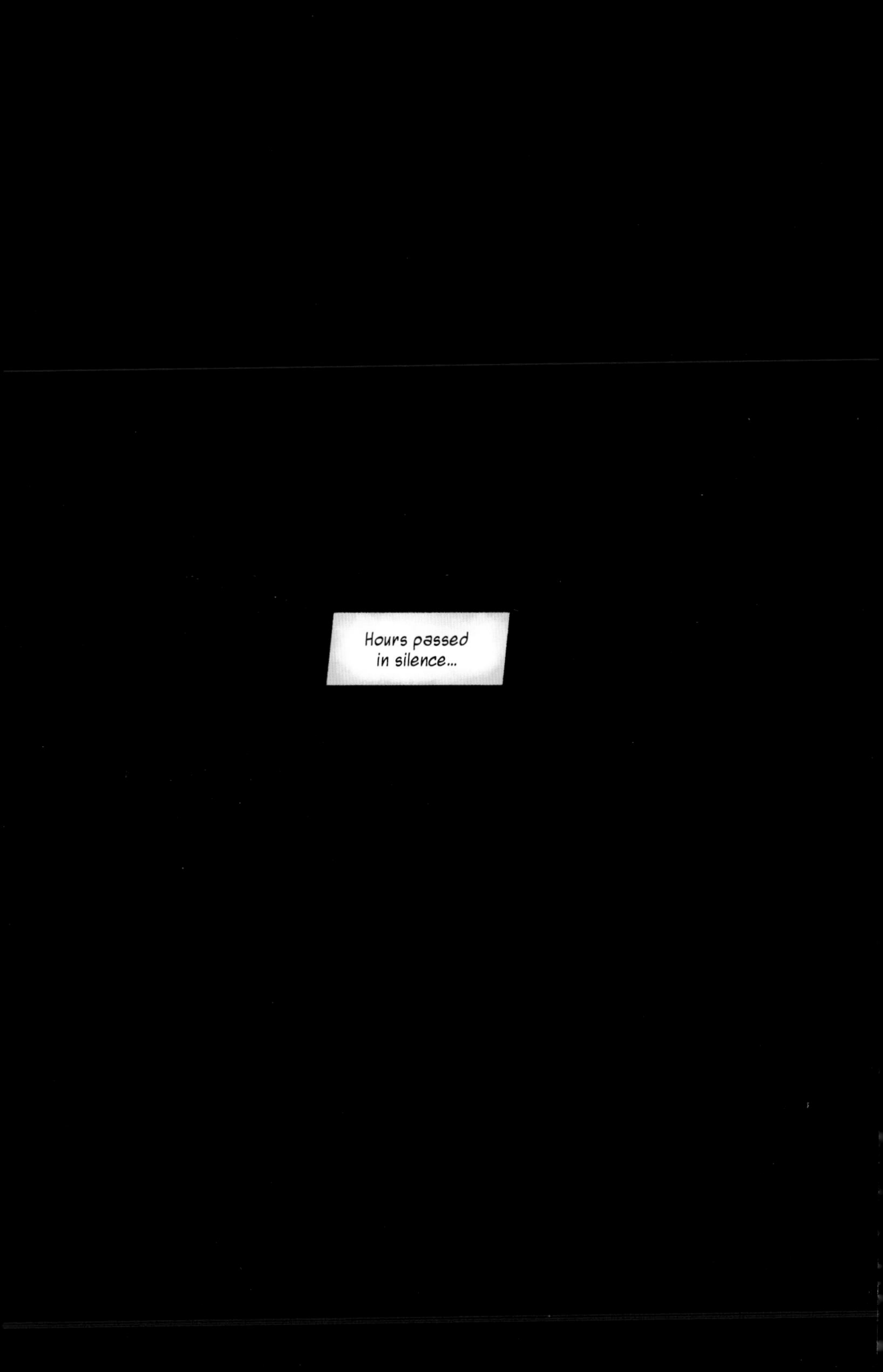

Hours passed
in silence...

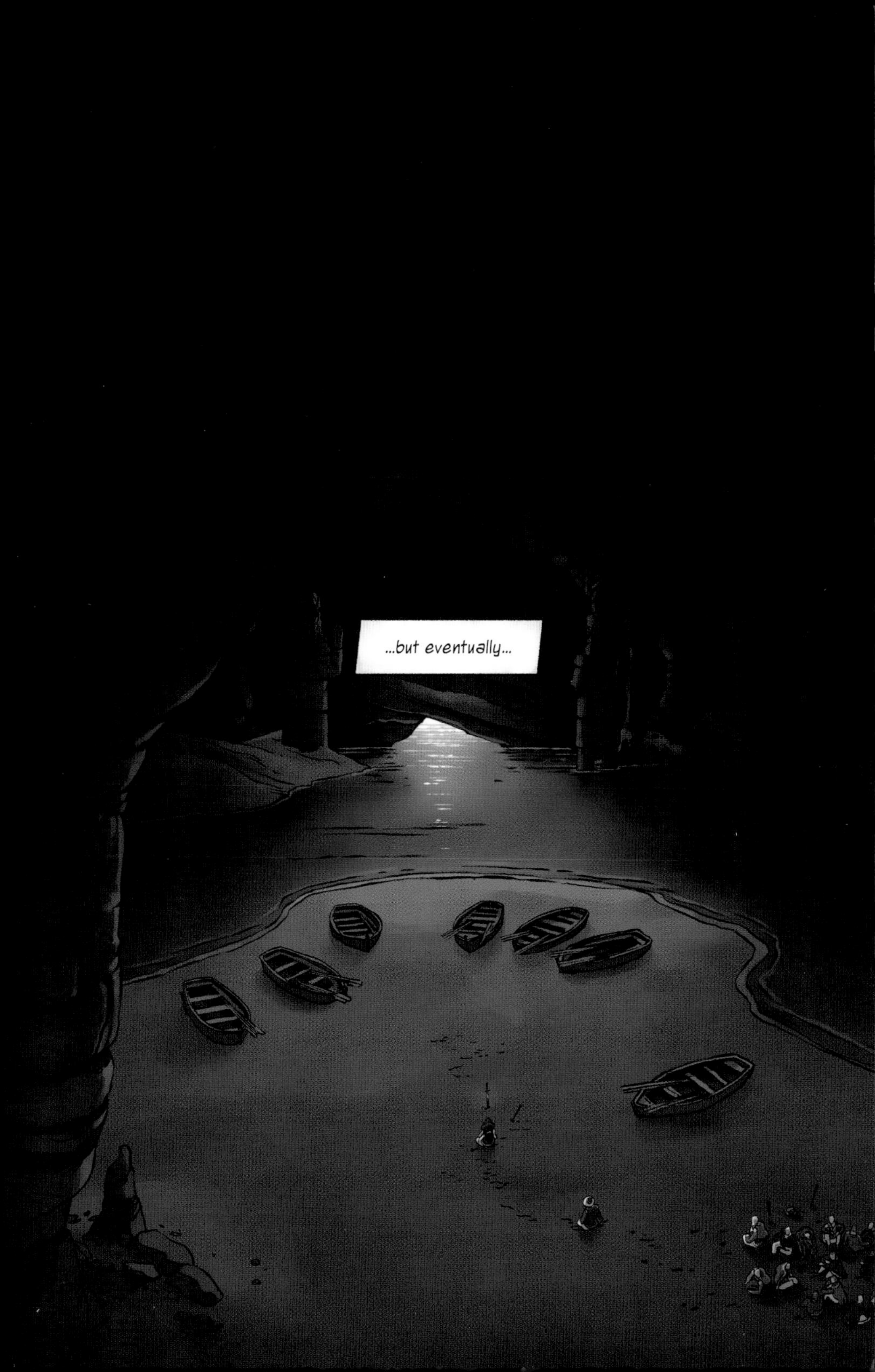
...but eventually...

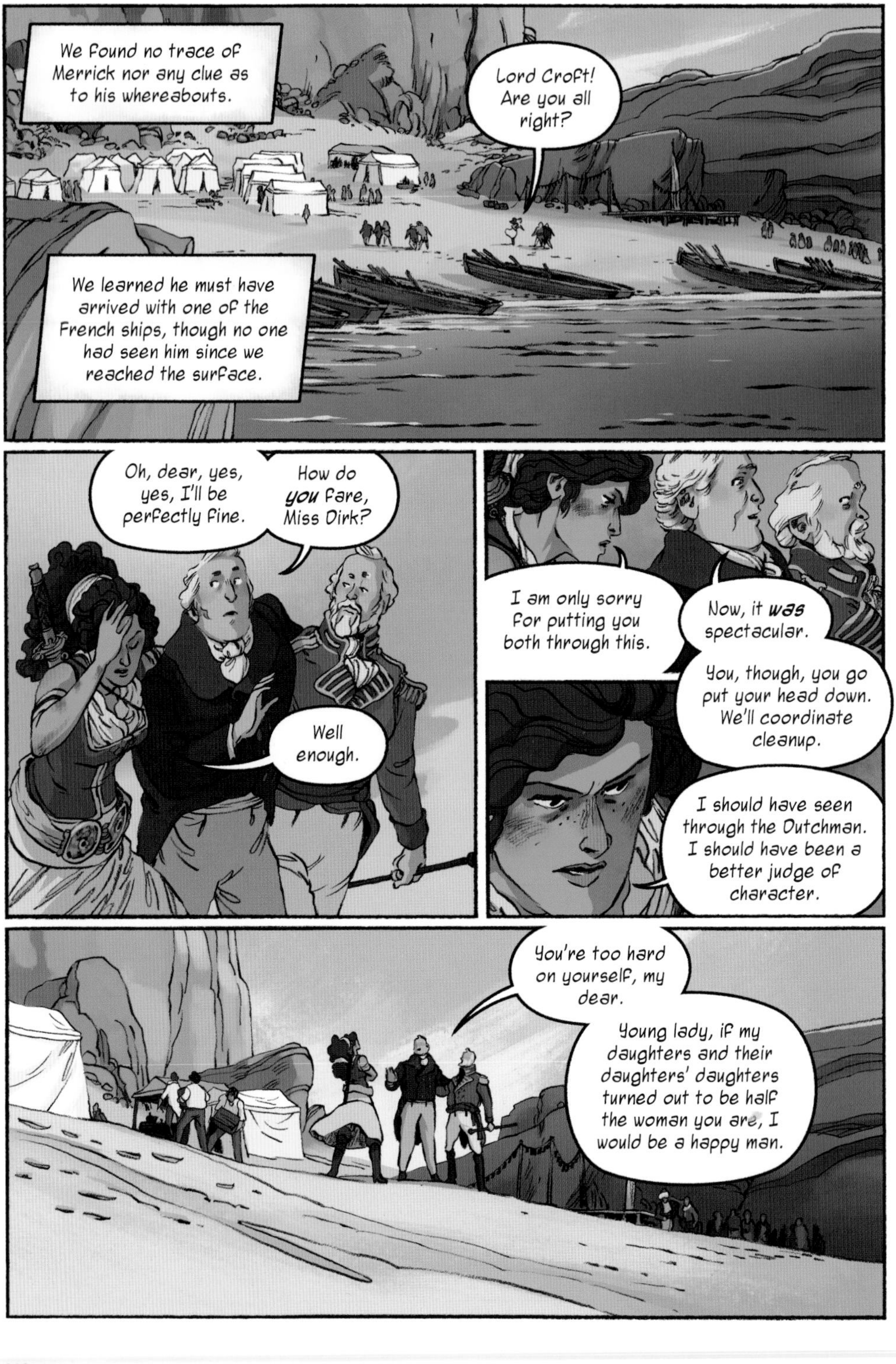
We found no trace of Merrick nor any clue as to his whereabouts.
Lord Croft! Are you all right?
We learned he must have arrived with one of the French ships, though no one had seen him since we reached the surface.
Oh, dear, yes, yes, I'll be perfectly fine.
How do *you* fare, Miss Dirk?
Well enough.
I am only sorry for putting you both through this.
Now, it *was* spectacular.
You, though, you go put your head down. We'll coordinate cleanup.
I should have seen through the Dutchman. I should have been a better judge of character.
You're too hard on yourself, my dear.
Young lady, if my daughters and their daughters' daughters turned out to be half the woman you are, I would be a happy man.

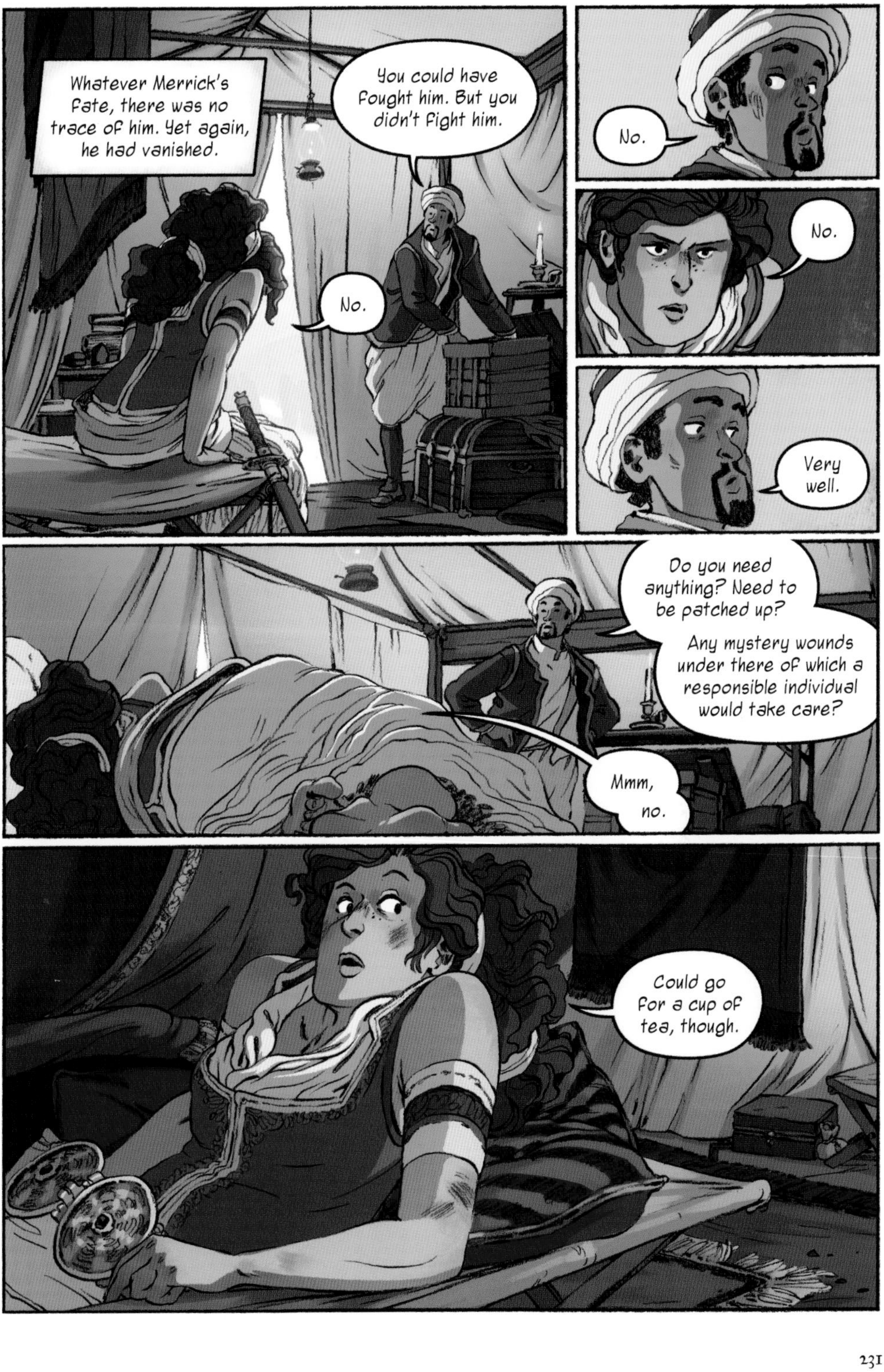
Whatever Merrick's fate, there was no trace of him. Yet again, he had vanished.
You could have fought him. But you didn't fight him.
No.
No.
No.
Very well.
Do you need anything? Need to be patched up?
Any mystery wounds under there of which a responsible individual would take care?
Mmm, no.
Could go for a cup of tea, though.

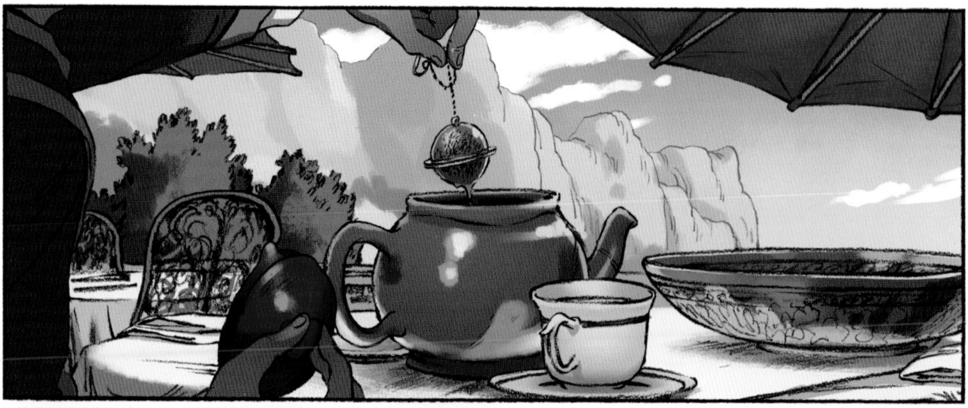

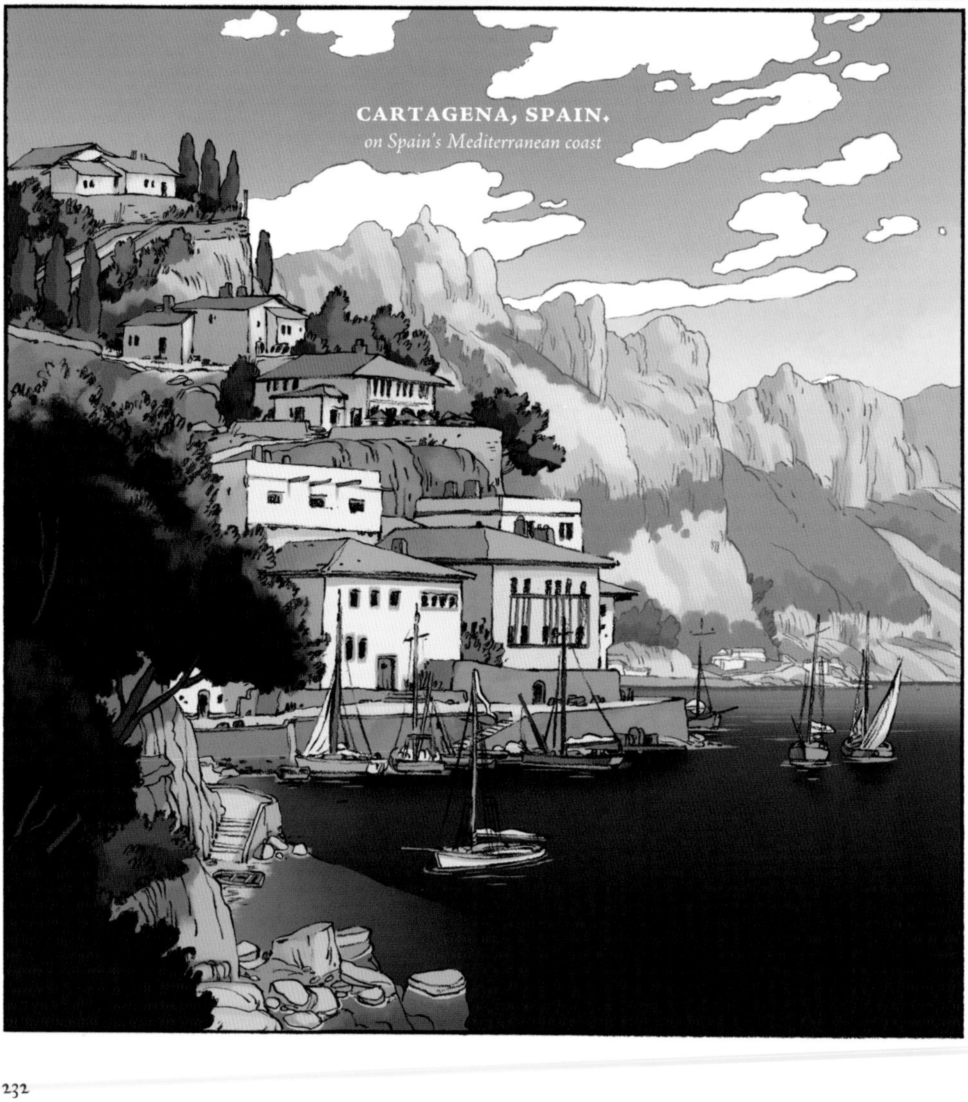
CARTAGENA, SPAIN.
on Spain's Mediterranean coast

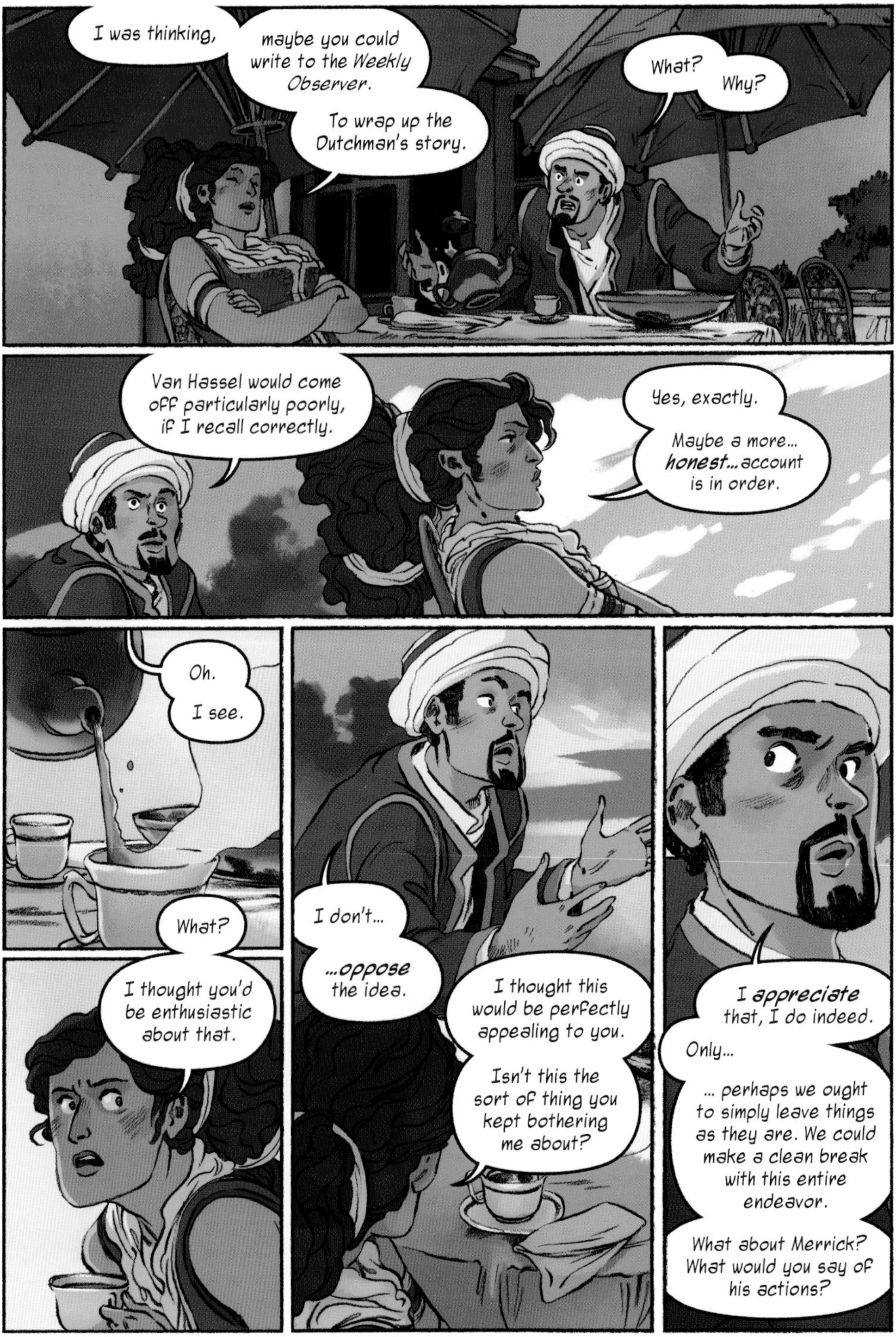
I was thinking,
maybe you could write to the *Weekly Observer*.
To wrap up the Dutchman's story.
What?
Why?
Van Hassel would come off particularly poorly, if I recall correctly.
Yes, exactly.
Maybe a more... ***honest...*** account is in order.
Oh.
I see.
What?
I thought you'd be enthusiastic about that.
I don't...
***...oppose*** the idea.
I thought this would be perfectly appealing to you.
Isn't this the sort of thing you kept bothering me about?
I ***appreciate*** that, I do indeed.
Only...
... perhaps we ought to simply leave things as they are. We could make a clean break with this entire endeavor.
What about Merrick? What would you say of his actions?

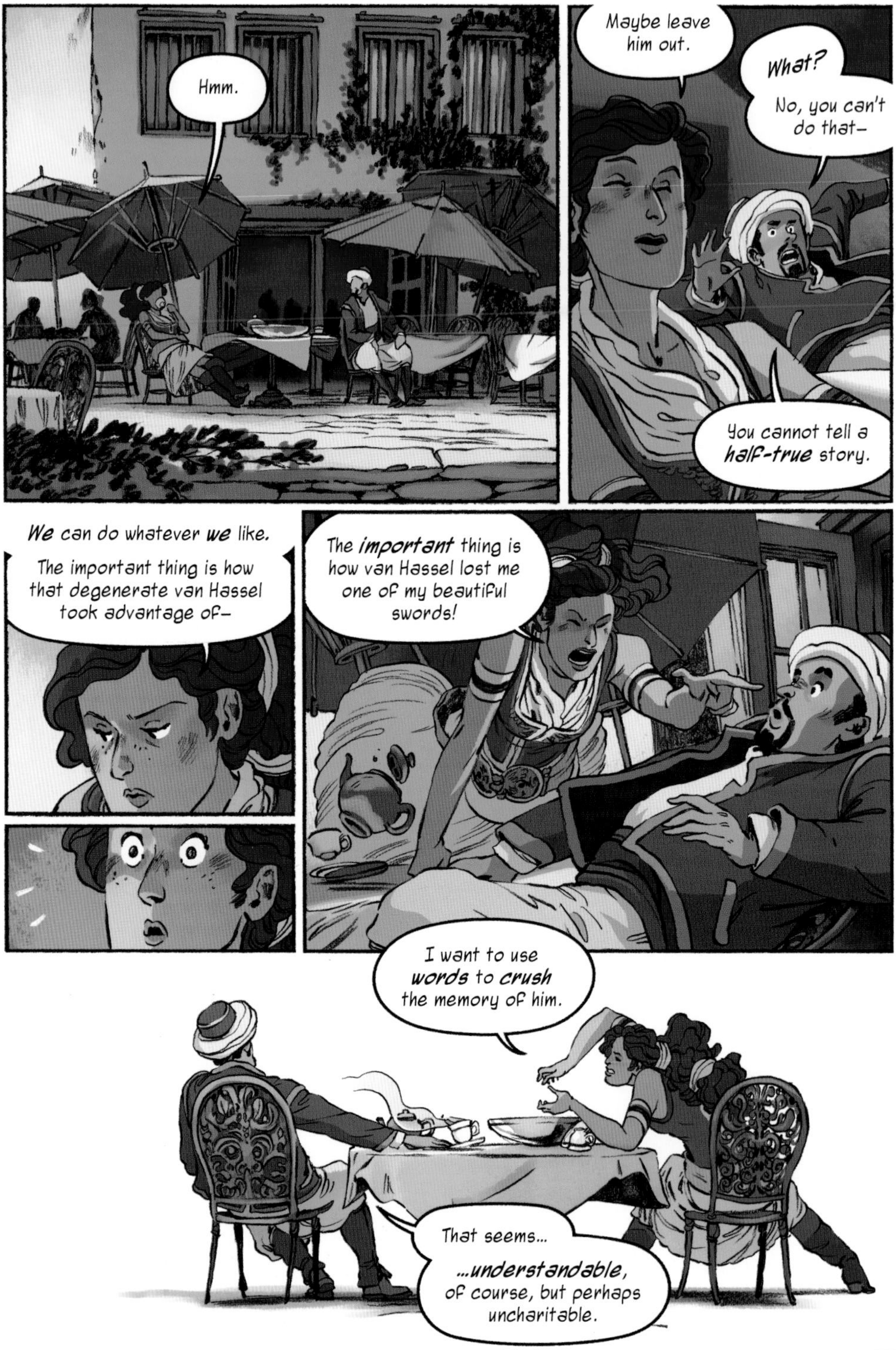
Hmm.
Maybe leave him out.
What? No, you can't do that—
You cannot tell a half-true story.
We can do whatever we like. The important thing is how that degenerate van Hassel took advantage of—
The important thing is how van Hassel lost me one of my beautiful swords!
I want to use words to crush the memory of him.
That seems... ...understandable, of course, but perhaps uncharitable.

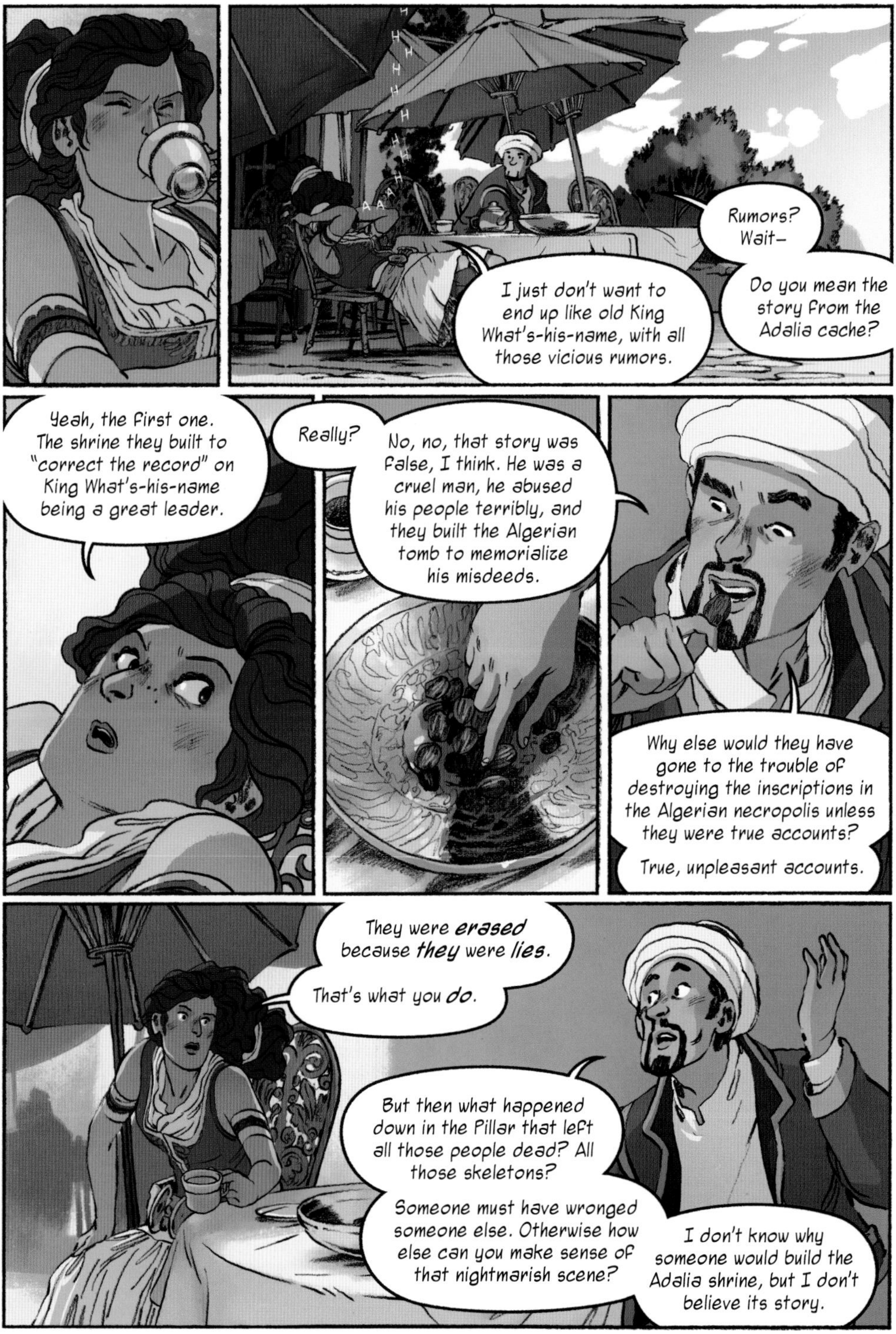

HHHHHHHHAAA
Rumors? Wait—
I just don't want to end up like old King What's-his-name, with all those vicious rumors.
Do you mean the story from the Adalia cache?
Yeah, the first one. The shrine they built to "correct the record" on King What's-his-name being a great leader.
Really?
No, no, that story was false, I think. He was a cruel man, he abused his people terribly, and they built the Algerian tomb to memorialize his misdeeds.
Why else would they have gone to the trouble of destroying the inscriptions in the Algerian necropolis unless they were true accounts?
True, unpleasant accounts.
They were *erased* because *they* were *lies*.
That's what you *do*.
But then what happened down in the Pillar that left all those people dead? All those skeletons?
Someone must have wronged someone else. Otherwise how else can you make sense of that nightmarish scene?
I don't know why someone would build the Adalia shrine, but I don't believe its story.

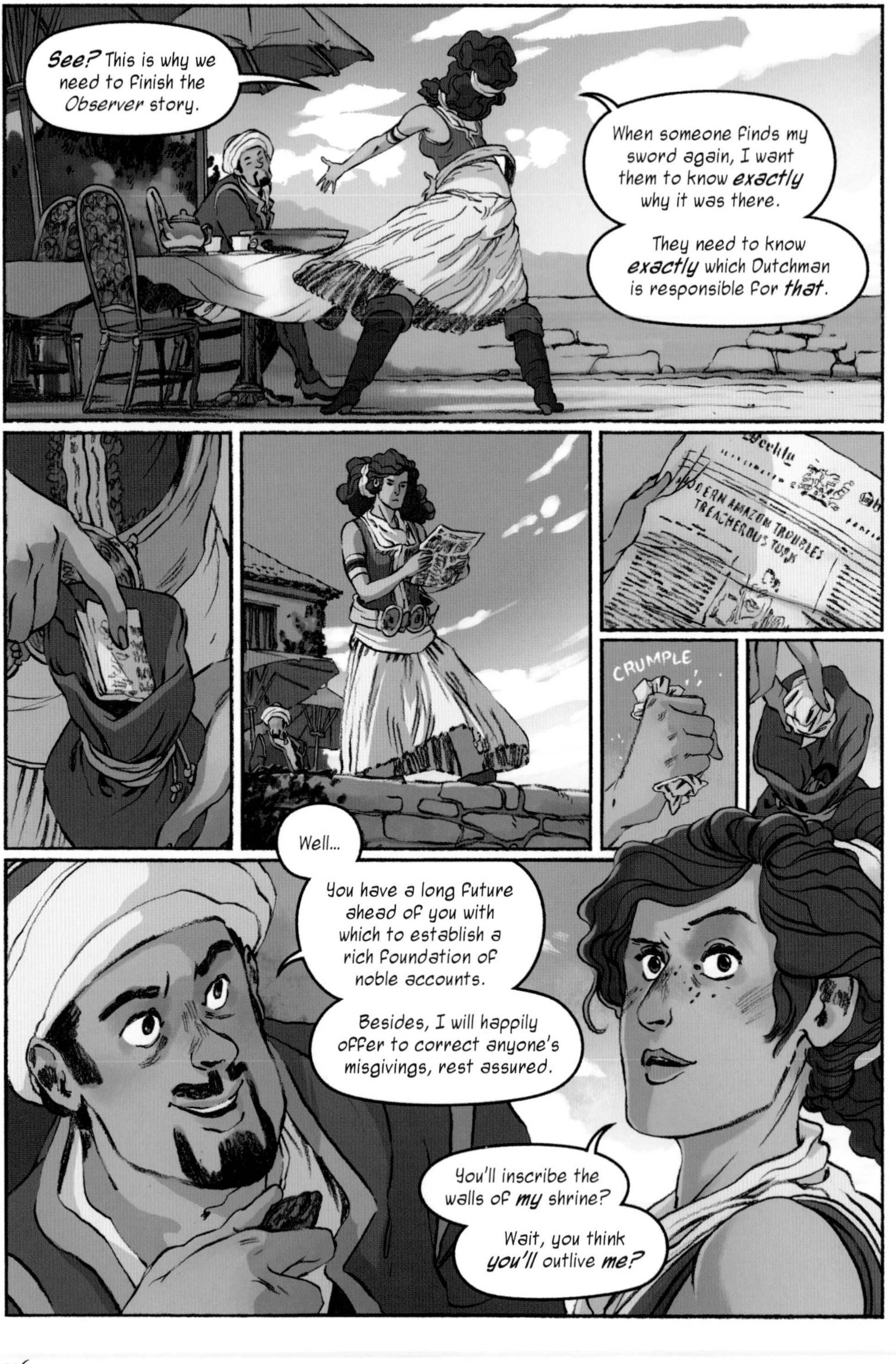

See? This is why we need to finish the Observer story.
When someone finds my sword again, I want them to know exactly why it was there.
They need to know exactly which Dutchman is responsible for that.
ODERN AMAZON TROUBLES
TREACHEROUS TURK
CRUMPLE
Well...
You have a long future ahead of you with which to establish a rich foundation of noble accounts.
Besides, I will happily offer to correct anyone's misgivings, rest assured.
You'll inscribe the walls of my shrine?
Wait, you think you'll outlive me?

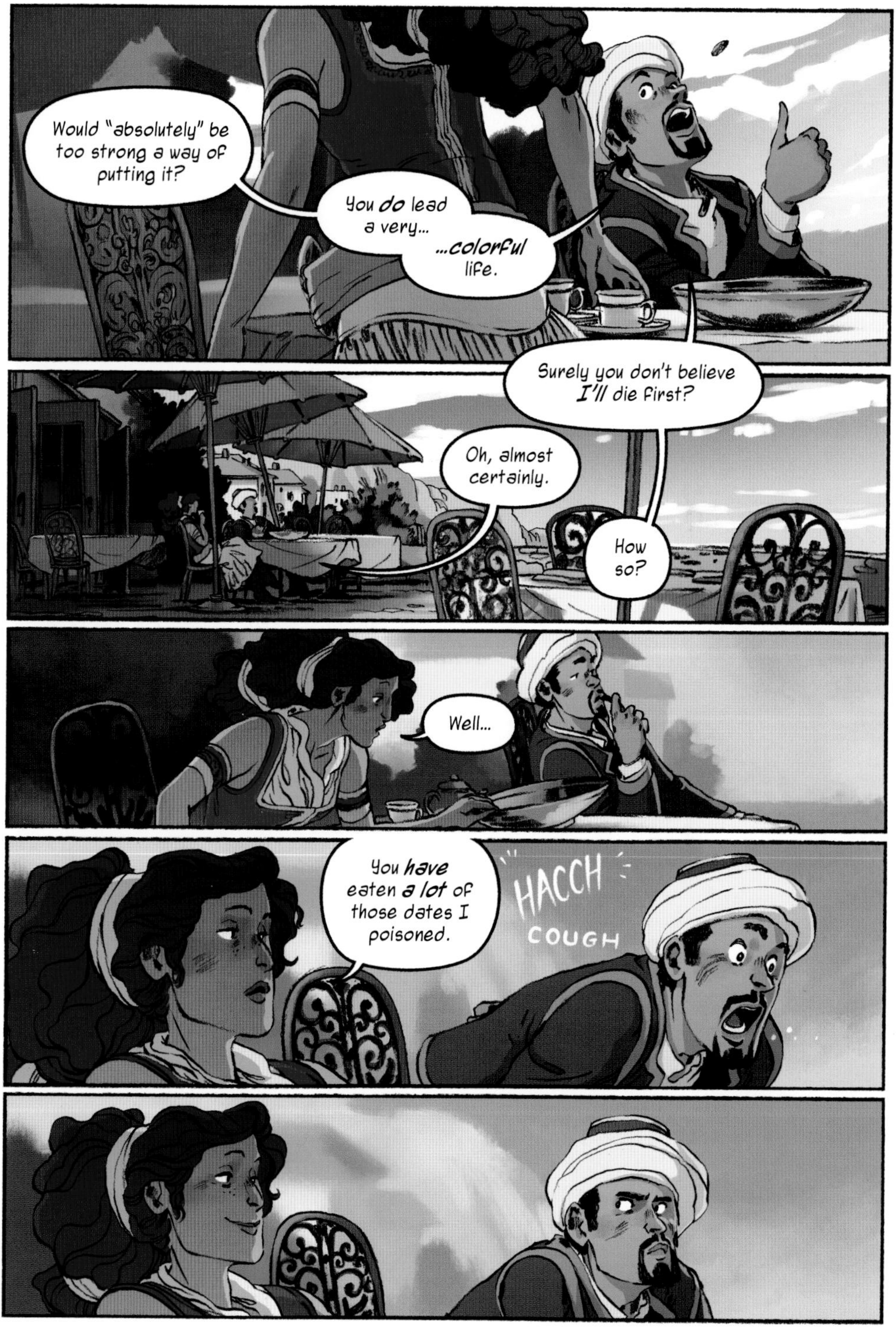
Would "absolutely" be too strong a way of putting it?
You *do* lead a very...
...*colorful* life.
Surely you don't believe *I'll* die first?
Oh, almost certainly.
How so?
Well...
You *have* eaten *a lot* of those dates I poisoned.
HACCH
COUGH

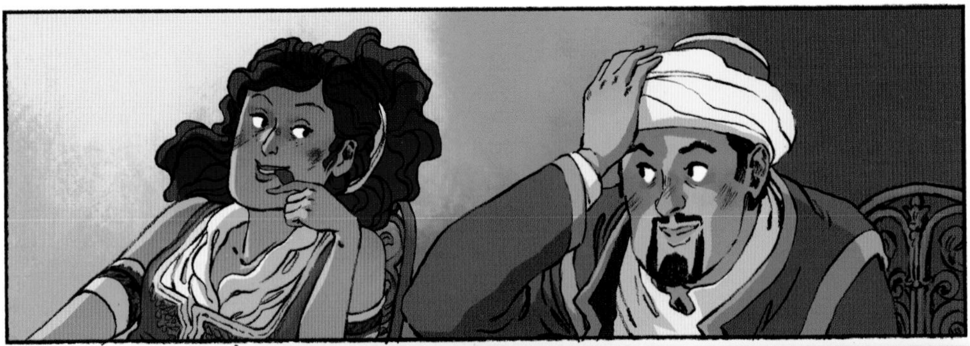

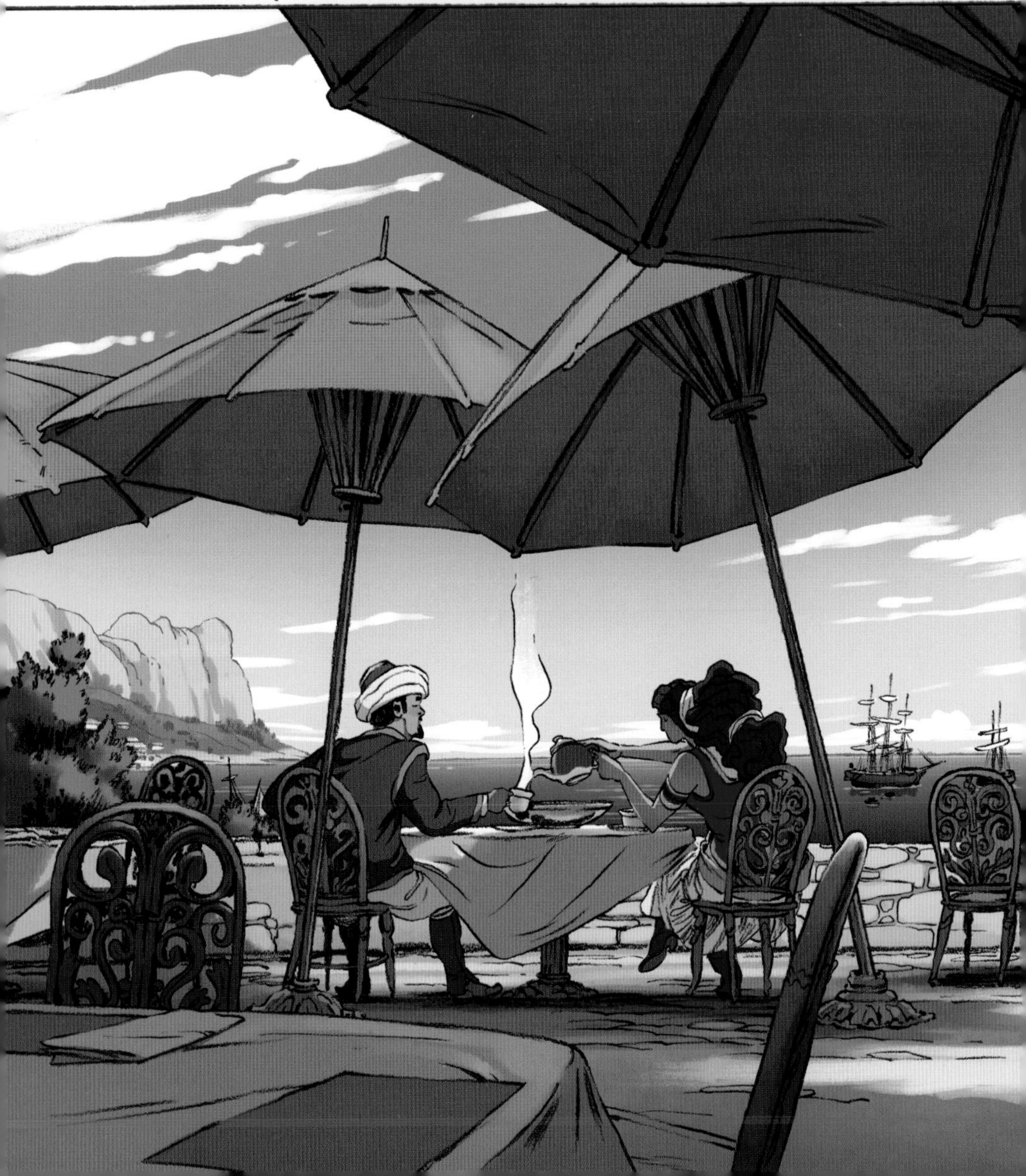

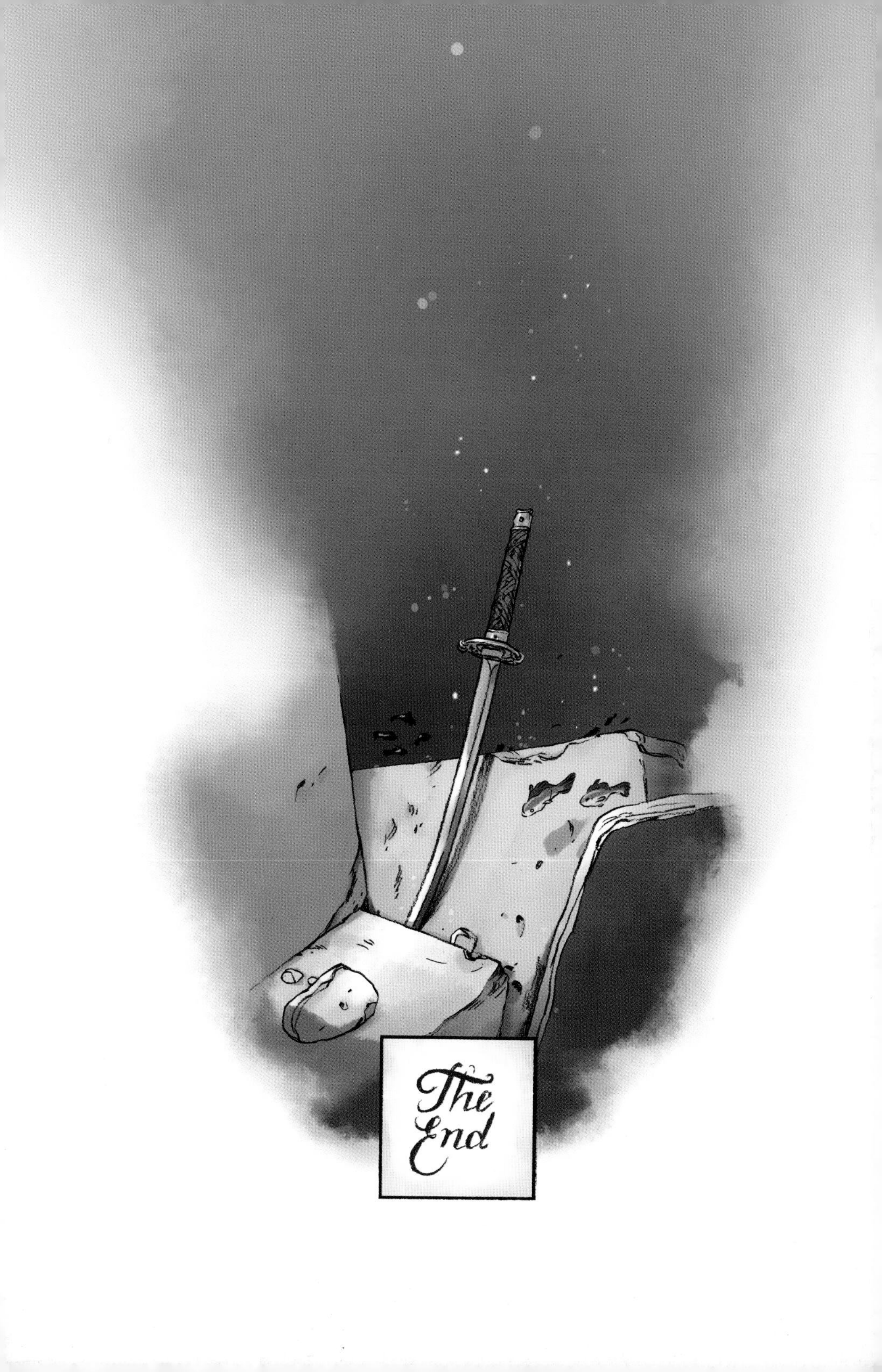
The End

# Delilah Dirk
### and the
## PILLARS of HERCULES

*A Complete Do-It-Yourself Guide*

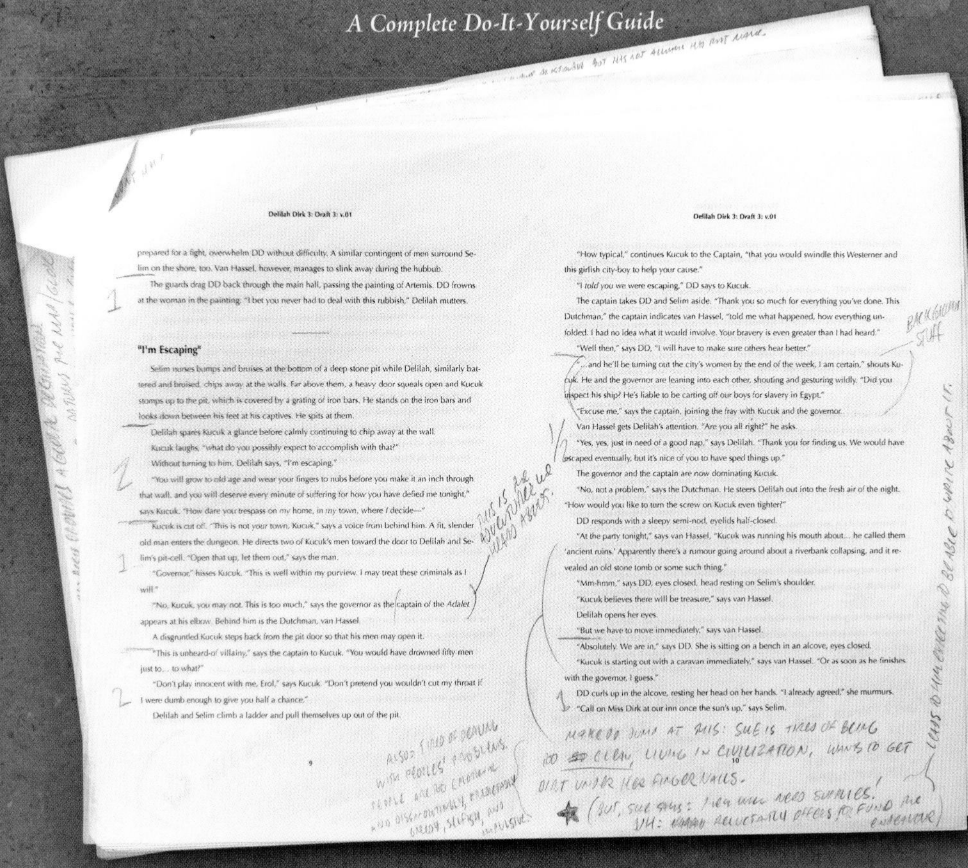

prepared for a fight, overwhelm DD without difficulty. A similar contingent of men surround Selim on the shore, too. Van Hassel, however, manages to slink away during the hubbub.

The guards drag DD back through the main hall, passing the painting of Artemis. DD frowns at the woman in the painting. "I bet you never had to deal with this rubbish," Delilah mutters.

## "I'm Escaping"

Selim nurses bumps and bruises at the bottom of a deep stone pit while Delilah, similarly battered and bruised, chips away at the walls. Far above them, a heavy door squeals open and Kucuk stomps up to the pit, which is covered by a grating of iron bars. He stands on the iron bars and looks down between his feet at his captives. He spits at them.

Delilah spares Kucuk a glance before calmly continuing to chip away at the wall.

Kucuk laughs, "what do you possibly expect to accomplish with that?"

Without turning to him, Delilah says, "I'm escaping."

"You will grow to old age and wear your fingers to nubs before you make it an inch through that wall, and you will deserve every minute of suffering for how you have defied me tonight," says Kucuk. "How dare you trespass on my home, in my town, where I decide—"

Kucuk is cut off. "This is not your town, Kucuk," says a voice from behind him. A fit, slender old man enters the dungeon. He directs two of Kucuk's men toward the door to Delilah and Selim's pit-cell. "Open that up, let them out," says the man.

"Governor," hisses Kucuk. "This is well within my purview. I may treat these criminals as I will."

"No, Kucuk, you may not. This is too much," says the governor as the captain of the *Adalet* appears at his elbow. Behind him is the Dutchman, van Hassel.

A disgruntled Kucuk steps back from the pit door so that his men may open it.

"This is unheard-of villainy," says the captain to Kucuk. "You would have drowned fifty men just to... to what?"

"Don't play innocent with me, Erol," says Kucuk. "Don't pretend you wouldn't cut my throat if I were dumb enough to give you half a chance."

Delilah and Selim climb a ladder and pull themselves up out of the pit.

"How typical," continues Kucuk to the Captain, "that you would swindle this Westerner and this girlish city-boy to help your cause."

"I *told* you we were escaping," DD says to Kucuk.

The captain takes DD and Selim aside. "Thank you so much for everything you've done. This Dutchman," the captain indicates van Hassel, "told me what happened, how everything unfolded. I had no idea what it would involve. Your bravery is even greater than I had heard."

"Well then," says DD, "I will have to make sure others hear better."

"...and he'll be turning out the city's women by the end of the week, I am certain," shouts Kucuk. He and the governor are leaning into each other, shouting and gesturing wildly. "Did you inspect his ship? He's liable to be carting off our boys for slavery in Egypt."

"Excuse me," says the captain, joining the fray with Kucuk and the governor.

Van Hassel gets Delilah's attention. "Are you all right?" he asks.

"Yes, yes, just in need of a good nap," says Delilah. "Thank you for finding us. We would have escaped eventually, but it's nice of you to have sped things up."

The governor and the captain are now dominating Kucuk.

"No, not a problem," says the Dutchman. He steers Delilah out into the fresh air of the night. "How would you like to turn the screw on Kucuk even tighter?"

DD responds with a sleepy semi-nod, eyelids half-closed.

"At the party tonight," says van Hassel, "Kucuk was running his mouth about... he called them 'ancient ruins.' Apparently there's a rumour going around about a riverbank collapsing, and it revealed an old stone tomb or some such thing."

"Mm-hmm," says DD, eyes closed, head resting on Selim's shoulder.

"Kucuk believes there will be treasure," says van Hassel.

Delilah opens her eyes.

"But we have to move immediately," says van Hassel.

"Absolutely. We are in," says DD. She is sitting on a bench in an alcove, eyes closed.

"Kucuk is starting out with a caravan immediately," says van Hassel. "Or as soon as he finishes with the governor, I guess."

DD curls up in the alcove, resting her head on her hands. "I already agreed," she murmurs.

"Call on Miss Dirk at our inn once the sun's up," says Selim.

10

*Handwritten marginal notes:*

MAKE DD JUMP AT THIS: SHE IS TIRED OF BEING TOO CLEAN, LIVING IN CIVILIZATION, WANTS TO GET DIRT UNDER HER FINGERNAILS.

(BUT, SHE SAYS: THEY WILL NEED SUPPLIES! VH: KUCUK RELUCTANTLY OFFERS TO FUND THE EXPEDITION)

ALSO TIRED OF DEALING WITH PEOPLE'S PROBLEMS. PEOPLE ARE NO CHALLENGE AND DISHEARTENINGLY, EVERYBODY GREEDY, SELFISH, AND IMPULSIVE.

BACKGROUND STUFF

# I. WRITE THE STORY

This book started out as a 25,000-word manuscript. Writing might be my favorite part of the process, and once I'm done I have a complete, beginning-to-end, bird's-eye view of the story. It's easy to rearrange and manipulate scenes without having to invest time drawing and re-drawing. It's like trying to change a sculpture when the clay is wet versus once you've fired and glazed it; at this point, the clay is still very wet, very easy and cheap to modify.

"A combination of both, I would say," says Delilah as van Hassel makes notes in his notebook. "Though it was hard to tell. I was distracted by the foam spraying from his mouth." Tired and parched though they were, nothing would interrupt van Hassel from recording a juicy story.

Hearing their exchange, Selim rolls his eyes and sighs.

"The last thing I heard about the devil was an unconfirmed rumour that he had disappeared into the French countryside," says Delilah. "How he could have tracked me down out here is... I don't know. It defies explanation."

Delilah looks to Selim, assessing him and the likelihood of him having told anyone. No; Selim wouldn't have told anyone.

Selim looks to van Hassel. Delilah, in turn, looks to van Hassel. Here, now, is an unknown quantity.

In an instant, Delilah grabs van Hassel by the collar with both hands. "This is your doing! Who did you tell!" she demands.

"No one!" says a cowed van Hassel. "I have told no one!" he stammers under Delilah's furious snorting nostrils. "Maybe I wrote to someone, maybe I told him. But only one person."

## Van Hassel and Merrick Business in Algiers

"Yes, one person," says Delilah, chapped lips, haggard-looking, back in Algiers, holding two issues of The Weekly Observer, one of which has her illustration on the cover. "One person who happens to publish a news magazine."

"Upon our return to Algiers," narrates Selim, "a letter from Delilah's uncle was waiting, accompanied by two issues of The Weekly Observer. Uncle had been curious, surprised to find how explicitly Miss Dirk's movements and plans had been depicted and how she had allowed herself to be written about in such a public forum."

"This," says Delilah, "is how Merrick knew where to find us. Because, 'and so we set sail, to the storied Necropolis of Djemmorah, sun-bleached sepulchre of sovereigns, surrounded by the searing sands of the Sahara. What wonders and mysteries await? Miss Dirk will return, only in the pages of The Weekly Observer!"

Van Hassel is seated in a small, fragile chair, looking terrified. They are on the top floor of a small apartment, exposed to the open night air. Selim stands before the door, blocking any at-

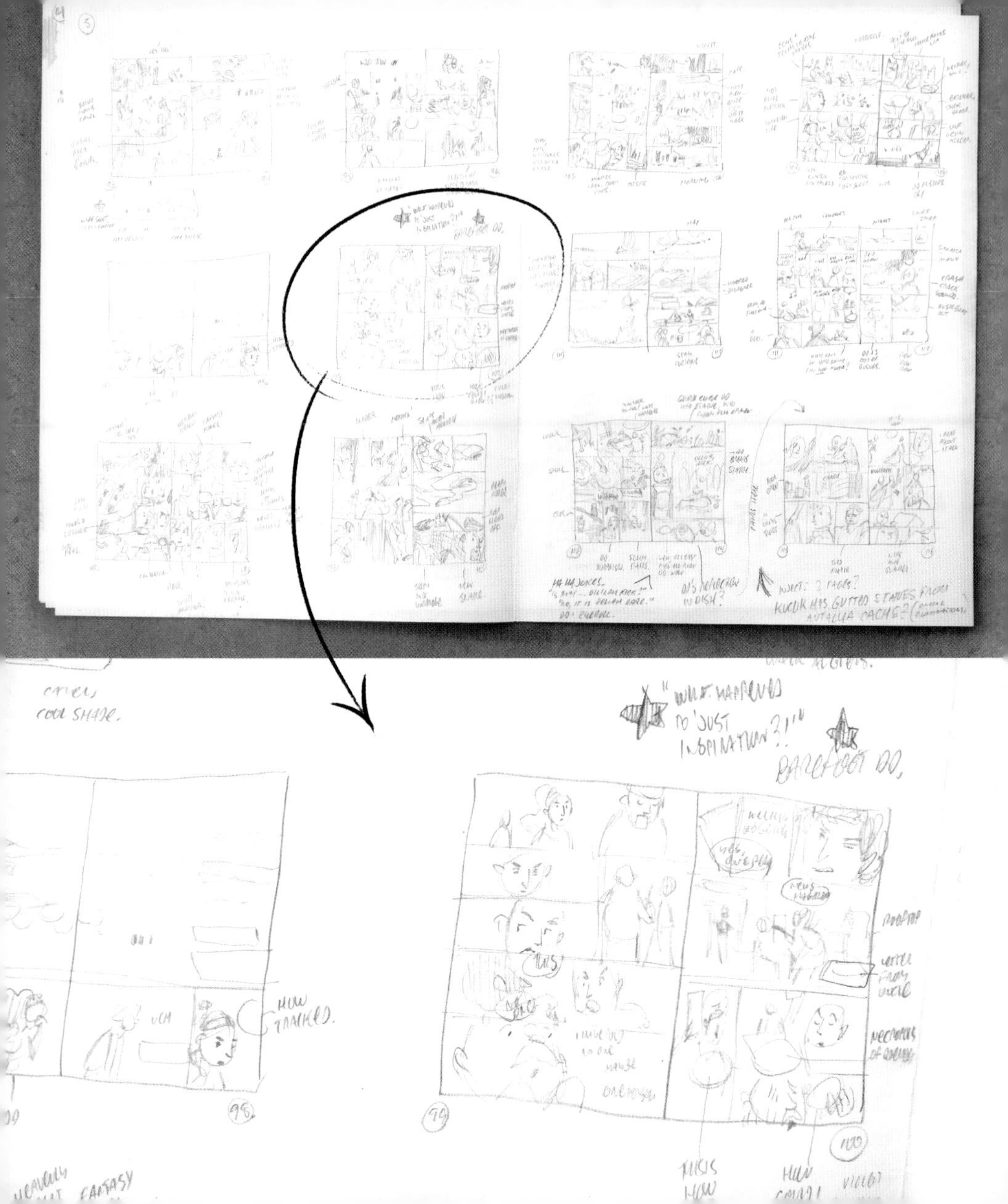
"WHAT HAPPENED TO 'JUST INSPIRATION'?!"
BAREFOOT DD.
INSERT: 2 PAGES?
KUCUK HAS GUTTED STATUES FROM ANTALYA CACHE?
DD'S REFLECTION IN DISH?
COOL SHADE.
HOW TRACKED.
ROOFTOP
FANTASY

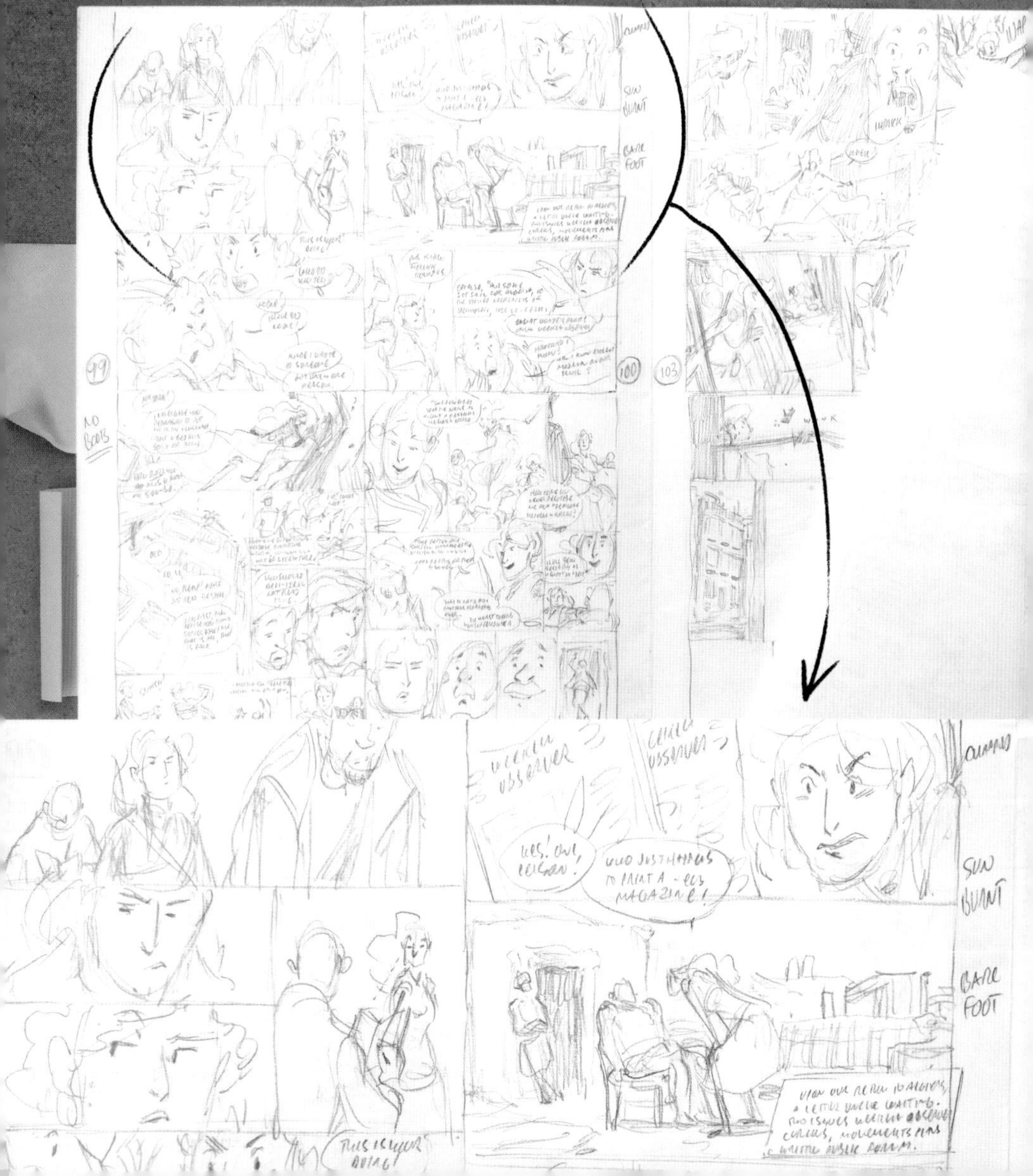
99
100
103
NO BOOBS
WEEKLY OBSERVER
SUN BURNT
BARE FOOT

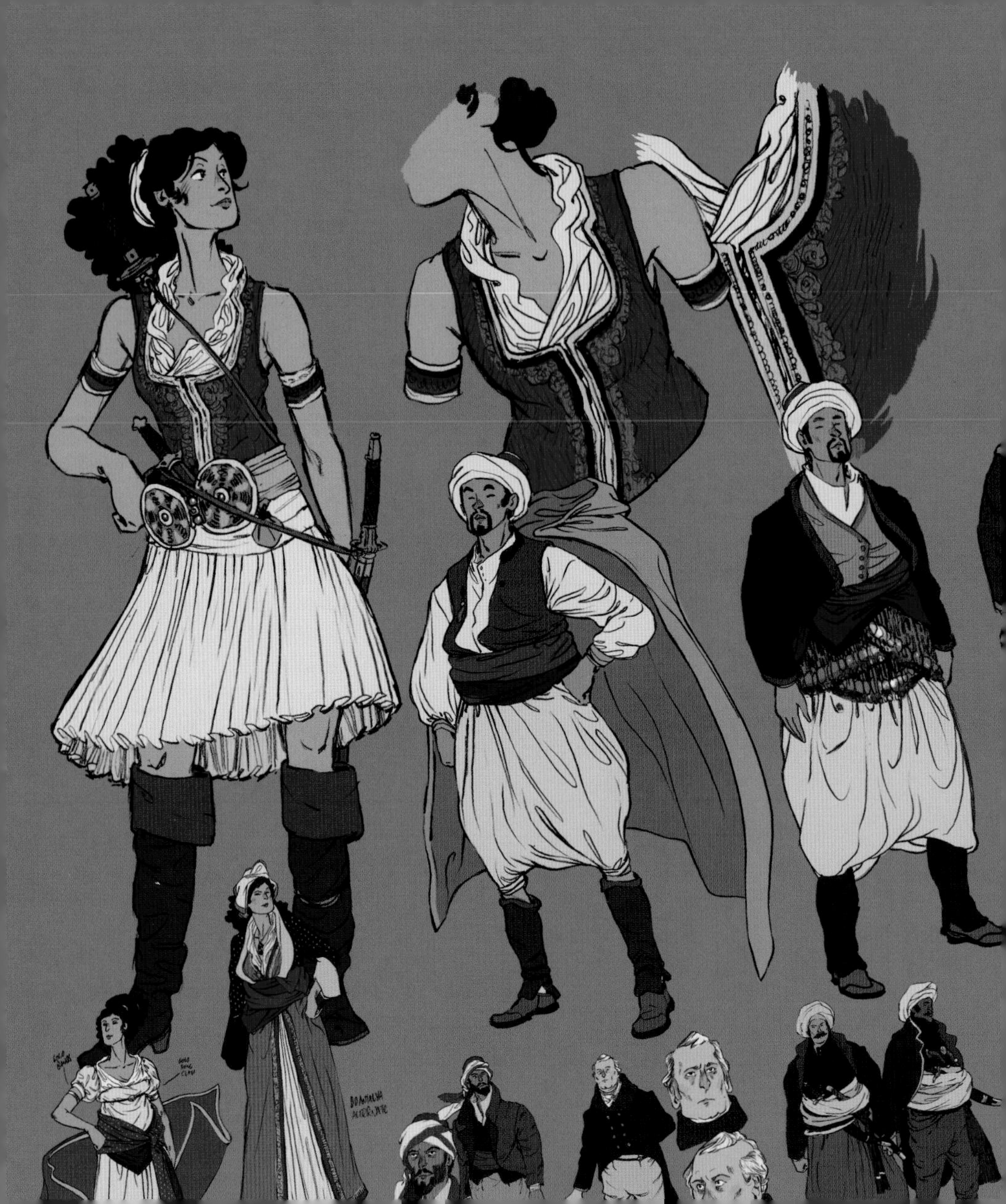

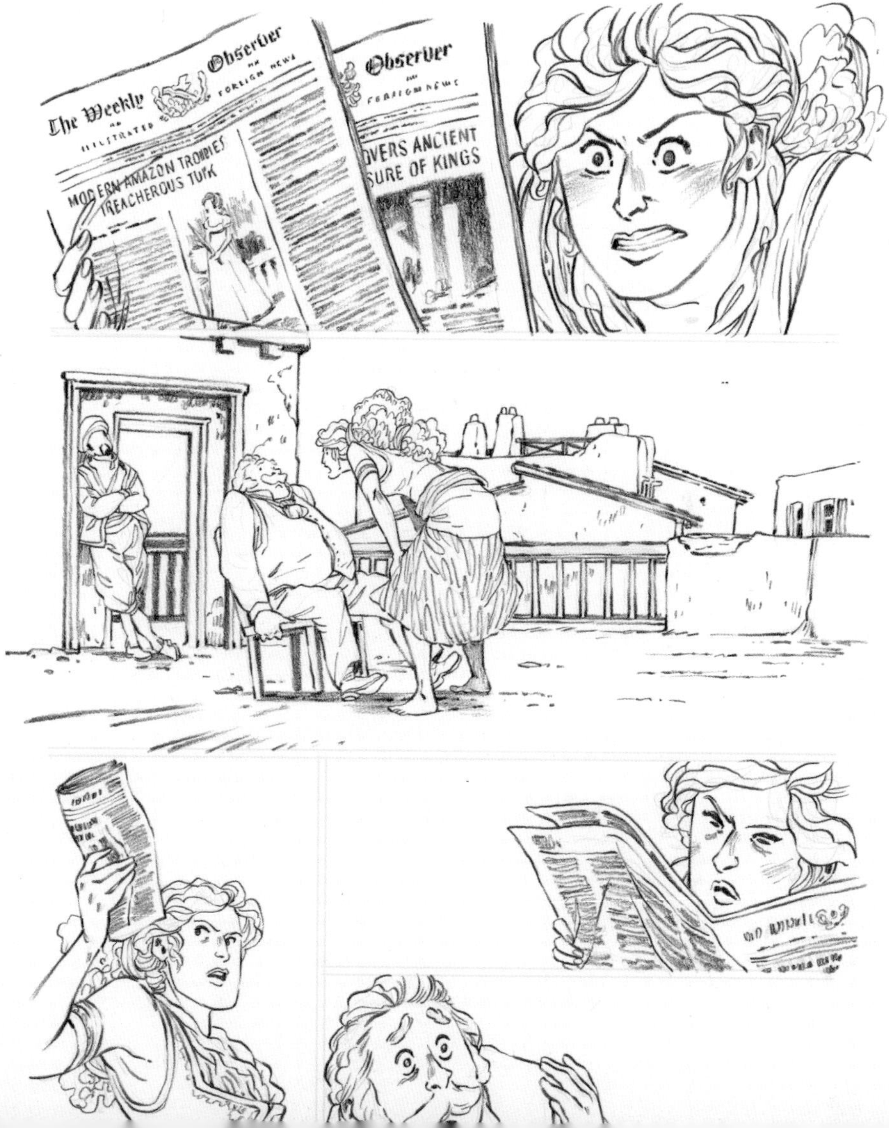
The Weekly Observer
An Illustrated
Foreign News
MODERN AMAZON TROUNCES TREACHEROUS TURK
Observer
Foreign News
OVERS ANCIENT
SURE OF KINGS

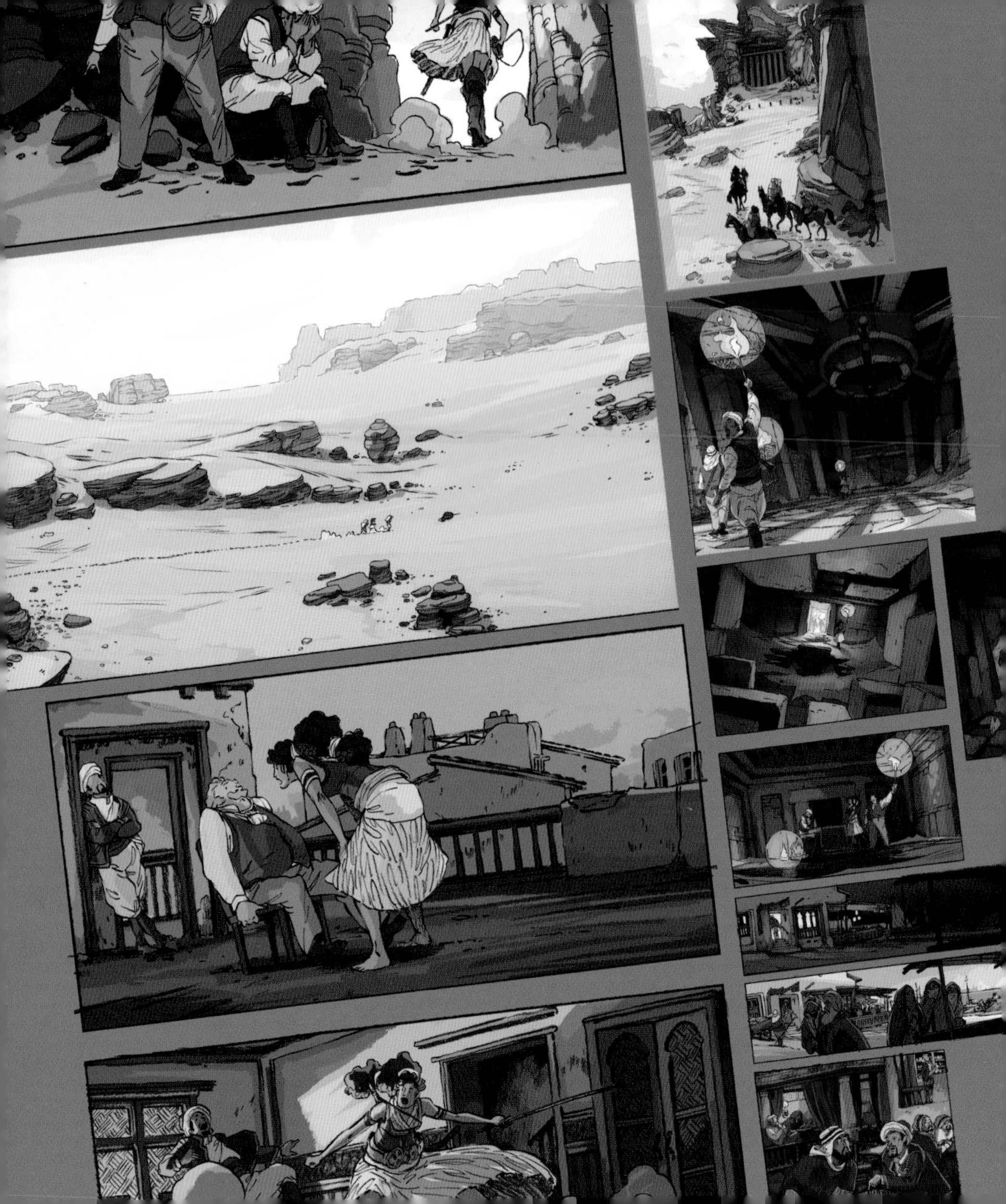

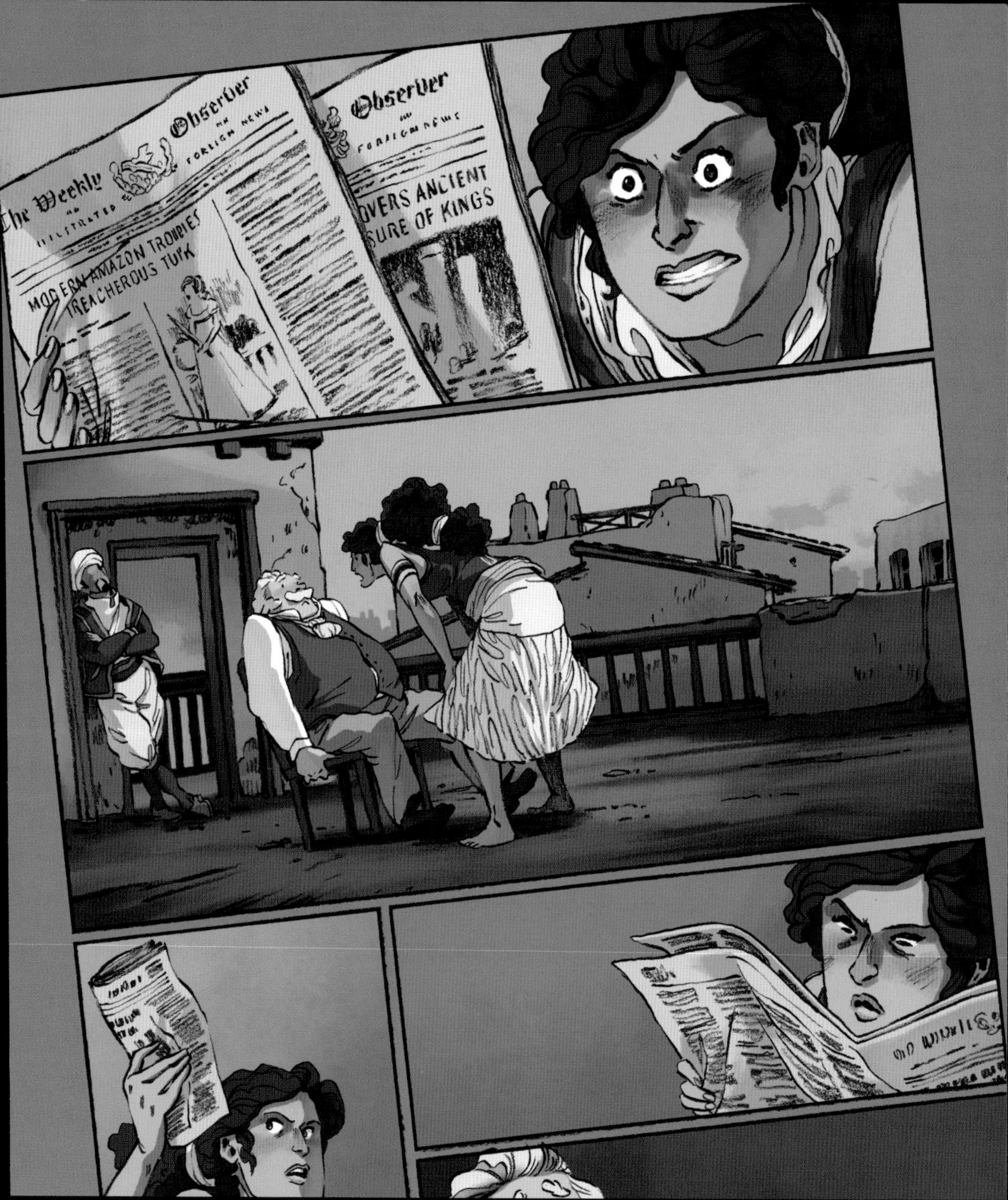
The Weekly
Observer
MODERN AMAZON TROPHIES
TREACHEROUS TURK
Observer
OVERS ANCIENT
SURE OF KINGS

## 7. PREPARE FOR AND, FINALLY, 8. COLOR THAT COMIC

Color preparation (often called"flatting") is the digital equivalent of using masking fluid with watercolours or a stencil for spraypainting: image elements are isolated so that it's easy to go in and slap down paint. Once that's done, it's just a matter of going in and painting all the finishing touches: rendering the sky, making DD's lips look chapped, etcetera.

Dear reader, I hope you have enjoyed this thick comic book.

I believe it goes almost without saying that this story plays fast and loose with elements that you or I might recognize from, say, *history*, and/or *the real world as we know it.* As an author, I admit to having exercised a brazen "have your cake and eat it, too" attitude toward the inclusion of historical elements in The Pillars of Hercules. It should be obvious, however, that the great bulk of this book—more so than *The King's Shilling* and perhaps more so than *The Turkish Lieutenant*—is composed of fantastical ingredients.

Where the hull of this story occasionally trades paint with the wharf of historical fact, I made considerable efforts to be accurate and respectful in representing said historical elements. And, of course, in many other respects I have chosen to sail far away from the shores of reality. I hope it is evident in the story which tack I have taken in each circumstance. When an element seems as though it ought to be true to history but I have erred in its representation, I can only ask for your forgiveness. It is my sincerest wish to present to you a world which is internally consistent, and if I have offered an element which fends you away from this quality, dear reader, I apologize and hope it has not considerably lessened your enjoyment of this work.

I feel a great affection for this time period and its occupants. I welcome any communication through which I can increase my understanding thereof. If you are able to shine a lantern into what appears, evidently, to be a darker corner of my awareness, please do not hesitate to get in touch. Contact me via any one of the many means available at www.delilahdirk.com.

**ACKNOWLEDGMENTS**

First and foremost, I cannot understate the the importance of Sarah Haddleton's contribution to the making of this book. It would not exist if I did not have the privilege of her support, which took many forms—many tangible, many less so. Sarah, you are the mysterious and unknowable mechanisms powering the ancient mythical city of my heart. Sarah claims to be the inspiration for Delilah Dirk, but Delilah shares only a portion of her thoughtfulness and caring. The two are, however, united by their affinity for sensible footwear.

For providing valuable objective feedback on early drafts, I am indebted to Hamish van der Ven, Michael Swanston, Katy Campbell, Kenny Park, and Michael Harris.

For designing a pair of phony ancient alphabets, my thanks to Sarah Airriess.

In early 2017, it became apparent that if I were to attempt to single-handedly color every page of this book, it would not likely be delivered to my publisher within my own lifetime. And so, for responding to my urgent (some might say "panicked") call for assistance and for their painstaking work, I am indebted to Sarah Airriess (yes, again), Jarad Greene, Beth Morrell, Amanda Scurti, and one Brian Cliff. *Yes*, dear reader, *my dad.*

I am grateful to Calista Brill and Robyn Chapman for their enthusiasm, support, and valuable editorial guidance.

Thank you to my wonderful literary agent, Bernadette Baker-Baughman, for her faith and persistence.

Finally, thank you to the Canada Council for the Arts and the British Columbia Arts Council for supporting this work, and to Michael Harris and Kate Beaton for their enthusiasm and input as I prepared my proposals.

Canada Council    Conseil des arts
for the Arts      du Canada

Tony Cliff acknowledges the support of the Canada Council for the Arts, which last year invested $153 million to bring the arts to Canadians throughout the country.

Tony Cliff remercions le Conseil des arts du Canada de son soutien. L'an dernier, le Conseil a investi 153 millions de dollars pour mettre de l'art dans la vie des Canadiennes et des Canadiens de tout le pays.

BRITISH COLUMBIA    BRITISH COLUMBIA
ARTS COUNCIL
An agency of the Province of British Columbia

First Second

Copyright © 2018 by Tony Cliff

Produced primarily using pencil on paper with intermediate digital processes and digital lettering and coloring.

Published by First Second
First Second is an imprint of Roaring Brook Press,
a division of Holtzbrinck Publishing Holdings Limited Partnership
175 Fifth Avenue, New York, NY 10010

Library of Congress Control Number: 2017946150

ISBN 978-1-62672-804-2

Our books may be purchased in bulk for promotional, educational, or business use. Please contact your local bookseller or the Macmillan Corporate and Premium Sales Department at (800) 221-7945 ext. 5442 or by e-mail at MacmillanSpecialMarkets@macmillan.com.

First edition, 2018
Book design by Taylor Esposito

Printed in China by 1010 Printing International Limited, North Point, Hong Kong
10 9 8 7 6 5 4 3 2 1